The Best of

ROALD DAHL

ALSO BY ROALD DAHL

AUTOBIOGRAPHY
Boy
Going Solo

NOVEL
My Uncle Oswald

SHORT STORIES
Over to You
Someone Like You
Kiss Kiss
Twenty-Nine Kisses from Roald Dahl
Switch Bitch
Tales of the Unexpected
More Tales of the Unexpected
Ah, Sweet Mystery of Life

POETRY
Revolting Rhymes
Rhyme Stew

CHILDREN'S BOOKS
James and the Giant Peach
Charlie and the Chocolate Factory
The Magic Finger
Fantastic Mr. Fox
Charlie and the Great Glass Elevator
Danny, the Champion of the World
The Wonderful World of Henry Sugar and Six More
The Enormous Crocodile
The Twits
George's Marvellous Medicine
The BFG
Dirty Beasts
The Witches
The Giraffe, the Pelly and Me
Matilda

The Best of

ROALD DAHL

VINTAGE BOOKS

A Division of Random House, Inc.

New York

Vintage Books Edition, July 1990

Library of Congress Cataloging-in-Publication Data
Dahl, Roald.
[Short stories. Selections]
The best of Roald Dahl
p. cm.
"A Vintage original, May 1978"—T.p. verso.
ISBN 0-679-72991-7
I. Title.
PR6054.A35A6   1990
823'.914—dc20   89-40734
CIP

Manufactured in the United States of America
79B86

Contents

The Best of

ROALD DAHL

Madame Rosette

1945

"Oh jesus, this is wonderful," said the Stag.

He was lying back in the bath with a scotch and soda in one hand and a cigarette in the other. The water was right up to the brim and he was keeping it warm by turning the tap with his toes.

He raised his head and took a little sip of his whiskey, then he lay back and closed his eyes.

"For God's sake, get out," said a voice from the next room. "Come on, Stag, you've had over an hour." Stuffy was sitting on the edge of the bed with no clothes on, drinking slowly and waiting his turn.

The Stag said, "All right. I'm letting the water out now," and he stretched out a leg and flipped up the plug with his toes.

Stuffy stood up and wandered into the bathroom, holding his drink in his hand. The Stag lay in the bath for a few moments more, then, balancing his glass carefully on the soap rack, he stood up and reached for a towel. His body was short and square, with strong thick legs and exaggerated calf muscles. He had coarse curly ginger hair and a thin, rather pointed face covered with freckles. There was a layer of pale ginger hair on his chest.

"Jesus," he said, looking down into the bathtub, "I've brought half the desert with me."

Stuffy said, "Wash it out and let me get in. I haven't had a bath for five months."

This was back in the early days when we were fighting the Italians in Libya. One flew very hard in those days because there were not many pilots. They certainly could not send any out from England because there they were fighting the Battle of Britain. So one remained for long periods out in the desert, living the strange unnatural life of the desert, living in the same dirty little tent, washing and shaving every day in a mug full of one's own spat-out tooth water, all the time picking flies out of one's tea and out of one's food, having sandstorms which were as much in the tents as outside them so that placid men became bloody-minded and lost their tempers with their friends and with themselves; having dysentery and gippy tummy and mastoid and desert sores, having some bombs from the Italian S.79's, having no water and no women; having no flowers growing out of the ground; having very little except sand sand sand. One flew old Gloster Gladiators against the Italian C.R.42's, and when one was not flying, it was difficult to know what to do.

Occasionally one would catch scorpions, put them in empty petrol cans and match them against each other in fierce mortal combat. Always there would be a champion scorpion in the squadron, a sort of Joe Louis who was invincible and won all his fights. He would have a name; he would become famous and his training diet would be a great secret known only to the owner. Training diet was considered very important with scorpions. Some were trained on corned beef, some on a thing called Machonachies, which is an unpleasant canned meat stew, some on live beetles and there were others who were persuaded to take a little beer just before the fight, on the premise that it made the scorpion happy and gave him confidence. These last ones always lost. But there were great battles and great champions, and in the afternoons when the flying was over, one could often see a group of pilots and airmen standing around in a circle on the sand, bending over with their hands on their knees, watching the fight, exhorting the scorpions and shouting at them as people shout at boxers or wrestlers in a ring. Then there would be a victory, and the man who owned the winner would become excited. He would dance around in the sand yelling, waving his arms in the air and extolling in a loud voice the virtues of the victorious animal. The greatest scorpion of all was owned by a sergeant called Wishful who fed him only on marmalade. The animal had an unmentionable name, but he won forty-two consecutive fights and then died quietly in training just when Wishful was considering the problem of retiring him to stud.

So you can see that because there were no great pleasures while living in the desert, the small pleasures became great pleasures and the pleasures of children became the pleasures of grown men. That was true for everyone; for the pilots, the fitters, the riggers, the corporals who cooked the food and the men who kept the stores. It was true for the Stag and for Stuffy, so true that when the two of them wangled a forty-eight hour pass and a lift by air into Cairo, and when they got to the hotel, they were feeling about having a bath rather as you would feel on the first night of your honeymoon.

The Stag had dried himself and was lying on the bed with a towel round his waist, with his hands up behind his head, and Stuffy was in the bath, lying with his head against the back of the bath, groaning and sighing with ecstasy.

The Stag said, "Stuffy."

"Yes."

"What are we going to do now?"

"Women," said Stuffy. "We must find some women to take out to supper."

The Stag said, "Later. That can wait till later." It was early afternoon.

"I don't think it can wait," said Stuffy.

"Yes," said the Stag, "it can wait."

The Stag was very old and wise; he never rushed any fences. He was twenty-seven, much older than anyone else in the squadron, including the C.O., and his judgment was much respected by the others.

"Let's do a little shopping first," he said.

"Then what?" said the voice from the bathroom.

"Then we can consider the other situation."

There was a pause.

"Stag?"

"Yes."

"Do you know any women here?"

"I used to. I used to know a Turkish girl with very white skin called Wenka, and a Yugoslav girl who was six inches taller than I, called Kiki, and another who I think was Syrian. I can't remember her name."

"Ring them up," said Stuffy.

"I've done it. I did it while you were getting the whiskey. They've all gone. It isn't any good."

"It's never any good," Stuffy said.

The Stag said, "We'll go shopping first. There is plenty of time."

In an hour Stuffy got out of the bath. They both dressed themselves in clean khaki shorts and shirts and wandered downstairs, through the lobby of the hotel and out into the bright hot street. The Stag put on his sunglasses.

Stuffy said, "I know. I want a pair of sunglasses."

"All right. We'll go and buy some."

They stopped a gharri, got in and told the driver to go to Cicurel. Stuffy bought his sunglasses and the Stag bought some poker dice, then they wandered out again onto the hot crowded street.

"Did you see that girl?" said Stuffy.

"The one that sold us the sunglasses?"

"Yes. That dark one."

"Probably Turkish," said Stag.

Stuffy said, "I don't care what she was. She was terrific. Didn't you think she was terrific?"

They were walking along the Sharia Kasr-el-Nil with their hands in their pockets, and Stuffy was wearing the sunglasses which he had just bought. It was a hot dusty afternoon, and the sidewalk was crowded with Egyptians and Arabs and small boys with bare feet. The flies followed the small boys and buzzed around their eyes, trying to get at the inflammation which was in them, which was there because their mothers had done something terrible to those eyes when the boys were young, so that they would not be eligible for military conscription when they grew older. The small boys pattered along beside the Stag and Stuffy shouting, "Baksheesh, baksheesh," in shrill insistent voices, and the flies followed the small boys. There was the smell of Cairo, which is not like the smell of any other city. It comes not from any one thing or from any one place; it comes from everything everywhere; from the gutters and the sidewalks, from the houses and the shops and the things in the shops and the food cooking in the shops, from the horses and the dung of the horses in the streets and from the drains; it comes from the people and the way the sun bears down upon the people and from the way the sun bears down upon the gutters and the drains and the horses and the food and the refuse in the streets. It is a rare, pungent smell, like something which is sweet and rotting and hot and salty and bitter all at the same time, and it is never absent, even in the cool of the early morning.

The two pilots walked along slowly among the crowd.

"Didn't you think she was terrific?" said Stuffy. He wanted to know what the Stag thought.

"She was all right."

"Certainly she was all right. You know what, Stag?"

"What?"

"I would like to take that girl out tonight."

They crossed over a street and walked on a little further.

The Stag said, "Well, why don't you? Why don't you ring up Rosette?"

"Who in the hell's Rosette?"

"Madame Rosette," said the Stag. "She is a great woman."

They were passing a place called Tim's Bar. It was run by an Englishman called Tim Gilfillan who had been a quartermaster sergeant in the last war and who had somehow managed to get left behind in Cairo when the army went home.

"Tim's," said the Stag. "Let's go in."

There was no one inside except for Tim, who was arranging his bottles on shelves behind the bar.

"Well, well, well," he said, turning around. "Where you boys been all this time?"

"Hello, Tim."

He did not remember them, but he knew by their looks that they were in from the desert.

"How's my old friend Graziani?" he said, turning round and leaning his elbows on the counter.

"He's bloody close," said the Stag. "He's outside Mersah."

"What you flying now?"

"Gladiators."

"Hell, they had those here eight years ago."

"Same ones still here," said the Stag. "They're clapped out."

They got their whiskey and carried the glasses over to a table in the corner.

Stuffy said, "Who's this Rosette?"

The Stag took a long drink and put down the glass.

"She's a great woman," he said.

"Who is she?"

"She's a filthy old whore."

"All right," said Stuffy, "all right, but what about her?"

"Well," said Stag, "I'll tell you. Madame Rosette runs the biggest brothel in the world. It is said that she can get you any girl that you want in the whole of Cairo."

"Bullshit."

"No, it's true. You just ring her up and tell her where you saw the woman, where she was working, what shop and at which counter, together with an accurate description, and she will do the rest."

"Don't be such a bloody fool," said Stuffy.

"It's true. It's absolutely true. Thirty-three squadron told me about her."

"They were pulling your leg."

"All right. You go and look her up in the phone book."

"She wouldn't be in the phone book under that name."

"I'm telling you she is," said Stag. "Go and look her up under Rosette. You'll see I'm right."

Stuffy did not believe him, but he went over to Tim and asked him for a telephone directory and brought it back to the table. He opened it and turned the pages until he came to R-o-s. He ran his finger down the column. Roseppi . . . Rosery . . . Rosette. There it was, Rosette, Madame and the address and number, clearly printed in the book. The Stag was watching him.

"Got it?" he said.

"Yes, here it is. Madame Rosette."

"Well, why don't you go and ring her up?"

"What shall I say?"

The Stag looked down into his glass and poked the ice with his finger.

"Tell her you are a Colonel," he said. "Colonel Higgins; she mistrusts pilot officers. And tell her that you have seen a beautiful dark girl selling sunglasses at Cicurel's and that you would like, as you put it, to take her out to dinner."

"There isn't a telephone here."

"Oh yes there is. There's one over there."

Stuffy looked around and saw the telephone on the wall at the end of the bar.

"I haven't got a piastre piece."

"Well, I have," said Stag. He fished in his pocket and put a piastre on the table.

"Tim will hear everything I say."

"What the hell does that matter? He probably rings her up himself. You're windy," he added.

"You're a shit," said Stuffy.

Stuffy was just a child. He was nineteen; seven whole years younger than the Stag. He was fairly tall and he was thin, with a lot of black hair and a handsome wide-mouthed face which was coffee brown from the sun of the desert. He was unquestionably the finest pilot in the squadron, and already in these early days, his score was fourteen Italians confirmed destroyed. On the ground he moved slowly and lazily like a tired person and he thought slowly and lazily like a sleepy child, but when he was up in the air his mind was quick and his movements were quick, so quick that they were like reflex actions. It seemed, when he was on the ground, almost as though he was resting, as though he was dozing a little in order to make sure that when he got into the cockpit he would wake up fresh and quick, ready for that two hours of high concentration. But Stuffy was away from the airdrome now and he had something on his mind which had waked him up almost like flying. It might not last, but for the moment anyway, he was concentrating.

He looked again in the book for the number, got up and walked slowly over to the telephone. He put in the piastre, dialed the number and heard it ringing at the other end. The Stag was sitting at the table looking at him and Tim was still behind the bar arranging his bottles. Tim was only about five yards away and he was obviously going to listen to everything that was said. Stuffy felt rather foolish. He leaned against the bar and waited, hoping that no one would answer.

Then click, the receiver was lifted at the other end and he heard a woman's voice saying, "Allo."

He said, "Hello, is Madame Rosette there?" He was watching Tim. Tim went on arranging his bottles, pretending to take no notice, but Stuffy knew that he was listening.

"This ees Madame Rosette. Oo ees it?" Her voice was petulant and gritty. She sounded as if she did not want to be bothered with anyone just then.

Stuffy tried to sound casual. "This is Colonel Higgins."

"Colonel oo?"

"Colonel Higgins." He spelled it.

"Yes, Colonel. What do you want?" She sounded impatient. Obviously this was a woman who stood no nonsense. He still tried to sound casual.

"Well, Madame Rosette, I was wondering if you could help me over a little matter."

Stuffy was watching Tim. He was listening all right. You can always tell if someone is listening when he is pretending not to. He is careful not to make any noise about what he is doing and he pretends that he is concentrating very hard upon his job. Tim was like that now, moving the bottles quickly from one shelf to another, watching the bottles, making no noise, never looking around into the room. Over in the far corner the Stag was leaning forward with his elbows on the table, smoking a cigarette. He was watching Stuffy, enjoying the whole business and knowing that Stuffy was embarrassed because of Tim. Stuffy had to go on.

"I was wondering if you could help me," he said. "I was in Cicurel's today buying a pair of sunglasses and I saw a girl there whom I would very much like to take out to dinner."

"What's 'er name?" The hard, rasping voice was more businesslike than ever.

"I don't know," he said sheepishly.

"What's she look like?"

"Well, she's got dark hair, and tall and, well, she's very beautiful."

"What sort of a dress was she wearing?"

"Er, let me see. I think it was a kind of white dress with red flowers printed all over it." Then, as a brilliant afterthought, he added, "She had a red belt." He remembered that she had been wearing a shiny red belt.

There was a pause. Stuffy watched Tim who wasn't making any noise with the bottles; he was picking them up carefully and putting them down carefully.

Then the loud gritty voice again, "It may cost you a lot."

"That's all right." Suddenly he didn't like the conversation any more. He wanted to finish it and get away.

"Might cost you six pounds, might cost you eight or ten. I don't know till I've seen her. That all right?"

"Yes yes, that's all right."

"Where you living, Colonel?"

"Metropolitan Hotel," he said without thinking.

"All right, I give you a ring later." And she put down the receiver, bang.

Stuffy hung up, went slowly back to the table and sat down.

"Well," said Stag, "that was all right, wasn't it?"

"Yes, I suppose so."

"What did she say?"

"She said that she would call me back at the hotel."

"You mean she'll call Colonel Higgins at the hotel."

Stuffy said, "Oh Christ."

Stag said, "It's all right. We'll tell the desk that the Colonel is in our room and to put his calls through to us. What else did she say?"

"She said it may cost me a lot, six or ten pounds."

"Rosette will take ninety percent of it," said Stag. "She's a filthy old whore."

"How will she work it?" Stuffy said.

He was really a gentle person and now he was feeling worried about having started something which might become complicated.

"Well," said Stag, "she'll dispatch one of her pimps to locate the girl and find out who she is. If she's already on the books, then it's easy. If she isn't, the pimp will proposition her there and then over the counter at Cicurel's. If the girl tells him to go to hell, he'll up the price, and if she still tells him to go to hell, he'll up the price still more, and in the end she'll be tempted by the cash and probably agree. Then Rosette quotes you a price three times as high and takes the balance herself. You have to pay her, not the girl. Of course, after that the girl goes on Rosette's books, and once she's in her clutches she's finished. Next time Rosette will dictate the price and the girl will not be in a position to argue."

"Why?"

"Because if she refuses, Rosette will say, 'All right, my girl, I shall see that your employers, that's Cicurel's, are told about what you did last time, how you've been working for me and using their shop as a market place. Then they'll fire you.' That's what Rosette will say, and the wretched girl will be frightened and do what she's told."

Stuffy said, "Sounds like a nice person."

"Who?"

"Madame Rosette."

"Charming," said Stag. "She's a charming person."

It was hot. Stuffy wiped his face with his handkerchief.

"More whiskey," said Stag. "Hi, Tim, two more of those."

Tim brought the glasses over and put them on the table without saying anything. He picked up the empty glasses and went away at once. To Stuffy it seemed as though he was different from what he had been when they first came in. He wasn't cheery any more, he was quiet and offhand. There wasn't any more "Hi, you fellows, where you been all this time" about him now, and when he got back behind the counter, he turned his back and went on arranging the bottles.

The Stag said, "How much money you got?"

"Nine pounds, I think."

"May not be enough. You gave her a free hand, you know. You ought to have set a limit. She'll sting you now."

"I know," Stuffy said.

They went on drinking for a little while without talking. Then Stag said, "What you worrying about, Stuffy?"

"Nothing," he answered. "Nothing at all. Let's go back to the hotel. She may ring up."

They paid for their drinks and said goodbye to Tim, who nodded but didn't say anything. They went back to the Metropolitan and as they went past the desk, the Stag said to the clerk, "If a call comes in for Colonel Higgins, put it through to our room. He'll be there." The Egyptian said, "Yes, sir," and made a note of it.

In the bedroom, the Stag lay down on his bed and lit a cigarette. "And what am I going to do tonight?" he said.

Stuffy had been quiet all the way back to the hotel. He hadn't said a word. Now he sat down on the edge of the other bed with his hands still in his pockets and said, "Look, Stag, I'm not very keen on this Rosette deal any more. It may cost too much. Can't we put it off?"

The Stag sat up. "Hell no," he said. "You're committed. You can't fool about with Rosette like that. She's probably working on it at this moment. You can't back out now."

"I may not be able to afford it," Stuffy said.

"Well, wait and see."

Stuffy got up, went over to the parachute bag and took out the bottle of whiskey. He poured out two, filled the glasses with water from the tap in the bathroom, came back and gave one to the Stag.

"Stag," he said. "Ring up Rosette and tell her that Colonel Higgins has had to leave town urgently, to rejoin his regiment in the desert. Ring her up and tell her that. Say the Colonel asked you to deliver the message because he didn't have time."

"Ring her up yourself."

"She'd recognize my voice. Come on, Stag, you ring her."

"No," he said, "I won't."

"Listen," said Stuffy suddenly. It was the child Stuffy speaking. "I don't want to go out with that woman and I don't want to have any dealings with Madame Rosette tonight. We can think of something else."

The Stag looked up quickly. Then he said, "All right. I'll ring her."

He reached for the phone book, looked up her number and spoke it into the telephone. Stuffy heard him get her on the line and he heard him giving her the message from the Colonel. There was a pause, then the Stag said, "I'm sorry, Madame Rosette, but it's nothing to do with me. I'm merely delivering a message." Another pause; then the Stag said the same thing over again and that went on for quite a long time, until he must have got tired of it, because in the end he put down the receiver and lay back on his bed. He was roaring with laughter.

"The lousy old bitch," he said, and he laughed some more.

Stuffy said, "Was she angry?"

"Angry," said Stag. "Was she angry? You should have heard her. Wanted to know the Colonel's regiment and God knows what else and said he'd have to pay. She said you boys think you can fool around with me but you can't."

"Hooray," said Stuffy. "The filthy old whore."

"Now what are we going to do?" said the Stag. "It's six o'clock already."

"Let's go out and do a little drinking in some of those Gyppi places."

"Fine. We'll do a Gyppi pub crawl."

They had one more drink, then they went out. They went to a place called the Excelsior, then they went to a place called the Sphinx, then to a small place called by an Egyptian name, and by ten o'clock they were sitting happily in a place which hadn't got a name at all, drinking beer and watching a kind of stage show. At the Sphinx they had picked up a pilot from thirty-three squadron, who said that his name was William. He was about the same age as Stuffy, but his face was younger, for he had not been flying so long. It was especially around his mouth that he was younger. He had a round school-boy face and a small turned-up nose and his skin was brown from the desert.

The three of them sat happily in the place without a name drinking beer, because beer was the only thing that they served there. It was a long wooden room with an unpolished wooden sawdust floor and wooden tables and chairs. At the far end there was a raised wooden stage where there was a show going on. The room was full of Egyptians, sitting drinking black coffee with the red tarbooshes on their heads. There were two fat girls on the stage dressed in shiny silver pants and silver brassieres. One was waggling her bottom in time to the music. The other was waggling her bosom in time to the music. The bosom waggler was most skilful. She could waggle one bosom without waggling the other and sometimes she would waggle her bottom as well. The Egyptians were spellbound and kept giving her a big hand. The more they clapped the more she waggled and the more she waggled the faster the music played, and the faster the music played, the faster she waggled, faster and faster and faster, never losing the tempo, never losing the fixed brassy smile that was upon her face, and the Egyptians clapped more and more and louder and louder as the speed increased. Everyone was very happy.

When it was over William said, "Why do they always have those dreary fat women? Why don't they have beautiful women?"

The Stag said, "The Gyppies like them fat. They like them like that."

"Impossible," said Stuffy.

"It's true," Stag said. "It's an old business. It comes from the days when there used to be lots of famines here, and all the poor people were thin and all the rich people and the aristocracy were well fed and fat. If you got someone fat you couldn't go wrong; she was bound to be high-class."

"Bullshit," said Stuffy.

William said, "Well, we'll soon find out. I'm going to ask those Gyppies." He jerked his thumb towards two middle-aged Egyptians who were sitting at the next table, only about four feet away.

"No," said Stag. "No, William. We don't want them over here."

"Yes," said Stuffy.

"Yes," said William. "We've got to find out why the Gyppies like fat women."

He was not drunk. None of them was drunk, but they were happy with a fair amount of beer and whiskey, and William was the happiest. His brown schoolboy face was radiant with happiness, his turned-up nose seemed to have turned up a little more and he was probably relaxing for the first time in many weeks. He got up, took three paces over to the table of the Egyptians and stood in front of them, smiling.

"Gentlemen," he said, "my friends and I would be honored if you would join us at our table."

The Egyptians had dark greasy skin and podgy faces. They were wearing the red hats and one of them had a gold tooth. At first, when William addressed them, they looked a little alarmed. Then they caught on, looked at each other, grinned and nodded.

"Pleess," said one.

"Pleess," said the other, and they got up, shook hands with William and followed him over to where the Stag and Stuffy were sitting.

William said, "Meet my friends. This is the Stag. This is Stuffy. I am William."

The Stag and Stuffy stood up, they all shook hands, the Egyptians said "Pleess" once more and then everyone sat down.

The Stag knew that their religion forbade them to drink. "Have a coffee," he said.

The one with the gold tooth grinned broadly, raised his hands, palms upward and hunched his shoulders a little. "For me," he said, "I am accustomed. But for my frient," and he spread out his hands toward the other, "for my frient—I cannot speak."

The Stag looked at the friend. "Coffee?" he asked.

"Pleess," he answered. "I am accustomed."

"Good," said Stag. "Two coffees."

He called a waiter. "Two coffees," he said. "And, wait a minute. Stuffy, William, more beer?"

"For me," Stuffy said, "I am accustomed. But for my friend," and he turned toward William, "for my friend—I cannot speak."

William said, "Please. I am accustomed." None of them smiled.

The Stag said, "Good. Waiter, two coffees and three beers." The waiter fetched the order and the Stag paid. The Stag lifted his glass toward the Egyptians and said, "Bung ho."

"Bung ho," said Stuffy.

"Bung ho," said William.

The Egyptians seemed to understand and they lifted their coffee cups. "Pleess," said the one. "Thank you," said the other. They drank.

The Stag put down his glass and said, "It is an honor to be in your country."

"You like?"

"Yes," said the Stag. "Very fine."

The music had started again and the two fat women in silver tights were doing an encore. The encore was a knockout. It was surely the most remarkable exhibition of muscle control that has ever been witnessed; for although the bottom-waggler was still just waggling her bottom, the bosom-waggler was standing like an oak tree in the center of the stage with her arms above her head. Her left bosom she was rotating in a clockwise direction and her right bosom in an anticlockwise direction. At the same time she was waggling her bottom and it was all in time to the music. Gradually the music increased its speed, and as it got faster, the rotating and the waggling got faster and some of the Egyptians were so spellbound by the contra-rotating bosoms of the woman that they were unconsciously following the movements of the bosoms with their hands, holding their hands up in front of them and describing circles in the air. Everyone stamped their feet and screamed with delight and the two women on the stage continued to smile their fixed brassy smiles.

Then it was over. The applause gradually died down

"Remarkable," said the Stag.

"You like?"

"Please, it was remarkable."

"Those girls," said the one with the gold tooth, "very special."

William couldn't wait any longer. He leaned across the table and said, "Might I ask you a question?"

"Pleess," said Golden Tooth. "Pleess."

"Well," said William, "how do you like your women? Like this —slim?" and he demonstrated with his hands. "Or like this—fat?"

The gold tooth shone brightly behind a big grin. "For me, I like like this, fat," and a pair of podgy hands drew a big circle in the air.

"And your friend?" said William.

"For my frient," he answered, "I cannot speak."

"Pleess," said the friend. "Like this." He grinned and drew a fat girl in the air with his hands.

Stuffy said, "Why do you like them fat?"

Golden Tooth thought for a moment, then he said, "You like them slim, eh?"

"Please," said Stuffy. "I like them slim."

"Why you like them slim? You tell me."

Stuffy rubbed the back of his neck with the palm of his hand. "William," he said, "why do we like them slim?"

"For me," said William, "I am accustomed."

"So am I," Stuffy said. "But why?"

William considered. "I don't know," he said. "I don't know why we like them slim."

"Ha," said Golden Tooth, "You don't know." He leaned over the table toward William and said triumphantly, "And me, I do not know either."

But that wasn't good enough for William. "The Stag," he said, "says that all rich people in Egypt used to be fat and all poor people were thin."

"No," said Golden Tooth, "No no no. Look those girls up there. Very fat; very poor. Look queen of Egypt, Queen Farida. Very thin; very rich. Quite wrong."

"Yes, but what about years ago?" said William.

"What is this, years ago?"

William said, "Oh all right. Let's leave it.'

The Egyptians drank their coffee and made noises like the last bit of water running out of the bathtub. When they had finished, they got up to go.

"Going?" said the Stag.

"Pleess," said Golden Tooth.

William said, "Thank you." Stuffy said, "Pleess." The other Egyptian said, "Pleess," and the Stag said, "Thank you." They all shook hands and the Egyptians departed.

"Ropey types," said William.

"Very," said Stuffy. "Very ropey types."

The three of them sat on drinking happily until midnight, when the waiter came up and told them that the place was closing and that there were no more drinks. They were still not really drunk because they had been taking it slowly, but they were feeling healthy.

"He says we've got to go."

"All right. Where shall we go? Where shall we go, Stag?"

"I don't know. Where do you want to go?"

"Let's go to another place like this," said William. "This is a fine place."

There was a pause. Stuffy was stroking the back of his neck with his hand. "Stag," he said slowly, "I know where I want to go. I want to go to Madame Rosette's and I want to rescue all the girls there."

"Who's Madame Rosette?" William said.

"She's a great woman," said the Stag.

"She's a filthy old whore," said Stuffy.

"She's a lousy old bitch," said the Stag.

"All right," said William. "Let's go. But who is she?"

They told him who she was. They told him about their telephone calls and about Colonel Higgins, and William said, "Come on, let's go. Let's go and rescue all the girls."

They got up and left. When they went outside, they remembered that they were in a rather remote part of the town.

"We'll have to walk a bit," said Stag. "No gharries here."

It was a dark starry night with no moon. The street was narrow and blacked-out. It smelled strongly with the smell of Cairo. It was quiet as they walked along, and now and again they passed a man or sometimes two men standing back in the shadow of a house, leaning against the wall of the house, smoking.

"I say," said William, "ropey, what?"

"Very," said Stuffy. "Very bad types."

They walked on, the three of them walking abreast; square short ginger-haired Stag, tall dark Stuffy and tall young William who went barehead because he had lost his cap. They headed roughly toward the center of the town where they knew that they would find a gharri to take them on to Rosette.

Stuffy said, "Oh, won't the girls be pleased when we rescue them?"

"Jesus," said the Stag, "it ought to be a party."

"Does she actually keep them locked up?" William said.

"Well, no," said Stag. "Not exactly. But if we rescue them now, they won't have to work any more tonight anyway. You see, the girls she has at her place are nothing but ordinary shop girls who still work during the day in the shops. They have all of them made some mistake or other which Rosette either engineered or found out about, and now she has put the screws on them; she makes them come along in the evening. But they hate her and they do not depend on her for a living. They would kick her in the teeth if they got the chance."

Stuffy said, "We'll give them the chance."

They crossed over a street. William said, "How many girls will there be there, Stag?"

"I don't know. I suppose there might be thirty."

"Good God," said William. "This *will* be a party. Does she really treat them very badly?"

The Stag said, "Thirty-three squadron told me that she pays them nothing, about twenty akkers a night. She charges the customers a hundred or two hundred akkers each. Every girl earns for Rosette between five hundred and a thousand akkers every night."

"Good God," said William. "A thousand piastres a night and thirty girls. She must be a millionaire."

"She is. Someone calculated that not even counting her outside business, she makes the equivalent of about fifteen hundred pounds a week. That's, let me see, that's between five and six thousand pounds a month. Sixty thousand pounds a year."

Stuffy came out of his dream. "Jesus," he said, "Jesus Christ. The filthy old whore."

"The lousy old bitch," said William.

They were coming into a more civilized section of the town, but still there were no gharries.

The Stag said, "Did you hear about Mary's House?"

"What's Mary's House?" said William.

"It's a place in Alexandria. Mary is the Rosette of Alex."

"Lousy old bitch," said William.

"No," Stag said. "They say she's a good woman. But anyway, Mary's House was hit by a bomb last week. The navy was in port at the time and the place was full of sailors, nautic types."

"Killed?"

"Lots of them killed. And d'you know what happened? They posted them as killed in action."

"The Admiral is a gentleman," said Stuffy.

"Magnificent," said William.

Then they saw a gharri and hailed it.

Stuffy said, "We don't know the address."

"He'll know it," said Stag. "Madame Rosette," he said to the driver.

The driver grinned and nodded. Then William said, "I'm going to drive. Give me the reins, driver, and sit up here beside me and tell me where to go."

The driver protested vigorously, but when William gave him ten piastres, he gave him the reins. William sat high up on the driver's seat with the driver beside him. The Stag and Stuffy got in the back of the carriage.

"Take off," said Stuffy. William took off. The horses began to gallop.

"No good," shrieked the driver. "No good. Stop."

"Which way Rosette?" shouted William.

"Stop," shrieked the driver.

William was happy. "Rosette," he shouted. "Which way?"

The driver made a decision. He decided that the only way to stop this madman was to get him to his destination. "This way," he shrieked. "Left." William pulled hard on the left rein and the horses swerved around the corner. The gharri took it on one wheel.

"Too much bank," shouted Stuffy from the back seat.

"Which way now?" shouted William.

"Left," shrieked the driver. They took the next street to the left, then they took one to the right, two more to the left, then one to the right again and suddenly the driver yelled, "Here pleess, here Rosette. Stop."

William pulled hard on the reins and gradually the horses raised their heads with the pulling and slowed down to a trot.

"Where?" said William.

"Here," said the driver. "Pleess." He pointed to a house twenty yards ahead. William brought the horses to a stop right in front of it.

"Nice work, William," said Stuffy.

"Jesus," said the Stag. "That was quick."

"Marvelous," said William. "Wasn't it?" He was very happy.

The driver was sweating through his shirt and he was too frightened to be angry.

William said, "How much?"

"Pleess, twenty piastres."

William gave him forty and said, "Thank you very much. Fine horses." The little man took the money, jumped up onto the gharri and drove off. He was in a hurry to get away.

They were in another of those narrow, dark streets, but the houses, what they could see of them, looked huge and prosperous. The one which the driver had said was Rosette's was wide and thick and three stories high, built of grey concrete, and it had a large thick front door which stood wide open. As they went in, the Stag said, "Now leave this to me. I've got a plan."

Inside there was a cold grey dusty stone hall, lit by a bare electric light bulb in the ceiling, and there was a man standing in the hall. He was a mountain of a man, a huge Egyptian with a flat face and two cauliflower ears. In his wrestling days he had probably been billed as Abdul the Killer or The Poisonous Pasha, but now he wore a dirty white cotton suit.

The Stag said, "Good evening. Is Madame Rosette here?"

Abdul looked hard at the three pilots, hesitated, then said, "Madame Rosette top floor."

"Thank you," said Stag. "Thank you very much." Stuffy noticed that the Stag was being polite. There was always trouble for somebody when he was like that. Back in the squadron, when he was leading a flight, when they sighted the enemy and when there was going to be a battle, the Stag never gave an order without saying "Please" and he never received a message without saying "Thank you." He was saying "Thank you" now to Abdul.

They went up the bare stone steps which had iron railings. They went past the first landing and the second landing, and the place was as bare as a cave. At the top of the third flight of steps, there was no landing; it was walled off, and the stairs ran up to a door. The Stag pressed the bell. They waited a while, then a little panel in the door slid back and a pair of small black eyes peeked through. A woman's voice said, "What you boys want?" Both the Stag and

Stuffy recognized the voice from the telephone. The Stag said, "We would like to see Madame Rosette." He pronounced the Madame in the French way because he was being polite.

"You officers? Only officers here," said the voice. She had a voice like a broken board.

"Yes," said Stag. "We are officers."

"You don't look like officers. What kind of officers?"

"R.A.F."

There was a pause. The Stag knew that she was considering. She had probably had trouble with pilots before, and he hoped only that she would not see William and the light that was dancing in his eyes; for William was still feeling the way he had felt when he drove the gharri. Suddenly the panel closed and the door opened.

"All right, come in," she said. She was too greedy, this woman, even to pick her customers carefully.

They went in and there she was. Short, fat, greasy, with wisps of untidy black hair straggling over her forehead; a large, mud-colored face, a large wide nose and a small fish mouth, with just the trace of a black moustache above the mouth. She had on a loose black satin dress.

"Come into the office, boys," she said, and started to waddle down the passage to the left. It was a long wide passage, about fifty yards long and four or five yards wide. It ran through the middle of the house, parallel with the street, and as you came in from the stairs, you had to turn left along it. All the way down there were doors, about eight or ten of them on each side. If you turned right as you came in from the stairs, you ran into the end of the passage, but there was one door there too, and as the three of them walked in, they heard a babble of female voices from behind that door. The Stag noted that it was the girls' dressing room.

"This way, boys," said Rosette. She turned left and slopped down the passage, away from the door with the voices. The three followed her, Stag first, then Stuffy, then William, down the passage which had a red carpet on the floor and huge pink lampshades hanging from the ceiling. They got about halfway down the passage when there was a yell from the dressing room behind them. Rosette stopped and looked around.

"You go on, boys," she said, "into the office, last door on the left. I won't be a minute." She turned and went back toward the dressing-room door. They didn't go on. They stood and watched her, and just as she got to the door, it opened and a girl rushed out.

From where they stood, they could see that her fair hair was all over her face and that she had on an untidy-looking green evening dress. She saw Rosette in front of her and she stopped. They heard Rosette say something, something angry and quick spoken, and they heard the girl shout something back at her. They saw Rosette raise her right arm and they saw her hit the girl smack on the side of the face with the palm of her hand. They saw her draw back her hand and hit her again in the same place. She hit her hard. The girl put her hands up to her face and began to cry. Rosette opened the door of the dressing room and pushed her back inside.

"Jesus," said the Stag. "She's tough." William said, "So am I." Stuffy didn't say anything.

Rosette came back to them and said, "Come along, boys. Just a bit of trouble, that's all." She led them to the end of the passage and in through the last door on the left. This was the office. It was a medium-sized room with two red plush sofas, two or three red plush armchairs and a thick red carpet on the floor. In one corner was a small desk, and Rosette sat herself behind it, facing the room.

"Sit down, boys," she said.

The Stag took an armchair, Stuffy and William sat on a sofa.

"Well," she said, and her voice became sharp and urgent. "Let's do business."

The Stag leaned forward in his chair. His short ginger hair looked somehow wrong against the bright red plush. "Madame Rosette," he said, "it is a great pleasure to meet you. We have heard so much about you." Stuffy looked at the Stag. He was being polite again. Rosette look at him too, and her little black eyes were suspicious. "Believe me," the Stag went on, "we've really been looking forward to this for quite a time now."

His voice was so pleasant and he was so polite that Rosette took it.

"That's nice of you boys," she said. "You'll always have a good time here. I see to that. Now—business."

William couldn't wait any longer. He said slowly, "The Stag says that you're a great woman."

"Thanks, boys."

Stuffy said, "The Stag says that you're a filthy old whore."

William said quickly, "The Stag says that you're a lousy old bitch."

"And I know what I'm talking about," said the Stag.

Rosette jumped to her feet. "What's this?" she shrieked, and her face was no longer the color of mud; it was the color of red clay. The men did not move. They did not smile or laugh; they sat quite still, leaning forward a little in their seats, watching her.

Rosette had had trouble before, plenty of it, and she knew how to deal with it. But this was different. They didn't seem drunk, it wasn't about money and it wasn't about one of her girls. It was about herself and she didn't like it.

"Get out," she yelled. "Get out unless you want trouble." But they did not move.

For a moment she paused, then she stepped quickly from behind her desk and made for the door. But the Stag was there first and when she went for him, Stuffy and William each caught one of her arms from behind.

"We'll lock her in," said the Stag. "Let's get out."

Then she really started yelling and the words which she used cannot be written down on paper, for they were terrible words. They poured out of her small fish mouth in one long unbroken high-pitched stream, and little bits of spit and saliva came out with them. Stuffy and William pulled her back by the arms toward one of the big chairs and she fought and yelled like a large fat pig being dragged to the slaughter. They got her in front of the chair and gave her a quick push so that she fell backwards into it. Stuffy nipped across to her desk, bent down quickly and jerked the telephone cord from its connection. The Stag had the door open and all three of them were out of the room before Rosette had time to get up. The Stag had taken the key from the inside of the door, and now he locked it. The three of them stood outside in the passage.

"Jesus," said the Stag. "What a woman!"

"Mad as hell," William said. "Listen to her."

They stood outside in the passage and they listened. They heard her yelling, then she began banging on the door, but she went on yelling and her voice was not the voice of a woman, it was the voice of an enraged but articulate bull.

The Stag said, "Now quick. The girls. Follow me. And from now on you've got to act serious. You've got to act serious as hell."

He ran down the passage toward the dressing room, followed by Stuffy and William. Outside the door he stopped, the other two stopped and they could still hear Rosette yelling from her office. The Stag said, "Now don't say anything. Just act serious as hell," and he opened the door and went in.

There were about a dozen girls in the room. They all looked up.

They stopped talking and looked up at the Stag, who was standing in the doorway. The Stag clicked his heels and said, "This is the Military Police. *Les Gendarmes Militaires.*" He said it in a stern voice and with a straight face and he was standing there in the doorway at attention with his cap on his head. Stuffy and William stood behind him.

"This is the Military Police," he said again, and he produced his identification card and held it up between two fingers.

The girls didn't move or say anything. They stayed still in the middle of what they were doing and they were like a tableau because they stayed so still. One had been pulling on a stocking and she stayed like that, sitting on a chair with her leg out straight and the stocking up to her knee with her hands on the stocking. One had been doing her hair in front of a mirror and when she looked round she kept her hands up to her hair. One was standing up and had been applying lipstick and she raised her eyes to the Stag but still held the lipstick to her mouth. Several were just sitting around on plain wooden chairs, doing nothing, and they raised their heads and turned them to the door, but they went on sitting. Most of them were in some sort of shiny evening dress, one or two were half-clothed, but most of them were in shiny green or shiny blue or shiny red or shiny gold, and when they turned to look at the Stag, they were so still that they were like a tableau.

The Stag paused. Then he said, "I am to state on behalf of the authorities that they are sorry to disturb you. My apologies, mesd'moiselles. But it is necessary that you come with us for purposes of registration, et cetera. Afterwards you will be allowed to go. It is a mere formality. But now you must come, please. I have conversed with Madame."

The Stag stopped speaking, but still the girls did not move.

"Please," said the Stag, "get your coats. We are the military." He stepped aside and held open the door. Suddenly the tableau dissolved, the girls got up, puzzled and murmuring, and two or three of them moved toward the door. The others followed. The ones that were half-clothed quickly slipped into dresses, patted their hair with their hands and came too. None of them had coats.

"Count them," said the Stag to Stuffy as they filed out of the door. Stuffy counted them aloud and there were fourteen.

"Fourteen, sir," said Stuffy, who was trying to talk like a sergeant-major.

The Stag said, "Correct," and he turned to the girls who were crowded in the passage. "Now, mesd'moiselles, I have the list of your names from Madame, so please do not try to run away. And do not worry. This is merely a formality of the military."

William was out in the passage opening the door which led to the stairs, and he went out first. The girls followed and the Stag and Stuffy brought up the rear. The girls were quiet and puzzled and worried and a little frightened and they didn't talk, none of them talked except for a tall one with black hair who said, "Mon Dieu, a formality of the military. Mon Dieu, mon Dieu, what next." But that was all and they went on down. In the hall they met the Egyptian who had a flat face and two cauliflower ears. For a moment it looked as though there would be trouble. But the Stag waved his identification card in his face and said, "The Military Police," and the man was so surprised that he did nothing and let them pass.

And so they came out into the street and the Stag said, "It is necessary to walk a little way, but only a very little way," and they turned right and walked along the sidewalk with the Stag leading, Stuffy at the rear and William walking out on the road guarding the flank. There was some moon now. One could see quite well and William tried to keep in step with Stag and Stuffy tried to keep in step with William, and they swung their arms and held their heads up high and looked very military, and the whole thing was a sight to behold. Fourteen girls in shiny evening dresses, fourteen girls in the moonlight in shiny green, shiny blue, shiny red, shiny black and shiny gold, marching along the street with the Stag in front, William alongside and Stuffy at the rear. It was a sight to behold.

The girls had started chattering. The Stag could hear them, although he didn't look around. He marched on at the head of the column and when they came to the crossroads he turned right. The others followed and they had walked fifty yards down the block when they came to an Egyptian café. The Stag saw it and he saw the lights burning behind the blackout curtains. He turned around and shouted "Halt!" The girls stopped, but they went on chattering and anyone could see now that there was mutiny in the ranks. You can't make fourteen girls in high heels and shiny evening dresses march all over town with you at night, not for long anyway, not for long, even if it is a formality of the military. The Stag knew it and now he was speaking.

"Mesd'moiselles," he said, "listen to me." But there was mutiny in the ranks and they went on talking and the tall one with dark hair was saying, "Mon Dieu, what is this? What in hell's name sort of a thing is this, oh mon Dieu?"

"Quiet," said the Stag. "Quiet!" and the second time he shouted it as a command. The talking stopped.

"Mesd'moiselles," he said, and now he became polite. He talked to them in his best way and when the Stag was polite there wasn't anyone who didn't take it. It was an extraordinary thing because he could make a kind of smile with his voice without smiling with his lips. His voice smiled while his face remained serious. It was a most forcible thing because it gave people the impression that he was being serious about being nice.

"Mesd'moiselles," he said, and his voice was smiling. "With the military there always has to be formality. It is something unavoidable. It is something that I regret exceedingly. But there can be chivalry also. And you must know that with the R.A.F. there is great chivalry. So now it will be a pleasure if you will all come in here and take with us a glass of beer. It is the chivalry of the military." He stepped forward, opened the door of the café and said, "Oh for God's sake, let's have a drink. Who wants a drink?"

Suddenly the girls saw it all. They saw the whole thing as it was, all of them at once. It took them by surprise. For a second they considered. Then they looked at one another, then they looked at the Stag, then they looked around at Stuffy and at William, and when they looked at those two they caught their eyes and the laughter that was in them. All at once the girls began to laugh and William laughed and Stuffy laughed and they moved forward and poured into the café.

The tall one with dark hair took the Stag by the arm and said, "Mon Dieu, Military Police, mon Dieu, oh mon Dieu," and she threw her head back and laughed and the Stag laughed with her. William said, "It is the chivalry of the military," and they moved into the café.

The place was rather like the one that they had been in before, wooden and sawdusty, and there were a few coffee-drinking Egyptians sitting around with the red tarbooshes on their heads. William and Stuffy pushed three round tables together and fetched chairs. The girls sat down. The Egyptians at the other tables put down their coffee cups, turned around in their chairs and gaped. They gaped like so many fat muddy fish, and some of them shifted their chairs round facing the party so that they could get a better view and they went on gaping.

A waiter came up and the Stag said, "Seventeen beers. Bring us seventeen beers." The waiter said "Pleess" and went away.

As they sat waiting for the drinks the girls looked at the three pilots and the pilots looked at the girls. William said, "It is the chivalry of the military," and the tall dark girl said, "Mon Dieu, you are crazy people, oh mon Dieu."

The waiter brought the beer. William raised his glass and said, "To the chivalry of the military." The dark girl said, "Oh mon Dieu." Stuffy didn't say anything. He was busy looking around at the girls, sizing them up, trying to decide now which one he liked best so that he could go to work at once. The Stag was smiling and the girls were sitting there in their shiny evening dresses, shiny red, shiny gold, shiny blue, shiny green, shiny black and shiny silver, and once again it was almost a tableau, certainly it was a picture, and the girls were sitting there sipping their beer, seeming quite happy, not seeming suspicious any more because to them the whole thing now appeared exactly as it was and they understood.

"Jesus," said the Stag. He put down his glass and looked around him. "Oh Jesus, there's enough here for the whole squadron. How I wish the whole squadron was here!" He took another drink, stopped in the middle of it and put down his glass quickly. "I know what," he said. "Waiter, oh waiter."

"Pleess."

"Get me a big piece of paper and a pencil."

"Pleess." The waiter went away and came back with a sheet of paper. He took a pencil from behind his ear and handed it to the Stag. The Stag banged the table for silence.

"Mesd'moiselles," he said, "for the last time there is a formality. It is the last of all the formalities."

"Of the military," said William.

"Oh mon Dieu," said the dark girl.

"It is nothing," the Stag said. "You are required to write your name and your telephone number on this piece of paper. It is for my friends in the squadron. It is so that they can be as happy as I am now, but without the same trouble beforehand." The Stag's voice was smiling again. One could see that the girls liked his voice. "You would be very kind if you would do that," he went on, "for they too would like to meet you. It would be a pleasure."

"Wonderful," said William.

"Crazy," said the dark girl, but she wrote her name and number on the paper and passed it on. The Stag ordered another round of beer. The girls certainly looked funny sitting there in their dresses, but they were writing their names down on the paper. They looked happy and William particularly looked happy, but Stuffy looked serious because the problem of choosing was a weighty one and it was heavy on his mind. They were good-looking girls, young and good-looking, all different, completely different from each other because they were Greek and Syrian and French and Italian and light Egyptian and Yugoslav and many other things, but they were good-looking, all of them were good-looking and handsome.

The piece of paper had come back to the Stag now and they had all written on it; fourteen strangely written names and fourteen telephone numbers. The Stag looked at it slowly. "This will go on the squadron notice-board," he said, "and I will be regarded as a great benefactor."

William said, "It should go to headquarters. It should be mimeographed and circulated to all squadrons. It would be good for morale."

"Oh mon Dieu," said the dark girl. "You are crazy."

Slowly Stuffy got to his feet, picked up his chair, carried it round to the other side of the table and pushed it between two of the girls. All he said was, "Excuse me. Do you mind if I sit here?" At last he had made up his mind, and now he turned toward the one on his right and quietly went to work. She was very pretty; very dark and very pretty and she had plenty of shape. Stuffy began to talk to her, completely oblivious to the rest of the company, turning toward her and leaning his head on his hand. Watching him, it was not so difficult to understand why he was the greatest pilot in the squadron. He was a young concentrator, this Stuffy; an intense athletic concentrator who moved toward what he wanted in a dead straight line. He took hold of winding roads and carefully he made them straight, then he moved over them with great speed and nothing stopped him. He was like that, and now he was talking to the pretty girl but no one could hear what he was saying.

Meanwhile the Stag was thinking. He was thinking about the next move, and when everyone was getting toward the end of their third beer, he banged the table again for silence.

"Mesd'moiselles," he said, "it will be a pleasure for us to escort you home. I will take five of you,"—he had worked it all out— "Stuffy will take five, and Jamface will take four. We will take three gharries and I will take five of you in mine and I will drop you home one at a time."

William said, "It is the chivalry of the military."

"Stuffy," said the Stag. "Stuffy, is that all right? You take five. It's up to you whom you drop off last."

Stuffy looked around. "Yes," he said. "Oh yes. That suits me."

"William, you take four. Drop them home one by one; you understand."

"Perfectly," said William. "Oh perfectly."

They all got up and moved toward the door. The tall one with dark hair took the Stag's arm and said, "You take me?"

"Yes," he answered. "I take you."

'You drop me off last?"

'Yes. I drop you off last."

"Oh mon Dieu," she said. "That will be fine."

Outside they got three gharries and they split up into parties. Stuffy was moving quickly. He got his girls into the carriage quickly, climbed in after them and the Stag saw the gharry drive off down the street. Then he saw William's gharry move off, but it seemed to start away with a sudden jerk, with the horses breaking into a gallop at once. The Stag looked again and he saw William perched high up on the driver's seat with the reins in his hands.

The Stag said, "Let's go," and his five girls got into their gharry. It was a squash, but everyone got in. The Stag sat back in his seat and then he felt an arm pushing up and under and linking with his. It was the tall one with dark hair. He turned and looked at her.

"Hello," he said. "Hello, you."

"Ah," she whispered. "You are such goddam crazy people." And the Stag felt a warmness inside him and he began to hum a little tune as the gharry rattled on through the dark streets.

Man from the South

1948

IT was getting on toward six o'clock so I thought I'd buy myself a beer and go out and sit in a deck chair by the swimming pool and have a little evening sun.

I went to the bar and got the beer and carried it outside and wandered down the garden toward the pool.

It was a fine garden with lawns and beds of azaleas and tall coconut palms, and the wind was blowing strongly through the tops of the palm trees making the leaves hiss and crackle as though they were on fire. I could see the clusters of big brown nuts hanging down underneath the leaves.

There were plenty of deck chairs around the swimming pool and there were white tables and huge brightly colored umbrellas and sunburned men and women sitting around in bathing suits. In the pool itself there were three or four girls and about a dozen boys, all splashing about and making a lot of noise and throwing a large rubber ball at one another.

I stood watching them. The girls were English girls from the hotel. The boys I didn't know about, but they sounded American and I thought they were probably naval cadets who'd come ashore from the U.S. naval training vessel which had arrived in harbor that morning.

I went over and sat down under a yellow umbrella where there were four empty seats, and I poured my beer and settled back comfortably with a cigarette.

It was very pleasant sitting there in the sunshine with beer and cigarette. It was pleasant to sit and watch the bathers splashing about in the green water.

The American sailors were getting on nicely with the English girls. They'd reached the stage where they were diving under the water and tipping them up by their legs.

Just then I noticed a small, oldish man walking briskly around the edge of the pool. He was immaculately dressed in a white suit and he walked very quickly with little bouncing strides, pushing himself high up onto his toes with each step. He had on a large creamy Panama hat, and he came bouncing along the side of the pool, looking at the people and the chairs.

He stopped beside me and smiled, showing two rows of very small, uneven teeth, slightly tarnished. I smiled back.

"Excuse pleess, but may I sit here?"

"Certainly," I said. "Go ahead."

He bobbed around to the back of the chair and inspected it for safety, then he sat down and crossed his legs. His white buckskin shoes had little holes punched all over them for ventilation.

"A fine evening," he said. "They are all evenings fine here in Jamaica." I couldn't tell if the accent was Italian or Spanish, but I felt fairly sure he was some sort of a South American. And old too, when you saw him close. Probably around sixty-eight or seventy.

"Yes," I said. "It is wonderful here, isn't it?"

"And who, might I ask, are all dese? Dese is no hotel people." He was pointing at the bathers in the pool.

"I think they're American sailors," I told him. "They're Americans who are learning to be sailors."

"Of course dey are Americans. Who else in de world is going to make as much noise at dat? You are not American, no?"

"No," I said. "I am not."

Suddenly one of the American cadets was standing in front of us. He was dripping wet from the pool and one of the English girls was standing there with him.

"Are these chairs taken?" he said.

"No," I answered.

"Mind if I sit down?"

"Go ahead."

"Thanks," he said. He had a towel in his hand and when he sat down he unrolled it and produced a pack of cigarettes and a lighter. He offered the cigarettes to the girl and she refused; then he offered them to me and I took one. The little man said, "Tank you, no, but I tink I have a cigar." He pulled out a crocodile case and got himself a cigar, then he produced a knife which had a small scissors in it and he snipped the end off the cigar.

"Here, let me give you a light." The American boy held up his lighter.

"Dat will not work in dis wind."

"Sure, it'll work. It always works."

The little man removed his unlighted cigar from his mouth, cocked his head on one side and looked at the boy.

"*All*-ways?" he said slowly.

"Sure, it never fails. Not with me anyway."

The little man's head was still cocked over on one side and he was still watching the boy. "Well, well. So you say dis famous lighter it never fails. Iss dat you say?"

"Sure," the boy said. "That's right." He was about nineteen or twenty with a long freckled face and a rather sharp birdlike nose. His chest was not very sunburned and there were freckles there too, and a few wisps of pale-reddish hair. He was holding the lighter in his right hand, ready to flip the wheel. "It never fails," he said, smiling now because he was purposely exaggerating his little boast. "I promise you it never fails."

"One momint, pleess." The hand that held the cigar came up high, palm outward, as though it were stopping traffic. "Now juss one momint." He had a curiously soft, toneless voice and he kept looking at the boy all the time.

"Shall we not perhaps make a little bet on dat?" He smiled at the boy. "Shall we not make a little bet on whether your lighter lights?"

"Sure, I'll bet," the boy said. "Why not?"

"You like to bet?"

"Sure, I'll always bet."

The man paused and examined his cigar, and I must say I didn't much like the way he was behaving. It seemed he was already trying to make something out of this, and to embarrass the boy, and at the same time I had the feeling he was relishing a private little secret all his own.

He looked up again at the boy and said slowly, "I like to bet, too. Why we don't have a good bet on dis ting? A good big bet."

"Now wait a minute," the boy said. "I can't do that. But I'll bet you a quarter. I'll even bet you a dollar, or whatever it is over here —some shillings, I guess."

The little man waved his hand again. "Listen to me. Now we have some fun. We make a bet. Den we go up to my room here in de hotel where iss no wind and I bet you you cannot light dis famous lighter of yours ten times running without missing once."

"I'll bet I can," the boy said.

"All right. Good. We make a bet, yes?"

"Sure. I'll bet you a buck."

"No, no. I make you very good bet. I am rich man and I am sporting man also. Listen to me. Outside de hotel iss my car. Iss very fine car. American car from your country. Cadillac—"

"Hey, now. Wait a minute." The boy leaned back in his deck chair and he laughed. "I can't put up that sort of property. This is crazy."

"Not crazy at all. You strike lighter successfully ten times running and Cadillac is yours. You like to have dis Cadillac, yes?"

"Sure, I'd like to have a Cadillac." The boy was still grinning.

"All right. Fine. We make a bet and I put up my Cadillac."

"And what do I put up?"

The little man carefully removed the red band from his still unlighted cigar. "I never ask you, my friend, to bet something you cannot afford. You understand?"

"Then what do I bet?"

"I make it very easy for you, yes?"

"Okay. You make it easy."

"Some small ting you can afford to give away, and if you did happen to lose it you would not feel too bad. Right?"

"Such as what?"

"Such as, perhaps, de little finger of your left hand."

"My *what!*" The boy stopped grinning.

"Yes. Why not? You win, you take de car. You looss, I take de finger."

"I don't get it. How d'you mean, you take the finger?"

"I chop it off."

"Jumping jeepers! That's a crazy bet. I think I'll just make it a dollar."

The little man leaned back, spread out his hands palms upward and gave a tiny contemptuous shrug of the shoulders. "Well, well, well," he said. "I do not understand. You say it lights but you will not bet. Den we forget it, yes?"

The boy sat quite still, staring at the bathers in the pool. Then he remembered suddenly he hadn't lighted his cigarette. He put it between his lips, cupped his hands around the lighter and flipped the wheel. The wick lighted and burned with a small, steady, yellow flame and the way he held his hands the wind didn't get to it at all.

"Could I have a light, too?" I said.

"Gee, I'm sorry. I forgot you didn't have one."

I held out my hand for the lighter, but he stood up and came over to do it for me.

"Thank you," I said, and he returned to his seat.

"You having a good time?" I asked.

"Fine," he answered. "It's pretty nice here."

There was a silence then, and I could see that the little man had succeeded in disturbing the boy with his absurd proposal. He was sitting there very still, and it was obvious that a small tension was beginning to build up inside him. Then he started shifting about in his seat, and rubbing his chest, and stroking the back of his neck, and finally he placed both hands on his knees and began tap-tapping with his fingers against the knee-caps. Soon he was tapping with one of his feet as well.

"Now just let me check up on this bet of yours," he said at last. "You say we go up to your room and if I make this lighter light ten times running I win a Cadillac. If it misses just once then I forfeit the little finger of my left hand. Is that right?"

"Certainly. Dat is de bet. But I think you are afraid."

"What do we do if I lose? Do I have to hold my finger out while you chop it off?"

"Oh, no! Dat would be no good. And you might be tempted to refuse to hold it out. What I should do I should tie one of your hands to de table before we started and I should stand dere with a knife ready to go *chop* de momint your lighter missed."

"What year is the Cadillac?" the boy asked.

"Excuse. I not understand."

"What year—how old is the Cadillac?"

"Ah! How old? Yes. It is last year. Quite new car. But I see you are not betting man. Americans never are."

The boy paused for just a moment and he glanced first at the English girl, then at me. "Yes," he said sharply. "I'll bet you."

"Good!" The little man clapped his hands together quietly, once. "Fine," he said. "We do it now. And you, sir," he turned to me, "you would perhaps be good enough to, what you call it, to— to referee." He had pale, almost colorless eyes with tiny bright black pupils.

"Well," I said. "I think it's a crazy bet. I don't think I like it very much."

"Nor do I," said the English girl. It was the first time she'd spoken. "I think it's a stupid, ridiculous bet."

"Are you serious about cutting off this boy's finger if he loses?" I said.

"Certainly I am. Also about giving him Cadillac if he win. Come now. We go to my room."

He stood up. "You like to put on some clothes first?" he said.

"No," the boy answered. "I'll come like this." Then he turned to me. "I'd consider it a favor if you'd come along and referee."

"All right," I said. "I'll come along, but I don't like the bet."

"You come too," he said to the girl. "You come and watch."

The little man led the way back through the garden to the hotel. He was animated now, and excited, and that seemed to make him bounce up higher than ever on his toes as he walked along.

"I live in annex," he said. "You like to see car first? Iss just here."

He took us to where we could see the front driveway of the hotel and he stopped and pointed to a sleek pale-green Cadillac parked close by.

"Dere she iss. De green one. You like?"

"Say, that's a nice car," the boy said.

"All right. Now we go up and see if you can win her."

We followed him into the annex and up one flight of stairs. He unlocked his door and we all trooped into what was a large pleasant double bedroom. There was a woman's dressing gown lying across the bottom of one of the beds.

"First," he said, "we 'ave a little Martini."

The drinks were on a small table in the far corner, all ready to be mixed, and there was a shaker and ice and plenty of glasses. He began to make the Martini, but meanwhile he'd rung the bell and now there was a knock on the door and a coloured maid came in.

"Ah!" he said, putting down the bottle of gin, taking a wallet from his pocket and pulling out a pound note. "You will do something for me now, pleess." He gave the maid the pound.

"You keep dat," he said. "And now we are going to play a little game in here and I want you to go off and find for me two—no tree tings. I want some nails; I want a hammer, and I want a chopping knife, a butcher's chopping knife which you can borrow from de kitchen. You can get, yes?"

"A *chopping knife!*" The maid opened her eyes wide and clasped her hands in front of her. "You mean a *real* chopping knife?"

"Yes, yes, of course. Come on now, pleess. You can find dose tings surely for me."

"Yes, sir, I'll try, sir. Surely I'll try to get them." And she went.

The little man handed round the Martinis. We stood there and sipped them, the boy with the long freckled face and the pointed nose, bare-bodied except for a pair of faded brown bathing shorts; the English girl, a large-boned, fair-haired girl wearing a pale blue bathing suit, who watched the boy over the top of her glass all the time; the little man with the colourless eyes standing there in his immaculate white suit drinking his Martini and looking at the girl in her pale blue bathing dress. I didn't know what to make of it all. The man seemed serious about the bet and he seemed serious about the business of cutting off the finger. But hell, what if the boy lost? Then we'd have to rush him to the hospital in the Cadillac that he hadn't won. That would be a fine thing. Now wouldn't that be a really fine thing? It would be a damn silly unnecessary thing so far as I could see.

"Don't you think this is rather a silly bet?" I said.

"I think it's a fine bet," the boy answered. He had already downed one large Martini.

"I think it's a stupid, ridiculous bet," the girl said. "What'll happen if you lose?"

"It won't matter. Come to think of it, I can't remember ever in my life having had any use for the little finger on my left hand. Here he is." The boy took hold of the finger. "Here he is and he hasn't ever done a thing for me yet. So why shouldn't I bet him. I think it's a fine bet."

The little man smiled and picked up the shaker and refilled our glasses.

"Before we begin," he said, "I will present to de—to de referee de key of de car." He produced a car key from his pocket and gave it to me. "De papers," he said, "de owning papers and insurance are in de pocket of de car."

Then the colored maid came in again. In one hand she carried a small chopper, the kind used by butchers for chopping meat bones, and in the other a hammer and a bag of nails.

"Good! You get dem all. Tank you, tank you. Now you can go." He waited until the maid had closed the door, then he put the implements on one of the beds and said, "Now we prepare ourselves, yes?" And to the boy, "Help me, pleess, with dis table. We carry it out a little."

It was the usual kind of hotel writing desk, just a plain rectangular table about four feet by three with a blotting pad, ink, pens and paper. They carried it out into the room away from the wall, and removed the writing things.

"And now," he said, "a chair." He picked up a chair and placed it beside the table. He was very brisk and very animated, like a person organizing games at a children's party. "And now de nails. I must put in de nails." He fetched the nails and he began to hammer them into the top of the table.

We stood there, the boy, the girl, and I, holding Martinis in our hands, watching the little man at work. We watched him hammer two nails into the table, about six inches apart. He didn't hammer them right home; he allowed a small part of each one to stick up. Then he tested them for firmness with his fingers.

Anyone would think the son of a bitch had done this before, I told myself. He never hesitates. Table, nails, hammer, kitchen chopper. He knows exactly what he needs and how to arrange it.

"And now," he said, "all we want is some string." He found some string. "All right, at last we are ready. Will you pleess to sit here at de table," he said to the boy.

The boy put his glass away and sat down.

"Now place de left hand between dese two nails. De nails are only so I can tie your hand in place. All right, good. Now I tie your hand secure to de table—so."

He wound the string around the boy's wrist, then several times around the wide part of the hand, then he fastened it tight to the nails. He made a good job of it and when he'd finished there wasn't any question about the boy being able to draw his hand away But he could move his fingers.

"Now pleess, clench de fist, all except for de little finger. You must leave de little finger out, lying on de table.

"*Ex*-cellent! *Ex*-cellent! Now we are ready. Wid your right hand you manipulate de lighter. But one momint, pleess."

He skipped over to the bed and picked up the chopper. He came back and stood beside the table with the chopper in his hand.

"We are all ready?" he said. "Mister referee, you must say to begin."

The English girl was standing there in her pale blue bathing costume right behind the boy's chair. She was just standing there, not saying anything. The boy was sitting quite still, holding the lighter in his right hand, looking at the chopper. The little man was looking at me.

"Are you ready?" I asked the boy.

"I'm ready."

"And you?" to the little man.

"Quite ready," he said and he lifted the chopper up in the air and held it there about two feet above the boy's finger, ready to chop. The boy watched it, but he didn't flinch and his mouth didn't move at all. He merely raised his eyebrows and frowned.

"All right," I said. "Go ahead."

The boy said, "Will you please count aloud the number of times I light it."

"Yes," I said. "I'll do that."

With his thumb he raised the top of the lighter, and again with the thumb he gave the wheel a sharp flick. The flint sparked and the wick caught fire and burned with a small yellow flame.

"One!" I called.

He didn't blow the flame out; he closed the top of the lighter on it and he waited for perhaps five seconds before opening it again.

He flicked the wheel very strongly and once more there was a small flame burning on the wick.

"Two!"

No one else said anything. The boy kept his eyes on the lighter. The little man held the chopper up in the air and he too was watching the lighter.

"Three!"

"Four!"

"Five!"

"Six!"

"Seven!" Obviously it was one of those lighters that worked. The flint gave a big spark and the wick was the right length. I watched the thumb snapping the top down onto the flame. Then a pause. Then the thumb raising the top once more. This was an all-thumb operation. The thumb did everything. I took a breath, ready to say eight. The thumb flicked the wheel. The flint sparked. The little flame appeared.

"Eight!" I said, and as I said it the door opened. We all turned and we saw a woman standing in the doorway, a small, black-haired woman, rather old, who stood there for about two seconds then rushed forward shouting, "Carlos! Carlos!" She grabbed his wrist, took the chopper from him, threw it on the bed, took hold of the little man by the lapels of his white suit and began shaking him very vigorously, talking to him fast and loud and fiercely all the time in some Spanish-sounding language. She shook him so fast you couldn't see him any more. He became a faint, misty, quickly moving outline, like the spokes of a turning wheel.

Then she sloved down and the little man came into view again and she hauled him across the room and pushed him backward onto one of the beds. He sat on the edge of it blinking his eyes and testing his head to see if it would still turn on his neck.

"I am so sorry," the woman said. "I am so terribly sorry that this should happen." She spoke almost perfect English.

"It is too bad," she went on. "I suppose it is really my fault. For ten minutes I leave him alone to go and have my hair washed and I come back and he is at it again." She looked sorry and deeply concerned.

The boy was untying his hand from the table. The English girl and I stood there and said nothing.

"He is a menace," the woman said. "Down where we live at home he has taken altogether forty-seven fingers from different people, and he has lost eleven cars. In the end they threatened to have him put away somewhere. That's why I brought him up here."

"We were only having a little bet," mumbled the little man from the bed.

"I suppose he bet you a car," the woman said.

"Yes," the boy answered. "A Cadillac."

"He has no car. It's mine. And that makes it worse," she said, "that he should bet you when he has nothing to bet with. I am ashamed and very sorry about it all." She seemed an awfully nice woman.

"Well," I said, "then here's the key of your car." I put it on the table.

"We were only having a little bet," mumbled the little man.

"He hasn't anything left to bet with," the woman said. "He hasn't a thing in the world. Not a thing. As a matter of fact I myself won it all from him a long while ago. It took time, a lot of time, and it was hard work, but I won it all in the end." She looked up at the boy and she smiled, a slow sad smile, and she came over and put out a hand to take the key from the table.

I can see it now, that hand of hers; it had only one finger on it, and a thumb.

The Sound Machine

1949

It was a warm summer evening and Klausner walked quickly through the front gate and around the side of the house and into the garden at the back. He went on down the garden until he came to a wooden shed and he unlocked the door, went inside and closed the door behind him.

The interior of the shed was an unpainted room. Against one wall, on the left, there was a long wooden workbench, and on it, among a littering of wires and batteries and small sharp tools, there stood a black box about three feet long, the shape of a child's coffin.

Klausner moved across the room to the box. The top of the box was open, and he bent down and began to poke and peer inside it among a mass of different-coloured wires and silver tubes. He picked up a piece of paper that lay beside the box, studied it carefully, put it down, peered inside the box and started running his fingers along the wires, tugging gently at them to test the connections, glancing back at the paper, then into the box, then at the paper again, checking each wire. He did this for perhaps an hour.

Then he put a hand around to the front of the box where there were three dials, and he began to twiddle them, watching at the same time the movement of the mechanism inside the box. All the while he kept speaking softly to himself, nodding his head, smiling sometimes, his hands always moving, the fingers moving swiftly, deftly, inside the box, his mouth twisting into curious shapes when a thing was delicate or difficult to do, saying, "Yes . . . Yes. . . . And now this one . . . Yes. . . . Yes . . . But is this right? Is it—where's my diagram?. . . . Ah, yes . . . Of course . . . Yes, yes . . . That's right . . . And now . . . Good. . . . Good. . . . Yes . . . Yes, yes, yes." His concentration was intense; his movements were quick; there was an air of urgency about the way he worked, of breathlessness, of strong suppressed excitement.

Suddenly he heard footsteps on the gravel path outside and he straightened and turned swiftly as the door opened and a tall man came in. It was Scott. It was only Scott, the doctor.

"Well, well, well," the Doctor said. "So this is where you hide yourself in the evenings."

"Hullo, Scott," Klausner said.

"I happened to be passing," the Doctor told him, "so I dropped in to see how you were. There was no one in the house, so I came on down here. How's that throat of yours been behaving?"

"It's all right. It's fine."

"Now I'm here I might as well have a look at it."

"Please don't trouble. I'm quite cured. I'm fine."

The Doctor began to feel the tension in the room. He looked at the black box on the bench; then he looked at the man. "You've got your hat on," he said.

"Oh, have I?" Klausner reached up, removed the hat and put it on the bench.

The Doctor came up closer and bent down to look into the box. "What's this?" he said. "Making a radio?"

"No. Just fooling around."

"It's got rather complicated-looking innards."

"Yes." Klausner seemed tense and distracted.

"What is it?" the Doctor asked. "It's rather a frightening-looking thing, isn't it?"

"It's just an idea."

"Yes?"

"It has to do with sound, that's all."

"Good heavens, man! Don't you get enough of that sort of thing all day in your work?"

"I like sound."

"So it seems." The Doctor went to the door, turned, and said, "Well, I won't disturb you. Glad your throat's not worrying you any more." But he kept standing there, looking at the box, intrigued by the remarkable complexity of its inside, curious to know what this strange patient of his was up to. "What's it really for?" he asked. "You've made me inquisitive."

Klausner looked down at the box, then at the Doctor, and he reached up and began gently to scratch the lobe of his right ear. There was a pause. The Doctor stood by the door, waiting, smiling.

"All right, I'll tell you, if you're interested." There was another pause, and the Doctor could see that Klausner was having trouble about how to begin.

He was shifting from one foot to the other, tugging at the lobe of his ear, looking at his feet, and then at last, slowly, he said, "Well, it's like this . . . the theory is very simple, really. The human ear . . . You know that it can't hear everything. There are sounds that are so low-pitched or so high-pitched that it can't hear them."

"Yes," the Doctor said. "Yes."

"Well, speaking very roughly, any note so high that it has more than fifteen thousand vibrations a second—we can't hear it. Dogs have better ears than us. You know you can buy a whistle whose note is so high-pitched that you can't hear it at all. But a dog can hear it."

"Yes, I've seen one," the Doctor said.

"Of course you have. And up the scale, higher than the note of that whistle, there is another note—a vibration if you like, but I prefer to think of it as a note. You can't hear that one either. And above that there is another and another rising right up the scale for ever and ever and ever, an endless succession of notes . . . an infinity of notes . . . there is a note—if only ours ears could hear it—so high that it vibrates a million times a second . . . and another a million times as high as that . . . and on and on, higher and higher, as far as numbers go, which is . . . infinity . . . eternity . . . beyond the stars."

Klausner was becoming more animated every moment. He was a small frail man, nervous and twitchy, with always moving hands. His large head inclined toward his left shoulder as though his neck were not quite strong enough to support it rigidly. His face was smooth and pale, almost white, and the pale grey eyes that blinked and peered from behind a pair of steel spectacles were bewildered, unfocussed, remote. He was a frail, nervous, twitchy little man, a moth of a man, dreamy and distracted; suddenly fluttering and animated; and now the Doctor, looking at that strange pale face and those pale grey eyes, felt that somehow there was about this little person a quality of distance, of immense, immeasurable distance, as though the mind were far away from where the body was.

The Doctor waited for him to go on. Klausner sighed and clasped his hands tightly together. "I believe," he said, speaking more slowly now, "that there is a whole world of sound about us all the time that we cannot hear. It is possible that up there in those high-pitched inaudible regions there is a new exciting music being made, with subtle harmonies and fierce grinding discords, a music so powerful that it would drive us mad if only our ears were tuned to hear the sound of it. There may be anything . . . for all we know there may—"

"Yes," the Doctor said. "But it's not very probable."

"Why not? Why not?" Klausner pointed to a fly sitting on a small roll of copper wire on the workbench. "You see that fly? What sort of a noise is that fly making now? None—that one can hear. But for all we know the creature may be whistling like mad on a very high note, or barking or croaking or singing a song. It's got a mouth, hasn't it? It's got a throat!"

The Doctor looked at the fly and he smiled. He was still standing by the door with his hand on the doorknob. "Well," he said. "So you're going to check up on that?"

"Some time ago," Klausner said, "I made a simple instrument that proved to me the existence of many odd inaudible sounds. Often I have sat and watched the needle of my instrument recording the presence of sound vibrations in the air when I myself could hear nothing. And *those* are the sounds I want to listen to. I want to know where they come from and who or what is making them."

"And that machine on the table there," the Doctor said, "is that going to allow you to hear these noises?"

"It may. Who knows? So far, I've had no luck. But I've made some changes in it and tonight I'm ready for another trial. This machine," he said, touching it with his hands, "is designed to pick up sound vibrations that are too high-pitched for reception by the human ear, and to convert them to a scale of audible tones. I tune it in, almost like a radio."

"How d'you mean?"

"It isn't complicated. Say I wish to listen to the squeak of a bat. That's a fairly high-pitched sound—about thirty thousand vibrations a second. The average human ear can't quite hear it. Now, if there were a bat flying around this room and I tuned in to thirty thousand on my machine, I would hear the squeaking of that bat very clearly. I would even hear the correct note—F sharp, or B flat, or whatever it might be—but merely at a much *lower pitch*. Don't you understand?"

The Doctor looked at the long black coffin-box. "And you're going to try it tonight?"

"Yes."

"Well, I wish you luck." He glanced at his watch. "My goodness!" he said. "I must fly. Goodbye, and thank you for telling me. I must call again sometime and find out what happened." The Doctor went out and closed the door behind him.

For a while longer, Klausner fussed about with the wires in the black box; then he straightened up and in a soft excited whisper said,

"Now we'll try again . . . We'll take it out into the garden this time
. . . and then perhaps . . . perhaps . . . the reception will be better.
Lift it up now . . . carefully. . . . Oh, my God, it's heavy!" He carried
the box to the door, found that he couldn't open the door without
putting it down, carried it back, put it on the bench, opened the
door, and then carried it with some difficulty into the garden. He
placed the box carefully on a small wooden table that stood on the
lawn. He returned to the shed and fetched a pair of earphones. He
plugged the wire connections from the earphones into the machine
and put the earphones over his ears. The movements of his hands
were quick and precise. He was excited, and breathed loudly and
quickly through his mouth. He kept on talking to himself with little
words of comfort and encouragement, as though he were afraid—
afraid that the machine might not work and afraid also of what might
happen if it did.

He stood there in the garden beside the wooden table, so pale,
small, and thin that he looked like an ancient, consumptive, bespec-
tacled child. The sun had gone down. There was no wind, no sound
at all. From where he stood, he could see over a low fence into the
next garden, and there was a woman walking down the garden with
a flower basket on her arm. He watched her for a while without
thinking about her at all. Then he turned to the box on the table and
pressed a switch on its front. He put his left hand on the volume
control and his right hand on the knob that moved a needle across
a large central dial, like the wave-length dial of a radio. The dial was
marked with many numbers, in a series of bands, starting at 15,000
and going on up to 1,000,000.

And now he was bending forward over the machine. His head
was cocked to one side in a tense listening attitude. His right hand
was beginning to turn the knob. The needle was travelling slowly
across the dial, so slowly he could hardly see it move, and in the
earphones he could hear a faint, spasmodic crackling.

Behind this crackling sound he could hear a distant humming
tone which was the noise of the machine itself, but that was all. As
he listened, he became conscious of a curious sensation, a feeling that
his ears were stretching out away from his head, that each ear was
connected to his head by a thin stiff wire, like a tentacle, and that
the wires were lengthening, that the ears were going up and up
toward a secret and forbidden territory, a dangerous ultrasonic region where ears had never been before and had no right to be.

The little needle crept slowly across the dial, and suddenly he heard a shriek, a frightful piercing shriek, and he jumped and dropped his hands, catching hold of the edge of the table. He stared around him as if expecting to see the person who had shrieked. There was no one in sight except the woman in the garden next door, and it was certainly not she. She was bending down, cutting yellow roses and putting them in her basket.

Again it came—a throatless, inhuman shriek, sharp and short, very clear and cold. The note itself possessed a minor, metallic quality that he had never heard before. Klausner looked around him, searching instinctively for the source of the noise. The woman next door was the only living thing in sight. He saw her reach down, take a rose stem in the fingers of one hand and snip the stem with a pair of scissors. Again he heard the scream.

It came at the exact moment when the rose stem was cut.

At this point, the woman straightened up, put the scissors in the basket with the roses and turned to walk away.

"Mrs. Saunders!" Klausner shouted, his voice shrill with excitement. "Oh, Mrs. Saunders!"

And looking round, the woman saw her neighbor standing on his lawn—a fantastic, arm-waving little person with a pair of earphones on his head—calling to her in a voice so high and loud that she became alarmed.

"Cut another one! Please cut another one quickly!"

She stood still, staring at him. "Why, Mr. Klausner," she said, "what's the matter?"

"Please do as I ask," he said. "Cut just one more rose!"

Mrs. Saunders had always believed her neighbor to be a rather peculiar person; now it seemed that he had gone completely crazy. She wondered whether she should run into the house and fetch her husband. No, she thought. No, he's harmless. I'll just humor him. "Certainly, Mr. Klausner, if you like," she said. She took her scissors from the basket, bent down and snipped another rose.

Again Klausner heard that frightful, throatless shriek in the earphones; again it came at the exact moment the rose stem was cut. He took off the earphones and ran to the fence that separated the two gardens. "All right," he said. "That's enough. No more. Please, no more."

The woman stood there, a yellow rose in one hand, clippers in the other, looking at him.

"I'm going to tell you something, Mrs. Saunders," he said, "something that you won't believe." He put his hands on top of the fence and peered at her intently through his thick spectacles. "You have, this evening, cut a basketful of roses. You have with a sharp pair of scissors cut through the stems of living things, and each rose that you cut screamed in the most terrible way. Did you know that, Mrs. Saunders?"

"No," she said. "I certainly didn't know that."

"It happens to be true," he said. He was breathing rather rapidly, but he was trying to control his excitement. "I heard them shrieking. Each time you cut one, I heard the cry of pain. A very high-pitched sound, approximately one hundred and thirty-two thousand vibrations a second. You couldn't possibly have heard it yourself. But *I* heard it."

"Did you really, Mr. Klausner?" She decided she would make a dash for the house in about five seconds.

"You might say," he went on, "that a rosebush has no nervous system to feel with, no throat to cry with. You'd be right. It hasn't. Not like ours, anyway. But *how do you know, Mrs. Saunders*"—and here he leaned far over the fence and spoke in a fierce whisper—*"how do you know* that a rosebush doesn't feel as much pain when someone cuts its stem in two as you would feel if someone cut your wrist off with a garden shears? *How do you know that?* It's *alive,* isn't it?"

"Yes, Mr. Klausner. Oh yes—and good night." Quickly she turned and ran up the garden to her house. Klausner went back to the table. He put on the earphones and stood for a while listening. He could still hear the faint crackling sound and the humming noise of the machine, but nothing more. He bent down and took hold of a small white daisy growing on the lawn. He took it between thumb and forefinger and slowly pulled it upward and sideways until the stem broke.

From the moment that he started pulling to the moment when the stem broke, he heard—he distinctly heard in the earphones—a faint high-pitched cry, curiously inanimate. He took another daisy and did it again. Once more he heard the cry, but he wasn't so sure now that it expressed *pain.* No, it wasn't pain; it was surprise. Or was it? It didn't really express any of the feelings or emotions known to a human being. It was just a cry, a neutral, stony cry—a single emotionless note, expressing nothing. It had been the same with the roses. He had been wrong in calling it a cry of pain. A flower probably didn't feel pain. It felt something else which we didn't know about—something called toin or spurl or plinuckment, or anything you like.

He stood up and removed the earphones. It was getting dark and he could see pricks of light shining in the windows of the houses all around him. Carefully he picked up the black box from the table, carried it into the shed and put it on the workbench. Then he went out, locked the door behind him and walked up to the house.

The next morning Klausner was up as soon as it was light. He dressed and went straight to the shed. He picked up the machine and carried it outside, clasping it to his chest with both hands, walking unsteadily under its weight. He went past the house, out through the front gate, and across the road to the park. There he paused and looked around him; then he went on until he came to a large tree, a beech tree, and he placed the machine on the ground close to the trunk of the tree. Quickly he went back to the house and got an axe from the coal cellar and carried it across the road into the park. He put the axe on the ground beside the tree.

Then he looked around him again, peering nervously through his thick glasses in every direction. There was no one about. It was six in the morning.

He put the earphones on his head and switched on the machine. He listened for a moment to the faint familiar humming sound; then he picked up the axe, took a stance with his legs wide apart and swung the axe as hard as he could at the base of the tree trunk. The blade cut deep into the wood and stuck there, and at the instant of impact he heard a most extraordinary noise in the earphones. It was a new noise, unlike any he had heard before—a harsh, noteless, enormous noise, a growling, low-pitched, screaming sound, not quick and short like the noise of the roses, but drawn out like a sob, lasting for fully a minute, loudest at the moment when the axe struck, fading gradually fainter and fainter until it was gone.

Klausner stared in horror at the place where the blade of the axe had sunk into the woodflesh of the tree; then gently he took the axe handle, worked the blade loose and threw the thing on the ground. With his fingers he touched the gash that the axe had made in the wood, touching the edges of the gash, trying to press them together to close the wound, and he kept saying, "Tree . . . oh tree . . . I am sorry . . . I am so sorry . . . but it will heal . . . it will heal fine . . ."

For a while he stood there with his hands upon the trunk of the great tree; then suddenly he turned away and hurried off out of the park, across the road, through the front gate and back into his house. He went to the telephone, consulted the book, dialed a number and waited. He held the receiver tightly in his left hand and tapped the table impatiently with his right. He heard the telephone buzzing at the other end, and then the click of a lifted receiver and a man's voice, a sleepy voice, saying: "Hullo. Yes."

"Dr. Scott?" he said.

"Yes. Speaking."

"Dr. Scott. You must come at once—quickly please."

"Who is it speaking?"

"Klausner here, and you remember what I told you last night about my experience with sound, and how I hoped I might—"

"Yes, yes, of course, but what's the matter? Are you ill?"

"No, I'm not ill, but—"

"It's half past six in the morning," the Doctor said, "and you call me, but you are not ill."

"Please come. Come quickly. I want someone to hear it. It's driving me mad! I can't believe it . . ."

The Doctor heard the frantic, almost hysterical note in the man's voice, the same note he was used to hearing in the voices of people who called up and said, "There's been an accident. Come quickly." He said slowly, "You really want me to get out of bed and come over now?"

"Yes now. At once please."

"All right then, I'll come."

Klausner sat down beside the telephone and waited. He tried to remember what the shriek of the tree had sounded like, but he couldn't. He could remember only that it had been enormous and frightful and that it had made him feel sick with horror. He tried to imagine what sort of noise a human would make if he had to stand anchored to the ground while someone deliberately swung a small sharp thing at his leg so that the blade cut in deep and wedged itself in the cut. Same sort of noise perhaps? No. Quite different. The noise of the tree was worse than any known human noise because of that frightening, toneless, throatless quality. He began to wonder about other living things, and he thought immediately of a field of wheat, a field of wheat standing up straight and yellow and alive, with the mower going through it, cutting the stems, five hundred stems a second, every second. Oh, my God, what would *that* noise be like? Five hundred wheat plants screaming together, and every second another five hundred being cut and screaming and—no, he thought, I do not want to go to a wheat field with my machine. I would never eat bread after that. But what about potatoes and cabbages and carrots and onions? And what about apples? Ah, no.

Apples are all right. They fall off naturally when they are ripe. Apples are all right if you let them fall off instead of tearing them from the tree branch. But not vegetables. Not a potato for example. A potato would surely shriek; so would a carrot and an onion and a cabbage. . . .

He heard the click of the front-gate latch and he jumped up and went out and saw the tall doctor coming down the patch, little black bag in hand.

"Well," the Doctor said. "Well, what's all the trouble?"

"Come with me, Doctor. I want you to hear it. I called you because you're the only one I've told. It's over the road in the park. Will you come now?"

The Doctor looked at him. He seemed calmer now. There was no sign of madness or hysteria; he was merely disturbed and excited.

They went across the road into the park and Klausner led the way to the great beech tree at the foot of which stood the long black coffin-box of the machine—and the axe.

"Why did you bring it out here?" the Doctor asked.

"I wanted a tree. There aren't any big trees in the garden."

"And why the axe?"

"You'll see in a moment. But now please put on these earphones and listen. Listen carefully and tell me afterwards precisely what you hear. I want to make quite sure . . ."

The Doctor smiled and took the earphones and put them over his ears.

Klausner bent down and flicked the switch on the panel of the machine; then he picked up the axe and took his stance with his legs apart, ready to swing. For a moment he paused. "Can you hear anything?" he said to the Doctor.

"Can I what?"

"Can you *hear* anything?"

"Just a humming noise."

Klausner stood there with the axe in his hands trying to bring himself to swing, but the thought of the noise that the tree would make made him pause again.

"What are you waiting for?" the Doctor asked.

"Nothing," Klausner answered, and then he lifted the axe and swung it at the tree; and as he swung, he thought he felt, he could swear he felt a movement of the ground on which he stood. He felt a slight shifting of the earth beneath his feet as though the roots of the tree were moving underneath the soil, but it was too late to check the blow and the axe blade struck the tree and wedged deep into the wood. At that moment, high overhead, there was the cracking sound of wood splintering and the swishing sound of leaves brushing against other leaves and they both looked up and the Doctor cried, "Watch out! Run, man! Quickly run!"

The Doctor had ripped off the earphones and was running away fast, but Klausner stood spellbound, staring up at the great branch, sixty feet long at least, that was bending slowly downward, breaking and crackling and splintering at its thickest point, where it joined the main trunk of the tree. The branch came crashing down and Klausner leapt aside just in time. It fell upon the machine and smashed it into pieces.

"Great heavens!" shouted the Doctor as he came running back. "That was a near one! I thought it had got you!"

Klausner was staring at the tree. His large head was leaning to one side and upon his smooth white face there was a tense, horrified expression. Slowly he walked up to the tree and gently he prized the blade loose from the trunk.

"Did you hear it?" he said, turning to the Doctor. His voice was barely audible.

The Doctor was still out of breath from the running and the excitement. "Hear what?"

"In the earphones. Did you hear anything when the axe struck?"

The Doctor began to rub the back of his neck. "Well," he said, "as a matter of fact . . ." He paused and frowned and bit his lower lip. "No, I'm not sure. I couldn't be sure. I don't suppose I had the earphones on for more than a second after the axe struck."

"Yes yes, but what did you hear?"

"I don't know," the Doctor said. "I don't know what I heard. Probably the noise of the branch breaking." He was speaking rapidly, rather irritably.

"What did it sound like?" Klausner leaned forward slightly, staring hard at the Doctor. *"Exactly* what did it sound like?"

"Oh hell!" the Doctor said. "I really don't know. I was more interested in getting out of the way. Let's leave it."

"Dr. Scott, *what-did-it-sound-like?"*

"For God's sake, how could I tell, what with half the tree falling on me and having to run for my life?" The Doctor certainly seemed nervous. Klausner had sensed it now. He stood quite still, staring at the Doctor, and for fully half a minute he didn't speak. The Doctor moved his feet, shrugged his shoulders and half turned to go. "Well," he said, "We'd better get back."

"Look," said the little man, and now his smooth white face became suddenly suffused with color. "Look," he said, "you stitch this up." He pointed to the last gash that the axe had made in the tree trunk. "You stitch this up quickly."

"Don't be silly," the Doctor said.

"You do as I say. Stitch it up." Klausner was gripping the axe handle and he spoke softly, in a curious, almost a threatening tone.

"Don't be silly," the Doctor said. "I can't stitch through wood. Come on. Let's get back."

"So you can't stitch through wood?"

"No, of course not."

"Have you got any iodine in your bag?"

"What if I have?"

"Then paint the cut with iodine. It'll sting, but that can't be helped."

"Now look," the Doctor said, and again he turned as if to go. "Let's not be ridiculous. Let's get back to the house and then . . ."

"Paint-the-cut-with-iodine."

The Doctor hesitated. He saw Klausner's hands tightening on the handle of the axe. He decided that his only alternative was to run away fast, and he certainly wasn't going to do that.

"All right," he said. "I'll paint it with iodine."

He got his black bag which was lying on the grass about ten yards away, opened it and took out a bottle of iodine and some cotton wool. He went up to the tree trunk, uncorked the bottle, tipped some of the iodine onto the cotton wool, bent down and began to dab it into the cut. He kept one eye on Klausner who was standing motionless with the axe in his hands, watching him.

"Make sure you get it right in."

"Yes," the Doctor said.

"Now do the other one, the one just above it!"

The Doctor did as he was told.

"There you are," he said. "It's done."

He straightened up and surveyed his work in a very serious manner. "That should do nicely."

Klausner came closer and gravely examined the two wounds.

"Yes," he said, nodding his huge head slowly up and down. "Yes, that will do nicely." He stepped back a pace. "You'll come and look at them again tomorrow?"

"Oh yes," the Doctor said. "Of course."

"And put some more iodine on?"

"If necessary, yes."

"Thank you, Doctor," Klausner said, and he nodded his head again and he dropped the axe and all at once he smiled, a wild excited smile, and quickly the Doctor went over to him and gently he took him by the arm and he said, "Come on, we must go now," and suddenly they were walking away, the two of them, walking silently, rather hurriedly across the park, over the road, back to the house.

Taste

1951

THERE were six of us to dinner that night at Mike Schofield's house in London: Mike and his wife and daughter, my wife and I, and a man called Richard Pratt.

Richard Pratt was a famous gourmet. He was president of a small society known as the Epicures, and each month he circulated privately to its members a pamphlet on food and wines. He organized dinners where sumptuous dishes and rare wines were served. He refused to smoke for fear of harming his palate, and when discussing a wine, he had a curious, rather droll habit of referring to it as though it were a living being. "A prudent wine," he would say, "rather diffident and evasive, but quite prudent." Or, "a good-humoured wine, benevolent and cheerful—slightly obscene, perhaps, but nonetheless good-humoured."

I had been to dinner at Mike's twice before when Richard Pratt was there, and on each occasion Mike and his wife had gone out of their way to produce a special meal for the famous gourmet. And this one, clearly, was to be no exception. The moment we entered the dining room, I could see that the table was laid for a feast. The tall candles, the yellow roses, the quantity of shining silver, the three wineglasses to each person, and above all, the faint scent of roasting meat from the kitchen brought the first warm oozings of saliva to my mouth.

As we sat down, I remembered that on both Richard Pratt's previous visits Mike had played a little betting game with him over the claret, challenging him to name its breed and its vintage. Pratt had replied that that should not be too difficult provided it was one of the great years. Mike had then bet him a case of the wine in question that he could not do it. Pratt had accepted, and had won both times. Tonight I felt sure that the little game would be played over again, for Mike was quite willing to lose the bet in order to prove that his wine was good enough to be recognized, and Pratt, for his part, seemed to take a grave, restrained pleasure in displaying his knowledge.

The meal began with a plate of whitebait, fried very crisp in butter, and to go with it there was a Moselle. Mike got up and poured the wine himself, and when he sat down again, I could see that he was watching Richard Pratt. He had set the bottle in front of me so that I could read the label. It said, "Geierslay Ohligsberg, 1945." He leaned over and whispered to me that Geierslay was a tiny village in the Moselle, almost unknown outside Germany. He said that this wine we were drinking was something unusual, that the output of the vineyard was so small that it was almost impossible for a stranger to get any of it. He had visited Geierslay personally the previous summer in order to obtain the few dozen bottles that they had finally allowed him to have.

"I doubt anyone else in the country has any of it at the moment," he said. I saw him glance again at Richard Pratt. "Great thing about Moselle," he continued, raising his voice, "it's the perfect wine to serve before a claret. A lot of people serve a Rhine wine instead, but that's because they don't know any better. A Rhine wine will kill a delicate claret, you know that? It's barbaric to serve a Rhine before a claret. But a Moselle—ah!—a Moselle is exactly right."

Mike Schofield was an amiable, middle-aged man. But he was a stock-broker. To be precise, he was a jobber in the stock market, and like a number of his kind, he seemed to be somewhat embarrassed, almost ashamed to find that he had made so much money with so slight a talent. In his heart he knew that he was not really much more than a bookmaker—an unctuous, infinitely respectable, secretly unscrupulous bookmaker—and he knew that his friends knew it, too. So he was seeking now to become a man of culture, to cultivate a literary and aesthetic taste, to collect paintings, music, books, and all the rest of it. His little sermon about Rhine wine and Moselle was a part of this thing, this culture that he sought.

"A charming little wine, don't you think?" he said. He was still watching Richard Pratt. I could see him give a rapid furtive glance down the table each time he dropped his head to take a mouthful of whitebait. I could almost *feel* him waiting for the moment when Pratt would take his first sip, and look up from his glass with a smile of pleasure, of astonishment, perhaps even of wonder, and then there would be a discussion and Mike would tell him about the village of Geierslay.

But Richard Pratt did not taste his wine. He was completely engrossed in conversation with Mike's eighteen-year-old daughter, Louise. He was half turned toward her, smiling at her, telling her, so far as I could gather, some story about a chef in a Paris restaurant. As he spoke, he leaned closer and closer to her, seeming in his eagerness almost to impinge upon her, and the poor girl leaned as far as she could away from him, nodding politely, rather desperately, and looking not at his face but at the topmost button of his dinner jacket.

We finished our fish, and the maid came around removing the plates. When she came to Pratt, she saw that he had not yet touched his food, so she hesitated, and Pratt noticed her. Her waved her away, broke off his conversation, and quickly began to eat, popping the little crisp brown fish quickly into his mouth with rapid jabbing movements of his fork. Then, when he had finished, he reached for his glass, and in two short swallows he tipped the wine down his throat and turned immediately to resume his conversation with Louise Schofield.

Mike saw it all. I was conscious of him sitting there, very still, containing himself, looking at his guest. His round jovial face seemed to loosen slightly and to sag, but he contained himself and was still and said nothing.

Soon the maid came forward with the second course. This was a large roast of beef. She placed it on the table in front of Mike who stood up and carved it, cutting the slices very thin, laying them gently on the plates for the maid to take around. When he had served everyone, including himself, he put down the carving knife and leaned forward with both hands on the edge of the table.

"Now," he said, speaking to all of us but looking at Richard Pratt. "Now for the claret. I must go and fetch the claret, if you'll excuse me."

"You go and fetch it, Mike?" I said. "Where is it?"

"In my study, with the cork out—breathing."

"Why the study?"

"Acquiring room temperature, of course. It's been there twenty-four hours."

"But why the study?"

"It's the best place in the house. Richard helped me choose it last time he was here."

At the sound of his name, Pratt looked around.

"That's right, isn't it?" Mike said.

"Yes," Pratt answered, nodding gravely. "That's right."

"On top of the green filing cabinet in my study," Mike said. "That's the place we chose. A good draft-free spot in a room with an even temperature. Excuse me now, will you, while I fetch it."

The thought of another wine to play with had restored his humor, and he hurried out the door, to return a minute later more slowly, walking softly, holding in both hands a wine basket in which a dark bottle lay. The label was out of sight, facing downward. "Now!" he cried as he came toward the table. "What about this one, Richard? You'll never name this one!"

Richard Pratt turned slowly and looked up at Mike; then his eyes travelled down to the bottle nestling in its small wicker basket, and he raised his eyebrows, a slight, supercilious arching of the brows, and with it a pushing outward of the wet lower lip, suddenly imperious and ugly.

"You'll never get it," Mike said. "Not in a hundred years."

"A claret?" Richard Pratt asked, condescending.

"Of course."

"I assume, then, that it's from one of the smaller vineyards?"

"Maybe it is, Richard. And then again, maybe it isn't."

"But it's a good year? One of the great years?"

"Yes, I guarantee that."

"Then it shouldn't be too difficult," Richard Pratt said, drawling his words, looking exceedingly bored. Except that, to me, there was something strange about his drawling and his boredom: between the eyes a shadow of something evil, and in his bearing an intentness that gave me a faint sense of uneasiness as I watched him.

"This one is really rather difficult," Mike said, "I won't force you to bet on this one."

"Indeed. And why not?" Again the slow arching of the brows, the cool, intent look.

"Because it's difficult."

"That's not very complimentary to me, you know."

"My dear man," Mike said, "I'll bet you with pleasure, if that's what you wish."

"It shouldn't be too hard to name it."

"You mean you want to bet?"

"I'm perfectly willing to bet," Richard Pratt said.

"All right, then, we'll have the usual. A case of the wine itself."

"You don't think I'll be able to name it, do you?"

"As a matter of fact, and with all due respect, I don't," Mike said. He was making some effort to remain polite, but Pratt was not bothering overmuch to conceal his contempt for the whole proceeding. And yet, curiously, his next question seemed to betray a certain interest.

"You like to increase the bet?"

"No, Richard. A case is plenty."

"Would you like to bet fifty cases?"

"That would be silly."

Mike stood very still behind his chair at the head of the table, carefully holding the bottle in its ridiculous wicker basket. There was a trace of whiteness around his nostrils now, and his mouth was shut very tight.

Pratt was lolling back in his chair, looking up at him, the eyebrows raised, the eyes half closed, a little smile touching the corners of his lips. And again I saw, or thought I saw, something distinctly disturbing about the man's face, that shadow of intentness between the eyes, and in the eyes themselves, right in their centers where it was black, a small slow spark of shrewdness, hiding.

"So you don't want to increase the bet?"

"As far as I'm concerned, old man, I don't give a damn," Mike said. "I'll bet you anything you like."

The three women and I sat quietly, watching the two men. Mike's wife was becoming annoyed; her mouth had gone sour and I felt that at any moment she was going to interrupt. Our roast beef lay before us on our plates, slowly steaming.

"So you'll bet me anything I like?"

"That's what I told you. I'll bet you anything you damn well please, if you want to make an issue out of it."

"Even ten thousand pounds?"

"Certainly I will, if that's the way you want it." Mike was more confident now. He knew quite well that he could call any sum Pratt cared to mention.

"So you say I can name the bet?" Pratt asked again.

"That's what I said."

There was a pause while Pratt looked slowly around the table, first at me, then at the three women, each in turn. He appeared to be reminding us that we were witness to the offer.

"Mike!" Mrs. Schofield said. "Mike, why don't we stop this nonsense and eat our food. It's getting cold."

"But it isn't nonsense," Pratt told her evenly. "We're making a little bet."

I noticed the maid standing in the background holding a dish of vegetables, wondering whether to come forward with them or not.

"All right, then," Pratt said. "I'll tell you what I want you to bet."

"Come on, then," Mike said, rather reckless. "I don't give a damn what it is—you're on."

Pratt nodded, and again the little smile moved the corners of his lips, and then, quite slowly, looking at Mike all the time, he said, "I want you to bet me the hand of your daughter in marriage."

Louise Schofield gave a jump. "Hey!" she cried. "No! That's not funny! Look here, Daddy, that's not funny at all."

"No, dear," her mother said. "They're only joking."

"I'm not joking," Richard Pratt said.

"It's ridiculous," Mike said. He was off balance again now.

"You said you'd bet anything I liked."

"I meant money."

"You didn't *say* money."

"That's what I meant."

"Then it's a pity you didn't say it. But anyway, if you wish to go back on your offer, that's quite all right with me."

"It's not a question of going back on my offer, old man. It's a no-bet anyway, because you can't match the stake. You yourself don't happen to have a daughter to put up against mine in case you lose. And if you had, I wouldn't want to marry her."

"I'm glad of that, dear," his wife said.

"I'll put up anything you like," Pratt announced. "My house, for example. How about my house?"

"Which one?" Mike asked, joking now.

"The country one."

"Why not the other one as well?"

"All right then, if you wish it. Both my houses."

At that point I saw Mike pause. He took a step forward and placed the bottle in its basket gently down on the table. He moved the saltcellar to one side, then the pepper, and then he picked up his knife, studied the blade thoughtfully for a moment, and put it down again. His daughter, too, had seen him pause.

"Now, Daddy!" she cried. "Don't be *absurd!* It's *too* silly for words. I refuse to be betted on like this."

"Quite right, dear," her mother said. "Stop it at once, Mike, and sit down and eat your food."

Mike ignored her. He looked over at his daughter and he

smiled, a slow, fatherly, protective smile. But in his eyes, suddenly, there glimmered a little triumph. "You know," he said, smiling as he spoke. "You know, Louise, we ought to think about this a bit."

"Now, stop it, Daddy! I refuse even to listen to you! Why, I've never heard anything so ridiculous in my life!"

"No, seriously, my dear. Just wait a moment and hear what I have to say."

"But I don't *want* to hear it."

"Louise! Please! It's like this. Richard here, has offered us a serious bet. He is the one who wants to make it, not me. And if he loses, he will have to hand over a considerable amount of property. Now, wait a minute, my dear, don't interrupt. The point is this. *He cannot possibly win.*"

"He seems to think he can."

"Now listen to me, because I know what I'm talking about. The expert, when tasting a claret—so long as it is not one of the famous great wines like Lafite or Latour—can only get a certain way toward naming the vineyard. He can, of course, tell you the Bordeaux district from which the wine comes, whether it is from St. Emilion, Pomerol, Graves, or Médoc. But then each district has several communes, little counties, and each county has many, many small vineyards. It is impossible for a man to differentiate between them all by taste and smell alone. I don't mind telling you that this one I've got here is a wine from a small vineyard that is surrounded by many other small vineyards, and he'll never get it. It's impossible."

"You can't be sure of that," his daughter said.

"I'm telling you I can. Though I say it myself, I understand quite a bit about this wine business, you know. And anyway, heavens alive, girl, I'm your father and you don't think I'd let you in for—for something you didn't want, do you? I'm trying to make you some money."

"Mike!" his wife said sharply. "Stop it now, Mike, please!"

Again he ignored her. "If you will take this bet," he said to his daughter, "in ten minutes you will be the owner of two large houses."

"But I don't want two large houses, Daddy."

"Then sell them. Sell them back to him on the spot. I'll arrange all that for you. And then, just think of it, my dear, you'll be rich! You'll be independent for the rest of your life!"

"Oh, Daddy, I don't like it. I think it's silly."

"So do I," the mother said. She jerked her head briskly up and down as she spoke, like a hen. "You ought to be ashamed of yourself, Michael, ever suggesting such a thing! Your own daughter, too!"

Mike didn't even look at her. "Take it!" he said eagerly, staring hard at the girl. "Take it, quick! I'll guarantee you won't lose."

"But I don't like it, Daddy."

"Come on, girl. Take it!"

Mike was pushing her hard. He was leaning toward her, fixing her with two hard bright eyes, and it was not easy for the daughter to resist him.

"But what if I lose?"

"I keep telling you, you can't lose. I'll guarantee it."

"Oh, Daddy, must I?"

"I'm making you a fortune. So come on now. What do you say, Louise? All right?"

For the last time, she hesitated. Then she gave a helpless little shrug of the shoulders and said, "Oh, all right, then. Just so long as you swear there's no danger of losing."

"Good!" Mike cried. "That's fine! Then it's a bet!"

"Yes," Richard Pratt said, looking at the girl. "It's a bet."

Immediately, Mike picked up the wine, tipped the first thimbleful into his own glass, then skipped excitedly around the table filling up the others. Now everyone was watching Richard Pratt, watching his face as he reached slowly for his glass with his right hand and lifted it to his nose. The man was about fifty years old and he did not have a pleasant face. Somehow, it was all mouth—mouth and lips —the full, wet lips of the professional gourmet, the lower lip hanging downward in the center, a pendulous, permanently open taster's lip, shaped open to receive the rim of a glass or a morsel of food. Like a keyhole, I thought, watching it; his mouth is like a large wet keyhole.

Slowly he lifted the glass to his nose. The point of the nose entered the glass and moved over the surface of the wine, delicately sniffing. He swirled the wine gently around in the glass to receive the bouquet. His concentration was intense. He had closed his eyes, and now the whole top half of his body, the head and neck and chest, seemed to become a kind of huge sensitive smelling-machine, receiving, filtering, analysing the message from the sniffing nose.

Mike, I noticed, was lounging in his chair, apparently unconcerned, but he was watching every move. Mrs. Schofield, the wife, sat prim and upright at the other end of the table, looking straight ahead, her face tight with disapproval. The daughter, Louise, had shifted her chair away a little, and sidewise, facing the gourmet, and she, like her father, was watching closely.

For at least a minute, the smelling process continued; then, without opening his eyes or moving his head, Pratt lowered the glass to his mouth and tipped in almost half the contents. He paused, his mouth full of wine, getting the first taste; then he permitted some of it to trickle down his throat and I saw his Adam's apple move as it passed by. But most of it he retained in his mouth. And now, without swallowing again, he drew in through his lips a thin breath of air which mingled with the fumes of the wine in the mouth and passed on down into his lungs. He held the breath, blew it out through his nose, and finally began to roll the wine around under the tongue, and chewed it, actually chewed it with his teeth as though it were bread.

It was a solemn, impressive performance, and I must say he did it well.

"Um," he said, putting down the glass, running a pink tongue over his lips. "Um—yes. A very interesting little wine—gentle and gracious, almost feminine in the aftertaste."

There was an excess of saliva in his mouth, and as he spoke he spat an occasional bright speck of it onto the table.

"Now we can start to eliminate," he said. "You will pardon me for doing this carefully, but there is much at stake. Normally I would perhaps take a bit of a chance, leaping forward quickly and landing right in the middle of the vineyard of my choice. But this time—I must move cautiously this time, must I not?" He looked up at Mike and he smiled, a thick-lipped, wet-lipped smile. Mike did not smile back.

"First, then, which district in Bordeaux does this wine come from? That is not too difficult to guess. It is far too light in the body to be from either St. Emilion or Graves. It is obviously a Médoc. There's no doubt about *that*.

"Now—from which commune in Médoc does it come? That also, by elimination, should not be too difficult to decide. Margaux? No. It cannot be Margaux. It has not the violent bouquet of a Margaux. Pauillac? It cannot be Pauillac, either. It is too tender, too gentle and wistful for a Pauillac. The wine of Pauillac has a character that is almost imperious in its taste. And also, to me, a Pauillac contains just a little pith, a curious, dusty, pithy flavor that the grape acquires from the soil of the district. No, no. This—this is a very gentle wine, demure and bashful in the first taste, emerging shyly but quite graciously in the second. A little arch, perhaps, in the second taste, and a little naughty also, teasing the tongue with a trace, just a trace, of tannin. Then, in the aftertaste, delightful—consoling and feminine, with a certain blithely generous quality that one associates only with the wines of the commune of St. Julien. Unmistakably this is a St. Julien."

He leaned back in his chair, held his hands up level with his chest, and placed the fingertips carefully together. He was becoming ridiculously pompous, but I thought that some of it was deliberate, simply to mock his host. I found myself waiting rather tensely for him to go on. The girl Louise was lighting a cigarette. Pratt heard the match strike and he turned on her, flaring suddenly with real anger. "Please!" he said. "Please don't do that! It's a disgusting habit, to smoke at table!"

She looked up at him, still holding the burning match in one hand, the big slow eyes settling on his face, resting there a moment, moving away again, slow and contemptuous. She bent her head and blew out the match, but continued to hold the unlighted cigarette in her fingers.

"I'm sorry, my dear," Pratt said, "but I simply cannot have smoking at table."

She didn't look at him again.

"Now, let me see—where were we?" he said. "Ah, yes. This wine is from Bordeaux, from the commune of St. Julien, in the district of Médoc. So far, so good. But now we come to the more difficult part—the name of the vineyard itself. For in St. Julien there are many vineyards, and as our host so rightly remarked earlier on, there is often not much difference between the wine of one and the wine of another. But we shall see."

He paused again, closing his eyes. "I am trying to establish the 'growth,' " he said. "If I can do that, it will be half the battle. Now, let me see. This wine is obviously not from a first-growth vineyard —nor even a second. It is not a great wine. The quality, the—the —what do you call it?—the radiance, the power, is lacking. But a third growth—that it could be. And yet I doubt it. We know it is a good year—our host has said so—and this is probably flattering it a little bit. I must be careful. I must be very careful here."

He picked up his glass and took another small sip.

"Yes," he said, sucking his lips, "I was right. It is a fourth growth. Now I am sure of it. A fourth growth from a very good year —from a great year, in fact. And that's what made it taste for a moment like a third—or even a second-growth wine. Good! That's better! Now we are closing in! What are the fourth-growth vineyards in the commune of St. Julien?"

Again he paused, took up his glass, and held the rim against that sagging, pendulous lower lip of his. Then I saw the tongue shoot out, pink and narrow, the tip of it dipping into the wine, withdrawing swiftly again—a repulsive sight. When he lowered the glass, his eyes remained closed, the face concentrated, only the lips moving, sliding over each other like two pieces of wet, spongy rubber.

"There it is again!" he cried. "Tannin in the middle taste, and the quick astringent squeeze upon the tongue. Yes, yes, of course! Now I have it! This wine comes from one of those small vineyards around Beychevelle. I remember now. The Beychevelle district, and the river and the little harbor that has silted up so the wine ships can no longer use it. Beychevelle . . . could it actually be a Beychevelle itself? No, I don't think so. Not quite. But it is somewhere very close. Château Talbot? Could it be Talbot? Yes, it could. Wait one moment."

He sipped the wine again, and out of the side of my eye I noticed Mike Schofield and how he was leaning farther and farther forward over the table, his mouth slightly open, his small eyes fixed upon Richard Pratt.

"No. I was wrong. It was not a Talbot. A Talbot comes forward to you just a little quicker than this one; the fruit is nearer to the surface. If it is a '34, which I believe it is, then it couldn't be Talbot. Well, well. Let me think. It is not a Beychevelle and it is not a Talbot, and yet—yet it is so close to both of them, so close, that the vineyard must be almost in between. Now, which could that be?"

He hesitated, and we waited, watching his face. Everyone, even Mike's wife, was watching him now. I heard the maid put down the dish of vegetables on the sideboard behind me, gently, so as not to disturb the silence.

"Ah!" he cried. "I have it! Yes, I think I have it!"

For the last time, he sipped the wine. Then, still holding the glass up near his mouth, he turned to Mike and he smiled, a slow, silky smile, and he said, "You know what this is? This is the little Château Branaire-Ducru."

Mike sat tight, not moving.

"And the year, 1934."

We all looked at Mike, waiting for him to turn the bottle around in its basket and show the label.

"Is that your final answer?" Mike said

"Yes, I think so."

"Well, is it or isn't it?"

"Yes, it is."

"What was the name again?"

"Château Branaire-Ducru. Pretty little vineyard. Lovely old château. Know it quite well. Can't think why I didn't recognize it at once."

"Come on, Daddy," the girl said. "Turn it round and let's have a peek. I want my two houses."

"Just a minute," Mike said. "Wait just a minute." He was sitting very quiet, bewildered-looking, and his face was becoming puffy and pale, as though all the force was draining slowly out of him.

"Michael!" his wife called sharply from the other end of the table. "What's the matter?"

"Keep out of this, Margaret, will you please."

Richard Pratt was looking at Mike, smiling with his mouth, his eyes small and bright. Mike was not looking at anyone.

"Daddy!" the daughter cried, agonized. "But, Daddy, you don't mean to say he's guessed it right!"

"Now, stop worrying, my dear," Mike said. "There's nothing to worry about."

I think it was more to get away from his family than anything else that Mike then turned to Richard Pratt and said, "I'll tell you what, Richard. I think you and I better slip off into the next room and have a little chat?"

"I don't want a little chat," Pratt said. "All I want is to see the label on that bottle." He knew he was a winner now; he had the bearing, the quiet arrogance of a winner, and I could see that he was prepared to become thoroughly nasty if there was any trouble. "What are you waiting for?" he said to Mike. "Go on and turn it round."

Then this happened: The maid, the tiny, erect figure of the maid in her white-and-black uniform, was standing beside Richard Pratt, holding something out in her hand. "I believe these are yours, sir," she said.

Pratt glanced around, saw the pair of thin horn-rimmed spectacles that she held out to him, and for a moment he hesitated. "Are they? Perhaps they are. I don't know."

"Yes sir, they're yours." The maid was an elderly woman—nearer seventy than sixty—a faithful family retainer of many years' standing. She put the spectacles down on the table beside him.

Without thanking her, Pratt took them up and slipped them into his top pocket, behind the white handkerchief.

But the maid didn't go away. She remained standing beside and slightly behind Richard Pratt, and there was something so unusual in her manner and in the way she stood there, small, motionless, and erect, that I for one found myself watching her with a sudden apprehension. Her old gray face had a frosty, determined look, the lips were compressed, the little chin was out, and the hands were clasped together tight before her. The curious cap on her head and the flash of white down the front of her uniform made her seem like some tiny, ruffled, white-breasted bird.

"You left them in Mr. Scofield's study," she said. Her voice was unnaturally, deliberately polite. "On top of the green filing cabinet in his study, sir, when you happened to go in there by yourself before dinner."

It took a few moments for the full meaning of her words to penetrate, and in the silence that followed I became aware of Mike and how he was slowly drawing himself up in his chair, and the color coming to his face, and the eyes opening wide, and the curl of the mouth, and the dangerous little patch of whiteness beginning to spread around the area of the nostrils.

"Now, Michael!" his wife said. "Keep calm now, Michael, dear! Keep calm!"

Dip in the Pool

1952

On the morning of the third day, the sea calmed. Even the most delicate passengers—those who had not been seen around the ship since sailing time—emerged from their cabins and crept up onto the sun deck where the deck steward gave them chairs and tucked rugs around their legs and left them lying in rows, their faces upturned to the pale, almost heatless January sun.

It had been moderately rough the first two days, and this sudden calm and the sense of comfort that it brought created a more genial atmosphere over the whole ship. By the time evening came, the passengers, with twelve hours of good weather behind them, were beginning to feel confident, and at eight o'clock that night the main dining room was filled with people eating and drinking with the assured, complacent air of seasoned sailors.

The meal was not half over when the passengers became aware, by a slight friction between their bodies and the seats of their chairs, that the big ship had actually started rolling again. It was very gentle at first, just a slow, lazy leaning to one side, then to the other, but it was enough to cause a subtle, immediate change of mood over the whole room. A few of the passengers glanced up from their food, hesitating, waiting, almost listening for the next roll, smiling nervously, little secret glimmers of apprehension in their eyes. Some were completely unruffled, some were openly smug, a number of the smug ones making jokes about food and weather in order to torture the few who were beginning to suffer. The movement of the ship then became rapidly more and more violent, and only five or six minutes after the first roll had been noticed, she was swinging heavily from side to side, the passengers bracing themselves in their chairs, leaning against the pull as in a car cornering.

At last the really bad roll came, and Mr. William Botibol, sitting at the purser's table, saw his plate of poached turbot with hollandaise sauce sliding suddenly away from under his fork. There was a flutter of excitement, everybody reaching for plates and wineglasses. Mrs. Renshaw, seated at the purser's right, gave a little scream and clutched that gentleman's arm.

"Going to be a dirty night," the purser said, looking at Mrs. Renshaw. "I think it's blowing up for a very dirty night." There was just the faintest suggestion of relish in the way he said it.

A steward came hurrying up and sprinkled water on the tablecloth between the plates. The excitement subsided. Most of the passengers continued with their meal. A small number, including Mrs. Renshaw, got carefully to their feet and threaded their ways with a kind of concealed haste between the tables and through the doorway.

"Well," the purser said, "there she goes." He glanced around with approval at the remainder of his flock who were sitting quiet, looking complacent, their faces reflecting openly that extraordinary pride that travellers seem to take in being recognized as "good sailors."

When the eating was finished and the coffee had been served, Mr. Botibol, who had been unusually grave and thoughtful since the rolling started, suddenly stood up and carried his cup of coffee around to Mrs. Renshaw's vacant place, next to the purser. He seated himself in her chair, then immediately leaned over and began to whisper urgently in the purser's ear. "Excuse me," he said, "but could you tell me something please?"

The purser, small and fat and red, bent forward to listen. "What's the trouble, Mr. Botibol?"

"What I want to know is this." The man's face was anxious and the purser was watching it. "What I want to know is will the captain already have made his estimate on the day's run—you know, for the auction pool? I mean before it began to get rough like this?"

The purser, who had prepared himself to receive a personal confidence, smiled and leaned back in his seat to relax his full belly. "I should say so—yes," he answered. He didn't bother to whisper his reply, although automatically he lowered his voice, as one does when answering a whisperer.

"About how long ago do you think he did it?"

"Some time this afternoon. He usually does it in the afternoon."

"About what time?"

"Oh, I don't know. Around four o'clock I should guess."

"Now tell me another thing. How does the captain decide

which number it shall be? Does he take a lot of trouble over that?"

The purser looked at the anxious frowning face of Mr. Botibol and he smiled, knowing quite well what the man was driving at. "Well, you see, the captain has a little conference with the navigating officer, and they study the weather and a lot of other things, and then they make their estimate."

Mr. Botibol nodded, pondering this answer for a moment. Then he said, "Do you think the captain knew there was bad weather coming today?"

"I couldn't tell you," the purser replied. He was looking into the small black eyes of the other man, seeing the two single little sparks of excitement dancing in their centers. "I really couldn't tell you, Mr. Botibol. I wouldn't know."

"If this gets any worse it might be worth buying some of the low numbers. What do you think?" The whispering was more urgent, more anxious now.

"Perhaps it will," the purser said. "I doubt the old man allowed for a really rough night. It was pretty calm this afternoon when he made his estimate."

The others at the table had become silent and were trying to hear, watching the purser with that intent, half-cocked, listening look that you can see also at the race track when they are trying to overhear a trainer talking about his chance: the slightly open lips, the upstretched eyebrows, the head forward and cocked a little to one side—that desperately straining, half-hypnotized, listening look that comes to all of them when they are hearing something straight from the horse's mouth.

"Now suppose *you* were allowed to buy a number, which one would *you* choose today?" Mr. Botibol whispered.

"I don't know what the range is yet," the purser patiently answered. "They don't announce the range till the auction starts after dinner. And I'm really not very good at it anyway. I'm only the purser, you know."

At that point Mr. Botibol stood up. "Excuse me, all," he said, and he walked carefully away over the swaying floor between the other tables, and twice he had to catch hold of the back of a chair to steady himself against the ship's roll.

"The sun deck, please," he said to the elevator man.

The wind caught him full in the face as he stepped out onto the open deck. He staggered and grabbed hold of the rail and held on tight with both hands, and he stood there looking out over the darkening sea where the great waves were welling up high and white horses were riding against the wind with plumes of spray behind them as they went.

"Pretty bad out there, wasn't it, sir?" the elevator man said on the way down.

Mr. Botibol was combing his hair back into place with a small red comb. "Do you think we've slackened speed at all on account of the weather?" he asked.

"Oh my word yes, sir. We slacked off considerable since this started. You got to slacken off speed in weather like this or you'll be throwing the passengers all over the ship."

Down in the smoking room people were already gathering for the auction. They were grouping themselves politely around the various tables, the men a little stiff in their dinner jackets, a little pink and overshaved and stiff beside their cool, white-armed women. Mr. Botibol took a chair close to the auctioneer's table. He crossed his legs, folded his arms, and settled himself in his seat with the rather desperate air of a man who has made a tremendous decision and refuses to be frightened.

The pool, he was telling himself, would probably be around seven thousand dollars. That was almost exactly what it had been the last two days with the numbers selling for between three and four hundred apiece. Being a British ship they did it in pounds, but he liked to do his thinking in his own currency. Seven thousand dollars was plenty of money. My goodness yes! And what he would do he would get them to pay him in hundred-dollar bills and he would take it ashore in the inside pocket of his jacket. No problem there. And right away, yes right away, he would buy a Lincoln convertible. He would pick it up on the way from the ship and drive it home just for the pleasure of seeing Ethel's face when she came out the front door and looked at it. Wouldn't that be something, to see Ethel's face when he glided up to the door in a brand-new pale-green Lincoln convertible! Hello Ethel honey, he would say, speaking very casual. I just thought I'd get you a little present. I saw it in the window as I went by, so I thought of you and how you were always wanting one. You like it, honey? he would say. You like the colour? And then he would watch her face.

The auctioneer was standing up behind his table now. "Ladies and gentlemen!" he shouted. "The captain has estimated the day's run, ending midday tomorrow, at five hundred and fifteen miles. As usual we will take the ten numbers on either side of it to make up the range. That makes it five hundred and five to five hundred and twenty-five. And of course for those who think the true figure will be still farther away, there'll be 'low field' and 'high field' sold separately as well. Now, we'll draw the first number out of the hat . . . here we are . . . five hundred and twelve?"

The room became quiet. The people sat still in their chairs, all eyes watching the auctioneer. There was a certain tension in the air, and as the bids got higher, the tension grew. This wasn't a game or a joke; you could be sure of that by the way one man would look across at another who had raised his bid—smiling perhaps, but only the lips smiling, the eyes bright and absolutely cold.

Number five hundred and twelve was knocked down for one hundred and ten pounds. The next three or four numbers fetched roughly the same amount.

The ship was rolling heavily, and each time she went over, the wooden panelling on the walls creaked as if it were going to split. The passengers held on to the arms of their chairs, concentrating upon the auction.

"Low field!" the auctioneer called out. "The next number is low field."

Mr. Botibol sat up very straight and tense. He would wait, he had decided, until the others had finished bidding, then he would jump in and make the last bid. He had figured that there must be at least five hundred dollars in his account at the bank at home, probably nearer six. That was about two hundred pounds—over two hundred. This ticket wouldn't fetch more than that.

"As you all know," the auctioneer was saying, "low field covers every number *below* the smallest number in the range, in this case every number below five hundred and five. So, if you think this ship is going to cover less than five hundred and five miles in the twenty-four hours ending at noon tomorrow, you better get in and buy this number. So what am I bid?"

It went clear up to one hundred and thirty pounds. Others besides Mr. Botibol seemed to have noticed that the weather was rough. One hundred and forty . . . fifty . . . There it stopped. The auctioneer raised his hammer.

"Going at one hundred and fifty . . ."

"Sixty!" Mr. Botibol called, and every face in the room turned and looked at him.

"Seventy!"

"Eighty!" Mr. Botibol called.

"Ninety!"

"Two hundred!" Mr. Botibol called. He wasn't stopping now —for anyone.

There was a pause.

"Any advance on two hundred pounds?"

Sit still, he told himself. Sit absolutely still and don't look up. Hold your breath. No one's going to bid you up so long as you hold your breath.

"Going for two hundred pounds . . ." The auctioneer had a pink bald head and there were little beads of sweat sparkling on top of it. "Going . . ." Mr. Botibol held his breath. "Going . . . Gone!" The man banged the hammer on the table. Mr. Botibol wrote out a check and handed it to the auctioneer's assistant, then he settled back in his chair to wait for the finish. He did not want to go to bed before he knew how much there was in the pool.

They added it up after the last number had been sold and it came to twenty-one hundred-odd pounds. That was around six thousand dollars. Ninety per cent to go to the winner, ten per cent to seamen's charities. Ninety per cent of six thousand was five thousand four hundred. Well—that was enough. He could buy the Lincoln convertible and there would be something left over, too. With this gratifying thought he went off, happy and excited, to his cabin.

When Mr. Botibol awoke the next morning he lay quite still for several minutes with his eyes shut, listening for the sound of the gale, waiting for the roll of the ship. There was no sound of any gale and the ship was not rolling. He jumped up and peered out of the porthole. The sea—Oh Jesus God—was smooth as glass, the great ship was moving through it fast, obviously making up for time lost during the night. Mr. Botibol turned away and sat slowly down on the edge of his bunk. A fine electricity of fear was beginning to prickle under the skin of his stomach. He hadn't a hope now. One of the higher numbers was certain to win it after this.

"Oh my God," he said aloud. "What shall I do?"

What, for example, would Ethel say? It was simply not possible to tell her that he had spent almost all of their two years' savings on a ticket in the ship's pool. Nor was it possible to keep the matter secret. To do that he would have to tell her to stop drawing checks. And what about the monthly installments on the television set and the Encyclopaedia Britannica? Already he could see the anger and contempt in the woman's eyes, the blue becoming gray and the eyes themselves narrowing as they always did when there was anger in them.

"Oh my God. What *shall* I do?"

There was no point in pretending that he had the slightest chance now—not unless the goddam ship started to go backward. They'd have to put her in reverse and go full speed astern and keep right on going if he was to have any chance of winning it now. Well, maybe he should ask the captain to do just that. Offer him ten per cent of the profits. Offer him more if he wanted it. Mr. Botibol started to giggle. Then very suddenly he stopped, his eyes and mouth both opening wide in a kind of shocked surprise. For it was at this moment that the idea came. It hit him hard and quick, and he jumped up from his bed, terribly excited, ran over to the porthole and looked out again. Well, he thought, why not? Why ever not? The sea was calm and he wouldn't have any trouble keeping afloat until they picked him up. He had a vague feeling that someone had done this thing before, but that didn't prevent him from doing it again. The ship would have to stop and lower a boat, and the boat would have to go back maybe half a mile to get him, and then it would have to return to the ship and be hoisted back on board. It would take at least an hour, the whole thing. An hour was about thirty miles. It would knock thirty miles off the day's run. That would do it. "Low field" would be sure to win it then. Just so long as he made certain someone saw him falling over; but that would be simple to arrange. And he'd better wear light clothes, something easy to swim in. Sports clothes, that was it. He would dress as though he were going up to play some deck tennis—just a shirt and a pair of shorts and tennis shoes. And leave his watch behind. What was the time? Nine-fifteen. The sooner the better, then. Do it now and get it over with. Have to do it soon, because the time limit was midday.

Mr. Botibol was both frightened and excited when he stepped out onto the sundeck in his sports clothes. His small body was wide at the hips, tapering upward to extremely narrow sloping shoulders, so that it resembled, in shape at any rate, a bollard. His white skinny legs were covered with black hairs, and he came cautiously out on deck, treading softly in his tennis shoes. Nervously he looked around him. There was only one other person in sight, an elderly woman with very thick ankles and immense buttocks who was leaning over the rail staring at the sea. She was wearing a coat of Persian lamb and the collar was turned up so Mr. Botibol couldn't see her face.

He stood still, examining her carefully from a distance. Yes, he told himself, she would probably do. She would probably give the alarm just as quickly as anyone else. But wait one minute, take your time, William Botibol, take your time. Remember what you told yourself a few minutes ago in the cabin when you were changing? You remember that?

The thought of leaping off a ship into the ocean a thousand miles from the nearest land had made Mr. Botibol—a cautious man at the best of times—unusually advertent. He was by no means satisfied yet that this woman he saw before him was *absolutely certain* to give the alarm when he made his jump. In his opinion there were two possible reasons why she might fail him. Firstly, she might be deaf and blind. It was not very probable, but on the other hand it *might* be so, and why take a chance? All he had to do was check it by talking to her for a moment beforehand. Secondly—and this will demonstrate how suspicious the mind of a man can become when it is working through self-preservation and fear—secondly, it had occurred to him that the woman might herself be the owner of one of the high numbers in the pool and as such would have a sound financial reason for not wishing to stop the ship. Mr. Botibol recalled that people had killed their fellows for far less than six thousand dollars. It was happening every day in the newspapers. So why take a chance on that either? Check on it first. Be sure of your facts. Find out about it by a little polite conversation. Then, provided that the woman appeared also to be a pleasant, kindly human being, the thing was a cinch and he could leap overboard with a light heart.

Mr. Botibol advanced casually toward the woman and took up a position beside her, leaning on the rail. "Hullo," he said pleasantly.

She turned and smiled at him, a surprisingly lovely, almost a beautiful smile, although the face itself was very plain. "Hullo," she answered him.

Check, Mr. Botibol told himself, on the first question. She is neither blind nor deaf. "Tell me," he said, coming straight to the point, "what did you think of the auction last night?"

"Auction?" she asked, frowning. "Auction? What auction?"

"You know, that silly old thing they have in the lounge after dinner, selling numbers on the ship's daily run. I just wondered what you thought about it."

She shook her head, and again she smiled, a sweet and pleasant smile that had in it perhaps the trace of an apology. "I'm very lazy," she said. "I always go to bed early. I have my dinner in bed. It's so restful to have dinner in bed."

Mr. Botibol smiled back at her and began to edge away. "Got to go and get my exercise now," he said. "Never miss my exercise in the morning. It was nice seeing you. Very nice seeing you . . ." He retreated about ten paces, and the woman let him go without looking around.

Everything was now in order. The sea was calm, he was lightly dressed for swimming, there were almost certainly no man-eating sharks in this part of the Atlantic, and there was this pleasant kindly old woman to give the alarm. It was a question now only of whether the ship would be delayed long enough to swing the balance in his favor. Almost certainly it would. In any event, he could do a little to help in that direction himself. He could make a few difficulties about getting hauled up into the lifeboat. Swim around a bit, back away from them surreptitiously as they tried to come up close to fish him out. Every minute, every second gained would help him win. He began to move forward again to the rail, but now a new fear assailed him. Would he get caught in the propeller? He had heard about that happening to persons falling off the sides of big ships. But then, he wasn't going to fall, he was going to jump, and that was a very different thing. Provided he jumped out far enough he would be sure to clear the propeller.

Mr. Botibol advanced slowly to a position at the rail about twenty yards away from the woman. She wasn't looking at him now. So much the better. He didn't want her watching him as he jumped off. So long as no one was watching he would be able to say afterward that he had slipped and fallen by accident. He peered over the side of the ship. It was a long, long drop. Come to think of it now, he might easily hurt himself badly if he hit the water flat. Wasn't there someone who once split his stomach open that way, doing a belly flop from the high dive? He must jump straight and land feet first. Go in like a knife. Yes sir. The water seemed cold and deep and gray and it made him shiver to look at it. But it was now or never. Be a man, William Botibol, be a man. All right then . . . now . . . here goes . . .

He climbed up onto the wide wooden toprail, stood there poised, balancing for three terrifying seconds, then he leaped—he leaped up and out as far as he could go and at the same time he shouted *"Help!"*

"Help! Help!" he shouted as he fell. Then he hit the water and went under.

When the first shout for help sounded, the woman who was

leaning on the rail started up and gave a little jump of surprise. She looked around quickly and saw sailing past her through the air this small man dressed in white shorts and tennis shoes, spread-eagled and shouting as he went. For a moment she looked as though she weren't quite sure what she ought to do: throw a life belt, run away and give the alarm, or simply turn and yell. She drew back a pace from the rail and swung half around facing up to the bridge, and for this brief moment she remained motionless, tense, undecided. Then almost at once she seemed to relax, and she leaned forward far over the rail, staring at the water where it was turbulent in the ship's wake. Soon a tiny round black head appeared in the foam, an arm was raised about it, once, twice, vigorously waving, and a small faraway voice was heard calling something that was difficult to understand. The woman leaned still farther over the rail, trying to keep the little bobbing black speck in sight, but soon, so very soon, it was such a long way away that she couldn't even be sure it was there at all.

After a while another woman came out on deck. This one was bony and angular, and she wore horn-rimmed spectacles. She spotted the first woman and walked over to her, treading the deck in the deliberate, military fashion of all spinsters.

"So *there* you are," she said.

The woman with the fat ankles turned and looked at her, but said nothing.

"I've been searching for you," the bony one continued. "Searching all over."

"It's very odd," the woman with the fat ankles said. "A man dived overboard just now, with his clothes on."

"Nonsense!"

"Oh yes. He said he wanted to get some exercise and he dived in and didn't even bother to take his clothes off."

"You better come down now," the bony woman said. Her mouth had suddenly become firm, her whole face sharp and alert, and she spoke less kindly than before. "And don't you ever go wandering about on deck alone like this again. You know quite well you're meant to wait for me."

"Yes, Maggie," the woman with the fat ankles answered, and again she smiled, a tender, trusting smile, and she took the hand of the other one and allowed herself to be led away across the deck.

"Such a nice man," she said. "He waved to me."

Skin

1952

THAT year—1946—winter was a long time going. Although it was April, a freezing wind blew through the streets of the city, and overhead the snow clouds moved across the sky.

The old man who was called Drioli shuffled painfully along the sidewalk of the Rue de Rivoli. He was cold and miserable, huddled up like a hedgehog in a filthy black coat, only his eyes and the top of his head visible above the turned-up collar.

The door of a café opened and the faint whiff of roasting chicken brought a pain of yearning to the top of his stomach. He moved on, glancing without any interest at the things in the shopwindows—perfume, silk ties and shirts, diamonds, porcelain, antique furniture, finely bound books. Then a picture gallery. He had always liked picture galleries. This one had a single canvas on display in the window. He stopped to look at it. He turned to go on. He checked, looked back; and now, suddenly, there came to him a slight uneasiness, a movement of the memory, a distant recollection of something, somewhere, he had seen before. He looked again. It was a landscape, a clump of trees leaning madly over to one side as if blown by a tremendous wind, the sky swirling and twisting all around. Attached to the frame there was a little plaque, and on this it said: "CHAÏM SOUTINE (1894–1943)."

Drioli stared at the picture, wondering vaguely what there was about it that seemed familiar. Crazy painting, he thought. Very strange and crazy—but I like it . . . Chaïm Soutine . . . Soutine . . . "By God!" he cried suddenly. "My little Kalmuck, that's who it is! My little Kalmuck with a picture in the finest shop in Paris! Just imagine that!"

The old man pressed his face closer to the window. He could remember the boy—yes, quite clearly he could remember him. But when? When? The rest of it was not so easy to recollect. It was so long ago. How long? Twenty—no, more like thirty years, wasn't it? Wait a minute. Yes—it was the year before the war, the first war, 1913. That was it. And this Soutine, this ugly little Kalmuck, a sullen brooding boy whom he had liked—almost loved—for no reason at all that he could think of except that he could paint.

And how he could paint! It was coming back more clearly now —the street, the line of refuse cans along the length of it, the rotten smell, the brown cats walking delicately over the refuse, and then the women, moist fat women sitting on the doorsteps with their feet upon the cobblestones of the street. Which street? Where was it the boy had lived?

The Cité Falguière, that was it! The old man nodded his head several times, pleased to have remembered the name. Then there was the studio with the single chair in it, and the filthy red couch that the boy had used for sleeping; the drunken parties, the cheap white wine, the furious quarrels, and always, always the bitter sullen face of the boy brooding over his work.

It was odd, Drioli thought, how easily it all came back to him now, how each single small remembered fact seemed instantly to remind him of another.

There was that nonsense with the tattoo, for instance. Now, *that* was a mad thing if ever there was one. How had it started? Ah, yes —he had got rich one day, that was it, and he had bought lots of wine. He could see himself now as he entered the studio with the parcel of bottles under his arm—the boy sitting before the easel, and his (Drioli's) own wife standing in the center of the room, posing for her picture.

"Tonight we shall celebrate," he said. "We shall have a little celebration, us three."

"What is it that we celebrate?" the boy asked without looking up. "Is it that you have decided to divorce your wife so she can marry me?"

"No," Drioli said. "We celebrate because today I have made a great sum of money with my work."

"And I have made nothing. We can celebrate that also."

"If you like." Drioli was standing by the table unwrapping the parcel. He felt tired and he wanted to get at the wine. Nine clients in one day was all very nice, but it could play hell with a man's eyes. He had never done as many as nine before. Nine boozy soldiers— and the remarkable thing was that no fewer than seven of them had been able to pay in cash. This had made him extremely rich. But the work was terrible on the eyes. Drioli's eyes were half closed from fatigue, the whites streaked with little connecting lines of red; and about an inch behind each eyeball there was a small concentration of pain. But it was evening now and he was wealthy as a pig, and in the parcel there were three bottles—one for his wife, one for his friend, and one for him. He had found the corkscrew and was drawing the corks from the bottles, each making a small plop as it came out.

The boy put down his brush. "Oh Christ," he said. "How can one work with all this going on?"

The girl came across the room to look at the painting. Drioli came over also, holding a bottle in one hand, a glass in the other.

"No!" the boy shouted, blazing up suddenly. "Please—no!" He snatched the canvas from the easel and stood it against the wall. But Drioli had seen it.

"I like it."

"It's terrible."

"It's marvellous. Like all the others that you do, it's marvellous. I love them all."

"The trouble is," the boy said, scowling, "that in themselves they are not nourishing. I cannot eat them."

"But still they are marvellous." Drioli handed him a tumbler full of the pale-yellow wine. "Drink it," he said. "It will make you happy."

Never, he thought, had he known a more unhappy person, or one with a gloomier face. He had spotted him in a café some seven months before, drinking alone, and because he had looked like a Russian or some sort of an Asiatic, Drioli had sat down at his table and talked.

"You are a Russian?"

"Yes."

"Where from?"

"Minsk."

Drioli had jumped up and embraced him, crying that he too had been born in that city.

"It wasn't actually Minsk," the boy had said. "But quite near."

"Where?"

"Smilovichi, about twelve miles away."

"Smilovichi!" Drioli had shouted, embracing him again. "I walked there several times when I was a boy." Then he had sat down again, staring affectionately at the other's face. "You know," he had said, "you don't look like a western Russian. You're like a Tartar, or a Kalmuck. You look exactly like a Kalmuck."

Now, standing in the studio, Drioli looked again at the boy as he took the glass of wine and tipped it down his throat in one swallow. Yes, he did have a face like a Kalmuck—very broad and high-cheeked, with a wide coarse nose. This broadness of the cheeks was accentuated by the ears which stood out sharply from the head. And then he had the narrow eyes, the black hair, the thick sullen mouth of a Kalmuck; but the hands—the hands were always a surprise, so small and white like a lady's, with tiny thin fingers.

"Give me some more," the boy said. "If we are to celebrate, then let us do it properly."

Drioli distributed the wine and sat himself on a chair. The boy sat on the old couch with Drioli's wife. The three bottles were placed on the floor between them.

"Tonight we shall drink as much as we possibly can," Drioli said. "I am exceptionally rich. I think perhaps I should go out now and buy some more bottles. How many shall I get?"

"Six more," the boy said. "Two for each."

"Good. I shall go now and fetch them."

"And I will help you."

In the nearest café Drioli bought six bottles of white wine, and they carried them back to the studio. They placed them on the floor in two rows, and Drioli fetched the corkscrew and pulled the corks, all six of them; then they sat down again and continued to drink.

"It is only the very wealthy," Drioli said, "who can afford to celebrate in this manner."

"That is true," the boy said. "Isn't that true, Josie?"

"Of course."

"How do you feel, Josie?"

"Fine."

"Will you leave Drioli and marry me?"

"No."

"Beautiful wine," Drioli said. "It is a privilege to drink it."

Slowly, methodically, they set about getting themselves drunk. The process was routine, but all the same there was a certain ceremony to be observed, and a gravity to be maintained, and a great number of things to be said, then said again—and the wine must be praised, and the slowness was important too, so that there would be time to savour the three delicious stages of transition, especially (for Drioli) the one when he began to float and his feet did not really belong to him. That was the best period of them all—when he could look down at his feet and they were so far away that he would wonder what crazy person they might belong to and why they were lying around on the floor like that, in the distance.

After a while, he got up to switch on the light. He was surprised to see that the feet came with him when he did this, especially because he couldn't feel them touching the ground. It gave him a pleasant sensation of walking on air. Then he began wandering around the room, peeking slyly at the canvases stacked against the walls.

"Listen," he said at length. "I have an idea." He came across and stood before the couch, swaying gently. "Listen, my little Kalmuck."

"What?"

"I have a tremendous idea. Are you listening?"

"I'm listening to Josie."

"Listen to me, *please*. You are my friend—my ugly little Kalmuck from Minsk—and to me you are such an artist that I would like to have a picture, a lovely picture—"

"Have them all. Take all you can find, but do not interrupt me when I am talking with your wife."

"No, no. Now listen. I mean a picture that I can have with me always . . . forever . . . wherever I go . . . whatever happens . . . but always with me . . . a picture by you." He reached forward and shook the boy's knee. "Now listen to me, *please.*"

"Listen to him," the girl said.

"It is this. I want you to paint a picture on my skin, on my back. Then I want you to tattoo over what you have painted so that it will be there always."

"You have crazy ideas."

"I will teach you how to use the tattoo. It is easy. A child could do it."

"I am not a child."

"*Please . . .*"

"You are quite mad. What is it you want?" The painter looked up into the slow, dark, wine-bright eyes of the other man. "What in heaven's name is it you want?"

"You could do it easily! You could! You could!"

"You mean with the tattoo?"

"Yes, with the tattoo! I will teach you in two minutes!"

"Impossible!"

"Are you saying I don't know what I'm talking about?"

No, the boy could not possibly be saying that because if anyone knew about the tattoo it was he—Drioli. Had he not, only last month, covered a man's whole belly with the most wonderful and delicate design composed entirely of flowers? What about the client who had had so much hair upon his chest that he had done him a picture of a grizzly bear so designed that the hair on the chest became the furry coat of the bear? Could he not draw the likeness of a lady and position it with such subtlety upon a man's arm that when the muscle of the arm was flexed the lady came to life and performed some astonishing contortions?

"All I am saying," the boy told him, "is that you are drunk and this is a drunken idea."

"We could have Josie for a model. A study of Josie upon my back. Am I not entitled to a picture of my wife upon my back?"

"Of Josie?"

"Yes." Drioli knew he only had to mention his wife and the boy's thick brown lips would loosen and begin to quiver.

"No," the girl said.

"Darling Josie, *please.* Take this bottle and finish it, then you will feel more generous. It is an enormous idea. Never in my life have I had such an idea before."

"What idea?"

"That he should make a picture of you upon my back. Am I not entitled to that?"

"A picture of me?"

"A nude study," the boy said. "It is an agreeable idea."

"Not nude," the girl said.

"It is an enormous idea," Drioli said.

"It's a damn crazy idea," the girl said.

"It is in any event an idea," the boy said. "It is an idea that calls for a celebration."

They emptied another bottle among them. Then the boy said, "It is no good. I could not possibly manage the tattoo. Instead, I will paint this picture on your back and you will have it with you so long as you do not take a bath and wash it off. If you never take a bath again in your life then you will have it always, as long as you live."

"No," Drioli said.

"Yes—and on the day that you decide to take a bath I will know that you do not any longer value my picture. It will be a test of your admiration for my art."

"I do not like the idea," the girl said. "His admiration for your art is so great that he would be unclean for many years. Let us have the tattoo. But not nude."

"Then just the head," Drioli said.

"I could not manage it."

"It is immensely simple. I will undertake to teach you in two minutes. You will see. I shall go now and fetch the instruments. The needles and the inks. I have inks of many different colors—as many different colors as you have paints, and far more beautiful. . . ."

"It is impossible."

"I have many inks. Have I not many different colors of inks, Josie?"

"Yes."

"You will see," Drioli said. "I will go now and fetch them." He got up from his chair and walked unsteadily, but with determination, out of the room.

In half an hour Drioli was back. "I have brought everything," he cried, waving a brown suitcase. "All the necessities of the tattooist are here in this bag."

He placed the bag on the table, opened it, and laid out the electric needles and the small bottles of colored inks. He plugged in the electric needle, then he took the instrument in his hand and pressed a switch. It made a buzzing sound and the quarter inch of needle that projected from the end of it began to vibrate swiftly up and down. He threw off his jacket and rolled up his left sleeve. "Now look. Watch me and I will show you how easy it is. I will make a design on my arm, here."

His forearm was already covered with blue markings, but he selected a small clear patch of skin upon which to demonstrate.

"First, I choose my ink—let us use ordinary blue—and I dip the point of my needle in the ink . . . so . . . and I hold the needle up straight and I run it lightly over the surface of the skin . . . like this . . . and with the little motor and the electricity, the needle jumps up and down and punctures the skin and the ink goes in and there you are . . . See how easy it is . . . see how I draw a picture of a greyhound here upon my arm . . ."

The boy was intrigued. "Now let *me* practice a little—on your arm."

With the buzzing needle he began to draw blue lines upon Drioli's arm. "It is simple," he said. "It is like drawing with pen and ink. There is no difference except that it is slower."

"There is nothing to it. Are you ready? Shall we begin?"

"At once."

"The model!" cried Drioli. "Come on, Josie!" He was in a bustle of enthusiasm now, tottering around the room arranging everything, like a child preparing for some exciting game. "Where will you have her? Where shall she stand?"

"Let her be standing there, by my dressing table. Let her be brushing her hair. I will paint her with her hair down over her shoulders and her brushing it."

"Tremendous. You are a genius."

Reluctantly, the girl walked over and stood by the dressing table, carrying her glass of wine with her.

Drioli pulled off his shirt and stepped out of his trousers. He retained only his underpants and his socks and shoes, and he stood there, swaying gently from side to side, his small body firm, white-skinned, almost hairless. "Now," he said, "I am the canvas. Where will you place your canvas?"

"As always, upon the easel."

"Don't be crazy. I am the canvas."

"Then place yourself upon the easel. That is where you belong."

"How can I?"

"Are you the canvas or are you not the canvas?"

"I am the canvas. Already I begin to feel like a canvas."

"Then place yourself upon the easel. There should be no difficulty."

"Truly, it is not possible."

"Then sit on the chair. Sit back to front, then you can lean your drunken head against the back of it. Hurry now, for I am about to commence."

"I am ready. I am waiting."

"First," the boy said, "I shall make an ordinary painting. Then, if it pleases me, I shall tattoo over it." With a wide brush he began to paint upon the naked skin of the man's back.

"Ayee! Ayee!" Drioli screamed. "A monstrous centipede is marching down my spine!"

"Be still now! Be still!" The boy worked rapidly, applying the paint only in a thin blue wash so that it would not afterward interfere with the process of tattooing. His concentration, as soon as he began to paint, was so great that it appeared somehow to supersede his drunkenness. He applied the brush strokes with quick short jabs of the arm, holding the wrist stiff, and in less than half an hour it was finished.

"All right. That's all," he said to the girl, who immediately returned to the couch, lay down, and fell asleep.

Drioli remained awake. He watched the boy take up the needle and dip it in the ink; then he felt the sharp tickling sting as it touched the skin of his back. The pain, which was unpleasant but never extreme, kept him from going to sleep. By following the track of the needle and by watching the different colors of ink that the boy was using, Drioli amused himself trying to visualize what was going on behind him. The boy worked with an astonishing intensity. He appeared to have become completely absorbed in the little machine and in the unusual effects it was able to produce.

Far into the small hours of the morning the machine buzzed and the boy worked. Drioli could remember that when the artist finally stepped back and said, "It is finished," there was daylight outside and the sound of people walking in the street.

"I want to see it," Drioli said. The boy held up a mirror, at an angle, and Drioli craned his neck to look.

"Good God" he cried. It was a startling sight. The whole of his back, from the top of the shoulders to the base of the spine, was a blaze of color—gold and green and blue and black and scarlet. The tattoo was applied so heavily it looked almost like an impasto. The boy had followed as closely as possible the original brush strokes, filling them in solid, and it was marvellous the way he had made use of the spine and the protrusion of the shoulder blades so that they became part of the composition. What is more, he had somehow managed to achieve—even with this slow process—a certain spontaneity. The portrait was quite alive; it contained much of that twisted, tortured, quality so characteristic of Soutine's other work. It was not a good likeness. It was a mood rather than a likeness, the model's face vague and tipsy, the background swirling around her head in a mass of dark-green curling strokes.

"It's tremendous!"

"I rather like it myself." The boy stood back, examining it critically. "You know," he added, "I think it's good enough for me to sign." And taking up the buzzer again, he inscribed his name in red ink on the right-hand side, over the place where Drioli's kidney was.

The old man who was called Drioli was standing in a sort of trance, staring at the painting in the window of the picture-dealer's shop. It had been so long ago, all that—almost as though it had happened in another life.

And the boy? What had become of him? He could remember

now that after returning from the war—the first war—he had missed him and had questioned Josie.

"Where is my little Kalmuck?"

"He is gone," she had answered. "I do not know where, but I heard it said that a dealer had taken him up and sent him away to Céret to make more paintings."

"Perhaps he will return."

"Perhaps he will. Who knows?"

That was the last time they had mentioned him. Shortly afterward they had moved to Le Havre where there were more sailors and business was better. The old man smiled as he remembered Le Havre. Those were the pleasant years, the years between the wars, with the small shop near the docks and the comfortable rooms and always enough work, with every day three, four, five sailors coming and wanting pictures on their arms. Those were truly the pleasant years.

Then had come the second war, and Josie being killed, and the Germans arriving, and that was the finish of his business. No one had wanted pictures on their arms any more after that. And by that time he was too old for any other kind of work. In desperation he had made his way back to Paris, hoping vaguely that things would be easier in the big city. But they were not.

And now, after the war was over, he possessed neither the means nor the energy to start up his small business again. It wasn't very easy for an old man to know what to do, especially when one did not like to beg. Yet how else could he keep alive?

Well, he thought, still staring at the picture. So that is my little Kalmuck. And how quickly the sight of one small object such as this can stir the memory. Up to a few moments ago he had even forgotten that he had a tattoo on his back. It had been ages since he had thought about it. He put his face closer to the window and looked into the gallery. On the walls he could see many other pictures and all seemed to be the work of the same artist. There were a great number of people strolling around. Obviously it was a special exhibition.

On a sudden impulse, Drioli turned, pushed open the door of the gallery and went in.

It was a long room with a thick wine-colored carpet, and by God how beautiful and warm it was! There were all these people strolling about looking at the pictures, well-washed, dignified people, each of whom held a catalogue in the hand. Drioli stood just inside the door, nervously glancing around, wondering whether he dared go forward and mingle with this crowd. But before he had had time to gather his courage, he heard a voice beside him saying, "What is it you want?"

The speaker wore a black morning coat. He was plump and short and had a very white face. It was a flabby face with so much flesh upon it that the cheeks hung down on either side of the mouth in two fleshy collops, spanielwise. He came up close to Drioli and said again, "What is it you want?"

Drioli stood still.

"If you please," the man was saying, "take yourself out of my gallery."

"Am I not permitted to look at the pictures?"

"I have asked you to leave."

Drioli stood his ground. He felt suddenly, overwhelmingly outraged.

"Let us not have trouble," the man was saying. "Come on now, this way." He put a fat white paw on Drioli's arm and began to push him firmly to the door.

That did it. "Take your goddam hands off me!" Drioli shouted. His voice rang clear down the long gallery and all the heads jerked around as one—all the startled faces stared down the length of the room at the person who had made this noise. A flunky came running over to help, and the two men tried to hustle Drioli through the door. The people stood still, watching the struggle. Their faces expressed only a mild interest, and seemed to be saying, "It's all right. There's no danger to us. It's being taken care of."

"I, too!" Drioli was shouting. "I, too, have a picture by this painter! He was my friend and I have a picture which he gave me!"

"He's mad."

"A lunatic. A raving lunatic."

"Someone should call the police."

With a rapid twist of the body Drioli suddenly jumped clear of the two men, and before anyone could stop him he was running down the gallery shouting, "I'll show you! I'll show you! I'll show you!" He flung off his overcoat, then his jacket and shirt, and he turned so that his naked back was toward the people.

"There!" he cried, breathing quickly. "You see? There it is!"

There was a sudden absolute silence in the room, each person arrested in what he was doing, standing motionless in a kind of shocked, uneasy bewilderment. They were staring at the tattooed picture. It was still there, the colors as bright as ever, but the old man's back was thinner now, the shoulder blades protruded more sharply, and the effect, though not great, was to give the picture a curiously wrinkled, squashed appearance.

Somebody said, "My God, but it is!"

Then came the excitement and the noise of voices as the people surged forward to crowd around the old man.

"It is unmistakable!"

"His early manner, yes?"

"It is fantastic, fantastic!"

"And look, it is signed!"

"Bend your shoulders forward, my friend, so that the picture stretches out flat."

"Old one, when was this done?"

"In 1913," Drioli said, without turning around. "In the autumn of 1913."

"Who taught Soutine to tattoo?"

"I taught him."

"And the woman?"

"She was my wife."

The gallery owner was pushing through the crowd toward Drioli. He was calm now, deadly serious, making a smile with his mouth. "Monsieur," he said, "I will buy it." Drioli could see the loose fat upon the face vibrating as he moved his jaw. "I said I will buy it, Monsieur."

"How can you buy it?" Drioli asked softly.

"I will give two hundred thousand francs for it." The dealer's eyes were small and dark, the wings of his broad nose-base were beginning to quiver.

"Don't do it!" someone murmured in the crowd. "It is worth twenty times as much."

Drioli opened his mouth to speak. No words came, so he shut it; then he opened it again and said slowly, "But how can I sell it?" He lifted his hands, let them drop loosely to his sides. "Monsieur, how can I possibly sell it?" All the sadness in the world was in his voice.

"Yes!" they were saying in the crowd. "How can he sell it? It is a part of himself!"

"Listen," the dealer said, coming up close. "I will help you. I will make you rich. Together we shall make some private arrangement over this picture, no?"

Drioli watched him with slow, apprehensive eyes. "But how can you buy it, Monsieur? What will you do with it when you have bought it? Where will you keep it? Where will you keep it tonight? And where tomorrow?"

"Ah, where will I keep it? Yes, where will I keep it? Now, where will I keep it? Well, now . . ." The dealer stroked the bridge of his nose with a fat white finger. "It would seem," he said, "that if I take the picture, I take you also. That is a disadvantage." He paused and stroked his nose again. "The picture itself is of no value until you are dead. How old are you, my friend?"

"Sixty-one."

"But you are perhaps not very robust, no?" The dealer lowered the hand from his nose and looked Drioli up and down, slowly, like a farmer appraising an old horse.

"I do not like this," Drioli said, edging away. "Quite honestly, Monsieur, I do not like it." He edged straight into the arms of a tall man who put out his hands and caught him gently by the shoulders. Drioli glanced around and apologized. The man smiled down at him, patting one of the old fellow's naked shoulders reassuringly with a hand encased in a canary-colored glove.

"Listen, my friend," the stranger said, still smiling. "Do you like to swim and to bask yourself in the sun?"

Drioli looked up at him, rather startled.

"Do you like fine food and red wine from the great châteaux of Bordeaux?" The man was still smiling, showing strong white teeth with flash of gold among them. He spoke in a soft coaxing manner, one gloved hand still resting on Drioli's shoulder. "Do you like such things?"

"Well—yes," Drioli answered, still greatly perplexed. "Of course."

"And the company of beautiful women?"

"Why not?"

"And a cupboard full of suits and shirts made to your own personal measurements? It would seem that you are a little lacking for clothes."

Drioli watched this suave man, waiting for the rest of the proposition.

"Have you ever had a shoe constructed especially for your own foot?"

"No."

"You would like that?"

"Well . . ."

"And a man who will shave you in the mornings and trim your hair?"

Drioli simply stood and gaped.

"And a plump attractive girl to manicure the nails of your fingers?"

Someone in the crowd giggled.

"And a bell beside your bed to summon a maid to bring your breakfast in the morning? Would you like these things, my friend? Do they appeal to you?"

Drioli stood still and looked at him.

"You see, I am the owner of the Hotel Bristol in Cannes. I now invite you to come down there and live as my guest for the rest of your life in luxury and comfort." The man paused, allowing his listener time to savor this cheerful prospect.

"Your only duty—shall I call it your pleasure—will be to spend your time on my beach in bathing trunks, walking among my guests, sunning yourself, swimming, drinking cocktails. You would like that?"

There was no answer.

"Don't you see—all the guests will thus be able to observe this fascinating picture by Soutine. You will become famous, and men will say, 'Look, there is the fellow with ten million francs upon his back.' You like this idea, Monsieur? It pleases you?"

Drioli looked up at the tall man in the canary gloves, still wondering whether this was some sort of a joke. "It is a comical idea," he said slowly. "But do you really mean it?"

"Of course I mean it."

"Wait," the dealer interrupted. "See here, old one. Here is the answer to our problem. I will buy the picture, and I will arrange with a surgeon to remove the skin from your back, and then you will be able to go off on your own and enjoy the great sum of money I shall give you for it."

"With no skin on my back?"

"No, no, please! You misunderstand. This surgeon will put a new piece of skin in the place of the old one. It is simple."

"Could he do that?"

"There is nothing to it."

"Impossible!" said the man with the canary gloves. "He's too old for such a major skin-grafting operation. It would kill him. It would kill you, my friend."

"It would kill me?"

"Naturally. You would never survive. Only the picture would come through."

"In the name of God!" Drioli cried. He looked around aghast at the faces of the people watching him, and in the silence that followed, another man's voice, speaking quietly from the back of the group, could be heard saying, "Perhaps, if one were to offer this old man enough money, he might consent to kill himself on the spot. Who knows?" A few people sniggered. The dealer moved his feet uneasily on the carpet.

Then the hand in the canary glove was tapping Drioli again upon the shoulder. "Come on," the man was saying, smiling his broad white smile. "You and I will go and have a good dinner and we can talk about it some more while we eat. How's that? Are you hungry?"

Drioli watched him, frowning. He didn't like the man's long flexible neck, or the way he craned it forward at you when he spoke, like a snake.

"Roast duck and Chambertin," the man was saying. He put a rich succulent accent on the words, splashing them out with his tongue. "And perhaps a soufflé aux marrons, light and frothy."

Drioli's eyes turned up toward the ceiling, his lips became loose and wet. One could see the poor old fellow beginning literally to drool at the mouth.

"How do you like your duck?" the man went on. "Do you like it very brown and crisp outside, or shall it be . . ."

"I am coming," Drioli said quickly. Already he had picked up his shirt and was pulling it frantically over his head. "Wait for me, Monsieur. I am coming." And within a minute he had disappeared out of the gallery with his new patron.

It wasn't more than a few weeks later that a picture by Soutine, of a woman's head, painted in an unusual manner, nicely framed and heavily varnished, turned up for sale in Buenos Aires. That—and the fact that there is no hotel in Cannes called Bristol—causes one to wonder a little, and to pray for the old man's health, and to hope fervently that wherever he may be at this moment, there is a plump attractive girl to manicure the nails of his fingers, and a maid to bring him his breakfast in bed in the mornings.

Edward the Conqueror

1953

LOUISA, holding a dishcloth in her hand, stepped out the kitchen door at the back of the house into the cool October sunshine.

"Edward!" she called. "*Ed-ward!* Lunch is ready!"

She paused a moment, listening; then she strolled out onto the lawn and continued across it—a little shadow attending her—skirting the rose bed and touching the sundial lightly with one finger as she went by. She moved rather gracefully for a woman who was small and plump, with a lilt in her walk and a gentle swinging of the shoulders and the arms. She passed under the mulberry tree onto the brick path, then went all the way along the path until she came to the place where she could look down into the dip at the end of this large garden.

"*Edward!* Lunch!"

She could see him now, about eighty yards away, down in the dip on the edge of the wood—the tallish narrow figure in khaki slacks and dark-green sweater, working beside a big bonfire with a fork in his hands, pitching brambles onto the top of the fire. It was blazing fiercely, with orange flames and clouds of milky smoke, and the smoke was drifting back over the garden with a wonderful scent of autumn and burning leaves.

Louisa went down the slope toward her husband. Had she wanted, she could easily have called again and made herself heard, but there was something about a first-class bonfire that impelled her toward it, right up close so she could feel the heat and listen to it burn.

"Lunch," she said, approaching.

"Oh, hello. All right—yes. I'm coming."

"*What* a good fire."

"I've decided to clear this place right out," her husband said. "I'm sick and tired of all these brambles." His long face was wet with perspiration. There were small beads of it clinging all over his moustache like dew, and two little rivers were running down his throat onto the turtleneck of the sweater.

"You better be careful you don't overdo it, Edward."

"Louisa, I do wish you'd stop treating me as though I were eighty. A bit of exercise never did anyone any harm."

"Yes, dear, I know. Oh, Edward! Look! Look!"

The man turned and looked at Louisa, who was pointing now to the far side of the bonfire.

"Look, Edward! The cat!"

Sitting on the ground, so close to the fire that the flames sometimes seemed actually to be touching it, was a large cat of a most unusual colour. It stayed quite still, with its head on one side and its nose in the air, watching the man and woman with a cool yellow eye.

"It'll get burnt!" Louisa cried, and she dropped the dishcloth and darted swiftly in and grabbed it with both hands, whisking it away and putting it on the grass well clear of the flames.

"You crazy cat," she said, dusting off her hands. "What's the matter with you?"

"Cats know what they're doing," the husband said. "You'll never find a cat doing something it doesn't want. Not cats."

"Whose is it? You ever seen it before?"

"No, I never have. Damn peculiar colour."

The cat had seated itself on the grass and was regarding them with a sidewise look. There was a veiled inward expression about the eyes, something curiously omniscient and pensive, and around the nose a most delicate air of contempt, as though the sight of these two middle-aged persons—the one small, plump, and rosy, the other lean and extremely sweaty—were a matter of some surprise but very little importance. For a cat, it certainly had an unusual colour—a pure silvery grey with no blue in it at all—and the hair was very long and silky.

Louisa bent down and stroked its head. "You must go home," she said. "Be a good cat now and go on home to where you belong."

The man and wife started to stroll back up the hill toward the house. The cat got up and followed, at a distance first, but edging closer and closer as they went along. Soon it was alongside them, then it was ahead, leading the way across the lawn to the house, and walking as though it owned the whole place, holding its tail straight up in the air, like a mast.

"Go home," the man said. "Go on home. We don't want you."

But when they reached the house, it came in with them, and Louisa gave it some milk in the kitchen. During lunch, it hopped up onto the spare chair between them and sat through the meal with its head just above the level of the table, watching the proceedings with those dark-yellow eyes which kept moving slowly from the woman to the man and back again.

"I don't like this cat," Edward said.

"Oh, I think it's a beautiful cat. I do hope it stays a little while."

"Now, listen to me, Louisa. The creature can't possibly stay here. It belongs to someone else. It's lost. And if it's still trying to hang around this afternoon, you'd better take it to the police. They'll see it gets home."

After lunch, Edward returned to his gardening. Louisa, as usual, went to the piano. She was a competent pianist and a genuine music-lover, and almost every afternoon she spent an hour or so playing for herself. The cat was now lying on the sofa, and she paused to stroke it as she went by. It opened its eyes, looked at her a moment, then closed them again and went back to sleep.

"You're an awfully nice cat," she said. "And such a beautiful colour. I wish I could keep you." Then her fingers, moving over the fur on the cat's head, came into contact with a small lump, a little growth just above the right eye.

"Poor cat," she said. "You've got bumps on your beautiful face. You must be getting old."

She went over and sat down on the long piano bench, but she didn't immediately start to play. One of her special little pleasures was to make every day a kind of concert day, with a carefully ar-ranged programme which she worked out in detail before she began. She never liked to break her enjoyment by having to stop while she wondered what to play next. All she wanted was a brief pause after each piece while the audience clapped enthusiastically and called for more. It was so much nicer to imagine an audience, and now and again while she was playing—on the lucky days, that is—the room would begin to swim and fade and darken, and she would see nothing but row upon row of seats and a sea of white faces upturned toward her, listening with a rapt and adoring concentra-tion.

Sometimes she played from memory, sometimes from music. Today she would play from memory; that was the way she felt. And what should the programme be? She sat before the piano with her small hands clasped on her lap, a plump rosy little person with a round and still quite pretty face, her hair done up in a neat bun at the back of her head. By looking slightly to the right, she could see the cat curled up asleep on the sofa, and its silvery-grey coat was beautiful against the purple of the cushion. How about some Bach to begin with? Or, better still, Vivaldi. The Bach adaptation for organ of the D minor Concerto Grosso. Yes—that first. Then perhaps a little Schumann. *Carnaval?* That would be fun. And after that —well, a touch of Liszt for a change. One of the *Petrarch Sonnets*. The second one—that was the loveliest—the E major. Then another Schumann, another of his gay ones—*Kinderscenen.* And lastly, for the encore, a Brahms waltz, or maybe two of them if she felt like it.

Vivaldi, Schumann, Liszt, Schumann, Brahms. A very nice programme, one that she could play easily without the music. She moved herself a little closer to the piano and paused a moment while someone in the audience—already she could feel that this was one of the lucky days—while someone in the audience had his last cough; then, with the slow grace that accompanied nearly all her movements, she lifted her hands to the keyboard and began to play.

She wasn't, at that particular moment, watching the cat at all— as a matter of fact she had forgotten its presence—but as the first deep notes of the Vivaldi sounded softly in the room, she became aware, out of the corner of one eye, of a sudden flurry, a flash of movement on the sofa to her right. She stopped playing at once. "What is it?" she said, turning to the cat. "What's the matter?"

The animal, who a few seconds before had been sleeping peacefully, was now sitting bolt upright on the sofa, very tense, the whole body aquiver, ears up and eyes wide open, staring at the piano.

"Did I frighten you?" she asked gently. "Perhaps you've never heard music before."

No, she told herself. I don't think that's what it is. On second thought, it seemed to her that the cat's attitude was not one of fear. There was no shrinking or backing away. If anything, there was a leaning forward, a kind of eagerness about the creature, and the face —well, there was rather an odd expression on the face, something of a mixture between surprise and shock. Of course, the face of a cat is a small and fairly expressionless thing, but if you watch carefully the eyes and ears working together, and particularly that little area of mobile skin below the ears and slightly to one side, you can occasionally see the reflection of very powerful emotions. Louisa was watching the face closely now, and because she was curious to see what would happen a second time, she reached out her hands to the keyboard and began again to play the Vivaldi.

This time the cat was ready for it, and all that happened to begin with was a small extra tensing of the body. But as the music swelled and quickened into that first exciting rhythm of the introduction to the fugue, a strange look that amounted almost to ecstasy began to settle upon the creature's face. The ears, which up to then had been pricked up straight, were gradually drawn back, the eyelids drooped, the head went over to one side, and at that moment Louisa could have sworn that the animal was actually *appreciating* the work.

What she saw (or thought she saw) was something she had noticed many times on the faces of people listening very closely to a piece of music. When the sound takes complete hold of them and drowns them in itself, a peculiar, intensely ecstatic look comes over them that you can recognize as easily as a smile. So far as Louisa could see, the cat was now wearing almost exactly this kind of look.

Louisa finished the fugue, then played the siciliana, and all the way through she kept watching the cat on the sofa. The final proof for her that the animal was listening came at the end, when the music stopped. It blinked, stirred itself a little, stretched a leg, settled into a more comfortable position, took a quick glance round the room, then looked expectantly in her direction. It was precisely the way a concert-goer reacts when the music momentarily releases him in the pause between two movements of a symphony. The behaviour was so thoroughly human it gave her a queer agitated feeling in the chest.

"You like that?" she asked. "You like Vivaldi?"

The moment she'd spoken, she felt ridiculous, but not—and this to her was a trifle sinister—not quite so ridiculous as she knew she should have felt.

Well, there was nothing for it now except to go straight ahead with the next number on the programme, which was *Carnaval.* As soon as she began to play, the cat again stiffened and sat up straighter; then, as it became slowly and blissfully saturated with the sound, it relapsed into that queer melting mood of ecstasy that seemed to have something to do with drowning and with dreaming. It was really an extravagant sight—quite a comical one, too—to see this silvery cat sitting on the sofa and being carried away like this. And what made it more screwy than ever, Louisa thought, was the fact that this music, which the animal seemed to be enjoying so much, was manifestly too *difficult,* too *classical,* to be appreciated by the majority of humans in the world.

Maybe, she thought, the creature's not really enjoying it at all. Maybe it's a sort of hypnotic reaction, like with snakes. After all, if you can charm a snake with music, then why not a cat? Except that millions of cats hear the stuff every day of their lives, on radio and gramophone and piano, and, as far as she knew, there'd never yet been a case of one behaving like this. This one was acting as though it were following every single note. It was certainly a fantastic thing.

But was it not also a wonderful thing? Indeed it was. In fact, unless she was much mistaken, it was a kind of miracle, one of those animal miracles that happen about once every hundred years.

"I could see you *loved* that one," she said when the piece was over. "Although I'm sorry I didn't play it any too well today. Which did you like best—the Vivaldi or the Schumann?"

The cat made no reply, so Louisa, fearing she might lose the attention of her listener, went straight into the next part of the programme—Liszt's second *Petrarch Sonnet.*

And now an extraordinary thing happened. She hadn't played more than three or four bars when the animal's whiskers began perceptibly to twitch. Slowly it drew itself up to an extra height, laid its head on one side, then on the other, and stared into space with a kind of frowning concentrated look that seemed to say, "What's this? Don't tell me. I know it so well, but just for the moment I don't seem to be able to place it." Louisa was fascinated, and with her little mouth half open and half smiling, she continued to play, waiting to see what on earth was going to happen next.

The cat stood up, walked to one end of the sofa, sat down again, listened some more; then all at once it bounded to the floor and leaped up onto the piano bench beside her. There it sat, listening intently to the lovely sonnet, not dreamily this time, but very erect, the large yellow eyes fixed upon Louisa's fingers.

"Well!" she said as she struck the last chord. "So you came up to sit beside me, did you? You like this better than the sofa? All right, I'll let you stay, but you must keep still and not jump about." She put out a hand and stroked the cat softly along the back, from head to tail. "That was Liszt," she went on. "Mind you, he can sometimes be quite horribly vulgar, but in things like this he's really charming."

She was beginning to enjoy this odd animal pantomime, so she went straight on into the next item on the programme, Schumann's *Kinderscenen.*

She hadn't been playing for more than a minute or two when

she realized that the cat had again moved, and was now back in its old place on the sofa. She'd been watching her hands at the time, and presumably that was why she hadn't even noticed its going; all the same, it must have been an extremely swift and silent move. The cat was still staring at her, still apparently attending closely to the music, and yet it seemed to Louisa that there was not now the same rapturous enthusiasm there'd been during the previous piece, the Liszt. In addition, the act of leaving the stool and returning to the sofa appeared in itself to be a mild but positive gesture of disappointment.

"What's the matter?" she asked when it was over. "What's wrong with Schumann? What's so marvellous about Liszt?" The cat looked straight back at her with those yellow eyes that had small jet-black bars lying vertically in their centres.

This, she told herself, is really beginning to get interesting—a trifle spooky, too, when she came to think of it. But one look at the cat sitting there on the sofa, so bright and attentive, so obviously waiting for more music, quickly reassured her.

"All right," she said. "I'll tell you what I'm going to do. I'm going to alter my programme specially for you. You seem to like Liszt so much, I'll give you another."

She hesitated, searching her memory for a good Liszt; then softly she began to play one of the twelve little pieces from *Der Weihnachtsbaum*. She was now watching the cat very closely, and the first thing she noticed was that the whiskers again began to twitch. It jumped down to the carpet, stood still a moment, inclining its head, quivering with excitement, and then, with a slow, silky stride, it walked around the piano, hopped up on the bench, and sat down beside her.

They were in the middle of all this when Edward came in from the garden.

"Edward!" Louisa cried, jumping up. "Oh, Edward, darling! Listen to this! Listen what's happened!"

"What is it now?" he said. "I'd like some tea." He had one of those narrow, sharp-nosed, faintly magenta faces, and the sweat was making it shine as though it were a long wet grape.

"It's the cat!" Louisa cried, pointing to it sitting quietly on the piano bench. "Just *wait* till you hear what's happened!"

"I thought I told you to take it to the police."

"But, Edward, *listen* to me. This is *terribly* exciting. This is a *musical* cat."

"Oh, yes?"

"This cat can appreciate music, and it can understand it too."

"Now stop this nonsense, Louisa, and let's for God's sake have some tea. I'm hot and tired from cutting brambles and building bonfires." He sat down in an armchair, took a cigarette from a box beside him, and lit it with an immense patent lighter that stood near the box.

"What you don't understand," Louisa said, "is that something extremely exciting has been happening here in our own house while you were out, something that may even be . . . well . . . almost momentous."

"I'm quite sure of that."

"Edward, *please!*"

Louisa was standing by the piano, her little pink face pinker than ever, a scarlet rose high up on each cheek. "If you want to know," she said, "I'll tell you what I think."

"I'm listening, dear."

"I think it might be possible that we are at this moment sitting in the presence of—" She stopped, as though suddenly sensing the absurdity of the thought.

"Yes?"

"You may think it silly, Edward, but it's honestly what I think."

"In the presence of who, for heaven's sake?"

"Of Franz Liszt himself!"

Her husband took a long slow pull at his cigarette and blew the smoke up at the ceiling. He had the tight-skinned, concave cheeks of a man who has worn a full set of dentures for many years, and every time he sucked at a cigarette, the cheeks went in even more, and the bones of his face stood out like a skeleton's. "I don't get you," he said.

"Edward, listen to me. From what I've seen this afternoon with my own eyes, it really looks as though this might actually be some sort of a reincarnation."

"You mean this lousy cat?"

"Don't talk like that, dear, please."

"You're not ill, are you, Louisa?"

"I'm perfectly all right, thank you very much. I'm a bit confused —I don't mind admitting it, but who wouldn't be after what's just happened? Edward, I swear to you—"

"What *did* happen, if I may ask?"

Louisa told him, and all the while she was speaking, her husband lay sprawled in the chair with his legs stretched out in front of him, sucking at his cigarette and blowing the smoke up at the ceiling. There was a thin cynical smile on his mouth.

"I don't see anything very unusual about that," he said when it was over. "All it is—it's a trick cat. It's been taught tricks, that's all."

"Don't be so silly, Edward. Every time I play Liszt, he gets all excited and comes running over to sit on the stool beside me. But only for Liszt, and nobody can teach a cat the difference between Liszt and Schumann. You don't even know it yourself. But this one can do it every single time. Quite obscure Liszt, too."

"Twice," the husband said. "He's only done it twice."

"Twice is enough."

"Let's see him do it again. Come on."

"No," Louisa said. "Definitely not. Because if this *is* Liszt, as I believe it is, or anyway the soul of Liszt or whatever it is that comes back, then it's certainly not right or even very kind to put him through a lot of silly undignified tests."

"My dear woman! This is a *cat*—a rather stupid grey cat that nearly got its coat singed by the bonfire this morning in the garden. And anyway, what do you know about reincarnation?"

"If his soul is there, that's enough for me," Louisa said firmly. "That's all that counts."

"Come on, then. Let's see him perform. Let's see him tell the difference between his own stuff and someone else's."

"No, Edward. I've told you before, I refuse to put him through any more silly circus tests. He's had quite enough of that for one day. But I'll tell you what I *will* do. I'll play him a little more of his own music."

"A fat lot that'll prove."

"You watch. And one thing is certain—as soon as he recognizes it, he'll refuse to budge off that bench where he's sitting now."

Louisa went to the music shelf, took down a book of Liszt, thumbed through it quickly, and chose another of his finger compositions—the B minor Sonata. She had meant to play only the first part of the work, but once she got started and saw how the cat was sitting there literally quivering with pleasure and watching her hands with that rapturous concentrated look, she didn't have the heart to stop. She played it all the way through. When it was finished, she glanced up at her husband and smiled. "There you are," she said. "You can't tell me he wasn't absolutely *loving* it."

"He just likes the noise, that's all."

"He was *loving* it. Weren't you, darling?" she said, lifting the cat in her arms. "Oh, my goodness, if only he could talk. Just think of it, dear—he met Beethoven in his youth! He knew Schubert and Mendelssohn and Schumann and Berlioz and Grieg and Delacroix and Ingres and Heine and Balzac. And let me see . . . My heavens, he was Wagner's father-in-law! I'm holding Wagner's father-in-law in my arms!"

"Louisa!" her husband said sharply, sitting up straight. "Pull yourself together." There was a new edge to his voice now, and he spoke louder.

Louisa glanced up quickly. "Edward, I do believe you're jealous!"

"Oh, sure, sure I'm jealous—of a lousy grey cat!"

"Then don't be so grumpy and cynical about it all. If you're going to behave like this, the best thing you can do is to go back to your gardening and leave the two of us together in peace. That will be best for all of us, won't it, darling?" she said, addressing the cat, stroking its head. "And later on this evening, we shall have some more music together, you and I, some more of your own work. Oh, yes," she said, kissing the creature several times on the neck, "and we might have a little Chopin, too. You needn't tell me—I happen to know you adore Chopin. You used to be great friends with him, didn't you, darling? As a matter of fact—if I remember rightly—it was in Chopin's apartment that you met the great love of your life, Madame Something-or-Other. Had three illegitimate children by her, too, didn't you? Yes, you did, you naughty thing, and don't go trying to deny it. So you shall have some Chopin," she said, kissing the cat again, "and that'll probably bring back all sorts of lovely memories to you, won't it?"

"Louisa, stop this at once!"

"Oh, don't be so stuffy, Edward."

"You're behaving like a perfect idiot, woman. And anyway, you forget we're going out this evening, to Bill and Betty's for canasta."

"Oh, but I couldn't *possibly* go out now. There's no question of that."

Edward got up slowly from his chair, then bent down and stubbed his cigarette hard into the ashtray. "Tell me something," he said quietly. "You don't really believe this—this twaddle you're talking, do you?"

"But of *course* I do. I don't think there's any question about it now. And, what's more, I consider that it puts a tremendous responsibility upon us, Edward—upon both of us. You as well."

"You know what I think," he said. "I think you ought to see a doctor. And damn quick, too."

With that, he turned and stalked out of the room, through the French windows, back into the garden.

Louisa watched him striding across the lawn toward his bonfire and his brambles, and she waited until he was out of sight before she turned and ran to the front door, still carrying the cat.

Soon she was in the car, driving to town.

She parked in front of the library, locked the cat in the car, hurried up the steps into the building, and headed straight for the reference room. There she began searching the cards for books on two subjects—REINCARNATION and LISZT.

Under REINCARNATION she found something called *Recurring Earth-Lives—How and Why,* by a man called F. Milton Willis, published in 1921. Under LISZT she found two biographical volumes. She took out all three books, returned to the car, and drove home.

Back in the house, she placed the cat on the sofa, sat herself down beside it with her three books, and prepared to do some serious reading. She would begin, she decided, with Mr. F. Milton Willis's work. The volume was thin and a trifle soiled, but it had a good heavy feel to it, and the author's name had an authoritative ring.

The doctrine of reincarnation, she read, states that spiritual souls pass from higher to higher forms of animals. "A man can, for instance, no more be reborn as an animal than an adult can re-become a child."

She read this again. But how did he know? How could he be so sure? He couldn't. No one could possibly be certain about a thing like that. At the same time, the statement took a good deal of the wind out of her sails.

"Around the centre of consciousness of each of us, there are, besides the dense outer body, four other bodies, invisible to the eye of flesh, but perfectly visible to people whose faculties of perception of superphysical things have undergone the requisite development. . . ."

She didn't understand that one at all, but she read on, and soon she came to an interesting passage that told how long a soul usually stayed away from the earth before returning in someone else's body. The time varied according to type, and Mr. Willis gave the following breakdown:

Drunkards and the unemployable	40/50	YEARS
Unskilled labourers	60/100	"
Skilled workers	100/200	"
The bourgeoisie	200/300	"
The upper-middle classes	500	"
The highest class of gentleman		
farmers	600/1000	"
Those in the Path of Initiation	1500/2000	"

Quickly she referred to one of the other books, to find out how long Liszt had been dead. It said he died in Bayreuth in 1886. That was sixty-seven years ago. Therefore, according to Mr. Willis, he'd have to have been an unskilled labourer to come back so soon. That didn't seem to fit at all. On the other hand, she didn't think much of the author's methods of grading. According to him, "the highest class of gentleman farmer" was just about the most superior being on the earth. Red jackets and stirrup cups and the bloody, sadistic murder of the fox. No, she thought, that isn't right. It was a pleasure to find herself beginning to doubt Mr. Willis.

Later in the book, she came upon a list of some of the more famous reincarnations. Epictetus, she was told, returned to earth as Ralph Waldo Emerson. Cicero came back as Gladstone, Alfred the Great as Queen Victoria, William the Conqueror as Lord Kitchener. Ashoka Vardhana, King of India in 272 B.C., came back as Colonel Henry Steel Olcott, an esteemed American lawyer. Pythagoras returned as Master Koot Hoomi, the gentleman who founded the Theosophical Society with Mme Blavatsky and Colonel H. S. Olcott (the esteemed American lawyer, alias Ashoka Vardhana, King of India). It didn't say who Mme Blavatsky had been. But "Theodore Roosevelt," it said, "has for numbers of incarnations played great parts as a leader of men. . . . From him descended the royal line of ancient Chaldea, he having been, about 30,000 B.C., appointed Governor of Chaldea by the Ego we know as Caesar who was then ruler of Persia. . . . Roosevelt and Caesar have been together time after time as military and administrative leaders; at one time, many thousands of years ago, they were husband and wife. . . ."

That was enough for Louisa. Mr. F. Milton Willis was clearly nothing but a guesser. She was not impressed by his dogmatic assertions. The fellow was probably on the right track, but his pronouncements were extravagant, especially the first one of all, about animals. Soon she hoped to be able to confound the whole Theosophical

Society with her proof that man could indeed reappear as a lower animal. Also that he did not have to be an unskilled labourer to come back within a hundred years.

She now turned to one of the Liszt biographies, and she was glancing through it casually when her husband came in again from the garden.

"What are you doing now?" he asked.

"Oh—just checking up a little here and there. Listen, my dear, did you know that Theodore Roosevelt once was Caesar's wife?"

"Louisa," he said, "look—why don't we stop this nonsense? I don't like to see you making a fool of yourself like this. Just give me that goddam cat and I'll take it to the police station myself."

Louisa didn't seem to hear him. She was staring open-mouthed at a picture of Liszt in the book that lay on her lap. "My God!" she cried. "Edward, look!"

"What?"

"Look! The warts on his face! I forgot all about them! He had these great warts on his face and it was a famous thing. Even his students used to cultivate little tufts of hair on their own faces in the same spots, just to be like him."

"What's that got to do with it?"

"Nothing. I mean not the students. But the warts have."

"Oh, Christ," the man said. "Oh, Christ God Almighty."

"The cat has them, too! Look, I'll show you."

She took the animal onto her lap and began examining its face. "There! There's one! And there's another! Wait a minute! I do believe they're in the same places! Where's that picture?"

It was a famous portrait of the musician in his old age, showing the fine powerful face framed in a mass of long grey hair that covered his ears and came halfway down his neck. On the face itself, each large wart had been faithfully reproduced, and there were five of them in all.

"Now, in the picture there's *one* above the right eyebrow." She looked above the right eyebrow of the cat. "Yes! It's there! In exactly the same place! And another on the left, at the top of the nose. That one's there, too! And one just below it on the cheek. And two fairly close together under the chin on the right side. Edward! Edward! Come and look! They're exactly the same."

"It doesn't prove a thing."

She looked up at her husband who was standing in the centre of the room in his green sweater and khaki slacks, still perspiring freely. "You're scared, aren't you, Edward? Scared of losing your precious dignity and having people think you might be making a fool of yourself just for once."

"I refuse to get hysterical about it, that's all."

Louisa turned back to the book and began reading some more. "This is interesting," she said. "It says here that Liszt loved all of Chopin's works except one—the Scherzo in B flat minor. Apparently he hated that. He called it the 'Governess Scherzo,' and said that it ought to be reserved solely for people in that profession."

"So what?"

"Edward, listen. As you insist on being so horrid about all this, I'll tell you what I'm going to do. I'm going to play this scherzo right now and you can stay here and see what happens."

"And then maybe you will deign to get us some supper."

Louisa got up and took from the shelf a large green volume containing all of Chopin's works. "Here it is. Oh yes, I remember it. It *is* rather awful. Now, listen—or, rather, watch. Watch to see what he does."

She placed the music on the piano and sat down. Her husband remained standing. He had his hands in his pockets and a cigarette in his mouth, and in spite of himself he was watching the cat, which was now dozing on the sofa. When Louisa began to play, the first effect was as dramatic as ever. The animal jumped up as though it had been stung, and it stood motionless for at least a minute, the ears pricked up, the whole body quivering. Then it became restless and began to walk back and forth along the length of the sofa. Finally, it hopped down onto the floor, and with its nose and tail held high in the air, it marched slowly, majestically, from the room.

"There!" Louisa cried, jumping up and running after it. "That does it! That really proves it!" She came back carrying the cat which she put down again on the sofa. Her whole face was shining with excitement now, her fists were clenched white, and the little bun on top of her head was loosening and going over to one side. "What about it, Edward? What d'you think?" She was laughing nervously as she spoke.

"I must say it was quite amusing."

"*Amusing!* My dear Edward, it's the most wonderful thing that's ever happened! Oh, goodness me!" she cried, picking up the cat again and hugging it to her bosom. "Isn't it marvellous to think we've got Franz Liszt staying in the house?"

"Now, Louisa. Don't let's get hysterical."

"I can't help it, I simply can't. And to *imagine* that he's actually going to live with us for always!"

"I beg your pardon?"

"Oh, Edward! I can hardly talk from excitement. And d'you know what I'm going to do next? Every musician in the whole world is going to want to meet him, that's a fact, and ask him about the people he knew—about Beethoven and Chopin and Schubert—"

"He can't talk," her husband said.

"Well—all right. But they're going to want to meet him anyway, just to see him and touch him and to play their own music to him, modern music he's never heard before."

"He wasn't that great. Now, if it had been Bach or Beethoven . . ."

"Don't interrupt, Edward, please. So what I'm going to do is to notify all the important living composers everywhere. It's my duty. I'll tell them Liszt is here, and invite them to visit him. And you know what? They'll come flying in from every corner of the earth!"

"To see a grey cat?"

"Darling, it's the same thing. It's *him.* No one cares what he *looks* like. Oh, Edward, it'll be the most exciting thing there ever was!"

"They'll think you're mad."

"You wait and see." She was holding the cat in her arms and petting it tenderly but looking across at her husband, who now walked over to the French windows and stood there staring out into the garden. The evening was beginning, and the lawn was turning slowly from green to black, and in the distance he could see the smoke from his bonfire rising straight up in a white column.

"No," he said, without turning round, "I'm not having it. Not in this house. It'll make us both look perfect fools."

"Edward, what do you mean?"

"Just what I say. I absolutely refuse to have you stirring up a lot of publicity about a foolish thing like this. You happen to have found a trick cat. O.K.—that's fine. Keep it, if it pleases you. I don't mind. But I don't wish you to go any further than that. Do you understand me, Louisa?"

"Further than what?"

"I don't want to hear any more of this crazy talk. You're acting like a lunatic."

Louisa put the cat slowly down on the sofa. Then slowly she raised herself to her full small height and took one pace forward.

"*Damn* you, Edward!" she shouted, stamping her foot. "For the first time in our lives something really exciting comes along and you're scared to death of having anything to do with it because someone may laugh at you! That's right, isn't it? You can't deny it, can you?"

"Louisa," her husband said. "That's quite enough of that. Pull yourself together now and stop this at once." He walked over and took a cigarette from the box on the table, then lit it with the enormous patent lighter. His wife stood watching him, and now the tears were beginning to trickle out of the inside corners of her eyes, making two little shiny rivers where they ran through the powder on her cheeks.

"We've been having too many of these scenes just lately, Louisa," he was saying. "No no, don't interrupt. Listen to me. I make full allowance for the fact that this may be an awkward time of life for you, and that—"

"Oh, my God! You idiot! You pompous idiot! Can't you see that this is different, this is—this is something miraculous? Can't you see *that?*"

At that point, he came across the room and took her firmly by the shoulders. He had the freshly lit cigarette between his lips, and she could see faint contours on his skin where the heavy perspiration had dried in patches. "Listen," he said. "I'm hungry. I've given up my golf and I've been working all day in the garden, and I'm tired and hungry and I want some supper. So do you. Off you go now to the kitchen and get us both something good to eat."

Louisa stepped back and put both hands to her mouth. "My heavens!" she cried. "I forgot all about it. He must be absolutely famished. Except for some milk, I haven't given him a thing to eat since he arrived."

"Who?"

"Why, *him,* of course. I must go at once and cook something really special. I wish I knew what his favourite dishes used to be. What do you think he would like best, Edward?"

"*Goddam* it, Louisa!"

"Now, Edward, please. I'm going to handle this *my* way just for once. You stay here," she said, bending down and touching the cat gently with her fingers. "I won't be long."

Louisa went into the kitchen and stood for a moment, wondering what special dish she might prepare. How about a soufflé? A nice cheese soufflé? Yes, that would be rather special. Of course, Edward didn't much care for them, but that couldn't be helped.

She was only a fair cook, and she couldn't be sure of always having a soufflé come out well, but she took extra trouble this time and waited a long while to make certain the oven had heated fully to the correct temperature. While the soufflé was baking and she was searching around for something to go with it, it occurred to her that Liszt had probably never in his life tasted either avocado pears or grapefruit, so she decided to give him both of them at once in a salad. It would be fun to watch his reaction. It really would.

When it was all ready, she put it on a tray and carried it into the living-room. At the exact moment she entered, she saw her husband coming in through the French windows from the garden.

"Here's his supper," she said, putting it on the table and turning toward the sofa. "Where is he?"

Her husband closed the garden door behind him and walked across the room to get himself a cigarette.

"Edward, where is he?"

"Who?"

"You know who."

"Ah, yes. Yes, that's right. Well—I'll tell you." He was bending forward to light the cigarette, and his hands were cupped around the enormous patent lighter. He glanced up and saw Louisa looking at him—at his shoes and the bottoms of his khaki slacks, which were damp from walking in long grass.

"I just went out to see how the bonfire was going," he said.

Her eyes travelled slowly upward and rested on his hands.

"It's still burning fine," he went on. "I think it'll keep going all night."

But the way she was staring made him uncomfortable.

"What is it?" he said, lowering the lighter. Then he looked down and noticed for the first time the long thin scratch that ran diagonally clear across the back of one hand, from the knuckle to the wrist.

"*Edward!*"

"Yes," he said, "I know. Those brambles are terrible. They tear you to pieces. Now, just a minute, Louisa. What's the matter?"

"*Edward!*"

"Oh, for God's sake, woman, sit down and keep calm. There's nothing to get worked up about. Louisa! Louisa, *sit down!*"

Lamb to the Slaughter

1953

THE room was warm and clean, the curtains drawn, the two table lamps alight—hers and the one by the empty chair opposite. On the sideboard behind her, two tall glasses, soda water, whiskey. Fresh ice cubes in the Thermos bucket.

Mary Maloney was waiting for her husband to come home from work.

Now and again she would glance up at the clock, but without anxiety, merely to please herself with the thought that each minute gone by made it nearer the time when he would come. There was a slow smiling air about her, and about everything she did. The drop of the head as she bent over her sewing was curiously tranquil. Her skin—for this was her sixth month with child—had acquired a wonderful translucent quality, the mouth was soft, and the eyes, with their new placid look, seemed larger, darker than before.

When the clock said ten minutes to five, she began to listen, and a few moments later, punctually as always, she heard the tires on the gravel outside, and the car door slamming, the footsteps passing the window, the key turning in the lock. She laid aside her sewing, stood up, and went forward to kiss him as he came in.

"Hullo darling," she said.

"Hullo," he answered.

She took his coat and hung it in the closet. Then she walked over and made the drinks, a strongish one for him, a weak one for herself; and soon she was back again in her chair with the sewing, and he in the other, opposite, holding the tall glass with both his hands, rocking it so the ice cubes tinkled against the side.

For her, this was always a blissful time of day. She knew he didn't want to speak much until the first drink was finished, and she, on her side, was content to sit quietly, enjoying his company after the long hours alone in the house. She loved to luxuriate in the presence of this man, and to feel—almost as a sunbather feels the sun —that warm male glow that came out of him to her when they were alone together. She loved him for the way he sat loosely in a chair, for the way he came in a door, or moved slowly across the room with long strides. She loved the intent, far look in his eyes when they rested on her, the funny shape of the mouth, and especially the way he remained silent about his tiredness, sitting still with himself until the whiskey had taken some of it away.

"Tired darling?"

"Yes," he said. "I'm tired." And as he spoke, he did an unusual thing. He lifted his glass and drained it in one swallow although there was still half of it, at least half of it left. She wasn't really watching him, but she knew what he had done because she heard the ice cubes falling back against the bottom of the empty glass when he lowered his arm. He paused a moment, leaning forward in the chair, then he got up and went slowly over to fetch himself another.

"I'll get it!" she cried, jumping up.

"Sit down," he said.

When he came back, she noticed that the new drink was dark amber with the quantity of whiskey in it.

"Darling, shall I get your slippers?"

"No."

She watched him as he began to sip the dark yellow drink, and she could see little oily swirls in the liquid because it was so strong.

"I think it's a shame," she said, "that when a policeman gets to be as senior as you, they keep him walking about on his feet all day long."

He didn't answer, so she bent her head again and went on with her sewing; but each time he lifted the drink to his lips, she heard the ice cubes clinking against the side of the glass.

"Darling," she said. "Would you like me to get you some cheese? I haven't made any supper because it's Thursday."

"No," he said.

"If you're too tired to eat out," she went on, "it's still not too late. There's plenty of meat and stuff in the freezer, and you can have it right here and not even move out of the chair."

Her eyes waited on him for an answer, a smile, a little nod, but he made no sign.

"Anyway," she went on, "I'll get you some cheese and crackers first."

"I don't want it," he said.

She moved uneasily in her chair, the large eyes still watching his face. "But you *must* have supper. I can easily do it here. I'd like to do it. We can have lamb chops. Or pork. Anything you want. Everything's in the freezer."

"Forget it," he said.

"But darling, you *must* eat! I'll fix it anyway, and then you can have it or not, as you like."

She stood up and placed her sewing on the table by the lamp.

"Sit down," he said. "Just for a minute, sit down."

It wasn't till then that she began to get frightened.

"Go on," he said. "Sit down."

She lowered herself back slowly into the chair, watching him all the time with those large, bewildered eyes. He had finished the second drink and was staring down into the glass, frowning.

"Listen," he said. "I've got something to tell you."

"What is it, darling? What's the matter?"

He had now become absolutely motionless, and he kept his head down so that the light from the lamp beside him fell across the upper part of his face, leaving the chin and mouth in shadow. She noticed there was a little muscle moving near the corner of his left eye.

"This is going to be a bit of a shock to you, I'm afraid," he said. "But I've thought about it a good deal and I've decided the only thing to do is tell you right away. I hope you won't blame me too much."

And he told her. It didn't take long, four or five minutes at most, and she sat very still through it all, watching him with a kind of dazed horror as he went further and further away from her with each word.

"So there it is," he added. "And I know it's kind of a bad time to be telling you, but there simply wasn't any other way. Of course I'll give you money and see you're looked after. But there needn't really be any fuss. I hope not anyway. It wouldn't be very good for my job."

Her first instinct was not to believe any of it, to reject it all. It occurred to her that perhaps he hadn't even spoken, that she herself had imagined the whole thing. Maybe, if she went about her business and acted as though she hadn't been listening, then later, when she sort of woke up again, she might find none of it had ever happened.

"I'll get the supper," she managed to whisper, and this time he didn't stop her.

When she walked across the room she couldn't feel her feet

touching the floor. She couldn't feel anything at all—except a slight nausea and a desire to vomit. Everything was automatic now—down the steps to the cellar, the light switch, the deep freeze, the hand inside the cabinet taking hold of the first object it met. She lifted it out, and looked at it. It was wrapped in paper, so she took off the paper and looked at it again.

A leg of lamb.

All right then, they would have lamb for supper. She carried it upstairs, holding the thin bone-end of it with both her hands, and as she went through the living-room, she saw him standing over by the window with his back to her, and she stopped.

"For God's sake," he said, hearing her, but not turning round. "Don't make supper for me. I'm going out."

At that point, Mary Maloney simply walked up behind him and without any pause she swung the big frozen leg of lamb high in the air and brought it down as hard as she could on the back of his head.

She might just as well have hit him with a steel club.

She stepped back a pace, waiting, and the funny thing was that he remained standing there for at least four or five seconds, gently swaying. Then he crashed to the carpet.

The violence of the crash, the noise, the small table overturning, helped bring her out of the shock. She came out slowly, feeling cold and surprised, and she stood for a while blinking at the body, still holding the ridiculous piece of meat tight with both hands.

All right, she told herself. So I've killed him.

It was extraordinary, now, how clear her mind became all of a sudden. She began thinking very fast. As the wife of a detective, she knew quite well what the penalty would be. That was fine. It made no difference to her. In fact, it would be a relief. On the other hand, what about the child? What were the laws about murderers with unborn children? Did they kill them both—mother and child? Or did they wait until the tenth month? What did they do?

Mary Maloney didn't know. And she certainly wasn't prepared to take a chance.

She carried the meat into the kitchen, placed it in a pan, turned the oven on high, and shoved it inside. Then she washed her hands and ran upstairs to the bedroom. She sat down before the mirror, tidied her hair, touched up her lips and face. She tried a smile. It came out rather peculiar. She tried again.

"Hullo Sam," she said brightly, aloud.

The voice sounded peculiar too.

"I want some potatoes please, Sam. Yes, and I think a can of peas."

That was better. Both the smile and the voice were coming out better now. She rehearsed it several times more. Then she ran downstairs, took her coat, went out the back door, down the garden, into the street.

It wasn't six o'clock yet and the lights were still on in the grocery shop.

"Hullo Sam," she said brightly, smiling at the man behind the counter.

"Why, good evening, Mrs. Maloney. How're *you?*"

"I want some potatoes please, Sam. Yes, and I think a can of peas."

The man turned and reached up behind him on the shelf for the peas.

"Patrick's decided he's tired and doesn't want to eat out tonight," she told him. "We usually go out Thursdays, you know, and now he's caught me without any vegetables in the house."

"Then how about meat, Mrs. Maloney?"

"No, I've got meat, thanks. I got a nice leg of lamb from the freezer."

"Oh."

"I don't much like cooking it frozen, Sam, but I'm taking a chance on it this time. You think it'll be all right?"

"Personally," the grocer said, "I don't believe it makes any difference. You want these Idaho potatoes?"

"Oh yes, that'll be fine. Two of those."

"Anything else?" The grocer cocked his head on one side, looking at her pleasantly. "How about afterwards? What you going to give him for afterwards?"

"Well—what would you suggest, Sam?"

The man glanced around his shop. "How about a nice big slice of cheesecake? I know he likes that."

"Perfect," she said. "He loves it."

And when it was all wrapped and she had paid, she put on her brightest smile and said, "Thank you, Sam. Goodnight."

"Goodnight, Mrs. Maloney. And thank *you.*"

And now, she told herself as she hurried back, all she was doing now, she was returning home to her husband and he was waiting for his supper; and she must cook it good, and make it as tasty as possible because the poor man was tired; and if, when she entered the house, she happened to find anything unusual, or tragic, or terrible, then naturally it would be a shock and she'd become frantic with grief and horror. Mind you, she wasn't *expecting* to find anything. She was just going home with the vegetables. Mrs. Patrick Maloney going home with the vegetables on Thursday evening to cook supper for her husband.

That's the way, she told herself. Do everything right and natural. Keep things absolutely natural and there'll be no need for any acting at all.

Therefore, when she entered the kitchen by the back door, she was humming a little tune to herself and smiling.

"Patrick!" she called. "How are you, darling?"

She put the parcel down on the table and went through into the living room; and when she saw him lying there on the floor with his legs doubled up and one arm twisted back underneath his body, it really was rather a shock. All the old love and longing for him welled up inside her, and she ran over to him, knelt down beside him, and began to cry her heart out. It was easy. No acting was necessary.

A few minutes later she got up and went to the phone. She knew the number of the police station, and when the man at the other end answered, she cried to him, "Quick! Come quick! Patrick's dead!"

"Who's speaking?"

"Mrs. Maloney. Mrs. Patrick Maloney."

"You mean Patrick Maloney's dead?"

"I think so," she sobbed. "He's lying on the floor and I think he's dead."

"Be right over," the man said.

The car came very quickly, and when she opened the front door, two policemen walked in. She knew them both—she knew nearly all the men at that precinct—and she fell right into Jack Noonan's arms, weeping hysterically. He put her gently into a chair, then went over to join the other one, who was called O'Malley, kneeling by the body.

"Is he dead?" she cried.

"I'm afraid he is. What happened?"

Briefly, she told her story about going out to the grocer and coming back to find him on the floor. While she was talking, crying and talking, Noonan discovered a small patch of congealed blood on the dead man's head. He showed it to O'Malley who got up at once and hurried to the phone.

Soon, other men began to come into the house. First a doctor, then two detectives, one of whom she knew by name. Later, a police photographer arrived and took pictures, and a man who knew about fingerprints. There was a great deal of whispering and muttering beside the corpse, and the detectives kept asking her a lot of questions. But they always treated her kindly. She told her story again, this time right from the beginning, when Patrick had come in, and she was sewing, and he was tired, so tired he hadn't wanted to go out for supper. She told how she'd put the meat in the oven—"it's there now, cooking"—and how she'd slipped out to the grocer for vegetables, and come back to find him lying on the floor.

"Which grocer?" one of the detectives asked.

She told him, and he turned and whispered something to the other detective who immediately went outside into the street.

In fifteen minutes he was back with a page of notes, and there was more whispering, and through her sobbing she heard a few of the whispered phrases—". . . acted quite normal . . . very cheerful . . . wanted to give him a good supper . . . peas . . . cheesecake . . . impossible that she . . ."

After a while, the photographer and the doctor departed and two other men came in and took the corpse away on a stretcher. Then the fingerprint man went away. The two detectives remained, and so did the two policemen. They were exceptionally nice to her, and Jack Noonan asked if she wouldn't rather go somewhere else, to her sister's house perhaps, or to his own wife who would take care of her and put her up for the night.

No, she said. She didn't feel she could move even a yard at the moment. Would they mind awfully if she stayed just where she was until she felt better. She didn't feel too good at the moment, she really didn't.

Then hadn't she better lie down on the bed? Jack Noonan asked.

No, she said. She'd like to stay right where she was, in this chair. A little later perhaps, when she felt better, she would move.

So they left her there while they went about their business, searching the house. Occasionally one of the detectives asked her another question. Sometimes Jack Noonan spoke at her gently as he passed by. Her husband, he told her, had been killed by a blow on the back of the head administered with a heavy blunt instrument, almost certainly a large piece of metal. They were looking for the weapon. The murderer may have taken it with him, but on the other hand he may've thrown it away or hidden it somewhere on the premises.

"It's the old story," he said. "Get the weapon, and you've got the man."

Later, one of the detectives came up and sat beside her. Did she know, he asked, of anything in the house that could've been used as the weapon? Would she mind having a look around to see if anything was missing—a very big spanner, for example, or a heavy metal vase.

They didn't have any heavy metal vases, she said.

"Or a big spanner?"

She didn't think they had a big spanner. But there might be some things like that in the garage.

The search went on. She knew that there were other policemen in the garden all around the house. She could hear their footsteps on the gravel outside, and sometimes she saw the flash of a torch through a chink in the curtains. It began to get late, nearly nine she noticed by the clock on the mantle. The four men searching the rooms seemed to be growing weary, a trifle exasperated.

"Jack," she said, the next time Seargeant Noonan went by. "Would you mind giving me a drink?"

"Sure I'll give you a drink. You mean this whiskey?"

"Yes please. But just a small one. It might make me feel better."

He handed her the glass.

"Why don't you have one yourself," she said. "You must be awfully tired. Please do. You've been very good to me."

"Well," he answered. "It's not strictly allowed, but I might take just a drop to keep me going."

One by one the others came in and were persuaded to take a little nip of whiskey. They stood around rather awkwardly with the drinks in their hands, uncomfortable in her presence, trying to say consoling things to her. Sergeant Noonan wandered into the kitchen, came out quickly and said, "Look, Mrs. Maloney. You know that oven of yours is still on, and the meat still inside."

"Oh *dear* me!" she cried. "So it is!"

"I better turn it off for you, hadn't I?"

"Will you do that, Jack? Thank you so much."

When the sergeant returned the second time, she looked at him with her large, dark, tearful eyes. "Jack Noonan," she said.

"Yes?"

"Would you do me a small favour—you and these others?"

"We can try, Mrs. Maloney."

"Well," she said. "Here you all are, and good friends of dear

Patrick's too, and helping to catch the man who killed him. You must be terribly hungry by now because it's long past your supper-time, and I know Patrick would never forgive me, God bless his soul, if I allowed you to remain in his house without offering you decent hospitality. Why don't you eat up that lamb that's in the oven. It'll be cooked just right by now."

"Wouldn't dream of it," Sergeant Noonan said.

"Please," she begged. "Please eat it. Personally I couldn't touch a thing, certainly not what's been in the house when he was here. But it's all right for you. It'd be a favour to me if you'd eat it up. Then you can go on with your work again afterwards."

There was a good deal of hesitating among the four policemen, but they were clearly hungry, and in the end they were persuaded to go into the kitchen and help themselves. The woman stayed where she was, listening to them through the open door, and she could hear them speaking among themselves, their voices thick and sloppy because their mouths were full of meat.

"Have some more, Charlie?"

"No. Better not finish it."

"She *wants* us to finish it. She said so. Be doing her a favour."

"Okay then. Give me some more."

"That's a hell of a big club the guy must've used to hit poor Patrick," one of them was saying. "The doc says his skull was smashed all to pieces just like from a sledgehammer."

"That's why it ought to be easy to find."

"Exactly what I say."

"Whoever done it, they're not going to be carrying a thing like that around with them longer than they need."

One of them belched.

"Personally, I think it's right here on the premises."

"Probably right under our very noses. What you think, Jack?"

And in the other room, Mary Maloney began to giggle.

Galloping Foxley

1953

Five days a week, for thirty-six years, I have travelled the eight-twelve train to the City. It is never unduly crowded, and it takes me right in to Cannon Street Station, only an eleven and a half minute walk from the door of my office in Austin Friars.

I have always liked the process of commuting; every phase of the little journey is a pleasure to me. There is a regularity about it that is agreeable and comforting to a person of habit, and in addition, it serves as a sort of slipway along which I am gently but firmly launched into the waters of daily business routine.

Ours is a smallish country station and only nineteen or twenty people gather there to catch the eight-twelve. We are a group that rarely changes, and when occasionally a new face appears on the platform it causes a certain disclamatory, protestant ripple, like a new bird in a cage of canaries.

But normally, when I arrive in the morning with my usual four minutes to spare, there they all are, these good, solid, steadfast people, standing in their right places with their right umbrellas and hats and ties and faces and their newspapers under their arms, as unchanged and unchangeable through the years as the furniture in my own living-room. I like that.

I like also my corner seat by the window and reading *The Times* to the noise and motion of the train. This part of it lasts thirty-two minutes and it seems to soothe both my brain and my fretful old body like a good long massage. Believe me, there's nothing like routine and regularity for preserving one's peace of mind. I have now made this morning journey nearly ten thousand times in all, and I enjoy it more and more every day. Also (irrelevant, but interesting), I have become a sort of clock. I can tell at once if we are running two, three, or four minutes late, and I never have to look up to know which station we are stopped at.

The walk at the other end from Cannon Street to my office is neither too long nor too short—a healthy little perambulation along streets crowded with fellow commuters all proceeding to their places of work on the same orderly schedule as myself. It gives me a sense of assurance to be moving among these dependable, dignified people who stick to their jobs and don't go gadding about all over the world. Their lives, like my own, are regulated nicely by the minute hand of an accurate watch, and very often our paths cross at the same times and places on the street each day.

For example, as I turn the corner into St. Swithin's Lane, I invariably come head on with a genteel middle-aged lady who wears silver pince-nez and carries a black briefcase in her hand—a first-rate accountant, I should say, or possibly an executive in the textile industry. When I cross over Threadneedle Street by the traffic lights, nine times out of ten I pass a gentleman who wears a different garden flower in his button-hole each day. He dresses in black trousers and grey spats and is clearly a punctual and meticulous person, probably a banker, or perhaps a solicitor like myself; and several times in the last twenty-five years, as we have hurried past one another across the street, our eyes have met in a fleeting glance of mutual approval and respect.

At least half the faces I pass on this little walk are now familiar to me. And good faces they are too, my kind of faces, my kind of people—sound, sedulous, businesslike folk with none of that restlessness and glittering eye about them that you see in all these so-called clever types who want to tip the world upside down with their Labour Governments and socialized medicines and all the rest of it.

So you can see that I am, in every sense of the words, a contented commuter. Or would it be more accurate to say that I *was* a contented commuter? At the time when I wrote the little autobiographical sketch you have just read—intending to circulate it among the staff of my office as an exhortation and an example—I was giving a perfectly true account of my feelings. But that was a whole week ago, and since then something rather peculiar has happened. As a matter of fact, it started to happen last Tuesday, the very morning that I was carrying the rough draft up to Town in my pocket; and this, to me, was so timely and coincidental that I can only believe it to have been the work of God. God had read my little essay and he had said to himself, "This man Perkins is becoming over-complacent. It is high time I taught him a lesson." I honestly believe that's what happened.

As I say, it was last Tuesday, the Tuesday after Easter, a warm yellow spring morning, and I was striding onto the platform of our small country station with *The Times* tucked under my arm and the draft of "The Contented Commuter" in my pocket, when I immediately became aware that something was wrong. I could actually *feel* that curious little ripple of protest running along the ranks of my fellow commuters. I stopped and glanced around.

The stranger was standing plumb in the middle of the platform, feet apart and arms folded, looking for all the world as though he owned the whole place. He was a biggish, thickset man, and even from behind he somehow managed to convey a powerful impression of arrogance and oil. Very definitely, he was not one of us. He carried a cane instead of an umbrella, his shoes were brown instead of black, the grey hat was cocked at a ridiculous angle, and in one way and another there seemed to be an excess of silk and polish about his person. More than this I did not care to observe. I walked straight past him with my face to the sky, adding, I sincerely hope, a touch of real frost to an atmosphere that was already cool.

The train came in. And now, try if you can to imagine my horror when the new man actually followed me into *my own* compartment! Nobody has done this to me for fifteen years. My colleagues always respect my seniority. One of my special little pleasures is to have the place to myself for at least one, sometimes two or even three stations. But here, if you please, was this fellow, this stranger, straddling the seat opposite and blowing his nose and rustling *The Daily Mail* and lighting a disgusting pipe.

I lowered my *Times* and stole a glance at his face. I suppose he was about the same age as me—sixty-two or three—but he had one of those unpleasantly handsome, brown, leathery countenances that you see nowadays in advertisements for men's shirts—the lion shooter and the polo player and the Everest climber and the tropical explorer and the racing yachtsman all rolled into one; dark eyebrows, steely eyes, strong white teeth clamping the stem of a pipe. Personally, I mistrust all handsome men. The superficial pleasures of this life come too easily to them, and they seem to walk the world as though they themselves were personally responsible for their own good looks. I don't mind a *woman* being pretty. That's different. But in a man, I'm sorry, but somehow or other I find it downright offensive. Anyway, here was this one sitting right opposite me in the carriage, and I was looking at him over the top of my *Times* when suddenly he glanced up and our eyes met.

"D'you mind the pipe?" he asked, holding it up in his fingers. That was all he said. But the sound of his voice had a sudden and extraordinary effect upon me. In fact, I think I jumped. Then I sort of froze up and sat staring at him for at least a minute before I got a hold of myself and made an answer.

"This is a smoker," I said, "so you may do as you please."

"I just thought I'd ask."

There it was again, that curiously crisp, familiar voice, clipping its words and spitting them out very hard and small like a little quick-firing gun shooting out raspberry seeds. Where had I heard it before? And why did every word seem to strike upon some tiny tender spot far back in my memory? Good heavens, I thought. Pull yourself together. What sort of nonsense is this?

The stranger returned to his paper. I pretended to do the same. But by this time I was properly put out and I couldn't concentrate at all. Instead, I kept stealing glances at him over the top of the editorial page. It was really an intolerable face, vulgarly, almost lasciviously handsome, with an oily salacious sheen all over the skin. But had I or had I not seen it before sometime in my life? I began to think I had, because now, even when I looked at it I felt a peculiar kind of discomfort that I cannot quite describe—something to do with pain and with violence, perhaps even with fear.

We spoke no more during the journey, but you can well imagine that by then my whole routine had been thoroughly upset. My day was ruined; and more than one of my clerks at the office felt the sharper edge of my tongue, particularly after luncheon when my digestion started acting up on me as well.

The next morning, there he was again standing in the middle of the platform with his cane and his pipe and his silk scarf and his nauseatingly handsome face. I walked past him and approached a certain Mr. Grummitt, a stockbroker who has been commuting with me for over twenty-eight years. I can't say I've ever had an actual conversation with him before—we are rather a reserved lot on our station—but a crisis like this will usually break the ice.

"Grummitt," I whispered. "Who's this bounder?"

"Search me," Grummitt said.

"Pretty unpleasant."

"Very."

"Not going to be a regular, I trust."

"Oh God," Grummitt said.

Then the train came in.

This time, to my great relief, the man got into another compartment.

But the following morning I had him with me again.

"Well," he said, settling back in the seat directly opposite. "It's a *topping* day." And once again I felt that slow uneasy stirring of the memory, stronger than ever this time, closer to the surface but not yet quite within my reach.

Then came Friday, the last day of the week. I remember it had rained as I drove to the station, but it was one of those warm sparkling April showers that last only five or six minutes, and when I walked onto the platform, all the umbrellas were rolled up and the sun was shining and there were big white clouds floating in the sky. In spite of this, I felt depressed. There was no pleasure in this journey for me any longer. I knew the stranger would be there. And sure enough, he was, standing with his legs apart just as though he owned the place and this time swinging his cane casually back and forth through the air.

The cane! That did it! I stopped like I'd been shot.

"It's Foxley!" I cried under my breath. "Galloping Foxley! And still swinging his cane!"

I stepped closer to get a better look. I tell you I've never had such a shock in all my life. It was Foxley all right. Bruce Foxley or Galloping Foxley as we used to call him. And the last time I'd seen him, let me see—it was at school and I was no more than twelve or thirteen years old.

At that point the train came in, and heaven help me if he didn't get into my compartment once again. He put his hat and cane up on the rack, then turned and sat down and began lighting his pipe. He glanced up at me through the smoke with those rather small cold eyes and he said, *"Ripping* day, isn't it. Just like summer."

There was no mistaking the voice now. It hadn't changed at all. Except that the things I had been used to hearing it say were different.

"All right Perkins," it used to say. "All right you nasty little boy. I am about to beat you again."

How long ago was that? It must be nearly fifty years. Extraordinary, though, how little the features had altered. Still the same arrogant tilt of the chin, the flaring nostrils, the contemptuous staring eyes that were too small and a shade too close together for comfort; still the same habit of thrusting his face forward at you, impinging on you, pushing you into a corner, and even the hair I could remember—coarse and slightly wavy, with just a trace of oil all over it, like a well-tossed salad. He used to keep a bottle of green hair mixture on the side table in his study—when you have to dust a room you get to know and to hate all the objects in it—and this bottle had the royal coat of arms on the label and the name of a shop in Bond Street, and under that, in small print, it said "By Appointment—Hairdressers To His Majesty King Edward VII." I can remember that particularly because it seemed so funny that a shop should want to boast about being hairdresser to someone who was practically bald—even a monarch.

And now I watched Foxley settle back in his seat and begin reading his paper. It was a curious sensation, sitting only a yard away from this man who fifty years before had made me so miserable that I had once contemplated suicide. He hadn't recognized *me;* there wasn't much danger of that because of my mustache. I felt fairly sure I was safe and could sit there and watch him all I wanted.

Looking back on it, there seems little doubt that I suffered very badly at the hands of Bruce Foxley my first year in school, and strangely enough, the unwitting cause of it all was my father. I was twelve and a half when I first went off to this fine old Public School. That was, let me see, in 1907. My father, who wore a silk topper and morning coat, escorted me to the station, and I can remember how we were standing on the platform among piles of wooden tuck-boxes and trunks and what seemed like thousands of very large boys milling about and talking and shouting at one another, when suddenly somebody who was wanting to get by us gave my father a great push from behind and nearly knocked him off his feet.

My father, who was a small, courteous, dignified person, turned around with surprising speed and seized the culprit by the wrist.

"Don't they teach you better manners than that at this school, young man," he said.

The boy, at least a head taller than my father, looked down at him with a cold, arrogant-laughing glare, and said nothing.

"It seems to me," my father said, staring back at him, "that an apology would be in order."

But the boy just kept on looking down his nose at my father with this funny little arrogant smile at the corners of his mouth, and his chin kept coming further and further out.

"You strike me as being an impudent and ill-mannered boy," my father went on. "And I can only pray that you are an exception in your school. I would not wish for any son of mine to pick up such habits."

At this point, the big boy inclined his head slightly in my direction, and a pair of small, cold, rather close together eyes looked down into mine. I was not particularly frightened at the time; I knew nothing about the power of senior boys over junior boys at Public Schools; and I can remember that I looked straight back at him in support of my father, whom I adored and respected.

When my father started to say something more, the boy simply turned away and sauntered slowly down the platform into the crowd.

Bruce Foxley never forgot this episode; and of course the really unlucky thing about it for me was that when I arrived at school I found myself in the same "house" as him. Even worse than that— I was in his study. He was doing his last year, and he was a prefect —a "boazer" we called it—and as such he was officially permitted to beat any of the fags in the house. But being in his study, I automatically became his own particular, personal slave. I was his valet and cook and maid and errand-boy, and it was my duty to see that he never lifted a finger for himself unless absolutely necessary. In no society that I know of in the world is a servant imposed upon to the extent that we wretched little fags were imposed upon by the boazers at school. In frosty or snowy weather I even had to sit on the seat of the lavatory (which was in an unheated outhouse) every morning after breakfast to warm it before Foxley came along.

I could remember how he used to saunter across the room in his loose-jointed, elegant way, and if a chair were in his path he would knock it aside and I would have to run over and pick it up. He wore silk shirts and always had a silk handkerchief tucked up his sleeve, and his shoes were made by someone called Lobb (who also had a Royal crest). They were pointed shoes, and it was my duty to rub the leather with a bone for fifteen minutes each day to make it shine.

But the worst memories of all had to do with the changing-room.

I could see myself now, a small pale shrimp of a boy standing just inside the door of this huge room in my pyjamas and bedroom slippers and brown camel hair dressing-gown. A single bright electric bulb was hanging on a flex from the ceiling, and all around the walls the black and yellow football shirts with their sweaty smell filling the room, and the voice, the clipped, pip-spitting voice was saying, "So which is it to be this time? Six with the dressing-gown on—or four with it off?"

I never could bring myself to answer this question. I would simply stand there staring down at the dirty floor-planks, dizzy with fear and unable to think of anything except that this other larger boy would soon start smashing away at me with his long, thin, white stick, slowly, scientifically, skillfully, legally, and with apparent relish, and I would bleed. Five hours earlier, I had failed to get the fire to light in his study. I had spent my pocket money on a box of special firelighters and I had held a newspaper across the chimney opening to make a draught and I had knelt down in front of it and blown my guts out into the bottom of the grate; but the coals would not burn.

"If you're too obstinate to answer," the voice was saying, "then I'll have to decide for you."

I wanted desperately to answer because I knew which one I had to choose. It's the first thing you learn when you arrive. Always keep the dressing-gown *on* and take the extra strokes. Otherwise you're almost certain to get cut. Even three with it on is better than one with it off.

"Take it off then and get into the far corner and touch your toes. I'm going to give you four."

Slowly I would take it off and lay it on the ledge above the boot-lockers. And slowly I would walk over to the far corner, cold and naked now in my cotton pyjamas, treading softly and seeing everything around me suddenly very bright and flat and far away, like a magic lantern picture, and very big, and very unreal, and sort of swimming through the water in my eyes.

"Go on and touch your toes. Tighter—much tighter than that."

Then he would walk down to the far end of the changing-room and I would be watching him upside down between my legs, and he would disappear through a doorway that led down two steps into what we called "the basin-passage." This was a stone-floored corridor with wash basins along one wall, and beyond it was the bathroom. When Foxley disappeared I knew he was walking down to the far end of the basin-passage. Foxley always did that. Then, in the distance, but echoing loud among the basins and the tiles, I would hear the noise of his shoes on the stone floor as he started galloping forward, and through my legs I would see him leaping up the two steps into the changing-room and come bounding toward me with his face thrust forward and the cane held high in the air. This was the moment when I shut my eyes and waited for the crack and told myself that whatever happened I must not straighten up.

Anyone who has been properly beaten will tell you that the real pain does not come until about eight or ten seconds after the stroke. The stroke itself is merely a loud crack and a sort of blunt thud against your backside, numbing you completely. (I'm told a bullet wound does the same.) But later on, oh my heavens, it feels like someone is laying a red hot poker right across your naked buttocks and it is absolutely impossible to prevent yourself from reaching back and clutching it with your fingers.

Foxley knew all about this time lag, and the slow walk back over a distance that must altogether have been fifteen yards gave each stroke plenty of time to reach the peak of its pain before the next one was delivered.

On the fourth stroke I would invariably straighten up. I couldn't help it. It was an automatic defense reaction from a body that had had as much as it could stand.

"You flinched," Foxley would say. "That one doesn't count. Go on—down you get."

The next time I would remember to grip my ankles.

Afterwards, he would watch me as I walked over—very stiff now and holding by backside—to put on my dressing-gown, but I would always try to keep turned away from him so he couldn't see my face. And when I went out, it would be, "Hey you! Come back!"

I was in the passage then, and I would stop and turn and stand in the doorway, waiting.

"Come here. Come on, come back here. Now—haven't you forgotten something?"

All I could think of at that moment was the excruciating burning pain in my behind.

"You strike me as being an impudent and ill-mannered boy," he would say, imitating my father's voice. "Don't they teach you better manners than that at this school?"

"Thank . . . you," I would stammer. "Thank . . . you . . . for the beating."

And then back up the dark stairs to the dormitory and it became much better then because it was all over and the pain was going and the others were clustering round and treating me with a certain rough sympathy born of having gone through the same thing themselves, many times.

"Hey Perkins, let's have a look."

"How many d'you get?"

"Five, wasn't it. We heard them easily from here."

"Come on, man. Let's see the marks."

I would take down my pyjamas and stand there while this group of experts solemnly examined the damage.

"Rather far apart, aren't they? Not quite up to Foxley's usual standard."

"Two of them are close. Actually touching. Look—these two are beauties!"

"That low one was a rotten shot."

"Did he go right down the basin-passage to start his run?"

"You got an extra one for flinching, didn't you?"

"By golly, old Foxley's really got it in for *you*, Perkins."

"Bleeding a bit too. Better wash it, you know."

Then the door would open and Foxley would be there, and everyone would scatter and pretend to be doing his teeth or saying his prayers while I was left standing in the centre of the room with my pants down.

"What's going on here?" Foxley would say, taking a quick look at his own handiwork. "You—Perkins! Put your pyjamas on properly and get into bed."

And that was the end of a day.

Through the week, I never had a moment of time to myself. If Foxley saw me in the study taking up a novel or perhaps opening my stamp album, he would immediately find something for me to do One of his favourites, especially when it was raining outside, was, "Oh Perkins, I think a bunch of wild irises would look rather nice on my desk, don't you?"

Wild irises grew only around Orange Ponds. Orange Ponds was two miles down the road and half a mile across the fields. I would get up from my chair, put on my raincoat and my straw hat, take my umbrella—my brolly—and set off on this long and lonely trek. The straw hat had to be worn at all times outdoors, but it was easily destroyed by rain; therefore the brolly was necessary to protect the hat. On the other hand, you can't keep a brolly over your head while scrambling about on a woody bank looking for irises, so to save my hat from ruin I would put it on the ground under my brolly while I searched for the flowers. In this way, I caught many colds.

But the most dreaded day was Sunday. Sunday was for cleaning the study, and how well I can remember the terror of those mornings, the frantic dusting and scrubbing, and then the waiting for Foxley to come in to inspect.

"Finished?" he would ask.

"I . . . I think so."

Then he would stroll over to the drawer of his desk and take out a single white glove, fitting it slowly onto his right hand, pushing each finger well home, and I would stand there watching and trembling as he moved around the room running his white-gloved forefinger along the picture tops, the skirting, the shelves, the window sills, the lamp shades. I never took my eyes off that finger. For me it was an instrument of doom. Nearly always, it managed to discover some tiny crack that I had overlooked or perhaps hadn't even thought about; and when this happened Foxley would turn slowly around, smiling that dangerous little smile that wasn't a smile, holding up the white finger so that I should see for myself the thin smudge of dust that lay along the side of it.

"Well," he would say. "So you're a lazy little boy. Aren't you?"

No answer.

"Aren't you?"

"I thought I dusted it all."

"Are you or are you not a nasty, lazy little boy?"

"Y-yes."

"But your father wouldn't want you to grow up like that, would he? Your father is very particular about manners, is he not?"

No answer.

"I asked you, is your father particular about manners?"

"Perhaps—yes."

"Therefore I will be doing him a favour if I punish you, won't I?"

"I don't know."

"Won't I?"

"Y-yes."

"We will meet later then, after prayers, in the changing-room."

The rest of the day would be spent in an agony of waiting for the evening to come.

Oh my goodness, how it was all coming back to me now. Sunday was also letter-writing time. "Dear Mummy and Daddy—thank you very much for your letter. I hope you are both well. I am, except I have got a cold because I got caught in the rain but it will soon be over. Yesterday we played Shrewsbury and beat them 4–2. I watched and Foxley who you know is the head of our house scored one of our goals. Thank you very much for the cake. With love from William."

I usually went to the lavatory to write my letter, or to the boot-hole, or the bathroom—any place out of Foxley's way. But I had to watch the time. Tea was at four-thirty and Foxley's toast had to be ready. Every day I had to make toast for Foxley, and on weekdays there were no fires allowed in the studies so all the fags, each making toast for his own study-holder, would have to crowd around the one small fire in the library, jockeying for position with his toasting-fork. Under these conditions, I still had to see that Foxley's toast was (1) very crisp (2) not burned at all (3) hot and ready exactly on time. To fail in any one of these requirements was a "beatable offense."

"Hey you! What's this?"

"It's toast."

"Is this really your idea of toast?"

"Well . . ."

"You're too idle to make it right, aren't you?"

"I try to make it."

"You know what they do to an idle horse, Perkins?"

"No."

"Are you a horse?"

"No."

"Well—anyway you're an ass—ha, ha—so I think you qualify. I'll be seeing you later."

Oh, the agony of those days. To burn Foxley's toast was a "beatable offense." So was forgetting to take the mud off Foxley's football boots. So was failing to hang up Foxley's football clothes. So was rolling up Foxley's brolly the wrong way round. So was banging the study door when Foxey was working. So was filling Foxley's bath too hot for him. So was not cleaning the buttons properly on Foxley's O.T.C. uniform. So was making those blue metal-polish smudges on the uniform itself. So was failing to shine the *soles* of Foxley's shoes. So was leaving Foxley's study untidy at any time. In fact, so far as Foxley was concerned, I was practically a beatable offense myself.

I glanced out the window. My goodness, we were nearly there. I must have been dreaming away like this for quite a while, and I hadn't even opened my *Times.* Foxley was still leaning back in the corner seat opposite me reading his *Daily Mail,* and through a cloud of blue smoke from his pipe I could see the top half of his face over the newspaper, the small bright eyes, the corrugated forehead, the wavy, slightly oily hair.

Looking at him now, after all that time, was a peculiar and rather exciting experience. I knew he was no longer dangerous, but the old memories were still there and I didn't feel altogether comfortable in his presence. It was something like being inside the cage with a tame tiger.

What nonsense is this? I asked myself. Don't be so stupid. My heavens, if you wanted to you could go ahead and tell him exactly what you thought of him and he couldn't touch you. Hey—that was an idea!

Except that—well—after all, was it worth it? I was too old for that sort of thing now, and I wasn't sure that I really felt much anger toward him anyway.

So what should I do? I couldn't sit there staring at him like an idiot.

At that point, a little impish fancy began to take a hold of me. What I would like to do, I told myself, would be to lean across and tap him lightly on the knee and tell him who I was. Then I would watch his face. After that, I would begin talking about our school-days together, making it just loud enough for the other people in the carriage to hear. I would remind him playfully of some of the things he used to do to me, and perhaps even describe the changing-room beatings so as to embarrass him a trifle. A bit of teasing and discomfort wouldn't do him any harm. And it would do *me* an awful lot of good.

Suddenly he glanced up and caught me staring at him. It was the second time this had happened, and I noticed a flicker of irritation in his eyes.

All right, I told myself. Here we go. But keep it pleasant and sociable and polite. It'll be much more effective that way, more embarrassing for him.

So I smiled at him and gave him a courteous little nod. Then, raising my voice, I said, "I do hope you'll excuse me. I'd like to introduce myself." I was leaning forward, watching him closely so as not to miss the reaction. "My name is Perkins—William Perkins —and I was at Repton in 1907."

The others in the carriage were sitting very still, and I could sense that they were all listening and waiting to see what would happen next.

"I'm glad to meet you," he said, lowering the paper to his lap. "Mine's Fortescue—Jocelyn Fortescue, Eton, 1916."

The Way Up to Heaven

1954

ALL her life, Mrs. Foster had had an almost pathological fear of missing a train, a plane, a boat, or even a theatre curtain. In other respects, she was not a particularly nervous woman, but the mere thought of being late on occasions like these would throw her into such a state of nerves that she would begin to twitch. It was nothing much—just a tiny vellicating muscle in the corner of the left eye, like a secret wink—but the annoying thing was that it refused to disappear until an hour or so after the train or plane or whatever it was had been safely caught.

It is really extraordinary how in certain people a simple apprehension about a thing like catching a train can grow into a serious obsession. At least half an hour before it was time to leave the house for the station, Mrs. Foster would step out of the elevator all ready to go, with hat and coat and gloves, and then, being quite unable to sit down, she would flutter and fidget about from room to room until her husband, who must have been well aware of her state, finally emerged from his privacy and suggested in a cool dry voice that perhaps they had better get going now, had they not?

Mr. Foster may possibly have had a right to be irritated by this foolishness of his wife's, but he could have had no excuse for increasing her misery by keeping her waiting unnecessarily. Mind you, it is by no means certain that this is what he did, yet whenever they were to go somewhere, his timing was so accurate—just a minute or two late, you understand—and his manner so bland that it was hard to believe he wasn't purposely inflicting a nasty private little torture of his own on the unhappy lady. And one thing he must have known —that she would never dare to call out and tell him to hurry. He had disciplined her too well for that. He must also have known that if he was prepared to wait even beyond the last moment of safety, he could drive her nearly into hysterics. On one or two special occasions in the later years of their married life, it seemed almost as though he had *wanted* to miss the train simply in order to intensify the poor woman's suffering.

Assuming (though one cannot be sure) that the husband was guilty, what made his attitude doubly unreasonable was the fact that, with the exception of this one small irrepressible foible, Mrs. Foster was and always had been a good and loving wife. For over thirty years, she had served him loyally and well. There was no doubt about this. Even she, a very modest woman, was aware of it, and although she had for years refused to let herself believe that Mr. Foster would ever consciously torment her, there had been times recently when she had caught herself beginning to wonder.

Mr. Eugene Foster, who was nearly seventy years old, lived with his wife in a large six-story house on East Sixty-second Street, and they had four servants. It was a gloomy place, and few people came to visit them. But on this particular morning in January, the house had come alive and there was a great deal of bustling about. One maid was distributing bundles of dust sheets to every room, while another was draping them over the furniture. The butler was bringing down suitcases and putting them in the hall. The cook kept popping up from the kitchen to have a word with the butler, and Mrs. Foster herself, in an old-fashioned fur coat and with a black hat on the top of her head, was flying from room to room and pretending to supervise these operations. Actually, she was thinking of nothing at all except that she was going to miss her plane if her husband didn't come out of his study soon and get ready.

"What time is it, Walker?" she said to the butler as she passed him.

"It's ten minutes past nine, Madam."

"And has the car come?"

"Yes, Madam, it's waiting. I'm just going to put the luggage in now."

"It takes an hour to get to Idlewild," she said. "My plane leaves at eleven. I have to be there half an hour beforehand for the formalities. I shall be late. I just *know* I'm going to be late."

"I think you have plenty of time, Madam," the butler said kindly. "I warned Mr. Foster that you must leave at nine fifteen. There's still another five minutes."

"Yes, Walker, I know, I know. But get the luggage in quickly, will you please?"

She began walking up and down the hall, and whenever the

butler came by, she asked him the time. This, she kept telling herself, was the *one* plane she must not miss. It had taken months to persuade her husband to allow her to go. If she missed it, he might easily decide that she should cancel the whole thing. And the trouble was that he insisted on coming to the airport to see her off.

"Dear God," she said aloud, "I'm going to miss it. I know, I know, I *know* I'm going to miss it." The little muscle beside the left eye was twitching madly now. The eyes themselves were very close to tears.

"What time is it, Walker?"

"It's eighteen minutes past, Madam."

"Now I really *will* miss it!" she cried. "Oh, I wish he would come!"

This was an important journey for Mrs. Foster. She was going all alone to Paris to visit her daughter, her only child, who was married to a Frenchman. Mrs. Foster didn't care much for the Frenchman, but she was fond of her daughter, and, more than that, she had developed a great yearning to set eyes on her three grandchildren. She knew them only from the many photographs that she had received and that she kept putting up all over the house. They were beautiful, these children. She doted on them, and each time a new picture arrived, she would carry it away and sit with it for a long time, staring at it lovingly and searching the small faces for signs of that old satisfying blood likeness that meant so much. And now, lately, she had come more and more to feel that she did not really wish to live out her days in a place where she could not be near these children, and have them visit her, and take them for walks, and buy them presents, and watch them grow. She knew, of course, that it was wrong and in a way disloyal to have thoughts like these while her husband was still alive. She knew also that although he was no longer active in his many enterprises, he would never consent to leave New York and live in Paris. It was a miracle that he had ever agreed to let her fly over there alone for six weeks to visit them. But, oh, how she wished she could live there always, and be close to them!

"Walker, what time is it?"

"Twenty-two minutes past, Madam."

As he spoke, a door opened and Mr. Foster came into the hall. He stood for a moment, looking intently at his wife, and she looked back at him—at this diminutive but still quite dapper old man with the huge bearded face that bore such an astonishing resemblance to those old photographs of Andrew Carnegie.

"Well," he said, "I suppose perhaps we'd better get going fairly soon if you want to catch that plane."

"*Yes, dear—yes!* Everything's ready. The car's waiting."

"That's good," he said. With his head over to one side, he was watching her closely. He had a peculiar way of cocking the head and then moving it in a series of small, rapid jerks. Because of this and because he was clasping his hands up high in front of him, near the chest, he was somehow like a squirrel standing there—a quick clever old squirrel from the Park.

"Here's Walker with your coat, dear. Put it on."

"I'll be with you in a moment," he said. "I'm just going to wash my hands."

She waited for him, and the tall butler stood beside her, holding the coat and the hat.

"Walker, will I miss it?"

"No, Madam," the butler said. "I think you'll make it all right."

Then Mr. Foster appeared again, and the butler helped him on with his coat. Mrs. Foster hurried outside and got into the hired Cadillac. Her husband came after her, but he walked down the steps of the house slowly, pausing halfway to observe the sky and to sniff the cold morning air.

"It looks a bit foggy," he said as he sat down beside her in the car. "And it's always worse out there at the airport. I shouldn't be surprised if the flight's cancelled already."

"Don't say that, dear—*please.*"

They didn't speak again until the car had crossed over the river to Long Island.

"I arranged everything with the servants," Mr. Foster said. "They're all going off today. I gave them half pay for six weeks and told Walker I'd send him a telegram when we wanted them back."

"Yes," she said. "He told me."

"I'll move into the club tonight. It'll be a nice change staying at the club."

"Yes, dear. I'll write to you."

"I'll call in at the house occasionally to see that everything's all right and to pick up the mail."

"But don't you really think Walker should stay there all the time to look after things?" she asked meekly.

"Nonsense. It's quite unnecessary. And anyway, I'd have to pay him full wages."

"Oh yes," she said. "Of course."

"What's more, you never know what people get up to when they're left alone in a house," Mr. Foster announced, and with that he took out a cigar and, after snipping off the end with a silver cutter, lit it with a gold lighter.

She sat still in the car with her hands clasped together tight under the rug.

"Will you write to me?" she asked.

"I'll see," he said. "But I doubt it. You know I don't hold with letter-writing unless there's something specific to say."

"Yes, dear, I know. So don't you bother."

They drove on, along Queens Boulevard, and as they approached the flat marshland on which Idlewild is built, the fog began to thicken and the car had to slow down.

"Oh dear!" cried Mrs. Foster. "I'm *sure* I'm going to miss it now! What time is it?"

"Stop fussing," the old man said. "It doesn't matter anyway. It's bound to be cancelled now. They never fly in this sort of weather. I don't know why you bothered to come out."

She couldn't be sure, but it seemed to her that there was suddenly a new note in his voice, and she turned to look at him. It was difficult to observe any change in his expression under all that hair. The mouth was what counted. She wished, as she had so often before, that she could see the mouth clearly. The eyes never showed anything except when he was in a rage.

"Of course," he went on, "if by any chance it *does* go, then I agree with you—you'll be certain to miss it now. Why don't you resign yourself to that?"

She turned away and peered through the window at the fog. It seemed to be getting thicker as they went along, and now she could only just make out the edge of the road and the margin of grassland beyond it. She knew that her husband was still looking at her. She glanced back at him again, and this time she noticed with a kind of horror that he was staring intently at the little place in the corner of her left eye where she could feel the muscle twitching.

"Won't you?" he said.

"Won't I what?"

"Be sure to miss it now if it goes. We can't drive fast in this muck."

He didn't speak to her any more after that. The car crawled on and on. The driver had a yellow lamp directed onto the edge of the road, and this helped him to keep going. Other lights, some white and some yellow, kept coming out of the fog toward them, and there was an especially bright one that followed close behind them all the time.

Suddenly, the driver stopped the car.

"There!" Mr. Foster cried. "We're stuck. I knew it."

"No, sir," the driver said, turning round. "We made it. This is the airport."

Without a word, Mrs. Foster jumped out and hurried through the main entrance into the building. There was a mass of people inside, mostly disconsolate passengers standing around the ticket counters. She pushed her way through and spoke to the clerk.

"Yes," he said. "Your flight is temporarily postponed. But please don't go away. We're expecting this weather to clear any moment."

She went back to her husband who was still sitting in the car and told him the news. "But don't you wait, dear," she said. "There's no sense in that."

"I won't," he answered. "So long as the driver can get me back. Can you get me back, driver?"

"I think so," the man said.

"Is the luggage out?"

"Yes, sir."

"Goodbye, dear," Mrs. Foster said, leaning into the car and giving her husband a small kiss on the coarse grey fur of his cheek.

"Goodbye," he answered. "Have a good trip."

The car drove off, and Mrs. Foster was left alone.

The rest of the day was a sort of nightmare for her. She sat for hour after hour on a bench, as close to the airline counter as possible, and every thirty minutes or so she would get up and ask the clerk if the situation had changed. She always received the same reply—that she must continue to wait, because the fog might blow away at any moment. It wasn't until after six in the evening that the loud-speakers finally announced that the flight had been postponed until eleven o'clock the next morning.

Mrs. Foster didn't quite know what to do when she heard this news. She stayed sitting on her bench for at least another half-hour, wondering, in a tired, hazy sort of way, where she might go to spend the night. She hated to leave the airport. She didn't wish to see her husband. She was terrified that in one way or another he would eventually manage to prevent her from getting to France. She would have liked to remain just where she was, sitting on the bench the whole night through. That would be the safest. But she was already exhausted, and it didn't take her long to realize that this was a ridiculous thing for an elderly lady to do. So in the end she went to a phone and called the house.

Her husband, who was on the point of leaving for the club, answered it himself. She told him the news, and asked whether the servants were still there.

"They've all gone," he said.

"In that case, dear, I'll just get myself a room somewhere for the night. And don't you bother yourself about it at all."

"That would be foolish," he said. "You've got a large house here at your disposal. Use it."

"But, dear, it's *empty.*"

"Then I'll stay with you myself."

"There's no food in the house. There's nothing."

"Then eat before you come in. Don't be so stupid, woman. Everything you do, you seem to want to make a fuss about it."

"Yes," she said. "I'm sorry. I'll get myself a sandwich here, and then I'll come on in."

Outside, the fog had cleared a little, but it was still a long, slow drive in the taxi, and she didn't arrive back at the house on Sixty-second Street until fairly late.

Her husband emerged from his study when he heard her coming in. "Well," he said, standing by the study door, "how was Paris?"

"We leave at eleven in the morning," she answered. "It's definite."

"You mean if the fog clears."

"It's clearing now. There's a wind coming up."

"You look tired," he said. "You must have had an anxious day."

"It wasn't very comfortable. I think I'll go straight to bed."

"I've ordered a car for the morning," he said. "Nine o'clock."

"Oh, thank you, dear. And I certainly hope you're not going to bother to come all the way out again to see me off."

"No," he said slowly. "I don't think I will. But there's no reason why you shouldn't drop me at the club on your way."

She looked at him, and at that moment he seemed to be standing a long way off from her, beyond some borderline. He was suddenly so small and far away that she couldn't be sure what he was doing, or what he was thinking, or even what he was.

"The club is downtown," she said. "It isn't on the way to the airport."

"But you'll have plenty of time, my dear. Don't you want to drop me at the club?"

"Oh, yes—of course."

"That's good. Then I'll see you in the morning at nine."

She went up to her bedroom on the third floor, and she was so exhausted from her day that she fell asleep soon after she lay down.

Next morning, Mrs. Foster was up early, and by eight thirty she was downstairs and ready to leave.

Shortly after nine, her husband appeared. "Did you make any coffee?" he asked.

"No, dear. I thought you'd get a nice breakfast at the club. The car is here. It's been waiting. I'm all ready to go."

They were standing in the hall—they always seemed to be meeting in the hall nowadays—she with her hat and coat and purse, he in a curiously cut Edwardian jacket with high lapels.

"Your luggage?"

"It's at the airport."

"Ah yes," he said. "Of course. And if you're going to take me to the club first, I suppose we'd better get going fairly soon, hadn't we?"

"Yes!" she cried. "Oh, yes—*please!*"

"I'm just going to get a few cigars. I'll be right with you. You get in the car."

She turned and went out to where the chauffeur was standing, and he opened the car door for her as she approached.

"What time is it?" she asked him.

"About nine fifteen."

Mr. Foster came out five minutes later, and watching him as he walked slowly down the steps, she noticed that his legs were like goat's legs in those narrow stovepipe trousers that he wore. As on the day before, he paused halfway down to sniff the air and to examine the sky. The weather was still not quite clear, but there was a wisp of sun coming through the mist.

"Perhaps you'll be lucky this time," he said as he settled himself beside her in the car.

"Hurry, please," she said to the chauffeur. "Don't bother about the rug. I'll arrange the rug. Please get going. I'm late."

The man went back to his seat behind the wheel and started the engine.

"Just a moment!" Mr. Foster said suddenly. "Hold it a moment, chauffeur, will you?"

"What is it, dear?" She saw him searching the pockets of his overcoat.

"I had a little present I wanted you to take to Ellen," he said. "Now, where on earth is it? I'm sure I had it in my hand as I came down."

"I never saw you carrying anything. What sort of present?"

"A little box wrapped up in white paper. I forgot to give it to you yesterday. I don't want to forget it today."

"A little box!" Mrs. Foster cried. "I never saw any little box!" She began hunting frantically in the back of the car.

Her husband continued searching through the pockets of his coat. Then he unbuttoned the coat and felt around in his jacket. "Confound it," he said, "I must've left it in my bedroom. I won't be a moment."

"Oh, *please!*" she cried. "We haven't got time! *Please* leave it! You can mail it. It's only one of those silly combs anyway. You're always giving her combs."

"And what's wrong with combs, may I ask?" he said, furious that she should have forgotten herself for once.

"Nothing, dear, I'm sure. But . . ."

"Stay here!" he commanded. "I'm going to get it."

"Be quick, dear! Oh, *please* be quick!"

She sat still, waiting and waiting.

"Chauffeur, what time is it?"

The man had a wristwatch, which he consulted. "I make it nearly nine thirty."

"Can we get to the airport in an hour?"

"Just about."

At this point, Mrs. Foster suddenly spotted a corner of something white wedged down in the crack of the seat on the side where her husband had been sitting. She reached over and pulled out a small paper-wrapped box, and at the same time she couldn't help noticing that it was wedged down firm and deep, as though with the help of a pushing hand.

"Here it is!" she cried. "I've found it! Oh dear, and now he'll be up there forever searching for it! Chauffeur, quickly—run in and call him down, will you please?"

The chauffeur, a man with a small rebellious Irish mouth, didn't care very much for any of this, but he climbed out of the car and went up the steps to the front door of the house. Then he turned and came back. "Door's locked," he announced. "You got a key?"

"Yes—wait a minute." She began hunting madly in her purse. The little face was screwed up tight with anxiety, the lips pushed outward like a spout.

"Here it is! No—I'll go myself. It'll be quicker. I know where he'll be."

She hurried out of the car and up the steps to the front door, holding the key in one hand. She slid the key into the keyhole and was about to turn it—and then she stopped. Her head came up, and she stood there absolutely motionless, her whole body arrested right in the middle of all this hurry to turn the key and get into the house, and she waited—five, six, seven, eight, nine, ten seconds, she waited. The way she was standing there, with her head in the air and the body so tense, it seemed as though she were listening for the repetition of some sound that she had heard a moment before from a place far away inside the house.

Yes—quite obviously she was listening. Her whole attitude was a *listening* one. She appeared actually to be moving one of her ears closer and closer to the door. Now it was right up against the door, and for still another few seconds she remained in that position, head up, ear to door, hand on key, about to enter but not entering, trying instead, or so it seemed, to hear and to analyse these sounds that were coming faintly from this place deep within the house.

Then, all at once, she sprang to life again. She withdrew the key from the door and came running back down the steps.

"It's too late!" she cried to the chauffeur. "I can't wait for him, I simply can't. I'll miss the plane. Hurry now, driver, hurry! To the airport!"

The chauffeur, had he been watching her closely, might have noticed that her face had turned absolutely white and that the whole expression had suddenly altered. There was no longer that rather soft and silly look. A peculiar hardness had settled itself upon the features. The little mouth, usually so flabby, was now tight and thin, the eyes were bright, and the voice, when she spoke, carried a new note of authority.

"Hurry, driver, hurry!"

"Isn't your husband travelling with you?" the man asked, astonished.

"Certainly not! I was only going to drop him at the club. It won't matter He'll understand. He'll get a cab. Don't sit there talking, man. *Get going!* I've got a plane to catch for Paris!"

With Mrs. Foster urging him from the back seat, the man drove fast all the way, and she caught her plane with a few minutes to spare. Soon she was high up over the Atlantic, reclining comfortably in her airplane chair, listening to the hum of the motors, heading for Paris at last. The new mood was still with her. She felt remarkably strong and, in a queer sort of way, wonderful. She was a trifle breathless with it all, but this was more from pure astonishment at what she had done than anything else, and as the plane flew farther and farther away from New York and East Sixty-second Street, a great sense of calmness began to settle upon her. By the time she reached Paris, she was just as strong and cool and calm as she could wish.

She met her grandchildren, and they were even more beautiful in the flesh than in their photographs. They were like angels, she told herself, so beautiful they were. And every day she took them for walks, and fed them cakes, and bought them presents, and told them charming stories.

Once a week, on Tuesdays, she wrote a letter to her husband— a nice, chatty letter—full of news and gossip, which always ended with the words "Now be sure to take your meals regularly, dear, although this is something I'm afraid you may not be doing when I'm not with you."

When the six weeks were up, everybody was sad that she had to return to America, to her husband. Everybody, that is, except her. Surprisingly, she didn't seem to mind as much as one might have expected, and when she kissed them all goodbye, there was something in her manner and in the things she said that appeared to hint at the possibility of a return in the not too distant future.

However, like the faithful wife she was, she did not overstay her time. Exactly six weeks after she had arrived, she sent a cable to her husband and caught the plane back to New York.

Arriving at Idlewild, Mrs. Foster was interested to observe that there was no car to meet her. It is possible that she might even have been a little amused. But she was extremely calm and did not overtip the porter who helped her into a taxi with her baggage.

New York was colder than Paris, and there were lumps of dirty snow lying in the gutters of the streets. The taxi drew up before the house on Sixty-second Street, and Mrs. Foster persuaded the driver to carry her two large cases to the top of the steps. Then she paid him off and rang the bell. She waited, but there was no answer. Just to make sure, she rang again, and she could hear it tinkling shrilly far away in the pantry, at the back of the house. But still no one came.

So she took out her own key and opened the door herself.

The first thing she saw as she entered was a great pile of mail lying on the floor where it had fallen after being slipped through the letter hole. The place was dark and cold. A dust sheet was still draped over the grandfather clock. In spite of the cold, the atmosphere was peculiarly oppressive, and there was a faint but curious odor in the air that she had never smelled before.

She walked quickly across the hall and disappeared for a moment around the corner to the left, at the back. There was something deliberate and purposeful about this action; she had the air of a woman who is off to investigate a rumor or to confirm a suspicion. And when she returned a few seconds later, there was a little glimmer of satisfaction on her face.

She paused in the center of the hall, as though wondering what to do next. Then, suddenly, she turned and went across into her husband's study. On the desk she found his address book, and after hunting through it for a while she picked up the phone and dialled a number.

"Hello," she said. "Listen—this is Nine East Sixty-second Street. . . . Yes, that's right. Could you send someone round as soon as possible, do you think? Yes, it seems to be stuck between the second and third floors. At least, that's where the indicator's pointing. . . . Right away? Oh, that's very kind of you. You see, my legs aren't any too good for walking up a lot of stairs. Thank you so much. Goodbye."

She replaced the receiver and sat there at her husband's desk, patiently waiting for the man who would be coming soon to repair the elevator.

Parson's Pleasure

1958

MR. Boggis was driving the car slowly, leaning back comfortably in the seat with one elbow resting on the sill of the open window. How beautiful the countryside, he thought; how pleasant to see a sign or two of summer once again. The primroses especially. And the hawthorn. The hawthorn was exploding white and pink and red along the hedges and the primroses were growing underneath in little clumps, and it was beautiful.

He took one hand off the wheel and lit himself a cigarette. The best thing now, he told himself, would be to make for the top of Brill Hill. He could see it about half a mile ahead. And that must be the village of Brill, that cluster of cottages among the trees right on the very summit. Excellent. Not many of his Sunday sections had a nice elevation like that to work from.

He drove up the hill and stopped the car just short of the summit on the outskirts of the village. Then he got out and looked around. Down below, the countryside was spread out before him like a huge green carpet. He could see for miles. It was perfect. He took a pad and pencil from his pocket, leaned against the back of the car, and allowed his practised eye to travel slowly over the landscape.

He could see one medium farmhouse over on the right, back in the fields, with a track leading to it from the road. There was another larger one beyond it. There was a house surrounded by tall elms that looked as though it might be a Queen Anne, and there were two likely farms away over on the left. Five places in all. That was about the lot in this direction.

Mr. Boggis drew a rough sketch on his pad showing the position of each so that he'd be able to find them easily when he was down below, then he got back into the car and drove up through the village to the other side of the hill. From there he spotted six more possibles—five farms and one big white Georgian house. He studied the Georgian house through his binoculars. It had a clean prosperous look, and the garden was well ordered. That was a pity. He ruled it out immediately. There was no point in calling on the prosperous.

In this square then, in this section, there were ten possibles in all. Ten was a nice number, Mr. Boggis told himself. Just the right amount for a leisurely afternoon's work. What time was it now? Twelve o'clock. He would have liked a pint of beer in the pub before he started, but on Sundays they didn't open until one. Very well, he would have it later. He glanced at the notes on his pad. He decided to take the Queen Anne first, the house with the elms. It had looked nicely dilapidated through the binoculars. The people there could probably do with some money. He was always lucky with Queen Annes, anyway. Mr. Boggis climbed back into the car, released the handbrake, and began cruising slowly down the hill without the engine.

Apart from the fact that he was at this moment disguised in the uniform of a clergyman, there was nothing very sinister about Mr. Cyril Boggis. By trade he was a dealer in antique furniture, with his own shop and showroom in the King's Road, Chelsea. His premises were not large, and generally he didn't do a great deal of business, but because he always bought cheap, very very cheap, and sold very very dear, he managed to make quite a tidy little income every year. He was a talented salesman, and when buying or selling a piece he could slide smoothly into whichever mood suited the client best. He could become grave and charming for the aged, obsequious for the rich, sober for the godly, masterful for the weak, mischievous for the widow, arch and saucy for the spinster. He was well aware of his gift, using it shamelessly on every possible occasion; and often, at the end of a unusually good performance, it was as much as he could do to prevent himself from turning aside and taking a bow or two as the thundering applause of the audience went rolling through the theatre.

In spite of this rather clownish quality of his, Mr. Boggis was not a fool. In fact, it was said of him by some that he probably knew as much about French, English, and Italian furniture as anyone else in London. He also had surprisingly good taste, and he was quick to recognize and reject an ungraceful design, however genuine the article might be. His real love, naturally, was for the work of the great eighteenth-century English designers, Ince, Mayhew, Chippendale, Robert Adam, Manwaring, Inigo Jones, Hepplewhite, Kent, Johnson, George Smith, Lock, Sheraton, and the rest of them, but even with these he occasionally drew the line. He refused, for example, to allow a single piece from Chippendale's Chinese or Gothic period to come into his showroom, and the same was true of some of the heavier Italian designs of Robert Adam.

During the past few years, Mr. Boggis had achieved considerable fame among his friends in the trade by his ability to produce unusual and often quite rare items with astonishing regularity. Apparently the man had a source of supply that was almost inexhaustible, a sort of private warehouse, and it seemed that all he had to do was to drive out to it once a week and help himself. Whenever they asked him where he got the stuff, he would smile knowingly and wink and murmur something about a little secret.

The idea behind Mr. Boggis's little secret was a simple one, and it had come to him as a result of something that had happened on a certain Sunday afternoon nearly nine years before, while he was driving in the country.

He had gone out in the morning to visit his old mother, who lived in Sevenoaks, and on the way back the fanbelt on his car had broken, causing the engine to overheat and the water to boil away. He had got out of the car and walked to the nearest house, a smallish farm building about fifty years off the road, and had asked the woman who answered the door if he could please have a jug of water.

While he was waiting for her to fetch it, he happened to glance in through the door to the living-room, and there, not five yards from where he was standing, he spotted something that made him so excited the sweat began to come out all over the top of his head. It was a large oak armchair of a type that he had only seen once before in his life. Each arm, as well as the panel at the back, was supported by a row of eight beautifully turned spindles. The back panel itself was decorated by an inlay of the most delicate floral design, and the head of a duck was carved to lie along half the length of either arm. Good God, he thought. This thing is late fifteenth century!

He poked his head in further through the door, and there, by heavens, was another of them on the other side of the fireplace!

He couldn't be sure, but two chairs like that must be worth at least a thousand pounds up in London. And oh, what beauties they were!

When the woman returned, Mr. Boggis introduced himself and straight away asked if she would like to sell her chairs.

Dear me, she said. But why on earth should she want to sell her chairs?

No reason at all, except that he might be willing to give her a pretty nice price.

And how much would he give? They were definitely not for sale, but just out of curiosity, just for fun, you know, how much would he give?

Thirty-five pounds.

How much?

Thirty-five pounds.

Dear me, thirty-five pounds. Well, well, that was very interesting. She'd always thought they were valuable. They were very old. They were very comfortable too. She couldn't possibly do without them, not possibly. No, they were not for sale but thank you very much all the same.

They weren't really so very old, Mr. Boggis told her, and they wouldn't be at all easy to sell, but it just happened that he had a client who rather liked that sort of thing. Maybe he could go up another two pounds—call it thirty-seven. How about that?

They bargained for half an hour, and of course in the end Mr. Boggis got the chairs and agreed to pay her something less than a twentieth of their value.

That evening, driving back to London in his old station-wagon with the two fabulous chairs tucked away snugly in the back, Mr. Boggis had suddenly been struck by what seemed to him to be a most remarkable idea.

Look here, he said. If there is good stuff in one farmhouse, then why not in others? Why shouldn't he search for it? Why shouldn't he comb the countryside? He could do it on Sundays. In that way, it wouldn't interfere with his work at all. He never knew what to do with his Sundays.

So Mr. Boggis bought maps, large scale maps of all the counties around London, and with a fine pen he divided each of them up into a series of squares. Each of these squares covered an actual area of five miles by five, which was about as much territory, he estimated, as he could cope with on a single Sunday, were he to comb it thoroughly. He didn't want the towns and the villages. It was the comparatively isolated places, the large farmhouses and the rather dilapidated country mansions, that he was looking for; and in this way, if he did one square each Sunday, fifty-two squares a year, he would gradually cover every farm and every country house in the home counties.

But obviously there was a bit more to it than that. Country folk are a suspicious lot. So are the impoverished rich. You can't go about ringing their bells and expecting them to show you around their houses just for the asking, because they won't do it. That way you would never get beyond the front door. How then was he to gain admittance? Perhaps it would be best if he didn't let them know he was a dealer at all. He could be the telephone man, the plumber, the gas inspector. He could even be a clergyman. . . .

From this point on, the whole scheme began to take on a more practical aspect. Mr. Boggis ordered a large quantity of superior cards on which the following legend was engraved:

THE REVEREND
CYRIL WINNINGTON BOGGIS

President of the Society	*In association with*
for the Preservation of	*The Victoria and*
Rare Furniture	*Albert Museum*

From now on, every Sunday, he was going to be a nice old parson spending his holiday travelling around on a labour of love for the "Society," compiling an inventory of the treasures that lay hidden in the country homes of England. And who in the world was going to kick him out when they heard that one?

Nobody.

And then, once he was inside, if he happened to spot something he really wanted, well—he knew a hundred different ways of dealing with that.

Rather to Mr. Boggis's surprise, the scheme worked. In fact, the friendliness with which he was received in one house after another through the countryside was, in the beginning, quite embarrassing, even to him. A slice of cold pie, a glass of port, a cup of tea, a basket of plums, even a full sit-down Sunday dinner with the family, such things were constantly being pressed upon him. Sooner or later, of course, there had been some bad moments and a number of unpleasant incidents, but then nine years is more than four hundred Sundays, and that adds up to a great quantity of houses visited. All in all, it had been an interesting, exciting, and lucrative business.

And now it was another Sunday and Mr. Boggis was operating in the county of Buckinghamshire, in one of the most northerly squares on his map, about ten miles from Oxford, and as he drove down the hill and headed for his first house, the dilapidated Queen Anne, he began to get the feeling that this was going to be one of his lucky days.

He parked the car about a hundred yards from the gates and got out to walk the rest of the way. He never liked people to see his car until after a deal was completed. A dear old clergyman and a large station-wagon somehow never seemed quite right together. Also the short walk gave him time to examine the property closely from the outside and to assume the mood most likely to be suitable for the occasion.

Mr. Boggis strode briskly up the drive. He was a small fat-legged man with a belly. The face was round and rosy, quite perfect for the part, and the two large brown eyes that bulged out at you from this rosy face gave an impression of gentle imbecility. He was dressed in a black suit with the usual parson's dog-collar round his neck, and on his head a soft black hat. He carried an old oak walking-stick which lent him, in his opinion, a rather rustic easy-going air.

He approached the front door and rang the bell. He heard the sound of footsteps in the hall and the door opened and suddenly there stood before him, or rather above him, a gigantic woman dressed in riding-breeches. Even through the smoke of her cigarette he could smell the powerful odour of stables and horse manure that clung about her.

"Yes?" she asked, looking at him suspiciously. "What is it you want?"

Mr. Boggis, who half expected her to whinny any moment, raised his hat, made a little bow, and handed her his card. "I do apologize for bothering you," he said, and then he waited, watching her face as she read the message.

"I don't understand," she said, handing back the card. "What is it you want?"

Mr. Boggis explained about the Society for the Preservation of Rare Furniture.

"This wouldn't by any chance be something to do with the Socialist Party?" she asked, staring at him fiercely from under a pair of pale bushy brows.

From then on, it was easy. A Tory in riding-breeches, male or female, was always a sitting duck for Mr. Boggis. He spent two minutes delivering an impassioned eulogy on the extreme Right Wing Conservative Party, then two more denouncing the Socialists. As a clincher, he made particular reference to the Bill that the

Socialists had once introduced for the abolition of bloodsports in the country, and went on to inform his listener that his idea of heaven —"though you better not tell the bishop, my dear"—was a place where one could hunt the fox, the stag, and the hare with large packs of tireless hounds from morn till night every day of the week, including Sundays.

Watching her as he spoke, he could see the magic beginning to do its work. The woman was grinning now, showing Mr. Boggis a set of enormous, slightly yellow teeth. "Madam," he cried, "I beg of you, *please* don't get me started on Socialism." At that point, she let out a great guffaw of laughter, raised an enormous red hand, and slapped him so hard on the shoulder that he nearly went over.

"Come in!" she shouted. "I don't know what the hell you want, but come on in!"

Unfortunately, and rather surprisingly, there was nothing of any value in the whole house, and Mr. Boggis, who never wasted time on barren territory, soon made his excuses and took his leave. The whole visit had taken less than fifteen minutes, and that, he told himself as he climbed back into his car and started off for the next place, was exactly as it should be.

From now on, it was all farmhouses, and the nearest was about half a mile up the road. It was a large half-timbered brick building of considerable age, and there was a magnificent pear tree still in blossom covering almost the whole of the south wall.

Mr. Boggis knocked on the door. He waited, but no one came. He knocked again, but still there was no answer, so he wandered around the back to look for the farmer among the cowsheds. There was no one there either. He guessed that they must all still be in church, so he began peering in the windows to see if he could spot anything interesting. There was nothing in the dining-room. Nothing in the library either. He tried the next window, the living-room, and there, right under his nose, in the little alcove that the window made, he saw a beautiful thing, a semicircular card-table in mahogany, richly veneered, and in the style of Hepplewhite, built around 1780.

"Ah-ha," he said aloud, pressing his face hard against glass. "Well done, Boggis."

But that was not all. There was a chair there as well, a single chair, and if he were not mistaken it was of an even finer quality than the table. Another Hepplewhite, wasn't it? And oh, what a beauty! The lattices on the back were finely carved with the honeysuckle, the husk, and the paterae, the caning on the seat was original, the legs were very gracefully turned and the two back ones had that peculiar outward splay that meant so much. It was an exquisite chair. "Before this day is done," Mr. Boggis said softly, "I shall have the pleasure of sitting down upon that lovely seat." He never bought a chair without doing this. It was a favourite test of his, and it was always an intriguing sight to see him lowering himself delicately into the seat, waiting for the "give," expertly gauging the precise but infinitesimal degree of shrinkage that the years had caused in the mortice and dovetail joints.

But there was no hurry, he told himself. He would return here later. He had the whole afternoon before him.

The next farm was situated some way back in the fields, and in order to keep his car out of sight, Mr. Boggis had to leave it on the road and walk about six hundred yards along a straight track that led directly into the back yard of the farmhouse. This place, he noticed as he approached, was a good deal smaller than the last, and he didn't hold out much hope for it. It looked rambling and dirty, and some of the sheds were clearly in bad repair.

There were three men standing in a close group in a corner of the yard, and one of them had two large black greyhounds with him, on leashes. When the men caught sight of Mr. Boggis walking forward in his black suit and parson's collar, they stopped talking and seemed suddenly to stiffen and freeze, becoming absolutely still, motionless, three faces turned toward him, watching him suspiciously as he approached.

The oldest of the three was a stumpy man with a wide frog mouth and small shifty eyes, and although Mr. Boggis didn't know it, his name was Rummins and he was the owner of the farm.

The tall youth beside him, who appeared to have something wrong with one eye, was Bert, the son of Rummins.

The shortish flat-faced man with a narrow corrugated brow and immensely broad shoulders was Claud. Claud had dropped in on Rummins in the hope of getting a piece of pork or ham out of him from the pig that had been killed the day before. Claud knew about the killing—the noise of it had carried far across the fields—and he also knew that a man should have a government permit to do that sort of thing, and that Rummins didn't have one.

"Good afternoon," Mr. Boggis said. "Isn't it a lovely day."

None of the three men moved. At that moment they were all thinking precisely the same thing—that somehow or other this clergyman, who was certainly not the local fellow, had been sent to poke his nose into their business and to report what he found to the government.

"What beautiful dogs," Mr. Boggis said. "I must say I've never been greyhound-racing myself, but they tell me it's a fascinating sport."

Again the silence, and Mr. Boggis glanced quickly from Rummins to Bert, then to Claud, then back again to Rummins, and he noticed that each of them had the same peculiar expression on his face, something between a jeer and a challenge, with a contemptuous curl to the mouth, and a sneer around the nose.

"Might I enquire if you are the owner?" Mr. Boggis asked, undaunted, addressing himself to Rummins.

"What is it you want?"

"I do apologize for troubling you, especially on a Sunday."

Mr. Boggis offered his card and Rummins took it and held it up close to his face. The other two didn't move, but their eyes swivelled over to one side, trying to see.

"And what exactly might you be wanting?" Rummins asked.

For the second time that morning, Mr. Boggis explained at some length the aims and ideals of the Society for the Preservation of Rare Furniture.

"We don't have any," Rummins told him when it was over. "You're wasting your time."

"Now, just a minute, sir," Mr. Boggis said, raising a finger. "The last man who said that to me was an old farmer down in Sussex, and when he finally let me into his house, d'you know what I found? A dirty-looking old chair in the corner of the kitchen, and it turned out to be worth *four hundred pounds!* I showed him how to sell it, and he bought himself a new tractor with the money."

"What on earth are you talking about?" Claud said. "There ain't no chair in the world worth four hundred pound."

"Excuse me," Mr. Boggis answered primly, "but there are plenty of chairs in England worth more than twice that figure. And you know where they are? They're tucked away in the farms and cottages all over the country, with the owners using them as steps and ladders and standing on them with hobnailed boots to reach a pot of jam out of the top cupboard or to hang a picture. This is the truth I'm telling you, my friends."

Rummins shifted uneasily on his feet. "You mean to say all you want to do is go inside and stand there in the middle of the room and look around?"

"Exactly," Mr. Boggis said. He was at last beginning to sense what the trouble might be. "I don't want to pry into your cupboards or into your larder. I just want to look at the furniture to see if you happen to have any treasures here, and then I can write about them in our Society magazine."

·"You know what I think?" Rummins said, fixing him with his small wicked eyes. "I think you're after buying the stuff yourself. Why else would you be going to all this trouble?"

"Oh, dear me. I only wish I had the money. Of course, if I saw something that I took a great fancy to, and it wasn't beyond my means, I might be tempted to make an offer. But alas, that rarely happens."

"Well," Rummins said, "I don't suppose there's any harm in your taking a look around if that's all you want." He led the way across the yard to the back door of the farmhouse, and Mr. Boggis followed him; so did the son, Bert, and Claud with his two dogs. They went through the kitchen, where the only furniture was a cheap deal table with a dead chicken lying on it, and they emerged into a fairly large, exceedingly filthy living-room.

And there it was! Mr. Boggis saw it at once, and he stopped dead in his tracks and gave a little shrill gasp of shock. Then he stood there for five, ten, fifteen seconds at least, staring like an idiot, unable to believe, not daring to believe what he saw before him. It *couldn't* be true, not possibly! But the longer he stared, the more true it began to seem. After all, there it was standing against the wall right in front of him, as real and as solid as the house itself. And who in the world could possibly make a mistake about a thing like that? Admittedly it was painted white, but that made not the slightest difference. Some idiot had done that. The paint could easily be stripped off. But good God! Just look at it! And in a place like this!

At that point, Mr. Boggis became aware of the three men, Rummins, Bert, and Claud, standing together in a group over by the fireplace, watching him intently. They had seen him stop and gasp and stare, and they must have seen his face turning red, or maybe it was white, but in any event they had seen enough to spoil the whole goddam business if he didn't do something about it quick. In a flash, Mr. Boggis clapped one hand over his heart, staggered to the nearest chair, and collapsed into it, breathing heavily.

"What's the matter with you?" Claud asked.

"It's nothing," he gasped. "I'll be all right in a minute. Please —a glass of water. It's my heart."

Bert fetched him the water, handed it to him, and stayed close beside him, staring down at him with a fatuous leer on his face.

"I thought maybe you were looking at something," Rummins said. The wide frog-mouth widened a fraction further into a crafty grin, showing the stubs of several broken teeth.

"No, no," Mr. Boggis said. "Oh dear me, no. It's just my heart. I'm so sorry. It happens every now and then. But it goes away quite quickly. I'll be all right in a couple of minutes."

He *must* have time to think, he told himself. More important still, he must have time to compose himself thoroughly before he said another word. Take it gently, Boggis. And whatever you do, keep calm. These people may be ignorant, but they are not stupid. They are suspicious and wary and sly. And if it is really true—no it *can't* be, it *can't* be true. . . .

He was holding one hand up over his eyes in a gesture of pain, and now, very carefully, secretly, he made a little crack between two of the fingers and peeked through.

Sure enough, the thing was still there, and on this occasion he took a good long look at it. Yes—he had been right the first time! There wasn't the slightest doubt about it! It was really unbelievable!

What he saw was a piece of furniture that any expert would have given almost anything to acquire. To a layman, it might not have appeared particularly impressive, especially when covered over as it was with dirty white paint, but to Mr. Boggis it was a dealer's dream. He knew, as does every other dealer in Europe and America, that among the most celebrated and coveted examples of eighteenth-century English furniture in existence are the three famous pieces known as "The Chippendale Commodes." He knew their history backwards—that the first was "discovered" in 1920, in a house at Moreton-on-the-Marsh, and was sold at Sotheby's the same year; that the other two turned up in the same auction rooms a year later, both coming out of Rainham Hall, Norfolk. They all fetched enormous prices. He couldn't quite remember the exact figure for the first one, or even the second, but he knew for certain that the last one to be sold had fetched thirty-nine hundred guineas. And that was in 1921! Today the same piece would surely be worth ten thousand pounds. Some man, Mr. Boggis couldn't remember his name, had made a study of these commodes fairly recently and had proved that all three must have come from the same workshop, for the veneers were all from the same log, and the same set of templates had been used in the construction of each. No invoices had been found for any of them, but all the experts were agreed that these three commodes could have been executed only by Thomas Chippendale himself, with his own hands, at the most exalted period in his career.

And here, Mr. Boggis kept telling himself as he peered cautiously through the crack in his fingers, here was the fourth Chippendale Commode! And *he* had found it! He would be rich! He would also be famous! Each of the other three was known throughout the furniture world by a special name—The Chastleton Commode, The First Rainham Commode, The Second Rainham Commode. This one would go down in history as The Boggis Commode! Just imagine the faces of the boys up there in London when they got a look at it tomorrow morning! And the luscious offers coming in from the big fellows over in the West End—Frank Partridge, Mallett, Jetley, and the rest of them! There would be a picture of it in *The Times,* and it would say, "The very fine Chippendale Commode which was recently discovered by Mr. Cyril Boggis, a London dealer. . . ." Dear God, what a stir he was going to make!

This one here, Mr. Boggis thought, was almost exactly similar to the Second Rainham Commode. (All three, the Chastleton and the two Rainhams, differed from one another in a number of small ways.) It was a most impressive handsome affair built in the French rococo style of Chippendale's Director period, a kind of large fat chest-of-drawers set upon four carved and fluted legs that raised it about a foot from the ground. There were six drawers in all, two long ones in the middle and two shorter ones on either side. The serpentine front was magnificently ornamented along the top and sides and bottom, and also vertically between each set of drawers, with intricate carvings of festoons and scrolls and clusters. The brass handles, although partly obscured by white paint, appeared to be superb. It was, of course, a rather "heavy" piece, but the design had been executed with such elegance and grace that the heaviness was in no way offensive.

"How're you feeling now?" Mr. Boggis heard someone saying.

"Thank you, thank you, I'm much better already. It passes quickly. My doctor says it's nothing to worry about really so long as I rest for a few minutes whenever it happens. Ah yes," he said, raising himself slowly to his feet. "That's better. I'm all right now."

A trifle unsteadily, he began to move around the room examining the furniture, one piece at a time, commenting upon it briefly. He could see at once that apart from the commode it was a very poor lot.

"Nice oak table," he said. "But I'm afraid it's not old enough to be of any interest. Good comfortable chairs, but quite modern, yes, quite modern. Now this cupboard, well, it's rather attractive, but again, not valuable. This chest-of-drawers"—he walked casually past the Chippendale Commode and gave it a little contemptuous flip with his fingers—"worth a few pounds, I dare say, but no more. A rather crude reproduction, I'm afraid. Probably made in Victorian times. Did you paint it white?"

"Yes," Rummins said. "Bert did it."

"A very wise move. It's considerably less offensive in white."

"That's a strong piece of furniture," Rummins said. "Some nice carving on it too."

"Machine-carved," Mr. Boggis answered superbly, bending down to examine the exquisite craftsmanship. "You can tell it a mile off. But still, I suppose it's quite pretty in its way. It has its points."

He began to saunter off, then he checked himself and turned slowly back again. He placed the tip of one finger against the point of his chin, laid his head over to one side, and frowned as though deep in thought.

"You know what?" he said, looking at the commode, speaking so casually that his voice kept trailing off. "I've just remembered . . . I've been wanting a set of legs something like that for a long time. I've got a rather curious table in my own little home, one of those low things that people put in front of the sofa, sort of a coffee-table, and last Michaelmas, when I moved house, the foolish movers damaged the legs in the most shocking way. I'm very fond of that table. I always keep my big Bible on it, and all my sermon notes."

He paused, stroking his chin with the finger. "Now I was just thinking. These legs on your chest-of-drawers might be very suitable. Yes, they might indeed. They could easily be cut off and fixed onto my table."

He looked around and saw the three men standing absolutely still, watching him suspiciously, three pairs of eyes, all different but equally mistrusting, small pig-eyes for Rummins, large slow eyes for Claud, and two odd eyes for Bert, one of them very queer and boiled and misty pale, with a little black dot in the centre, like a fish-eye on a plate.

Mr. Boggis smiled and shook his head. "Come, come, what on earth am I saying? I'm talking as though I owned the piece myself. I do apologize "

"What you mean to say is you'd like to buy it," Rummins said.

"Well..." Mr. Boggis glanced back at the commode, frowning. "I'm not sure. I might . . . and then again . . . on second thoughts . . . no . . . I think it might be a bit too much trouble. It's not worth it. I'd better leave it."

"How much were you thinking of offering?" Rummins asked.

"Not much, I'm afraid. You see, this is not a genuine antique. It's merely a reproduction."

"I'm not so sure about that," Rummins told him. "It's been in *here* over twenty years, and before that it was up at the Manor House. I bought it there myself at auction when the old Squire died. You can't tell me that thing's new."

"It's not exactly new, but it's certainly not more than about sixty years old."

"It's more than that," Rummins said. "Bert, where's that bit of paper you once found at the back of one of them drawers? That old bill."

The boy looked vacantly at his father.

Mr. Boggis opened his mouth, then quickly shut it again without uttering a sound. He was beginning literally to shake with excitement, and to calm himself he walked over to the window and stared out at a plump brown hen pecking around for stray grains of corn in the yard.

"It was in the back of that drawer underneath all them rabbit-snares," Rummins was saying. "Go on and fetch it out and show it to the parson."

When Bert went forward to the commode, Mr. Boggis turned round again. He couldn't stand not watching him. He saw him pull out one of the big middle drawers, and he noticed the beautiful smooth way in which the drawer slid open. He saw Bert's hand dipping inside and rummaging around among a lot of wires and strings.

"You mean this?" Bert lifted out a piece of folded yellowing paper and carried it over to the father, who unfolded it and held it up close to his face.

"You can't tell me this writing ain't bloody old," Rummins said, and he held the paper out to Mr. Boggis, whose whole arm was shaking as he took it. It was brittle and it crackled slightly between his fingers. The writing was in a long sloping copper-plate hand:

Edward Montagu, Esq. *Dr.*

To Thos. Chippendale

A large mahogany Commode Table of exceeding fine wood, very rich carvd, set upon fluted legs, two very neat shapd long drawers in the middle part and two ditto on each side, with rich chasd Brass Handles and Ornaments, the whole compleatly finished in the most exquisite taste £87

Mr. Boggis was holding onto himself tight and fighting to suppress the excitement that was spinning round inside him and making him dizzy. Oh God, it was wonderful! With the invoice, the value had climbed even higher. What in heaven's name would it fetch now? Twelve thousand pounds? Fourteen? Maybe fifteen or even twenty? Who knows?

Oh, boy!

He tossed the paper contemptuously onto the table and said quietly, "It's exactly what I told you, a Victorian reproduction. This is simply the invoice that the seller—the man who made it and passed it off as an antique—gave to his client. I've seen lots of them. You'll notice that he doesn't say he made it himself. That would give the game away."

"Say what you like," Rummins announced, "but that's an old piece of paper."

"Of course it is, my dear friend. It's Victorian, late Victorian. About eighteen ninety. Sixty or seventy years old. I've seen hundreds of them. That was a time when masses of cabinet-makers did nothing else but apply themselves to faking the fine furniture of the century before."

"Listen, Parson," Rummins said, pointing at him with a thick dirty finger, "I'm not saying as how you may not know a fair bit about this furniture business, but what I *am* saying is this: How on earth can you be so mighty sure it's a fake when you haven't even seen what it looks like underneath all that paint?"

"Come here," Mr. Boggis said. "Come over here and I'll show you." He stood beside the commode and waited for them to gather round. "Now, anyone got a knife?"

Claud produced a horn-handled pocket knife, and Mr. Boggis took it and opened the smallest blade. Then, working with apparent casualness but actually with extreme care, he began chipping off the white paint from a small area on the top of the commode. The paint flaked away cleanly from the old hard varnish underneath, and when he had cleared away about three square inches, he stepped back and said, "Now, take a look at that!"

It was beautiful—a warm little patch of mahogany, glowing like a topaz, rich and dark with the true colour of its two hundred years.

"What's wrong with it?" Rummins asked.

"It's processed! Anyone can see that!"

"How can you see it, Mister? You tell us."

"Well, I must say that's a trifle difficult to explain. It's chiefly a matter of experience. My experience tells me that without the slightest doubt this wood has been processed with lime. That's what they use for mahogany, to give it that dark aged colour. For oak, they use potash salts, and for walnut it's nitric acid, but for mahogany it's always lime."

The three men moved a little closer to peer at the wood. There was a slight stirring of interest among them now. It was always intriguing to hear about some new form of crookery or deception.

"Look closely at the grain. You see that touch of orange in among the dark red-brown. That's the sign of lime."

They leaned forward, their noses close to the wood, first Rummins, then Claud, then Bert.

"And then there's the patina," Mr. Boggins continued.

"The what?"

He explained to them the meaning of this word as applied to furniture.

"My dear friends, you've no idea the trouble these rascals will go to to imitate the hard beautiful bronze-like appearance of genuine patina. It's terrible, really terrible, and it makes me quite sick to speak of it!" He was spitting each word sharply off the tip of the tongue and making a sour mouth to show his extreme distaste. The men waited, hoping for more secrets.

"The time and trouble that some mortals will go to in order to deceive the innocent!" Mr. Boggis cried. "It's perfectly disgusting! D'you know what they did here, my friends? I can recognize it clearly. I can almost *see* them doing it, the long, complicated ritual of rubbing the wood with linseed oil, coating it over with French polish that has been cunningly coloured, brushing it down with pumice-stone and oil, beeswaxing it with a wax that contains dirt and dust, and finally giving it the heat treatment to crack the polish so that it looks like two-hundred-year-old varnish! It really upsets me to contemplate such knavery!"

The three men continued to gaze at the little patch of dark wood.

"Feel it!" Mr. Boggis ordered. "Put your fingers on it! There, how does it feel, warm or cold?"

"Feels cold," Rummins said.

"Exactly, my friend! It happens to be a fact that faked patina is always cold to the touch. Real patina has a curiously warm feel to it."

"This feels normal," Rummins said, ready to argue.

"No, sir, it's cold. But of course it takes an experienced and sensitive finger-tip to pass a positive judgment. You couldn't really be expected to judge this any more than I could be expected to judge the quality of your barley. Everything in life, my dear sir, is experience."

The men were staring at this queer moon-faced clergyman with the bulging eyes, not quite so suspiciously now because he did seem to know a bit about his subject. But they were still a long way from trusting him.

Mr. Boggis bent down and pointed to one of the metal drawer-handles on the commode. "This is another place where the fakers go to work," he said. "Old brass normally has a colour and character all of its own. Did you know that?"

They stared at him, hoping for still more secrets.

"But the trouble is that they've become exceedingly skilled at matching it. In fact it's almost impossible to tell the difference between "genuine old" and "faked old." I don't mind admitting that it has me guessing. So there's not really any point in our scraping the paint off these handles. We wouldn't be any the wiser."

"How can you possibly make new brass look like old?" Claud said. "Brass doesn't rust, you know."

"You are quite right, my friend. But these scoundrels have their own secret methods."

"Such as what?" Claud asked. Any information of this nature was valuable, in his opinion. One never knew when it might come in handy.

"All they have to do," Mr. Boggis said, "is to place these handles overnight in a box of mahogany shavings saturated in sal ammoniac. The sal ammoniac turns the metal green, but if you rub off the green, you will find underneath it a fine soft silvery-warm lustre, a lustre identical to that which comes with very old brass. Oh, it is so bestial, the things they do! With iron they have another trick."

"What do they do with iron?" Claud asked, fascinated.

"Iron's easy," Mr. Boggis said. "Iron locks and plates and hinges are simply buried in common salt and they come out all rusted and pitted in no time."

"All right," Rummins said. "So you admit you can't tell about the handles. For all you know, they may be hundreds and hundreds of years old. Correct?"

"Ah," Mr. Boggis whispered, fixing Rummins with two big bulging brown eyes. "That's where you're wrong. Watch this."

From his jacket pocket, he took out a small screwdriver. At the same time, although none of them saw him do it, he also took out a little brass screw which he kept well hidden in the palm of his hand. Then he selected one of the screws in the commode—there were four to each handle—and began carefully scraping all traces of white paint from its head. When he had done this, he started slowly to unscrew it.

"If this is a genuine old brass screw from the eighteenth century," he was saying, "the spiral will be slightly uneven and you'll be able to see quite easily that it has been hand-cut with a file. But if this brasswork is faked from more recent times, Victorian or later, then obviously the screw will be of the same period. It will be a mass-produced, machine-made article. Anyone can recognize a machine-made screw. Well, we shall see."

It was not difficult, as he put his hands over the old screw and drew it out, for Mr. Boggis to substitute the new one hidden in his palm. This was another little trick of his, and through the years it had proved a most rewarding one. The pockets of his clergyman's jacket were always stocked with a quantity of cheap brass screws of various sizes.

"There you are," he said, handing the modern screw to Rummins. "Take a look at that. Notice the exact evenness of the spiral? See it? Of course you do. It's just a cheap common little screw that you yourself could buy today in any ironmonger's in the country."

The screw was handed round from the one to the other, each examining it carefully. Even Rummins was impressed now.

Mr. Boggis put the screwdriver back in his pocket together with the fine hand-cut screw that he'd taken from the commode, and then he turned and walked slowly past the three men toward the door.

"My dear friends," he said, pausing at the entrance to the kitchen, "it was so good of you to let me peep inside your little home —so kind. I do hope I haven't been a terrible old bore."

Rummins glanced up from examining the screw. "You didn't tell us what you were going to offer," he said.

"Ah," Mr. Boggis said. "That's quite right. I didn't, did I? Well, to tell you the honest truth, I think it's all a bit too much trouble. I think I'll leave it."

"How much would you give?"

"You mean that you really wish to part with it?"

"I didn't say I wished to part with it. I asked you how much."

Mr. Boggis looked across at the commode, and he laid his head first to one side, then to the other, and he frowned, and pushed out his lips, and shrugged his shoulders, and gave a little scornful wave of the hand as though to say the thing was hardly worth thinking about really, was it?

"Shall we say . . . ten pounds. I think that would be fair."

"Ten pounds!" Rummins cried. "Don't be so ridiculous, Parson, *please!*"

"It's worth more'n that for firewood!" Claud said, disgusted.

"Look here at the bill!" Rummins went on, stabbing that precious document so fiercely with his dirty forefinger that Mr. Boggis became alarmed. "It tells you exactly what it cost! Eighty-seven pounds! And that's when it was new. Now it's antique it's worth double!"

"If you'll pardon me, no, sir, it's not. It's a second-hand reproduction. But I'll tell you what, my friend—I'm being rather reckless, I can't help it—I'll go up as high as fifteen pounds. How's that?"

"Make it fifty," Rummins said.

A delicious little quiver like needles ran all the way down the back of Mr. Boggis's legs and then under the soles of his feet. He had it now. It was his. No question about that. But the habit of buying cheap, as cheap as it was humanly possible to buy, acquired by years of necessity and practice, was too strong in him now to permit him to give in so easily.

"My dear man," he whispered softly, "I only *want* the legs. Possibly I could find some use for the drawers later on, but the rest of it, the carcass itself, as your friend so rightly said, it's firewood, that's all."

"Make it thirty-five," Rummins said.

"I *couldn't*, sir, I *couldn't!* It's not worth it. And I simply mustn't allow myself to haggle like this about a price. It's all wrong. I'll make you one final offer, and then I must go. Twenty pounds."

"I'll take it," Rummins snapped. "It's yours."

"Oh dear," Mr. Boggis said, clasping his hands. "There I go again. I should never have started this in the first place."

"You can't back out now, Parson. A deal's a deal."

"Yes, yes, I know."

"How're you going to take it?"

"Well, let me see. Perhaps if I were to drive my car up into the yard, you gentlemen would be kind enough to help me load it?"

"In a car? This thing'll never go in a car! You'll need a truck for this!"

"I don't think so. Anyway, we'll see. My car's on the road. I'll be back in a jiffy. We'll manage it somehow, I'm sure."

Mr. Boggis walked out into the yard and through the gate and then down the long track that led across the field toward the road. He found himself giggling quite uncontrollably, and there was a feeling inside him as though hundreds and hundreds of tiny bubbles were rising up from his stomach and bursting merrily in the top of his head, like sparkling-water. All the buttercups in the field were suddenly turning into golden sovereigns, glistening in the sunlight. The ground was littered with them, and he swung off the track onto the grass so that he could walk among them and tread on them and hear the little metallic tinkle they made as he kicked them around with his toes. He was finding it difficult to stop himself from breaking into a run. But clergymen never run; they walk slowly. Walk slowly, Boggis. Keep calm, Boggis. There's no hurry now. The commode is yours! Yours for twenty pounds, and it's worth fifteen or twenty thousand! The Boggis Commode! In ten minutes it'll be loaded into your car—it'll go in easily—and you'll be driving back to London and singing all the way! Mr. Boggis driving the Boggis Commode home in the Boggis car. Historic occasion. What *wouldn't* a newspaperman give to get a picture of that! Should he arrange it? Perhaps he should. Wait and see. Oh, glorious day! Oh, lovely sunny summer day! Oh, glory be!

Back in the farmhouse, Rummins was saying, "Fancy that old bastard giving twenty pound for a load of junk like this."

"You did very nicely, Mr. Rummins," Claud told him. "You think he'll pay you?"

"We don't put it in the car till he do."

"And what if it won't go in the car?" Claud asked. "You know what I think, Mr. Rummins? You want my honest opinion? I think the bloody thing's too big to go in the car. And then what happens? Then he's going to say to hell with it and just drive off without it and you'll never see him again. Nor the money either. He didn't seem all that keen on having it, you know."

Rummins paused to consider this new and rather alarming prospect.

"How can a thing like that possibly go in a car?" Claud went on relentlessly. "A parson never has a big car anyway. You ever seen a parson with a big car, Mr. Rummins?"

"Can't say I have."

"Exactly! And now listen to me. I've got an idea. He told us, didn't he, that it was only the legs he was wanting. Right? So all we've got to do is to cut 'em off quick right here on the spot before he comes back, then it'll be sure to go in the car. All we're doing is saving him the trouble of cutting them off himself when he gets home. How about it, Mr. Rummins?" Claud's flat bovine face glimmered with a mawkish pride

"It's not such a bad idea at that," Rummins said, looking at the commode "In fact it's a bloody good idea. Come on then, we'll have to hurry. You and Bert carry it out into the yard I'll get the saw Take the drawers out first "

Within a couple of minutes, Claud and Bert had carried the commode outside and had laid it upside down in the yard amidst the chicken droppings and cow dung and mud. In the distance, halfway across the field, they could see a small black figure striding along the path toward the road. They paused to watch. There was something rather comical about the way in which this figure was conducting itself. Every now and again it would break into a trot, then it did a kind of hop skip and jump, and once it seemed as though the sound of a cheerful song came rippling faintly to them from across the meadow.

"I reckon he's balmy," Claud said, and Bert grinned darkly, rolling his misty eye slowly round in its socket.

Rummins came waddling over from the shed, squat and frog-like, carrying a long saw. Claud took the saw away from him and went to work.

"Cut 'em close," Rummins said. "Don't forget he's going to use 'em on another table."

The mahogany was hard and very dry, and as Claud worked, a fine red dust sprayed out from the edge of the saw and fell softly to the ground. One by one, the legs came off, and when they were all severed, Bert stooped down and arranged them carefully in a row.

Claud stepped back to survey the results of his labour. There was a longish pause.

"Just let me ask you one question, Mr. Rummins," he said slowly. "Even now, could *you* put that enormous thing into the back of a car?"

"Not unless it was a van."

"Correct!" Claud cried. "And parsons don't have vans, you know. All they've got usually is piddling little Morris Eights or Austin Sevens."

"The legs is all he wants," Rummins said. "If the rest of it won't go in, then he can leave it. He can't complain. He's got the legs."

"Now you know better'n that, Mr. Rummins," Claud said patiently. "You know damn well he's going to start knocking the price if he don't get every single bit of this into the car. A parson's just as cunning as the rest of 'em when it comes to money, don't you make any mistake about that. Especially this old boy. So why don't we give him his firewood now and be done with it. Where d'you keep the axe?"

"I reckon that's fair enough," Rummins said. "Bert, go fetch the axe."

Bert went into the shed and fetched a tall woodcutter's axe and gave it to Claud. Claud spat on the palms of his hands and rubbed them together. Then, with a long-armed high-swinging action, he began fiercely attacking the legless carcase of the commode.

It was hard work, and it took several minutes before he had the whole thing more or less smashed to pieces.

"I'll tell you one thing," he said, straightening up, wiping his brow. "That was a bloody good carpenter put this job together and I don't care what the parson says."

"We're just in time!" Rummins called out. "Here he comes!"

The Landlady

1959

BILLY WEAVER had travelled down from London on the slow afternoon train, with a change at Reading on the way, and by the time he got to Bath it was about nine o'clock in the evening and the moon was coming up out of a clear starry sky over the houses opposite the station entrance. But the air was deadly cold and the wind was like a flat blade of ice on his cheeks.

"Excuse me," he said, "but is there a fairly cheap hotel not too far away from here?"

"Try The Bell and Dragon," the porter answered, pointing down the road. "They might take you in. It's about a quarter of a mile along on the other side."

Billy thanked him and picked up his suitcase and set out to walk the quarter-mile to The Bell and Dragon. He had never been to Bath before. He didn't know anyone who lived there. But Mr. Greenslade at the Head Office in London had told him it was a splendid town. "Find your own lodgings," he had said, "and then go along and report to the Branch Manager as soon as you've got yourself settled."

Billy was seventeen years old. He was wearing a new navy-blue overcoat, a new brown trilby hat, and a new brown suit, and he was feeling fine. He walked briskly down the street. He was trying to do everything briskly these days. Briskness, he had decided, was *the* one common characteristic of all successful businessmen. The big shots up at Head Office were absolutely fantastically brisk all the time. They were amazing.

There were no shops on this wide street that he was walking along, only a line of tall houses on each side, all of them identical. They had porches and pillars and four or five steps going up to their front doors, and it was obvious that once upon a time they had been very swanky residences. But now, even in the darkness, he could see that the paint was peeling from the woodwork on their doors and windows, and that the handsome white façades were cracked and blotchy from neglect.

Suddenly, in a downstairs window that was brilliantly illuminated by a street-lamp not six yards away, Billy caught sight of a printed notice propped up against the glass in one of the upper panes. It said BED AND BREAKFAST. There was a vase of yellow chrysanthemums, tall and beautiful, standing just underneath the notice.

He stopped walking. He moved a bit closer. Green curtains (some sort of velvety material) were hanging down on either side of the window. The chrysanthemums looked wonderful beside them. He went right up and peered through the glass into the room, and the first thing he saw was a bright fire burning in the hearth. On the carpet in front of the fire, a pretty little dachshund was curled up asleep with its nose tucked into its belly. The room itself, so far as he could see in the half-darkness, was filled with pleasant furniture. There was a baby-grand piano and a big sofa and several plump armchairs; and in one corner he spotted a large parrot in a cage. Animals were usually a good sign in a place like this, Billy told himself; and all in all, it looked to him as though it would be a pretty decent house to stay in. Certainly it would be more comfortable than The Bell and Dragon.

On the other hand, a pub would be more congenial than a boarding-house. There would be beer and darts in the evenings, and lots of people to talk to, and it would probably be a good bit cheaper, too. He had stayed a couple of nights in a pub once before and he had liked it. He had never stayed in any boarding-houses, and, to be perfectly honest, he was a tiny bit frightened of them. The name itself conjured up images of watery cabbage, rapacious landladies, and a powerful smell of kippers in the living-room.

After dithering about like this in the cold for two or three minutes, Billy decided that he would walk on and take a look at The Bell and Dragon before making up his mind. He turned to go.

And now a queer thing happened to him. He was in the act of stepping back and turning away from the window when all at once his eye was caught and held in the most peculiar manner by the small notice that was there. BED AND BREAKFAST, it said. BED AND BREAKFAST, BED AND BREAKFAST, BED AND BREAKFAST. Each word was like a large black eye staring at him through the glass, holding him, compelling him, forcing him to stay where he was and not to walk away from that house, and the next thing he knew, he was actually moving across from the window to the front door of the house, climbing the steps that led up to it, and reaching for the bell.

He pressed the bell. Far away in a back room he heard it ringing, and then *at once*—it must have been at once because he hadn't even had time to take his finger from the bell-button—the door swung open and a woman was standing there

Normally you ring the bell and you have at least a half-minute's wait before the door opens. But this dame was like a jack-in-the-box He pressed the bell—and out she popped! It made him jump

She was about forty-five or fifty years old, and the moment she saw him, she gave him a warm welcoming smile.

"Please come in," she said pleasantly. She stepped aside, holding the door wide open, and Billy found himself automatically starting forward. The compulsion or, more accurately, the desire to follow after her into that house was extraordinarily strong.

"I saw the notice in the window," he said, holding himself back.

"Yes, I know."

"I was wondering about a room."

"It's *all* ready for you, my dear," she said. She had a round pink face and very gentle blue eyes.

"I was on my way to The Bell and Dragon," Billy told her. "But the notice in your window just happened to catch my eye."

"My dear boy," she said, "why don't you come in out of the cold?"

"How much do you charge?"

"Five and sixpence a night, including breakfast."

It was fantastically cheap. It was less than half of what he had been willing to pay.

"If that is too much," she added, "then perhaps I can reduce it just a tiny bit. Do you desire an egg for breakfast? Eggs are expensive at the moment. It would be sixpence less without the egg."

"Five and sixpence is fine," he answered. "I should like very much to stay here."

"I knew you would. Do come in."

She seemed terribly nice. She looked exactly like the mother of one's best school-friend welcoming one into the house to stay for the Christmas holidays. Billy took off his hat, and stepped over the threshold.

"Just hang it there," she said, "and let me help you with your coat."

There were no other hats or coats in the hall. There were no umbrellas, no walking-sticks—nothing.

"We have it *all* to ourselves," she said, smiling at him over her shoulder as she led the way upstairs. "You see, it isn't very often I have the pleasure of taking a visitor into my little nest."

The old girl is slightly dotty, Billy told himself. But at five and sixpence a night, who gives a damn about that? "I should've thought you'd be simply swamped with applicants," he said politely.

"Oh, I am, my dear, I am, of course I am. But the trouble is that I'm inclined to be just a teeny weeny bit choosy and particular—if you see what I mean."

"Ah, yes."

"But I'm always ready. Everything is always ready day and night in this house just on the off-chance that an acceptable young gentleman will come along. And it is such a pleasure, my dear, such a very great pleasure when now and again I open the door and I see someone standing there who is just *exactly* right." She was halfway up the stairs, and she paused with one hand on the stair-rail, turning her head and smiling down at him with pale lips. "Like you," she added, and her blue eyes travelled slowly all the way down the length of Billy's body, to his feet, and then up again.

On the second-floor landing she said to him, "This floor is mine."

They climbed up another flight. "And this one is *all* yours," she said. "Here's your room. I do hope you'll like it." She took him into a small but charming front bedroom, switching on the light as she went in.

"The morning sun comes right in the window, Mr. Perkins. It *is* Mr. Perkins, isn't it?"

"No," he said. "It's Weaver."

"Mr. Weaver. How nice. I've put a water-bottle between the sheets to air them out, Mr. Weaver. It's such a comfort to have a hot water-bottle in a strange bed with clean sheets, don't you agree? And you may light the gas fire at any time if you feel chilly."

"Thank you," Billy said. "Thank you ever so much." He noticed that the bedspread had been taken off the bed, and that the bedclothes had been neatly turned back on one side, all ready for someone to get in.

"I'm so glad you appeared," she said, looking earnestly into his face. "I was beginning to get worried."

"That's all right," Billy answered brightly. "You mustn't worry about me." He put his suitcase on the chair and started to open it.

"And what about supper, my dear? Did you manage to get anything to eat before you came here?"

"I'm not a bit hungry, thank you," he said. "I think I'll just go to bed as soon as possible because tomorrow I've got to get up rather early and report to the office."

"Very well, then. I'll leave you now so that you can unpack. But before you go to bed, would you be kind enough to pop into the sitting-room on the ground floor and sign the book? Everyone has to do that because it's the law of the land, and we don't want to go breaking any laws at *this* stage in the proceedings, do we?" She gave him a little wave of the hand and went quickly out of the room and closed the door.

Now, the fact that his landlady appeared to be slightly off her rocker didn't worry Billy in the least. After all, she not only was harmless—there was no question about that—but she was also quite obviously a kind and generous soul. He guessed that she had probably lost a son in the war, or something like that, and had never gotten over it.

So a few minutes later, after unpacking his suitcase and washing his hands, he trotted downstairs to the ground floor and entered the living-room. His landlady wasn't there, but the fire was glowing in the hearth, and the little dachshund was still sleeping soundly in front of it. The room was wonderfully warm and cosy. I'm a lucky fellow, he thought, rubbing his hands. This is a bit of all right.

He found the guest-book lying open on the piano, so he took out his pen and wrote down his name and address. There were only two other entries above his on the page, and, as one always does with guest-books, he started to read them. One was a Christopher Mulholland from Cardiff. The other was Gregory W. Temple from Bristol.

That's funny, he thought suddenly. Christopher Mulholland. It rings a bell.

Now where on earth had he heard that rather unusual name before?

Was it a boy at school? No. Was it one of his sister's numerous young men, perhaps, or a friend of his father's? No, no, it wasn't any of those. He glanced down again at the book.

Christopher Mulholland　　*231 Cathedral Road, Cardiff*
Gregory W. Temple　　*27 Sycamore Drive, Bristol*

As a matter of fact, now he came to think of it, he wasn't at all sure that the second name didn't have almost as much of a familiar ring about it as the first.

"Gregory Temple?" he said aloud, searching his memory. "Christopher Mulholland? . . ."

"Such charming boys," a voice behind him answered, and he turned and saw his landlady sailing into the room with a large silver tea-tray in her hands. She was holding it well out in front of her, and rather high up, as though the tray were a pair of reins on a frisky horse.

"They sound somehow familiar," he said.

"They do? How interesting."

"I'm almost positive I've heard those names before somewhere. Isn't that odd? Maybe it was in the newspapers. They weren't famous in any way, were they? I mean famous cricketers or footballers or something like that?"

"Famous," she said, setting the tea-tray down on the low table in front of the sofa. "Oh no, I don't think they were famous. But they were incredibly handsome, both of them, I can promise you that. They were tall and young and handsome, my dear, just exactly like you."

Once more, Billy glanced down at the book. "Look here," he said, noticing the dates. "This last entry is over two years old."

"It is?"

"Yes, indeed. And Christopher Mulholland's is nearly a year before that—more than *three years* ago."

"Dear me," she said, shaking her head and heaving a dainty little sigh. "I would never have thought it. How time does fly away from us all, doesn't it, Mr. Wilkins?"

"It's Weaver," Billy said. "W-e-a-v-e-r."

"Oh, of course it is!" she cried, sitting down on the sofa. "How silly of me. I do apologize. In one ear and out the other, that's me, Mr. Weaver."

"You know something?" Billy said. "Something that's really quite extraordinary about all this?"

"No, dear, I don't."

"Well, you see, both of these names—Mulholland and Temple —I not only seem to remember each one of them separately, so to speak, but somehow or other, in some peculiar way, they both appear to be sort of connected together as well. As though they were both famous for the same sort of thing, if you see what I mean—like

. . . well . . . like Dempsey and Tunney, for example, or Churchill and Roosevelt.''

"How amusing," she said. "But come over here now, dear, and sit down beside me on the sofa and I'll give you a nice cup of tea and a ginger biscuit before you go to bed."

"You really shouldn't bother," Billy said. "I didn't mean you to do anything like that." He stood by the piano, watching her as she fussed about with the cups and saucers. He noticed that she had small, white, quickly moving hands, and red finger-nails.

"I'm almost positive it was in the newspapers I saw them," Billy said. "I'll think of it in a second. I'm sure I will."

There is nothing more tantalizing than a thing like this that lingers just outside the borders of one's memory. He hated to give up.

"Now wait a minute," he said. "Wait just a minute. Mulholland . . . Christopher Mulholland . . . wasn't *that* the name of the Eton schoolboy who was on a walking-tour through the West Country, and then all of a sudden . . ."

"Milk?" she said. "And sugar?"

"Yes, please. And then all of a sudden . . ."

"Eton schoolboy?" she said. "Oh no, my dear, that can't possibly be right because *my* Mr. Mulholland was certainly not an Eton schoolboy when he came to me. He was a Cambridge undergraduate. Come over here now and sit next to me and warm yourself in front of this lovely fire. Come on. Your tea's all ready for you." She patted the empty place beside her on the sofa, and she sat there smiling at Billy and waiting for him to come over.

He crossed the room slowly, and sat down on the edge of the sofa. She placed his teacup on the table in front of him.

"*There* we are," she said. "How nice and cosy this is, isn't it?"

Billy started sipping his tea. She did the same. For half a minute or so, neither of them spoke. But Billy knew that she was looking at him. Her body was half turned toward him, and he could feel her eyes resting on his face, watching him over the rim of her teacup. Now and again, he caught a whiff of a peculiar smell that seemed to emanate directly from her person. It was not in the least unpleasant, and it reminded him—well, he wasn't quite sure what it reminded him of. Pickled walnuts? New leather? Or was it the corridors of a hospital?

At length, she said, "Mr. Mulholland was a great one for his tea. Never in my life have I seen anyone drink as much tea as dear, sweet Mr. Mulholland."

"I suppose he left fairly recently," Billy said. He was still puzzling his head about the two names. He was positive now that he had seen them in the newspapers—in the headlines.

"Left?" she said, arching her brows. "But my dear boy, he never left. He's still here. Mr. Temple is also here. They're on the fourth floor, both of them together."

Billy set his cup down slowly on the table and stared at his landlady. She smiled back at him, and then she put out one of her white hands and patted him comfortingly on the knee. "How old are you, my dear?" she asked.

"Seventeen."

"Seventeen!" she cried. "Oh, it's the perfect age! Mr. Mulholland was also seventeen. But I think he was a trifle shorter than you are; in fact I'm sure he was, and his teeth weren't *quite* so white. You have the most beautiful teeth, Mr. Weaver, did you know that?"

"They're not as good as they look," Billy said. "They've got simply masses of fillings in them at the back."

"Mr. Temple, of course, was a little older," she said, ignoring his remark. "He was actually twenty-eight. And yet I never would have guessed it if he hadn't told me, never in my whole life. There wasn't a *blemish* on his body."

"A what?" Billy said.

"His skin was *just* like a baby's."

There was a pause. Billy picked up his teacup and took another sip of his tea, then he set it down again gently in its saucer. He waited for her to say something else, but she seemed to have lapsed into another of her silences. He sat there staring straight ahead of him into the far corner of the room, biting his lower lip.

"That parrot," he said at last. "You know something? It had me completely fooled when I first saw it through the window. I could have sworn it was alive."

"Alas, no longer."

"It's most terribly clever the way it's been done," he said. "It doesn't look in the least bit dead. Who did it?"

"I did."

"*You* did?"

"Of course," she said. "And have you met my little Basil as well?" She nodded toward the dachshund curled up so comfortably in front of the fire. Billy looked at it. And suddenly, he realized that this animal had all the time been just as silent and motionless as the parrot. He put out a hand and touched it gently on the top of its back. The back was hard and cold, and when he pushed the hair to one side with his fingers, he could see the skin underneath, greyish-black and dry and perfectly preserved.

"Good gracious me," he said. "How absolutely fascinating." He turned away from the dog and stared with deep admiration at the little woman beside him on the sofa. "It must be most awfully difficult to do a thing like that."

"Not in the least," she said. "I stuff *all* my little pets myself when they pass away. Will you have another cup of tea?"

"No, thank you," Billy said. The tea tasted faintly of bitter almonds, and he didn't much care for it.

"You did sign the book, didn't you?"

"Oh, yes."

"That's good. Because later on, if I happen to forget what you were called, then I could always come down here and look it up. I still do that almost every day with Mr. Mulholland and Mr. . . . Mr. . . ."

"Temple," Billy said. "Gregory Temple. Excuse my asking, but haven't there been *any* other guests here except them in the last two or three years?"

Holding her teacup high in one hand, inclining her head slightly to the left, she looked up at him out of the corners of her eyes and gave him another gentle little smile.

"No, my dear," she said. "Only you."

William and Mary

1959

WILLIAM PEARL did not leave a great deal of money when he died, and his will was a simple one. With the exception of a few small bequests to relatives, he left all his property to his wife.

The solicitor and Mrs. Pearl went over it together in the solicitor's office, and when the business was completed, the widow got up to leave. At that point, the solicitor took a sealed envelope from the folder on his desk and held it out to his client.

"I have been instructed to give you this," he said. "Your husband sent it to us shortly before he passed away." The solicitor was pale and prim, and out of respect for a widow he kept his head on one side as he spoke, looking downward. "It appears that it might be something personal, Mrs. Pearl. No doubt you'd like to take it home with you and read it in privacy."

Mrs. Pearl accepted the envelope and went out into the street. She paused on the pavement, feeling the thing with her fingers. A letter of farewell from William? Probably, yes. A formal letter. It was bound to be formal—stiff and formal. The man was incapable of acting otherwise. He had never done anything informal in his life.

My dear Mary, I trust that you will not permit my departure from this world to upset you too much, but that you will continue to observe those precepts which have guided you so well during our partnership together. Be diligent and dignified in all things. Be thrifty with your money. Be very careful that you do not . . . et cetera, et cetera.

A typical William letter.

Or was it possible that he might have broken down at the last moment and written her something beautiful? Maybe this was a beautiful tender message, a sort of love letter, a lovely warm note of thanks to her for giving him thirty years of her life and for ironing a million shirts and cooking a million meals and making a million beds, something that she could read over and over again, once a day at least, and she would keep it for ever in the box on her dressing-table together with her brooches.

There is no knowing what people will do when they are about to die, Mrs. Pearl told herself, and she tucked the envelope under her arm and hurried home.

She let herself in the front door and went straight to the living-room and sat down on the sofa without removing her hat or coat. Then she opened the envelope and drew out the contents. These consisted, she saw, of some fifteen or twenty sheets of lined white paper, folded over once and held together at the top left-hand corner by a clip. Each sheet was covered with the small, neat, forward-sloping writing that she knew so well, but when she noticed how much of it there was, and in what a neat businesslike manner it was written, and how the first page didn't even begin in the nice way a letter should, she began to get suspicious.

She looked away. She lit herself a cigarette. She took one puff and laid the cigarette in the ashtray.

If this is about what I am beginning to suspect it is about, she told herself, then I don't want to read it.

Can one refuse to read a letter from the dead?

Yes.

Well . . .

She glanced over at William's empty chair on the other side of the fireplace. It was a big brown leather armchair, and there was a depression on the seat of it, made by his buttocks over the years. Higher up, on the backrest, there was a dark oval stain on the leather where his head had rested. He used to sit reading in that chair and she would be opposite him on the sofa, sewing on buttons or mend-ing socks or putting a patch on the elbow of one of his jackets, and every now and then a pair of eyes would glance up from the book and settle on her, watchful, but strangely impersonal, as if calculating something. She had never liked those eyes. They were ice blue, cold, small, and rather close together, with two deep vertical lines of disapproval dividing them. All her life they had been watching her. And even now, after a week alone in the house, she sometimes had an uneasy feeling that they were still there, following her around, staring at her from doorways, from empty chairs, through a window at night.

Slowly she reached into her handbag and took out her spectacles and put them on. Then, holding the pages up high in front of her so that they caught the late afternoon light from the window behind, she started to read:

THIS NOTE, *my dear Mary,* is entirely for you, and will be given you shortly after I am gone.

Do not be alarmed by the sight of all this writing. It is nothing but an attempt on my part to explain to you precisely what Landy is going to do to me, and why I have agreed that he should do it, and what are his theories and his hopes. You are my wife and you have a right to know these things. In fact you *must* know them. During the past few days I have tried very hard to speak with you about Landy, but you have steadfastly refused to give me a hearing. This, as I have already told you, is a very foolish attitude to take, and I find it not entirely an unselfish one either. It stems mostly from ignorance, and I am absolutely convinced that if only you were made aware of all the facts, you would immediately change your view. That is why I am hoping that when I am no longer with you, and your mind is less distracted, you will consent to listen to me more carefully through these pages. I swear to you that when you have read my story, your sense of antipathy will vanish, and enthusiasm will take its place. I even dare to hope that you will become a little proud of what I have done.

As you read on, you must forgive me, if you will, for the coolness of my style, but this is the only way I know of getting my message over to you clearly. You see, as my time draws near, it is natural that I begin to brim with every kind of sentimentality under the sun. Each day I grow more extravagantly wistful, especially in the evenings, and unless I watch myself closely my emotions will be overflowing onto these pages.

I have a wish, for example, to write something about you and what a satisfactory wife you have been to me through the years, and I am promising myself that if there is time, and I still have the strength, I shall do that next.

I have a yearning also to speak about this Oxford of mine where I have been living and teaching for the past seventeen years, to tell something about the glory of the place and to explain, if I can, a little of what it has meant to have been allowed to work in its midst. All the things and places that I loved so well keep crowding in on me now in this gloomy bedroom. They are bright and beautiful as they always were, and today, for some reason, I can see them more clearly than ever. The path around the lake in the gardens of Worcester

College, where Lovelace used to walk. The gateway at Pembroke. The view westward over the town from Magdalen Tower. The great hall at Christchurch. The little rockery at St. Johns where I have counted more than a dozen varieties of campanula, including the rare and dainty C. Waldsteiniana. But there, you see! I haven't even begun and already I'm falling into the trap. So let me get started now; and let you read it slowly, my dear, without any of that sense of sorrow or disapproval that might otherwise embarrass your understanding. Promise me now that you will read it slowly, and that you will put yourself in a cool and patient frame of mind before you begin.

The details of the illness that struck me down so suddenly in my middle life are known to you. I need not waste time upon them— except to admit at once how foolish I was not to have gone earlier to my doctor. Cancer is one of the few remaining diseases that these modern drugs cannot cure. A surgeon can operate if it has not spread too far; but with me, not only did I leave it too late, but the thing had the effrontery to attack me in the pancreas, making both surgery and survival equally impossible.

So here I was with somewhere between one and six months left to live, growing more melancholy every hour—and then, all of a sudden, in comes Landy.

That was six weeks ago, on a Tuesday morning, very early, long before your visiting time, and the moment he entered I knew there was some sort of madness in the wind. He didn't creep in on his toes, sheepish and embarrassed, not knowing what to say, like all my other visitors. He came in strong and smiling, and he strode up to the bed and stood there looking down at me with a wild bright glimmer in his eyes, and he said, "William, my boy, this is perfect. You're just the one I want!"

Perhaps I should explain to you here that although John Landy has never been to our house, and you have seldom if ever met him, I myself have been friendly with him for at least nine years. I am, of course, primarily a teacher of philosophy, but as you know I've lately been dabbling a good deal in psychology as well. Landy's interests and mine have therefore slightly overlapped. He is a magnificent neurosurgeon, one of the finest, and recently he has been kind enough to let me study the results of some of his work, especially the varying effects of prefrontal lobotomies upon different types of psychopath. So you can see that when he suddenly burst in on me Tuesday morning, we were by no means strangers to one another

"Look," he said, pulling up a chair beside the bed. "In a few weeks you're going to be dead. Correct?"

Coming from Landy, the question didn't seem especially unkind. In a way it was refreshing to have a visitor brave enough to touch upon the forbidden subject.

"You're going to expire right here in this room, and then they'll take you out and cremate you."

"Bury me," I said.

"That's even worse. And then what? Do you believe you'll go to heaven?"

"I doubt it," I said, "though it would be comforting to think so."

"Or hell, perhaps?"

"I don't really see why they should send me there."

"You never know, my dear William."

"What's all this about?" I asked.

"Well," he said, and I could see him watching me carefully, "personally, I don't believe that after you're dead you'll ever hear of yourself again—unless . . ." and here he paused and smiled and leaned closer ". . . unless, of course, you have the sense to put yourself into my hands. Would you care to consider a proposition?"

The way he was staring at me, and studying me, and appraising me with a queer kind of hungriness, I might have been a piece of prime beef on the counter and he had bought it and was waiting for them to wrap it up.

"I'm really serious about it, William. Would you care to consider a proposition?"

"I don't know what you're talking about."

"Then listen and I'll tell you. Will you listen to me?"

"Go on then, if you like. I doubt I've got very much to lose by hearing it."

"On the contrary, you have a great deal to gain—especially *after you're dead.*"

I am sure he was expecting me to jump when he said this, but for some reason I was ready for it. I lay quite still, watching his face and that slow white smile of his that always revealed the gold clasp of an upper denture curled around the canine on the left side of his mouth.

"This is a thing, William, that I've been working on quietly for some years. One or two others here at the hospital have been helping me, especially Morrison, and we've completed a number of fairly successful trials with laboratory animals. I'm at the stage now where

I'm ready to have a go with a man. It's a big idea, and it may sound a bit farfetched at first, but from a surgical point of view there doesn't seem to be any reason why it shouldn't be more or less practicable."

Landy leaned forward and placed both his hands on the edge of my bed. He has a good face, handsome in a bony sort of way, and with none of the usual doctor's look about it. You know that look, most of them have it. It glimmers at you out of their eyeballs like a dull electric sign and it reads *Only I can save you.* But John Landy's eyes were wide and bright and little sparks of excitement were dancing in the centres of them.

"Quite a long time ago," he said, "I saw a short medical film that had been brought over from Russia. It was a rather gruesome thing, but interesting. It showed a dog's head completely severed from the body, but with the normal blood supply being maintained through the arteries and veins by means of an artificial heart. Now the thing is this: that dog's head, sitting there all alone on a sort of tray, was *alive.* The brain was functioning. They proved it by several tests. For example, when food was smeared on the dog's lips, the tongue would come out and lick it away; and the eyes would follow a person moving across the room.

"It seemed reasonable to conclude from this that the head and the brain did not need to be attached to the rest of the body in order to remain alive—provided, of course, that a supply of properly oxygenated blood could be maintained.

"Now then. My own thought, which grew out of seeing this film, was to remove the brain from the skull of a human and keep it alive and functioning as an independent unit for an unlimited period after he is dead. *Your* brain, for example, after *you* are dead."

"I don't like that," I said.

"Don't interrupt, William. Let me finish. So far as I can tell from subsequent experiments, the brain is a peculiarly self-supporting object. It manufactures its own cerebrospinal fluid. The magic processes of thought and memory which go on inside it are manifestly not impaired by the absence of limbs or trunk or even of skull, provided, as I say, that you keep pumping in the right kind of oxygenated blood under the proper conditions.

"My dear William, just think for a moment of your own brain. It is in perfect shape. It is crammed full of a lifetime of learning. It has taken you years of work to make it what it is. It is just beginning to give out some first-rate original ideas. Yet soon it is going to have to die along with the rest of your body simply because your silly little pancreas is lousy with cancer."

"No thank you," I said to him. "You can stop there. It's a repulsive idea, and even if you could do it, which I doubt, it would be quite pointless. What possible use is there in keeping my brain alive if I couldn't talk or see or hear or feel? Personally, I can think of nothing more unpleasant."

"I believe that you *would* be able to communicate with us," Landy said. "And we might even succeed in giving you a certain amount of vision. But let's take this slowly. I'll come to all that later on. The fact remains that you're going to die fairly soon whatever happens; and my plans would not involve touching you at all until *after* you are dead. Come now, William. No true philosopher could object to lending his dead body to the cause of science."

"That's not putting it quite straight," I answered. "It seems to me there'd be some doubt as to whether I were dead or alive by the time you'd finished with me."

"Well," he said, smiling a little, "I suppose you're right about that. But I don't think you ought to turn me down quite so quickly, before you know a bit more about it."

"I said I don't want to hear it."

"Have a cigarette," he said, holding out his case.

"I don't smoke, you know that."

He took one himself and lit it with a tiny silver lighter that was no bigger than a shilling piece. "A present from the people who make my instruments," he said. "Ingenious, isn't it?"

I examined the lighter, then handed it back.

"May I go on?" he asked.

"I'd rather you didn't."

"Just lie still and listen. I think you'll find it quite interesting."

There were some blue grapes on a plate beside my bed. I put the plate on my chest and began eating the grapes.

"At the very moment of death," Landy said, "I should have to be standing by so that I could step in immediately and try to keep your brain alive."

"You mean leaving it in the head?"

"To start with, yes. I'd have to."

"And where would you put it after that?"

"If you want to know, in a sort of basin."

"Are you really serious about this?"

"Certainly I'm serious."

"All right. Go on."

"I suppose you know that when the heart stops and the brain is deprived of fresh blood and oxygen, its tissues die very rapidly. Anything from four to six minutes and the whole thing's dead. Even after three minutes you may get a certain amount of damage. So I should have to work rapidly to prevent this from happening. But with the help of the machine, it should all be quite simple."

"What machine?"

"The artificial heart. We've got a nice adaptation here of the one originally devised by Alexis Carrel and Lindbergh. It oxygenates the blood, keeps it at the right temperature, pumps it in at the right pressure, and does a number of other little necessary things. It's really not at all complicated."

"Tell me what you would do at the moment of death," I said. "What is the first thing you would do?"

"Do you know anything about the vascular and venous arrangements of the brain?"

"No."

"Then listen. It's not difficult. The blood supply to the brain is derived from two main sources, the internal carotid arteries and the vertebral arteries. There are two of each, making four arteries in all. Got that?"

"Yes."

"And the return system is even simpler. The blood is drained away by only two large veins, the internal jugulars. So you have four arteries going up—they go up the neck, of course—and two veins coming down. Around the brain itself they naturally branch out into other channels, but those don't concern us. We never touch them."

"All right," I said. "Imagine that I've just died. Now what would you do?"

"I should immediately open your neck and locate the four arteries, the carotids and the vertebrals. I should then perfuse them, which means that I'd stick a large hollow needle into each. These four needles would be connected by tubes to the artificial heart.

"Then, working quickly, I would dissect out both the left and right internal jugular veins and hitch these also to the heart machine to complete the circuit. Now switch on the machine, which is already primed with the right type of blood, and there you are. The circulation through your brain would be restored."

"I'd be like that Russian dog."

"I don't think you would. For one thing, you'd certainly lose consciousness when you died, and I very much doubt whether you would come to again for quite a long time—if indeed you came to at all. But, conscious or not, you'd be in a rather interesting position, wouldn't you? You'd have a cold dead body and a living brain."

Landy paused to savour this delightful prospect. The man was so entranced and bemused by the whole idea that he evidently found it impossible to believe I might not be feeling the same way.

"We could now afford to take our time," he said. "And believe me, we'd need it. The first thing we'd do would be to wheel you to the operating-room, accompanied of course by the machine, which must never stop pumping. The next problem . . ."

"All right," I said. "That's enough. I don't have to hear the details."

"Oh but you must," he said. "It is important that you should know precisely what is going to happen to you all the way through. You see, afterwards, when you regain consciousness, it will be much more satisfactory from your point of view if you are able to remember exactly *where* you are and *how* you came to be there. If only for your own peace of mind you should know that. You agree?"

I lay still on the bed, watching him.

"So the next problem would be to remove your brain, intact and undamaged, from your dead body. The body is useless. In fact it has already started to decay. The skull and the face are also useless. They are both encumbrances and I don't want them around. All I want is the brain, the clean beautiful brain, alive and perfect. So when I get you on the table I will take a saw, a small oscillating saw, and with this I shall proceed to remove the whole vault of your skull. You'd still be unconscious at that point so I wouldn't have to bother with anaesthetic."

"Like hell you wouldn't," I said.

"You'd be out cold, I promise you that, William. Don't forget you *died* just a few minutes before."

"Nobody's sawing off the top of my skull without an anaesthetic," I said.

Landy shrugged his shoulders. "It makes no difference to me," he said. "I'll be glad to give you a little procaine if you want it. If it will make you any happier I'll infiltrate the whole scalp with procaine, the whole head, from the neck up."

"Thanks very much," I said.

"You know," he went on, "it's extraordinary what sometimes happens. Only last week a man was brought in unconscious, and I opened his head without any anaesthetic at all and removed a small blood clot. I was still working inside the skull when he woke up and began talking.

" 'Where am I?' he asked.

" 'You're in hospital.'

" 'Well,' he said. 'Fancy that.'

" 'Tell me,' I asked him, 'is this bothering you, what I'm doing?'

" 'No,' he answered. 'Not at all. What *are* you doing?'

" 'I'm just removing a blood clot from your brain.'

" 'You *are?*'

" 'Just lie still. Don't move. I'm nearly finished.'

" 'So that's the bastard been giving me all those headaches,' the man said."

Landy paused and smiled, remembering the occasion. "That's word for word what the man said," he went on, "although the next day he couldn't even recollect the incident. It's a funny thing, the brain."

"I'll have the procaine," I said.

"As you wish, William. And now, as I say, I'd take a small oscillating saw and carefully remove your complete calvarium—the whole vault of the skull. This would expose the top half of the brain, or rather the outer covering in which it is wrapped. You may or may not know that there are three separate coverings around the brain itself—the outer one called the dura mater or dura, the middle one called the arachnoid, and the inner one called the pia mater or pia. Most laymen seem to have the idea that the brain is a naked thing floating around in fluid in your head. But it isn't. It's wrapped up neatly in these three strong coverings, and the cerebrospinal fluid actually flows within the little gap between the two inner coverings, known as the subarachnoid space. As I told you before, this fluid is manufactured by the brain, and it drains off into the venous system by osmosis.

"I myself would leave all three coverings—don't they have lovely names, the dura, the arachnoid, and the pia?—I'd leave them all intact. There are many reasons for this, not least among them being the fact that within the dura run the venous channels that drain the blood from the brain into the jugular.

"Now," he went on, "we've got the upper half of your skull off so that the top of the brain, wrapped in its outer covering, is exposed. The next step is the really tricky one: to release the whole package so that it can be lifted cleanly away, leaving the stubs of the four supply arteries and the two veins hanging underneath ready to be re-connected to the machine. This is an immensely lengthy and complicated business involving the delicate chipping away of much bone, the severing of many nerves, and the cutting and tying of numerous blood vessels. The only way I could do it with any hope of success would be by taking a rongeur and slowly biting off the rest of your skull, peeling it off downward like an orange until the sides and underneath of the brain covering are fully exposed. The problems involved are highly technical and I won't go into them, but I feel fairly sure that the work can be done. It's simply a question of surgical skill and patience. And don't forget that I'd have plenty of time, as much as I wanted, because the artificial heart would be continually pumping away alongside the operating-table, keeping the brain alive.

"Now, let's assume that I've succeeded in peeling off your skull and removing everything else that surrounds the sides of the brain. That leaves it connected to the body only at the base, mainly by the spinal column and by the two large veins and the four arteries that are supplying it with blood. So what next?

"I would sever the spinal column just above the first cervical vertebra, taking great care not to harm the two vertebral arteries which are in that area. But you must remember that the dura or outer covering is open at this place to receive the spinal column, so I'd have to close this opening by sewing the edges of the dura together. There'd be no problem there.

"At this point, I would be ready for the final move. To one side, on a table, I'd have a basin of a special shape, and this would be filled with what we call Ringer's Solution. That is a special kind of fluid we use for irrigation in neurosurgery. I would now cut the brain completely loose by severing the supply arteries and the veins. Then I would simply pick it up in my hands and transfer it to the basin. This would be the only other time during the whole proceeding when the blood flow would be cut off; but once it was in the basin, it wouldn't take a moment to re-connect the stubs of the arteries and veins to the artificial heart.

"So there you are," Landy said. "Your brain is now in the basin, and still alive, and there isn't any reason why it shouldn't stay alive for a very long time, years and years perhaps, provided we looked after the blood and the machine."

"But would it *function?*"

"My dear William, how should I know? I can't even tell you

whether it would ever regain consciousness "

"And if it did?"

"There now! That would be fascinating!"

"Would it?" I said, and I must admit I had my doubts.

"Of course it would! Lying there with all your thinking pro cesses working beautifully, and your memory as well . . ."

"And not being able to see or feel or smell or hear or talk," I said.

"Ah!" he cried. "I knew I'd forgotten something! I never told you about the eye. Listen. I am going to try to leave one of your optic nerves intact, as well as the eye itself. The optic nerve is a little thing about the thickness of a clinical thermometer and about two inches in length as it stretches between the brain and the eye. The beauty of it is that it's not really a nerve at all. It's an outpouching of the brain itself, and the dura or brain covering extends along it and is attached to the eyeball. The back of the eye is therefore in very close contact with the brain, and cerebrospinal fluid flows right up to it.

"All this suits my purpose very well, and makes it reasonable to suppose that I could succeed in preserving one of your eyes. I've already constructed a small plastic case to contain the eyeball, instead of your own socket, and when the brain is in the basin, submerged in Ringer's Solution, the eyeball in its case will float on the surface of the liquid."

"Staring at the ceiling," I said.

"I suppose so, yes. I'm afraid there wouldn't be any muscles there to move it around. But it might be sort of fun to lie there so quietly and comfortably peering out at the world from your basin."

"Hilarious," I said. "How about leaving me an ear as well?"

"I'd rather not try an ear this time.'

"I want an ear," I said. "I insist upon an ear."

"No."

"I want to listen to Bach."

"You don't understand how difficult it would be," Landy said gently. "The hearing apparatus—the cochlea, as it's called—is a far more delicate mechanism than the eye. What's more, it is encased in bone. So is a part of the auditory nerve that connects it with the brain. I couldn't possibly chisel the whole thing out intact."

"Couldn't you leave it encased in the bone and bring the bone to the basin?"

"No," he said firmly. "This thing is complicated enough already. And anyway, if the eye works, it doesn't matter all that much about your hearing. We can always hold up messages for you to read. You really must leave me to decide what is possible and what isn't."

"I haven't yet said that I'm going to do it."

"I know, William, I know."

"I'm not sure I fancy the idea very much."

"Would you rather be dead, altogether?"

"Perhaps I would. I don't know yet. I wouldn't be able to talk, would I?"

"Of course not."

"Then how would I communicate with you? How would you know that I'm conscious?"

"It would be easy for us to know whether or not you regain consciousness," Landy said. "The ordinary electroencephalograph could tell us that. We'd attach the electrodes directly to the frontal lobes of your brain, there in the basin."

"And you could actually tell?"

"Oh, definitely. Any hospital could do that part of it."

"But *I* couldn't communicate with *you*."

"As a matter of fact," Landy said, "I believe you could. There's a man up in London called Wertheimer who's doing some interesting work on the subject of thought communication, and I've been in touch with him. You know, don't you, that the thinking brain throws off electrical and chemical discharges? And that these discharges go out in the form of waves, rather like radio waves?"

"I know a bit about it," I said.

"Well, Wertheimer has constructed an apparatus somewhat similar to the encephalograph, though far more sensitive, and he maintains that within certain narrow limits it can help him to interpret the actual things that a brain is thinking. It produces a kind of graph which is apparently decipherable into words or thoughts. Would you like me to ask Wertheimer to come and see you?"

"No," I said. Landy was already taking it for granted that I was going to go through with this business, and I resented his attitude. "Go away now and leave me alone," I told him. "You won't get anywhere by trying to rush me."

He stood up at once and crossed to the door.

"One question," I said.

He paused with a hand on the doorknob. "Yes, William?"

"Simply this. Do you yourself honestly believe that when my brain is in that basin, my mind will be able to function exactly as it is doing at present? Do you believe that I will be able to think and reason as I can now? And will the power of memory remain?"

"I don't see why not," he answered. "It's the same brain. It's alive. It's undamaged. In fact, it's completely untouched. We haven't even opened the dura. The big difference, of course, would be that we've severed every single nerve that leads into it—except for the one optic nerve—and this means that your thinking would no longer be influenced by your senses. You'd be living in an extraordinarily pure and detached world. Nothing to bother you at all, not even pain. You couldn't possibly feel pain because there wouldn't be any nerves to feel it with. In a way, it would be an almost perfect situation. No worries or fears or pains or hunger or thirst. Not even any desires. Just your memories and your thoughts, and if the remaining eye happened to function, then you could read books as well. It all sounds rather pleasant to me."

"It does, does it?"

"Yes, William, it does. And particularly for a Doctor of Philosophy. It would be a tremendous experience. You'd be able to reflect upon the ways of the world with a detachment and a serenity that no man had ever attained before. And who knows what might not happen then! Great thoughts and solutions might come to you, great ideas that could revolutionize our way of life! Try to imagine, if you can, the degree of concentration that you'd be able to achieve!"

"And the frustration," I said.

"Nonsense. There couldn't be any frustration. You can't have frustration without desire, and you couldn't possibly have any desire. Not physical desire, anyway."

"I should certainly be capable of remembering my previous life in the world, and I might desire to return to it."

"What, to this mess! Out of your comfortable basin and back into this madhouse!"

"Answer one more question," I said. "How long do you believe you could keep it alive?"

"The brain? Who knows? Possibly for years and years. The conditions would be ideal. Most of the factors that cause deterioration would be absent, thanks to the artificial heart. The blood-pressure would remain constant at all times, an impossible condition in real life. The temperature would also be constant. The chemical composition of the blood would be near perfect. There would be no impurities in it, no virus, no bacteria, nothing. Of course it's foolish to guess, but I believe that a brain might live for two or three hundred years in circumstances like these. Goodbye for now," he said. "I'll drop in and see you tomorrow." He went out quickly, leaving me, as you might guess, in a fairly disturbed state of mind.

My immediate reaction after he had gone was one of revulsion toward the whole business. Somehow, it wasn't at all nice. There was something basically repulsive about the idea that I myself, with all my mental faculties intact, should be reduced to a small slimy grey blob lying in a pool of water. It was monstrous, obscene, unholy. Another thing that bothered me was the feeling of helplessness that I was bound to experience once Landy had got me into the basin. There could be no going back after that, no way of protesting or explaining. I would be committed for as long as they could keep me alive.

And what, for example, if I could not stand it? What if it turned out to be terribly painful? What if I became hysterical?

No legs to run away on. No voice to scream with. Nothing. I'd just have to grin and bear it for the next two centuries.

No mouth to grin with either.

At this point, a curious thought struck me, and it was this: Does not a man who has had a leg amputated often suffer from the delusion that the leg is still there? Does he not tell the nurse that the toes he doesn't have any more are itching like mad, and so on and so forth? I seemed to have heard something to that effect quite recently.

Very well. On the same premise, was it not possible that my brain, lying there alone in that basin, might not suffer from a similar delusion in regard to my body? In which case, all my usual aches and pains could come flooding over me and I wouldn't even be able to take an aspirin to relieve them. One moment I might be imagining that I had the most excruciating cramp in my leg, or a violent indigestion, and a few minutes later, I might easily get the feeling that my poor bladder—you know me—was so full that if I didn't get to emptying it soon it would burst.

Heaven forbid.

I lay there for a long time thinking these horrid thoughts. Then quite suddenly, round about midday, my mood began to change. I became less concerned with the unpleasant aspect of the affair and found myself able to examine Landy's proposals in a more reasonable light. Was there not, after all, I asked myself, something a bit comforting in the thought that my brain might not necessarily have to die and disappear in a few weeks' time? There was indeed. I am rather proud of my brain. It is a sensitive, lucid, and uberous organ. It contains a prodigious store of information, and it is still capable of producing imaginative and original theories. As brains go, it is a damn good one, though I say it myself. Whereas my body, my poor old body, the thing that Landy wants to throw away—well, even you, my dear Mary, will have to agree with me that there is really nothing about *that* which is worth preserving any more.

I was lying on my back eating a grape. Delicious it was, and there were three little seeds in it which I took out of my mouth and placed on the edge of the plate.

"I'm going to do it," I said quietly. "Yes, by God, I'm going to do it. When Landy comes back to see me tomorrow I shall tell him straight out that I'm going to do it."

It was as quick as that. And from then on, I began to feel very much better. I surprised everyone by gobbling an enormous lunch, and shortly after that you came in to visit me as usual.

But how well I looked, you told me. How bright and well and chirpy. Had anything happened? Was there some good news?

Yes, I said, there was. And then, if you remember, I bade you sit down and make yourself comfortable, and I started out immediately to explain to you as gently as I could what was in the wind.

Alas, you would have none of it. I had hardly begun telling you the barest details when you flew into a fury and said that the thing was revolting, disgusting, horrible, unthinkable, and when I tried to go on, you marched out of the room.

Well, Mary, as you know, I have tried to discuss this subject with you many times since then, but you have consistently refused to give me a hearing. Hence this note, and I can only hope that you will have the good sense to permit yourself to read it. It has taken me a long time to write. Two weeks have gone by since I started to scribble the first sentence, and I'm now a good deal weaker than I was then. I doubt I have the strength to say much more. Certainly I won't say goodbye, because there's a chance, just a tiny chance, that if Landy succeeds in his work I may actually *see* you again later, that is if you can bring yourself to come and visit me.

I am giving orders that these pages shall not be delivered to you until a week after I am gone. By now, therefore, as you sit reading them, seven days have already elapsed since Landy did the deed. You yourself may even know what the outcome has been. If you don't, if you have purposely kept yourself apart and have refused to have anything to do with it—which I suspect may be the case—please change your mind now and give Landy a call to see how things went with me. That is the least you can do. I have told him that he may expect to hear from you on the seventh day.

Your faithful husband
William

P.S. Be good when I am gone, and always remember that it is harder to be a widow than a wife. Do not drink cocktails. Do not waste money. Do not smoke cigarettes. Do not eat pastry. Do not use lipstick. Do not buy a television apparatus. Keep my rose beds and my rockery well weeded in the summers. And incidentally I suggest that you have the telephone disconnected now that I shall have no further use for it.

W.

Mrs. Pearl laid the last page of the manuscript slowly down on the sofa beside her. Her little mouth was pursed up tight and there was a whiteness around her nostrils.

But really! You would think a widow was entitled to a bit of peace after all these years.

The whole thing was just too awful to think about. Beastly and awful. It gave her the shudders.

She reached for her bag and found herself another cigarette. She lit it, inhaling the smoke deeply and blowing it out in clouds all over the room. Through the smoke she could see her lovely television set, brand new, lustrous, huge, crouching defiantly but also a little self-consciously on top of what used to be William's worktable.

What would he say, she wondered, if he could see that now?

She paused, to remember the last time he had caught her smoking a cigarette. That was about a year ago, and she was sitting in the kitchen by the open window having a quick one before he came home from work. She'd had the radio on loud playing dance music and she had turned round to pour herself another cup of coffee and there he was standing in the doorway, huge and grim, staring down at her with those awful eyes, a little black dot of fury blazing in the centre of each.

For four weeks after that, he had paid the housekeeping bills himself and given her no money at all, but of course he wasn't to know that she had over six pounds stashed away in a soap-flake carton in the cupboard under the sink.

"What is it?" she had said to him once during supper. "Are you worried about me getting lung cancer?"

"I am not," he had answered.

"Then why can't I smoke?"

"Because I disapprove, that's why."

He had also disapproved of children, and as a result they had never had any of them either.

Where was he now, this William of hers, the great disapprover?

Landy would be expecting her to call up. Did she *have* to call Landy?

Well, not really, no.

She finished her cigarette, then lit another one immediately from the old stub. She looked at the telephone that was sitting on the worktable beside the television set. William had asked her to call. He had specifically requested that she telephone Landy as soon as she had read the letter. She hesitated, fighting hard now against that old ingrained sense of duty that she didn't quite yet dare to shake off. Then, slowly, she got to her feet and crossed over to the phone on the worktable. She found a number in the book, dialled it, and waited.

"I want to speak to Dr. Landy, please."

"Who is calling?"

"Mrs. Pearl. Mrs. William Pearl."

"One moment, please."

Almost at once, Landy was on the other end of the wire.

"Mrs. Pearl?"

"This is Mrs. Pearl."

There was a slight pause.

"I am so glad you called at last, Mrs. Pearl. You are quite well, I hope?" The voice was quiet, unemotional, courteous. "I wonder if you would care to come over here to the hospital? Then we can have a little chat. I expect you are very eager to know how it all came out."

She didn't answer.

"I can tell you now that everything went pretty smoothly, one way and another. Far better, in fact, than I was entitled to hope. It is not only alive, Mrs. Pearl, it is conscious. It recovered consciousness on the second day. Isn't that interesting?"

She waited for him to go on.

"And the eye is seeing. We are sure of that because we get an immediate change in the deflections on the encephalograph when we hold something up in front of it. And now we're giving it the newspaper to read every day."

"Which newspaper?" Mrs. Pearl asked sharply.

"The Daily Mirror. The headlines are larger."

"He hates *The Mirror.* Give him *The Times."*

There was a pause, then the doctor said, "Very well, Mrs. Pearl. We'll give it *The Times.* We naturally want to do all we can to keep it happy."

"Him," she said. "Not *it. Him!"*

"Him," the doctor said. "Yes, I beg your pardon. To keep him happy. That's one reason why I suggested you should come along here as soon as possible. I think it would be good for him to see you. You could indicate how delighted you were to be with him again—smile at him and blow him a kiss and all that sort of thing. It's bound to be a comfort to him to know that you are standing by."

There was a long pause.

"Well," Mrs. Pearl said at last, her voice suddenly very meek and tired. "I suppose I had better come on over and see how he is."

"Good. I knew you would. I'll wait here for you. Come straight up to my office on the second floor. Goodbye."

Half an hour later, Mrs. Pearl was at the hospital.

"You mustn't be surprised by what he looks like," Landy said as he walked beside her down a corridor.

"No, I won't."

"It's bound to be a bit of a shock to you at first. He's not very prepossessing in his present state, I'm afraid."

"I didn't marry him for his looks, Doctor."

Landy turned and stared at her. What a queer little woman this was, he thought, with her large eyes and her sullen, resentful air. Her features, which must have been quite pleasant once, had now gone completely. The mouth was slack, the cheeks loose and flabby, and the whole face gave the impression of having slowly but surely sagged to pieces through years and years of joyless married life. They walked on for a while in silence.

"Take your time when you get inside," Landy said. "He won't know you're in there until you place your face directly above his eye. The eye is always open, but he can't move it at all, so the field of vision is very narrow. At present we have it looking straight up at the ceiling. And of course he can't hear anything. We can talk together as much as we like. It's in here."

Landy opened a door and ushered her into a small square room.

"I wouldn't go too close yet," he said, putting a hand on her arm. "Stay back here a moment with me until you get used to it all."

There was a biggish white enamel bowl about the size of a washbasin standing on a high white table in the centre of the room, and there were half a dozen thin plastic tubes coming out of it. These tubes were connected with a whole lot of glass piping in which you could see the blood flowing to and from the heart machine. The machine itself made a soft rhythmic pulsing sound.

"He's in there," Landy said, pointing to the basin, which was too high for her to see into. "Come just a little closer. Not too near."

He led her two paces forward.

By stretching her neck, Mrs. Pearl could now see the surface of the liquid inside the basin. It was clear and still, and on it there floated a small oval capsule, about the size of a pigeon's egg.

"That's the eye in there," Landy said. "Can you see it?"

"Yes."

"So far as we can tell, it is still in perfect condition. It's his right eye, and the plastic container has a lens on it similar to the one he used in his own spectacles. At this moment he's probably seeing quite as well as he did before."

"The ceiling isn't much to look at," Mrs. Pearl said.

"Don't worry about that. We're in the process of working out a whole programme to keep him amused, but we don't want to go too quickly at first."

"Give him a good book."

"We will, we will. Are you feeling all right, Mrs. Pearl?"

"Yes."

"Then we'll go forward a little more, shall we, and you'll be able to see the whole thing."

He led her forward until they were standing only a couple of yards from the table, and now she could see right down into the basin.

"There you are," Landy said. "That's William."

He was far larger than she had imagined he would be, and darker in colour. With all the ridges and creases running over his surface, he reminded her of nothing so much as an enormous pickled walnut. She could see the stubs of the four big arteries and the two veins coming out from the base of him and the neat way in which they were joined to the plastic tubes; and with each throb of the heart machine, all the tubes gave a little jerk in unison as the blood was pushed through them.

"You'll have to lean over," Landy said, "and put your pretty face right above the eye. He'll see you then, and you can smile at him and blow him a kiss. If I were you I'd say a few nice things as well. He won't actually hear them, but I'm sure he'll get the general idea."

"He hates people blowing kisses at him," Mrs. Pearl said. "I'll do it my own way if you don't mind." She stepped up to the edge of the table, leaned forward until her face was directly over the basin, and looked straight down into William's eye.

"Hallo, dear," she whispered. "It's me—Mary."

The eye, bright as ever, stared back at her with a peculiar, fixed intensity.

"How are you, dear?" she said.

The plastic capsule was transparent all the way round so that the whole of the eyeball was visible. The optic nerve connecting the underside of it to the brain looked like a short length of grey spaghetti.

"Are you feeling all right, William?"

It was a queer sensation peering into her husband's eye when there was no face to go with it. All she had to look at was the eye, and she kept staring at it, and gradually it grew bigger and bigger, and in the end it was the only thing that she could see—a sort of face in itself. There was a network of tiny red veins running over the white surface of the eyeball, and in the ice-blue of the iris there were three or four rather pretty darkish streaks radiating from the pupil in the centre. The pupil was large and black, with a little spark of light reflecting from one side of it.

"I got your letter, dear, and came over at once to see how you were. Dr. Landy says you are doing wonderfully well. Perhaps if I talk slowly you can understand a little of what I am saying by reading my lips."

There was no doubt that the eye was watching her.

"They are doing everything possible to take care of you, dear. This marvellous machine thing here is pumping away all the time and I'm sure it's a lot better than those silly old hearts all the rest of us have. Ours are liable to break down any moment, but yours will go on for ever."

She was studying the eye closely, trying to discover what there was about it that gave it such an unusual appearance.

"You seem fine, dear, just fine. Really you do."

It looked ever so much nicer, this eye, than either of his eyes used to look, she told herself. There was a softness about it somewhere, a calm, kindly quality that she had never seen before. Maybe it had to do with the dot in the very centre, the pupil. William's pupils used always to be tiny black pinheads. They used to glint at you, stabbing into your brain, seeing right through you, and they always knew at once what you were up to and even what you were thinking. But this one she was looking at now was large and soft and gentle, almost cowlike.

"Are you quite sure he's conscious?" she asked, not looking up.

"Oh yes, completely," Landy said.

"And he *can* see me?"

"Perfectly."

"Isn't that marvellous? I expect he's wondering what happened."

"Not at all. He knows perfectly well where he is and why he's there. He can't possibly have forgotten that."

"You mean he *knows* he's in this basin?"

"Of course. And if only he had the power of speech, he would probably be able to carry on a perfectly normal conversation with you this very minute. So far as I can see, there should be absolutely no difference mentally between this William here and the one you used to know back home."

"Good *gracious* me," Mrs. Pearl said, and she paused to consider this intriguing aspect.

You know what, she told herself, looking behind the eye now and staring hard at the great grey pulpy walnut that lay so placidly under the water. I'm not at all sure that I don't prefer him as he is at present. In fact, I believe that I could live very comfortably with this kind of a William. I could cope with this one.

"Quiet, isn't he?" she said.

"Naturally he's quiet."

No arguments and criticisms, she thought, no constant admonitions, no rules to obey, no ban on smoking cigarettes, no pair of cold disapproving eyes watching me over the top of a book in the evenings, no shirts to wash and iron, no meals to cook—nothing but the throb of the heart machine, which was rather a soothing sound anyway and certainly not loud enough to interfere with television.

"Doctor," she said. "I do believe I'm suddenly getting to feel the most enormous affection for him. Does that sound queer?"

"I think it's quite understandable."

"He looks so helpless and silent lying there under the water in his little basin."

"Yes, I know."

"He's like a baby, that's what he's like. He's exactly like a little baby."

Landy stood still behind her, watching.

"There," she said softly, peering into the basin. "From now on Mary's going to look after you *all* by herself and you've nothing to worry about in the world. When can I have him back home, Doctor?"

"I beg your pardon?"

"I said when can I have him back—back in my own house?"

"You're joking," Landy said.

She turned her head slowly around and looked directly at him. "Why should I joke?" she asked. Her face was bright, her eyes round and bright as two diamonds.

"He couldn't possibly be moved."

"I don't see why not."

"This is an experiment, Mrs. Pearl."

"It's my husband, Dr. Landy."

A funny little nervous half-smile appeared on Landy's mouth. "Well . . ." he said.

"It *is* my husband, you know." There was no anger in her voice. She spoke quietly, as though merely reminding him of a simple fact.

"That's rather a tricky point," Landy said, wetting his lips. "You're a widow now, Mrs. Pearl. I think you must resign yourself to that fact."

She turned away suddenly from the table and crossed over to the window. "I mean it," she said, fishing in her bag for a cigarette. "I want him back."

Landy watched her as she put the cigarette between her lips and lit it. Unless he were very much mistaken, there was something a bit odd about this woman, he thought. She seemed almost pleased to have her husband over there in the basin.

He tried to imagine what his own feelings would be if it were *his* wife's brain lying there and *her* eye staring up at him out of that capsule.

He wouldn't like it.

"Shall we go back to my room now?" he said.

She was standing by the window, apparently quite calm and relaxed, puffing her cigarette.

"Yes, all right."

On her way past the table she stopped and leaned over the basin once more. "Mary's leaving now, sweetheart," she said. "And don't you worry about a single thing, you understand? We're going to get you right back home where we can look after you properly just as soon as we possibly can. And listen, dear . . ." At this point she paused and carried the cigarette to her lips, intending to take a puff.

Instantly the eye flashed.

She was looking straight into it at the time, and right in the centre of it she saw a tiny but brilliant flash of light, and the pupil contracted into a minute black pinpoint of absolute fury.

At first she didn't move. She stood bending over the basin, holding the cigarette up to her mouth, watching the eye.

Then very slowly, deliberately, she put the cigarette between her lips and took a long suck. She inhaled deeply, and she held the smoke inside her lungs for three or four seconds; then suddenly, *whoosh,* out it came through her nostrils in two thin jets which struck the water in the basin and billowed out over the surface in a thick blue cloud, enveloping the eye.

Landy was over by the door, with his back to her, waiting. "Come on, Mrs. Pearl," he called.

"Don't look so cross, William," she said softly. "It isn't any good looking cross."

Landy turned his head to see what she was doing.

"Not any more it isn't," she whispered. "Because from now on, my pet, you're going to do just exactly what Mary tells you. Do you understand that?"

"Mrs. Pearl," Landy said, moving toward her.

"So don't be a naughty boy again, will you, my precious," she said, taking another pull at the cigarette. "Naughty boys are liable to get punished most severely nowadays, you ought to know that."

Landy was beside her now, and he took her by the arm and began drawing her firmly but gently away from the table.

"Goodbye, darling," she called. "I'll be back soon."

"That's enough, Mrs. Pearl."

"Isn't he sweet?" she cried, looking up at Landy with big bright eyes. "Isn't he darling? I just can't wait to get him home."

Mrs. Bixby and
the Colonel's Coat

1959

AMERICA is the land of opportunity for women. Already they own about eighty-five per cent of the wealth of the nation. Soon they will have it all. Divorce has become a lucrative process, simple to arrange and easy to forget; and ambitious females can repeat it as often as they please and parlay their winnings to astronomical figures. The husband's death also brings satisfactory rewards and some ladies prefer to rely upon this method. They know that the waiting period will not be unduly protracted, for overwork and hypertension are bound to get the poor devil before long, and he will die at his desk with a bottle of benzedrines in one hand and a packet of tranquilizers in the other.

Succeeding generations of youthful American males are not deterred in the slightest by this terrifying pattern of divorce and death. The higher the divorce rate climbs, the more eager they become. Young men marry like mice, almost before they have reached the age of puberty, and a large proportion of them have at least two ex-wives on the payroll by the time they are thirty-six years old. To support these ladies in the manner to which they are accustomed, the men must work like slaves, which is of course precisely what they are. But now at last, as they approach their premature middle age, a sense of disillusionment and fear begins to creep slowly into their hearts, and in the evenings they take to huddling together in little groups, in clubs and bars, drinking their whiskies and swallowing their pills, and trying to comfort one another with stories.

The basic theme of these stories never varies. There are always three main characters—the husband, the wife, and the dirty dog. The husband is a decent clean-living man, working hard at his job. The wife is cunning, deceitful, and lecherous, and she is invariably up to some sort of jiggery-pokery with the dirty dog. The husband is too good a man even to suspect her. Things look black for the husband. Will the poor man ever find out? Must he be a cuckold for the rest of his life? Yes, he must. But wait! Suddenly, by a brilliant manoeuvre, the husband completely turns the tables on his monstrous spouse. The woman is flabbergasted, stupified, humiliated, defeated. The audience of men around the bar smiles quietly to itself and takes a little comfort from the fantasy.

There are many of these stories going around, these wonderful wishful-thinking dreamworld inventions of the unhappy male, but most of them are too fatuous to be worth repeating, and far too fruity to be put down on paper. There is one, however, that seems to be superior to the rest, particularly as it has the merit of being true. It is extremely popular with twice- or thrice-bitten males in search of solace, and if you are one of them, and if you haven't heard it before, you may enjoy the way it comes out. The story is called "Mrs. Bixby and the Colonel's Coat," and it goes something like this:

Dr. and Mrs. Bixby lived in a smallish apartment somewhere in New York City. Dr. Bixby was a dentist who made an average income. Mrs. Bixby was a big vigorous woman with a wet mouth. Once a month, always on Friday afternoons, Mrs. Bixby would board the train at Pennsylvania Station and travel to Baltimore to visit her old aunt. She would spend the night with the aunt and return to New York on the following day in time to cook supper for her husband. Dr. Bixby accepted this arrangement good-naturedly. He knew that Aunt Maude lived in Baltimore, and that his wife was very fond of the old lady, and certainly it would be unreasonable to deny either of them the pleasure of a monthly meeting.

"Just so long as you don't ever expect me to accompany you," Dr. Bixby had said in the beginning.

"Of course not, darling," Mrs. Bixby had answered. "After all, she is not *your* aunt. She's mine."

So far so good.

As it turned out, however, the aunt was little more than a convenient alibi for Mrs. Bixby. The dirty dog, in the shape of a gentleman known as the Colonel, was lurking slyly in the background, and our heroine spent the greater part of her Baltimore time in this scoundrel's company. The Colonel was exceedingly wealthy. He lived in a charming house on the outskirts of the town. No wife or family encumbered him, only a few discreet and loyal servants, and in Mrs. Bixby's absence he consoled himself by riding his horses and hunting the fox.

Year after year, this pleasant alliance between Mrs. Bixby and the Colonel continued without a hitch. They met so seldom—twelve times a year is not much when you come to think of it—that there was little or no chance of their growing bored with one another. On the contrary, the long wait between meetings only made the heart grow fonder, and each separate occasion became an exciting reunion.

"Tally-ho!" the Colonel would cry each time he met her at the station in the big car. "My dear, I'd almost forgotten how ravishing you looked. Let's go to earth."

Eight years went by.

It was just before Christmas, and Mrs. Bixby was standing on the station in Baltimore waiting for the train to take her back to New York. This particular visit which had just ended had been more than usually agreeable, and she was in a cheerful mood. But then the Colonel's company always did that to her these days. The man had a way of making her feel that she was altogether a rather remarkable woman, a person of subtle and exotic talents, fascinating beyond measure; and what a very different thing that was from the dentist husband at home who never succeeded in making her feel that she was anything but a sort of eternal patient, someone who dwelt in the waiting-room, silent among the magazines, seldom if ever nowadays to be called in to suffer the finicky precise ministrations of those clean pink hands.

"The Colonel asked me to give you this," a voice beside her said. She turned and saw Wilkins, the Colonel's groom, a small wizened dwarf with grey skin, and he was pushing a large flattish cardboard box into her arms.

"Good gracious me!" she cried, all of a flutter. "My heavens, what an enormous box! What is it, Wilkins? Was there a message? Did he send me a message?"

"No message," the groom said, and he walked away.

As soon as she was on the train, Mrs. Bixby carried the box into the privacy of the Ladies' Room and locked the door. How exciting this was! A Christmas present from the Colonel. She started to undo the string. "I'll bet it's a dress," she said aloud. "It might even be two dresses. Or it might be a whole lot of beautiful underclothes. I won't look. I'll just feel around and try to guess what it is. I'll try to guess the colour as well, and exactly what it looks like. Also how much it cost."

She shut her eyes tight and slowly lifted off the lid. Then she put one hand down into the box. There was some tissue paper on top; she could feel it and hear it rustling. There was also an envelope or a card of some sort. She ignored this and began burrowing underneath the tissue paper, the fingers reaching out delicately, like tendrils.

"My God," she cried suddenly. "It can't be true!"

She opened her eyes wide and stared at the coat. Then she pounced on it and lifted it out of the box. Thick layers of fur made a lovely noise against the tissue paper as they unfolded, and when she held it up and saw it hanging to its full length, it was so beautiful it took her breath away.

Never had she seen mink like this before. It *was* mink, wasn't it? Yes, of course it was. But what a glorious colour! The fur was almost pure black. At first she thought it *was* black; but when she held it closer to the window she saw that there was a touch of blue in it as well, a deep rich blue, like cobalt. Quickly she looked at the label. It said simply, WILD LABRADOR MINK. There was nothing else, no sign of where it had been bought or anything. But that, she told herself, was probably the Colonel's doing. The wily old fox was making darn sure he didn't leave any tracks. Good for him. But what in the world could it have cost? She hardly dared to think. Four, five, six thousand dollars? Possibly more.

She just couldn't take her eyes off it. Nor, for that matter, could she wait to try it on. Quickly she slipped off her own plain red coat. She was panting a little now, she couldn't help it, and her eyes were stretched very wide. But oh God, the feel of that fur! And those huge wide sleeves with their thick turned-up cuffs! Who was it had once told her that they always used female skins for the arms and male skins for the rest of the coat? Someone had told her that. Joan Rutfield, probably; though how *Joan* would know anything about *mink* she couldn't imagine.

The great black coat seemed to slide onto her almost of its own accord, like a second skin. Oh boy! It was the queerest feeling! She glanced into the mirror. It was fantastic. Her whole personality had suddenly changed completely. She looked dazzling, radiant, rich, brilliant, voluptuous, all at the same time. And the sense of power that it gave her! In this coat she could walk into any place she wanted and people would come scurrying around her like rabbits. The whole thing was just too wonderful for words!

Mrs. Bixby picked up the envelope that was still lying in the box. She opened it and pulled out the Colonel's letter:

I once heard you saying you were fond of mink so I got you this. I'm told it's a good one. Please accept it with my sincere good wishes as a parting gift. For my own personal reasons I shall not be able to see you any more. Goodbye and good luck.

Well!

Imagine that!

Right out of the blue, just when she was feeling so happy.

No more Colonel.

What a dreadful shock.

She would miss him enormously.

Slowly, Mrs. Bixby began stroking the lovely soft black fur of the coat.

What you lose on the swings you get back on the roundabouts.

She smiled and folded the letter, meaning to tear it up and throw it out the window, but in folding it she noticed that there was something written on the other side:

P.S. Just tell them that nice generous aunt of yours gave it to you for Christmas.

Mrs. Bixby's mouth, at that moment stretched wide in a silky smile, snapped back like a piece of elastic.

"The man must be mad!" she cried. "Aunt Maude doesn't have that sort of money. She couldn't possibly give me this."

But if Aunt Maude didn't give it to her, then who did?

Oh God! In the excitement of finding the coat and trying it on, she had completely overlooked this vital aspect.

In a couple of hours she would be in New York. Ten minutes after that she would be home, and the husband would be there to greet her; and even a man like Cyril, dwelling as he did in a dark phlegmy world of root canals, bicuspids, and caries, would start asking a few questions if his wife suddenly waltzed in from a weekend wearing a six-thousand-dollar mink coat.

You know what I think, she told herself. I think that goddam Colonel has done this on purpose just to torture me. He knew perfectly well Aunt Maude didn't have enough money to buy this. He knew I wouldn't be able to keep it.

But the thought of parting with it now was more than Mrs. Bixby could bear.

"I've *got* to have this coat!" she said aloud. "I've got to have this coat! I've got to have this coat!"

Very well, my dear. You shall have the coat. But don't panic. Sit still and keep calm and start thinking. You're a clever girl, aren't you? You've fooled him before. The man never has been able to see much further than the end of his own probe, you know that. So just sit absolutely still and *think*. There's lots of time.

Two and a half hours later, Mrs. Bixby stepped off the train at Pennsylvania Station and walked quickly to the exit. She was wearing her old red coat again now and carrying the cardboard box in her arms. She signalled for a taxi.

"Driver," she said, "would you know of a pawnbroker that's still open around here?"

The man behind the wheel raised his brows and looked back at her, amused.

"Plenty along Sixth Avenue," he answered.

"Stop at the first one you see, then, will you please?" She got in and was driven away.

Soon the taxi pulled up outside a shop that had three brass balls hanging over the entrance.

"Wait for me, please," Mrs. Bixby said to the driver, and she got out of the taxi and entered the shop.

There was an enormous cat crouching on the counter eating fishheads out of a white saucer. The animal looked up at Mrs. Bixby with bright yellow eyes, then looked away again and went on eating. Mrs. Bixby stood by the counter, as far away from the cat as possible, waiting for someone to come, staring at the watches, the shoe buckles, the enamel brooches, the old binoculars, the broken spectacles, the false teeth. Why did they always pawn their teeth, she wondered.

"Yes?" the proprietor said, emerging from a dark place in the back of the shop.

"Oh, good evening," Mrs. Bixby said. She began to untie the string around the box. The man went up to the cat and started stroking it along the top of its back, and the cat went on eating the fishheads.

"Isn't it silly of me?" Mrs. Bixby said. "I've gone and lost my pocketbook, and this being Saturday, the banks are all closed until Monday and I've simply got to have some money for the weekend. This is quite a valuable coat, but I'm not asking much. I only want to borrow enough on it to tide me over till Monday. Then I'll come back and redeem it."

The man waited, and said nothing. But when she pulled out the mink and allowed the beautiful thick fur to fall over the counter, his eyebrows went up and he drew his hand away from the cat and came over to look at it. He picked it up and held it out in front of him.

"If only I had a watch on me or a ring," Mrs. Bixby said, "I'd give you that instead. But the fact is I don't have a thing with me other than this coat." She spread out her fingers for him to see.

"It looks new," the man said, fondling the soft fur.

"Oh yes, it is. But, as I said, I only want to borrow enough to tide me over till Monday. How about fifty dollars?"

"I'll loan you fifty dollars."

"It's worth a hundred times more than that, but I know you'll take good care of it until I return."

The man went over to a drawer and fetched a ticket and placed it on the counter. The ticket looked like one of those labels you tie onto the handle of your suitcase, the same shape and size exactly, and the same stiff brownish paper. But it was perforated across the middle so that you could tear it in two, and both halves were identical.

"Name?" he asked.

"Leave that out. And the address."

She saw the man pause, and she saw the nib of the pen hovering over the dotted line, waiting.

"You don't *have* to put the name and address, do you?"

The man shrugged and shook his head and the pen-nib moved on down to the next line.

"It's just that I'd rather not," Mrs. Bixby said. "It's purely personal."

"You'd better not lose this ticket, then."

"I won't lose it."

"You realize that anyone who gets hold of it can come in and claim the article?"

"Yes, I know that."

"Simply on the number."

"Yes, I know."

"What do you want me to put for a description."

"No description either, thank you. It's not necessary. Just put the amount I'm borrowing."

The pen-nib hesitated again, hovering over the dotted line beside the word ARTICLE.

"I think you ought to put a description. A description is always a help if you want to sell the ticket. You never know, you might want to sell it sometime."

"I don't want to sell it."

"You might have to. Lots of people do."

"Look," Mrs. Bixby said. "I'm not broke, if that's what you mean. I simply lost my purse. Don't you understand?"

"You have it your own way then," the man said. "It's your coat."

At this point an unpleasant thought struck Mrs. Bixby. "Tell me something," she said. "If I don't have a description on my ticket, how can I be sure you'll give me back the coat and not something else when I return?"

"It goes in the books."

"But all I've got is a number. So actually you could hand me any old thing you wanted, isn't that so?"

"Do you want a description or don't you?" the man asked.

"No," she said. "I trust you."

The man wrote "fifty dollars" opposite the word VALUE on both sections of the ticket, then he tore it in half along the perforations and slid the lower portion across the counter. He took a wallet from the inside pocket of his jacket and extracted five ten-dollar bills. "The interest is three per cent a month," he said.

"Yes, all right. And thank you. You'll take good care of it, won't you?"

The man nodded but said nothing.

"Shall I put it back in the box for you?"

"No," the man said.

Mrs. Bixby turned and went out of the shop onto the street where the taxi was waiting. Ten minutes later, she was home.

"Darling," she said as she bent over and kissed her husband. "Did you miss me?"

Cyril Bixby laid down the evening paper and glanced at the watch on his wrist. "It's twelve and a half minutes past six," he said. "You're a bit late, aren't you?"

"I know. It's those dreadful trains. Aunt Maude sent you her love as usual. I'm dying for a drink, aren't you?"

The husband folded his newspaper into a neat rectangle and placed it on the arm of his chair. Then he stood up and crossed over to the sideboard. His wife remained in the centre of the room pulling off her gloves, watching him carefully, wondering how long she ought to wait. He had his back to her now, bending forward to measure the gin, putting his face right up close to the measurer and peering into it as though it were a patient's mouth.

It was funny how small he always looked after the Colonel. The

Colonel was huge and bristly, and when you were near to him he smelled faintly of horseradish. This one was small and neat and bony and he didn't really smell of anything at all, except peppermint drops, which he sucked to keep his breath nice for the patients.

"See what I've bought for measuring the vermouth," he said, holding up a calibrated glass beaker. "I can get it to the nearest milligram with this."

"Darling, how clever."

I really must try to make him change the way he dresses, she told herself. His suits are just too ridiculous for words. There had been a time when she thought they were wonderful, those Edwardian jackets with high lapels and six buttons down the front, but now they merely seemed absurd. So did the narrow stovepipe trousers. You had to have a special sort of face to wear things like that, and Cyril just didn't have it. His was a long bony countenance with a narrow nose and a slightly prognathous jaw, and when you saw it coming up out of the top of one of those tightly fitting old-fashioned suits it looked like a caricature of Sam Weller. He probably thought it looked like Beau Brummel. It was a fact that in the office he invariably greeted female patients with his white coat unbuttoned so that they would catch a glimpse of the trappings underneath; and in some obscure way this was obviously meant to convey the impression that he was a bit of a dog. But Mrs. Bixby knew better. The plumage was a bluff. It meant nothing. It reminded her of an aging peacock strutting on the lawn with only half its feathers left. Or one of those fatuous self-fertilizing flowers—like the dandelion. A dandelion never has to get fertilized for the setting of its seed, and all those brilliant yellow petals are just a waste of time, a boast, a masquerade. What's that word the biologists use? Subsexual. A dandelion is subsexual. So, for that matter, are the summer broods of water fleas. It sounds a bit like Lewis Carroll, she thought—water fleas and dandelions and dentists.

"Thank you, darling," she said, taking the martini and seating herself on the sofa with her handbag on her lap. "And what did *you* do last night?"

"I stayed on in the office and cast a few inlays. I also got my accounts up to date."

"Now really, Cyril, I think it's high time you let other people do your donkey work for you. You're much too important for that sort of thing. Why don't you give the inlays to the mechanic?"

"I prefer to do them myself. I'm extremely proud of my inlays."

"I know you are, darling, and I think they're absolutely wonderful. They're the best inlays in the whole world. But I don't want you to burn yourself out. And why doesn't that Pulteney woman do the accounts? That's part of her job, isn't it?"

"She does do them. But I have to price everything up first. She doesn't know who's rich and who isn't."

"This martini is perfect," Mrs. Bixby said, setting down her glass on the side table. "Quite perfect." She opened her bag and took out a handkerchief as if to blow her nose. "Oh look!" she cried, seeing the ticket. "I forgot to show you this! I found it just now on the seat of my taxi. It's got a number on it, and I thought it might be a lottery ticket or something, so I kept it."

She handed the small piece of stiff brown paper to her husband, who took it in his fingers and began examining it minutely from all angles, as though it were a suspect tooth.

"You know what this is?" he said slowly.

"No dear, I don't."

"It's a pawn ticket."

"A what?"

"A ticket from a pawnbroker. Here's the name and address of the shop—somewhere on Sixth Avenue."

"Oh dear, I *am* disappointed. I was hoping it might be a ticket for the Irish Sweep."

"There's no reason to be disappointed," Cyril Bixby said. "As a matter of fact this could be rather amusing."

"Why could it be amusing, darling?"

He began explaining to her exactly how a pawn ticket worked, with particular reference to the fact that anyone possessing the ticket was entitled to claim the article. She listened patiently until he had finished his lecture.

"You think it's worth claiming?" she asked.

"I think it's worth finding out what it is. You see this figure of fifty dollars that's written here? You know what that means?"

"No, dear, what does it mean?"

"It means that the item in question is almost certain to be something quite valuable."

"You mean it'll be worth fifty dollars?"

"More like five hundred."

"Five hundred!"

"Don't you understand?" he said. "A pawnbroker never gives you more than about a tenth of the real value."

"Good gracious! I never knew that."

"There's a lot of things you don't know, my dear. Now you listen to me. Seeing that there's no name and address of the owner . . ."

"But surely there's something to say who it belongs to?"

"Not a thing. People often do that. They don't want anyone to know they've been to a pawnbroker. They're ashamed of it."

"Then you think we can keep it?"

"Of course we can keep it. This is now *our* ticket."

"You mean *my* ticket," Mrs. Bixby said firmly. "I found it."

"My dear girl, what *does* it matter? The important thing is that we are now in a position to go and redeem it any time we like for only fifty dollars. How about that?"

"Oh, what fun!" she cried. "I think it's terribly exciting, especially when we don't even know what it is. It could be *anything,* isn't that right, Cyril? Absolutely anything!"

"It could indeed, although it's most likely to be either a ring or a watch."

"But wouldn't it be marvellous if it was a *real* treasure? I mean something *really* old, like a wonderful old vase or a Roman statue."

"There's no knowing what it might be, my dear. We shall just have to wait and see."

"I think it's absolutely fascinating! Give me the ticket and I'll rush over first thing Monday morning and find out!"

"I think I'd better do that."

"Oh no!" she cried. "Let *me* do it!"

"I think not. I'll pick it up on my way to work."

"But it's *my* ticket! *Please* let me do it, Cyril! Why should *you* have all the fun?"

"You don't know these pawnbrokers, my dear. You're liable to get cheated."

"I wouldn't get cheated, honestly I wouldn't. Give it to me, please."

"Also you have to have fifty dollars," he said, smiling. "You have to pay out fifty dollars in cash before they'll give it to you."

"I've got that," she said. "I think."

"I'd rather you didn't handle it, if you don't mind."

"But Cyril, *I found* it. It's mine. Whatever it is, it's mine, isn't that right?"

"Of course it's yours, my dear. There's no need to get so worked up about it."

"I'm not. I'm just excited, that's all."

"I suppose it hasn't occurred to you that this might be something entirely masculine—a pocket-watch, for example, or a set of shirt-studs. It isn't only women that go to pawnbrokers, you know."

"In that case I'll give it to you for Christmas," Mrs. Bixby said magnanimously. "I'll be delighted. But if it's a woman's thing, I want it myself. Is that agreed?"

"That sounds very fair. Why don't you come with me when I collect it?"

Mrs. Bixby was about to say yes to this, but caught herself just in time. She had no wish to be greeted like an old customer by the pawnbroker in her husband's presence.

"No," she said slowly. "I don't think I will. You see, it'll be even more thrilling if I stay behind and wait. Oh, I do hope it isn't going to be something that neither of us wants."

"You've got a point there," he said. "If I don't think it's worth fifty dollars, I won't even take it."

"But you said it would be worth five hundred."

"I'm quite sure it will. Don't worry."

"Oh, Cyril, I can hardly wait! Isn't it exciting?"

"It's amusing," he said, slipping the ticket into his waistcoat pocket. "There's no doubt about that."

Monday morning came at last, and after breakfast Mrs. Bixby followed her husband to the door and helped him on with his coat.

"Don't work too hard, darling," she said.

"No, all right."

"Home at six?"

"I hope so."

"Are you going to have time to go to that pawnbroker?" she asked.

"My God, I forgot all about it. I'll take a cab and go there now. It's on my way."

"You haven't lost the ticket, have you?"

"I hope not," he said, feeling in his waistcoat pocket. "No, here it is."

"And you have enough money?"

"Just about."

"Darling," she said, standing close to him and straightening his tie, which was perfectly straight. "If it happens to be something nice, something you think I might like, will you telephone me as soon as you get to the office?"

"If you want me to, yes."

"You know, I'm sort of hoping it'll be something for you, Cyril. I'd much rather it was for you than for me."

"That's very generous of you, my dear. Now I must run."

About an hour later, when the telephone rang, Mrs. Bixby was across the room so fast she had the receiver off the hook before the first ring had finished.

"I got it!" he said.

"You did! Oh, Cyril, what was it? Was it something good?"

"Good!" he cried. "It's fantastic! You wait till you get your eyes on this! You'll swoon!"

"Darling, what is it? Tell me quick!"

"You're a lucky girl, that's what you are."

"It's for me, then?"

"Of course it's for you. Though how in the world it ever got to be pawned for only fifty dollars I'll be damned if I know. Someone's crazy."

"Cyril! Stop keeping me in suspense! I can't bear it!"

"You'll go mad when you see it."

"What is it?"

"Try to guess."

Mrs. Bixby paused. Be careful, she told herself. Be very careful now.

"A necklace," she said.

"Wrong."

"A diamond ring."

"You're not even warm. I'll give you a hint. It's something you can wear."

"Something I can wear? You mean like a hat?"

"No, it's not a hat," he said, laughing.

"For goodness sake, Cyril! Why don't you tell me?"

"Because I want it to be a surprise. I'll bring it home with me this evening."

"You'll do nothing of the sort!" she cried. "I'm coming right down there to get it now!"

"I'd rather you didn't do that."

"Don't be so silly, darling. Why shouldn't I come?"

"Because I'm too busy. You'll disorganize my whole morning schedule. I'm half an hour behind already."

"Then I'll come in the lunch hour. All right?"

"I'm not having a lunch hour. Oh well, come at one thirty then, while I'm having a sandwich. Goodbye."

At half past one precisely, Mrs. Bixby arrived at Dr. Bixby's place of business and rang the bell. Her husband, in his white den-tist's coat, opened the door himself.

"Oh, Cyril, I'm so excited!"

"So you should be. You're a lucky girl, did you know that?" He led her down the passage and into the surgery.

"Go and have your lunch, Miss Pulteney," he said to the assistant, who was busy putting instruments into the sterilizer. "You can finish that when you come back." He waited until the girl had gone, then he walked over to a closet that he used for hanging up his clothes and stood in front of it, pointing with his finger. "It's in there," he said. "Now—shut your eyes."

Mrs. Bixby did as she was told. Then she took a deep breath and held it, and in the silence that followed she could hear him opening the cupboard door and there was a soft swishing sound as he pulled out a garment from among the other things hanging there.

"All right! You can look!"

"I don't dare to," she said, laughing.

"Go on. Take a peek."

Coyly, beginning to giggle, she raised one eyelid a fraction of an inch, just enough to give her a dark blurry view of the man standing there in his white overalls holding something up in the air.

"Mink!" he cried. "Real mink!"

At the sound of the magic word she opened her eyes quick, and at the same time she actually started forward in order to clasp the coat in her arms.

But there was no coat. There was only a ridiculous little fur neckpiece dangling from her husband's hand.

"Feast your eyes on that!" he said, waving it in front of her face.

Mrs. Bixby put a hand up to her mouth and started backing away. I'm going to scream, she told herself. I just know it. I'm going to scream.

"What's the matter, my dear? Don't you like it?" He stopped waving the fur and stood staring at her, waiting for her to say something.

"Why yes," she stammered. "I . . . I . . . think it's . . . it's lovely . . . really lovely."

"Quite took your breath away for a moment there, didn't it?"

"Yes, it did."

"Magnificent quality," he said. "Fine colour, too. You know something, my dear? I reckon a piece like this would cost you two or three hundred dollars at least if you had to buy it in a shop."

"I don't doubt it."

There were two skins, two narrow mangy-looking skins with their heads still on them and glass beads in their eye sockets and little paws hanging down. One of them had the rear end of the other in its mouth, biting it.

"Here," he said. "Try it on." He leaned forward and draped the thing around her neck, then stepped back to admire. "It's perfect. It really suits you. It isn't everyone who has mink, my dear."

"No, it isn't."

"Better leave it behind when you go shopping or they'll all think we're millionaires and start charging us double."

"I'll try to remember that, Cyril."

"I'm afraid you mustn't expect anything else for Christmas. Fifty dollars was rather more than I was going to spend anyway."

He turned away and went over to the basin and began washing his hands. "Run along now, my dear, and buy yourself a nice lunch. I'd take you out myself but I've got old man Gorman in the waiting-room with a broken clasp on his denture."

Mrs. Bixby moved toward the door.

I'm going to kill that pawnbroker, she told herself. I'm going right back there to the shop this very minute and I'm going to throw this filthy neckpiece right in his face and if he refuses to give me back my coat I'm going to kill him.

"Did I tell you I was going to be late home tonight?" Cyril Bixby said, still washing his hands.

"No."

"It'll probably be at least eight thirty the way things look at the moment. It may even be nine."

"Yes, all right. Goodbye." Mrs. Bixby went out, slamming the door behind her.

At that precise moment, Miss Pulteney, the secretary-assistant, came sailing past her down the corridor on her way to lunch.

"Isn't it a gorgeous day?" Miss Pulteney said as she went by, flashing a smile. There was lilt in her walk, a little whiff of perfume attending her, and she looked like a queen, just exactly like a queen in the beautiful black mink coat that the Colonel had given to Mrs. Bixby.

Royal Jelly

1959

"It worries me to death, Albert, it really does," Mrs. Taylor said.

She kept her eyes fixed on the baby who was now lying absolutely motionless in the crook of her left arm.

"I just know there's something wrong."

The skin on the baby's face had a pearly translucent quality, and was stretched very tightly over the bones.

"Try again," Albert Taylor said.

"It won't do any good."

"You have to keep trying, Mabel," he said.

She lifted the bottle out of the saucepan of hot water and shook a few drops of milk onto the inside of her wrist, testing for temperature.

"Come on," she whispered. "Come on, my baby. Wake up and take a bit more of this."

There was a small lamp on the table close by that made a soft yellow glow all around her.

"Please," she said. "Take just a weeny bit more."

The husband watched her over the top of his magazine. She was half dead with exhaustion, he could see that, and the pale oval face, usually so grave and serene, had taken on a kind of pinched and desperate look. But even so, the drop of her head as she gazed down at the child was curiously beautiful.

"You see," she murmured. "It's no good. She won't have it."

She held the bottle up to the light, squinting at the calibrations.

"One ounce again. That's all she's taken. No—it isn't even that. It's only three quarters. It's not enough to keep body and soul together, Albert, it really isn't. It worries me to death."

"I know," he said.

"If only they could *find out* what was wrong."

"There's nothing wrong, Mabel. It's just a matter of time."

"Of course there's something wrong."

"Dr. Robinson says no."

"Look," she said, standing up. "You can't tell me it's natural for a six-weeks-old child to weigh less, less by more than *two whole pounds* than she did when she was born! Just look at those legs! They're nothing but skin and bone!"

The tiny baby lay limply on her arm, not moving.

"Dr. Robinson said you was to stop worrying, Mabel. So did that other one."

"Ha!" she said. "Isn't that wonderful! I'm to stop worrying!"

"Now, Mabel."

"What does he want me to do? Treat it as some sort of a joke?"

"He didn't say that."

"I hate doctors! I hate them all!" she cried, and she swung away from him and walked quickly out of the room toward the stairs, carrying the baby with her.

Albert Taylor stayed where he was and let her go.

In a little while he heard her moving about in the bedroom directly over his head, quick nervous footsteps going tap tap tap on the linoleum above. Soon the footsteps would stop, and then he would have to get up and follow her, and when he went into the bedroom he would find her sitting beside the cot as usual, staring at the child and crying softly to herself and refusing to move.

"She's starving, Albert," she would say.

"Of course she's not starving."

"She *is* starving. I know she is. And Albert?"

"Yes?"

"I believe you know it too, but you won't admit it. Isn't that right?"

Every night now it was like this.

Last week they had taken the child back to the hospital, and the doctor had examined it carefully and told them that there was nothing the matter.

"It took us nine years to get this baby, Doctor," Mabel had said. "I think it would kill me if anything should happen to her."

That was six days ago and since then it had lost another five ounces.

But worrying about it wasn't going to help anybody, Albert Taylor told himself. One simply had to trust the doctor on a thing like this. He picked up the magazine that was still lying on his lap and glanced idly down the list of contents to see what it had to offer this week:

All his life Albert Taylor had been fascinated by anything that had to do with bees. As a small boy he used often to catch them in his bare hands and go running with them into the house to show to his mother, and sometimes he would put them on his face and let them crawl about over his cheeks and neck, and the astonishing thing about it all was that he never got stung. On the contrary, the bees seemed to enjoy being with him. They never tried to fly away, and to get rid of them he would have to brush them off gently with his fingers. Even then they would frequently return and settle again on his arm or hand or knee, any place where the skin was bare.

His father, who was a bricklayer, said there must be some witch's stench about the boy, something noxious that came oozing out through the pores of the skin, and that no good would ever come of it, hypnotizing insects like that. But the mother said it was a gift given him by God, and even went so far as to compare him with St. Francis and the birds.

As he grew older, Albert Taylor's fascination with bees developed into an obsession, and by the time he was twelve he had built his first hive. The following summer he had captured his first swarm. Two years later, at the age of fourteen, he had no less than five hives standing neatly in a row against the fence in his father's small back yard, and already—apart from the normal task of producing honey —he was practising the delicate and complicated business of rearing his own queens, grafting larvae into artificial cell cups, and all the rest of it.

He never had to use smoke when there was work to do inside a hive, and he never wore gloves on his hands or a net over his head. Clearly there was some strange sympathy between this boy and the bees, and down in the village, in the shops and pubs, they began to speak about him with a certain kind of respect, and people started coming up to the house to buy his honey.

When he was eighteen, he had rented one acre of rough pasture alongside a cherry orchard down the valley about a mile from the village, and there he had set out to establish his own business. Now, eleven years later, he was still in the same spot, but he had six acres of ground instead of one, two hundred and forty well-stocked hives, and a small house that he'd built mainly with his own hands. He had married at the age of twenty and that, apart from the fact that it had taken them over nine years to get a child, had also been a success. In fact, everything had gone pretty well for Albert until this strange little baby girl came along and started frightening them out of their wits by refusing to eat properly and losing weight every day.

He looked up from the magazine and began thinking about his daughter.

This evening, for instance, when she had opened her eyes at the beginning of the feed, he had gazed into them and seen something that frightened him to death—a kind of misty vacant stare, as though the eyes themselves were not connected to the brain at all but were just lying loose in their sockets like a couple of small grey marbles.

Did those doctors really know what they were talking about?

He reached for an ashtray and started slowly picking the ashes out from the bowl of his pipe with a matchstick.

One could always take her along to another hospital, somewhere in Oxford perhaps. He might suggest that to Mabel when he went upstairs.

He could still hear her moving around in the bedroom, but she must have taken off her shoes now and put on slippers because the noise was very faint.

He switched his attention back to the magazine and went on with his reading. He finished an article called "Experiences in the Control of Nosema," then turned over the page and began reading the next one, "The Latest on Royal Jelly." He doubted very much whether there would be anything in this that he didn't know already:

What is this wonderful substance called royal jelly?

He reached for the tin of tobacco on the table beside him and began filling his pipe, still reading.

Royal jelly is a glandular secretion produced by the nurse bees to feed the larvae immediately they have hatched from the egg. The pharingeal glands of bees produce this substance in much the same way as the mammary glands of vertebrates produce milk. The fact is of great biological interest because no other insects in the world are known to have evolved such a process.

All old stuff, he told himself, but for want of anything better to do, he continued to read.

Royal jelly is fed in concentrated form to all bee larvae for the first three days after hatching from the egg; but beyond that point, for all those who are destined to become drones or workers, this precious food is greatly diluted with honey and pollen. On the other hand, the larvae which are destined to become queens are fed throughout the whole of their larval period on a concentrated diet of pure royal jelly. Hence the name.

Above him, up in the bedroom, the noise of the footsteps had stopped altogether. The house was quiet. He struck a match and put it to his pipe.

Royal jelly must be a substance of tremendous nourishing power, for on this diet alone, the honey-bee larva increases in weight fifteen hundred times in five days.

That was probably about right, he thought, although for some reason it had never occurred to him to consider larval growth in terms of weight before.

This is as if a seven-and-a-half-pound baby should increase in that time to five tons.

Albert Taylor stopped and read that sentence again.

He read it a third time.

This is as if a seven-and-a-half-pound baby . . .

"Mabel!" he cried, jumping up from his chair. "Mabel! Come here!"

He went out into the hall and stood at the foot of the stairs calling for her to come down.

There was no answer.

He ran up the stairs and switched on the light on the landing. The bedroom door was closed. He crossed the landing and opened it and stood in the doorway looking into the dark room. "Mabel," he said. "Come downstairs a moment, will you please? I've just had a bit of an idea. It's about the baby."

The light from the landing behind him cast a faint glow over the bed and he could see her dimly now, lying on her stomach with her face buried in the pillow and her arms up over her head. She was crying again.

"Mabel," he said, going over to her, touching her shoulder. "Please come down a moment. This may be important."

"Go away," she said. "Leave me alone."

"Don't you want to hear about my idea?"

"Oh, Albert, I'm *tired,*" she sobbed. "I'm so tired I don't know what I'm doing any more. I don't think I can go on. I don't think I can stand it."

There was a pause. Albert Taylor turned away from her and walked slowly over to the cradle where the baby was lying, and peered in. It was too dark for him to see the child's face, but when he bent down close he could hear the sound of breathing, very faint and quick. "What time is the next feed?" he asked.

"Two o'clock, I suppose."

"And the one after that?"

"Six in the morning."

"I'll do them both," he said. "You go to sleep."

She didn't answer.

"You get properly into bed, Mabel, and go straight to sleep, you understand? And stop worrying. I'm taking over completely for the next twelve hours. You'll give yourself a nervous breakdown going on like this."

"Yes," she said. "I know."

"I'm taking the nipper and myself *and* the alarm clock into the spare room this very moment, so you just lie down and relax and forget all about us. Right?" Already he was pushing the cradle out through the door.

"Oh, Albert," she sobbed.

"Don't you worry about a thing. Leave it to me."

"Albert . . ."

"Yes?"

"I love you, Albert."

"I love you too, Mabel. Now go to sleep."

Albert Taylor didn't see his wife again until nearly eleven o'clock the next morning.

"Good *gracious* me!" she cried, rushing down the stairs in dressing-gown and slippers. "Albert! Just look at the time! I must have slept twelve hours at least! Is everything all right? What happened?"

He was sitting quietly in his armchair, smoking a pipe and reading the morning paper. The baby was in a sort of carrier cot on the floor at his feet, sleeping.

"Hullo, dear," he said, smiling.

She ran over to the cot and looked in. "Did she take anything, Albert? How many times have you fed her? She was due for another one at ten o'clock, did you know that?"

Albert Taylor folded the newspaper neatly into a square and put it away on the side table. "I fed her at two in the morning," he said, "and she took about half an ounce, no more. I fed her again at six and she did a bit better that time, two ounces . . ."

"*Two ounces!* Oh, Albert, that's marvellous!"

"And we just finished the last feed ten minutes ago. There's the bottle on the mantelpiece. Only one ounce left. She drank three. How's that?" He was grinning proudly, delighted with his achievement.

The woman quickly got down on her knees and peered at the baby.

"Don't she look better?" he asked eagerly. "Don't she look fatter in the face?"

"It may sound silly," the wife said, "but I actually think she does. Oh, Albert, you're a marvel! How did you do it?"

"She's turning the corner," he said. "That's all it is. Just like the doctor prophesied, she's turning the corner."

"I pray to God you're right, Albert."

"Of course I'm right. From now on, you watch her go."

The woman was gazing lovingly at the baby.

"You look a lot better yourself too, Mabel."

"I feel wonderful. I'm sorry about last night."

"Let's keep it this way," he said. "I'll do all the night feeds in future. You do the day ones."

She looked up at him across the cot, frowning. "No," she said. "Oh no, I wouldn't allow you to do that."

"I don't want you to have a breakdown, Mabel."

"I won't, not now I've had some sleep."

"Much better we share it."

"No, Albert. This is my job and I intend to do it. Last night won't happen again."

There was a pause. Albert Taylor took the pipe out of his mouth and examined the grain on the bowl. "All right," he said. "In that case I'll just relieve you of the donkey work, I'll do all the sterilising and the mixing of the food and getting everything ready. That'll help you a bit, anyway."

She looked at him carefully, wondering what could have come over him all of a sudden.

"You see, Mabel, I've been thinking . . ."

"Yes, dear."

"I've been thinking that up until last night I've never even raised a finger to help you with this baby."

"That isn't true."

"Oh yes it is. So I've decided that from now on I'm going to do *my* share of the work. I'm going to be the feed-mixer and the bottle-steriliser. Right?"

"It's very sweet of you, dear, but I really don't think it's necessary. . . ."

"Come on!" he cried. "Don't change the luck! I done it the last three times and just *look* what happened! When's the next one? Two o'clock, isn't it?"

"Yes."

"It's all mixed," he said. "Everything's all mixed and ready and all you've got to do when the time comes is to go out there to the larder and take it off the shelf and warm it up. That's *some* help, isn't it?"

The woman got up off her knees and went over to him and kissed him on the cheek. "You're such a nice man," she said. "I love you more and more every day I know you."

Later, in the middle of the afternoon, when Albert was outside in the sunshine working among the hives, he heard her calling to him from the house.

"Albert!" she shouted. "Albert, come here!" She was running through the buttercups toward him.

He started forward to meet her, wondering what was wrong.

"Oh, Albert! Guess what!"

"What?"

"I've just finished giving her the two-o'clock feed and she's taken the whole lot!"

"No!"

"Every drop of it! Oh, Albert, I'm so happy! She's going to be all right! She's turned the corner just like you said!" She came up to him and threw her arms around his neck and hugged him, and he clapped her on the back and laughed and said what a marvellous little mother she was.

"Will you come in and watch the next one and see if she does it again, Albert?"

He told her he wouldn't miss it for anything, and she hugged him again, then turned and ran back to the house, skipping over the grass and singing all the way.

Naturally, there was a certain amount of suspense in the air as the time approached for the six-o'clock feed. By five thirty both parents were already seated in the living-room waiting for the moment to arrive. The bottle with the milk formula in it was standing in a saucepan of warm water on the mantelpiece. The baby was asleep in its carrier cot on the sofa.

At twenty minutes to six it woke up and started screaming its head off.

"There you are!" Mrs. Taylor cried. "She's asking for the bottle. Pick her up quick, Albert, and hand her to me here. Give me the bottle first."

He gave her the bottle, then placed the baby on the woman's lap. Cautiously, she touched the baby's lips with the end of the nipple. The baby seized the nipple between its gums and began to suck ravenously with a rapid powerful action.

"Oh, Albert, isn't it wonderful?" she said, laughing.

"It's terrific, Mabel."

In seven or eight minutes, the entire contents of the bottle had disappeared down the baby's throat.

"You clever girl," Mrs. Taylor said. "Four ounces again."

Albert Taylor was leaning forward in his chair, peering intently into the baby's face. "You know what?" he said. "She even seems as though she's put on a touch of weight already. What do you think?"

The mother looked down at the child.

"Don't she seem bigger and fatter to you, Mabel, than she was yesterday?"

"Maybe she does, Albert. I'm not sure. Although actually there couldn't be any *real* gain in such a short time as this. The important thing is that she's eating normally."

"She's turned the corner," Albert said. "I don't think you need worry about her any more."

"I certainly won't."

"You want me to go up and fetch the cradle back into our own bedroom, Mabel?"

"Yes, please," she said.

Albert went upstairs and moved the cradle. The woman followed with the baby, and after changing its nappy, she laid it gently down on its bed. Then she covered it with sheet and blanket.

"Doesn't she look lovely, Albert?" she whispered. "Isn't that the most beautiful baby you've ever seen in your *entire* life?"

"Leave her be now, Mabel," he said. "Come on downstairs and cook us a bit of supper. We both deserve it."

After they had finished eating, the parents settled themselves in armchairs in the living-room, Albert with his magazine and his pipe,

Mrs. Taylor with her knitting. But this was a very different scene from the one of the night before. Suddenly, all tensions had vanished. Mrs. Taylor's handsome oval face was glowing with pleasure, her cheeks were pink, her eyes were sparkling bright, and her mouth was fixed in a little dreamy smile of pure content. Every now and again she would glance up from her knitting and gaze affectionately at her husband. Occasionally, she would stop the clicking of her needles altogether for a few seconds and sit quite still, looking at the ceiling, listening for a cry or a whimper from upstairs. But all was quiet.

"Albert," she said after a while.

"Yes, dear?"

"What was it you were going to tell me last night when you came rushing up to the bedroom? You said you had an idea for the baby."

Albert Taylor lowered the magazine onto his lap and gave her a long sly look.

"Did I?" he said.

"Yes." She waited for him to go on, but he didn't.

"What's the big joke?" she asked. "Why are you grinning like that?"

"It's a joke all right," he said.

"Tell it to me, dear."

"I'm not sure I ought to," he said. "You might call me a liar."

She had seldom seen him looking so pleased with himself as he was now, and she smiled back at him, egging him on.

"I'd just like to see your face when you hear it, Mabel, that's all."

"Albert, what *is* all this?"

He paused, refusing to be hurried.

"You do think the baby's better, don't you?" he asked.

"Of course I do."

"You agree with me that all of a sudden she's feeding marvellously and looking one-hundred-per-cent different?"

"I do, Albert, yes."

"That's good," he said, the grin widening. "You see, it's me that did it."

"Did what?"

"I cured the baby."

"Yes, dear, I'm sure you did." Mrs. Taylor went right on with her knitting.

"You don't believe me, do you?"

"Of course I believe you, Albert. I give you all the credit, every bit of it."

"Then how did I do it?"

"Well," she said, pausing a moment to think. "I suppose it's simply that you're a brilliant feed-mixer. Ever since you started mixing the feeds she's got better and better."

"You mean there's some sort of an art in mixing the feeds?"

"Apparently there is." She was knitting away and smiling quietly to herself, thinking how funny men were

"I'll tell you a secret," he said. "You're absolutely right. Although, mind you, it isn't so much *how* you mix it that counts. It's what you put in. You realize that, don't you, Mabel?"

Mrs. Taylor stopped knitting and looked up sharply at her husband. "Albert," she said, "don't tell me you've been putting things into that child's milk?"

He sat there grinning.

"Well, have you or haven't you?"

"It's possible," he said.

"I don't believe it."

He had a strange fierce way of grinning that showed his teeth.

"Albert," she said. "Stop playing with me like this."

"Yes, dear, all right."

"You haven't *really* put anything into her milk, have you? Answer me properly, Albert. This could be serious with such a tiny baby."

"The answer is yes, Mabel."

"*Albert Taylor!* How could you?"

"Now don't get excited," he said. "I'll tell you all about it if you really want me to, but for heaven's sake keep your hair on."

"It was beer!" she cried. "I just know it was beer!"

"Don't be so daft, Mabel, please."

"Then what was it?"

Albert laid his pipe down carefully on the table beside him and leaned back in his chair. "Tell me," he said, "did you ever by any chance happen to hear me mentioning something called royal jelly?"

"I did not."

"It's magic," he said. "Pure magic. And last night I suddenly got the idea that if I was to put some of this into the baby's milk . . ."

"How *dare* you!"

"Now, Mabel, you don't even know what it is yet."

"I don't care what it is," she said. "You can't go putting foreign bodies like that into a tiny baby's milk. You must be mad."

"It's perfectly harmless, Mabel, otherwise I wouldn't have done it. It comes from bees."

"I might have guessed that."

"And it's so precious that practically no one can afford to take it. When they do, it's only one little drop at a time."

"And how much did you give to our baby, might I ask?"

"Ah," he said, "that's the whole point. That's where the difference lies. I reckon that our baby, just in the last four feeds, has already swallowed about fifty times as much royal jelly as anyone else in the world has ever swallowed before. How about that?"

"Albert, stop pulling my leg."

"I swear it," he said proudly.

She sat there staring at him, her brow wrinkled, her mouth slightly open.

"You know what this stuff actually costs, Mabel, if you want to buy it? There's a place in America advertising it for sale this very moment for something like five hundred dollars a pound jar! *Five hundred dollars!* That's more than gold, you know!"

She hadn't the faintest idea what he was talking about.

"I'll prove it," he said, and he jumped up and went across to the large bookcase where he kept all his literature about bees. On the top shelf, the back numbers of *The American Bee Journal* were neatly stacked alongside those of *The British Bee Journal, Beecraft,* and other magazines. He took down the last issue of *The American Bee Journal* and turned to a page of small classified advertisements at the back.

"Here you are," he said. "Exactly as I told you. 'We sell royal jelly—$480 per lb. jar wholesale.' "

He handed her the magazine so she could read it herself.

"Now do you believe me? This is an actual shop in New York, Mabel. It says so."

"It doesn't say you can go stirring it into the milk of a practically new-born baby," she said. "I don't know what's come over you, Albert, I really don't."

"It's curing her, isn't it?"

"I'm not so sure about that, now."

"Don't be so damn silly, Mabel. You know it is."

"Then why haven't other people done it with *their* babies?"

"I keep telling you," he said. "It's too expensive. Practically nobody in the world can afford to buy royal jelly just for *eating* except maybe one or two multimillionaries. The people who buy it are the big companies that make women's face creams and things like that. They're using it as a stunt. They mix a tiny pinch of it into a big jar of face cream and it's selling like hot cakes for absolutely enormous prices. They claim it takes out the wrinkles."

"And does it?"

"Now how on earth would I know that, Mabel? Anyway," he said, returning to his chair, "that's not the point. The point is this. It's done so much good to our little baby just in the last few hours that I think we ought to go right on giving it to her. Now don't interrupt, Mabel. Let me finish. I've got two hundred and forty hives out there and if I turn over maybe a hundred of them to making royal jelly, we ought to be able to supply her with all she wants."

"Albert Taylor," the woman said, stretching her eyes wide and staring at him. "Have you gone out of your mind?"

"Just hear me through, will you please?"

"I forbid it," she said, "absolutely. You're not to give my baby another drop of that horrid jelly, you understand?"

"Now, Mabel . . ."

"And quite apart from that, we had a shocking honey crop last year, and if you go fooling around with those hives now, there's no telling what might not happen."

"There's nothing wrong with my hives, Mabel."

"You know very well we had only half the normal crop last year."

"Do me a favour, will you?" he said. "Let me explain some of the marvellous things this stuff does."

"You haven't even told me what it is yet."

"All right, Mabel. I'll do that too. Will you listen? Will you give me a chance to explain it?"

She sighed and picked up her knitting once more. "I suppose you might as well get it off your chest, Albert. Go on and tell me."

He paused, a bit uncertain now how to begin. It wasn't going to be easy to explain something like this to a person with no detailed knowledge of apiculture at all.

"You know, don't you," he said, "that each colony has only one queen?"

"Yes."

"And that this queen lays all the eggs?"

"Yes, dear. That much I know."

"All right. Now the queen can actually lay two different kinds of eggs. You didn't know that, but she can. It's what we call one of the miracles of the hive. She can lay eggs that produce drones, and she can lay eggs that produce workers. Now if that isn't a miracle, Mabel, I don't know what is."

"Yes, Albert, all right."

"The drones are the males. We don't have to worry about them. The workers are all females. So is the queen, of course. But the workers are unsexed females, if you see what I mean. Their organs are completely undeveloped, whereas the queen is tremendously sexy. She can actually lay her own weight in eggs in a single day."

He hesitated, marshalling his thoughts.

"Now what happens is this. The queen crawls around on the comb and lays her eggs in what we call cells. You know all those hundreds of little holes you see in a honeycomb? Well, a brood comb is just about the same except the cells don't have honey in them, they have eggs. She lays one egg to each cell, and in three days each of these eggs hatches out into a tiny grub. We call it a larva.

"Now, as soon as this larva appears, the nurse bees—they're young workers—all crowd round and start feeding it like mad. And you know what they feed it on?"

"Royal jelly," Mabel answered patiently.

"Right!" he cried. "That's exactly what they do feed it on. They get this stuff out of a gland in their heads and they start pumping it into the cell to feed the larva. And what happens then?"

He paused dramatically, blinking at her with his small watery-grey eyes. Then he turned slowly in his chair and reached for the magazine that he had been reading the night before.

"You want to know what happens then?" he asked, wetting his lips.

"I can hardly wait."

" 'Royal jelly,' " he read aloud, " 'must be a substance of tremendous nourishing power, for on this diet alone, the honey-bee larva increases in weight *fifteen hundred times* in five days!' "

"How much?"

"Fifteen hundred times, Mabel. And you know what that means if you put it in terms of a human being? It means," he said, lowering his voice, leaning forward, fixing her with those small pale eyes, "it means that in five days a baby weighing seven and a half pounds to start off with would increase in weight to *five tons!"*

For the second time, Mrs. Taylor stopped knitting.

"Now you mustn't take that too literally, Mabel."

"Who says I mustn't?"

"It's just a scientific way of putting it, that's all."

"Very well, Albert. Go on."

"But that's only half the story," he said. "There's more to come. The really amazing thing about royal jelly, I haven't told you yet. I'm going to show you now how it can transform a plain dull-looking little worker bee with practically no sex organs at all into a great big beautiful fertile queen."

"Are you saying our baby is dull-looking and plain?" she asked sharply.

"Now don't go putting words into my mouth, Mabel, please. Just listen to this. Did you know that the queen bee and the worker bee, although they are completely different when they grow up, are both hatched out of exactly the same kind of egg?"

"I don't believe that," she said.

"It's true as I'm sitting here, Mabel, honest it is. Any time the bees want a queen to hatch out of the egg instead of a worker, they can do it."

"How?"

"Ah," he said, shaking a thick forefinger in her direction. "That's just what I'm coming to. That's the secret of the whole thing. Now—what do *you* think it is, Mabel, that makes this miracle happen?"

"Royal jelly," she answered. "You already told me."

"Royal jelly it is!" he cried, clapping his hands and bouncing up on his seat. His big round face was glowing with excitement now, and two vivid patches of scarlet had appeared high up on each cheek.

"Here's how it works. I'll put it very simply for you. The bees want a new queen. So they build an extra-large cell, a queen cell we call it, and they get the old queen to lay one of her eggs in there. The other one thousand nine hundred and ninety-nine eggs she lays in ordinary worker cells. Now. As soon as these eggs hatch out into larvae, the nurse bees rally round and start pumping in the royal jelly. All of them get it, workers as well as queen. But here's the vital thing, Mabel, so listen carefully. Here's where the difference comes. The worker larvae only receive this special marvellous food for the *first three days* of their larval life. After that they have a complete change of diet. What really happens is they get weaned, except that it's not like an ordinary weaning because it's so sudden. After the third day they're put straight away onto more or less routine bees' food—a mixture of honey and pollen—and then about two weeks later they emerge from the cells as workers.

"But not so the larva in the queen cell! This one gets royal jelly *all the way through its larval life*. The nurse bees simply pour it into the cell, so much so in fact that the little larva is literally floating in it. And that's what makes it into a queen!"

"You can't prove it," she said.

"Don't talk so damn silly, Mabel, please. Thousands of people have proved it time and time again, famous scientists in every country in the world. All you have to do is take a larva out of a worker cell and put it in a queen cell—that's what we call grafting—and just so long as the nurse bees keep it well supplied with royal jelly, then presto!—it'll grow up into a queen! And what makes it more marvellous still is the absolutely enormous difference between a queen and a worker when they grow up. The abdomen is a different shape. The sting is different. The legs are different. The . . ."

"In what way are the legs different?" she asked, testing him.

"The legs? Well, the workers have little pollen baskets on their legs for carrying the pollen. The queen has none. Now here's another thing. The queen has fully developed sex organs. The workers don't. And most amazing of all, Mabel, the queen lives for an average of four to six years. The worker hardly lives that many months. And all this difference simply because one of them got royal jelly and the other didn't!"

"It's pretty hard to believe," she said, "that a food can do all that."

"Of course it's hard to believe. It's another of the miracles of the hive. In fact it's the biggest ruddy miracle of them all. It's such a hell of a big miracle that it's baffled the greatest men of science for hundreds of years. Wait a moment. Stay there. Don't move."

Again he jumped up and went over to the bookcase and started rummaging among the books and magazines.

"I'm going to find you a few of the reports. Here we are. Here's one of them. Listen to this." He started reading aloud from a copy of the *American Bee Journal*:

" 'Living in Toronto at the head of a fine research laboratory given to him by the people of Canada in recognition of his truly great contribution to humanity in the discovery of insulin, Dr. Frederick A. Banting became curious about royal jelly. He requested his staff to do a basic fractional analysis. . . .' "

He paused.

"Well, there's no need to read it all, but here's what happened. Dr. Banting and his people took some royal jelly from queen cells that contained two-day-old larvae, and then they started analyzing it. And what d'you think they found?

"They found," he said, "that royal jelly contained phenols, sterols, glycerils, dextrose, *and*—now here it comes—and eighty to eighty-five per cent *unidentified* acids!"

He stood beside the bookcase with the magazine in his hand, smiling a funny little furtive smile of triumph, and his wife watched him, bewildered.

He was not a tall man; he had a thick plump pulpy-looking body that was built close to the ground on abbreviated legs. The legs were slightly bowed. The head was huge and round, covered with bristly short-cut hair, and the greater part of the face—now that he had given up shaving altogether—was hidden by a brownish yellow fuzz about an inch long. In one way and another, he was rather grotesque to look at, there was no denying that.

"Eighty to eighty-five per cent," he said, "unidentified acids. Isn't that fantastic?" He turned back to the bookshelf and began hunting through the other magazines.

"What does it mean, unidentified acids?"

"That's the whole point! No one knows! Not even Banting could find out. You've heard of Banting?"

"No."

"He just happens to be about the most famous living doctor in the world today, that's all."

Looking at him now as he buzzed around in front of the bookcase with his bristly head and his hairy face and his plump pulpy body, she couldn't help thinking that somehow, in some curious way, there was a touch of the bee about this man. She had often seen women grow to look like the horses that they rode, and she had noticed that people who bred birds or bull terriers or pomeranians frequently resembled in some small but startling manner the creature of their choice. But up until now it had never occurred to her that her husband might look like a bee. It shocked her a bit.

"And did Banting ever try to eat it," she asked, "this royal jelly?"

"Of course he didn't eat it, Mabel. He didn't have enough for that. It's too precious."

"You know something?" she said, staring at him but smiling a little all the same. "You're getting to look just a teeny bit like a bee yourself, did you know that?"

He turned and looked at her.

"I suppose it's the beard mostly," she said. "I do wish you'd stop wearing it. Even the colour is sort of bee-ish, don't you think?"

"What the hell are you talking about, Mabel?"

"Albert," she said. "Your language."

"Do you want to hear any more of this or don't you?"

"Yes, dear, I'm sorry. I was only joking. Do go on."

He turned away again and pulled another magazine out of the bookcase and began leafing through the pages. "Now just listen to this, Mabel. 'In 1939, Heyl experimented with twenty-one-day-old rats, injecting them with royal jelly in varying amounts. As a result, he found a precocious follicular development of the ovaries directly in proportion to the quantity of royal jelly injected.' "

"There!" she cried. "I knew it!"

"Knew what?"

"I knew something terrible would happen."

"Nonsense. There's nothing wrong with that. Now here's another, Mabel. 'Still and Burdett found that a male rat which hitherto had been unable to breed, upon receiving a minute daily dose of royal jelly, became a father many times over.' "

"Albert," she cried, "this stuff is *much* too strong to give to a baby! I don't like it at all."

"Nonsense, Mabel."

"Then why do they only try it out on rats, tell me that? Why don't some of these famous scientists take it themselves? They're too clever, that's why. Do you think Dr. Banting is going to risk finishing up with precious ovaries? Not him."

"But they *have* given it to people, Mabel. Here's a whole article about it. Listen." He turned the page and again began reading from the magazine. " 'In Mexico, in 1953, a group of enlightened physicians began prescribing minute doses of royal jelly for such things as cerebral neuritis, arthritis, diabetes, autointoxication from tobacco, impotence in men, asthma, croup, and gout.   . There are stacks of signed testimonials. . . . A celebrated stockbroker in Mexico City contracted a particularly stubborn case of psoriasis. He became physically unattractive. His clients began to forsake him. His business began to suffer. In desperation he turned to royal jelly—one drop with every meal—and presto!—he was cured in a fortnight. A waiter in the Café Jena, also in Mexico City, reported that his father, after taking minute doses of this wonder substance in capsule form, sired a healthy boy child at the age of ninety. A bullfight promoter in Acapulco, finding himself landed with a rather lethargic-looking bull, injected it with one gram of royal jelly (an excessive dose) just before it entered the arena. Thereupon, the beast became so swift and savage that it promptly dispatched two picadors, three horses, and a matador, and finally . . .' "

"Listen!" Mrs. Taylor said, interrupting him. "I think the baby's crying."

Albert glanced up from his reading. Sure enough, a lusty yelling noise was coming from the bedroom above.

"She must be hungry," he said.

His wife looked at the clock. "Good gracious me!" she cried, jumping up. "It's past her time again already! You mix the feed, Albert, quickly, while I bring her down! But hurry! I don't want to keep her waiting."

In half a minute, Mrs. Taylor was back, carrying the screaming infant in her arms. She was flustered now, still quite unaccustomed to the ghastly nonstop racket that a healthy baby makes when it wants its food. "Do be quick, Albert!" she called, settling herself in the armchair and arranging the child on her lap. "Please hurry!"

Albert entered from the kitchen and handed her the bottle of warm milk. "It's just right," he said. "You don't have to test it."

She hitched the baby's head a little higher in the crook of her arm, then pushed the rubber teat straight into the wide-open yelling mouth. The baby grabbed the teat and began to suck. The yelling stopped. Mrs. Taylor relaxed.

"Oh, Albert, isn't she lovely?"

"She's terrific, Mabel—thanks to royal jelly."

"Now, dear, I don't want to hear another word about that nasty stuff. It frightens me to death."

"You're making a big mistake," he said.

"We'll see about that."

The baby went on sucking the bottle.

"I do believe she's going to finish the whole lot again, Albert."

"I'm sure she is," he said.

And a few minutes later, the milk was all gone.

"Oh, what a good girl you are!" Mrs. Taylor cried, as very gently she started to withdraw the nipple. The baby sensed what she was doing and sucked harder, trying to hold on. The woman gave a quick little tug, and *plop*, out it came.

"Waa! Waa! Waa! Waa! Waa!" the baby yelled.

"Nasty old wind," Mrs. Taylor said, hoisting the child onto her shoulder and patting its back.

It belched twice in quick succession

"There you are, my darling, you'll be all right now."

For a few seconds, the yelling stopped. Then it started again.

"Keep belching her," Albert said. "She's drunk it too quick."

His wife lifted the baby back onto her shoulder. She rubbed its spine. She changed it from one shoulder to the other. She lay it on its stomach on her lap. She sat it up on her knee. But it didn't belch again, and the yelling became louder and more insistent every minute.

"Good for the lungs," Albert Taylor said, grinning. "That's the way they exercise their lungs, Mabel, did you know that?"

"There, there, there," the wife said, kissing it all over the face. "There, there, there."

They waited another five minutes, but not for one moment did the screaming stop.

"Change the nappy," Albert said. "It's got a wet nappy, that's all it is." He fetched a clean one from the kitchen, and Mrs. Taylor took the old one off and put the new one on.

This made no difference at all.

"Waa! Waa! Waa! Waa! Waa!" the baby yelled.

"You didn't stick the safety pin through the skin, did you, Mabel?"

"Of course I didn't," she said, feeling under the nappy with her fingers to make sure.

The parents sat opposite one another in their armchairs, smiling nervously, watching the baby on the mother's lap, waiting for it to tire and stop screaming.

"You know what?" Albert Taylor said at last.

"What?"

"I'll bet she's still hungry. I'll bet all she wants is another swig at that bottle. How about me fetching her an extra lot?"

"I don't think we ought to do that, Albert."

"It'll do her good," he said, getting up from his chair. "I'm going to warm her up a second helping."

He went into the kitchen, and was away several minutes. When he returned he was holding a bottle brimful of milk.

"I made her a double," he announced. "Eight ounces. Just in case."

"Albert! Are you mad! Don't you know it's just as bad to overfeed as it is to underfeed?"

"You don't have to give her the lot, Mabel. You can stop any time you like. Go on," he said, standing over her. "Give her a drink."

Mrs. Taylor began to tease the baby's upper lip with the end of the nipple. The tiny mouth closed like a trap over the rubber teat and suddenly there was silence in the room. The baby's whole body relaxed and a look of absolute bliss came over its face as it started to drink.

"There you are, Mabel! What did I tell you?"

The woman didn't answer.

"She's ravenous, that's what she is. Just look at her suck."

Mrs. Taylor was watching the level of the milk in the bottle. It was dropping fast, and before long three or four ounces out of the eight had disappeared.

"There," she said. "That'll do."

"You can't pull it away now, Mabel."

"Yes, dear. I must."

"Go on, woman. Give her the rest and stop fussing."

"But *Albert* . . ."

"She's famished, can't you see that? Go on, my beauty," he said. "You finish that bottle."

"I don't like it, Albert," the wife said, but she didn't pull the bottle away.

"She's making up for lost time, Mabel, that's all she's doing."

Five minutes later the bottle was empty. Slowly, Mrs. Taylor withdrew the nipple, and this time there was no protest from the baby, no sound at all. It lay peacefully on the mother's lap, the eyes glazed with contentment, the mouth half open, the lips smeared with milk.

"Twelve whole ounces, Mabel!" Albert Taylor said. "Three times the normal amount! Isn't that amazing!"

The woman was staring down at the baby. And now the old anxious tight-lipped look of the frightened mother was slowly returning to her face.

"What's the matter with *you?*" Albert asked. "You're not worried by that, are you? You can't expect her to get back to normal on a lousy four ounces, don't be ridiculous."

"Come here, Albert," she said.

"What?"

"I said come here."

He went over and stood beside her.

"Take a good look and tell me if you see anything different."

He peered closely at the baby. "She seems bigger, Mabel, if that's what you mean. Bigger and fatter."

"Hold her," she ordered. "Go on, pick her up."

He reached out and lifted the baby up off the mother's lap. "Good God!" he cried. "She weighs a ton!"

"Exactly."

"Now isn't that marvellous!" he cried, beaming. "I'll bet she must almost be back to normal already!"

"It frightens me, Albert. It's too quick."

"Nonsense, woman."

"It's that disgusting jelly that's done it," she said. "I hate the stuff."

"There's nothing disgusting about royal jelly," he answered, indignant.

"Don't be a fool, Albert! You think it's *normal* for a child to start putting on weight at this speed?"

"You're never satisfied!" he cried. "You're scared stiff when she's losing and now you're absolutely terrified because she's gaining! What's the matter with you, Mabel?"

The woman got up from her chair with the baby in her arms and started toward the door. "All I can say is," she said, "it's lucky I'm here to see you don't give her any more of it, that's all I can say." She went out, and Albert watched her through the open door as she crossed the hall to the foot of the stairs and started to ascend, and when she reached the third or fourth step she suddenly stopped and stood quite still for several seconds as though remembering something. Then she turned and came down again rather quickly and re-entered the room.

"Albert," she said.

"Yes?"

"I assume there wasn't any royal jelly in this last feed we've just given her?"

"I don't see why you should assume that, Mabel."

"Albert!"

"What's wrong?" he asked, soft and innocent.

"How *dare* you!" she cried.

Albert Taylor's great bearded face took on a pained and puzzled look. "I think you ought to be very glad she's got another big dose of it inside her," he said. "Honest I do. And this *is* a big dose, Mabel, believe you me."

The woman was standing just inside the doorway clasping the

sleeping baby in her arms and staring at her husband with huge eyes. She stood very erect, her body absolutely stiff with fury, her face paler, more tight-lipped than ever.

"You mark my words," Albert was saying, "you're going to have a nipper there soon that'll win first prize in any baby show in the *entire* country. Hey, why don't you weigh her now and see what she is? You want me to get the scales, Mabel, so you can weigh her?"

The woman walked straight over to the large table in the centre of the room and laid the baby down and quickly started taking off its clothes. "Yes!" she snapped. "Get the scales!" Off came the little nightgown, then the undervest.

Then she unpinned the nappy and she drew it away and the baby lay naked on the table.

"But Mabel!" Albert cried. "It's a miracle! She's fat as a puppy!"

Indeed, the amount of flesh the child had put on since the day before was astounding. The small sunken chest with the rib-bones showing all over it was now plump and round as a barrel, and the belly was bulging high in the air. Curiously, though, the arms and legs did not seem to have grown in proportion. Still short and skinny, they looked like little sticks protruding from a ball of fat.

"Look!" Albert said. "She's even beginning to get a bit of fuzz on the tummy to keep her warm!" He put out a hand and was about to run the tips of his fingers over the powdering of silky yellowy-brown hairs that had suddenly appeared on the baby's stomach.

"Don't you touch her!" the woman cried. She turned and faced him, her eyes blazing, and she looked suddenly like some kind of a little fighting bird with her neck arched over toward him as though she were about to fly at his face and peck his eyes out

"Now wait a minute," he said, retreating.

"You must be mad!" she cried.

"Now wait just one minute, Mabel, will you please, because if you're still thinking this stuff is dangerous . . . That *is* what you're thinking, isn't it? All right, then. Listen carefully. I shall now proceed to *prove* to you once and for all, Mabel, that royal jelly is absolutely harmless to human beings, even in enormous doses. For example— why do you think we had only half the usual honey crop last sum mer? Tell me that."

His retreat, walking backwards, had taken him three or four yards away from her, where he seemed to feel more comfortable.

"The reason we had only half the usual crop last summer," he said slowly, lowering his voice, "was because I turned one hundred of my hives over to the production of royal jelly."

"You *what?*"

"Ah," he whispered. "I thought that might surprise you a bit. And I've been making it ever since right under your very nose." His small eyes were glinting at her, and a slow sly smile was creeping around the corners of his mouth.

"You'll never guess the reason, either," he said. "I've been afraid to mention it up to now because I thought it might . . . well . . . sort of embarrass you."

There was a slight pause. He had his hands clasped high in front of him, level with his chest, and he was rubbing one palm against the other, making a soft scraping noise.

"You remember that bit I read you out of the magazine? That bit about the rat? Let me see now, how does it go? 'Still and Burdett found that a male rat which hitherto had been unable to breed . . .' " He hesitated, the grin widening, showing his teeth.

"You get the message, Mabel?"

She stood quite still, facing him.

"The very first time I ever read that sentence, Mabel, I jumped straight out of my chair and I said to myself if it'll work with a lousy rat, I said, then there's no reason on earth why it shouldn't work with Albert Taylor."

He paused again, craning his head forward and turning one ear slightly in his wife's direction, waiting for her to say something. But she didn't.

"And here's another thing," he went on. "It made me feel so absolutely marvellous, Mabel, and so sort of completely different to what I was before that I went right on taking it even after you'd announced the joyful tidings. *Buckets* of it I must have swallowed during the last twelve months."

The big heavy haunted-looking eyes of the woman were moving intently over the man's face and neck. There was no skin showing at all on the neck, not even at the sides below the ears. The whole of it, to a point where it disappeared into the collar of the shirt, was covered all the way around with those shortish silky hairs, yellowly black.

"Mind you," he said, turning away from her, gazing lovingly now at the baby, "it's going to work far better on a tiny infant than on a fully developed man like me. You've only got to look at her to see that, don't you agree?"

The woman's eyes travelled slowly downward and settled on the baby. The baby was lying naked on the table, fat and white and comatose, like some gigantic grub that was approaching the end of its larval life and would soon emerge into the world complete with mandibles and wings.

"Why don't you cover her up, Mabel?" he said. "We don't want our little queen to catch a cold."

Georgy Porgy

1959

WITHOUT in any way wishing to blow my own trumpet, I think that I can claim to being in most respects a moderately well-matured and rounded individual. I have travelled a good deal. I am adequately read. I speak Greek and Latin. I dabble in science. I can tolerate a mildly liberal attitude in the politics of others. I have compiled a volume of notes upon the evolution of the madrigal in the fifteenth century. I have witnessed the death of a large number of persons in their beds; and in addition, I have influenced, at least I hope I have, the lives of quite a few others by the spoken word delivered from the pulpit.

Yet in spite of all this, I must confess that I have never in my life—well, how shall I put it?—I have never really had anything much to do with women.

To be perfectly honest, up until three weeks ago I had never so much as laid a finger on one of them except perhaps to help her over a stile or something like that when the occasion demanded. And even then I always tried to ensure that I touched only the shoulder or the waist or some other place where the skin was covered, because the one thing I never could stand was actual contact between my skin and theirs. Skin touching skin, my skin, that is, touching the skin of a female, whether it were leg, neck, face, hand, or merely finger, was so repugnant to me that I invariably greeted a lady with my hands clasped firmly behind my back to avoid the inevitable handshake.

I could go further than that and say that any sort of physical contact with them, even when the skin wasn't bare, would disturb me considerably. If a woman stood close to me in a queue so that our bodies touched, or if she squeezed in beside me on a bus seat, hip to hip and thigh to thigh, my cheeks would begin burning like mad and little prickles of sweat would start coming out all over the crown of my head.

This condition is all very well in a schoolboy who has just reached the age of puberty. With him it is simply Dame Nature's way of putting on the brakes and holding the lad back until he is old enough to behave himself like a gentleman. I approve of that.

But there was no reason on God's earth why I, at the ripe old age of thirty-one, should continue to suffer a similar embarrassment. I was well trained to resist temptation, and I was certainly not given to vulgar passions.

Had I been even the slightest bit ashamed of my own personal appearance, then that might possibly have explained the whole thing. But I was not. On the contrary, and though I say it myself, the fates had been rather kind to me in that regard. I stood exactly five and a half feet tall in my stockinged feet, and my shoulders, though they sloped downward a little from the neck, were nicely in balance with my small neat frame. (Personally, I've always thought that a little slope on the shoulder lends a subtle and faintly aesthetic air to a man who is not overly tall, don't you agree?) My features were regular, my teeth were in excellent condition (protruding only a smallish amount from the upper jaw), and my hair, which was an unusually brilliant ginger-red, grew thickly all over my scalp. Good heavens above, I had seen men who were perfect shrimps in comparison with me displaying an astonishing aplomb in their dealings with the fairer sex. And oh, how I envied them! How I longed to do likewise—to be able to share in a few of those pleasant little rituals of contact that I observed continually taking place between men and women—the touching of hands, the peck on the cheek, the linking of arms, the pressure of knee against knee or foot against foot under the dining-table, and most of all, the full-blown violent embrace that comes when two of them join together on the floor—for a dance.

But such things were not for me. Alas, I had to spend my time avoiding them instead. And this, my friends, was easier said than done, even for a humble curate in a small country region far from the fleshpots of the metropolis.

My flock, you understand, contained an inordinate number of ladies. There were scores of them in the parish, and the unfortunate thing about it was that at least sixty per cent of them were spinsters, completely untamed by the benevolent influence of holy matrimony.

I tell you I was jumpy as a squirrel.

One would have thought that with all the careful training my mother had given me as a child, I should have been capable of taking this sort of thing well in my stride; and no doubt I would have done if only she had lived long enough to complete my education. But alas, she was killed when I was still quite young.

She was a wonderful woman, my mother. She used to wear huge bracelets on her wrists, five or six of them at a time, with all sorts of things hanging from them and tinkling against each other as she moved. It didn't matter where she was, you could always find her by listening for the noise of those bracelets. It was better than a cowbell. And in the evenings she used to sit on the sofa in her black trousers with her feet tucked up underneath her, smoking endless cigarettes from a long black holder. And I'd be crouching on the floor, watching her.

"You want to taste my martini, George?" she used to ask.

"Now stop it, Clare," my father would say. "If you're not careful you'll stunt the boy's growth."

"Go on," she said. "Don't be frightened of it. Drink it."

I always did everything my mother told me.

"That's enough," my father said. "He only has to know what it tastes like."

"Please don't interfere, Boris. This is *very* important."

My mother had a theory that nothing in the world should be kept secret from a child. Show him everything. Make him *experience* it.

"I'm not going to have any boy of mine going around whispering dirty secrets with other children and having to guess about this thing and that simply because no one will tell him."

Tell him everything. Make him listen.

"Come over here, George, and I'll tell you what there is to know about God."

She never read stories to me at night before I went to bed; she just "told" me things instead. And every evening it was something different.

"Come over here, George, because now I'm going to tell you about Mohammed."

She would be sitting on the sofa in her black trousers with her legs crossed and her feet tucked up underneath her, and she'd beckon to me in a queer languorous manner with the hand that held the long black cigarette-holder, and the bangles would start jingling all the way up her arm.

"If you must have a religion I suppose Mohammedanism is as good as any of them. It's all based on keeping healthy. You have lots of wives, and you mustn't ever smoke or drink."

"Why mustn't you smoke or drink, Mummy?"

"Because if you've got lots of wives you have to keep healthy and virile."

"What is virile?"

"I'll go into that tomorrow, my pet. Let's deal with one subject at a time. Another thing about the Mohammedan is that he never never gets constipated."

"Now, Clare," my father would say, looking up from his book. "Stick to the facts."

"My dear Boris, you don't know anything about it. Now if only *you* would try bending forward and touching the ground with your forehead morning, noon, and night every day, facing Mecca, you might have a bit less trouble in that direction yourself."

I used to love listening to her, even though I could only understand about half of what she was saying. She really was telling me secrets, and there wasn't anything more exciting than that.

"Come over here, George, and I'll tell you precisely how your father makes his money."

"Now, Clare, that's quite enough."

"Nonsense, darling. Why make a *secret* out of it with the child? He'll only imagine something much much worse."

I was exactly ten years old when she started giving me detailed lectures on the subject of sex. This was the biggest secret of them all, and therefore the most enthralling.

"Come over here, George, because now I'm going to tell you how you came into this world, right from the very beginning."

I saw my father glance up quietly, and open his mouth wide the way he did when he was going to say something vital, but my mother was already fixing him with those brilliant shining eyes of hers, and he went slowly back to his book without uttering a sound.

"Your poor father is embarrassed," she said, and she gave me her private smile, the one that she gave to nobody else, only to me —the one-sided smile where just one corner of her mouth lifted slowly upward until it made a lovely long wrinkle that stretched right up to the eye itself, and became a sort of wink-smile instead.

"Embarrassment, my pet, is the one thing that I want you never to feel. And don't think for a moment that your father is embarrassed only because of *you.*"

My father started wriggling about in his chair.

"My God, he's even embarrassed about things like that when he's alone with me, his own wife."

"About things like what?" I asked.

At that point my father got up and quietly left the room.

I think it must have been about a week after this that my mother was killed. It may possibly have been a little later, ten days or a fortnight, I can't be sure. All I know is that we were getting near the end of this particular series of "talks" when it happened; and because I myself was personally involved in the brief chain of events that led up to her death, I can still remember every single detail of that curious night just as clearly as if it were yesterday. I can switch it on in my memory any time I like and run it through in front of my eyes exactly as though it were the reel of a cinema film; and it never varies. It always ends at precisely the same place, no more and no less, and it always begins in the same peculiarly sudden way, with the screen in darkness, and my mother's voice somewhere above me, calling my name:

"George! Wake up, George, wake up!"

And then there is a bright electric light dazzling in my eyes, and right from the very centre of it, but far away, the voice is still calling to me:

"George, wake up and get out of bed and put your dressing-gown on! Quickly! You're coming downstairs. There's something I want you to see. Come on, child, come on! Hurry up! And put your slippers on. We're going outside."

"Outside?"

"Don't argue with me, George. Just do as you're told." I am so sleepy I can hardly see to walk, but my mother takes me firmly by the hand and leads me downstairs and out through the front door into the night where the cold air is like a sponge of water in my face, and I open my eyes wide and see the lawn all sparkling with frost and the cedar tree with its tremendous arms standing black against a thin small moon. And overhead a great mass of stars is wheeling up into the sky.

We hurry across the lawn, my mother and I, her bracelets all jingling like mad and me having to trot to keep up with her. Each step I take I can feel the crisp frosty grass crunching softly underfoot.

"Josephine has just started having her babies," my mother says. "It's a perfect opportunity. You shall watch the whole process."

There is a light burning in the garage when we get there, and we go inside. My father isn't there, nor is the car, and the place seems huge and bare, and the concrete floor is freezing cold through the soles of my bedroom slippers. Josephine is reclining on a heap of straw inside the low wire cage in one corner of the room—a large blue rabbit with small pink eyes that watch us suspiciously as we go toward her. The husband, whose name is Napoleon, is now in a separate cage in the opposite corner, and I notice that he is standing up on his hind legs scratching impatiently at the netting.

"Look!" my mother cries. "She's just having the first one! It's almost out!"

We both creep closer to Josephine, and I squat down beside the cage with my face right up against the wire. I am fascinated. Here is one rabbit coming out of another. It is magical and rather splendid. It is also very quick.

"Look how it comes out all neatly wrapped up in its own little cellophane bag!" my mother is saying.

"And just look how she's taking care of it now! The poor darling doesn't have a face-flannel, and even if she did she couldn't hold it in her paws, so she's washing it with her tongue instead."

The mother rabbit rolls her small pink eyes anxiously in our direction, and then I see her shifting position in the straw so that her body is between us and the young one.

"Come round the other side," my mother says. "The silly thing has moved. I do believe she's trying to hide her baby from us."

We go around the other side of the cage. The rabbit follows us with her eyes. A couple of yards away the buck is prancing madly up and down, clawing at the wire.

"Why is Napoleon so excited?" I ask.

"I don't know, dear. Don't you bother about him. Watch Josephine. I expect she'll be having another one soon. Look how carefully she's washing that little baby! She's treating it just like a human mother treats hers! Isn't it funny to think that I did almost exactly the same sort of thing to you once?"

The big blue doe is still watching us, and now, again, she pushes the baby away with her nose and rolls slowly over to face the other way. Then she goes on with her licking and cleaning.

"Isn't it wonderful how a mother knows instinctively just what she has to do?" my mother says. "Now you just imagine, my pet, that that baby is *you*, and Josephine is *me*—wait a minute, come back over here again so you can get a better look."

We creep back around the cage to keep the baby in view.

"See how she's fondling it and kissing it all over! There! She's *really* kissing it now, isn't she! Exactly like me and you!"

I peer closer. It seems a queer way of kissing to me.

"Look!" I scream. "She's eating it!"

And sure enough, the head of the baby rabbit is now disappearing swiftly into the mother's mouth.

"Mummy! Quick!"

But almost before the sound of my scream has died away, the whole of that tiny pink body has vanished down the mother's throat.

I swing quickly around, and the next thing I know I'm looking straight into my own mother's face, not six inches above me, and no doubt she is trying to say something or it may be that she is too astonished to say anything, but all I see is the mouth, the huge red mouth opening wider and wider and wider until it is just a great big round gaping hole with a black black centre, and I scream again, and this time I can't stop. Then suddenly out come her hands, and I can feel her skin touching mine, the long cold fingers closing tightly over my fists, and I jump back and jerk myself free and rush blindly out into the night. I run down the drive and through the front gates, screaming all the way, and then, above the noise of my own voice I can hear the jingle of bracelets coming up behind me in the dark, getting louder and louder as she keeps gaining on me all the way down the long hill to the bottom of the lane and over the bridge onto the main road where the cars are streaming by at sixty miles an hour with headlights blazing.

Then somewhere behind me I hear a screech of tires skidding on the road surface, and then there is silence, and I notice suddenly that the bracelets aren't jingling behind me any more.

Poor Mother.

If only she could have lived a little longer.

I admit that she gave me a nasty fright with those rabbits, but it wasn't her fault, and anyway queer things like that were always happening between her and me. I had come to regard them as a sort of toughening process that did me more good than harm. But if only she could have lived long enough to complete my education, I'm sure I should never have had all that trouble I was telling you about a few minutes ago.

I want to get on with that now. I didn't mean to begin talking about my mother. She doesn't have anything to do with what I originally started out to say. I won't mention her again.

I was telling you about the spinsters in my parish. It's an ugly word, isn't it—spinster? It conjures up the vision either of a stringy old hen with a puckered mouth or of a huge ribald monster shouting around the house in riding-breeches. But these were not like that at all. They were a clean, healthy, well-built group of females, the majority of them highly bred and surprisingly wealthy, and I feel sure that the average unmarried man would have been gratified to have them around.

In the beginning, when I first came to the vicarage, I didn't have too bad a time. I enjoyed a measure of protection, of course, by reason of my calling and my cloth. In addition, I myself adopted a cool dignified attitude that was calculated to discourage familiarity. For a few months, therefore, I was able to move freely among my parishioners, and no one took the liberty of linking her arm in mine at a charity bazaar, or of touching my fingers with hers as she passed me the cruet at suppertime. I was very happy. I was feeling better than I had in years. Even that little nervous habit I had of flicking my earlobe with my forefinger when I talked began to disappear.

This was what I call my first period, and it extended over approximately six months. Then came trouble.

I suppose I should have known that a healthy male like myself couldn't hope to evade embroilment indefinitely simply by keeping a fair distance between himself and the ladies. It just doesn't work. If anything it has the opposite effect.

I would see them eying me covertly across the room at a whist drive, whispering to one another, nodding, running their tongues over their lips, sucking at their cigarettes, plotting the best approach, but always whispering, and sometimes I overheard snatches of their talk—"What a shy person . . . he's just a trifle nervous, isn't he . . . he's much too tense . . . he needs companionship . . . he wants loosening up . . . we must teach him how to relax." And then slowly, as the weeks went by, they began to stalk me. I knew they were doing it. I could feel it happening although at first they did nothing definite to give themselves away.

That was my second period. It lasted for the best part of a year and was very trying indeed. But it was paradise compared with the third and final phase.

For now, instead of sniping at me sporadically from far away, the attackers suddenly came charging out of the wood with bayonets fixed. It was terrible, frightening. Nothing is more calculated to unnerve a man than the swift unexpected assault. Yet I am not a coward. I will stand my ground against any single individual of my own size under any circumstances. But this onslaught, I am now convinced, was conducted by vast numbers operating as one skilfully co-ordinated unit.

The first offender was Miss Elphinstone, a large woman with moles. I had dropped in on her during the afternoon to solicit a contribution toward a new set of bellows for the organ, and after some pleasant conversation in the library she had graciously handed me a cheque for two guineas. I told her not to bother to see me to the door and I went out into the hall to get my hat. I was about to reach for it when all at once—she must have come tip-toeing up behind me—all at once I felt a bare arm sliding through mine, and one second later her fingers were entwined in my own, and she was squeezing my hand hard, in out, in out, as though it were the bulb of a throat-spray.

"Are you really so Very Reverend as you're always pretending to be?" she whispered.

Well!

All I can tell you is that when that arm of hers came sliding in under mine, it felt exactly as though a cobra was coiling itself around my wrist. I leaped away, pulled open the front door, and fled down the drive without looking back.

The very next day we held a jumble sale in the village hall (again to raise money for the new bellows), and toward the end of it I was standing in a corner quietly drinking a cup of tea and keeping an eye on the villagers crowding round the stalls when all of a sudden I heard a voice beside me saying, "Dear me, what a hungry look you have in those eyes of yours." The next instant a long curvaceous body was leaning up against mine and a hand with red fingernails was trying to push a thick slice of coconut cake into my mouth.

"Miss Prattley," I cried. "Please!"

But she'd got me up against the wall, and with a teacup in one hand and a saucer in the other I was powerless to resist. I felt the sweat breaking out all over me and if my mouth hadn't quickly become full of the cake she was pushing into it, I honestly believe I would have started to scream.

A nasty incident, that one; but there was worse to come.

The next day it was Miss Unwin. Now Miss Unwin happened to be a close friend of Miss Elphinstone's *and* of Miss Prattley's, and this of course should have been enough to make me very cautious. Yet who would have thought that she of all people, Miss Unwin, that quiet gentle little mouse who only a few weeks before had presented me with a new hassock exquisitely worked in needlepoint with her own hands, who would have thought that *she* would ever have taken a liberty with anyone? So when she asked me to accompany her down to the crypt to show her the Saxon murals, it never entered my head that there was devilry afoot. But there was.

I don't propose to describe this encounter; it was too painful. And the ones which followed were no less savage. Nearly every day from then on, some new outrageous incident would take place. I became a nervous wreck. At times I hardly knew what I was doing. I started reading the burial service at young Gladys Pitcher's wedding. I dropped Mrs. Harris's new baby into the font during the christening and gave it a nasty ducking. An uncomfortable rash that I hadn't had in over two years reappeared on the side of my neck, and that annoying business with my earlobe came back worse than ever before. Even my hair began coming out in my comb. The faster I retreated, the faster they came after me. Women are like that. Nothing stimulates them quite so much as a display of modesty or shyness in a man. And they became doubly persistent if underneath it all they happen to detect—and here I have a most difficult confession to make—if they happen to detect, as they did in me, a little secret gleam of longing shining in the backs of the eyes.

You see, actually I was mad about women.

Yes, I know. You will find this hard to believe after all that I have said, but it was perfectly true. You must understand that it was only when they touched me with their fingers or pushed up against me with their bodies that I became alarmed. Providing they remained at a safe distance, I could watch them for hours on end with the same peculiar fascination that you yourself might experience in watching a creature you couldn't bear to touch—an octopus, for example, or a long poisonous snake. I loved the smooth white look of a bare arm emerging from a sleeve, curiously naked like a peeled banana. I could get enormously excited just from watching a girl walk across the room in a tight dress; and I particularly enjoyed the back view of a pair of legs when the feet were in rather high heels —the wonderful braced-up look behind the knees, with the legs themselves very taut as though they were made of strong elastic stretched out almost to breaking-point, but not quite. Sometimes, in Lady Birdwell's drawing-room, sitting near the window on a summer's afternoon, I would glance over the rim of my teacup toward the swimming-pool and become agitated beyond measure by the sight of a little patch of sunburned stomach bulging between the top and bottom of a two-piece bathing-suit.

There is nothing wrong in having thoughts like these. All men harbour them from time to time. But they did give me a terrible sense of guilt. Is it me, I kept asking myself, who is unwittingly responsible for the shameless way in which these ladies are now behaving? Is it the gleam in my eye (which I cannot control) that is constantly rousing their passions and egging them on? Am I unconsciously giving them what is sometimes known as the come-hither signal every time I glance their way? Am I?

Or is this brutal conduct of theirs inherent in the very nature of the female?

I had a pretty fair idea of the answer to this question, but that was not good enough for me. I happen to possess a conscience that can never be consoled by guesswork; it has to have proof. I simply had to find out who was really the guilty party in this case—me or them, and with this object in view, I now decided to perform a simple experiment of my own invention, using Snelling's rats.

A year or so previously I had had some trouble with an objectionable choirboy named Billy Snelling. On three consecutive Sundays this youth had brought a pair of white rats into church and had let them loose on the floor during my sermon. In the end I had confiscated the animals and carried them home and placed them in a box in the shed at the bottom of the vicarage garden. Purely for humane reasons I had then proceeded to feed them, and as a result, but without any further encouragement from me, the creatures began to multiply very rapidly. The two became five, and the five became twelve.

It was at this point that I decided to use them for research purposes. There were exactly equal numbers of males and females, six of each, so that conditions were ideal.

I first isolated the sexes, putting them into two separate cages, and I left them like that for three whole weeks. Now a rat is a very lascivious animal, and any zoologist will tell you that for them this is an inordinately long period of separation. At a guess I would say that one week of enforced celibacy for a rat is equal to approximately one year of the same treatment for someone like Miss Elphinstone or Miss Prattley; so you can see that I was doing a pretty fair job in reproducing actual conditions.

When the three weeks were up, I took a large box that was divided across the centre by a little fence, and I placed the females on one side and the males on the other. The fence consisted of nothing more than three single strands of naked wire, one inch apart, but there was a powerful electric current running through the wires.

To add a touch of reality to the proceedings, I gave each female a name. The largest one, who also had the longest whiskers, was Miss Elphinstone. The one with a short thick tail was Miss Prattley. The smallest of them all was Miss Unwin, and so on. The males, all six of them, were *ME*.

I now pulled up a chair and sat back to watch the result.

All rats are suspicious by nature, and when I first put the two sexes together in the box with only the wire between them, neither side made a move. The males stared hard at the females through the fence. The females stared back, waiting for the males to come forward. I could see that both sides were tense with yearning. Whiskers quivered and noses twitched and occasionally a long tail would flick sharply against the wall of the box.

After a while, the first male detached himself from his group and advanced gingerly toward the fence, his belly close to the ground. He touched a wire and was immediately electrocuted. The remaining eleven rats froze, motionless.

There followed a period of nine and a half minutes during which neither side moved; but I noticed that while all the males were now staring at the dead body of their colleague, the females had eyes only for the males.

Then suddenly Miss Prattley with the short tail could stand it no longer. She came bounding forward, hit the wire, and dropped dead.

The males pressed their bodies closer to the ground and gazed thoughtfully at the two corpses by the fence. The females also seemed to be quite shaken, and there was another wait, with neither side moving.

Now it was Miss Unwin who began to show signs of impatience. She snorted audibly and twitched a pink mobile nose-end from side to side, then suddenly she started jerking her body quickly up and down as though she were doing pushups. She glanced round at her remaining four companions, raised her tail high in the air as much as to say "Here I go, girls," and with that she advanced briskly to the wire, pushed her head through it, and was killed.

Sixteen minutes later, Miss Foster made her first move. Miss Foster was a woman in the village who bred cats, and recently she had had the effrontery to put up a large sign outside her house in the High Street, saying FOSTER'S CATTERY. Through long association with the creatures she herself seemed to have acquired all their most noxious characteristics, and whenever she came near me in a room I could detect, even through the smoke of her Russian cigarette, a faint but pungent aroma of cat. She had never struck me as having much control over her baser instincts, and it was with some satisfaction, therefore, that I watched her now as she foolishly took her own life in a last desperate plunge toward the masculine sex.

A Miss Montgomery-Smith came next, a small determined woman who had once tried to make me believe that she had been engaged to a bishop. She died trying to creep on her belly under the lowest wire, and I must say I thought this a very fair reflection upon the way in which she lived her life.

And still the five remaining males stayed motionless, waiting.

The fifth female to go was Miss Plumley. She was a devious one who was continually slipping little messages addressed to me into the collection bag. Only the Sunday before, I had been in the vestry counting the money after morning service and had come across one of them tucked inside a folded ten-shilling note. *Your poor throat sounded hoarse today during the sermon,* it said. *Let me bring you a bottle of my own cherry pectoral to soothe it down. Most affectionately, Eunice Plumley.*

Miss Plumley ambled slowly up to the wire, sniffed the centre strand with the tip of her nose, came a fraction too close, and received two hundred and forty volts of alternating current through her body.

The five males stayed where they were, watching the slaughter.

And now only Miss Elphinstone remained on the feminine side.

For a full half-hour neither she nor any of the others made a move. Finally one of the males stirred himself slightly, took a step forward, hesitated, thought better of it, and slowly sank back into a crouch on the floor.

This must have frustrated Miss Elphinstone beyond measure, for suddenly, with eyes blazing, she rushed forward and took a flying leap at the wire. It was a spectacular jump and she nearly cleared it; but one of her hind legs grazed the top strand, and thus she also perished with the rest of her sex.

I cannot tell you how much good it did me to watch this simple and, though I say it myself, this rather ingenious experiment. In one stroke I had laid open the incredibly lascivious, stop-at-nothing nature of the female. My own sex was vindicated; my own conscience was cleared. In a trice, all those awkward little flashes of guilt from which I had continually been suffering flew out the window. I felt suddenly very strong and serene in the knowledge of my own innocence.

For a few moments I toyed with the absurd idea of electrifying the black iron railings that ran around the vicarage garden; or perhaps just the gate would be enough. Then I would sit back comfortably in a chair in the library and watch through the window as the real Misses Elphinstone and Prattley and Unwin came forward one after the other and paid the final penalty for pestering an innocent male.

Such foolish thoughts!

What I must actually do now, I told myself, was to weave around me a sort of invisible electric fence constructed entirely out of my own personal moral fibre. Behind this I would sit in perfect safety while the enemy, one after another, flung themselves against the wire.

I would begin by cultivating a brusque manner. I would speak crisply to all women, and refrain from smiling at them. I would no longer step back a pace when one of them advanced upon me. I would stand my ground and glare at her, and if she said something that I considered suggestive, I would make a sharp retort.

It was in this mood that I set off the very next day to attend Lady Birdwell's tennis party.

I was not a player myself, but her ladyship had graciously invited me to drop in and mingle with the guests when play was over at six o'clock. I believe she thought that it lent a certain tone to a gathering to have a clergyman present, and she was probably hoping to persuade me to repeat the performance I gave the last time I was there, when I sat at the piano for a full hour and a quarter after supper and entertained the guests with a detailed description of the evolution of the madrigal through the centuries.

I arrived at the gates on my cycle promptly at six o'clock and pedalled up the long drive toward the house. This was the first week of June, and the rhododendrons were massed in great banks of pink and purple all the way along on either side. I was feeling unusually blithe and dauntless. The previous day's experiment with the rats had made it impossible now for anyone to take me by surprise. I knew exactly what to expect and I was armed accordingly. All around me the little fence was up.

"Ah, good evening, Vicar," Lady Birdwell cried, advancing upon me with both arms outstretched.

I stood my ground and looked her straight in the eye. "How's Birdwell?" I said. "Still up in the city?"

I doubt whether she had ever before in her life heard Lord Birdwell referred to thus by someone who had never even met him.

It stopped her dead in her tracks. She looked at me queerly and didn't seem to know how to answer.

"I'll take a seat if I may," I said, and walked past her toward the terrace where a group of nine or ten guests were settled comfortably in cane chairs, sipping their drinks. They were mostly women, the usual crowd, all of them dressed in white tennis clothes, and as I strode in among them, my own sober black suiting seemed to give me, I thought, just the right amount of separateness for the occasion.

The ladies greeted me with smiles. I nodded to them and sat down in a vacant chair, but I didn't smile back.

"I think perhaps I'd better finish my story another time," Miss Elphinstone was saying. "I don't believe the vicar would approve." She giggled and gave me an arch look. I knew she was waiting for me to come out with my usual little nervous laugh and to say my usual little sentence about how broad-minded I was; but I did nothing of the sort. I simply raised one side of my upper lip until it shaped itself into a tiny curl of contempt (I had practised in the mirror that morning), and then I said sharply, in a loud voice, *"Mens sano in corpore sana."*

"What's that?" she cried. "Come again, Vicar."

"A clean mind in a healthy body," I answered "It's a family motto."

There was an odd kind of silence for quite a long time after this. I could see the women exchanging glances with one another, frowning, shaking their heads.

"The vicar's in the dumps," Miss Foster announced. She was the one who bred cats. "I think the vicar needs a drink."

"Thank you," I said, "but I never imbibe. You know that."

"Then do let me fetch you a nice cooling glass of fruit cup?"

This last sentence came softly and rather suddenly from someone just behind me, to my right, and there was a note of such genuine concern in the speaker's voice that I turned around

I saw a lady of singular beauty whom I had met only once before, about a month ago. Her name was Miss Roach, and I remembered that she had struck me then as being a person far out of the usual run. I had been particularly impressed by her gentle and reticent nature; and the fact that I had felt comfortable in her presence proved beyond doubt that she was not the sort of person who would try to impinge herself upon me in any way.

"I'm sure you must be tired after cycling all that distance," she was saying now

I swivelled right round in my chair and looked at her carefully. She was certainly a striking person—unusually muscular for a woman, with broad shoulders and powerful arms and a huge calf bulging on each leg. The flush of the afternoon's exertions was still upon her, and her face glowed with a healthy red sheen.

"Thank you so much, Miss Roach," I said, "but I never touch alcohol in any form. Maybe a small glass of lemon squash . . ."

"The fruit cup is only made of fruit, Padre."

How I loved a person who called me "Padre." The word has a military ring about it that conjures up visions of stern discipline and officer rank.

"Fruit cup?" Miss Elphinstone said. "It's harmless."

"My dear man, it's nothing but vitamin C," Miss Foster said.

"Much better for you than fizzy lemonade," Lady Birdwell said. "Carbon dioxide attacks the lining of the stomach."

"I'll get you some," Miss Roach said, smiling at me pleasantly. It was a good open smile, and there wasn't a trace of guile or mischief from one corner of the mouth to the other.

She stood up and walked over to the drink table. I saw her slicing an orange, then an apple, then a cucumber, then a grape, and dropping the pieces into a glass. Then she poured in a large quantity of liquid from a bottle whose label I couldn't quite read without my spectacles, but I fancied that I saw the name JIM on it, or TIM, or PIM, or some such word.

"I hope there's enough left," Lady Birdwell called out. "Those greedy children of mine do love it so."

"Plenty," Miss Roach answered, and she brought the drink to me and set it on the table.

Even without tasting it I could easily understand why children adored it. The liquid itself was dark amber-red and there were great hunks of fruit floating around among the ice cubes; and on top of it all, Miss Roach had placed a sprig of mint. I guessed that the mint had been put there specially for me, to take some of the sweetness away and to lend a touch of grown-upness to a concoction that was otherwise so obviously for youngsters.

"Too sticky for you, Padre?"

"It's delectable," I said, sipping it. "Quite perfect."

It seemed a pity to gulp it down quickly after all the trouble Miss Roach had taken to make it, but it was so refreshing I couldn't resist.

"Do let me make you another?"

I liked the way she waited until I had set the glass on the table, instead of trying to take it out of my hand

"I wouldn't eat the mint if I were you," Miss Elphinstone said.

"I'd better get another bottle from the house," Lady Birdwell called out. "You're going to need it, Mildred."

"Do that," Miss Roach replied. "I drink gallons of the stuff myself," she went on, speaking to me. "And I don't think you'd say that I'm exactly what you might call emaciated."

"No indeed," I answered fervently. I was watching her again as she mixed me another brew, noticing how the muscles rippled under the skin of the arm that raised the bottle. Her neck also was uncommonly fine when seen from behind; not thin and stringy like the necks of a lot of these so-called modern beauties, but thick and strong with a slight ridge running down either side where the sinews bulged. It wasn't easy to guess the age of a person like this, but I doubted whether she could have been more than forty-eight or -nine.

I had just finished my second big glass of fruit cup when I began to experience a most peculiar sensation. I seemed to be floating up out of my chair, and hundreds of little warm waves came washing in under me, lifting me higher and higher. I felt as buoyant as a bubble, and everything around me seemed to be bobbing up and down and swirling gently from side to side. It was all very pleasant, and I was overcome by an almost irresistible desire to break into song.

"Feeling happy?" Miss Roach's voice sounded miles and miles away, and when I turned to look at her, I was astonished to see how near to me she really was. She, also, was bobbing up and down.

"Terrific," I answered. "I'm feeling absolutely terrific."

Her face was large and pink, and it was so close to me now that I could see the pale carpet of fuzz covering both her cheeks, and the way the sunlight caught each tiny separate hair and made it shine like gold. All of a sudden I found myself wanting to put out a hand and stroke those cheeks of hers with my fingers. To tell the truth, I wouldn't have objected in the least if she had tried to do the same to me.

"Listen," she said softly. "How about the two of us taking a little stroll down the garden to see the lupins?"

"Fine," I answered. "Lovely. Anything you say."

There is a small Georgian summer-house alongside the croquet lawn in Lady Birdwell's garden, and the very next thing I knew, I was sitting inside it on a kind of chaise longue and Miss Roach was beside me. I was still bobbing up and down, and so was she, and so, for that matter, was the summer-house, but I was feeling wonderful. I asked Miss Roach if she would like me to give her a song.

"Not now," she said, encircling me with her arms and squeezing my chest against hers so hard that it hurt.

"Don't," I said, melting.

"That's better," she kept saying. "That's much better, isn't it?"

Had Miss Roach or any other female tried to do this sort of thing to me an hour before, I don't quite know what would have happened. I think I would probably have fainted. I might even have died. But here I was now, the same old me, actually relishing the contact of those enormous bare arms against my body! Also—and this was the most amazing thing of all—I was beginning to feel the urge to reciprocate.

I took the lobe of her left ear between my thumb and forefinger, and tugged it playfully.

"Naughty boy," she said.

I tugged harder and squeezed it a bit at the same time. This roused her to such a pitch that she began to grunt and snort like a hog. Her breathing became loud and stertorous

"Kiss me," she ordered

"What?" I said.

"Come on, kiss me."

At that moment, I saw her mouth. I saw this great mouth of hers coming slowly down on top of me, starting to open, and coming closer and closer, and opening wider and wider; and suddenly my whole stomach began to roll right over inside me and I went stiff with terror

"No!" I shrieked. "Don't!"

I can only tell you that I had never in all my life seen anything more terrifying than that mouth. I simply could not *stand* it coming at me like that. Had it been a red-hot iron someone was pushing into my face I wouldn't have been nearly so petrified, I swear I wouldn't. The strong arms were around me, pinning me down so that I couldn't move, and the mouth kept getting larger and larger, and then all at once it was right on top of me, huge and wet and cavernous, and the next second—I was inside it.

I was right inside this enormous mouth, lying on my stomach along the length of the tongue, with my feet somewhere around the back of the throat; and I knew instinctively that unless I got myself out again at once I was going to be swallowed alive—just like that baby rabbit. I could feel my legs being drawn down the throat by some kind of suction, and quickly I threw up my arms and grabbed hold of the lower front teeth and held on for dear life. My head was near the mouth-entrance, and I could actually look right out between

the lips and see a little patch of the world outside—sunlight shining
on the polished wooden floor of the summer-house, and on the floor
itself a gigantic foot in a white tennis shoe.

I had a good grip with my fingers on the edge of the teeth, and
in spite of the suction, I was managing to haul myself up slowly
toward the daylight when suddenly the upper teeth came down on
my knuckles and started chopping away at them so fiercely I had to
let go. I went sliding back down the throat, feet first, clutching madly
at this and that as I went, but everything was so smooth and slippery
I couldn't get a grip. I glimpsed a bright flash of gold on the left as
I slid past the last of the molars, and then three inches farther on I
saw what must have been the uvula above me, dangling like a thick
red stalactite from the roof of the throat. I grabbed at it with both
hands but the thing slithered through my fingers and I went on
down.

I remember screaming for help, but I could barely hear the
sound of my own voice above the noise of the wind that was caused
by the throat-owner's breathing. There seemed to be a gale blowing
all the time, a queer erratic gale that blew alternately very cold (as
the air came in) and very hot (as it went out again).

I managed to get my elbows hooked over a sharp fleshy ridge
—I presume the epiglottis—and for a brief moment I hung there,
defying the suction and scrabbling with my feet to find a foothold
on the wall of the larynx; but the throat gave a huge heaving swallow
that jerked me away, and down I went again.

From then on, there was nothing else for me to catch hold of,
and down and down I went until soon my legs were dangling below
me in the upper reaches of the stomach, and I could feel the slow
powerful pulsing of peristalsis dragging away at my ankles, pulling
me down and down and down. . . .

Far above me, outside in the open air, I could hear the distant
babble of women's voices:

"It's not true. . . ."

"But my dear Mildred, how awful.   "

"The man must be mad. . . ."

"Your poor mouth, just look at it. . . ."

"A sex maniac . . ."

"A sadist . . ."

"Someone ought to write to the bishop. . . ."

And then Miss Roach's voice, louder than the others, swearing
and screeching like a parakeet:

"He's damn lucky I didn't kill him, the little bastard! . . . I said to him, listen, I said, if ever I happen to want any of my teeth extracted, I'll go to a dentist, not to a goddam vicar. . . . It isn't as though I'd given him any encouragement either! . . ."

"Where is he now, Mildred?"

"God knows. In the bloody summer-house, I suppose."

"Hey girls, let's go and root him out!"

Oh dear, oh dear. Looking back on it all now, some three weeks later, I don't know how I ever came through the nightmare of that awful afternoon without taking leave of my senses.

A gang of witches like that is a very dangerous thing to fool around with, and had they managed to catch me in the summer-house right then and there when their blood was up, they would likely as not have torn me limb from limb on the spot.

Either that, or I should have been frog-marched down to the police station with Lady Birdwell and Miss Roach leading the procession through the main street of the village.

But of course they didn't catch me.

They didn't catch me then, and they haven't caught me yet, and if my luck continues to hold, I think I've got a fair chance of evading them altogether—or anyway for a few months, until they forget about the whole affair.

As you might guess, I am having to keep entirely to myself and to take no part in public affairs or social life. I find that writing is a most salutary occupation at a time like this, and I spend many hours each day playing with sentences. I regard each sentence as a little wheel, and my ambition lately has been to gather several hundred of them together at once and to fit them all end to end, with the cogs interlocking, like gears, but each wheel a different size, each turning at a different speed. Now and again I try to put a really big one right next to a very small one in such a way that the big one, turning slowly, will make the small one spin so fast that it hums. Very tricky, that.

I also sing madrigals in the evenings, but I miss my own harpsichord terribly.

All the same, this isn't such a bad place, and I have made myself as comfortable as I possibly can. It is a small chamber situated in what is almost certainly the primary section of the duodenal loop, just before it begins to run vertically downward in front of the right kidney. The floor is quite level—indeed it was the first level place I came to during that horrible descent down Miss Roach's throat—and that's the only reason I managed to stop at all. Above me, I can see a pulpy sort of opening that I take to be the pylorus, where the stomach enters the small intestine (I can still remember some of those diagrams my mother used to show me), and below me, there is a funny little hole in the wall where the pancreatic duct enters the lower section of the duodenum.

It is all a trifle bizarre for a man of conservative tastes like myself. Personally I prefer oak furniture and parquet flooring. But there is anyway one thing here that pleases me greatly, and that is the walls. They are lovely and soft, like a sort of padding, and the advantage of this is that I can bounce up against them as much as I wish without hurting myself.

There are several other people about, which is rather surprising, but thank God they are every one of them males. For some reason or other, they all wear white coats, and they bustle around pretending to be very busy and important. In actual fact, they are an uncommonly ignorant bunch of fellows. They don't even seem to realize where they *are*. I try to tell them, but they refuse to listen. Sometimes I get so angry and frustrated with them that I lose my temper and start to shout; and then a sly mistrustful look comes over their faces and they begin backing slowly away, and saying, "Now then. Take it easy. Take it easy, Vicar, there's a good boy. Take it easy."

What sort of talk is that?

But there is one oldish man—he comes in to see me every morning after breakfast—who appears to live slightly closer to reality than the others. He is civil and dignified, and I imagine he is lonely because he likes nothing better than to sit quietly in my room and listen to me talk. The only trouble is that whenever we get onto the subject of our whereabouts, he starts telling me that he's going to help me to escape. He said it again this morning, and we had quite an argument about it.

"But can't you see," I said patiently, "I don't *want* to escape."

"My dear Vicar, why ever not?"

"I keep telling you—because they're all searching for me outside."

"Who?"

"Miss Elphinstone and Miss Roach and Miss Prattley and all the rest of them."

"What nonsense."

"Oh yes they are! And I imagine they're after *you* as well, but you won't admit it."

"No, my friend, they are not after me."

"Then may I ask precisely what you are doing down here?"

A bit of a stumper for him, that one. I could see he didn't know how to answer it.

"I'll bet you were fooling around with Miss Roach and got yourself swallowed up just the same as I did. I'll bet that's exactly what happened, only you're ashamed to admit it."

He looked suddenly so wan and defeated when I said this that I felt sorry for him.

"Would you like me to sing you a song?" I asked.

But he got up without answering and went quietly out into the corridor.

"Cheer up," I called after him. "Don't be depressed. There is always some balm in Gilead."

Genesis and Catastrophe

1959

A True Story

"Everything is normal," the doctor was saying. "Just lie back and relax." His voice was miles away in the distance and he seemed to be shouting at her. "You have a son."

"What?"

"You have a fine son. You understand that, don't you? A fine son. Did you hear him crying?"

"Is he all right, Doctor?"

"Of course he is all right."

"Please let me see him."

"You'll see him in a moment."

"You are certain he is all right?"

"I am quite certain."

"Is he still crying?"

"Try to rest. There is nothing to worry about."

"Why has he stopped crying, Doctor? What happened?"

"Don't excite yourself, please. Everything is normal."

"I want to see him. Please let me see him."

"Dear lady," the doctor said, patting her hand. "You have a fine strong healthy child. Don't you believe me when I tell you that?"

"What is the woman over there doing to him?"

"Your baby is being made to look pretty for you," the doctor said. "We are giving him a little wash, that is all. You must spare us a moment or two for that."

"You swear he is all right?"

"I swear it. Now lie back and relax. Close your eyes. Go on, close your eyes. That's right. That's better. Good girl . . ."

"I have prayed and prayed that he will live, Doctor."

"Of course he will live. What are you talking about?"

"The others didn't."

"What?"

"None of my other ones lived, Doctor."

The doctor stood beside the bed looking down at the pale exhausted face of the young woman. He had never seen her before today. She and her husband were new people in the town. The innkeeper's wife, who had come up to assist in the delivery, had told him that the husband worked at the local customs-house on the border and that the two of them had arrived quite suddenly at the inn with one trunk and one suitcase about three months ago. The husband was a drunkard, the innkeeper's wife had said, an arrogant, overbearing, bullying little drunkard, but the young woman was gentle and religious. And she was very sad. She never smiled. In the few weeks that she had been here, the innkeeper's wife had never once seen her smile. Also there was a rumour that this was the husband's third marriage, that one wife had died and that the other had divorced him for unsavoury reasons. But that was only a rumour.

The doctor bent down and pulled the sheet up a little higher over the patient's chest. "You have nothing to worry about," he said gently. "This is a perfectly normal baby."

"That's exactly what they told me about the others. But I lost them all, Doctor. In the last eighteen months I have lost all three of my children, so you mustn't blame me for being anxious."

"Three?"

"This is my fourth . . . in four years."

The doctor shifted his feet uneasily on the bare floor.

"I don't think you know what it means, Doctor, to lose them all, all three of them, slowly, separately, one by one. I keep seeing them. I can see Gustav's face now as clearly as if he were lying here beside me in the bed. Gustav was a lovely boy, Doctor. But he was always ill. It is terrible when they are always ill and there is nothing you can do to help them."

"I know."

The woman opened her eyes, stared up at the doctor for a few seconds, then closed them again.

"My little girl was called Ida. She died a few days before Christmas. That is only four months ago. I just wish you could have seen Ida, Doctor."

"You have a new one now."

"But Ida was so beautiful."

"Yes," the doctor said. "I know."

"How can you know?" she cried.

"I am sure that she was a lovely child. But this new one is also like that." The doctor turned away from the bed and walked over to the window and stood there looking out. It was a wet grey April afternoon, and across the street he could see the red roofs of the houses and the huge raindrops splashing on the tiles.

"Ida was two years old, Doctor . . . and she was so beautiful I was never able to take my eyes off her from the time I dressed her in the morning until she was safe in bed again at night. I used to live in holy terror of something happening to that child. Gustav had gone and my little Otto had also gone and she was all I had left. Sometimes I used to get up in the night and creep over to the cradle and put my ear close to her mouth just to make sure that she was breathing."

"Try to rest," the doctor said, going back to the bed. "Please try to rest." The woman's face was white and bloodless, and there was a slight bluish-grey tinge around the nostrils and the mouth. A few strands of damp hair hung down over her forehead, sticking to the skin.

"When she died . I was already pregnant again when that happened, Doctor. This new one was a good four months on its way when Ida died. 'I don't want it!' I shouted after the funeral. 'I won't have it! I have buried enough children!' And my husband . he was strolling among the guests with a big glass of beer in his hand . . he turned around quickly and said, 'I have news for you, Klara, I have good news.' Can you imagine that, Doctor? We have just buried our third child and he stands there with a glass of beer in his hand and tells me that he has good news. 'Today I have been posted to Braunau,' he says, 'so you can start packing at once. This will be a new start for you, Klara,' he says. 'It will be a new place and you can have a new doctor. . . .' "

"Please don't talk any more."

"You *are* the new doctor, aren't you, Doctor?"

"That's right."

"And here we are in Braunau."

"Yes."

"I am frightened, Doctor."

"Try not to be frightened."

"What chance can the fourth one have now?"

"You must stop thinking like that."

"I can't help it. I am certain there is something inherited that causes my children to die in this way. There must be."

"That is nonsense "

"Do you know what my husband said to me when Otto was born, Doctor? He came into the room and he looked into the cradle where Otto was lying and he said, 'Why do *all* my children have to be so small and weak?' "

"I am sure he didn't say that."

"He put his head right into Otto's cradle as though he were examining a tiny insect and he said, 'All I am saying is why can't they be better *specimens?* That's all I am saying.' And three days after that, Otto was dead. We baptized him quickly on the third day and he died the same evening. And then Gustav died. And then Ida died. All of them died, Doctor . . . and suddenly the whole house was empty. . . ."

"Don't think about it now."

"Is this one so very small?"

"He is a normal child."

"But small?"

"He is a little small, perhaps. But the small ones are often a lot tougher than the big ones. Just imagine, Frau Hitler, this time next year he will be almost learning how to walk. Isn't that a lovely thought?"

She didn't answer this.

"And two years from now he will probably be talking his head off and driving you crazy with his chatter. Have you settled on a name for him yet?"

"A name?"

"Yes."

"I don't know. I'm not sure. I think my husband said that if it was a boy we were going to call him Adolfus."

"That means he would be called Adolf."

"Yes. My husband likes Adolf because it has a certain similarity to Alois. My husband is called Alois."

"Excellent."

"Oh no!" she cried, starting up suddenly from the pillow. "That's the same question they asked me when Otto was born! It means he is going to die! You are going to baptize him at once!"

"Now, now," the doctor said, taking her gently by the shoulders. "You are quite wrong. I promise you you are wrong. I was simply being an inquisitive old man, that is all. I love talking about names. I think Adolfus is a particularly fine name. It is one of my favourites. And look—here he comes now."

The innkeeper's wife, carrying the baby high up on her enormous bosom, came sailing across the room towards the bed "Here is the little beauty!" she cried, beaming. "Would you like to hold him, my dear? Shall I put him beside you?"

"Is he well wrapped?" the doctor asked. "It is extremely cold in here."

"Certainly he is well wrapped."

The baby was tightly swaddled in a white woollen shawl, and only the tiny pink head protruded. The innkeeper's wife placed him gently on the bed beside the mother. "There you are," she said. "Now you can lie there and look at him to your heart's content."

"I think you will like him," the doctor said, smiling. "He is a fine little baby."

"He has the most lovely hands!" the innkeeper's wife exclaimed. "Such long delicate fingers!"

The mother didn't move. She didn't even turn her head to look.

"Go on!" cried the innkeeper's wife. "He won't bite you!"

"I am frightened to look. I don't dare to believe that I have another baby and that he is all right."

"Don't be so stupid "

Slowly, the mother turned her head and looked at the small, incredibly serene face that lay on the pillow beside her

"Is this my baby?"

"Of course "

"Oh . . . oh .   but he is beautiful.'

The doctor turned away and went over to the table and began putting his things into his bag. The mother lay on the bed gazing at the child and smiling and touching him and making little noises of pleasure. "Hello, Adolfus," she whispered. "Hello, my little Adolf . . ."

"Ssshh!" said the innkeeper's wife. "Listen! I think your husband is coming."

The doctor walked over to the door and opened it and looked out into the corridor

"Herr Hitler?"

"Yes "

"Come in, please."

A small man in a dark-green uniform stepped softly into the room and looked around him.

"Congratulations," the doctor said. "You have a son."

The man had a pair of enormous whiskers meticulously groomed after the manner of the Emperor Franz Josef, and he smelled strongly of beer. "A son?"

"Yes "

"How is he?"

"He is fine. So is your wife."

"Good." The father turned and walked with a curious little prancing stride over to the bed where his wife was lying. "Well, Klara," he said, smiling through his whiskers. "How did it go?" He bent down to take a look at the baby. Then he bent lower. In a series of quick jerky movements, he bent lower and lower until his face was only about twelve inches from the baby's head. The wife lay sideways on the pillow, staring up at him with a kind of supplicating look.

"He has the most marvellous pair of lungs," the innkeeper's wife announced. "You should have heard him screaming just after he came into this world."

"But my God, Klara . . ."

"What is it, dear?"

"This one is even smaller than Otto was!"

The doctor took a couple of quick paces forward. "There is nothing wrong with that child," he said.

Slowly, the husband straightened up and turned away from the bed and looked at the doctor. He seemed bewildered and stricken. "It's no good lying, Doctor," he said. "I know what it means. It's going to be the same all over again."

"Now you listen to me," the doctor said.

"But do you *know* what happened to the others, Doctor?"

"You must forget about the others, Herr Hitler. Give this one a chance."

"But so small and weak!"

"My dear sir, he has only just been born."

"Even so . . ."

"What are you trying to do?" cried the innkeeper's wife. "Talk him into his grave?"

"That's enough!" the doctor said sharply.

The mother was weeping now. Great sobs were shaking her body.

The doctor walked over to the husband and put a hand on his shoulder. "Be good to her," he whispered. "Please. It is very important." Then he squeezed the husband's shoulder hard and began pushing him forward surreptitiously to the edge of the bed. The husband hesitated. The doctor squeezed harder, signalling to him urgently through fingers and thumb. At last, reluctantly, the husband bent down and kissed his wife lightly on the cheek.

"All right, Klara," he said. "Now stop crying."

"I have prayed so hard that he will live, Alois."

"Yes."

"Every day for months I have gone to the church and begged on my knees that this one will be allowed to live."

"Yes, Klara, I know."

"Three dead children is all that I can stand, don't you realize that?"

"Of course."

"He *must* live, Alois. He *must*, he *must* ... Oh God, be merciful unto him now. . . ."

Pig

1959

One

Once upon a time, in the City of New York, a beautiful baby boy was born into this world, and the joyful parents named him Lexington.

No sooner had the mother returned home from the hospital carrying Lexington in her arms than she said to her husband, "Darling, now you must take me out to a most marvellous restaurant for dinner so that we can celebrate the arrival of our son and heir."

Her husband embraced her tenderly and told her that any woman who could produce such a beautiful child as Lexington deserved to go absolutely any place she wanted. But was she strong enough yet, he enquired, to start running around the city late at night?

No, she said, she wasn't. But what the hell.

So that evening they both dressed themselves up in fancy clothes, and leaving little Lexington in care of a trained infant's nurse who was costing them twenty dollars a day and was Scottish into the bargain, they went out to the finest and most expensive restaurant in town. There they each ate a giant lobster and drank a bottle of champagne between them, and after that, they went on to a nightclub, where they drank another bottle of champagne and then sat holding hands for several hours while they recalled and discussed and admired each individual physical feature of their lovely newborn son.

They arrived back at their house on the East Side of Manhattan at around two o'clock in the morning and the husband paid off the taxi-driver and then began feeling in his pockets for the key to the front door. After a while, he announced that he must have left it in the pocket of his other suit, and he suggested they ring the bell and get the nurse to come down and let them in. An infant's nurse at twenty dollars a day must expect to be hauled out of bed occasionally in the night, the husband said.

So he rang the bell. They waited. Nothing happened. He rang it again, long and loud. They waited another minute. Then they both stepped back onto the street and shouted the nurse's name (McPottle) up at the nursery windows on the third floor, but there was still no response. The house was dark and silent. The wife began to grow apprehensive. Her baby was imprisoned in this place, she told herself. Alone with McPottle. And who was McPottle? They had known her for two days, that was all, and she had a thin mouth, a small disapproving eye, and a starchy bosom, and quite clearly she was in the habit of sleeping much too soundly for safety. If she couldn't hear the front-door bell, then how on earth did she expect to hear a baby crying? Why, this very second the poor thing might be swallowing its tongue or suffocating on its pillow.

"He doesn't use a pillow," the husband said. "You are not to worry. But I'll get you in if that's what you want." He was feeling rather superb after all the champagne, and now he bent down and undid the laces of one of his black patent-leather shoes, and took it off. Then, holding it by the toe, he flung it hard and straight right through the dining-room window on the ground floor.

"There you are," he said, grinning. "We'll deduct it from McPottle's wages."

He stepped forward and very carefully put a hand through the hole in the glass and released the catch. Then he raised the window.

"I shall lift you in first, little mother," he said, and he took his wife around the waist and lifted her off the ground. This brought her big red mouth up level with his own, and very close, so he started kissing her. He knew from experience that women like very much to be kissed in this position, with their bodies held tight and their legs dangling in the air, so he went on doing it for quite a long time, and she wiggled her feet, and made loud gulping noises down in her throat. Finally, the husband turned her round and began easing her gently through the open window into the dining-room. At this point, a police patrol car came nosing silently along the street toward them. It stopped about thirty yards away, and three cops of Irish extraction leaped out of the car and started running in the direction of the husband and wife, brandishing revolvers.

"Stick 'em up!" the cops shouted. "Stick 'em up!" But it was impossible for the husband to obey this order without letting go of his wife, and had he done this she would either have fallen to the ground or would have been left dangling half in and half out of the house, which is a terribly uncomfortable position for a woman; so he continued gallantly to push her upward and inward through the window. The cops, all of whom had received medals before for killing robbers, opened fire immediately, and although they were still running, and although the wife in particular was presenting them with a very small target indeed, they succeeded in scoring several direct hits on each body—sufficient anyway to prove fatal in both cases.

Thus, when he was no more than twelve days old, little Lexington became an orphan.

Two

The news of this killing, for which the three policemen subsequently received citations, was eagerly conveyed to all relatives of the deceased couple by newspaper reporters, and the next morning, the closest of these relatives, as well as a couple of undertakers, three lawyers, and a priest, climbed into taxis and set out for the house with the broken window. They assembled in the living-room, men and women both, and they sat around in a circle on the sofas and armchairs, smoking cigarettes and sipping sherry and debating what on earth should be done now with the baby upstairs, the orphan Lexington.

It soon became apparent that none of the relatives was particularly keen to assume responsibility for the child, and the discussions and arguments continued all through the day. Everybody declared an enormous, almost an irresistible desire to look after him, and would have done so with the greatest of pleasure were it not for the fact that their apartment was too small, or that they already had one baby and couldn't possibly afford another, or that they wouldn't know what to do with the poor little thing when they went abroad in the summer, or that they were getting on in years, which surely would be most unfair to the boy when he grew up, and so on and so forth. They all knew, of course, that the father had been heavily in debt for a long time and that the house was mortgaged and that consequently there would be no money at all to go with the child.

They were still arguing like mad at six in the evening when suddenly, in the middle of it all, an old aunt of the deceased father (her name was Glosspan) swept in from Virginia, and without even removing her hat and coat, not even pausing to sit down, ignoring all offers of a martini, a whisky, a sherry, she announced firmly to the assembled relatives that she herself intended to take sole charge of the infant boy from then on. What was more, she said, she would assume full financial responsibility on all counts, including education, and everyone else could go on back home where they belonged and give their consciences a rest. So saying, she trotted upstairs to the nursery and snatched Lexington from his cradle and swept out of the house with the baby clutched tightly in her arms, while the relatives simply sat and stared and smiled and looked relieved, and McPottle the nurse stood stiff with disapproval at the head of the stairs, her lips compressed, her arms folded across her starchy bosom.

And thus it was that the infant Lexington, when he was thirteen days old, left the City of New York and travelled southward to live with his Great Aunt Glosspan in the State of Virginia.

Three

Aunt Glosspan was nearly seventy when she became guardian to Lexington, but to look at her you would never have guessed it for one minute. She was as sprightly as a woman half her age, with a small, wrinkled, but still quite beautiful face and two lovely brown eyes that sparkled at you in the nicest way. She was also a spinster, though you would never have guessed that either, for there was nothing spinsterish about Aunt Glosspan. She was never bitter or gloomy or irritable; she didn't have a moustache; and she wasn't in the least bit jealous of other people, which in itself is something you can seldom say about either a spinster or a virgin lady, although of course it is not known for certain whether Aunt Glosspan qualified on both counts.

But she was an eccentric old woman, there was no doubt about that. For the past thirty years she had lived a strange isolated life all by herself in a tiny cottage high up on the slopes of the Blue Ridge Mountains, several miles from the nearest village. She had five acres of pasture, a plot for growing vegetables, a flower garden, three cows, a dozen hens, and a fine cockerel.

And now she had little Lexington as well.

She was a strict vegetarian and regarded the consumption of animal flesh as not only unhealthy and disgusting, but horribly cruel. She lived upon lovely clean foods like milk, butter, eggs, cheese, vegetables, nuts, herbs, and fruit, and she rejoiced in the conviction that no living creature would be slaughtered on her account, not even a shrimp. Once, when a brown hen of hers passed away in the prime of life from being eggbound, Aunt Glosspan was so distressed that she nearly gave up egg-eating altogether.

She knew not the first thing about babies, but that didn't worry her in the least. At the railway station in New York, while waiting for the train that would take her and Lexington back to Virginia, she bought six feeding-bottles, two dozen diapers, a box of safety pins, a carton of milk for the journey, and a small paper-covered book called *The Care of Infants.* What more could anyone want? And when the train got going, she fed the baby some milk, changed its nappies after a fashion, and laid it down on the seat to sleep. Then she read *The Care of Infants* from cover to cover.

"There is no problem here," she said, throwing the book out the window. "No problem at all."

And curiously enough there wasn't. Back home in the cottage everything went just as smoothly as could be. Little Lexington drank his milk and belched and yelled and slept exactly as a good baby should, and Aunt Glosspan glowed with joy whenever she looked at him, and showered him with kisses all day long.

Four

By the time he was six years old, young Lexington had grown into a most beautiful boy with long golden hair and deep blue eyes the colour of cornflowers. He was bright and cheerful, and already he was learning to help his old aunt in all sorts of different ways around the property, collecting the eggs from the chicken house, turning the handle of the butter churn, digging up potatoes in the vegetable garden, and searching for wild herbs on the side of the mountain. Soon, Aunt Glosspan told herself, she would have to start thinking about his education.

But she couldn't bear the thought of sending him away to school. She loved him so much now that it would kill her to be parted from him for any length of time. There was, of course, that village school down in the valley, but it was a dreadful-looking place, and if she sent him there she just knew they would start forcing him to eat meat the very first day he arrived.

"You know what, my darling?" she said to him one day when he was sitting on a stool in the kitchen watching her make cheese. "I don't really see why I shouldn't give you your lessons myself."

The boy looked up at her with his large blue eyes, and gave her a lovely trusting smile. "That would be nice," he said.

"And the very first thing I should do would be to teach you how to cook."

"I think I would like that, Aunt Glosspan."

"Whether you like it or not, you're going to have to learn some time," she said. "Vegetarians like us don't have nearly so many foods to choose from as ordinary people, and therefore they must learn to be doubly expert with what they have."

"Aunt Glosspan," the boy said, "what *do* ordinary people eat that we don't?"

"Animals," she answered, tossing her head in disgust.

"You mean *live* animals?"

"No," she said. "Dead ones."

The boy considered this for a moment.

"You mean when they die they *eat* them instead of *burying* them?"

"They don't wait for them to die, my pet. They kill them."

"How do they kill them, Aunt Glosspan?"

"They usually slit their throats with a knife."

"But what *kind* of animals?"

"Cows and pigs mostly, and sheep."

"Cows!" the boy cried. "You mean like Daisy and Snowdrop and Lily?"

"Exactly, my dear."

"But *how* do they eat them, Aunt Glosspan?"

"They cut them up into bits and they cook the bits. They like it best when it's all red and bloody and sticking to the bones. They love to eat lumps of cow's flesh with the blood oozing out of it."

"Pigs too?"

"They adore pigs."

"Lumps of bloody pig's meat," the boy said. "Imagine that. What else do they eat, Aunt Glosspan?"

"Chickens."

"Chickens!"

"Millions of them."

"Feathers and all?"

"No, dear, not the feathers. Now run along outside and get Aunt Glosspan a bunch of chives, will you, my darling?"

Shortly after that, the lessons began. They covered five subjects, reading, writing, geography, arithmetic, and cooking, but the latter was by far the most popular with both teacher and pupil. In fact, it very soon became apparent that young Lexington possessed a truly remarkable talent in this direction. He was a born cook. He was dextrous and quick. He could handle his pans like a juggler. He could slice a single potato into twenty paper-thin slivers in less time than it took his aunt to peel it. His palate was exquisitely sensitive, and he could taste a pot of strong onion soup and immediately detect the presence of a single tiny leaf of sage. In so young a boy, all this was a bit bewildering to Aunt Glosspan, and to tell the truth she didn't quite know what to make of it. But she was proud as proud could be, all the same, and predicted a brilliant future for the child.

"What a mercy it is," she said, "that I have such a wonderful little fellow to look after me in my dotage." And a couple of years later, she retired from the kitchen for good, leaving Lexington in sole charge of all household cooking. The boy was now ten years old, and Aunt Glosspan was nearly eighty.

Five

With the kitchen to himself, Lexington straight away began experimenting with dishes of his own invention. The old favourites no longer interested him. He had a violent urge to create. There were hundreds of fresh ideas in his head. "I will begin," he said, "by devising a chestnut soufflé." He made it and served it up for supper that very night. It was terrific. "You are a genius!" Aunt Glosspan cried, leaping up from her chair and kissing him on both cheeks. "You will make history!"

From then on, hardly a day went by without some new delectable creation being set upon the table. There was Brazil-nut soup, hominy cutlets, vegetable ragout, dandelion omelette, cream-cheese fritters, stuffed-cabbage surprise, stewed foggage, shallots *à la bonne femme,* beetroot mousse piquant, prunes Stroganoff, Dutch rarebit, turnips on horseback, flaming spruce-needle tarts, and many many other beautiful compositions. Never before in her life, Aunt Glosspan declared, had she tasted such food as this; and in the mornings, long before lunch was due, she would go out onto the porch and sit there in her rocking-chair, speculating about the coming meal, licking her chops, sniffing the aromas that came wafting out through the kitchen window.

"What's that you're making in there today, boy?" she would call out.

"Try to guess, Aunt Glosspan."

"Smells like a bit of salsify fritters to me," she would say, sniffing vigorously.

Then out he would come, this ten-year-old child, a little grin of triumph on his face, and in his hands a big steaming pot of the most heavenly stew made entirely of parsnips and lovage.

"You know what you ought to do," his aunt said to him, gobbling the stew. "You ought to set yourself down this very minute with paper and pencil and write a cooking-book."

He looked at her across the table, chewing his parsnips slowly.

"Why not?" she cried. "I've taught you how to write and I've taught you how to cook and now all you've got to do is put the two things together. You write a cooking-book, my darling, and it'll make you famous the whole world over."

"All right," he said. "I will."

And that very day, Lexington began writing the first page of that monumental work which was to occupy him for the rest of his life. He called it *Eat Good and Healthy*.

Six

Seven years later, by the time he was seventeen, he had recorded over nine thousand different recipes, all of them original, all of them delicious.

But now, suddenly, his labours were interrupted by the tragic death of Aunt Glosspan. She was afflicted in the night by a violent seizure, and Lexington, who had rushed into her bedroom to see what all the noise was about, found her lying on her bed yelling and cussing and twisting herself up into all manner of complicated knots. Indeed, she was a terrible sight to behold, and the agitated youth danced around her in his pyjamas, wringing his hands, and wondering what on earth he should do. Finally, in an effort to cool her down, he fetched a bucket of water from the pond in the cow field and tipped it over her head, but this only intensified the paroxysms, and the old lady expired within the hour.

"This is really too bad," the poor boy said, pinching her several times to make sure that she was dead. "And how sudden! How quick and sudden! Why only a few hours ago she seemed in the very best of spirits. She even took three large helpings of my most recent creation, devilled mushroomburgers, and told me how succulent it was."

After weeping bitterly for several minutes, for he had loved his aunt very much, he pulled himself together and carried her outside and buried her behind the cowshed.

The next day, while tidying up her belongings, he came across an envelope that was addressed to him in Aunt Glosspan's handwriting. He opened it and drew out two fifty-dollar bills and a letter. *Darling boy,* the letter said. *I know that you have never yet been down the mountain since you were thirteen days old, but as soon as I die you must put on a pair of shoes and a clean shirt and walk down to the village and find the doctor. Ask the doctor to give you a death certificate to prove that I am dead. Then take this certificate to my lawyer, a man called Mr. Samuel Zuckermann, who lives in New York City and who has a copy of my will. Mr. Zuckermann will arrange everything. The cash in this envelope is to pay the doctor for the certificate and to cover the cost of your journey to New York. Mr. Zuckermann will give you more money when you get there, and it is my earnest wish that you use it to further your researches into culinary and vegetarian matters, and that you continue to work upon that great book of yours until you are satisfied that it is complete in every way. Your loving aunt—Glosspan.*

Lexington, who had always done everything his aunt told him, pocketed the money, put on a pair of shoes and a clean shirt, and went down the mountain to the village where the doctor lived.

"Old Glosspan?" the doctor said. "My God, is *she* dead?"

"Certainly she's dead," the youth answered. "If you will come back home with me now I'll dig her up and you can see for yourself."

"How deep did you bury her?" the doctor asked.

"Six or seven feet down, I should think."

"And how long ago?"

"Oh, about eight hours."

"Then she's dead," the doctor announced. "Here's the certificate."

Seven

Our hero now set out for the City of New York to find Mr. Samuel Zuckermann. He travelled on foot, and he slept under hedges, and he lived on berries and wild herbs, and it took him sixteen days to reach the metropolis.

"What a fabulous place this is!" he cried as he stood at the corner of Fifty-seventh Street and Fifth Avenue, staring around him.

"There are no cows or chickens anywhere, and none of the women looks in the least like Aunt Glosspan."

As for Mr. Samuel Zuckermann, he looked like nothing that Lexington had ever seen before.

He was a small spongy man with livid jowls and a huge magenta nose, and when he smiled, bits of gold flashed at you marvellously from lots of different places inside his mouth. In his luxurious office, he shook Lexington warmly by the hand and congratulated him upon his aunt's death.

"I suppose you knew that your dearly beloved guardian was a woman of considerable wealth?" he said.

"You mean the cows and the chickens?"

"I mean half a million bucks," Mr. Zuckermann said.

"How much?"

"Half a million dollars, my boy. And she's left it all to you." Mr. Zuckermann leaned back in his chair and clasped his hands over his spongy paunch. At the same time, he began secretly working his right forefinger in through his waistcoat and under his shirt so as to scratch the skin around the circumference of his navel—a favourite exercise of his, and one that gave him a peculiar pleasure. "Of course, I shall have to deduct fifty per cent for my services," he said, "but that still leaves you with two hundred and fifty grand."

"I am rich!" Lexington cried. "This is wonderful! How soon can I have the money?"

"Well," Mr. Zuckermann said, "luckily for you, I happen to be on rather cordial terms with the tax authorities around here, and I am confident that I shall be able to persuade them to waive all death duties and back taxes."

"How kind you are," murmured Lexington.

"I should naturally have to give somebody a small honorarium."

"Whatever you say, Mr. Zuckermann."

"I think a hundred thousand would be sufficient."

"Good gracious, isn't that rather excessive?"

"Never undertip a tax-inspector or a policeman," Mr. Zuckermann said. "Remember that."

"But how much does it leave for me?" the youth asked meekly.

"One hundred and fifty thousand. But then you've got the funeral expenses to pay out of that."

"*Funeral* expenses?"

"You've got to pay the funeral parlour. Surely you know that?"

"But I buried her myself, Mr. Zuckermann, behind the cowshed."

"I don't doubt it," the lawyer said. "So what?"

"I never used a funeral parlour."

"Listen," Mr. Zuckermann said patiently. "You may not know it, but there is a law in this State which says that no beneficiary under a will may receive a single penny of his inheritance until the funeral parlour has been paid in full."

"You mean that's a *law?*"

"Certainly it's a law, and a very good one it is, too. The funeral parlour is one of our great national institutions. It must be protected at all cost."

Mr. Zuckermann himself, together with a group of public-spirited doctors, controlled a corporation that owned a chain of nine lavish funeral parlours in the city, not to mention a casket factory in Brooklyn and a post-graduate school for embalmers in Washington Heights. The celebration of death was therefore a deeply religious affair in Mr. Zuckermann's eyes. In fact, the whole business affected him profoundly, almost as profoundly, one might say, as the birth of Christ affected the shopkeeper.

"You had no right to go out and bury your aunt like that," he said. "None at all."

"I'm very sorry, Mr. Zuckermann."

"Why, it's downright subversive."

"I'll do whatever you say, Mr. Zuckermann. All I want to know is how much I'm going to get in the end, when everything's paid."

There was a pause. Mr. Zuckermann sighed and frowned and continued secretly to run the tip of his finger around the rim of his navel.

"Shall we say fifteen thousand?" he suggested, flashing a big gold smile. "That's a nice round figure."

"Can I take it with me this afternoon?"

"I don't see why not."

So Mr. Zuckermann summoned his chief cashier and told him to give Lexington fifteen thousand dollars out of the petty cash, and to obtain a receipt. The youth, who by this time was delighted to be getting anything at all, accepted the money gratefully and stowed it away in his knapsack. Then he shook Mr. Zuckermann warmly by the hand, thanked him for all his help, and went out of the office.

"The whole world is before me!" our hero cried as he emerged into the street. "I now have fifteen thousand dollars to see me through until my book is published. And after that, of course, I shall have a great deal more." He stood on the pavement, wondering which way to go. He turned left and began strolling slowly down the street, staring at the sights of the city.

"What a revolting smell," he said, sniffing the air. "I can't stand this." His delicate olfactory nerves, tuned to receive only the most delicious kitchen aromas, were being tortured by the stench of the diesel-oil fumes pouring out of the backs of the buses.

"I must get out of this place before my nose is ruined altogether," he said. "But first, I've simply got to have something to eat. I'm starving." The poor boy had had nothing but berries and wild herbs for the past two weeks, and now his stomach was yearning for solid food. I'd like a nice hominy cutlet, he told himself. Or maybe a few juicy salsify fritters.

He crossed the street and entered a small restaurant. The place was hot inside, and dark and silent. There was a strong smell of cooking-fat and cabbage water. The only other customer was a man with a brown hat on his head, crouching intently over his food, who did not look up as Lexington came in.

Our hero seated himself at a corner table and hung his knapsack on the back of his chair. This, he told himself, is going to be most interesting. In all my seventeen years I have tasted only the cooking of two people, Aunt Glosspan and myself—unless one counts Nurse McPottle, who must have heated my bottle a few times when I was an infant. But I am now about to sample the art of a new chef altogether, and perhaps, if I am lucky, I may pick up a couple of useful ideas for my book.

A waiter approached out of the shadows at the back, and stood beside the table.

"How do you do," Lexington said. "I should like a large hominy cutlet please. Do it twenty-five seconds each side, in a very hot skillet with sour cream, and sprinkle a pinch of lovage on it before serving—unless of course your chef knows of a more original method, in which case I should be delighted to try it."

The waiter laid his head over to one side and looked carefully at his customer. "You want the roast pork and cabbage?" he asked. "That's all we got left."

"Roast what and cabbage?"

The waiter took a soiled handkerchief from his trouser pocket and shook it open with a violent flourish, as though he were cracking a whip. Then he blew his nose loud and wet.

"You want it or don't you?" he said, wiping his nostrils.

"I haven't the foggiest idea what it is," Lexington replied, "but I should love to try it. You see, I am writing a cooking-book and . . ."

"One pork and cabbage!" the waiter shouted, and somewhere in the back of the restaurant, far away in the darkness, a voice answered him.

The waiter disappeared. Lexington reached into his knapsack for his personal knife and fork. These were a present from Aunt Glosspan, given him when he was six years old, made of solid silver, and he had never eaten with any other instruments since. While waiting for the food to arrive, he polished them lovingly with a piece of soft muslin.

Soon the waiter returned carrying a plate on which there lay a thick greyish-white slab of something hot. Lexington leaned forward anxiously to smell it as it was put down before him. His nostrils were wide open now to receive the scent, quivering and sniffing.

"But this is absolute heaven!" he exclaimed. "What an aroma! It's tremendous!"

The waiter stepped back a pace, watching his customer carefully.

"Never in my life have I smelled anything as rich and wonderful as this!" our hero cried, seizing his knife and fork. "What on earth is it made of?"

The man in the brown hat looked around and stared, then returned to his eating. The waiter was backing away toward the kitchen.

Lexington cut off a small piece of the meat, impaled it on his silver fork, and carried it up to his nose so as to smell it again. Then he popped it into his mouth and began to chew it slowly, his eyes half closed, his body tense.

"This is fantastic!" he cried. "It is a brand-new flavour! Oh, Glosspan, my beloved Aunt, how I wish you were with me now so you could taste this remarkable dish! Waiter! Come here at once! I want you!"

The astonished waiter was now watching from the other end of the room, and he seemed reluctant to move any closer.

"If you will come and talk to me I will give you a present," Lexington said, waving a hundred-dollar bill. "Please come over here and talk to me."

The waiter sidled cautiously back to the table, snatched away the money, and held it up close to his face, peering at it from all angles. Then he slipped it quickly into his pocket.

"What can I do for you, my friend?" he asked.

"Look," Lexington said. "If you will tell me what this delicious dish is made of, and exactly how it is prepared, I will give you another hundred."

"I already told you," the man said. "It's pork "

"And what exactly is pork?"

"You never had roast pork before?" the waiter asked, staring.

"For heaven's sake, man, tell me what it is and stop keeping me in suspense like this."

"It's pig," the waiter said. "You just bung it in the oven."

"Pig!"

"All pork is pig. Didn't you know that?"

"You mean *this* is *pig's meat?*"

"I guarantee it."

"But ... but ... that's impossible," the youth stammered. "Aunt Glosspan, who knew more about food than anyone else in the world, said that meat of any kind was disgusting, revolting, horrible, foul, nauseating, and beastly. And yet this piece that I have here on my plate is without a doubt the most delicious thing that I have ever tasted. Now how on earth do you explain that? Aunt Glosspan certainly wouldn't have told me it was revolting if it wasn't."

"Maybe your aunt didn't know how to cook it," the waiter said.

"Is that possible?"

"You're damn right it is. Especially with pork. Pork has to be very well done or you can't eat it."

"Eureka!" Lexington cried. "I'll bet that's exactly what happened! She did it wrong!" He handed the man another hundred-dollar bill. "Lead me to the kitchen," he said. "Introduce me to the genius who prepared this meat."

Lexington was at once taken into the kitchen, and there he met the cook who was an elderly man with a rash on one side of his neck.

"This will cost you another hundred," the waiter said.

Lexington was only too glad to oblige, but this time he gave the money to the cook. "Now listen to me," he said, "I have to admit that I am really rather confused by what the waiter has just been telling me. Are you quite positive that the delectable dish which I have just been eating was prepared from pig's flesh?"

The cook raised his right hand and began scratching the rash on his neck.

"Well," he said, looking at the waiter and giving him a sly wink, "all I can tell you is that I *think* it was pig's meat."

"You mean you're not sure?"

"One can't ever be sure."

"Then what else could it have been?"

"Well," the cook said, speaking very slowly and still staring at the waiter. "There's just a chance, you see, that it might have been a piece of human stuff."

"You mean a man?"

"Yes."

"Good heavens."

"Or a woman. It could have been either. They both taste the same."

"Well—now you really do surprise me," the youth declared.

"One lives and learns."

"Indeed one does."

"As a matter of fact, we've been getting an awful lot of it just lately from the butcher's in place of pork," the cook declared.

"Have you really?"

"The trouble is, it's almost impossible to tell which is which. They're both very good."

"The piece I had just now was simply superb."

"I'm glad you liked it," the cook said. "But to be quite honest, I think that was a bit of pig. In fact, I'm almost sure it was."

"You are?"

"Yes, I am."

"In that case, we shall have to assume that you are right," Lexington said. "So now will you please tell me—and here is another hundred dollars for your trouble—will you please tell me precisely how you prepared it?"

The cook, after pocketing the money, launched out upon a colourful description of how to roast a loin of pork, while the youth, not wanting to miss a single word of so great a recipe, sat down at the kitchen table and recorded every detail in his notebook.

"Is that all?" he asked when the cook had finished.

"That's all."

"But there must be more to it than that, surely?"

"You got to get a good piece of meat to start off with," the cook said. "That's half the battle. It's got to be a good hog and it's got to be butchered right, otherwise it'll turn out lousy whichever way you cook it."

"Show me how," Lexington said. "Butcher me one now so I can learn."

"We don't butcher pigs in the kitchen," the cook said. "That lot you just ate came from a packing-house over in the Bronx."

"Then give me the address!"

The cook gave him the address, and our hero, after thanking them both many times for all their kindnesses, rushed outside and leapt into a taxi and headed for the Bronx.

Eight

The packing-house was a big four-storey brick building, and the air around it smelled sweet and heavy, like musk. At the main entrance gates, there was a large notice which said VISITORS WEL-COME AT ANY TIME, and thus encouraged, Lexington walked through the gates and entered a cobbled yard which surrounded the building itself. He then followed a series of signposts (THIS WAY FOR THE GUIDED TOURS), and came eventually to a small corrugated-iron shed set well apart from the main building (VISI-TORS WAITING-ROOM). After knocking politely on the door, he went in.

There were six other people ahead of him in the waiting-room. There was a fat mother with her two little boys aged about nine and eleven. There was a bright-eyed young couple who looked as though they might be on their honeymoon. And there was a pale woman with long white gloves, who sat very upright, looking straight ahead, with her hands folded on her lap. Nobody spoke. Lexington won-dered whether they were all writing cooking-books, like himself, but when he put this question to them aloud, he got no answer. The grown-ups merely smiled mysteriously to themselves and shook their heads, and the two children stared at him as though they were seeing a lunatic.

Soon, the door opened and a man with a merry pink face popped his head into the room and said, "Next, please." The mother and the two boys got up and went out.

About ten minutes later, the same man returned. "Next, please," he said again, and the honeymoon couple jumped up and followed him outside.

Two new visitors came in and sat down—a middle-aged hus-band and a middle-aged wife, the wife carrying a wicker shopping-basket containing groceries.

"Next, please," said the guide, and the woman with the long white gloves got up and left.

Several more people came in and took their places on the stiff-backed wooden chairs.

Soon the guide returned for the third time, and now it was Lexington's turn to go outside.

"Follow me, please," the guide said, leading the youth across the yard toward the main building.

"How exciting this is!" Lexington cried, hopping from one foot to the other. "I only wish that my dear Aunt Glosspan could be with me now to see what I am going to see "

"I myself only do the preliminaries," the guide said "Then I shall hand you over to someone else "

"Anything you say," cried the ecstatic youth.

First they visited a large penned-in area at the back of the building where several hundred pigs were wandering around. "Here's where they start," the guide said. "And over there's where they go in."

"Where?"

"Right there." The guide pointed to a long wooden shed that stood against the outside wall of the factory. "We call it the shackling-pen. This way, please."

Three men wearing long rubber boots were driving a dozen pigs into the shackling-pen just as Lexington and the guide approached, so they all went in together.

"Now," the guide said, "watch how they shackle them."

Inside, the shed was simply a bare wooden room with no roof, but there was a steel cable with hooks on it that kept moving slowly along the length of one wall, parallel with the ground, about three feet up. When it reached the end of the shed, this cable suddenly changed direction and climbed vertically upward through the open roof toward the top floor of the main building.

The twelve pigs were huddled together at the far end of the pen, standing quietly, looking apprehensive. One of the men in rubber boots pulled a length of metal chain down from the wall and advanced upon the nearest animal, approaching it from the rear. Then he bent down and quickly looped one end of the chain around one of the animal's hind legs. The other end he attached to a hook on the moving cable as it went by. The cable kept moving. The chain tightened. The pig's leg was pulled up and back, and then the pig itself began to be dragged backwards. But it didn't fall down. It was rather a nimble pig, and somehow it managed to keep its balance on three legs, hopping from foot to foot and struggling against the pull of the chain, but going back and back all the time until at the end of the pen where the cable changed direction and went vertically upward, the creature was suddenly jerked off its feet and borne aloft. Shrill protests filled the air.

"Truly a fascinating process," Lexington said. "But what was that funny cracking noise it made as it went up?"

"Probably the leg," the guide answered "Either that or the pelvis."

"But doesn't that matter?"

"Why should it matter?" the guide asked. "You don't eat the bones."

The rubber-booted men were busy shackling the rest of the pigs, and one after another they were hooked to the moving cable and hoisted up through the roof, protesting loudly as they went.

"There's a good deal more to this recipe than just picking herbs," Lexington said. "Aunt Glosspan would never have made it."

At this point, while Lexington was gazing skyward at the last pig to go up, a man in rubber boots approached him quietly from behind and looped one end of a chain around the youth's own left ankle, hooking the other end to the moving belt. The next moment, before he had time to realize what was happening, our hero was jerked off his feet and dragged backwards along the concrete floor of the shackling-pen.

"Stop!" he cried. "Hold everything! My leg is caught!"

But nobody seemed to hear him, and five seconds later, the unhappy young man was jerked off the floor and hoisted vertically upward through the open roof of the pen, dangling upside down by one ankle, and wriggling like a fish.

"Help!" he shouted. "Help! There's been a frightful mistake! Stop the engines! Let me down!"

The guide removed a cigar from his mouth and looked up serenely at the rapidly ascending youth, but he said nothing. The men in rubber boots were already on their way out to collect the next batch of pigs.

"Oh save me!" our hero cried. "Let me down! Please let me down!" But he was now approaching the top floor of the building where the moving belt curled over like a snake and entered a large hole in the wall, a kind of doorway without a door; and there, on the threshold, waiting to greet him, clothed in a dark-stained yellow rubber apron, and looking for all the world like Saint Peter at the Gates of Heaven, the sticker stood.

Lexington saw him only from upside down, and very briefly at that, but even so he noticed at once the expression of absolute peace and benevolence on the man's face, the cheerful twinkle in the eyes, the little wistful smile, the dimples in his cheeks—and all this gave him hope.

"Hi there," the sticker said, smiling.

"Quick! Save me!" our hero cried.

"With pleasure," the sticker said, and taking Lexington gently by one ear with his left hand, he raised his right hand and deftly slit open the boy's jugular vein with a knife.

The belt moved on. Lexington went with it. Everything was still upside down and the blood was pouring out of his throat and getting into his eyes, but he could still see after a fashion, and he had a blurred impression of being in an enormously long room, and at the far end of the room there was a great smoking cauldron of water, and there were dark figures, half hidden in the steam, dancing around the edge of it, brandishing long poles. The conveyor-belt seemed to be travelling right over the top of the cauldron, and the pigs seemed to be dropping down one by one into the boiling water, and one of the pigs seemed to be wearing long white gloves on its front feet.

Suddenly our hero started to feel very sleepy, but it wasn't until his good strong heart had pumped the last drop of blood from his body that he passed on out of this, the best of all possible worlds, into the next.

The Visitor

NOT LONG AGO, a large wooden case was deposited at the door of my house by the railway delivery service. It was an unusually strong and well-constructed object, and made of some kind of dark red hardwood, not unlike mahogany. I lifted it with great difficulty onto a table in the garden, and examined it carefully. The stencilling on one side said that it had been shipped from Haifa by the m/v *Waverley Star,* but I could find no sender's name or address. I tried to think of somebody living in Haifa or thereabouts who might be wanting to send me a magnificent present. I could think of no one. I walked slowly to the toolshed, still pondering the matter deeply, and returned with a hammer and screwdriver. Then I began gently to prise open the top of the case.

Behold, it was filled with books! Extraordinary books! One by one, I lifted them all out (not yet looking inside any of them) and stacked them in three tall piles on the table. There were twenty-eight volumes altogether, and very beautiful they were indeed. Each of them was identically and superbly bound in rich green morocco, with the initials O.H.C. and a Roman numeral (I to XXVIII) tooled in gold upon the spine.

I took up the nearest volume, number XVI, and opened it. The unlined white pages were filled with a neat small handwriting in black ink. On the title page was written "1934." Nothing else. I took up another volume, number XXI. It contained more manuscript in the same handwriting, but on the title page it said "1939." I put it down and pulled out Vol. I, hoping to find a preface of some kind there, or perhaps the author's name. Instead, I found an envelope inside the cover. The envelope was addressed to me. I took out the letter it contained and glanced quickly at the signature. *Oswald Hendryks Cornelius,* it said.

It was Uncle Oswald!

No member of the family had heard from Uncle Oswald for over thirty years. This letter was dated March 10, 1964, and until its arrival, we could only assume that he still existed. Nothing was really known about him except that he lived in France, that he travelled a great deal, that he was a wealthy bachelor with unsavoury but glamorous habits who steadfastly refused to have anything to do with his own relatives. The rest was all rumour and hearsay, but the rumours were so splendid and the hearsay so exotic that Oswald had long since become a shining hero and a legend to us all

"My dear boy," the letter began, "I believe that you and your three sisters are my closest surviving blood relations. You are there-fore my rightful heirs, and because I have made no will, all that I leave behind me when I die will be yours. Alas, I have nothing to leave. I used to have quite a lot, and the fact that I have recently disposed of it all in my own way is none of your business. As consolation, though, I am sending you my private diaries. These, I think, ought to remain in the family. They cover all the best years of my life, and it will do you no harm to read them. But if you show them around or lend them out to strangers, you do so at your own great peril. If you publish them, then that, I should imagine, would be the end of both you and your publisher simultaneously. For you must understand that thousands of the heroines whom I mention in the diaries are still only half dead, and if you were foolish enough to splash their lilywhite reputations with scarlet print, they would have your head on a salver in two seconds flat, and probably roast it in the oven for good measure. So you'd better be careful. I only met you once. That was years ago, in 1921, when your family was living in that large ugly house in South Wales. I was your big uncle and you were a very small boy, about five years old. I don't suppose you remember the young Norwegian nursemaid you had then. A remarkably clean, well-built girl she was, and exquisitely shaped even in her uniform with its ridiculous starchy white shield conceal-ing her lovely bosom. The afternoon I was there, she was taking you for a walk in the woods to pick bluebells, and I asked if I might come along. And when we got well into the middle of the woods, I told you I'd give you a bar of chocolate if you could find your own way home. And you did (see Vol. III). You were a sensible child. Fare-well—Oswald Hendryks Cornelius."

The sudden arrival of the diaries caused much excitement in the family, and there was a rush to read them. We were not disap-pointed. It was astonishing stuff—hilarious, witty, exciting, and often quite touching as well. The man's vitality was unbelievable. He was always on the move, from city to city, from country to country, from woman to woman, and in between the women, he would be searching for spiders in Kashmir or tracking down a blue porcelain vase in Nanking. But the women always came first. Wherever he went, he left an endless trail of females in his wake, females ruffled and ravished beyond words, but purring like cats.

Twenty-eight volumes with exactly three hundred pages to each volume take a deal of reading, and there are precious few writers who could hold an audience over a distance like that. But Oswald did it. The narrative never seemed to lose its flavour, the pace seldom slackened, and almost without exception, every single entry, whether it was long or short, and whatever the subject, became a marvellous little individual story that was complete in itself. And at the end of it all, when the last page of the last volume had been read, one was left with the rather breathless feeling that this might just possibly be one of the major autobiographical works of our time.

If it were regarded solely as a chronicle of a man's amorous adventures, then without a doubt there was nothing to touch it. Casanova's *Memoirs* read like a parish magazine in comparison, and the famous lover himself, beside Oswald, appears positively undersexed.

There was social dynamite on every page; Oswald was right about that. But he was surely wrong in thinking that the explosions would all come from the women. What about their husbands, the humiliated cock-sparrows, the cuckolds? The cuckold, when aroused, is a very fierce bird indeed, and there would be thousands upon thousands of them rising up out of the bushes if The Cornelius Diaries, unabridged, saw the light of day while they were still alive. Publication, therefore, was right out of the question.

A pity, this. Such a pity, in fact, that I thought something ought to be done about it. So I sat down and reread the diaries from beginning to end in the hope that I might discover at least one complete passage which could be printed and published without involving both the publisher and myself in serious litigation. To my joy, I found no less than six. I showed them to a lawyer. He said he thought they *might* be "safe," but he wouldn't guarantee it. One of them—The Sinai Desert Episode—seemed "safer" than the other five, he added.

So I have decided to start with that one and to offer it for publication right away, at the end of this short preface. If it is accepted and all goes well, then perhaps I shall release one or two more.

The Sinai entry is from the last volume of all, Vol. XXVIII, and is dated August 24, 1946. In point of fact, it is the *very last entry* of the last volume of all, the last thing Oswald ever wrote, and we have no record of where he went or what he did after that date. One can only guess. You shall have the entry verbatim in a moment, but first of all, and so that you may more easily understand some of the things Oswald says and does in his story, let me try to tell you a little about the man himself. Out of the mass of confession and opinion contained in those twenty-eight volumes, there emerges a fairly clear picture of his character.

At the time of the Sinai episode, Oswald Hendryks Cornelius was fifty-one years old, and he had, of course, never been married. "I am afraid," he was in the habit of saying, "that I have been blessed, or should I call it burdened, with an uncommonly fastidious nature."

In some ways, this was true, but in others, and especially insofar as marriage was concerned, the statement was the exact opposite of the truth.

The real reason Oswald had refused to get married was simply that he had never in his life been able to confine his attentions to one particular woman for longer than the time it took to conquer her. When that was done, he lost interest and looked around for another victim.

A normal man would hardly consider this a valid reason for remaining single, but Oswald was not a normal man. He was not even a normally polygamous man. He was, to be honest, such a wanton and incorrigible philanderer that no bride on earth would have put up with him for more than a few days, let alone for the duration of a honeymoon—although heaven knows there were enough who would have been willing to give it a try.

He was a tall; narrow person with a fragile and faintly aesthetic air. His voice was soft, his manner was courteous, and at first sight he seemed more like a gentleman-in-waiting to the Queen than a celebrated rapscallion. He never discussed his amorous affairs with other men, and a stranger, though he might sit and talk with him all evening, would be unable to observe the slightest sign of deceit in Oswald's clear blue eyes. He was, in fact, precisely the sort of man that an anxious father would be likely to choose to escort his daughter safely home.

But sit Oswald beside a *woman,* a woman who interested him, and instantaneously his eyes would change, and as he looked at her, a small dangerous spark would begin dancing slowly in the very centre of each pupil; and then he would set about her with his conversation, talking to her rapidly and cleverly and almost certainly more wittily than anyone else had ever done before. This was a gift he had, a most singular talent, and when he put his mind to it, he could make his words coil themselves around and around the listener until they held her in some sort of a mild hypnotic spell.

But it wasn't only his fine talk and the look in his eyes that fascinated the women. It was also his nose. (In Vol. XIV, Oswald includes, with obvious relish, a note written to him by a certain lady in which she describes such things as this in great detail.) It appears that when Oswald was aroused, something odd would begin to happen around the edges of his nostrils, a tightening of the rims, a visible flaring which enlarged the nostril holes and revealed whole areas of the bright red skin inside. This created a queer, wild, animalistic impression, and although it may not sound particularly attractive when described on paper, its effect upon the ladies was electric.

Almost without exception, women were drawn toward Oswald. In the first place, he was a man who refused to be owned at any price, and this automatically made him desirable. Add to this the unusual combination of a first-rate intellect, an abundance of charm, and a reputation for excessive promiscuity, and you have a potent recipe.

Then again, and forgetting for a moment the disreputable and licentious angle, it should be noted that there were a number of other surprising facets to Oswald's character that in themselves made him a rather intriguing person. There was, for example, very little that he did not know about nineteenth-century Italian opera, and he had written a curious little manual upon the three composers Donizetti, Verdi, and Ponchielli. In it, he listed by name all the important mistresses that these men had had during their lives, and he went on to examine, in a most serious vein, the relationship between creative passion and carnal passion, and the influence of the one upon the other, particularly as it affected the works of these composers.

Chinese porcelain was another of Oswald's interests, and he was acknowledged as something of an international authority in this field. The blue vases of the Tchin-Hoa period were his special love, and he had a small but exquisite collection of these pieces.

He also collected spiders and walking-sticks.

His collection of spiders, or more accurately, his collection of

Arachnida, because it included scorpions and pedipalps, was possibly as comprehensive as any outside a museum, and his knowledge of the hundreds of genera and species was impressive. He maintained, incidentally (and probably correctly), that spiders' silk was superior in quality to the ordinary stuff spun by silkworms, and he never wore a tie that was made of any other material. He possessed about forty of these ties altogether, and in order to acquire them in the first place, and in order also to be able to add two new ties a year to his wardrobe, he had to keep thousands and thousands of *Arana* and *Epeira diademata* (the common English garden spiders) in an old conservatory in the garden of his country house outside Paris, where they bred and multiplied at approximately the same rate as they ate one another. From them, he collected the raw thread himself—no one else would enter that ghastly glasshouse—and sent it to Avignon, where it was reeled and thrown and scoured and dyed and made into cloth. From Avignon, the cloth was delivered directly to Sulka, who were enchanted by the whole business, and only too glad to fashion ties out of such a rare and wonderful material.

"But you can't *really* like spiders?" the women visitors would say to Oswald as he displayed his collection.

"Oh, but I adore them," he would answer. "Especially the females. They remind me so much of certain human females that I know. They remind me of my very favourite human females."

"What nonsense, darling."

"Nonsense? I think not."

"It's rather insulting."

"On the contrary, my dear, it is the greatest compliment I could pay. Did you not know, for instance, that the female spider is so savage in her love-making that the male is very lucky indeed if he escapes with his life at the end of it all. Only if he is exceedingly agile and marvelously ingenious will he get away in one piece."

"Now, *Oswald!*"

"And the crab spider, my beloved, the teeny-weeny little crab spider is so dangerously passionate that her lover has to tie her down with intricate loops and knots of his own thread before he dares to embrace her   "

"Oh, *stop* it, Oswald, this *minute!*" the women would cry, their eyes shining.

Oswald's collection of walking-sticks was something else again. Every one of them had belonged either to a distinguished or a disgusting person, and he kept them all in his Paris apartment, where they were displayed in two long racks standing against the walls of the passage (or should one call it the highway?) which led from the living-room to the bedroom. Each stick had its own little ivory label above it, saying Sibelius, Milton, King Farouk, Dickens, Robespierre, Puccini, Oscar Wilde, Franklin Roosevelt, Goebbels, Queen Victoria, Toulouse-Lautrec, Hindenburg, Tolstoy, Laval, Sarah Bernhardt, Goethe, Voroshiloff, Cezanne, Tojo . . . There must have been over a hundred of them in all, some very beautiful, some very plain, some with gold or silver tops, and some with curly handles.

"Take down the Tolstoy," Oswald would say to a pretty visitor. "Go on, take it down . . . that's right . . . and now . . . now rub your own palm gently over the knob that has been worn to a shine by the great man himself. Is it not rather wonderful, the mere contact of your skin with that spot?"

"It is, rather, isn't it."

"And now take the Goebbels and do the same thing. Do it properly, though. Allow your palm to fold tightly over the handle . . . good . . . and now . . . now lean your weight on it, lean hard, exactly as the little deformed doctor used to do . . . there . . . that's it . . . now stay like that for a minute or so and then tell me if you do not feel a thin finger of ice creeping all the way up your arm and into your chest."

"It's terrifying!"

"Of course it is. Some people pass out completely. They keel right over."

Nobody ever found it dull to be in Oswald's company, and perhaps that, more than anything else, was the reason for his success.

We come now to the Sinai episode. Oswald, during that month, had been amusing himself by motoring at a fairly leisurely pace down from Khartoum to Cairo. His car was a superlative prewar Lagonda which had been carefully stored in Switzerland during the war years, and as you can imagine, it was fitted with every kind of gadget under the sun. On the day before Sinai (August 23, 1946), he was in Cairo, staying at Shepheard's Hotel, and that evening, after a series of impudent manoeuvres, he had succeeded in getting hold of a Moorish lady of supposedly aristocratic descent, called Isabella. Isabella happened to be the jealously guarded mistress of none other than a certain notorious and dyspeptic Royal Personage (there was still a monarchy in Egypt then). This was a typically Oswaldian move.

But there was more to come. At midnight, he drove the lady out to Giza and persuaded her to climb with him in the moonlight right to the very top of the great pyramid of Cheops.

". . . There can be no safer place," he wrote in the diary, "nor a more romantic one, than the apex of a pyramid on a warm night when the moon is full. The passions are stirred not only by the magnificent view but also by that curious sensation of power that surges within the body whenever one surveys the world from a great height. And as for safety—this pyramid is exactly 481 feet high, which is 115 feet higher than the dome of St. Paul's Cathedral, and from the summit one can observe all the approaches with the greatest of ease. No other boudoir on earth can offer this facility. None has so many emergency exits, either, so that if some sinister figure should happen to come clambering up in pursuit on one side of the pyramid, one has only to slip calmly and quietly down the other . . ."

As it happened, Oswald had a very narrow squeak indeed that night. Somehow, the palace must have got word of the little affair, for Oswald, from his lofty moonlit pinnacle, suddenly observed *three* sinister figures, not one, closing in on three different sides, and starting to climb. But luckily for him, there is a fourth side to the great pyramid of Cheops, and by the time those Arab thugs had reached the top, the two lovers were already at the bottom and getting into the car.

The entry for August 24th takes up the story at exactly this point. It is reproduced here word for word and comma for comma as Oswald wrote it. Nothing has been altered or added or taken away:

August 24, 1946

"He'll chop off Isabella's head if he catch her now," Isabella said.

"Rubbish," I answered, but I reckoned she was probably right.

"He'll chop off Oswald's head, too," she said.

"Not mine, dear lady. I shall be a long way away from here when daylight comes. I'm heading straight up the Nile for Luxor immediately."

We were driving quickly away from the pyramids now. It was about two thirty A.M.

"To Luxor?" she said.

"Yes "

"And Isabella is going with you."

"No," I said.

"Yes," she said.

"It is against my principles to travel with a lady," I said.

I could see some lights ahead of us. They came from the Mena House Hotel, a place where tourists stay out in the desert, not far from the pyramids. I drove fairly close to the hotel and stopped the car.

"I'm going to drop you here," I said. "We had a fine time."

"So you won't take Isabella to Luxor?"

"I'm afraid not," I said. "Come on, hop it."

She started to get out of the car, then she paused with one foot on the road, and suddenly she swung round and poured out upon me a torrent of language so filthy yet so fluent that I had heard nothing like it from the lips of a lady since . . . well, since 1931, in Marrakesh, when the greedy old Duchess of Glasgow put her hand into a chocolate box and got nipped by a scorpion I happened to have placed there for safe-keeping (Vol. XIII, June 5th, 1931).

"You are disgusting," I said.

Isabella leapt out and slammed the door so hard the whole car jumped on its wheels. I drove off very fast. Thank heaven I was rid of her. I cannot abide bad manners in a pretty girl.

As I drove, I kept one eye on the mirror, but as yet no car seemed to be following me. When I came to the outskirts of Cairo, I began threading my way through the side roads, avoiding the centre of the city. I was not particularly worried. The royal watch-dogs were unlikely to carry the matter much further. All the same, it would have been foolhardy to go back to Shepheard's at this point. It wasn't necessary anyway, because all my baggage, except for a small valise, was with me in the car. I never leave suitcases behind me in my room when I go out of an evening in a foreign city. I like to be mobile.

I had no intention, of course, of going to Luxor. I wanted now to get away from Egypt altogether. I didn't like the country at all. Come to think of it, I never had. The place made me feel uncomfortable in my skin. It was the dirtiness of it all, I think, and the putrid smells. But then let us face it, it really is a rather squalid country; and I have a powerful suspicion, though I hate to say it, that the Egyptians wash themselves less thoroughly than any other peoples in the world—with the possible exception of the Mongolians. Certainly they do not wash their crockery to my taste. There was, believe it or not, a long, crusted, coffee-coloured lipmark stamped upon the rim of the cup they placed before me at breakfast yesterday. Ugh! It was repulsive! I kept staring at it and wondering whose slobbery lower lip had done the deed.

I was driving now through the narrow dirty streets of the eastern suburbs of Cairo. I knew precisely where I was going. I had made up my mind about that before I was even halfway down the pyramid with Isabella. I was going to Jerusalem. It was no distance to speak of, and it was a city that I always enjoyed. Furthermore, it was the quickest way out of Egypt. I would proceed as follows:

1. Cairo to Ismailia. About three hours driving. Sing an opera on the way, as usual. Arrive Ismailia 6–7 A.M. Take a room and have a two-hour sleep. Then shower, shave, and breakfast.

2. At 10 A.M., cross over the Suez Canal by the Ismailia bridge and take the desert road across Sinai to the Palestine border. Make a search for scorpions en route in the Sinai Desert. Time, about four hours, arriving Palestine border 2 P.M.

3. From there, continue straight on to Jerusalem via Beersheba, reaching the King David Hotel in time for cocktails and dinner.

It was several years since I had travelled that particular road, but I remembered that the Sinai Desert was an outstanding place for scorpions. I badly wanted another female opisthophthalmus, a large one. My present specimen had the fifth segment of its tail missing, and I was ashamed of it.

It didn't take me long to find the main road to Ismailia, and as soon as I was on it, I settled the Lagonda down to a steady sixty-five miles an hour. The road was narrow, but it had a smooth surface, and there was no traffic. The Delta country lay bleak and dismal around me in the moonlight, the flat treeless fields, the ditches running between, and the black black soil everywhere. It was inexpressibly dreary.

But it didn't worry *me.* I was no part of it. I was completely isolated in my own luxurious little shell, as snug as a hermit crab and travelling a lot faster. Oh, how I do love to be on the move, winging away to new people and new places and leaving the old ones far behind! Nothing in the world exhilarates me more than that. And how I despise the average citizen, who settles himself down upon one tiny spot of land with one asinine woman, to breed and stew and rot in that condition unto his life's end. And always with the same woman! I simply cannot *believe* that any man in his senses would put up with just one female day after day and year after year. Some of them, of course, don't. But millions pretend they do.

I myself have never, absolutely never permitted an intimate relationship to last for more than twelve hours. That is the farthest limit. Even eight hours is stretching it a bit, to my mind. Look what happened, for example, with Isabella. While we were upon the summit of the pyramid, she was a lady of scintillating parts, as pliant and playful as a puppy, and had I left her there to the mercy of those three Arab thugs, and skipped down on my own, all would have been well. But I foolishly stuck by her and helped her to descend, and as a result, the lovely lady turned into a vulgar screeching trollop, disgusting to behold.

What a world we live in! One gets no thanks these days for being chivalrous.

The Lagonda moved on smoothly through the night. Now for an opera. Which one should it be this time? I was in the mood for a Verdi. What about *Aida?* Of course! It must be *Aida*—the Egyptian opera! Most appropriate.

I began to sing. I was in exceptionally good voice tonight. I let myself go. It was delightful; and as I drove through the small town of Bilbeis, I was Aida herself, singing *"Numei pieta,"* the beautiful concluding passage of the first scene.

Half an hour later, at Zagazig, I was Amonasro begging the King of Egypt to save the Ethiopian captives with *"Ma tu, re, tu signore possente."*

Passing through El Abbasa, I was Rhadames, rendering *"Fuggiam gli adori nospiti,"* and now I opened all the windows of the car so that this incomparable love song might reach the ears of the fellaheen snoring in their hovels along the roadside, and perhaps mingle with their dreams.

As I pulled into Ismailia, it was six o'clock in the morning and the sun was already climbing high in a milky-blue heaven, but I myself was in the terrible sealed-up dungeon with Aida, singing *"O, terra, addio; addio valle di pianti!"*

How swiftly the journey had gone. I drove to an hotel. The staff was just beginning to stir. I stirred them up some more and got the best room available. The sheets and blanket on the bed looked as though they had been slept in by twenty-five unwashed Egyptians on twenty-five consecutive nights, and I tore them off with my own hands (which I scrubbed immediately afterward with antiseptic soap) and replaced them with my personal bedding. Then I set my alarm and slept soundly for two hours.

For breakfast I ordered a poached egg on a piece of toast. When the dish arrived—and I tell you, it makes my stomach curdle just to write about it—there was a *gleaming, curly, jet-black human hair*, three inches long, lying diagonally across the yolk of my poached egg. It was too much. I leapt up from the table and rushed out of the dining room. *"Addio!"* I cried, flinging some money at the cashier as I went by, *"addio valle di pianti!"* And with that I shook the filthy dust of the hotel from my feet.

Now for the Sinai Desert. What a welcome change that would be. A real desert is one of the least contaminated places on earth, and Sinai was no exception. The road across it was a narrow strip of black tarmac about a hundred and forty miles long, with only a single filling-station and a group of huts at the halfway mark, at a place called B'ir Rawd Salim. Otherwise there was nothing but pure uninhabited desert all the way. It would be very hot at this time of year, and it was essential to carry drinking water in case of a breakdown. I therefore pulled up outside a kind of general store in the main street of Ismailia to get my emergency canister refilled.

I went in and spoke to the proprietor. The man had a nasty case of trachoma. The granulation on the under surfaces of his eyelids was so acute that the lids themselves were raised right up off the eyeballs—a beastly sight. I asked him if he would sell me a gallon of *boiled* water. He thought I was mad, and madder still when I insisted on following him back into his grimy kitchen to make sure that he did things properly. He filled a kettle with tap-water and placed it on a paraffin stove. The stove had a tiny little smoky yellow flame. The proprietor seemed very proud of the stove and of its performance. He stood admiring it, his head on one side. Then he suggested that I might prefer to go back and wait in the shop. He would bring me the water, he said, when it was ready. I refused to leave. I stood there watching the kettle like a lion, waiting for the water to boil; and while I was doing this, the breakfast scene suddenly started coming back to me in all its horror—the egg, the yolk, and the hair. Whose hair was it that had lain embedded in the slimy yolk of my egg at breakfast? Undoubtedly it was the cook's hair. And when, pray, had the cook last washed his head? He had probably never washed his head. Very well, then. He was almost certainly verminous. But that in itself would not cause a hair to fall out. What *did* cause the cook's hair, then, to fall out onto my poached egg this morning as he transferred the egg from the pan to the plate? There is a reason for all things, and in this case the reason was obvious. The cook's scalp was infested with purulent seborrhoeic impetigo. And the hair itself, the long black hair that I might so easily have swallowed had I been less alert, was therefore swarming with millions and millions of living pathogenic cocci whose exact scientific name I have, happily, forgotten.

Can I, you ask, be absolutely sure that the cook had purulent seborrhoeic impetigo? Not absolutely sure—no. But if he hadn't, then he certainly had ringworm instead. And what did that mean? I knew only too well what it meant. It meant that ten million microsporons had been clinging and clustering around that awful hair, waiting to go into my mouth.

I began to feel sick.

"The water boils," the shopkeeper said triumphantly.

"Let it boil," I told him. "Give it eight minutes more. What is it you want me to get—typhus?"

Personally, I never drink plain water by itself if I can help it, however pure it may be. Plain water has no flavour at all. I take it, of course, as tea or as coffee, but even then I try to arrange for bottled Vichy or Malvern to be used in the preparation. I avoid tap-water. Tap-water is diabolical stuff. Often it is nothing more nor less than reclaimed sewage.

"Soon this water will be boiled away in steam," the proprietor said, grinning at me with green teeth.

I lifted the kettle myself and poured the contents into my canister.

Back in the shop, I bought six oranges, a small watermelon, and a slab of well-wrapped English chocolate. Then I returned to the Lagonda. Now at last I was away.

A few minutes later, I had crossed the sliding bridge that went over the Suez Canal just above Lake Timsah, and ahead of me lay the flat blazing desert and the little tarmac road stretching out before me like a black ribbon all the way to the horizon. I settled the Lagonda down to the usual steady sixty-five miles an hour, and I opened the windows wide. The air that came in was like the breath of an oven. The time was almost noon, and the sun was throwing its heat directly onto the roof of the car. My thermometer inside registered 103°. But as you know, a touch of warmth never bothers me so long as I am sitting still and am wearing suitable clothes—in this case a pair of cream-coloured linen slacks, a white Aertex shirt, and a spider's-silk tie of the loveliest rich moss-green. I felt perfectly comfortable and at peace with the world.

For a minute or two I played with the idea of performing another opera en route—I was in the mood for *La Gioconda*—but after singing a few bars of the opening chorus, I began to perspire slightly; so I rang down the curtain, and lit a cigarette instead.

I was now driving through some of the finest scorpion country in the world, and I was eager to stop and make a search before I reached the halfway filling-station at B'ir Rawd Salim. I had so far met not a single vehicle nor seen a living creature since leaving Ismailia an hour before. This pleased me. Sinai was authentic desert. I pulled up on the side of the road and switched off the engine. I was thirsty, so I ate an orange. Then I put my white topee on my head, and eased myself slowly out of the car, out of my comfortable hermit-crab shell, and into the sunlight. For a full minute I stood motionless in the middle of the road, blinki.ig at the brilliance of the surroundings.

There was a blazing sun, a vast hot sky, and beneath it all on every side a great pale sea of yellow sand that was not quite of this world. There were mountains now in the distance on the south side of the road, bare, pale, tanagra-coloured mountains faintly glazed with blue and purple, that rose up suddenly out of the desert and faded away in a haze of heat against the sky. The stillness was overpowering. There was no sound at all, no voice of bird or insect anywhere, and it gave me a queer godlike feeling to be standing there alone in the middle of such a splendid, hot, inhuman landscape —as though I were on another planet altogether, on Jupiter or Mars, or in some place more distant and desolate still, where never would the grass grow nor the clouds turn red.

I went to the boot of the car and took out my killing-box, my net, and my trowel. Then I stepped off the road into the soft burning sand. I walked slowly for about a hundred yards into the desert, my eyes searching the ground. I was not looking for scorpions but the lairs of scorpions. The scorpion is a cryptozoic and nocturnal creature that hides all through the day either under a stone or in a burrow, according to its type. Only after the sun has gone down does it come out to hunt for food.

The one I wanted, opisthophthalmus, was a burrower, so I wasted no time turning over stones. I searched only for burrows. After ten or fifteen minutes, I had found none; but already the heat was getting to be too much for me, and I decided reluctantly to return to the car. I walked back very slowly, still watching the ground, and I had reached the road and was in the act of stepping onto it when all at once, in the sand, not more than twelve inches from the edge of the tarmac, I caught sight of a scorpion's burrow.

I put the killing-box and the net on the ground beside me. Then, with my little trowel, I began very cautiously to scrape away the sand all around the hole. This was an operation that never failed to excite me. It was like a treasure hunt—a treasure hunt with just the right amount of danger accompanying it to stir the blood. I could feel my heart beating away in my chest as I probed deeper and deeper into the sand.

And suddenly . . . there she was!

Oh, my heavens, what a whopper! A gigantic female scorpion, not opisthophthalmus, as I saw immediately, but pandinus, the other large African burrower. And clinging to her back—this was too good to be true!—swarming all over her, were one, two, three, four, five . . . a total of fourteen tiny babies! The mother was six inches long at least! Her children were the size of small revolver bullets. She had seen me now, the first human she had ever seen in her life, and her pincers were wide open, her tail was curled high over her back like a question mark, ready to strike. I took up the net, and slid it swiftly underneath her, and scooped her up. She twisted and squirmed, striking wildly in all directions with the end of her tail. I saw a single large drop of venom fall through the mesh onto the sand. Quickly, I transferred her, together with all the offspring, to the killing-box, and closed the lid. Then I fetched the ether from the car, and poured it through the little gauze hole in the top of the box until the pad inside was well-soaked.

How splendid she would look in my collection! The babies would, of course, fall away from her as they died, but I would stick them on again with glue in more or less their correct positions; and then I would be the proud possessor of a huge female pandinus with her own fourteen offspring on her back! I was extremely pleased. I lifted the killing-box (I could feel her thrashing about furiously inside) and placed it in the boot, together with the net and trowel. Then I returned to my seat in the car, lit a cigarette, and drove on.

The more contented I am, the slower I drive. I drove quite slowly now, and it must have taken me nearly an hour more to reach B'ir Rawd Salim, the halfway station. It was a most unenticing place. On the left, there was a single gasoline pump and a wooden shack. On the right, there were three more shacks, each about the size of a potting-shed. The rest was desert. There was not a soul in sight. The time was twenty minutes before two in the afternoon, and the temperature inside the car was 106°.

What with the nonsense of getting the water boiled before

leaving Ismailia, I had forgotten completely to fill up with gasoline before leaving, and my gauge was now registering slightly less than two gallons. I'd cut it rather fine—but no matter. I pulled in alongside the pump, and waited. Nobody appeared. I pressed the horn button, and the four tuned horns on the Lagonda shouted their wonderful *"Son gia mille e tre!"* across the desert. Nobody appeared. I pressed again.

Son gia mille e tre

sang the horns. Mozart's phrase sounded magnificent in these surroundings. But still nobody appeared. The inhabitants of B'ir Rawd Salim didn't give a damn, it seemed, about my friend Don Giovanni and the one thousand and three women he had deflowered in Spain.

At last, after I had played the horns no less than six times, the door of the hut behind the gasoline pump opened and a tallish man emerged and stood on the threshold, doing up his buttons with both hands. He took his time over this, and not until he had finished did he glance up at the Lagonda. I looked back at him through my open window. I saw him take the first step in my direction . . . he took it very, very slowly . . . Then he took a second step . . .

My God! I thought at once. The spirochetes have got him!

He had the slow, wobbly walk, the loose-limbed, high-stepping gait of a man with locomotor ataxia. With each step he took, the front foot was raised high in the air before him and brought down violently to the ground, as though he were stamping on a dangerous insect.

I thought: I had better get out of here. I had better start the motor and get the hell out of here before he reaches me. But I knew I couldn't. I *had* to have the gasoline. I sat in the car staring at the awful creature as he came stamping laboriously over the sand. He must have had the revolting disease for years and years, otherwise it wouldn't have developed into ataxis. *Tabes dorsalis,* they call it in professional circles, and pathologically this means that the victim is suffering from degeneration of the posterior columns of the spinal cord. But ah my foes and oh my friends, it is really a lot worse than that; it is a slow and merciless consuming of the actual nerve fibres of the body by syphilitic toxins.

The man—the Arab, I shall call him—came right up to the door of my side of the car and peered in through the open window. I leaned away from him, praying that he would come not an inch closer. Without a doubt, he was one of the most blighted humans I had ever seen. His face had the eroded, eaten-away look of an old wood-carving when the worm has been at it, and the sight of it made me wonder how many other diseases the man was suffering from, besides syphilis.

"Salaam," he mumbled.

"Fill up the tank," I told him.

He didn't move. He was inspecting the interior of the Lagonda with great interest. A terrible feculent odour came wafting in from his direction.

"Come along!" I said sharply. "I want some gasoline!"

He looked at me and grinned. It was more of a leer than a grin, an insolent mocking leer that seemed to be saying, "I am the king of the gasoline pump at B'ir Rawd Salim! Touch me if you dare!" A fly had settled in the corner of one of his eyes. He made no attempt to brush it away.

"You want gasoline?" he said, taunting me.

I was about to swear at him, but I checked myself just in time, and answered politely, "Yes please, I would be very grateful."

He watched me slyly for a few moments to be sure I wasn't mocking him, then he nodded as though satisfied now with my behaviour. He turned away and started slowly toward the rear of the car. I reached into the door-pocket for my bottle of Glenmorangie. I poured myself a stiff one, and sat sipping it. That man's face had been within a yard of my own; his foetid breath had come pouring into the car . . . and who knows how many billions of airborne viruses might not have come pouring in with it? On such an occasion it is a fine thing to sterilise the mouth and throat with a drop of Highland whisky. The whisky is also a solace. I emptied the glass, and poured myself another. Soon I began to feel less alarmed. I noticed the watermelon lying on the seat beside me. I decided that a slice of it at this moment would be refreshing. I took my knife from its case and cut out a thick section. Then, with the point of the knife, I carefully picked out all the black seeds, using the rest of the melon as a receptacle.

I sat drinking the whisky and eating the melon. Both were delicious.

"Gasoline is done," the dreadful Arab said, appearing at the window. "I check water now, and oil."

I would have preferred him to keep his hands off the Lagonda altogether, but rather than risk an argument, I said nothing. He went clumping off toward the front of the car, and his walk reminded me of a drunken Hitler Stormtrooper doing the goosestep in very slow motion.

Tabes dorsalis, as I live and breathe.

The only other disease to induce that queer high-stepping gait is chronic beriberi. Well—he probably had that one, too. I cut myself another slice of watermelon, and concentrated for a minute or so on taking out the seeds with the knife. When I looked up again, I saw that the Arab had raised the bonnet of the car on the righthand side, and was bending over the engine. His head and shoulders were out of sight, and so were his hands and arms. What on earth was the man doing? The oil dipstick was on the other side. I rapped on the windshield. He seemed not to hear me. I put my head out of the window and shouted, "Hey! Come out of there!"

Slowly, he straightened up, and as he drew his right arm out of the bowels of the engine, I saw that he was holding in his fingers something that was long and black and curly and very thin.

"Good God!" I thought. "He's found a snake in there!"

He came round to the window, grinning at me and holding the object out for me to see; and only then, as I got a closer look, did I realize that it was not a snake at all—*it was the fan-belt of my Lagonda!*

All the awful implications of suddenly being stranded in this outlandish place with this disgusting man came flooding over me as I sat there staring dumbly at my broken fan-belt.

"You can see," the Arab was saying, "it was hanging on by a single thread. A good thing I noticed it."

I took it from him and examined it closely. "You cut it!" I cried.

"Cut it?" he answered softly. "Why should I cut it?"

To be perfectly honest, it was impossible for me to judge whether he had or had not cut it. If he had, then he had also taken the trouble to fray the severed ends with some instrument to make it look like an ordinary break. Even so, my guess was that he *had* cut it, and if I was right then the implications were more sinister than ever.

"I suppose you know I can't go on without a fan-belt?" I said.

He grinned again with that awful mutilated mouth, showing ulcerated gums. "If you go now," he said, "you will boil over in three minutes."

"So what do you suggest?"

"I shall get you another fan-belt."

"You will?"

"Of course. There is a telephone here, and if you will pay for the call, I will telephone to Ismailia. And if they haven't got one in Ismailia, I will telephone to Cairo. There is no problem."

"No problem!" I shouted, getting out of the car. "And when, pray, do you think the fan-belt is going to arrive in this ghastly place?"

"There is a mail-truck comes through every morning about ten o'clock. You would have it tomorrow."

The man had all the answers. He never even had to think before replying.

This bastard, I thought, *has cut fan-belts before.*

I was very alert now, and watching him closely.

"They will not have a fan-belt for a machine of this make in Ismailia," I said. "It would have to come from the agents in Cairo. I will telephone them myself." The fact that there was a telephone gave me some comfort. The telephone poles had followed the road all the way across the desert, and I could see the two wires leading into the hut from the nearest pole. "I will ask the agents in Cairo to set out immediately for this place in a special vehicle," I said.

The Arab looked along the road toward Cairo, some two hundred miles away. "Who is going to drive six hours here and six hours back to bring a fan-belt?" he said. "The mail will be just as quick."

"Show me the telephone," I said, starting toward the hut. Then a nasty thought struck me, and I stopped.

How could I possibly use this man's contaminated instrument? The earpiece would have to be pressed against my ear, and the mouthpiece would almost certainly touch my mouth; and I didn't give a damn what the doctors said about the impossibility of catching syphilis from remote contact. A syphilitic mouthpiece was a syphilitic mouthpiece, and you wouldn't catch *me* putting it anywhere near *my* lips, thank you very much. I wouldn't even enter his hut.

I stood there in the sizzling heat of the afternoon and looked at the Arab with his ghastly diseased face, and the Arab looked back at me, as cool and unruffled as you please.

"You want the telephone?" he asked.

"No," I said. "Can you read English?"

"Oh, yes."

"Very well. I shall write down for you the name of the agents and the name of this car, and also my own name. They know me there. You will then tell them what is wanted. And listen . . . tell them to dispatch a special car immediately at my expense. I will pay them well. And if they won't do that, tell them they *have* to get the fan-belt to Ismailia in time to catch the mail-truck. You understand?"

"There is no problem," the Arab said.

So I wrote down what was necessary on a piece of paper and gave it to him. He walked away with that slow, stamping tread toward the hut, and disappeared inside. I closed the bonnet of the car. Then I went back and sat in the driver's seat to think things out.

I poured myself another whisky, and lit a cigarette. There must be *some* traffic on this road. Somebody would surely come along before nightfall. But would that help me? No, it wouldn't—unless I were prepared to hitch a ride and leave the Lagonda and all my baggage behind to the tender mercies of the Arab. Was I prepared to do that? I didn't know. Probably yes. But if I were forced to stay the night, I would lock myself in the car and try to keep awake as much as possible. On no account would I enter the shack where that creature lived. Nor would I touch his food. I had whisky and water, and I had half a watermelon and a slab of chocolate. That was ample.

The heat was pretty bad. The thermometer in the car was still around 104°. It was hotter outside in the sun. I was perspiring freely. My God, what a place to get stranded in! And what a companion!

After about fifteen minutes, the Arab came out of the hut. I watched him all the way to the car.

"I talked to garage in Cairo," he said, pushing his face through the window. "Fan-belt will arrive tomorrow by mail-truck. Everything arranged."

"Did you ask them about sending it at once?"

"They said impossible," he answered.

"You're sure you asked them?"

He inclined his head to one side and gave me that sly insolent grin. I turned away and waited for him to go. He stayed where he was. "We have house for visitors," he said. "You can sleep there very nice. My wife will make food, but you will have to pay."

"Who else is here besides you and your wife?"

"Another man," he said. He waved an arm in the direction of the three shacks across the road, and I turned and saw a man standing in the doorway of the middle shack, a short wide man who was dressed in dirty khaki slacks and shirt. He was standing absolutely motionless in the shadow of the doorway, his arms dangling at his sides. He was looking at me.

"Who is he?" I said.

"Saleh."

"What does he do?"

"He helps."

"I will sleep in the car," I said. "And it will not be necessary for your wife to prepare food. I have my own." The Arab shrugged and turned away and started back toward the shack where the telephone was. I stayed in the car. What else could I do? It was just after two thirty. In three or four hours' time it would start to get a little cooler. Then I could take a stroll and maybe hunt up a few scorpions. Meanwhile, I had to make the best of things as they were. I reached into the back of the car where I kept my box of books and, without looking, I took out the first one I touched. The box contained thirty or forty of the best books in the world, and all of them could be reread a hundred times and would improve with each reading. It was immaterial which one I got. It turned out to be *The Natural History of Selborne*. I opened it at random . . .

". . . We had in this village more than twenty years ago an idiot boy, whom I well remember, who, from a child, showed a strong propensity to bees; they were his food, his amusement, his sole object. And as people of this cast have seldom more than one point of view, so this lad exerted all his few faculties on this one pursuit. In winter he dozed away his time, within his father's house, by the fireside, in a kind of torpid state, seldom departing from the chimney-corner; but in the summer he was all alert, and in quest of his game in the fields, and on sunny banks. Honey-bees, bumble-bees, wasps, were his prey wherever he found them; he had no apprehensions from their stings, but would seize them *nudis manibus,* and at once disarm them of their weapons, and suck their bodies for the sake of their honey-bags. Sometimes he would fill his bosom, between his shirt and his skin, with a number of these captives, and sometimes confine them to bottles. He was a very *merops apiaster,* or bee-bird, and very injurious to men that kept bees; for he would slide into their bee-gardens, and, sitting down before the stools, would rap with his fingers on the hives, and so take the bees as they came out. He has been known to overturn hives for the sake of honey, of which he is passionately fond. Where metheglin was making, he would linger around the tubs and vessels, begging a draught of what he called bee-wine. As he ran about, he used to make a humming noise with his lips, resembling the buzzing of bees . . ."

I glanced up from the book and looked around me. The motionless man across the road had disappeared. There was nobody in sight. The silence was eerie, and the stillness, the utter stillness and desolation of the place was profoundly oppressive. I knew I was being watched. I knew that every little move I made, every sip of whisky and every puff of a cigarette, was being carefully noticed. I detest violence and I never carry a weapon. But I could have done with one now. For a while, I toyed with the idea of starting the motor and driving on down the road until the engine boiled over. But how far would I get? Not very far in this heat and without a fan. One mile, perhaps, or two at the most . . .

No—to hell with it. I would stay where I was and read my book.

It must have been about an hour later that I noticed a small dark speck moving toward me along the road in the far distance, coming from the Jerusalem direction. I laid aside my book without taking my eyes away from the speck. I watched it growing bigger and bigger. It was travelling at a great speed, at a really amazing speed. I got out of the Lagonda and hurried to the side of the road and stood there, ready to signal the driver to stop.

Closer and closer it came, and when it was about a quarter of a mile away, it began to slow down. Suddenly, I noticed the shape of its radiator. It was a *Rolls-Royce!* I raised an arm and kept it raised, and the big green car with a man at the wheel pulled in off the road and stopped beside my Lagonda.

I felt absurdly elated. Had it been a Ford or a Morris, I would have been pleased enough, but I would not have been elated. The fact that it was a Rolls—a Bentley would have done equally well, or an Isotta, or another Lagonda—was a virtual guarantee that I would receive all the assistance I required; for whether you know it or not, there is a powerful brotherhood existing among people who own very costly automobiles. They respect one another automatically, and the reason they respect one another is simply that wealth respects wealth. In point of fact, there is nobody in the world that a very wealthy person respects more than another very wealthy person, and because of this, they naturally seek each other out wherever they go. Recognition signals of many kinds are used among them. With the female, the wearing of massive jewels is perhaps the most common; but the costly automobile is also much favoured, and is used by both sexes. It is a travelling placard, a public declaration of affluence, and as such, it is also a card of membership to that excellent unofficial society, the Very-Wealthy-People's Union. I am a member myself of long standing, and am delighted to be one. When I meet another member, as I was about to do now, I feel an immediate rapport. I respect him. We speak the same language. He is one of *us*. I had good reason, therefore, to be elated.

The driver of the Rolls climbed out and came toward me. He was a small dark man with olive skin, and he wore an immaculate white linen suit. Probably a Syrian, I thought. Just possibly a Greek. In the heat of the day he looked as cool as could be.

"Good afternoon," he said. "Are you having trouble?"

I greeted him, and then bit by bit, I told him everything that had happened.

"My dear fellow," he said in perfect English, "but my *dear fellow*, how very distressing. What rotten luck. This is no place to get stranded in."

"It isn't, is it?"

"And you say that a new fan-belt has definitely been ordered?"

"Yes," I answered, "if I can rely upon the proprietor of this establishment."

The Arab, who had emerged from his shack almost before the Rolls had come to a stop, now joined us, and the stranger proceeded to question him swiftly in Arabic about the steps he had taken on my behalf. It seemed to me that the two knew each other pretty well, and it was clear that the Arab was in great awe of the new arrival. He was practically crawling along the ground in his presence.

"Well—that seems to be all right," the stranger said at last, turning to me. "But quite obviously you won't be able to move on from here until tomorrow morning. Where were you headed for?"

"Jerusalem," I said. "And I don't relish the idea of spending the night in this infernal spot."

"I should say not, my dear man. That would be most uncomfortable." He smiled at me, showing exceptionally white teeth. Then he took out a cigarette case, and offered me a cigarette. The case was gold, and on the outside of it there was a thin line of green jade inlaid diagonally from corner to corner. It was a beautiful thing. I accepted the cigarette. He lit it for me, then lit his own.

The stranger took a long pull at his cigarette, inhaling deeply. Then he tilted back his head and blew the smoke up into the sun. "We shall both get heat-stroke if we stand around here much longer," he said. "Will you permit me to make a suggestion?"

"But of course."

"I do hope you won't consider it presumptuous, coming from a complete stranger . . ."

"Please . . ."

"You can't possibly remain here, so I suggest you come back and stay the night in my house."

There! The Rolls-Royce was smiling at the Lagonda—smiling at it as it would never have smiled at a Ford or a Morris!

"You mean in Ismailia?" I said.

"No, no," he answered, laughing. "I live just around the corner, just over there." He waved a hand in the direction he had come from.

"But surely you were going to Ismailia? I wouldn't want you to change your plans on my behalf."

"I wasn't going to Ismailia at all," he said. "I was coming down here to collect the mail. My house—and this may surprise you—is quite close to where we are standing. You see that mountain? That's Maghara. I'm immediately behind it."

I looked at the mountain. It lay about ten miles to the north, a yellow rocky lump, perhaps two thousand feet high. "Do you really mean that you have a house in the middle of all this . . . this wasteland?" I asked.

"You don't believe me?" he said, smiling.

"Of course I believe you," I answered. "Nothing surprises me any more. Except, perhaps," and here I smiled back at him, "except when I meet a stranger in the middle of the desert, and he treats me like a brother. I am overwhelmed by your offer."

"Nonsense, my dear fellow. My motives are entirely selfish. Civilised company is not easy to come by in these parts. I am quite thrilled at the thought of having a guest for dinner. Permit me to introduce myself—Abdul Aziz." He made a quick little bow.

"Oswald Cornelius," I said. "It is a great pleasure." We shook hands.

"I live partly in Beirut," he said.

"I live in Paris."

"Charming. And now—shall we go? Are you ready?"

"But my car," I said. "Can I leave it here safely?"

"Have no fear about that. Omar is a friend of mine. He's not much to look at, poor chap, but he won't let you down if you're with me. And the other one, Saleh, is a good mechanic. He'll fit your new fan-belt when it arrives tomorrow. I'll tell him now."

Saleh, the man from across the road, had walked over while we were talking. Mr. Aziz gave him his instructions. He then spoke to both men about guarding the Lagonda. He was brief and incisive.

Omar and Saleh stood bowing and scraping. I went across to the Lagonda to get a suitcase. I needed a change of clothes badly.

"Oh, by the way," Mr. Aziz called over to me, "I usually put on a black tie for dinner."

"Of course," I murmured, quickly pushing back my first choice of suitcase and taking another.

"I do it for the ladies mostly. They seem to like dressing themselves up for dinner."

I turned sharply and looked at him, but he was already getting into his car.

"Ready?" he said.

I took the suitcase and placed it in the back of the Rolls. Then I climbed into the front seat beside him, and we drove off.

During the drive, we talked casually about this and that. He told me that his business was in carpets. He had offices in Beirut and Damascus. His forefathers, he said, had been in the trade for hundreds of years.

I mentioned that I had a seventeenth-century Damascus carpet on the floor of my bedroom in Paris.

"You don't mean it!" he cried, nearly swerving off the road with excitement. "Is it silk and wool, with the warp made entirely of silk? And has it got a ground of gold and silver threads?"

"Yes," I said. "Exactly."

"But my dear fellow! You mustn't put a thing like that on the floor!"

"It is touched only by bare feet," I said.

That pleased him. It seemed that he loved carpets almost as much as I loved the blue vases of Tchin-Hoa.

Soon we turned left off the tarred road onto a hard stony track and headed straight over the desert toward the mountain. "This is my private driveway," Mr. Aziz said. "It is five miles long."

"You are even on the telephone," I said, noticing the poles that branched off the main road to follow his private drive.

And then suddenly a queer thought struck me.

That Arab at the filling-station . . . he also was on the tele phone . . .

Might not this, then, explain the fortuitous arrival of Mr. Aziz?

Was it possible that my lonely host had devised a clever method of shanghai-ing travellers off the road in order to provide himself with what he called "civilised company" for dinner? Had he, in fact, given the Arab standing instructions to immobilise the cars of all likely-looking persons one after the other as they came along? "Just cut the fan-belt, Omar. Then phone me up quick. But make sure it's a decent-looking fellow with a good car. Then I'll pop along and see if I think he's worth inviting to the house . . ."

It was ridiculous, of course.

"I think," my companion was saying, "that you are wondering why in the world I should choose to have a house out here in a place like this."

"Well, yes, I am a bit."

"Everyone does," he said.

"Everyone," I said.

"Yes," he said.

Well, well, I thought—everyone.

"I live here," he said, "because I have a peculiar affinity with the desert. I am drawn to it the same way as a sailor is drawn to the sea. Does that seem so very strange to you?"

"No," I answered, "it doesn't seem strange at all."

He paused and took a pull at his cigarette. Then he said, "That is one reason. But there is another. Are you a family man, Mr. Cornelius?"

"Unfortunately not," I answered cautiously.

"I am," he said. "I have a wife and a daughter. Both of them, in my eyes at any rate, are very beautiful. My daughter is just eighteen. She has been to an excellent boarding-school in England, and she is now . . ." he shrugged . . . "she is now just sitting around and waiting until she is old enough to get married. But this waiting period—what does one do with a beautiful young girl during that time? I can't let her loose. She is far too desirable for that. When I take her to Beirut, I see the men hanging around her like wolves waiting to pounce. It drives me nearly out of my mind. I know all about men, Mr. Cornelius. I know how they behave. It is true, of course, that I am not the only father who has had this problem. But the others seem somehow able to face it and accept it. They let their daughters go. They just turn them out of the house and look the other way. I cannot do that. I simply *cannot bring* myself to do it! I refuse to allow her to be mauled by every Achmed, Ali, and Hamil that comes along. And that, you see, is the other reason why I live in the desert—to protect my lovely child for a few more years from the wild beasts. Did you say that you had no family at all, Mr. Cornelius?"

"I'm afraid that's true."

"Oh." He seemed disappointed. "You mean you've never been married?"

"Well . . . no," I said. "No, I haven't." I waited for the next inevitable question. It came about a minute later.

"Have you never *wanted* to get married and have children?"

They all asked that one. It was simply another way of saying, "Are you, in that case, homosexual?"

"Once," I said. "Just once."

"What happened?"

"There was only one person ever in my life, Mr. Aziz . . . and after she went . . ." I sighed.

"You mean she died?"

I nodded, too choked up to answer.

"My dear fellow," he said. "Oh, I am so sorry. Forgive me for intruding."

We drove on for a while in silence.

"It's amazing," I murmured, "how one loses all interest in matters of the flesh after a thing like that. I suppose it's the shock. One never gets over it."

He nodded sympathetically, swallowing it all.

"So now I just travel around trying to forget. I've been doing it for years . . ."

We had reached the foot of Mount Maghara now and were following the track as it curved around the mountain toward the side that was invisible from the road—the north side. "As soon as we round the next bend you'll see the house," Mr. Aziz said.

We rounded the bend . . . and there it was! I blinked and stared, and I tell you that for the first few seconds I literally could not believe my eyes. I saw before me a white castle—I mean it—a *tall, white castle* with turrets and towers and little spires all over it, standing like a fairy-tale in the middle of a small splash of green vegetation on the lower slope of the blazing-hot, bare, yellow mountain! It was fantastic! It was straight out of Hans Christian Andersen or Grimm. I had seen plenty of romantic-looking Rhine and Loire valley castles in my time, but never before had I seen anything with such a slender, graceful, fairy-tale quality as this! The greenery, as I observed when we drew closer, was a pretty garden of lawns and date-palms, and there was a high white wall going all the way round to keep out the desert.

"Do you approve?" my host asked, smiling.

"It's fabulous!" I said. "It's like all the fairy-tale castles in the world made into one."

"That's exactly what it is!" he cried. "It's a fairy-tale castle! I built it especially for my daughter, my beautiful Princess."

And the beautiful Princess is imprisoned within its walls by her strict and jealous father, King Abdul Aziz, who refuses to allow her the pleasures of masculine company. But watch out, for here comes Prince Oswald Cornelius to the rescue! Unbeknownst to the King, he is going to ravish the beautiful Princess, and make her very happy.

"You have to admit it's different," Mr. Aziz said.

"It is that."

"It is also nice and private. I sleep very peacefully here. So does the Princess. No unpleasant young men are likely to come climbing in through *those* windows during the night."

"Quite so," I said.

"It used to be a small oasis," he went on. "I bought it from the government. We have ample water for the house, the swimming-pool, and three acres of garden."

We drove through the main gates, and I must say it was wonderful to come suddenly into a miniature paradise of green lawns and flowerbeds and palm-trees. Everything was in perfect order, and water-sprinklers were playing on the lawns. When we stopped at the front door of the house, two servants in spotless gallabiyahs and scarlet tarbooshes ran out immediately, one to each side of the car, to open the doors for us.

Two servants? But would both of them have come out like that unless they'd been expecting *two* people? I doubted it. More and more, it began to look as though my odd little theory about being shanghaied as a dinner guest was turning out to be correct. It was all very amusing.

My host ushered me in through the front door, and at once I got that lovely shivery feeling that comes over the skin as one walks suddenly out of intense heat into an air-conditioned room. I was standing in the hall. The floor was of green marble. On my right, there was a wide archway leading to a large room, and I received a fleeting impression of cool white walls, fine pictures, and superlative Louis XV furniture. What a place to find oneself in, in the middle of the Sinai Desert!

And now a woman was coming slowly down the stairs. My host had turned away to speak to the servants, and he didn't see her at once, so when she reached the bottom step, the woman paused, and she laid her naked arm like a white anaconda along the rail of the banister, and there she stood, looking at me as though she were Queen Semiramis on the steps of Babylon, and I was a candidate who might or might not be to her taste. Her hair was jet-black, and she had a figure that made me wet my lips.

When Mr. Aziz turned and saw her, he said, "Oh darling, there you are. I've brought you a guest. His car broke down at the filling-station—such rotten luck—so I asked him to come back and stay the night. Mr. Cornelius . . . my wife."

"How very nice," she said quietly, coming forward.

I took her hand and raised it to my lips. "I am overcome by your kindness, madame," I murmured. There was, upon that hand of hers, a diabolical perfume. It was almost exclusively animal. The subtle, sexy secretions of the sperm-whale, the male musk-deer, and the beaver were all there, pungent and obscene beyond words; they dominated the blend completely, and only faint traces of the clean vegetable oils—lemon, cajuput, and zeroli—were allowed to come through. It was superb! And another thing I noticed in the flash of that first moment was this: When I took her hand, she did not, as other women do, let it lie limply across my palm like a fillet of raw fish. Instead, she placed her thumb *underneath* my hand, with the fingers on top; and thus she was able to—and I swear she did—exert a gentle but suggestive pressure upon my hand as I administered the conventional kiss.

"Where is Diana?" asked Mr. Aziz.

"She's out by the pool," the woman said. And turning to me, "Would *you* like a swim, Mr. Cornelius? You must be roasted after hanging around that awful filling-station."

She had huge velvet eyes, so dark they were almost black, and when she smiled at me, the end of her nose moved upward, distending the nostrils.

There and then, Prince Oswald Cornelius decided that he cared not one whit about the beautiful Princess who was held captive in the castle by the jealous King. He would ravish the Queen instead.

"Well . . ." I said.

"I'm going to have one," Mr. Aziz said.

"Let's all have one," his wife said. "We'll lend you a pair of trunks."

I asked if I might go up to my room first and get out a clean shirt and clean slacks to put on after the swim, and my hostess said, "Yes, of course," and told one of the servants to show me the way. He took me up two flights of stairs, and we entered a large white bedroom which had in it an exceptionally large double-bed. There was a well-equipped bathroom leading off to one side, with a pale-blue bathtub and a bidet to match. Everywhere, things were scrupulously clean and very much to my liking. While the servant was unpacking my case, I went over to the window and looked out, and I saw the great blazing desert sweeping in like a yellow sea all the way from the horizon until it met the white garden wall just below me, and there, within the wall, I could see the swimming-pool, and beside the pool there was a girl lying on her back in the shade of a big pink parasol. The girl was wearing a white swimming-costume, and she was reading a book. She had long slim legs and black hair. She was the Princess.

What a set-up, I thought. The white castle, the comfort, the cleanliness, the air-conditioning, the two dazzlingly beautiful females, the watchdog husband, and a whole evening to work in! The situation was so perfectly designed for my entertainment that it would have been impossible to improve upon it. The problems that lay ahead appealed to me very much. A simple straightforward seduction did not amuse me any more. There was no artistry in that sort of thing; and I can assure you that had I been able, by waving a magic wand, to make Mr. Abdul Aziz, the jealous watchdog, disappear for the night, I would not have done so. I wanted no pyrrhic victories.

When I left the room, the servant accompanied me. We descended the first flight of stairs, and then, on the landing of the floor below my own, I paused and said casually, "Does the whole family sleep on this floor?"

"Oh, yes," the servant said. "That is the master's room there" —indicating a door—"and next to it is Mrs. Aziz. Miss Diana is opposite."

Three separate rooms. All very close together. Virtually impregnable. I tucked the information away in my mind and went on down to the pool. My host and hostess were there before me.

"This is my daughter, Diana," my host said.

The girl in the white swimming-suit stood up and I kissed her hand. "Hello, Mr. Cornelius," she said.

She was using the same heavy animal perfume as her mother— ambergris, musk, and castor! What a smell it had—bitchy, brazen, and marvellous! I sniffed at it like a dog. She was, I thought, even more beautiful than the parent, if that were possible. She had the same large velvety eyes, the same black hair, and the same shape of face; but her legs were unquestionably longer, and there was something about her body that gave it a slight edge over the older woman's: it was more sinuous, more snaky, and almost certain to be a good deal more flexible. But the older woman, who was probably thirty-seven and looked no more than twenty-five, had a spark in her eye that the daughter could not possibly match.

Eeny, meeny, miny, mo—just a little while ago, Prince Oswald had sworn that he would ravish the Queen alone, and to hell with the Princess. But now that he had seen the Princess in the flesh, he did not know which one to prefer. Both of them, in their different ways, held forth a promise of innumerable delights, the one innocent and eager, the other expert and voracious. The truth of the matter was that he would like to have them both —the Princess as an hors d'oeuvre, and the Queen as the main dish.

"Help yourself to a pair of trunks in the changing-room, Mr. Cornelius," Mrs. Aziz was saying, so I went into the hut and changed, and when I came out again the three of them were already splashing about in the water. I dived in and joined them. The water was so cold it made me gasp.

"I thought that would surprise you," Mr. Aziz said, laughing. "It's cooled. I keep it at sixty-five degrees. It's more refreshing in this climate."

Later, when the sun began dropping lower in the sky, we all sat around in our wet swimming-clothes while a servant brought us pale, ice-cold martinis, and it was at this point that I began, very slowly, very cautiously, to seduce the two ladies in my own particular fashion. Normally, when I am given a free hand, this is not especially difficult for me to do. The curious little talent that I happen to possess —the ability to hypnotise a woman with words—very seldom lets me down. It is not, of course, done only with words. The words themselves, the innocuous, superficial words, are spoken only by the mouth, whereas the real message, the improper and exciting promise, comes from all the limbs and organs of the body, and is transmitted through the eyes. More than that I cannot honestly tell you about how it is done. The point is that it works. It works like cantharides. I believe that I could sit down opposite the Pope's wife, if he had one, and within fifteen minutes, were I to try hard enough, she would be leaning toward me over the table with her lips apart and her eyes glazed with desire. It is a minor talent, not a great one, but I am nonetheless thankful to have had it bestowed upon me, and I have done my best at all times to see that it has not been wasted.

So the four of us, the two wondrous women, the little man, and myself, sat close together in a semi-circle beside the swimming-pool, lounging in deck-chairs and sipping our drinks and feeling the warm six o'clock sunshine upon our skin. I was in good form. I made them laugh a great deal. The story about the greedy old Duchess of Glasgow putting her hand in the chocolate box and getting nipped by one of my scorpions had the daughter falling out of her chair with mirth; and when I described in detail the interior of my spider breeding-house in the garden outside Paris, both ladies began wriggling with revulsion and pleasure.

It was at this stage that I noticed the eyes of Mr Abdul Aziz resting upon me in a good-humoured, twinkling kind of way. "Well, well," the eyes seemed to be saying, "we are glad to see that you are not quite so disinterested in women as you led us to believe in the car . . . Or is it, perhaps, that these congenial surroundings are helping you to forget that great sorrow of yours at last . ." Mr. Aziz smiled at me, showing his pure white teeth. It was a friendly smile. I gave him a friendly smile back. What a friendly little fellow he was. He was genuinely delighted to see me paying so much attention to the ladies. So far, then, so good.

I shall skip very quickly over the next few hours, for it was not until after midnight that anything really tremendous happened to me. A few brief notes will suffice to cover the intervening period:

At seven o'clock, we all left the swimming-pool and returned to the house to dress for dinner.

At eight o'clock, we assembled in the big living-room to drink another cocktail. The two ladies were both superbly turned out, and sparkling with jewels. Both of them wore low-cut, sleeveless evening-dresses which had come, without any doubt at all, from some great fashion house in Paris. My hostess was in black, her daughter in pale blue, and the scent of that intoxicating perfume was everywhere about them. What a pair they were! The older woman had that slight forward hunch to her shoulders which one sees only in the most passionate and practised of females; for in the same way as a horsey woman will become bandy-legged from sitting constantly upon a horse, so a woman of great passion will develop a curious roundness of the shoulders from continually embracing men. It is an occupational deformity, and the noblest of them all.

The daughter was not yet old enough to have acquired this singular badge of honour, but with her it was enough for me simply to stand back and observe the shape of her body and to notice the splendid sliding motion of her thighs underneath the tight silk dress as she wandered about the room. She had a line of tiny soft golden hairs growing all the way up the exposed length of her spine, and when I stood behind her it was difficult to resist the temptation of running my knuckles up and down those lovely vertebrae.

At eight thirty, we moved into the dining-room. The dinner that followed was a really magnificent affair, but I shall waste no time here describing food or wine. Throughout the meal I continued to play most delicately and insidiously upon the sensibilities of the women, employing every skill that I possessed; and by the time the dessert arrived, they were melting before my eyes like butter in the sun.

After dinner we returned to the living-room for coffee and brandy, and then, at my host's suggestion, we played a couple of rubbers of bridge.

By the end of the evening, I knew for certain that I had done my work well. The old magic had not let me down. Either of the two ladies, should circumstances permit, was mine for the asking. I was not deluding myself over this. It was a straightforward, obvious fact. It stood out a mile. The face of my hostess was bright with excitement, and whenever she looked at me across the card-table, those huge dark velvety eyes would grow bigger and bigger, and the nostrils would dilate, and the mouth would open slightly to reveal the tip of a moist pink tongue squeezing through between the teeth. It was a marvellously lascivious gesture, and more than once it caused me to trump my own trick. The daughter was less daring but equally direct. Each time her eyes met mine, and that was often enough, she would raise her brows just the tiniest fraction of a centimetre, as though asking a question; then she would make a quick sly little smile, supplying the answer.

"I think it's time we all went to bed," Mr. Aziz said, examining his watch. "It's after eleven. Come along, my dears."

Then a queer thing happened. At once, without a second's hesitation and without another glance in my direction, both ladies rose and made for the door! It was astonishing. It left me stunned. I didn't know what to make of it. It was the quickest thing I'd ever seen. And yet it wasn't as though Mr. Aziz had spoken angrily. His voice, to me at any rate, had sounded as pleasant as ever. But now he was already turning out the lights, indicating clearly that he wished me also to retire. What a blow! I had expected at least to receive a whisper from either the wife or the daughter before we separated for the night, just a quick three or four words telling me where to go and when; but instead, I was left standing like a fool beside the card table while the two ladies glided out of the room.

My host and I followed them up the stairs. On the landing of the first floor, the mother and daughter stood side by side, waiting for me.

"Goodnight, Mr. Cornelius," my hostess said.

"Goodnight, Mr. Cornelius," the daughter said.

"Goodnight, my dear fellow," Mr. Aziz said. "I do hope you have everything you want."

They turned away, and there was nothing for me to do but continue slowly, reluctantly, up the second flight of stairs to my own room. I entered it and closed the door. The heavy brocade curtains had already been drawn by one of the servants, but I parted them and leaned out the window to take a look at the night. The air was still and warm, and a brilliant moon was shining over the desert. Below me, the swimming-pool in the moonlight looked something like an enormous glass mirror lying flat on the lawn, and beside it I could see the four deck-chairs we had been sitting in earlier.

Well, well, I thought. What happens now?

One thing I knew I must not do in this house was to venture out of my room and go prowling around the corridors. That would be suicide. I had learned many years ago that there are three breeds of husband with whom one must never take unnecessary risks—the Bulgarian, the Greek, and the Syrian. None of them, for some reason, resents you flirting quite openly with his wife, but he will kill you at once if he catches you getting into her bed. Mr. Aziz was a Syrian. A degree of prudence was therefore essential, and if any move were going to be made now, it must be made not by me but by one of the two women, for only she (or they) would know precisely what was safe and what was dangerous. Yet I had to admit that after witnessing the way in which my host had called them both to heel four minutes ago, there was very little hope of further action in the near future. The trouble was, though, that I had gotten myself so infernally steamed up.

I undressed and took a long cold shower. That helped. Then, because I have never been able to sleep in the moonlight, I made sure that the curtains were tightly drawn together. I got into bed, and for the next hour or so I lay reading some more of Gilbert White's *Natural History of Selborne*. That also helped, and at last, somewhere between midnight and one A.M., there came a time when I was able to switch out the light and prepare myself for sleep without altogether too many regrets.

I was just beginning to doze off when I heard some tiny sounds. I recognised them at once. They were sounds that I had heard many times before in my life, and yet they were still, for me, the most thrilling and evocative in the whole world. They consisted of a series of little soft metallic noises, of metal grating gently against metal, and they were made, they were always made by somebody who was very slowly, very cautiously, turning the handle of one's door from the outside. Instantly, I became wide awake. But I did not move. I simply opened my eyes and stared in the direction of the door; and I can remember wishing at that moment for a gap in the curtain, for just a small thin shaft of moonlight to come in from outside so that I could at least catch a glimpse of the shadow of the lovely form that was about to enter. But the room was as dark as a dungeon.

I did not hear the door open. No hinge squeaked. But suddenly a little gust of air swept through the room and rustled the curtains, and a moment later I heard the soft thud of wood against wood as the door was carefully closed again. Then came the click of the latch as the handle was released.

Next, I heard feet tiptoeing toward me over the carpet.

For one horrible second, it occurred to me that this might just possibly be Mr. Abdul Aziz creeping in upon me with a long knife in his hand, but then all at once a warm extensile body was bending over mine, and a woman's voice was whispering in my ear, *"Don't make a sound!"*

"My dearest beloved," I said, wondering which one of them it was, "I knew you'd : . ." Instantly her hand came over my mouth.

"Please!" she whispered. *"Not another word!"*

I didn't argue. My lips had many better things to do than that. So had hers.

Here I must pause. This is not like me at all—I know that. But just for once, I wish to be excused a detailed description of the great scene that followed. I have my own reasons for this and I beg you to respect them. In any case, it will do you no harm to exercise your own imagination for a change, and if you wish, I will stimulate it a little by saying simply and truthfully that of the many thousands and thousands of women I have known in my time, none has transported me to greater extremes of ecstasy than this lady of the Sinai Desert. Her dexterity was amazing. Her passion was intense. Her range was unbelievable. At every turn, she was ready with some new and intricate manoeuvre. And to cap it all, she possessed the subtlest and most recondite style I have ever encountered. She was a great artist. She was a genius.

All this, you will probably say, indicated clearly that my visitor must have been the older woman. You would be wrong. It indicated nothing. True genius is a gift of birth. It has very little to do with age; and I can assure you I had no way of knowing for certain which of them it was in the darkness of that room. I wouldn't have bet a penny on it either way. At one moment, after some particularly boisterous cadenza, I would be convinced it was the wife. *It must be the wife!* Then suddenly the whole tempo would begin to change, and the melody would become so childlike and innocent that I found myself swearing it was the daughter. *It must be the daughter!*

Maddening it was not to know the true answer. It tantalised me. It also humbled me, for, after all, a connoisseur, a supreme connoisseur, should always be able to guess the vintage without seeing the label on the bottle. But this one really had me beat. At one point, I reached for cigarettes, intending to solve the mystery in the flare of a match, but her hand was on me in a flash, and cigarettes and matches both were snatched away and flung across the room. More than once, I began to whisper the question itself into her ear, but I never got three words out before the hand shot up again and smacked itself over my mouth. Rather violently, too.

Very well, I thought. Let it be for now. Tomorrow morning, downstairs in the daylight, I shall know for certain which one of you it was. I shall know by the glow on the face, by the way the eyes look back into mine, and by a hundred other little telltale signs. I shall also know by the marks that my teeth have made on the left side of the neck, above the dress line. A rather wily move, that one, I thought, and so perfectly timed—my vicious bite was administered during the height of her passion—that she never for one moment realised the significance of the act.

It was altogether a most memorable night, and at least four hours must have gone by before she gave me a final fierce embrace, and slipped out of the room as quickly as she had come in.

The next morning I did not awaken until after ten o'clock. I got out of bed and drew open the curtains. It was another brilliant, hot, desert day. I took a leisurely bath, then dressed myself as carefully as ever. I felt relaxed and chipper. It made me very happy to think that I could still summon a woman to my room with my eyes alone, even in middle-age. And what a woman! It would be fascinating to find out which one of them she was. I would soon know.

I made my way slowly down the two flights of stairs.

"Good morning, my dear fellow, good morning!" Mr. Aziz said, rising from a small desk he had been writing at in the living-room. "Did you have a good night?"

"Excellent, thank you," I answered, trying not to sound smug.

He came and stood close to me, smiling with his very white teeth. His shrewd little eyes rested on my face and moved over it slowly, as though searching for something.

"I have good news for you," he said. "They called up from B'ir Rawd Salim five minutes ago and said your new fan-belt had arrived by the mail-truck. Saleh is fitting it on now. It'll be ready in an hour. So when you've had some breakfast, I'll drive you over and you can be on your way."

I told him how grateful I was.

"We'll be sorry to see you go," he said. "It's been an immense pleasure for all of us having you drop in like this, an immense pleasure."

I had my breakfast alone in the dining-room. Afterward, I returned to the living-room to smoke a cigarette while my host continued writing at his desk.

"Do forgive me," he said. "I just have a couple of things to finish here. I won't be long. I've arranged for your case to be packed and put in the car, so you have nothing to worry about. Sit down and enjoy your cigarette. The ladies ought to be down any minute now."

The wife arrived first. She came sailing into the room looking more than ever like the dazzling Queen Semiramis of the Nile, and the first thing I noticed about her was the pale-green chiffon scarf knotted casually around her neck! Casually but carefully! So carefully that no part of the skin of the neck was visible. The woman went straight over to her husband and kissed him on the cheek. "Good morning, my darling," she said.

You cunning beautiful bitch, I thought.

"Good *morning,* Mr. Cornelius," she said gaily, coming over to sit in the chair opposite mine. "Did you have a good night? I do hope you had everything you wanted."

Never in my life have I seen such a sparkle in a woman's eyes as I saw in hers that morning, nor such a glow of pleasure in a woman's face.

"I had a very good night indeed, thank *you,*" I answered, showing her that I knew.

She smiled and lit a cigarette. I glanced over at Mr. Aziz, who was still writing away busily at the desk with his back to us. He wasn't paying the slightest attention to his wife or to me. He was, I thought, exactly like all the other poor cuckolds that I had ever created. Not one of them would believe that it could happen to him, not right under his own nose.

"Good morning, everybody!" cried the daughter, sweeping into the room. "Good morning, Daddy! Good morning, Mummy!" She gave them each a kiss. "Good morning, Mr. Cornelius!" She was wearing a pair of pink slacks and a rust-coloured blouse, and I'll be damned if she didn't also have a scarf tied carelessly but carefully around her neck! A chiffon scarf!

"Did you have a decent night?" she asked, perching herself like a young bride on the arm of my chair, arranging herself in such a way that one of her thighs rested against my forearm. I leaned back and looked at her closely. She looked back at me and winked. She actually winked! Her face was glowing and sparkling every bit as much as her mother's, and if anything, she seemed even more pleased with herself than the older woman.

I felt pretty confused. Only one of them had a bite mark to conceal, yet both of them had covered their necks with scarves. I conceded that this might be a coincidence, but on the face of it, it looked much more like a conspiracy to me. It looked as though they were both working closely together to keep me from discovering the truth. But what an extraordinary screwy business! And what was the purpose of it all? And in what other peculiar ways, might I ask, did they plot and plan together among themselves? Had they drawn lots or something the night before? Or did they simply take it in turns with visitors? I *must* come back again, I told myself, for another visit as soon as possible just to see what happens the next time. In fact, I might motor down specially from Jerusalem in a day or two. It would be easy, I reckoned, to get myself invited again.

"Are you ready, Mr. Cornelius?" Mr. Aziz said, rising from his desk.

"Quite ready," I answered.

The ladies, sleek and smiling, led the way outside to where the big green Rolls-Royce was waiting. I kissed their hands and murmured a million thanks to each of them. Then I got into the front seat beside my host, and we drove off. The mother and daughter waved. I lowered my window and waved back. Then we were out of the garden and into the desert, following the stony yellow track as it skirted the base of Mount Maghara, with the telegraph poles marching along beside us.

During the journey, my host and I conversed pleasantly about this and that. I was at pains to be as agreeable as possible because my one object now was to get myself invited to stay at the house again. If I didn't succeed in getting *him* to ask *me,* then *I* should have to ask *him.* I would do it at the last moment. "Goodbye, my dear friend," I would say, gripping him warmly by the throat. "May I have the pleasure of dropping in to see you again if I happen to be passing this way?" And of course he would say yes.

"Did you think I exaggerated when I told you my daughter was beautiful?" he asked me.

"You understated it," I said. "She's a raving beauty. I do congratulate you. But your wife is no less lovely. In fact, between the two of them they almost swept me off my feet," I added, laughing.

"I noticed that," he said, laughing with me. "They're a couple of very naughty girls. They do so love to flirt with other men. But why should I mind? There's no harm in flirting."

"None whatsoever," I said.

"I think it's gay and fun."

"It's charming," I said.

In less than half an hour we had reached the main Ismailia–Jerusalem road. Mr. Aziz turned the Rolls onto the black tarmac strip and headed for the filling-station at seventy miles an hour. In a few minutes we would be there. So now I tried moving a little closer to the subject of another visit, fishing gently for an invitation. "I can't get over your house," I said. "I think it's simply wonderful."

"It is nice, isn't it?"

"I suppose you're bound to get pretty lonely out there, on and off, just the three of you together?"

"It's no worse than anywhere else," he said. "People get lonely wherever they are. A desert, or a city—it doesn't make much difference, really. But we do have visitors, you know. You'd be surprised at the number of people who drop in from time to time. Like you, for instance. It was a great pleasure having you with us, my dear fellow."

"I shall never forget it," I said. "It is a rare thing to find kindness and hospitality of that order nowadays."

I waited for him to tell me that I must come again, but he didn't. A little silence sprang up between us, a slightly uneasy little silence. To bridge it, I said, "I think yours is the most thoughtful paternal gesture I've ever heard of in my life."

"Mine?"

"Yes. Building a house right out there in the back of beyond and living in it just for your daughter's sake, to protect her. I think it's remarkable."

I saw him smile, but he kept his eyes on the road and said nothing. The filling-station and the group of huts were now in sight about a mile ahead of us. The sun was high and it was getting hot inside the car.

"Not many fathers would put themselves out to that extent," I went on.

Again he smiled, but somewhat bashfully this time, I thought. And then he said, "I don't deserve *quite* as much credit as you like to give me, really I don't. To be absolutely honest with you, that pretty daughter of mine isn't the only reason for my living in such splendid isolation."

"I know that."

"You do?"

"You told me. You said the other reason was the desert. You loved it, you said, as a sailor loves the sea."

"So I did. And it's quite true. But there's still a third reason."

"Oh, and what is that?"

He didn't answer me. He sat quite still with his hands on the wheel and his eyes fixed on the road ahead.

"I'm sorry," I said. "I shouldn't have asked the question. It's none of my business."

"No, no, that's quite all right," he said. "Don't apologise."

I stared out of the window at the desert. "I think it's hotter than yesterday," I said. "It must be well over a hundred already."

"Yes."

I saw him shifting a little in his seat, as though trying to get comfortable, and then he said, "I don't really see why I shouldn't tell you the truth about that house. You don't strike me as being a gossip."

"Certainly not," I said.

We were close to the filling-station now, and he had slowed the car down almost to walking-speed to give himself time to say what he had to say. I could see the two Arabs standing beside my Lagonda, watching us.

"That daughter," he said at length, "the one you met—she isn't the only daughter I have."

"Oh, really?"

"I've got another who is five years older than she."

"And just as beautiful, no doubt," I said. "Where does she live? In Beirut?"

"No, she's in the house."

"In which house? Not the one we've just left?"

"Yes."

"But I never saw her!"

"Well," he said, turning suddenly to watch my face, "maybe not."

"But why?"

"She has leprosy."

I jumped.

"Yes, I know," he said, "it's a terrible thing. She has the worst kind, too, poor girl. It's called anaesthetic leprosy. It is highly resistant, and almost impossible to cure. If only it were the nodular variety, it would be much easier. But it isn't, and there you are. So when a visitor comes to the house, she keeps to her own apartment, on the third floor . . ."

The car must have pulled into the filling-station about then because the next thing I can remember was seeing Mr. Abdul Aziz sitting there looking at me with those small clever black eyes of his, and he was saying, "But my dear fellow, you mustn't alarm yourself like this. Calm yourself down, Mr. Cornelius, calm yourself down! There's absolutely nothing in the world for you to worry about. It is not a very contagious disease. You have to have the most *intimate* contact with the person in order to catch it . . ."

I got out of the car very slowly and stood in the sunshine. The Arab with the diseased face was grinning at me and saying, "Fan-belt all fixed now. Everything fine." I reached into my pocket for cigarettes, but my hand was shaking so violently I dropped the packet on the ground. I bent down and retrieved it. Then I got a cigarette out and managed to light it. When I looked up again, I saw the green Rolls-Royce already half a mile down the road, and going away fast.

Claud's Dog

The Ratcatcher · *1953*

In the afternoon the ratcatcher came to the filling-station. He came sidling up the driveway with a stealthy, soft-treading gait, making no noise at all with his feet on the gravel. He had an army knapsack slung over one shoulder and he was wearing an old-fashioned black jacket with large pockets. His brown corduroy trousers were tied around the knees with pieces of white string.

"Yes?" Claud asked, knowing very well who he was.

"Rodent operative." His small dark eyes moved swiftly over the premises.

"The ratcatcher?"

"That's me."

The man was lean and brown with a sharp face and two long sulphur-coloured teeth that protruded from the upper jaw, overlapping the lower lip, pressing it inward. The ears were thin and pointed and set far back on the head, near the nape of the neck. The eyes were almost black but when they looked at you there was a flash of yellow somewhere inside them.

"You've come very quick."

"Special orders from the Health Officer."

"And now you're going to catch all the rats?"

"Yep."

The kind of dark furtive eyes he had were those of an animal that lives its life peering out cautiously and forever from a hole in the ground.

"How are you going to catch em?"

"Ah-h-h," the ratman said darkly. "That's all accordin to where they is."

"Trap em, I suppose."

"Trap em!" he cried, disgusted. "You won't catch many rats that way! Rats isn't rabbits you know."

He held his face up high, sniffing the air with a nose that twitched perceptibly from side to side.

"No," he said, scornfully. "Trappin's no way to catch a rat. Rats is clever, let me tell you that. If you want to catch em, you got to know em. You got to know rats on this job."

I could see Claud staring at him with a certain fascination.

"They're more clever'n dogs, rats is."

"Get away."

"You know what they do? They watch you! All the time you're goin round preparin to catch em, they're sitting quietly in dark places, watchin you." The man crouched, stretching his stringy neck far forward.

"So what do you do?" Claud asked, fascinated.

"Ah! That's it you see. That's where you got to know rats."

"How d'you catch em?"

"There's ways," the ratman said, leering. "There's various ways."

He paused, nodding his repulsive head sagely up and down. "It's all dependin," he said, "on where they is. This ain't a sewer job, is it?"

"No, it's not a sewer job."

"Tricky things, sewer jobs. Yes," he said, delicately sniffing the air to the left of him with his mobile nose-end, "sewer jobs is very tricky things."

"Not especially, I shouldn't think."

"Oh-ho. You shouldn't, shouldn't you! Well, I'd like to see *you* do a sewer job! Just exactly how would *you* set about it, I'd like to know?"

"Nothing to it. I'd just poison em, that's all."

"And where exactly would you put the poison, might I ask?"

"Down the sewer. Where the hell you think I put it!"

"There!" the ratman cried, triumphant. "I knew it! Down the sewer! And you know what'd happen then? Get washed away, that's all. Sewer's like a river, y'know."

"That's what *you* say," Claud answered. "That's only what *you* say."

"It's facts."

"All right then, all right. So what would *you* do, Mr. Know-all?"

"That's exactly where you got to know rats, on a sewer job."

"Come on then, let's have it."

"Now listen. I'll tell you." The ratman advanced a step closer, his voice became secretive and confidential, the voice of a man divulging fabulous professional secrets. "You works on the understandin that a rat is a gnawin animal, see. Rats *gnaws*. Anything you give em, don't matter what it is, anything new they never seen before, and what do they do? They *gnaws* it. So now! There you are! You got a sewer job on your hands. And what d'you do?"

His voice had the soft throaty sound of a croaking frog and he seemed to speak all his words with an immense wet-lipped relish, as though they tasted good on the tongue. The accent was similar to Claud's, the broad soft accent of the Buckinghamshire countryside, but his voice was more throaty, the words more fruity in his mouth.

"All you do is you go down the sewer and you take along some ordinary paper bags, just ordinary brown paper bags, and these bags is filled with plaster of Paris powder. Nothin else. Then you suspend the bags from the roof of the sewer so they hang down not quite touching the water. See? Not quite touchin, and just high enough so a rat can reach em."

Claud was listening, rapt.

"There you are, y'see. Old rat comes swimmin along the sewer and sees the bag. He stops. He takes a sniff at it and it don't smell so bad anyway. So what's he do then?"

"He *gnaws* it," Claud cried, delighted.

"There! That's it! That's exackly it! He starts *gnawin* away at the bag and the bag breaks and the old rat gets a mouthful of powder for his pains."

"Well?"

"That does him."

"What? Kills him?"

"Yep. Kills him stony!"

"Plaster of Paris ain't poisonous, you know."

"Ah! There you are! That's exackly where you're wrong, see. This powder swells. When you wet it, it swells. Gets into the rat's tubes and swells right up and kills him quicker'n anythin in the world."

"*No!*"

"That's where you got to know rats."

The ratman's face glowed with a stealthy pride, and he rubbed his stringy fingers together, holding the hands up close to the face. Claud watched him, fascinated.

"Now—where's them rats?" The word "rats" came out of his mouth soft and throaty, with a rich fruity relish as though he were gargling with melted butter. "Let's take a look at them *rraats*."

"Over there in the hayrick across the road."

"Not in the house?" he asked, obviously disappointed.

"No. Only around the hayrick. Nowhere else."

"I'll wager they're in the house too. Like as not gettin in all your food in the night and spreadin disease and sickness. You got any disease here?" he asked, looking first at me, then at Claud.

"Everyone fine here."

"Quite sure?"

"Oh yes."

"You never know, you see. You could be sickenin for it weeks and weeks and not feel it. Then all of a sudden—bang!—and it's got you. That's why Doctor Arbuthnot's so particular. That's why he sent me out so quick, see. To stop the spreadin of disease."

He had now taken upon himself the mantle of the Health Officer. A most important rat he was now, deeply disappointed that we were not suffering from bubonic plague.

"I feel fine," Claud said, nervously.

The ratman searched his face again, but said nothing.

"And how are you goin to catch em in the hayrick?"

The ratman grinned, a crafty toothy grin. He reached down into his knapsack and withdrew a large tin which he held up level with his face. He peered around one side of it at Claud.

"Poison!" he whispered. But he pronounced it *pye-zn*, making it into a soft, dark, dangerous word. "Deadly *pye-zn*, that's what this is!" He was weighing the tin up and down in his hands as he spoke. "Enough here to kill a million men!"

"Terrifying," Claud said.

"Exackly it! They'd put you inside for six months if they caught you with even a spoonful of this," he said, wetting his lips with his tongue. He had a habit of craning his head forward on his neck as he spoke.

"Want to see?" he asked, taking a penny from his pocket, prising open the lid. "There now! There it is!" He spoke fondly, almost lovingly of the stuff, and he held it forward for Claud to look.

"Corn? Or barley is it?"

"It's oats. Soaked in deadly *pye-zn*. You take just one of them grains in your mouth and you'd be a gonner in five minutes!"

"Honest?"

"Yep. Never out of me sight, this tin."

He caressed it with his hands and gave it a little shake so that the oat grains rustled softly inside.

"But not today. Your rats don't get this today. They wouldn't have it anyway. That they wouldn't. There's where you got to know rats. Rats is suspicious. Terrible suspicious, rats is. So today they gets some nice clean tasty oats as'll do em no harm in the world. Fatten em, that's all it'll do. And tomorrow they gets the same again. And it'll taste so good there'll be all the rats in the districk comin along after a couple of days."

"Rather clever."

"You got to be clever on this job. You got to be cleverer'n a rat and that's sayin somethin."

"You've almost got to be a rat yourself," I said. It slipped out in error, before I had time to stop myself, and I couldn't really help it because I was looking at the man at the time. But the effect upon him was surprising.

"There!" he cried. "Now you got it! Now you really said somethin! A good ratter's got to be more like a rat than anythin else in the world! Cleverer even than a rat, and that's not an easy thing to be, let me tell you."

"Quite sure it's not."

"All right then, let's go. I haven't got all day, you know. There's Lady Leonora Benson asking for me urgent up there at the Manor."

"She got rats, too?"

"Everybody's got rats," the ratman said, and he ambled off down the driveway, across the road to the hayrick and we watched him go. The way he walked was so like a rat it made you wonder— that slow, almost a delicate ambling walk with a lot of give at the knees and no sound at all from the footsteps on the gravel. He hopped nimbly over the gate into the field, then walked quickly round the hayrick scattering handfuls of oats onto the ground.

The next day he returned and repeated the procedure.

The day after that he came again and this time he put down the poisoned oats. But he didn't scatter these; he placed them carefully in little piles at each corner of the rick.

"You got a dog?" he asked when he came back across the road on the third day after putting down the poison.

"Yes."

"Now if you want to see your dog die an orrible twistin death, all you got to do is let him in that gate sometime."

"We'll take care," Claud told him. "Don't you worry about that."

The next day he returned once more, this time to collect the dead.

"You got an old sack?" he asked. "Most likely we goin to need a sack to put em in."

He was puffed up and important now, the black eyes gleaming with pride. He was about to display the sensational results of his craft to the audience.

Claud fetched a sack and the three of us walked across the road, the ratman leading. Claud and I leaned over the gate, watching. The ratman prowled around the hayrick, bending over to inspect his little piles of poison.

"Somethin wrong here," he muttered. His voice was soft and angry.

He ambled over to another pile and got down on his knees to examine it closely.

"Somethin bloody wrong here."

"What's the matter?"

He didn't answer, but it was clear that the rats hadn't touched his bait.

"These are very clever rats here," I said.

"Exactly what I told him, Gordon. These aren't just no ordinary kind of rats you're dealing with here."

The ratman walked over to the gate. He was very annoyed and showed it on his face and around the nose and by the way the two yellow teeth were pressing down into the skin of his lower lip. "Don't give me that crap," he said, looking at me. "There's nothin wrong with these rats except somebody's feedin em. They got somethin juicy to eat somewhere and plenty of it. There's no rats in the world'll turn down oats unless their bellies is full to burstin."

"They're clever," Claud said.

The man turned away, disgusted. He knelt down again and began to scoop up the poisoned oats with a small shovel, tipping them carefully back into the tin. When he had done, all three of us walked back across the road.

The ratman stood near the petrol-pumps, a rather sorry, humble ratman now whose face was beginning to take on a brooding aspect. He had withdrawn into himself and was brooding in silence over his failure, the eyes veiled and wicked, the little tongue darting out to one side of the two yellow teeth, keeping the lips moist. It appeared to be essential that the lips should be kept moist. He looked up at me, a quick surreptitious glance, then over at Claud. His nose-end twitched, sniffing the air. He raised himself up and down a few times on his toes, swaying gently, and in a voice soft and secretive, he said:

"Want to see somethin?" He was obviously trying to retrieve his reputation.

"What?"

"Want to see somethin *amazin?*" As he said this he put his right hand into the deep poacher's pocket of his jacket and brought out a large live rat clasped tight between his fingers.

"Good God!"

"Ah! That's it, y'see!" He was crouching slightly now and craning his neck forward and leering at us and holding this enormous brown rat in his hands, one finger and thumb making a tight circle around the creature's neck, clamping its head rigid so it couldn't turn and bite.

"D'you usually carry rats around in your pockets?"

"Always got a rat or two about me somewhere."

With that he put his free hand into the other pocket and produced a small white ferret.

"Ferret," he said, holding it up by the neck.

The ferret seemed to know him and stayed still in his grasp.

"There's nothin'll kill a rat quicker'n a ferret. And there's nothin a rat's more frightened of either."

He brought his hands close together in front of him so that the ferret's nose was within six inches of the rat's face. The pink beady eyes of the ferret stared at the rat. The rat struggled, trying to edge away from the killer.

"Now," he said. "Watch!"

His khaki shirt was open at the neck and he lifted the rat and slipped it down inside his shirt, next to his skin. As soon as his hand was free, he unbuttoned his jacket at the front so that the audience could see the bulge the body of the rat made under his shirt. His belt prevented it from going down lower than his waist.

Then he slipped the ferret in after the rat.

Immediately there was a great commotion inside the shirt. It appeared that the rat was running around the man's body, being chased by the ferret. Six or seven times they went around, the small bulge chasing the larger one, gaining on it slightly each circuit and drawing closer and closer until at last the two bulges seemed to come together and there was a scuffle and a series of shrill shrieks.

Throughout this performance the ratman had stood absolutely still with legs apart, arms hanging loosely, the dark eyes resting on Claud's face. Now he reached one hand down into his shirt and pulled out the ferret; with the other he took out the dead rat. There were traces of blood around the white muzzle of the ferret.

"Not sure I liked that very much."

"You never seen anythin like it before, I'll bet you that."

"Can't really say I have."

"Like as not you'll get yourself a nasty little nip in the guts one of these days," Claud told him. But he was clearly impressed, and the ratman was becoming cocky again.

"Want to see somethin far more *amazin'n* that?" he asked. "You want to see somethin you'd never even *believe* unless you seen it with your own eyes?"

"Well?"

We were standing in the driveway out in front of the pumps and it was one of those pleasant warm November mornings. Two cars pulled in for petrol, one right after the other, and Claud went over and gave them what they wanted.

"You want to see?" the ratman asked.

I glanced at Claud, slightly apprehensive. "Yes," Claud said. "Come on then, let's see."

The ratman slipped the dead rat back into one pocket, the ferret into the other. Then he reached down into his knapsack and produced—if you please—a second live rat.

"Good Christ!" Claud said.

"Always got one or two rats about me somewhere," the man announced calmly. "You got to know rats on this job and if you want to know em you got to have em round you. This is a sewer rat, this is. An old sewer rat, clever as buggery. See him watchin me all the time, wonderin what I'm goin to do? See him?"

"Very unpleasant."

"What are you going to do?" I asked. I had a feeling I was going to like this one even less than the last.

"Fetch me a piece of string."

Claud fetched him a piece of string.

With his left hand, the man looped the string around one of the rat's hind legs. The rat struggled, trying to turn its head to see what was going on, but he held it tight around the neck with finger and thumb.

"Now!" he said, looking about him. "You got a table inside?"

"We don't want the rat inside the house," I said.

"Well—I need a table. Or somethin flat like a table."

"What about the bonnet of that car?" Claud said.

We walked over to the car and the man put the old sewer rat

on the bonnet. He attached the string to the windshield wiper so that the rat was now tethered.

At first it crouched, unmoving and suspicious, a big-bodied grey rat with bright black eyes and a scaly tail that lay in a long curl upon the car's bonnet. It was looking away from the ratman, but watching him sideways to see what he was going to do. The man stepped back a few paces and immediately the rat relaxed. It sat up on its haunches and began to lick the grey fur on its chest. Then it scratched its muzzle with both front paws. It seemed quite unconcerned about the three men standing nearby.

"Now—how about a little bet?" the ratman asked.

"We don't bet," I said.

"Just for fun. It's more fun if you bet."

"What d'you want to bet on?"

"I'll bet you I can kill that rat without usin my hands. I'll put my hands in my pockets and not use em."

"You'll kick it with your feet," Claud said.

It was apparent that the ratman was out to earn some money. I looked at the rat that was going to be killed and began to feel slightly sick, not so much because it was going to be killed but because it was going to be killed in a special way, with a considerable degree of relish.

"No," the ratman said. "No feet."

"Nor arms?" Claud asked.

"Nor arms. Nor legs, nor hands neither."

"You'll sit on it."

"No. No squashin."

"Let's see you do it."

"You bet me first. Bet me a quid."

"Don't be so bloody daft," Claud said. "Why should we give you a quid?"

"What'll you bet?"

"Nothin."

"All right. Then it's no go."

He made as if to untie the string from the windshield wiper.

"I'll bet you a shilling," Claud told him. The sick gastric sensation in my stomach was increasing, but there was an awful magnetism about this business and I found myself quite unable to walk away or even move.

"You too?"

"No," I said.

"What's the matter with you?" the ratman asked.

"I just don't want to bet you, that's all."

"So you want me to do this for a lousy shillin?"

"I don't want you to do it."

"Where's the money?" he said to Claud.

Claud put a shilling piece on the bonnet, near the radiator. The ratman produced two sixpences and laid them beside Claud's money. As he stretched out his hand to do this, the rat cringed, drawing its head back and flattening itself against the bonnet.

"Bet's on," the ratman said.

Claud and I stepped back a few paces. The ratman stepped forward. He put his hands in his pockets and inclined his body from the waist so that his face was on a level with the rat, about three feet away.

His eyes caught the eyes of the rat and held them. The rat was crouching, very tense, sensing extreme danger, but not yet frightened. The way it crouched, it seemed to me it was preparing to spring forward at the man's face; but there must have been some power in the ratman's eyes that prevented it from doing this, and subdued it, and then gradually frightened it so that it began to back away, dragging its body backward with slow crouching steps until the string tautened on its hind leg. It tried to struggle back further against the string, jerking its leg to free it. The man leaned forward toward the rat, following it with his face, watching it all the time with his eyes, and suddenly the rat panicked and leaped sideways in the air. The string pulled it up with a jerk that must almost have dislocated its leg.

It crouched again, in the middle of the bonnet, as far away as the string would allow, and it was properly frightened now, whiskers quivering, the long grey body tense with fear.

At this point, the ratman again began to move his face closer. Very slowly he did it, so slowly there wasn't really any movement to be seen at all except that the face just happened to be a fraction closer each time you looked. He never took his eyes from the rat. The tension was considerable and I wanted suddenly to cry out and tell him to stop. I wanted him to stop because it was making me feel sick inside, but I couldn't bring myself to say the word. Something extremely unpleasant was about to happen—I was sure of that. Something sinister and cruel and ratlike, and perhaps it really would make me sick. But I had to see it now.

The ratman's face was about eighteen inches from the rat.

Twelve inches. Then ten, or perhaps it was eight, and soon there was not more than the length of a man's hand separating their faces. The rat was pressing its body flat against the car-bonnet, tense and terrified. The ratman was also tense, but with a dangerous active tensity that was like a tight-wound spring. The shadow of a smile flickered around the skin of his mouth.

Then suddenly he struck.

He struck as a snake strikes, darting his head forward with one swift knifelike stroke that originated in the muscles of the lower body, and I had a momentary glimpse of his mouth opening very wide and two yellow teeth and the whole face contorted by the effort of mouth-opening.

More than that I did not care to see. I closed my eyes, and when I opened them again the rat was dead and the ratman was slipping the money into his pocket and spitting to clear his mouth.

"That's what they makes lickerish out of," he said. "Rat's blood is what the big factories and the chocolate-people use to make lickerish."

Again the relish, the wet-lipped, lip-smacking relish as he spoke the words, the throaty richness of his voice and the thick syrupy way he pronounced the word *lickerish.*

"No," he said, "there's nothin wrong with a drop of rat's blood."

"Don't talk so absolutely disgusting," Claud told him.

"Ah! But that's it, you see. You eaten it many a time. Penny sticks and lickerish bootlaces is all made from rat's blood."

"We don't want to hear about it, thank you."

"Boiled up, it is, in great cauldrons, bubblin and steamin and men stirrin it with long poles. That's one of the big secrets of the chocolate-makin factories, and no one knows about it—no one except the ratters supplyin the stuff."

Suddenly he noticed that his audience was no longer with him, that our faces were hostile and sick-looking and crimson with anger and disgust. He stopped abruptly, and without another word he turned and sloped off down the driveway out on to the road, moving with the slow, that almost delicate ambling walk that was like a rat prowling, making no noise with his footsteps even on the gravel of the driveway.

Rummins · *1953*

The sun was up over the hills now and the mist had cleared and it was wonderful to be striding along the road with the dog in the early morning, especially when it was autumn, with the leaves changing to gold and yellow and sometimes one of them breaking away and falling slowly, turning slowly over in the air, dropping noiselessly right in front of him onto the grass beside the road. There was a small wind up above, and he could hear the beeches rustling and murmuring like a crowd of people.

This was always the best time of the day for Claud Cubbage. He gazed approvingly at the rippling velvety hindquarters of the greyhound trotting in front of him.

"Jackie," he called softly. "Hey, Jackson. How you feeling, boy?"

The dog half turned at the sound of its name and gave a quick acknowledging wag of the tail.

There would never be another dog like this Jackie, he told himself. How beautiful the slim streamlining, the small pointed head, the yellow eyes, the black mobile nose. Beautiful the long neck, the way the deep brisket curved back and up out of sight into no stomach at all. See how he walked up on his toes, noiselessly, hardly touching the surface of the road at all.

"Jackson," he said. "Good old Jackson."

In the distance, Claud could see Rummins's farmhouse, small, narrow, and ancient, standing back behind the hedge on the right hand side.

I'll turn round there, he decided. That'll be enough for today.

Rummins, carrying a pail of milk across the yard, saw him coming down the road. He set the pail down slowly and came forward to the gate, leaning both arms on the topmost bar, waiting.

"Morning, Mr. Rummins," Claud said. It was necessary to be polite to Rummins because of eggs.

Rummins nodded and leaned over the gate, looking critically at the dog.

"Looks well," he said.

"He is well."

"When's he running?"

"I don't know, Mr. Rummins."

"Come on. When's he running?"

"He's only ten months yet, Mr. Rummins. He's not even schooled properly, honest."

The small beady eyes of Rummins peered suspiciously over the top of the gate. "I wouldn't mind betting a couple of quid you're having it off with him somewhere secret soon."

Claud moved his feet uncomfortably on the black road surface. He disliked very much this man with the wide frog mouth, the broken teeth, the shifty eyes; and most of all he disliked having to be polite to him because of eggs.

"That hayrick of yours opposite," he said, searching desperately for another subject. "It's full of rats."

"All hayrick's got rats."

"Not like this one. Matter of fact we've been having a touch of trouble with the authorities about that."

Rummins glanced up sharply. He didn't like trouble with the authorities. Any man who sells eggs blackmarket and kills pigs without a permit is wise to avoid contact with that sort of people.

"What kind of trouble?"

"They sent the ratcatcher along."

"You mean just for a few rats?"

"A few! Blimey, it's *swarming!*"

"Never."

"Honest it is, Mr. Rummins. There's hundreds of em."

"Didn't the ratcatcher catch em?"

"No."

"Why?"

"I reckon they're too artful."

Rummins began thoughtfully to explore the inner rim of one nostril with the end of his thumb, holding the noseflap between thumb and finger as he did so.

"I wouldn't give thank you for no ratcatchers," he said. "Ratcatchers is government men working for the soddin government and I wouldn't give thank you for 'em."

"Nor me, Mr. Rummins. All ratcatchers is slimy cunning creatures."

"Well," Rummins said, sliding fingers under his cap to scratch the head, "I was coming over soon anyway to fetch in that rick. Reckon I might just as well do it today as any other time. I don't want no government men nosing around my stuff thank you very much."

"Exactly, Mr. Rummins."

"We'll be over later—Bert and me." With that he turned and ambled off across the yard.

Around three in the afternoon, Rummins and Bert were seen riding slowly up the road in a cart drawn by a ponderous and magnificent black carthorse. Opposite the filling-station the cart turned off into the field and stopped near the hayrick.

"This ought to be worth seeing," I said. "Get the gun."

Claud fetched the rifle and slipped a cartridge into the breech.

I strolled across the road and leaned against the open gate. Rummins was on the top of the rick now and cutting away at the cord that bound the thatching. Bert remained in the cart, fingering the four-foot-long knife.

Bert had something wrong with one eye. It was pale grey all over, like a boiled fish-eye, and although it was motionless in its socket it appeared always to be looking at you and following you round the way the eyes of the people in some of those portraits do, in the museums. Wherever you stood and wherever Bert was looking, there was this faulty eye fixing you sideways with a cold stare, boiled and misty pale with a little black dot in the centre, like a fish-eye on a plate.

In his build he was the opposite of his father who was short and squat like a frog. Bert was a tall, reedy, boneless boy, loose at the joints, even the head loose upon the shoulders, falling sideways as though perhaps it was too heavy for the neck.

"You only made this rick last June," I said to him. "Why take it away so soon?"

"Dads wants it."

"Funny time to cut a new rick, November."

"Dad wants it," Bert repeated, and both his eyes, the sound one and the other stared down at me with a look of absolute vacuity.

"Going to all that trouble stacking it and thatching it and then pulling it down five months later."

"Dad wants it." Bert's nose was running and he kept wiping it with the back of his hand and wiping the back of the hand on his trousers.

"Come on Bert," Rummins called, and the boy climbed up onto the rick and stood in the place where the thatch had been removed. He took the knife and began to cut down into the tight-packed hay with an easy-swinging, sawing movement, holding the handle with both hands and rocking his body like a man sawing wood with a big saw. I could hear the crisp cutting noise of the blade against the dry hay and the noise becoming softer as the knife sank deeper into the rick.

"Claud's going to take a pot at the rats as they come out."

The man and the boy stopped abruptly and looked across the road at Claud who was leaning against the red pump with rifle in hand.

"Tell him to put that bloody rifle away," Rummins said.

"He's a good shot. He won't hit you."

"No one's potting no rats alongside of me, don't matter how good they are."

"You'll insult him."

"Tell him to put it away," Rummins said, slow and hostile. "I don't mind dogs nor sticks but I'll be buggered if I'll have rifles."

The two on the hayrick watched while Claud did as he was told, then they resumed their work in silence. Soon Bert came down into the cart, and reaching out with both hands he pulled a slice of solid hay away from the rick so that it dropped neatly into the cart beside him.

A rat, grey-black, with a long tail, came out of the base of the rick and ran into the hedge.

"A rat," I said.

"Kill it," Rummins said. "Why don't you get a stick and kill it?"

The alarm had been given now and the rats were coming out quicker, one or two of them every minute, fat and long-bodied, crouching close to the ground as they ran through the grass into the hedge. Whenever the horse saw one of them it twitched its ears and followed it with uneasy rolling eyes.

Bert had climbed back on top of the rick and was cutting out another bale. Watching him, I saw him suddenly stop, hesitate for perhaps a second, then again begin to cut, but very cautiously this time; and now I could hear a different sound, a muffled rasping noise as the blade of the knife grated against something hard.

Bert pulled out the knife and examined the blade, testing it with his thumb. He put it back, letting it down gingerly into the cut, feeling gently downward until it came again upon the hard object; and once more, when he made another cautious little sawing movement, there came that grating sound.

Rummins turned his head and looked over his shoulder at the boy. He was in the act of lifting an armful of loosened thatch, bending forward with both hands grasping the straw, but he stopped dead in the middle of what he was doing and looked at Bert. Bert remained still, hands holding the handle of the knife, a look of bewilderment on his face. Behind, the sky was a pale clear blue and the two figures up there on the hayrick stood out sharp and black like an etching against the paleness.

Then Rummins' voice, louder than usual, edged with an unmistakable apprehension that the loudness did nothing to conceal: "Some of them haymakers is too bloody careless what they put on a rick these days."

He paused, and again the silence, the men motionless, and across the road Claud leaning motionless against the red pump. It was so quiet suddenly we could hear a woman's voice far down the valley on the next farm calling the men to food.

Then Rummins again, shouting where there was no need to shout: "Go on, then! Go on an cut through it, Bert! A little stick of wood won't hurt the soddin knife!"

For some reason, as though perhaps scenting trouble, Claud came strolling across the road and joined me leaning on the gate. He didn't say anything, but both of us seemed to know that there was something disturbing about these two men, about the stillness that surrounded them and especially about Rummins himself. Rummins was frightened. Bert was frightened too. And now as I watched them, I became conscious of a small vague image moving just below the surface of my memory. I tried desperately to reach back and grasp it. Once I almost touched it, but it slipped away and when I went after it I found myself travelling back and back through many weeks, back into the yellow days of summer—the warm wind blowing down the valley from the south, the big beech trees heavy with their foliage, the fields turning to gold, the harvesting, the hay making, the rick—the building of the rick.

Instantly, I felt a fine electricity of fear running over the skin of my stomach.

Yes—the building of the rick. When was it we had built it? June? That was it, of course—a hot muggy day in June with the clouds low overhead and the air thick with the smell of thunder.

And Rummins had said, "Let's for God's sake get it in quick before the rain comes."

And Ole Jimmy had said, "There ain't going to be no rain. And there ain't no hurry either. You know very well when thunder's in the south it don't cross over into the valley."

Rummins, standing up in the cart handing out the pitchforks had not answered him. He was in a furious brooding temper because of his anxiety about getting in the hay before it rained.

"There ain't goin to be no rain before evenin," Ole Jimmy had repeated, looking at Rummins; and Rummins had stared back at him, the eyes glimmering with a slow anger.

All through the morning we had worked without a pause, loading the hay into the cart, trundling it across the field, pitching it out onto the slowly growing rick that stood over by the gate opposite the filling-station. We could hear the thunder in the south as it came toward us and moved away again. Then it seemed to return and remain stationary somewhere beyond the hills, rumbling intermittently. When we looked up we could see the clouds overhead moving and changing shape in the turbulence of the upper air; but on the ground it was hot and muggy and there was no breath of wind. We worked slowly, listlessly in the heat, shirts wet with sweat, faces shining.

Claud and I had worked beside Rummins on the rick itself, helping to shape it, and I could remember how very hot it had been and the flies around my face and the sweat pouring out everywhere; and especially I could remember the grim scowling presence of Rummins beside me, working with a desperate urgency and watching the sky and shouting at the men to hurry.

At noon, in spite of Rummins, we had knocked off for lunch.

Claud and I had sat down under the hedge with Ole Jimmy and another man called Wilson who was a soldier home on leave, and it was too hot to do much talking. Wilson had some bread and cheese and a canteen of cold tea. Ole Jimmy had a satchel that was an old gas-mask container, and in this, closely packed, standing upright with their necks protruding, were six pint bottles of beer.

"Come on," he said, offering a bottle to each of us.

"I'd like to buy one from you," Claud said, knowing very well the old man had little money.

"Take it."

"I must pay you."

"Don't be so daft. Drink it."

He was a very good old man, good and clean, with a clean pink face that he shaved each day. He had used to be a carpenter, but they retired him at the age of seventy and that was some years before. Then the Village Council, seeing him still active, had given him the job of looking after the newly built children's playground, of maintaining the swings and see-saws in good repair and also of acting as a kind of gentle watchdog, seeing that none of the kids hurt themselves or did anything foolish.

That was a fine job for an old man to have and everybody seemed pleased with the way things were going—until a certain Saturday night. That night Ole Jimmy had got drunk and gone reeling and singing down the middle of the High Street with such a howling noise that people got out of their beds to see what was going on below. The next morning they had sacked him saying he was a bum and a drunkard not fit to associate with young children on the playground.

But then an astonishing thing happened. The first day that he stayed away—a Monday it was—not one single child came near the playground.

Nor the next day, nor the one after that.

All week the swings and the see-saws and the high slide with steps going up to it stood deserted. Not a child went near them. Instead they followed Ole Jimmy out into a field behind the Rectory and played their games there with him watching; and the result of all this was that after a while the Council had had no alternative but to give the old man back his job.

He still had it now and he still got drunk and no one said anything about it any more. He left it only for a few days each year, at haymaking time. All his life Ole Jimmy had loved to go haymaking and he wasn't going to give it up yet.

"You want one?" he asked now, holding a bottle out to Wilson, the soldier.

"No thanks. I got tea."

"They say tea's good on a hot day."

"It is. Beer makes me sleepy."

"If you like," I said to Ole Jimmy, "we could walk across to the filling-station and I'll do you a couple of nice sandwiches? Would you like that?"

"Beer's plenty. There's more food in one bottle of beer, me lad, than twenty sandwiches."

He smiled at me, showing two rows of pale-pink, toothless gums, but it was a pleasant smile and there was nothing repulsive about the way the gums showed.

We sat for a while in silence. The soldier finished his bread and cheese and lay back on the ground, tilting his hat forward over his face. Ole Jimmy had drunk three bottles of beer, and now he offered the last to Claud and me.

"No thanks."

"No thanks. One's plenty for me."

The old man shrugged, unscrewed the stopper, tilted his head back and drank, pouring the beer into his mouth with the lips held open so the liquid ran smoothly without gurgling down his throat. He wore a hat that was of no colour at all and of no shape, and it did not fall off when he tilted back his head.

"Ain't Rummins goin to give that old horse a drink?" he asked, lowering the bottle, looking across the field at the great cart-horse that stood steaming between the shafts of the cart.

"Not Rummins."

"Horses is thirsty, just the same as us." Ole Jimmy paused, still looking at the horse. "You got a bucket of water in that place of yours there?"

"Of course."

"No reason why we shouldn't give the old horse a drink then, is there?"

"That's a very good idea. We'll give him a drink."

Claud and I both stood up and began walking toward the gate and I remember turning and calling back to the old man: "You quite sure you wouldn't like me to bring you a nice sandwich? Won't take a second to make."

He shook his head and waved the bottle at us and said something about taking himself a little nap. We went on through the gate over the road to the filling-station.

I suppose we stayed away for about an hour attending to customers and getting ourselves something to eat, and when at length we returned, Claud carrying the bucket of water, I noticed that the rick was at least six foot high.

"Some water for the old horse," Claud said, looking hard at Rummins who was up in the cart pitching hay onto the rick.

The horse put its head in the bucket, sucking and blowing gratefully at the water.

"Where's Ole Jimmy?" I asked. We wanted the old man to see the water because it had been his idea.

When I asked the question there was a moment, a brief moment when Rummins hesitated, pitchfork in mid-air, looking around him.

"I brought him a sandwich," I added.

"Bloody old fool drunk too much beer and gone off home to sleep," Rummins said.

I strolled along the hedge back to the place where we had been sitting with Ole Jimmy. The five empty bottles were lying there in the grass. So was the satchel. I picked up the satchel and carried it back to Rummins.

"I don't think Ole Jimmy's gone home, Mr. Rummins," I said, holding up the satchel by the long shoulder-band. Rummins glanced at it but made no reply. He was in a frenzy of haste now because the thunder was closer, the clouds blacker, the heat more oppressive than ever.

Carrying the satchel, I started back to the filling-station where I remained for the rest of the afternoon, serving customers. Toward evening, when the rain came, I glanced across the road and noticed that they had got the hay in and were laying a tarpaulin over the rick.

In a few days the thatcher arrived and took the tarpaulin off and made a roof of straw instead. He was a good thatcher and he made a fine roof with long straw, thick and well packed. The slope was nicely angled, the edges cleanly clipped, and it was a pleasure to look at it from the road or from the door of the filling-station.

All this came flooding back to me now as clearly as if it were yesterday—the building of the rick on that hot thundery day in June, the yellow field, the sweet woody smell of the hay; and Wilson the soldier, with tennis shoes on his feet, Bert with the boiled eye, Ole Jimmy with the clean old face, the pink naked gums; and Rummins, the broad dwarf, standing up in the cart scowling at the sky because he was anxious about the rain.

At this very moment, there he was again, this Rummins, crouching on top of the rick with a sheaf of thatch in his arms looking round at the son, the tall Bert, motionless also, both of them black like silhouettes against the sky, and once again I felt the fine electricity of fear as it came and went in little waves over the skin of my stomach.

"Go on and cut through it, Bert," Rummins said, speaking loudly.

Bert put pressure on the big knife and there was a high grating noise as the edge of the blade sawed across something hard. It was clear from Bert's face that he did not like what he was doing.

It took several minutes before the knife was through—then again at last the softer sound of the blade slicing the tight-packed hay and Bert's face turned sideways to the father, grinning with relief, nodding inanely.

"Go on and cut it out," Rummins said, and still he did not move. Bert made a second vertical cut the same depth as the first; then he got down and pulled the bale of hay so it came away cleanly from the rest of the rick like a chunk of cake, dropping into the cart at his feet.

Instantly, the boy seemed to freeze, staring stupidly at the newly exposed face of the rick, unable to believe or perhaps refusing to believe what this thing was that he had cut in two.

Rummins, who knew very well what it was, had turned away and was climbing quickly down the other side of the rick. He moved so fast he was through the gate and halfway across the road before Bert started to scream.

Mr. Hoddy · 1953

They got out of the car and went in the front door of Mr. Hoddy's house.

"I've an idea Dad's going to question you rather sharp tonight," Clarice whispered.

"About what, Clarice?"

"The usual stuff. Jobs and things like that. And whether you can support me in a fitting way."

"Jackie's going to do that," Claud said. "When Jackie wins there won't even be any need for any jobs . . ."

"Don't you ever mention Jackie to my dad, Claud Cubbage, or that'll be the end of it. If there's one thing in the world he can't abide it's greyhounds. Don't you ever forget that."

"Oh Christ," Claud said.

"Tell him something else—anything—anything to make him happy, see?" And with that she led Claud into the parlour.

Mr. Hoddy was a widower, a man with a prim sour mouth and an expression of eternal disapproval all over his face. He had the small, close-together teeth of his daughter Clarice, the same suspicious, inward look about the eyes, but none of her freshness and vitality; none of her warmth. He was a small sour apple of a man, grey-skinned and shrivelled, with a dozen or so surviving strands of black hair pasted across the dome of his bald head. But a very superior man was Mr. Hoddy, a grocer's assistant, one who wore a spotless white gown at his work, who handled large quantities of such precious commodities as butter and sugar, who was deferred to, even smiled at by every housewife in the village.

Claud Cubbage was never quite at his ease in this house and that was precisely as Mr. Hoddy intended it. They were sitting round the fire in the parlour with cups of tea in their hands, Mr. Hoddy in the best chair to the right of the fireplace, Claud and Clarice on the sofa, decorously separated by a wide space. The younger daughter, Ada, was on a hard upright chair to the left; and they made a little circle round the fire, a stiff, tense little circle, primly tea-sipping.

"Yes Mr. Hoddy," Claud was saying, "you can be quite sure both Gordon and me's got quite a number of nice little ideas up our sleeves this very moment. It's only a question of taking our time and making sure which is going to be the most profitable."

"What sort of ideas?" Mr. Hoddy asked, fixing Claud with his small, disapproving eyes.

"Ah, there you are now. That's it, you see." Claud shifted uncomfortably on the sofa. His blue lounge suit was tight around his chest, and it was especially tight between his legs, up in the crotch. The tightness in his crotch was actually painful to him and he wanted terribly to hitch it downward.

"This man you call Gordon, I thought he had a profitable business out there as it is," Mr. Hobby said. "Why does he want to change?"

"Absolutely right, Mr. Hoddy. It's a first-rate business. But it's a good thing to keep expanding, see. New ideas is what we're after. Something I can come in on as well and take a share of the profits."

"Such as what?"

Mr. Hoddy was eating a slice of currant cake, nibbling it round the edges, and his small mouth was like the mouth of a caterpillar biting a tiny curved slice out of the edge of a leaf.

"Such as what?" he asked again.

"There's long conferences, Mr. Hoddy, takes place every day between Gordon and me about these different matters of business."

"Such as what?" he repeated, relentless.

Clarice glanced sideways at Claud, encouraging. Claud turned his large slow eyes upon Mr. Hoddy, and he was silent. He wished Mr. Hoddy wouldn't push him around like this, always shooting questions at him and glaring at him and acting just exactly like he was the bloody adjutant or something.

"Such as what?" Mr. Hoddy said, and this time Claud knew that he was not going to let go. Also, his instinct warned him that the old man was trying to create a crisis.

"Well now," he said, breathing deep. "I don't really want to go into details until we got it properly worked out. All we're doing so far is turning our ideas over in our minds, see."

"All I'm asking," Mr. Hoddy said irritably, "is what *sort* of business are you contemplating? I presume that it's respectable?"

"Now *please,* Mr. Hoddy. You don't for one moment think we'd even so much as *consider* anything that wasn't absolutely and entirely respectable, do you?"

Mr. Hoddy grunted, stirring his tea slowly, watching Claud. Clarice sat mute and fearful on the sofa, gazing into the fire.

"I've never been in favour of starting a business," Mr. Hoddy pronounced, defending his own failure in that line. "A good respectable job is all a man should wish for. A respectable job in respectable surroundings. Too much hokey-pokey in business for my liking."

"The thing is this," Claud said, desperate now. "All I want is to provide my wife with everything she can possibly desire. A house to live in and furniture and a flower-garden and a washing-machine and all the best things in the world. That's what I want to do, and you can't do that on an ordinary wage, now can you? It's impossible to get enough money to do that unless you go into business, Mr. Hoddy. You'll surely agree with me there?"

Mr. Hoddy, who had worked for an ordinary wage all his life, didn't much like this point of view.

"And don't you think *I* provide everything my family wants, might I ask?"

"Oh yes and more!" Claud cried fervently. "But *you've* got a very superior job, Mr. Hoddy, and that makes all the difference."

"But what *sort* of business are you thinking of?" the man persisted.

Claud sipped his tea to give himself a little more time and he couldn't help wondering how the miserable old bastard's face would look if he simply up and told him the truth right there and then, if he'd said what we've got, Mr. Hoddy, if you really want to know, is a couple of greyhounds and one's a perfect ringer for the other and we're going to bring off the biggest goddam gamble in the history of flapping, see. He'd like to watch the old bastard's face if he said that, he really would.

They were all waiting for him to proceed now, sitting there with cups of tea in their hands staring at him and waiting for him to say something good. "Well," he said, speaking very slowly because he was thinking deep. "I've been pondering something a long time now, something as'll make more money even than Gordon's second hand cars or anything else come to that, and practically no expense involved." That's better, he told himself. Keep going along like that.

"And what might that be?"

"Something so queer, Mr. Hoddy, there isn't one in a million would even believe it."

"Well, what is it?" Mr. Hoddy placed his cup carefully on the little table beside him and leaned forward to listen. And Claud, watching him, knew more than ever that this man and all those like him were his enemies. It was the Mr. Hoddys were the trouble. They were all the same. He knew them all, with their clean ugly hands, their grey skin, their acrid mouths, their tendency to develop little round bulging bellies just below the waistcoat; and always the unctuous curl of the nose, the weak chin, the suspicious eyes that were dark and moved too quick. The Mr. Hoddys. Oh Christ.

"Well, what is it?"

"It's an absolute gold-mine Mr. Hoddy, honestly it is."

"I'll believe that when I hear it."

"It's a thing so simple and amazing most people wouldn't even bother to do it." He had it now—something he *had* actually been thinking seriously about for a long time, something he'd always wanted to do. He leaned across and put his tea-cup carefully on the table beside Mr. Hoddy's, then, not knowing what to do with his hands, placed them on his knees, palms downward.

"Well, come on, man, what is it?"

"It's maggots," Claud answered softly.

Mr. Hoddy jerked back as though someone had squirted water in his face. "Maggots!" he said, aghast. *"Maggots?* What on earth do you mean, maggots?" Claud had forgotten that this word was almost unmentionable in any self-respecting grocer's shop. Ada began to giggle, but Clarice glanced at her so malignantly the giggle died on her mouth.

"That's where the money is, starting a maggot-factory."

"Are you trying to be funny?"

"Honestly, Mr. Hoddy, it may sound a bit queer, and that's simply because you never heard of it before, but it's a little gold mine."

"A *maggot-factory!* Really now, Cubbage! Please be sensible!" Clarice wished her father wouldn't call him Cubbage.

"You never heard speak of a maggot-factory, Mr. Hoddy?"

"I certainly have not!"

"There's maggot-factories going now, real big companies with managers and directors and all, and you know what, Mr. Hoddy? They're making millions!"

"Nonsense, man."

"And you know why they're making millions?" Claud paused, but he did not notice now that his listener's face was slowly turning yellow. "It's because of the enormous demand for maggots, Mr. Hoddy."

At that moment, Mr. Hoddy was listening also to other voices, the voices of his customers across the counter—Mrs. Rabbits for instance, as he sliced off her ration of butter, Mrs. Rabbits with her brown moustache and always talking so loud and saying well well well; he could hear her now saying well well well Mr. Hoddy, so your Clarice got married last week, did she. Very nice too, I must say, and what was it you said her husband does, Mr. Hoddy?

He owns a maggot-factory, Mrs. Rabbits.

No thank you, he told himself, watching Claud with his small, hostile eyes. No thank you very much indeed. I don't want that.

"I can't say," he announced primly, "that I myself have ever had occasion to purchase a maggot."

"Now you come to mention it, Mr. Hoddy, nor have I. Nor has many other people we know. But let me ask you something else. How many times you had occasion to purchase . . . a crown wheel and pinion, for instance?"

This was a shrewd question and Claud permitted himself a slow mawkish smile.

"What's that got to do with maggots?"

"Exactly this—that certain people buy certain things, see. You never bought a crown wheel and pinion in your life, but that don't say there isn't men getting rich this very moment making them— because there is. It's the same with maggots!"

"Would you mind telling me who these unpleasant people are who buy maggots?"

"Maggots are bought by fishermen, Mr.. Hoddy. Amateur fishermen. There's thousands and thousands of fishermen all over the country going out every weekend fishing the rivers and all of them wanting maggots. Willing to pay good money for them, too. You go along the river there anywhere you like above Marlow on a Sunday and you'll see them *lining* the banks. Sitting there one beside the other simply *lining* the banks on both sides."

"Those men don't buy maggots. They go down the bottom of the garden and dig worms."

"Now that's just where you're wrong, Mr. Hoddy, if you'll allow me to say so. That's just where you're absolutely wrong. They want maggots, not worms."

"In that case they get their own maggots."

"They don't *want* to get their own maggots. Just imagine, Mr. Hoddy, it's Saturday afternoon and you're going out fishing and a nice clean tin of maggots arrives by post and all you've got to do is slip it in the fishing bag and away you go. You don't think fellers is going out digging for worms and hunting for maggots when they can have them delivered right to their very doorsteps like that just for a bob or two, do you?"

"And might I ask how you propose to run this maggot-factory of yours?" When he spoke the word maggot, it seemed as if he were spitting out a sour little pip from his mouth.

"Easiest thing in the world to run a maggot-factory." Claud was gaining confidence now and warming to his subject. "All you need is a couple of old oil drums and a few lumps of rotten meat or a sheep's head, and you put them in the oil drums and that's all you do. The flies do the rest "

Had he been watching Mr Hoddy's face he would probably have stopped there.

"Of course, it's not quite as easy as it sounds. What you've got to do next is feed up your maggots with special diet. Bran and milk. And then when they get big and fat you put them in pint tins and post them off to your customers. Five shillings a pint they fetch. *Five shillings a pint!*" he cried, slapping his knee. "You just imagine that, Mr. Hoddy! And they say one bluebottle'll lay twenty pints easy!"

He paused again, but merely to marshal his thoughts, for there was no stopping him now.

"And there's another thing, Mr Hoddy A good maggot-factory don't just breed ordinary maggots, you know. Every fisherman's got his own tastes. Maggots are commonest, but also there's lug worms. Some fishermen won't have nothing but lug worms. And of course there's coloured maggots. Ordinary maggots are white, but you get them all sorts of different colours by feeding them special foods, see. Red ones and green ones and black ones and you can even get blue ones if you know what to feed them. The most difficult thing of all in a maggot-factory is a blue maggot, Mr. Hoddy."

Claud stopped to catch his breath. He was having a vision now —the same vision that accompanied all his dreams of wealth—of an immense factory building with tall chimneys and hundreds of happy workers streaming in through the wide wrought iron gates and Claud himself sitting in his luxurious office directing operations with a calm and splendid assurance.

"There's people with brains studying these things this very minute," he went on. "So you got to jump in quick unless you want to get left out in the cold. That's the secret of big business, jumping in quick before all the others, Mr. Hoddy."

Clarice, Ada, and the father sat absolutely still looking straight ahead. None of them moved or spoke. Only Claud rushed on.

"Just so long as you make sure your maggots is alive when you post em. They've got to be wiggling, see. Maggots is no good unless they're wiggling. And when we really get going, when we've built up a little capital, then we'll put up some glasshouses."

Another pause, and Claud stroked his chin. "Now I expect you're all wondering why a person should want glasshouses in a maggot-factory. Well—I'll tell you. It's for the flies in the winter, see. Most important to take care of your flies in the winter."

"I think that's enough, thank you, Cubbage," Mr. Hoddy said suddenly.

Claud looked up and for the first time he saw the expression on the man's face. It stopped him cold.

"I don't want to hear any more about it," Mr. Hoddy said.

"All I'm trying to do, Mr. Hoddy," Claud cried, "is give your little girl everything she can possibly desire. That's all I'm thinking of night and day, Mr. Hoddy."

"Then all I hope is you'll be able to do it without the help of maggots."

"Dad!" Clarice cried, alarmed. "I simply won't have you talking to Claud like that."

"I'll talk to him how I wish, thank you, miss."

"I think it's time I was getting along," Claud said. "Goodnight."

Mr. Feasey · 1953

We were both up early when the big day came.

I wandered into the kitchen for a shave but Claud got dressed right away and went outside to arrange about the straw. The kitchen was a front room and through the window I could see the sun just coming up behind the line of trees on top of the ridge the other side of the valley.

Each time Claud came past the window with an armload of straw I noticed over the rim of the mirror the intent, breathless expression on his face, the great round bullet-head thrusting forward and the forehead wrinkled into deep corrugations right up to the hairline. I'd only seen this look on him once before and that was the evening he'd asked Clarice to marry him. Today he was so excited he even walked funny, treading softly as though the concrete around the filling-station were a shade too hot for the soles of his feet; and he kept packing more and more straw into the back of the van to make it comfortable for Jackie.

Then he came into the kitchen to fix breakfast, and I watched him put the pot of soup on the stove and begin stirring it. He had a long metal spoon and he kept on stirring and stirring all the time it was coming to the boil, and about every half minute he leaned forward and stuck his nose into that sickly-sweet steam of cooking horseflesh. Then he started putting extras into it—three peeled onions, a few young carrots, a cupful of stinging-nettle tops, a teaspoon of Valentines Meatjuice, twelve drops of codliver oil—and everything he touched was handled very gently with the ends of his big fat fingers as though it might have been a little fragment of Venetian glass. He took some minced horsemeat from the icebox, measured one handful into Jackie's bowl, three into the other, and when the soup was ready he shared it out between the two, pouring it over the meat.

It was the same ceremony I'd seen performed each morning for the past five months, but never with such intense and breathless concentration as this. There was no talk, not even a glance my way, and when he turned and went out again to fetch the dogs, even the back of his neck and the shoulders seemed to be whispering, "Oh Jesus, don't let anything go wrong, and especially don't let me *do* anything wrong today."

I heard him talking softly to the dogs in the pen as he put the leashes on them, and when he brought them around into the kitchen, they came in prancing and pulling to get at the breakfast, treading up and down with their front feet and waving their enormous tails from side to side, like whips.

"All right," Claud said, speaking at last. "Which is it?"

Most mornings he'd offer to bet me a pack of cigarettes, but there were bigger things at stake today and I knew all he wanted for the moment was a little extra reassurance.

He watched me as I walked once around the two beautiful, identical, tall, velvety-black dogs, and he moved aside, holding the leashes at arms' length to give me a better view.

"Jackie!" I said, trying the old trick that never worked. "Hey Jackie!" Two identical heads with identical expressions flicked around to look at me, four bright, identical, deep-yellow eyes stared into mine. There'd been a time when I fancied the eyes of one were a slightly darker yellow than those of the other. There'd also been a time when I thought I could recognise Jackie because of a deeper brisket and a shade more muscle on the hindquarters. But it wasn't so.

"Come on," Claud said. He was hoping that today of all days I would make a bad guess.

"This one," I said. "This is Jackie."

"Which?"

"This one on the left."

"There!" he cried, his whole face suddenly beaming. "You're wrong again!"

"I don't think I'm wrong."

"You're about as wrong as you could possibly be. And now listen, Gordon, and I'll tell you something. All these last weeks, every morning while you've been trying to pick him out—you know what?"

"What?"

"I've been keeping count. And the result is you haven't been right even *one-half* the time! You'd have done better tossing a coin!"

What he meant was that if I (who saw them every day and side by side) couldn't do it, why the hell should we be frightened of Mr Feasey. Claud knew Mr. Feasey was famous for spotting ringers, but he knew also that it could be very difficult to tell the difference between two dogs when there wasn't any.

He put the bowls of food on the floor, giving Jackie the one with the least meat because he was running today. When he stood back to watch them eat, the shadow of deep concern was back again on his face and the large pale eyes were staring at Jackie with the same rapt and melting look of love that up till recently had been reserved only for Clarice

"You see, Gordon," he said "It's just what I've always told you. For the last hundred years there's been all manner of ringers, some good and some bad, but in the whole history of dog-racing there's never been a ringer like this.'

"I hope you're right," I said, and my mind began travelling back to that freezing afternoon just before Christmas, four months ago, when Claud had asked to borrow the van and had driven away in the direction of Aylesbury without saying where he was going. I had assumed he was off to see Clarice, but late in the afternoon he had returned bringing with him this dog he said he'd bought off a man for thirty-five shillings.

"Is he fast?" I had said. We were standing out by the pumps and Claud was holding the dog on a leash and looking at him, and a few snowflakes were falling and settling on the dog's back. The motor of the van was still running.

"Fast!" Claud had said. "He's just about the slowest dog you ever saw in your whole life!"

"Then what you buy him for?"

"Well," he had said, the big bovine face secret and cunning, "it occurred to me that maybe he might possibly look a little bit like Jackie. What d'you think?"

"I suppose he does a bit, now you come to mention it."

He had handed me the leash and I had taken the new dog inside to dry him off while Claud had gone round to the pen to fetch his beloved. And when he returned and we put the two of them together for the first time, I can remember him stepping back and saying, "Oh, Jesus!" and standing dead still in front of them like he was seeing a phantom. Then he became very quick and quiet. He got down on his knees and began comparing them carefully point by point, and it was almost like the room was getting warmer and warmer the way I could feel his excitement growing every second through this long silent examination in which even the toenails and the dewclaws, eighteen on each dog, were matched alongside one another for colour.

"Look," he said at last, standing up. "Walk them up and down the room a few times, will you?" And then he had stayed there for quite five or six minutes leaning against the stove with his eyes half closed and his head on one side, watching them and frowning and chewing his lips. After that, as though he didn't believe what he had seen the first time, he had gone down again on his knees to recheck everything once more; but suddenly, in the middle of it he had jumped up and looked at me, his face fixed and tense, with a curious whiteness around the nostrils and the eyes. "All right," he had said, a little tremor in his voice. "You know what? We're home. We're rich."

And then the secret conferences between us in the kitchen, the detailed planning, the selection of the most suitable track, and finally every other Saturday, eight times in all, locking up my filling-station (losing a whole afternoon's custom) and driving the ringer all the way up to Oxford to a scruffy little track out in the fields near Headingley where the big money was played but which was actually nothing except a line of old posts and cord to mark the course, an upturned bicycle for pulling the dummy hare, and at the far end, in the distance, six traps and the starter. We had driven this ringer up there eight times over a period of sixteen weeks and entered him with Mr. Feasey and stood around on the edge of the crowd in freezing raining cold, waiting for his name to go up on the black-board in chalk. The Black Panther we called him. And when his time came, Claud would always lead him down to the traps and I would stand at the finish to catch him and keep him clear of the fighters, the gypsy dogs that the gypsies so often slipped in specially to tear another one to pieces at the end of a race.

But you know, there was something rather sad about taking this dog all the way up there so many times and letting him run and watching him and hoping and praying that whatever happened he would always come last. Of course the praying wasn't necessary and we never really had a moment's worry because the old fellow simply couldn't gallop and that's all there was to it. He run exactly like a crab. The only time he didn't come last was when a big fawn dog by the name of Amber Flash put his foot in a hole and broke a hock and finished on three legs. But even then ours only just beat him. So this way we got him right down to bottom grade with the scrub-bers, and the last time we were there all the bookies were laying him twenty or thirty to one and calling his name and begging people to back him.

Now at last, on this sunny April day, it was Jackie's turn to go instead. Claud said we mustn't run the ringer any more or Mr. Feasey might begin to get tired of him and throw him out altogether, he was so slow. Claud said this was the exact psychological time to have it off, and that Jackie would win it anything between thirty and fifty lengths.

He had raised Jackie from a pup and the dog was only fifteen months now, but he was a good fast runner. He'd never raced yet, but we knew he was fast from clocking him round the little private schooling track at Uxbridge where Claud had taken him every Sunday since he was seven months old—except once when he was having some inoculations. Claud said he probably wasn't fast enough to win top grade at Mr Feasey's, but where we'd got him now, in bottom grade with the scrubbers, he could fall over and get up again and still win it twenty—well, anyway ten or fifteen lengths, Claud said.

So all I had to do this morning was go to the bank in the village and draw out fifty pounds for myself and fifty for Claud which I would lend him as an advance against wages, and then at twelve o'clock lock up the filling-station and hang the notice on one of the pumps saying "GONE FOR THE DAY." Claud would shut the ringer in the pen at the back and put Jackie in the van and off we'd go. I won't say I was as excited as Claud, but there again, I didn't have all sorts of important things depending on it either, like buying a house and being able to get married. Nor was I almost *born* in a kennel with greyhounds like he was, walking about thinking of absolutely nothing else all day—except perhaps Clarice in the evenings. Personally, I had my own career as a filling-station owner to keep me busy, not to mention second-hand cars, but if Claud wanted to fool around with dogs that was all right with me, especially a thing like today—if it came off. As a matter of fact, I don't mind admitting that every time I thought about the money we were putting on and the money we might win, my stomach gave a little lurch.

The dogs had finished their breakfast now and Claud took them out for a short walk across the field opposite while I got dressed and fried the eggs. Afterwards, I went to the bank and drew out the money (all in ones), and the rest of the morning seemed to go very quickly serving customers.

At twelve sharp I locked up and hung the notice on the pump. Claud came around from the back leading Jackie and carrying a large suitcase made of reddish-brown cardboard.

"Suitcase?"

"For the money," Claud answered. "You said yourself no man can carry two thousand pound in his pockets."

It was a lovely yellow spring day with the buds bursting all along the hedges and the sun shining through the new pale green leaves on the big beech tree across the road. Jackie looked wonderful, with two big hard muscles the size of melons bulging on his hindquarters, his coat glistening like black velvet. While Claud was putting the suitcase in the van, the dog did a little prancing jig on his toes to show how fit he was, then he looked up at me and grinned, just like he knew he was off to the races to win two thousand pounds and a heap of glory. This Jackie had the widest most human-smiling grin I ever saw. Not only did he lift his upper lip, but he actually stretched the corners of his mouth so you could see every tooth in his head except perhaps one or two of the molars right at the back; and every time I saw him do it I found myself waiting to hear him start laughing out loud as well.

We got in the van and off we went. I was doing the driving. Claud was beside me and Jackie was standing up on the straw in the rear looking over our shoulders through the windshield. Claud kept turning round and trying to make him lie down so he wouldn't get thrown whenever we went round the sharp corners, but the dog was too excited to do anything except grin back at him and wave his enormous tail.

"You got the money, Gordon?" Claud was chain-smoking cigarettes and quite unable to sit still.

"Yes."

"Mine as well?"

"I got a hundred and five altogether. Five for the winder like you said, so he won't stop the hare and make it a no-race."

"Good," Claud said, rubbing his hands together hard as though he were freezing cold. "Good good good."

We drove through the little narrow High Street of Great Missenden and caught a glimpse of old Rummins going into The Nag's Head for his morning pint, then outside the village we turned left and climbed over the ridge of the Chilterns toward Princes Risborough, and from there it would only be twenty odd miles to Oxford.

And now a silence and a kind of tension began to come over us both. We sat very quiet, not speaking at all, each nursing his own fears and excitements, containing his anxiety. And Claud kept smoking his cigarettes and throwing them half finished out the window. Usually, on these trips, he talked his head off all the way there and back, all the things he'd done with dogs in his life, the jobs he'd pulled, the places he'd been, the money he'd won; and all the things other people had done with dogs, the thievery, the cruelty, the unbelievable trickery and cunning of owners at the flapping tracks. But today I don't think he was trusting himself to speak very much. At this point, for that matter, nor was I. I was sitting there watching the road and trying to keep my mind off the immediate future by thinking back on all that stuff Claud had told me about this curious greyhound racing racket.

I swear there wasn't a man alive who knew more about it than Claud did, and ever since we'd got the ringer and decide to pull this job, he'd taken it upon himself to give me an education in the business. By now, in theory at any rate, I suppose I knew nearly as much as him.

It had started during the very first strategy conference we'd had in the kitchen. I can remember it was the day after the ringer arrived and we were sitting there watching for customers through the window, and Claud was explaining to me all about what we'd have to do, and I was trying to follow him as best I could until finally there came one question I had to ask.

"What I don't see," I had said, "is why you use the ringer at all. Wouldn't it be safer if we use Jackie all the time and simply stop him the first half dozen races so he come last? Then when we're good and ready, we can let him go. Same result in the end, wouldn't it be, if we do it right? And no danger of being caught."

Well, as I say, that did it. Claud looked up at me quickly and said, "Hey! None of that! I'd just like you to know 'stopping's' something I never do. What's come over you, Gordon?" He seemed genuinely pained and shocked by what I had said.

"I don't see anything wrong with it."

"Now listen to me, Gordon. Stopping a good dog breaks his heart. A good dog knows he's fast, and seeing all the others out there in front and not being able to catch them—it breaks his heart, I tell you. And what's more, you wouldn't be making suggestions like that if you knew some of the tricks them fellers do to stop their dogs at the flapping tracks."

"Such as what, for example?" I had asked.

"Such as anything in the world almost, so long as it makes the dog go slower. And it takes a lot of stopping, a good greyhound does. Full of guts and so mad keen you can't even let them watch a race they'll tear the leash right out of your hand rearing to go. Many's the time I've seen one with a broken leg insisting on finishing the race."

He had paused then, looking at me thoughtfully with those large pale eyes, serious as hell and obviously thinking deep. "Maybe," he had said, "if we're going to do this job properly I'd better tell you a thing or two so's you'll know what we're up against."

"Go ahead and tell me," I had said. "I'd like to know."

For a moment he stared in silence out the window. "The main thing you got to remember," he had said darkly, "is that all these fellers going to the flapping tracks with dogs—they're artful. They're more artful than you could possibly imagine." Again he paused, marshalling his thoughts.

"Now take for example the different ways of stopping a dog. The first, the commonest, is strapping."

"Strapping?"

"Yes. Strapping em up. That's commonest. Pulling the muzzle-strap tight around their necks so they can't hardly breathe, see. A clever man knows just which hole on the strap to use and just how many lengths it'll take off his dog in a race. Usually a couple of notches is good for five or six lengths. Do it up real tight and he'll come last. I've known plenty of dogs collapse and die from being strapped up tight on a hot day. Strangulated, absolutely strangulated, and a very nasty thing it was too. Then again, some of em just tie two of the toes together with black cotton. Dog never runs well like that. Unbalances him."

"That doesn't sound too bad."

"Then there's others that put a piece of fresh-chewed gum up under their tails, right up close where the tail joins the body. And there's nothing funny about that," he had said, indignant. "The tail of a running dog goes up and down ever so slightly and the gum on the tail keeps sticking to the hairs on the backside, just where it's tenderest. No dog likes that, you know. Then there's sleeping pills. That's used a lot nowadays. They do it by weight, exactly like a doctor, and they measure the powder according to whether they want to slow him up five or ten or fifteen lengths. Those are just a few of the ordinary ways," he had said. "Actually they're nothing. Absolutely nothing compared with some of the other things that's done to hold a dog back in a race, especially by the gypsies. There's things the gypsies do that are almost too disgusting to mention, such as when they're just putting the dog in the trap, things you wouldn't hardly do to your worst enemies."

And when he had told me about those—which were, indeed, terrible things because they had to do with physical injury, quickly, painfully inflicted—then he had gone on to tell me what they did when they wanted the dog to win.

"There's just as terrible things done to make em go fast as to make em go slow," he had said softly, his face veiled and secret. "And perhaps the commonest of all is wintergreen. Whenever you see a dog going around with no hair on his back or little bald patches all over him—that's wintergreen. Just before the race they rub it hard into the skin. Sometimes it's Sloane's Liniment, but mostly it's wintergreen. Stings terrible. Stings so bad that all the old dog wants to do is run run run as fast as he possibly can to get away from the pain.

"Then there's special drugs they give with the needle. Mind you, that's the modern method and most of the spivs at the track are too ignorant to use it. It's the fellers coming down from London in the big cars with stadium dogs they've borrowed for the day by bribing the trainer—they're the ones use the needle."

I could remember him sitting there at the kitchen table with a cigarette dangling from his mouth and dropping his eyelids to keep out the smoke and looking at me through his wrinkled, nearly closed eyes, and saying, "What you've got to remember, Gordon, is this. There's nothing they won't do to make a dog win if they want him to. On the other hand, no dog can run faster than he's built, no matter what they do to him. So if we can get Jackie down into bottom grade, then we're home. No dog in bottom grade can get near him, not even with wintergreen and needles. Not even with ginger."

"Ginger?"

"Certainly. That's a common one, ginger is. What they do, they take a piece of raw ginger about the size of a walnut, and about five minutes before the off they slip it into the dog."

"You mean in his mouth? He eats it?"

"No," he had said. "Not in his mouth."

And so it had gone on. During each of the eight long trips we had subsequently made to the track with the ringer I had heard more and more about this charming sport—more, especially, about the methods of stopping them and making them go (even the names of the drugs and the quantities to use). I heard about "the rat treatment" (for nonchasers, to make them chase the dummy hare), where a rat is placed in a can which is then tied around the dog's neck. There's a small hole in the lid of the can just large enough for the rat to poke its head out and nip the dog. But the dog can't get at the rat, and so naturally he goes half crazy running around and being bitten in the neck, and the more he shakes the can the more the rat bites him. Finally, someone releases the rat, and the dog, who up to then was a nice docile tail-wagging animal who wouldn't hurt a mouse, pounces on it in a rage and tears it to pieces. Do this a few times, Claud had said—"mind you, I don't hold with it myself"—and the dog becomes a real killer who will chase anything, even the dummy hare.

We were over the Chilterns now and running down out of the beechwoods into the flat elm- and oak-tree country south of Oxford. Claud sat quietly beside me, nursing his nervousness and smoking cigarettes, and every two or three minutes he would turn round to see if Jackie was all right. The dog was at last lying down, and each time Claud turned round, he whispered something to him softly, and the dog acknowledged his words with a faint movement of the tail that made the straw rustle.

Soon we would be coming into Thame, the broad High Street where they penned the pigs and cows and sheep on market day, and where the Fair came once a year with the swings and roundabouts and bumping cars and gypsy caravans right there in the street in the middle of the town. Claud was born in Thame, and we'd never driven through it yet without him mentioning this fact.

"Well," he said as the first houses came into sight, "here's Thame. I was born and bred in Thame, you know, Gordon."

"You told me."

"Lots of funny things we used to do around here when we was nippers," he said, slightly nostalgic.

"I'm sure."

He paused, and I think more to relieve the tension building up inside him than anything else, he began talking about the years of his youth.

"There was a boy next door," he said. "Gilbert Gomm nis name was. Little sharp ferrety face and one leg a bit shorter'n the other. Shocking things him and me used to do together. You know one thing we done, Gordon?"

"What?"

"We'd go into the kitchen Saturday nights when Mum and Dad were at the pub, and we'd disconnect the pipe from the gas-ring and bubble the gas into a milk bottle full of water. Then we'd sit down and drink it out of teacups."

"Was that so good?"

"Good! It was absolutely disgusting! But we'd put lashings of sugar in and then it didn't taste so bad."

"Why did you drink it?"

Claud turned and looked at me, incredulous. "You mean you never drunk 'Snakes Water'!"

"Can't say I have."

"I thought everyone done that when they was kids! It intoxicates you, just like wine only worse, depending on how long you let the gas bubble through. We used to get reeling drunk together there in the kitchen Saturday nights and it was marvellous. Until one night Dad comes home early and catches us. I'll never forget that night as long as I live. There was me holding the milk bottle, and the gas bubbling through it lovely, and Gilbert kneeling on the floor ready to turn off the tap the moment I give the word, and in walks Dad."

"What did he say?"

"Oh Christ, Gordon, that was terrible. He didn't say one word, but he stands there by the door and he starts feeling for his belt, undoing the buckle very slow and pulling the belt slow out of his trousers, looking at me all the time. Great big feller he was, with great big hands like coalhammers and a black moustache and them little purple veins running all over his cheeks. Then he comes over quick and grabs me by the coat and lets me have it, hard as he can, using the end with the buckle on it and honest to God, Gordon, I thought he was going to kill me. But in the end he stops and then he puts on the belt again, slow and careful, buckling it up and tucking in the flap and belching with the beer he'd drunk. And then he walks out again back to the pub, still without saying a word. Worst hiding I ever had in my life."

"How old were you then?"

"Round about eight, I should think," Claud said.

As we drew closer to Oxford, he became silent again. He kept twisting his neck to see if Jackie was all right, to touch him, to stroke his head, and once he turned around and knelt on the seat to gather more straw around the dog, murmuring something about a draft. We drove around the fringe of Oxford and into a network of narrow country roads, and after a while we turned into a small bumpy lane and along this we began to overtake a thin stream of men and women all walking and cycling in the same direction. Some of the men were leading greyhounds. There was a large saloon car in front of us and through the rear window we could see a dog sitting on the back seat between two men.

"They come from all over," Claud said darkly. "That one there's probably come up special from London. Probably slipped him out from one of the big stadium kennels just for the afternoon. That could be a Derby dog probably, for all we know."

"Hope he's not running against Jackie."

"Don't worry," Claud said. "All new dogs automatically go in top grade. That's one rule Mr. Feasey's very particular about."

There was an open gate leading into a field, and Mr. Feasey's wife came forward to take our admission money before we drove in.

"He'd have her winding the bloody pedals too if she had the strength," Claud said. "Old Feasey don't employ more people than he has to."

I drove across the field and parked at the end of a line of cars along the top hedge. We both got out and Claud went quickly round the back to fetch Jackie. I stood beside the car, waiting. It was a very large field with a steepish slope on it, and we were at the top of the slope, looking down. In the distance I could see the six starting traps and the wooden posts marking the track which ran along the bottom of the field and turned sharp at right angles and came on up the hill toward the crowd, to the finish. Thirty yards beyond the finishing line stood the upturned bicycle for driving the hare. Because it is portable, this is the standard machine for hare-driving used at all flapping tracks. It comprises a flimsy wooden platform about eight feet high, supported on four poles knocked into the ground. On top of the platform there is fixed, upside down with wheels in the air, an ordinary old bicycle. The rear wheel is to the front, facing down the track, and from it the tire has been removed, leaving a concave metal rim. One end of the cord that pulls the hare is attached to this rim, and the winder (or hare driver), by straddling the bicycle at the back and turning the pedals with his hands, revolves the wheel and winds in the cord around the rim. This pulls the dummy hare toward him at any speed he likes up to forty miles an hour. After each race someone takes the dummy hare (with cord attached) all the way down to the starting traps again, thus unwinding the cord on the wheel, ready for a fresh start. From his high platform, the winder can watch the race and regulate the speed of the hare to keep it just ahead of the leading dog. He can also stop the hare any time he wants and make it a "no race" (if the wrong dog looks like winning) by suddenly turning the pedals backwards and getting the cord tangled up in the hub of the wheel. The other way of doing it is to slow down the hare suddenly, for perhaps one second, and that makes the lead dog automatically check a little so that the others catch up with him. He is an important man, the winder.

I could see Mr. Feasey's winder already standing atop his platform, a powerful looking man in a blue sweater, leaning on the bicycle and looking down at the crowd through the smoke of his cigarette.

There is a curious law in England which permits race meetings of this kind to be held only seven times a year over one piece of ground. That is why all Mr. Feasey's equipment was movable, and after the seventh meeting he would simply transfer to the next field. The law didn't bother him at all.

There was already a good crowd and the bookmakers were erecting their stands in a line over to the right. Claud had Jackie out of the van now and was leading him over to a group of people clustered around a small stocky man dressed in riding-breeches— Mr. Feasey himself. Each person in the group had a dog on a leash and Mr. Feasey kept writing names in a notebook that he held folded in his left hand. I sauntered over to watch.

"Which you got there?" Mr. Feasey said, pencil poised above the notebook.

"Midnight," a man said who was holding a black dog.

Mr. Feasey stepped back a pace and looked most carefully at the dog.

"Midnight. Right. I got him down."

"Jane," the next man said.

"Let me look. Jane . . . Jane . . . yes, all right."

"Soldier." This dog was led by a tall man with long teeth who wore a dark-blue, double-breasted lounge suit, shiny with wear, and when he said "Soldier" he began slowly to scratch the seat of his trousers with the hand that wasn't holding the leash.

Mr. Feasey bent down to examine the dog. The other man looked up at the sky.

"Take him away," Mr. Feasey said.

The man looked down quick and stopped scratching.

"Go on, take him away."

"Listen, Mr. Feasey," the man said, lisping slightly through his long teeth. "Now don't talk so bloody silly, *please.*"

"Go on and beat it, Larry, and stop wasting my time. You know as well as I do the Soldier's got two white toes on his off fore."

"Now look, Mr. Feasey," the man said. "You ain't even seen Soldier for six months at least."

"Come on now, Larry, and beat it. I haven't got time arguing with you." Mr. Feasey didn't appear the least angry. "Next," he said.

I saw Claud step forward leading Jackie. The large bovine face was fixed and wooden, the eyes staring at something about a yard above Mr. Feasey's head, and he was holding the leash so tight his knuckles were like a row of little white onions. I knew just how he was feeling. I felt the same way myself at that moment, and it was even worse when Mr. Feasey suddenly started laughing.

"Hey!" he cried. "Here's the Black Panther. Here's the champion."

"That's right, Mr. Feasey," Claud said.

"Well, I'll tell you," Mr. Feasey said, still grinning. "You can take him right back home where he come from. I don't want him."

"But look here, Mr. Feasey . . ."

"Six or eight times at least I've run him for you now and that's enough. Look—why don't you shoot him and have done with it?"

"Now listen, Mr. Feasey, *please.* Just once more and I'll never ask you again."

"Not even once! I got more dogs than I can handle here today. There's no room for crabs like that."

I thought Claud was going to cry.

"Now honest, Mr. Feasey," he said. "I been up at six every morning this past two weeks giving him roadwork and massage and buying him beefsteaks, and believe me he's a different dog absolutely than what he was last time he run."

The words "different dog" caused Mr. Feasey to jump like he'd been pricked with a hatpin. "What's that!" he cried. "Different dog!"

I'll say this for Claud, he kept his head. "See here, Mr. Feasey," he said. "I'll thank you not to go implying things to me. You know very well I didn't mean that."

"All right, all right. But just the same, you can take him away. There's no sense running dogs as slow as him. Take him home now, will you please, and don't hold up the whole meeting."

I was watching Claud. Claud was watching Mr. Feasey. Mr. Feasey was looking round for the next dog to enter up. Under his brown tweedy jacket he wore a yellow pullover, and this streak of yellow on his breast and his thin gaitered legs and the way he jerked his head from side to side made him seem like some sort of a little perky bird—a goldfinch, perhaps.

Claud took a step forward. His face was beginning to purple slightly with the outrage of it all and I could see his Adam's apple moving up and down as he swallowed.

"I'll tell you what I'll do, Mr. Feasey. I'm so absolutely sure this dog's improved I'll bet you a quid he don't finish last. There you are."

Mr. Feasey turned slowly around and looked at Claud. "You crackers?" he asked.

"I'll bet you a quid, there you are, just to prove what I'm saying."

It was a dangerous move, certain to cause suspicion, but Claud knew it was the only thing left to do. There was silence while Mr. Feasey bent down and examined the dog. I could see the way his eyes were moving slowly over the animal's whole body, part by part. There was something to admire in the man's thoroughness, and in his memory; something to fear also in this self-confident little rogue who held in his head the shape and colour and markings of perhaps several hundred different but very similar dogs. He never needed more than one little clue—a small scar, a splay toe, a trifle in at the hocks, a less pronounced wheelback, a slightly darker brindle—Mr. Feasey always remembered.

So I watched him now as he bent down over Jackie. His face was pink and fleshy, the mouth small and tight as though it couldn't stretch enough to make a smile, and the eyes were like two little cameras focussed sharply on the dog.

"Well," he said, straightening up. "It's the same dog anyway."

"I should hope so too!" Claud cried. "Just what sort of a fellow you think I am, Mr. Feasey?"

"I think you're crackers, that's what I think. But it's a nice easy way to make a quid. I suppose you forgot how Amber Flash nearly beat him on three legs last meeting?"

"This one wasn't fit then," Claud said. "He hadn't had beefsteak and massage and roadwork like I've been giving him lately. But look, Mr. Feasey, you're not to go sticking him in top grade just to win the bet. This is a bottom grade dog, Mr. Feasey. You know that."

Mr. Feasey laughed. The small button mouth opened into a tiny circle and he laughed and looked at the crowd who laughed with him. "Listen," he said, laying a hairy hand on Claud's shoulder. "I know my dogs. I don't have to do any fiddling around to win *this* quid. He goes in bottom."

"Right," Claud said. "That's a bet." He walked away with Jackie and I joined him.

"Jesus, Gordon, that was a near one!"

"Shook me."

"But we're in now," Claud said. He had that breathless look on his face again and he was walking about quick and funny, like the ground was burning his feet.

People were still coming through the gate into the field and there were easily three hundred of them now. Not a very nice crowd. Sharpnosed men and women with dirty faces and bad teeth and quick shifty eyes. The dregs of the big town. Oozing out like sewage from a cracked pipe and trickling along the road through the gate and making a smelly little pond of sewage at the top end of the

field. They were all there, all the spivs and the gypsies and the touts
and the dregs and the sewage and the scrapings and the scum from
the cracked drainpipes of the big town. Some with dogs, some
without. Dogs led about on pieces of string, miserable dogs with
hanging heads, thin mangy dogs with sores on their quarters (from
sleeping on board), sad old dogs with grey muzzles, doped dogs,
dogs stuffed with porridge to stop them winning, dogs walking
stiff-legged—one especially, a white one "Claud, why is that white
one walking so stiff-legged?"

"Which one?"

"That one over there."

"Ah yes, I see. Very probably because he's been hung."

"Hung?"

"Yes, hung. Suspended in a harness for twenty-four hours with
his legs dangling."

"Good God, but why?"

"To make him run slow, of course. Some people don't hold with
dope or stuffing or strapping up. So they hang em."

"I see."

"Either that," Claud said, "or they sandpaper them. Rub their
pads with rough sandpaper and take the skin off so it hurts when they
run."

"Yes, I see."

And then the fitter, brighter-looking dogs, the better fed
ones who get horsemeat every day, not pigswill or rusk and cabbage water, their coats shinier, their tails moving, pulling at their
leads, undoped, unstuffed, awaiting perhaps a more unpleasant
fate, the muzzle-strap to be tightened an extra four notches. *But
make sure he can breathe now, Jock. Don't choke him completely. Don't
let's have him collapse in the middle of the race. Just so he wheezes a bit,
see. Go on tightening it up an extra notch at a time until you can hear
him wheezing. You'll see his mouth open and he'll start breathing
heavy. Then it's just right, but not if his eyeballs is bulging. Watch out
for that, will you? Okay?*

Okay.

"Let's get away from the crowd, Gordon. It don't do Jackie no
good getting excited by all these other dogs."

We walked up the slope to where the cars were parked, then
back and forth in front of the line of cars, keeping the dog on the
move. Inside some of the cars I could see men sitting with their dogs,
and the men scowled at us through the windows as we went by.

"Watch out now, Gordon. We don't want any trouble."

"No, all right."

These were the best dogs of all, the secret ones kept in the cars and taken out quick just to be entered up (under some invented name) and put back again quick and held there till the last minute, then straight down to the traps and back again into the cars after the race so no nosey bastard gets too close a look. The trainer at the big stadium said so. *All right, he said. You can have him, but for Christsake don't let anybody recognise him. There's thousands of people know this dog, so you've got to be careful, see. And it'll cost you fifty pound.*

Very fast dogs these, but it doesn't much matter how fast they are they probably get the needle anyway, just to make sure. One and a half ccs. of ether, subcutaneous, done in the car, injected very slow. That'll put ten lengths on any dog. Or sometimes it's caffein, caffein in oil, or camphor. That makes them go too. The men in the big cars know all about that. And some of them know about whiskey. But that's intravenous. Not so easy when it's intravenous. Might miss the vein. All you got to do is miss the vein and it don't work and where are you then? So it's ether, or it's caffein, or it's camphor. *Don't give her too much of that stuff now, Jock. What does she weigh? Fifty-eight pounds. All right then, you know what the man told us. Wait a minute now. I got it written down on a piece of paper. Here it is. Point 1 of a cc. per 10 pounds bodyweight equals 5 lengths over 300 yards. Wait a minute now while I work it out. Oh Christ, you better guess it. Just guess it, Jock. It's be all right you'll find. Shouldn't be any trouble anyway because I picked the others in the race myself. Cost me a tenner to old Feasey. A bloody tenner I give him, and dear Mr. Feasey, I says, that's for your birthday and because I love you.*

Thank you ever so much, Mr. Feasey says. Thank you, my good and trusted friend.

And for stopping them, for the men in the big cars, it's chlorbutal. That's a beauty, chlorbutal, because you can give it the night before, especially to someone else's dog. Or Pethidine. Pethidine and Hyoscine mixed, whatever that may be.

"Lot of fine old English sporting gentry here," Claud said.

"Certainly are."

"Watch your pockets, Gordon. You got that money hidden away?"

We walked around the back of the line of cars—between the cars and the hedge—and I saw Jackie stiffen and begin to pull forward on the leash, advancing with a stiff crouching tread. About thirty yards away there were two men. One was holding a large fawn greyhound, the dog stiff and tense like Jackie. The other was holding a sack in his hands.

"Watch," Claud whispered, "they're giving him a kill."

Out of the sack onto the grass tumbled a small white rabbit, fluffy white, young, tame. It righted itself and sat still, crouching in the hunched up way rabbits crouch, its nose close to the ground. A frightened rabbit. Out of the sack so suddenly onto the grass with such a bump. Into the bright light. The dog was going mad with excitement now, jumping up against the leash, pawing the ground, throwing himself forward, whining. The rabbit saw the dog. It drew in its head and stayed still, paralyzed with fear. The man transferred his hold to the dog's collar, and the dog twisted and jumped and tried to get free. The other man pushed the rabbit with his foot but it was too terrified to move. He pushed it again, flicking it forward with his toe like a football, and the rabbit rolled over several times, righted itself and began to hop over the grass away from the dog. The other man released the dog which pounced with one huge pounce upon the rabbit, and then came the squeals, not very loud but shrill and anguished and lasting rather a long time.

"There you are," Claud said. "That's a kill."

"Not sure I liked it very much."

"I told you before, Gordon. Most of em does it. Keens the dog up before a race."

"I still don't like it."

"Nor me. But they all do it. Even in the big stadiums the trainers do it. Proper barbary I call it."

We strolled away, and below us on the slope of the hill the crowd was thickening and the bookies' stands with the names written on them in red and gold and blue were all erected now in a long line back of the crowd, each bookie already stationed on an upturned box beside his stand, a pack of numbered cards in one hand, a piece of chalk in the other, his clerk behind him with book and pencil. Then we saw Mr. Feasey walking over to a blackboard that was nailed to a post stuck in the ground.

"He's chalking up the first race," Claud said. "Come on, quick!"

We walked rapidly down the hill and joined the crowd. Mr. Feasey was writing the runners on the blackboard, copying names from his soft-covered notebook, and a little hush of suspense fell upon the crowd as they watched.

1. SALLY
2. THREE QUID
3. SNAILBOX LADY
4. BLACK PANTHER
5. WHISKEY
6. ROCKIT

"He's in it!" Claud whispered. "First race! Trap four! Now listen, Gordon! Give me a fiver quick to show the winder."

Claud could hardly speak from excitement. That patch of whiteness had returned around his nose and eyes, and when I handed him a five pound note, his whole arm was shaking as he took it. The man who was going to wind the bicycle pedals was still standing on top on the wooden platform in his blue jersey, smoking. Claud went over and stood below him, looking up.

"See this fiver," he said, talking softly, holding it folded small in the palm of his hand.

The man glanced at it without moving his head.

"Just so long as you wind her true this race, see. No stopping and no slowing down and run her fast. Right?"

The man didn't move but there was a slight, almost imperceptible lifting of the eybrows. Claud turned away.

"Now look, Gordon. Get the money on gradual, all in little bits like I told you. Just keep going down the line putting on little bits so you don't kill the price, see. And I'll be walking Jackie down very slow, as slow as I dare, to give you plenty of time. Right?"

"Right."

"And don't forget to be standing ready to catch him at the end of the race. Get him clear away from all them others when they start fighting for the hare. Grab a hold of him tight and don't let go till I come running up with the collar and lead. That Whiskey's a gypsy dog and he'll tear the leg off anything as gets in his way."

"Right," I said. "Here we go."

I saw Claud lead Jackie over to the finishing post and collect a yellow jacket with 4 written on it large. Also a muzzle. The other five runners were there too, the owners fussing around them, putting on their numbered jackets, adjusting their muzzles. Mr. Feasey was officiating, hopping about in his tight riding-breeches like an anxious perky bird, and once I saw him say something to Claud and laugh. Claud ignored him. Soon they would all start to lead the dogs down the track, the long walk down the hill and across to the far corner of the field to the starting-traps. It would take them ten minutes to walk it. I've got at least ten minutes, I told myself, and then I began to push my way through the crowd standing six or seven deep in front of the line of bookies.

"Even money Whiskey! Even money Whiskey! Five to two Sally! Even money Whiskey! Four to one Snailbox! Come on now! Hurry up, hurry up! Which is it?"

On every board all down the line the Black Panther was chalked up at twenty-five to one. I edged forward to the nearest book.

"Three pounds Black Panther," I said, holding out the money.

The man on the box had an inflamed magenta face and traces of some white substance around the corners of his mouth. He snatched the money and dropped it in his satchel. "Seventy-five pound to three Black Panther," he said. "Number forty-two." He handed me a ticket and his clerk recorded the bet.

I stepped back and wrote rapidly on the back of the ticket 75 to 3, then slipped it into the inside pocket of my jacket, with the money.

So long as I continued to spread the cash out thin like this, it ought to be all right. And anyway, on Claud's instructions, I'd made a point of betting a few pounds on the ringer every time he'd run so as not to arouse any suspicion when the real day arrived. Therefore, with some confidence, I went all the way down the line staking three pounds with each book. I didn't hurry, but I didn't waste any time either, and after each bet I wrote the amount on the back of the card before slipping it into my pocket. There were seventeen bookies. I had seventeen tickets and had laid out fifty-one pounds without disturbing the price one point. Forty-nine pounds left to get on. I glanced quickly down the hill. One owner and his dog had already reached the traps. The others were only twenty or thirty yards away. Except for Claud. Claud and Jackie were only halfway there. I could see Claud in his old khaki greatcoat sauntering slowly along with Jackie pulling ahead keenly on the leash, and once I saw him stop completely and bend down pretending to pick something up. When he went on again he seemed to have developed a limp so as to go slower still. I hurried back to the other end of the line to start again.

"Three pounds Black Panther."

The bookmaker, the one with the magenta face and the white substance around the mouth, glanced up sharply, remembering the last time, and in one swift almost graceful movement of the arm he licked his fingers and wiped the figure twenty-five neatly off the board. His wet fingers left a small dark patch opposite Black Panther's name.

"All right, you got one more seventy-five to three," he said. "But that's the lot." Then he raised his voice and shouted, "Fifteen to one Black Panther! Fifteens the Panther!"

All down the line the twenty-fives were wiped out and it was fifteen to one the Panther now. I took it quick, but by the time I was through the bookies had had enough and they weren't quoting him any more. They'd only taken six pounds each, but they stood to lose a hundred and fifty, and for them—small times bookies at a little country flapping-track—that was quite enough for one race, thank you very much. I felt pleased the way I'd managed it. Lots of tickets now. I took them out of my pockets and counted them and they were like a thin pack of cards in my hand. Thirty-three tickets in all. And what did we stand to win? Let me see . . . something over two thousand pounds. Claud had said he'd win it thirty lengths. Where was Claud now?

Far away down the hill I could see the khaki greatcoat standing by the traps and the big black dog alongside. All the other dogs were already in and the owners were beginning to walk away. Claud was bending down now, coaxing Jackie into number four, and then he was closing the door and turning away and beginning to run up the hill toward the crowd, the greatcoat flapping around him. He kept looking back over his shoulder as he ran.

Beside the traps the starter stood, and his hand was up waving a handkerchief. At the other end of the track, beyond the winning-post, quite close to where I stood, the man in the blue jersey was straddling the upturned bicycle on top of the wooden platform and he saw the signal and waved back and began to turn the pedals with his hands. Then a tiny white dot in the distance—the artificial hare that was in reality a football with a piece of white rabbit-skin tacked onto it—began to move away from the traps, accelerating fast. The traps went up and the dogs flew out. They flew out in a single dark lump, all together, as though it were one wide dog instead of six, and almost at once I saw Jackie drawing away from the field. I knew it was Jackie because of the colour. There weren't any other black dogs in the race. It was Jackie all right. Don't move, I told myself. Don't move a muscle or an eyelid or a toe or a fingertip. Stand quite still and don't move. Watch him going. Come on Jackson, boy! No, don't shout. It's unlucky to shout. And don't move. Be all over in twenty seconds. Round the sharp bend now and coming up the hill and he must be fifteen or twenty lengths clear. Easy twenty lengths. Don't count the lengths, it's unlucky. And don't move. Don't move your head. Watch him out of your eye-corners. Watch that Jackson go! He's really laying down to it now up that hill. He's won it now! He can't lose it now . . .

When I got over to him he was fighting the rabbit-skin and trying to pick it up in his mouth, but his muzzle wouldn't allow it, and the other dogs were pounding up behind him and suddenly they were all on top of him grabbing for the rabbit and I got hold of him round the neck and dragged him clear like Claud had said and knelt down on the grass and held him tight with both arms round his body. The other catchers were having a time all trying to grab their own dogs.

Then Claud was beside me, blowing heavily, unable to speak from blowing and excitement, removing Jackie's muzzle, putting on the collar and lead, and Mr. Feasey was there too, standing with hands on hips, the button mouth pursed up tight like a mushroom, the two little cameras staring at Jackie all over again.

"So that's the game, is it?" he said.

Claud was bending over the dog and acting like he hadn't heard.

"I don't want you here no more after this, you understand that?"

Claud went on fiddling with Jackie's collar.

I heard someone behind us saying, "That flat-faced bastard with the frown swung it properly on old Feasey this time." Someone else laughed. Mr. Feasey walked away. Claud straightened up and went over with Jackie to the hare driver in the blue jersey who had dismounted from his platform.

"Cigarette," Claud said, offering the pack.

The man took one, also the five pound note that was folded up small in Claud's fingers.

"Thanks," Claud said. "Thanks very much."

"Don't mention," the man said.

Then Claud turned to me. "You get it all on, Gordon?" He was jumping up and down and rubbing his hands and patting Jackie, and his lips trembled as he spoke.

"Yes. Half at twenty-fives, half at fifteens."

"Oh Christ, Gordon, that's marvellous. Wait here till I get the suitcase."

"You take Jackie," I said, "and go and sit in the car. I'll see you later."

There was nobody around the bookies now. I was the only one

with anything to collect, and I walked slowly with a sort of dancing stride and a wonderful bursting feeling in my chest, toward the first one in the line, the man with the magenta face and the white substance on his mouth. I stood in front of him and I took all the time I wanted going through my pack of tickets to find the two that were his. The name was Syd Pratchett. It was written up large across his board in gold letters on a scarlet field—"SYD PRATCHETT. THE BEST ODDS IN THE MIDLANDS. PROMPT SETTLEMENT."

I handed him the first ticket and said, "Seventy-eight pounds to come." It sounded so good I said it again, making a delicious little song of it. "Seventy-eight pounds to come on this one." I didn't mean to gloat over Mr. Pratchett. As a matter of fact, I was beginning to like him quite a lot. I even felt sorry for him having to fork out so much money. I hoped his wife and kids wouldn't suffer.

"Number forty-two," Mr. Pratchett said, turning to his clerk who held the big book. "Forty-two wants seventy-eight pound."

There was a pause while the clerk ran his finger down the column of recorded bets. He did this twice, then he looked up at the boss and began to shake his head.

"No," he said. "Don't pay. That ticket backed Snailbox Lady."

Mr. Pratchett, standing on his box, leaned over and peered down at the book. He seemed to be disturbed by what the clerk had said, and there was a look of genuine concern on the huge magenta face.

That clerk is a fool, I thought, and any moment now Mr. Pratchett's going to tell him so.

But when Mr. Pratchett turned back to me, the eyes had become narrow and hostile. "Now look Charley," he said softly. "Don't let's have any of that. You know very well you bet Snailbox. What's the idea?"

"I bet Black Panther," I said. "Two separate bets of three pounds each at twenty-five to one. Here's the second ticket."

This time he didn't even bother to check it with the book. "You bet Snailbox, Charley," he said. "I remember you coming round." With that, he turned away from me and started wiping the names of the last race runners off his board with a wet rag. Behind him, the clerk had closed the book and was lighting himself a cigarette. I stood watching them, and I could feel the sweat beginning to break through the skin all over my body.

"Let me see the book."

Mr. Pratchett blew his nose in the wet rag and dropped it to the ground. "Look," he said, "why don't you go away and stop annoy ing me?"

The point was this: a bookmaker's ticket, unlike a parimutual ticket, never has anything written on it regarding the nature of your bet. This is normal practice, the same at every racetrack in the country, whether it's the Silver Ring at Newmarket, the Royal Enclosure at Ascot, or a tiny country flapping track near Oxford. All you receive is a card bearing the bookie's name and a serial number. The wager is (or should be) recorded by the bookie's clerk in his book alongside the number of the ticket, but apart from that there is no evidence at all of how you betted.

"Go on," Mr. Pratchett was saying. "Hop it."

I stepped back a pace and glanced down the long line of bookmakers. None of them was looking my way. Each was standing motionless on his little wooden box beside his wooden placard, staring straight ahead into the crowd. I went up to the next one and presented a ticket.

"I had three pounds on Black Panther at twenty-five to one," I said firmly. "Seventy-eight pounds to come."

This man, who had a soft inflamed face, went through exactly the same routine as Mr. Pratchett, questioning his clerk, peering at the book, and giving me the same answers.

"Whatever's the matter with you?" he said quietly, speaking to me as though I were eight years old. "Trying such a silly thing as that."

This time I stepped well back. "You dirty thieving bastards!" I cried. "The whole lot of you!"

Automatically, as though they were puppets, all the heads down the line flicked round and looked at me. The expressions didn't alter. It was just the heads that moved, all seventeen of them, and seventeen pairs of cold glassy eyes looked down at me. There was not the faintest flicker of interest in any of them.

"Somebody spoke," they seemed to be saying. "We didn't hear it. It's quite a nice day today."

The crowd, sensing excitement, was beginning to move in around me. I ran back to Mr. Pratchett, right up close to him and poked him in the stomach with my finger. "You're a thief! A lousy rotten little thief!" I shouted.

The extraordinary thing was, Mr. Pratchett didn't seem to resent this at all.

"Well I never," he said. *"Look* who's talking."

Then suddenly the big face broke into a wide, frog-like grin, and he looked over at the crowd and shouted, *"Look* who's talking!"

All at once, everybody started to laugh. Down the line the bookies were coming to life and turning to each other and laughing and pointing at me and shouting, *"Look* who's talking! *Look* who's talking!" The crowd began to take up the cry as well, and I stood there on the grass alongside Mr. Pratchett with this wad of tickets as thick as a pack of cards in my hand, listening to them and feeling slightly hysterical. Over the heads of the people I could see Mr. Feasey beside his blackboard already chalking up the runners for the next race; and then beyond him, far away up the top of the field, I caught sight of Claud standing by the van, waiting for me with the suitcase in his hand.

It was time to go home.

The Champion of the World · *1959*

All day, in between serving customers, we had been crouching over the table in the office of the filling-station, preparing the raisins. They were plump and soft and swollen from being soaked in water, and when you nicked them with a razor-blade the skin sprang open and the jelly stuff inside squeezed out as easily as you could wish.

But we had a hundred and ninety-six of them to do altogether and the evening was nearly upon us before we had finished.

"Don't they look marvellous!" Claud cried, rubbing his hands together hard. "What time is it, Gordon?"

"Just after five."

Through the window we could see a station-wagon pulling up at the pumps with a woman at the wheel and about eight children in the back eating ice-creams.

"We ought to be moving soon," Claud said. "The whole thing'll be a washout if we don't arrive before sunset, you realize that." He was getting twitchy now. His face had the same flushed and pop-eyed look it got before a dog-race or when there was a date with Clarice in the evening.

We both went outside and Claud gave the woman the number of gallons she wanted. When she had gone, he remained standing in the middle of the driveway squinting anxiously up at the sun which was now only the width of a man's hand above the line of trees along the crest of the ridge on the far side of the valley

"All right," I said. "Lock up."

He went quickly from pump to pump, securing each nozzle in its holder with a small padlock.

"You'd better take off that yellow pullover," he said.

"Why should I?"

"You'll be shining like a bloody beacon out there in the moon light."

"I'll be all right "

"You will not," he said. "Take it off, Gordon, please. I'll see you in three minutes." He disappeared into his caravan behind the filling-station, and I went indoors and changed my yellow pullover for a blue one.

When we met again outside, Claud was dressed in a pair of black trousers and a dark-green turtleneck sweater. On his head he wore a brown cloth cap with the peak pulled down low over his eyes, and he looked like an apache actor out of a nightclub.

"What's under there?" I asked, seeing the bulge at his waistline.

He pulled up his sweater and showed me two thin but very large white cotton sacks which were bound neat and tight around his belly "To carry the stuff," he said darkly.

"I see."

"Let's go," he said,

"I still think we ought to take the car."

"It's too risky. They'll see it parked."

"But it's over three miles up to that wood."

"Yes," he said. "And I suppose you realize we can get six months in the clink if they catch us."

"You never told me that."

"Didn't I?"

"I'm not coming," I said. "It's not worth it."

"The walk will do you good, Gordon. Come on."

It was a calm sunny evening with little wisps of brilliant white cloud hanging motionless in the sky, and the valley was cool and very quiet as the two of us began walking together along the grass verge on the side of the road that ran between the hills toward Oxford.

"You got the raisins?" Claud asked.

"They're in my pocket."

"Good," he said. "Marvellous."

Ten minutes later we turned left off the main road into a narrow lane with high hedges on either side and from now on it was all uphill.

"How many keepers are there?" I asked.

"Three."

Claud threw away a half-finished cigarette. A minute later he lit another.

"I don't usually approve of new methods," he said. "Not on this sort of a job."

"Of course."

"But by God, Gordon, I think we're onto a hot one this time."

"You do?"

"There's no question about it."

"I hope you're right."

"It'll be a milestone in the history of poaching," he said. "But don't you go telling a single soul how we've done it, you understand. Because if this ever leaked out we'd have every bloody fool in the district doing the same thing and there wouldn't be a pheasant left."

"I won't say a word."

"You ought to be very proud of yourself," he went on. "There's been men with brains studying this problem for hundreds of years and not one of them's ever come up with anything even a quarter as artful as you have. Why didn't you tell me about it before?"

"You never invited my opinion," I said.

And that was the truth. In fact, up until the day before, Claud had never even offered to discuss with me the sacred subject of poaching. Often enough, on a summer's evening when work was finished, I had seen him with cap on head sliding quietly out of his caravan and disappearing up the road toward the woods; and sometimes, watching him through the window of the filling-station, I would find myself wondering exactly what he was going to do, what wily tricks he was going to practise all alone up there under the trees in the dead of night. He seldom came back until very late, and never, absolutely never did he bring any of the spoils with him personally on his return. But the following afternoon—and I couldn't imagine how he did it—there would always be a pheasant or a hare or a brace of partridges hanging up in the shed behind the filling-station for us to eat.

This summer he had been particularly active, and during the last couple of months he had stepped up the tempo to a point where he was going out four and sometimes five nights a week. But that was not all. It seemed to me that recently his whole attitude toward poaching had undergone a subtle and mysterious change. He was more purposeful about it now, more tight-lipped and intense than before, and I had the impression that this was not so much a game any longer as a crusade, a sort of private war that Claud was waging single-handed against an invisible and hated enemy

But who?

I wasn't sure about this, but I had a suspicion that it was none other than the famous Mr. Victor Hazel himself, the owner of the land and the pheasants. Mr. Hazel was a pie and sausage manufacturer with an unbelievably arrogant manner. He was rich beyond words, and his property stretched for miles along either side of the valley. He was a self-made man with no charm at all and precious few virtues. He loathed all persons of humble station, having once been one of them himself, and he strove desperately to mingle with what he believed were the right kind of folk. He hunted with the hounds and gave shooting-parties and wore fancy waistcoats, and every weekday he drove an enormous black Rolls-Royce past the filling-station on his way to the factory. As he flashed by, we would sometimes catch a glimpse of the great glistening butcher's face above the wheel, pink as a ham, all soft and inflamed from eating too much meat.

Anyway, yesterday afternoon, right out of the blue, Claud had suddenly said to me, "I'll be going on up to Hazel's woods again tonight. Why don't you come along?"

"Who, me?"

"It's about the last chance this year for pheasants," he had said. "The shooting-season opens Saturday and the birds'll be scattered all over the place after that—if there's any left."

"Why the sudden invitation?" I had asked, greatly suspicious.

"No special reason, Gordon. No reason at all."

"Is it risky?"

He hadn't answered this.

"I suppose you keep a gun or something hidden away up there?"

"A gun!" he cried, disgusted. "Nobody ever *shoots* pheasants, didn't you know that? You've only got to fire a *cap-pistol* in Hazel's woods and the keepers'll be on you."

"Then how do you do it?"

"Ah," he said, and the eyelids drooped over the eyes, veiled and secretive.

There was a long pause. Then he said, "Do you think you could keep your mouth shut if I was to tell you a thing or two?'

"Definitely."

"I've never told this to anyone else in my whole life, Gordon '

"I am greatly honoured," I said. "You can trust me com pletely."

He turned his head, fixing me with pale eyes. The eyes were large and wet and ox-like, and they were so near to me that I could see my own face reflected upside down in the centre of each.

"I am now about to let you in on the three best ways in the world of poaching a pheasant," he said. "And seeing that you're the guest on this little trip, I am going to give you the choice of which one you'd like us to use tonight. How's that?"

"There's a catch in this."

"There's no catch, Gordon. I swear it."

"All right, go on."

"Now, here's the thing," he said. "Here's the first big secret." He paused and took a long suck at his cigarette. "Pheasants," he whispered softly, "is *crazy* about raisins."

"Raisins?"

"Just ordinary raisins. It's like a mania with them. My dad dis. covered that more than forty years ago just like he discovered all three of these methods I'm about to describe to you now."

"I thought you said your dad was a drunk."

"Maybe he was. But he was also a great poacher, Gordon. Possibly the greatest there's ever been in the history of England. My dad studied poaching like a scientist."

"Is that so?"

"I mean it. I really mean it."

"I believe you."

"Do you know," he said, "my dad used to keep a whole flock of prime cockerels in the back yard purely for experimental pur-poses."

"Cockerels?"

"That's right. And whenever he thought up some new stunt for catching a pheasant, he'd try it out on a cockerel first to see how it worked. That's how he discovered about raisins. It's also how he invented the horsehair method."

Claud paused and glanced over his shoulder as though to make sure that there was nobody listening. "Here's how it's done," he said. "First you take a few raisins and you soak them overnight in water to make them nice and plump and juicy. Then you get a bit of good stiff horsehair and you cut it up into half-inch lengths. Then you push one of these lengths of horsehair through the middle of each raisin so that there's about an eighth of an inch of it sticking out on either side. You follow?"

"Yes."

"Now—the old pheasant comes along and eats one of these raisins. Right? And you're watching him from behind a tree. So what then?"

"I imagine it sticks in his throat."

"That's obvious, Gordon. But here's the amazing thing. Here's what my dad discovered. The moment this happens, the bird *never moves his feet again!* He becomes absolutely rooted to the spot, and there he stands pumping his silly neck up and down just like it was a piston, and all you've got to do is walk calmly out from the place where you're hiding and pick him up in your hands."

"I don't believe that."

"I swear it," he said. "Once a pheasant's had the horsehair you can fire a rifle in his ear and he won't even jump. It's just one of those unexplainable little things. But it takes a genius to discover it."

He paused, and there was a gleam of pride in his eye now as he dwelt for a moment or two upon the memory of his father, the great inventor.

"So that's Method Number One," he said. "Method Number Two is even more simple still. All you do is you have a fishing-line. Then you bait the hook with a raisin and you fish for the pheasant just like you fish for a fish. You pay out the line about fifty yards and you lie there on your stomach in the bushes waiting till you get a bite. Then you haul him in."

"I don't think your father invented that one."

"It's very popular with fishermen," he said, choosing not to hear me. "Keen fishermen who can't get down to the seaside as often as they want. It gives them a bit of the old thrill. The only trouble is it's rather noisy. The pheasant squawks like hell as you haul him in, and then every keeper in the wood comes running."

"What is Method Number Three?" I asked.

"Ah," he said. "Number Three's a real beauty. It was the last one my dad ever invented before he passed away."

"His final great work?"

"Exactly, Gordon. And I can even remember the very day it happened, a Sunday morning it was, and suddenly my dad comes into the kitchen holding a huge white cockerel in his hands and he says, 'I think I've got it.' There's a little smile on his face and a shine of glory in his eyes and he comes in very soft and quiet and he puts the bird down right in the middle of the kitchen table and he says, 'By God, I think I've got a good one this time.' 'A good what?' Mum says, looking up from the sink. 'Horace, take that filthy bird off my table.' The cockerel has a funny little paper hat over its head, like an ice-cream cone upside down, and my dad is pointing to it proudly 'Stroke him,' he says. 'He won't move an inch.' The cockerel starts scratching away at the paper hat with one of its feet, but the hat seems to be stuck on with glue and it won't come off. 'No bird in the world is going to run away once you cover up his eyes,' my dad says, and he starts poking the cockerel with his finger and pushing it around on the table, but it doesn't take the slightest bit of notice. 'You can have this one,' he says, talking to Mum. 'You can kill it and dish it up for dinner as a celebration of what I have just invented.' And then straight away he takes me by the arm and marches me quickly out the door and off we go over the fields and up into the big forest the other side of Haddenham which used to belong to the Duke of Buckingham, and in less than two hours we get five lovely fat pheasants with no more trouble than it takes to go out and buy them in a shop."

Claud paused for breath. His eyes were huge and moist and dreamy as they gazed back into the wonderful world of his youth.

"I don't quite follow this," I said. "How did he get the paper hats over the pheasants' heads up in the woods?"

"You'd never guess it."

"I'm sure I wouldn't."

"Then here it is. First of all you dig a little hole in the ground. Then you twist a piece of paper into the shape of a cone and you fit this into the hole, hollow end upward, like a cup. Then you smear the paper cup all around the inside with bird-lime and drop in a few raisins. At the same time you lay a trail of raisins along the ground leading up to it. Now—the old pheasant comes pecking along the trail, and when he gets to the hole he pops his head inside to gobble the raisins and the next thing he knows he's got a paper hat stuck over his eyes and he can't see a thing. Isn't it marvellous what some people think of, Gordon? Don't you agree?"

"Your dad was a genius," I said.

"Then take your pick. Choose whichever one of the three methods you fancy and we'll use it tonight."

"You don't think they're all just a trifle on the crude side, do you?"

"Crude!" he cried, aghast. "Oh my God! And who's been having roasted pheasant in the house nearly every single day for the last six months and not a penny to pay?"

He turned and walked away toward the door of the workshop. I could see that he was deeply pained by my remark.

"Wait a minute," I said. "Don't go."

"You want to come or don't you?"

"Yes, but let me ask you something first. I've just had a bit of an idea."

"Keep it," he said. "You are talking about a subject, you don't know the first thing about."

"Do you remember that bottle of sleeping-pills the doc gave me last month when I had a bad back?"

"What about them?"

"Is there any reason why those wouldn't work on a pheasant?"

Claud closed his eyes and shook his head pityingly from side to side.

"Wait," I said.

"It's not worth discussing," he said. "No pheasant in the world is going to swallow those lousy red capsules. Don't you know any better than that?"

"You are forgetting the raisins," I said. "Now listen to this. We take a raisin. Then we soak it till it swells. Then we make a tiny slit in one side of it with a razor-blade. Then we hollow it out a little. Then we open up one of my red capsules and pour all the powder into the raisin. Then we get a needle and cotton and very carefully we sew up the slit. Now . . ."

Out of the corner of my eye, I saw Claud's mouth slowly beginning to open.

"Now," I said. "We have a nice clean-looking raisin with two and a half grains of Seconal inside it, and let me tell *you* something now. That's enough dope to knock the average *man* unconscious, never mind about *birds!*"

I paused for ten seconds to allow the full impact of this to strike home.

"What's more, with this method we could operate on a really grand scale. We could prepare *twenty* raisins if we felt like it, and all we'd have to do is scatter them around the feeding-grounds at sunset and then walk away. Half an hour later we'd come back, and the pills would be beginning to work, and the pheasants would be up in the trees by then, roosting, and they'd be starting to feel groggy, and they'd be wobbling and trying to keep their balance, and soon every pheasant that had eaten *one single raisin* would keel over unconscious and fall to the ground. My dear boy, they'd be dropping out of the trees like apples, and all we'd have to do is walk around picking them up!"

Claud was staring at me, rapt.

"Oh Christ," he said softly.

"And they'd never catch us either. We'd simply stroll through the woods dropping a few raisins here and there as we went, and even if they were *watching* us they wouldn't notice anything."

"Gordon," he said, laying a hand on my knee and gazing at me with eyes large and bright as two stars. "If this thing works, it will *revolutionize* poaching."

"I'm glad to hear it."

"How many pills have you got left?" he asked.

"Forty-nine. There were fifty in the bottle and I've only used one."

"Forty-nine's not enough. We want at least two hundred."

"Are you mad!" I cried.

He walked slowly away and stood by the door with his back to me, gazing at the sky.

"Two hundred's the bare minimum," he said quietly. "There's really not much point in doing it unless we have two hundred."

What is it now, I wondered. What the hell's he trying to do?

"This is the last chance we'll have before the season opens," he said.

"I couldn't possibly get any more."

"You wouldn't want us to come back empty-handed, would you?"

"But why so *many?*"

Claude turned his head and looked at me with large innocent eyes. "Why not?" he said gently. "Do you have any objection?"

My God, I thought suddenly. The crazy bastard is out to wreck Mr. Victor Hazel's opening-day shooting-party.

"You get us two hundred of those pills," he said, "and then it'll be worth doing."

"I can't."

"You could try, couldn't you?"

Mr. Hazel's party took place on the first of October every year and it was a very famous event. Debilitated gentlemen in tweed suits, some with titles and some who were merely rich, motored in from miles around with their gun-bearers and dogs and wives, and all day long the noise of shooting rolled across the valley. There were always enough pheasants to go around, for each summer the woods were methodically restocked with dozens and dozens of young birds at incredible expense. I had heard it said that the cost of rearing and keeping each pheasant up to the time when it was ready to be shot was well over five pounds (which is approximately the price of two hundred loaves of bread). But to Mr. Hazel it was worth every penny of it. He became, if only for a few hours, a big cheese in a little world and even the Lord Lieutenant of the County slapped him on the back and tried to remember his first name when he said goodbye.

"How would it be if we just reduced the dose?" Claud asked. "Why couldn't we divide the contents of one capsule among four raisins?"

"I suppose you could if you wanted to."

"But would a quarter of a capsule be strong enough for each bird?"

One simply had to admire the man's nerve. It was dangerous enough to poach a single pheasant up in those woods at this time of year and here he was planning to knock off the bloody lot.

"A quarter would be plenty," I said.

"You're sure of that?"

"Work it out for yourself. It's all done by body-weight. You'd still be giving about twenty times more than is necessary."

"Then we'll quarter the dose," he said, rubbing his hands. He paused and calculated for a moment. "We'll have one hundred and ninety-six raisins!"

"Do you realize what that involves?" I said. "They'll take hours to prepare."

"What of it! he cried. "We'll go tomorrow instead. We'll soak the raisins overnight and then we'll have all morning and afternoon to get them ready "

And that was precisely what we did.

Now, twenty-four hours later, we were on our way. We had been walking steadily for about forty minutes and we were nearing the point where the lane curved around to the right and ran along the crest of the hill toward the big wood where the pheasants lived. There was about a mile to go.

"I don't suppose by any chance these keepers might be carrying guns?" I asked.

"All keepers carry guns," Claud said.

I had been afraid of that.

"It's for the vermin mostly."

"Ah."

"Of course there's no guarantee they won't take a pot at a poacher now and again."

"You're joking."

"Not at all. But they only do it from behind. Only when you're running away. They like to pepper you in the legs at about fifty yards."

"They can't do that!" I cried. "It's a criminal offence!"

"So is poaching," Claud said.

We walked on awhile in silence. The sun was below the high hedge on our right now and the lane was in shadow.

"You can consider yourself lucky this isn't thirty years ago," he went on. "They used to shoot you on sight in those days."

"Do you believe that?"

"I know it," he said. "Many's the night when I was a nipper I've gone into the kitchen and seen my old dad lying face downward on the table and Mum standing over him digging the grapeshot out of his buttocks with a potato knife."

"Stop," I said. "It makes me nervous."

"You believe me, don't you?"

"Yes, I believe you."

"Toward the end he was so covered in tiny little white scars he looked exactly like it was snowing."

"Yes," I said. "All right."

"Poacher's arse, they used to call it," Claud said. "And there wasn't a man in the whole village who didn't have a bit of it one way or another. But my dad was the champion."

"Good luck to him," I said.

"I wish to hell he was here now," Claud said, wistful. "He'd have given anything in the world to be coming with us on this job tonight."

"He could take my place," I said. "Gladly."

We had reached the crest of the hill and now we could see the wood ahead of us, huge and dark with the sun going down behind the trees and little sparks of gold shining through.

"You'd better let me have those raisins," Claud said.

I gave him the bag and he slid it gently into his trouser pocket.

"No talking once we're inside," he said. "Just follow me and try not to go snapping any branches."

Five minutes later we were there. The lane ran right up to the wood itself and then skirted the edge of it for about three hundred yards with only a little hedge between. Claud slipped through the hedge on all fours and I followed.

It was cool and dark inside the wood. No sunlight came in at all.

"This is spooky," I said.

"Ssshh!"

Claud was very tense. He was walking just ahead of me, picking his feet up high and putting them down gently on the moist ground. He kept his head moving all the time, the eyes sweeping slowly from side to side, searching for danger. I tried doing the same, but soon I began to see a keeper behind every tree, so I gave it up.

Then a large patch of sky appeared ahead of us in the roof of the forest and I knew that this must be the clearing. Claud had told me that the clearing was the place where the young birds were introduced into the woods in early July, where they were fed and watered and guarded by the keepers, and where many of them stayed from force of habit until the shooting began.

"There's always plenty of pheasants in the clearing," he had said.

"Keepers too, I suppose."

"Yes, but there's thick bushes all around and that helps."

We were now advancing in a series of quick crouching spurts, running from tree to tree and stopping and waiting and listening and running on again, and then at last we were kneeling safely behind a big clump of alder right on the edge of the clearing and Claud was grinning and nudging me in the ribs and pointing through the branches at the pheasants.

The place was absolutely stiff with birds. There must have been two hundred of them at least strutting around among the tree-stumps.

"You see what I mean?" Claud whispered.

It was an astonishing sight, a sort of poacher's dream come true. And how close they were! Some of them were not more than ten paces from where we knelt. The hens were plump and creamy-brown and they were so fat their breast-feathers almost brushed the ground as they walked. The cocks were slim and beautiful, with long tails and brilliant red patches around the eyes, like scarlet spectacles. I glanced at Claud. His big ox-like face was transfixed in ecstasy. The mouth was slightly open and the eyes had a kind of glazy look about them as they stared at the pheasants

I believe that all poachers react in roughly the same way as this on sighting game. They are like women who sight large emeralds in a jeweller's window, the only difference being that the women are less dignified in the methods they employ later on to acquire the loot. Poacher's arse is nothing to the punishment that a female is willing to endure.

"Ah-ha," Claud said softly. "You see the keeper?"

"Where?"

"Over the other side, by that big tree. Look carefully."

"My God!"

"It's all right. He can't see *us.*"

We crouched close to the ground, watching the keeper. He was a smallish man with a cap on his head and a gun under his arm. He never moved. He was like a little post standing there.

"Let's go," I whispered.

The keeper's face was shadowed by the peak of his cap, but it seemed to me that he was looking directly at us.

"I'm not staying here," I said.

"Hush," Claud said.

Slowly, never taking his eyes from the keeper, he reached into his pocket and brought out a single raisin. He placed it in the palm of his right hand, and then quickly, with a little flick of the wrist, he threw the raisin high into the air. I watched it as it went sailing over the bushes and I saw it land within a yard or so of two henbirds standing together beside an old tree-stump. Both birds turned their heads sharply at the drop of the raisin. Then one of them hopped over and made a quick peck at the ground and that must have been it.

I glanced up at the keeper. He hadn't moved.

Claud threw a second raisin into the clearing; then a third, and a fourth, and a fifth.

At this point, I saw the keeper turn away his head in order to survey the wood behind him.

Quick as a flash, Claud pulled the paper bag out of his pocket and tipped a huge pile of raisins into the cup of his right hand.

"Stop," I said.

But with a great sweep of the arm he flung the whole handful high over the bushes into the clearing.

They fell with a soft little patter, like raindrops on dry leaves, and every single pheasant in the place must either have seen them coming or heard them fall. There was a flurry of wings and a rush to find the treasure.

The keeper's head flicked round as though there were a spring inside his neck. The birds were all pecking away madly at the raisins. The keeper took two quick paces forward and for a moment I thought he was going in to investigate. But then he stopped, and his face came up and his eyes began travelling slowly around the perimeter of the clearing.

"Follow me," Claud whispered. "And *keep down.*" He started crawling away swiftly on all fours, like some kind of a monkey.

I went after him. He had his nose close to the ground and his huge tight buttocks were winking at the sky and it was easy to see now how poacher's arse had come to be an occupational disease among the fraternity.

We went along like this for about a hundred yards.

"Now run," Claud said.

We got to our feet and ran, and a few minutes later we emerged through the hedge into the lovely open safety of the lane.

"It went marvellous," Claud said, breathing heavily. "Didn't it go absolutely marvellous?" The big face was scarlet and glowing with triumph.

"It was a mess," I said.

"What!" he cried.

"Of course it was. We can't possibly go back now. That keeper knows there was someone there."

"He knows nothing," Claud said. "In another five minutes it'll be pitch dark inside the wood and he'll be sloping off home to his supper."

"I think I'll join him."

"You're a great poacher," Claud said. He sat down on the grassy bank under the hedge and lit a cigarette.

The sun had set now and the sky was a pale smoke blue, faintly glazed with yellow. In the wood behind us the shadows and the spaces in between the trees were turning from grey to black.

"How long does a sleeping-pill take to work?" Claud asked.

"Look out," I said. "There's someone coming."

The man had appeared suddenly and silently out of the dusk and he was only thirty yards away when I saw him.

"Another bloody keeper," Claud said.

We both looked at the keeper as he came down the lane toward us. He had a shotgun under his arm and there was a black Labrador walking at his heels. He stopped when he was a few paces away and the dog stopped with him and stayed behind him, watching us through the keeper's legs.

"Good evening," Claud said, nice and friendly.

This one was a tall bony man about forty with a swift eye and a hard cheek and hard dangerous hands.

"I know you," he said softly, coming closer. "I know the both of you."

Claud didn't answer this.

"You're from the fillin'-station. Right?"

His lips were thin and dry, with some sort of a brownish crust over them.

"You're Cubbage and Hawes and you're from the fillin'-station on the main road. Right?"

"What are we playing?" Claud said. "Twenty Questions?"

The keeper spat out a big gob of spit and I saw it go floating through the air and land with a plop on a patch of dry dust six inches from Claud's feet. It looked like a little baby oyster lying there.

"Beat it," the man said. "Go on. Get out."

Claud sat on the bank smoking his cigarette and looking at the gob of spit.

"Go on," the man said. "Get out."

When he spoke, the upper lip lifted above the gum and I could see a row of small discoloured teeth, one of them black, the others quince and ochre.

"This happens to be a public highway," Claud said. "Kindly do not molest us."

The keeper shifted the gun from his left arm to his right.

"You're loiterin'," he said, "with intent to commit a felony. I could run you in for that."

"No you couldn't," Claud said.

All this made me rather nervous.

"I've had my eye on you for some time," the keeper said, looking at Claud.

"It's getting late," I said. "Shall we stroll on?"

Claud flipped away his cigarette and got slowly to his feet. "All right," he said. "Let's go."

We wandered off down the lane the way we had come, leaving the keeper standing there, and soon the man was out of sight in the half-darkness behind us.

"That's the head keeper," Claud said. "His name is Rabbetts."

"Let's get the hell out," I said.

"Come in here," Claud said.

There was a gate on our left leading into a field and we climbed over it and sat down behind the hedge

"Mr. Rabbetts is also due for his supper," Claud said. "You mustn't worry about him."

We sat quietly behind the hedge waiting for the keeper to walk past us on his way home. A few stars were showing and a bright three-quarter moon was coming up over the hills behind us in the east.

"Here he is," Claud whispered. "Don't move."

The keeper came loping softly up the lane with the dog padding quick and soft-footed at his heels, and we watched them through the hedge as they went by.

"He won't be coming back tonight," Claud said.

"How do you know that?"

"A keeper never waits for you in the wood if he knows where you live. He goes to your house and hides outside and watches for you to come back."

"That's worse."

"No, it isn't, not if you dump the loot somewhere else before you go home. He can't touch you then."

"What about the other one, the one in the clearing?"

"He's gone too."

"You can't be sure of that."

"I've been studying these bastards for months, Gordon, honest I have. I know all their habits. There's no danger."

Reluctantly I followed him back into the wood. It was pitch dark in there now and very silent, and as we moved cautiously forward the noise of our footsteps seemed to go echoing around the walls of the forest as though we were walking in a cathedral.

"Here's where we threw the raisins," Claud said.

I peered through the bushes.

The clearing lay dim and milky in the moonlight

"You're quite sure the keeper's gone?"

"I *know* he's gone "

I could just see Claud's face under the peak of his cap, the pale lips, the soft pale cheeks, and the large eyes with a little spark of excitement dancing slowly in each

"Are they roosting?"

"Yes."

"Whereabouts?"

"All around. They don't go far."

"What do we do next?"

"We stay here and wait. I brought you a light," he added, and he handed me one of those small pocket flashlights shaped like a fountain-pen. "You may need it."

I was beginning to feel better. "Shall we see if we can spot some of them sitting in the trees?" I said.

"No."

"I should like to see how they look when they're roosting."

"This isn't a nature-study," Claud said. "Please be quiet."

We stood there for a long time waiting for something to happen.

"I've just had a nasty thought," I said. "If a bird can keep its balance on a branch when it's asleep, then surely there isn't any reason why the pills should make it fall down."

Claud looked at me quick.

"After all," I said, "it's not dead. It's still only sleeping."

"It's doped," Claud said.

"But that's just a *deeper* sort of sleep. Why should we expect it to fall down just because it's in a *deeper* sleep?"

There was a gloomy silence.

"We should've tried it with chickens," Claud said. "My dad would've done that."

"Your dad was a genius," I said.

At that moment there came a soft thump from the wood behind us.

"Hey!"

"Ssshh!"

We stood listening.

Thump.

"There's another!"

It was a deep muffled sound as though a bag of sand had been dropped from about shoulder height.

Thump!

"They're pheasants!" I cried

"Wait!"

"I'm sure they're pheasants!"

Thump! Thump!

"You're right!"

We ran back into the wood.

"Where were they?"

"Over here! Two of them were over here!"

"I thought they were this way."

"Keep looking!" Claud shouted "They can't be far "

We searched for about a minute

"Here's one!" he called.

When I got to him he was holding a magnificent cockbird in both hands. We examined it closely with out flashlights.

"It's doped to the gills," Claud said. "It's still alive, I can feel its heart, but it's doped to the bloody gills."

Thump!

"There's another!"

Thump! Thump!

"Two more!"

Thump!

Thump! Thump! Thump!

"Jesus Christ!"

Thump! Thump! Thump! Thump!

Thump! Thump!

All around us the pheasants were starting to rain down out of the trees. We began rushing around madly in the dark, sweeping the ground with our flashlights.

Thump! Thump! Thump! This lot fell almost on top of me. I was right under the tree as they came down and I found all three of them immediately—two cocks and a hen. They were limp and warm, the feathers wonderfully soft in the hand.

"Where shall I put them?" I called out. I was holding them by the legs.

"Lay them here, Gordon! Just pile them up here where it's light!"

Claud was standing on the edge of the clearing with the moonlight streaming down all over him and a great bunch of pheasants in each hand. His face was bright, his eyes big and bright and wonderful, and he was staring around him like a child who has just discovered that the whole world is made of chocolate.

Thump.

Thump! Thump!

"I don't like it," I said. "It's too many."

"It's beautiful!" he cried and he dumped the birds he was carrying and ran off to look for more.

Thump! Thump! Thump! Thump!

Thump!

It was easy to find them now. There were one or two lying under every tree. I quickly collected six more, three in each hand, and ran back and dumped them with the others. Then six more. Then six more after that.

And still they kept falling.

Claud was in a whirl of ecstasy now, dashing about like a mad ghost under the trees. I could see the beam of his flashlight waving around in the dark and each time he found a bird he gave a little yelp of triumph.

Thump! Thump! Thump!

"That bugger Hazel ought to hear this!" he called out.

"Don't shout," I said. "It frightens me."

"What's that?"

"Don't *shout*. There might be keepers."

"Screw the keepers!" he cried. "They're all eating!"

For three or four minutes, the pheasants kept on falling. Then suddenly they stopped.

"Keep searching!" Claud shouted. "There's plenty more on the ground!"

"Don't you think we ought to get out while the going's good?"

"No," he said.

We went on searching. Between us we looked under every tree within a hundred yards of the clearing, north, south, east, and west, and I think we found most of them in the end. At the collecting-point there was a pile of pheasants as big as a bonfire.

"It's a miracle," Claud was saying. "It's a bloody miracle." He was staring at them in a kind of trance.

"We'd better just take half a dozen each and get out quick," I said.

"I would like to count them, Gordon."

"There's no time for that."

"I must count them."

"No," I said. "Come on."

"One . . .

"Two . . .

"Three . . .

"Four . . ."

He began counting them very carefully, picking up each bird in turn and laying it carefully to one side. The moon was directly overhead now and the whole clearing was brilliantly illuminated.

"I'm not standing around here like this," I said. I walked back a few paces and hid myself in the shadows, waiting for him to finish.

"A hundred and seventeen . . . a hundred and eighteen . . . a hundred and nineteen . . . *a hundred and twenty!*" he cried. *"One hundred and twenty birds!* It's an all-time record!"

I didn't doubt it for a moment.

"The most my dad ever got in one night was fifteen and he was drunk for a week afterwards!"

"You're the champion of the world," I said. "Are you ready now?"

"One minute," he answered and he pulled up his sweater and proceeded to unwind the two big white cotton sacks from around his belly. "Here's yours," he said, handing one of them to me "Fill it up quick."

The light of the moon was so strong I could read the small print along the base of the sack. J. W. CRUMP, it said. KESTON FLOUR MILLS, LONDON S.W. 17.

"You don't think that bastard with the brown teeth is watching us this very moment from behind a tree?"

"There's no chance of that," Claud said. "He's down at the filling-station like I told you, waiting for us to come home."

We started loading the pheasants into the sacks. They were soft and floppy-necked and the skin underneath the feathers was still warm.

"There'll be a taxi waiting for us in the lane," Claud said.

"What?"

"I always go back in a taxi, Gordon, didn't you know that?"

I told him I didn't.

"A taxi is anonymous," Claud said. "Nobody knows who's inside a taxi except the driver. My dad taught me that."

"Which driver?"

"Charlie Kinch. He's only too glad to oblige."

We finished loading the pheasants and then we humped the sacks onto our shoulders and started staggering through the pitch-black wood toward the lane.

"I'm not walking all the way back to the village with this," I said. My sack had sixty birds inside it and it must have weighed a hundred-weight and a half at least.

"Charlie's never let me down yet," Claud said.

We came to the margin of the wood and peered through the hedge into the lane. Claud said, "Charlie boy" very softly and the old man behind the wheel of the taxi not five yards away poked his head out into the moonlight and gave us a sly toothless grin. We slid through the hedge, dragging the sacks after us along the ground.

"Hullo!" Charlie said. "What's this?"

"It's cabbages," Claud told him. "Open the door "

Two minutes later we were safely inside the taxi, cruising slowly down the hill toward the village

It was all over now bar the shouting. Claud was triumphant, bursting with pride and excitement, and he kept leaning forward and tapping Charlie Kinch on the shoulder and saying, 'How about it, Charlie? How about this for a haul?' and Charlie kept glancing back popeyed at the huge bulging sacks lying on the floor between us and saying, "Jesus Christ, man, how did you do it?"

"There's six brace of them for you, Charlie," Claud said And Charlie said, "I reckon pheasants is going to be a bit scarce up at Mr Victor Hazel's opening-day shoot this year," and Claud said, "I imagine they are, Charlie, I imagine they are."

"What in God's name are you going to do with a hundred and twenty pheasants?" I asked

"Put them in cold storage for the winter," Claud said. 'Put them in with the dogmeat in the deep-freeze at the filling-station '

"Not tonight, I trust?"

"No, Gordon, not tonight We leave them at Bessie s house tonight."

"Bessie who?"

"Bessie Organ."

"Bessie *Organ!*"

"Bessie always delivers my game, didn't you know that?'

"I don't know anything," I said. I was completely stunned. Mrs Organ was the wife of the Reverend Jack Organ, the local vicar

"Always choose a respectable woman to deliver your game ' Claud announced. "That's correct, Charlie, isn't it?'

"Bessie's a right smart girl,' Charlie said.

We were driving through the village now and the streetlamps were still on and the men were wandering home from the pubs. I saw Will Prattley letting himself in quietly by the side door of his fishmonger's shop and Mrs. Prattley's head was sticking out the window just above him, but he didn't know it.

"The vicar is very partial to roasted pheasant," Claud said

"He hangs it eighteen days, Charlie said, "then he gives it a couple of good shakes and all the feathers drop off."

The taxi turned left and swung in through the gates of the vicarage. There were no lights on in the house and nobody met us. Claud and I dumped the pheasants in the coalshed at the rear, and then we said goodbye to Charlie Kinch and walked back in the moonlight to the filling-station, empty-handed. Whether or not Mr

Rabbetts was watching us as we went in, I do not know. We saw no sign of him.

"Here she comes," Claud said to me the next morning.

"Who?"

"Bessie—Bessie Organ." He spoke the name proudly and with a slight proprietary air, as though he were a general referring to his bravest officer.

I followed him outside.

"Down there," he said, pointing.

Far away down the road I could see a small female figure advancing toward us.

"What's she pushing?" I asked.

Claud gave me a sly look.

"There's only one safe way of delivering game," he announced, "and that's under a baby."

"Yes," I murmured, "yes, of course."

"That'll be young Christopher Organ in there, aged one and a half. He's a lovely child, Gordon."

I could just make out the small dot of a baby sitting high up in the pram, which had its hood folded down.

"There's sixty or seventy pheasants at least under that little nipper," Claud said happily. "You just imagine that."

"You can't put sixty or seventy pheasants in a pram."

"You can if it's got a good deep well underneath it, and if you take out the mattress and pack them in tight, right up to the top. All you need then is a sheet. You'll be surprised how little room a pheasant takes up when it's limp."

We stood beside the pumps waiting for Bessie Organ to arrive. It was one of those warm windless September mornings with a darkening sky and a smell of thunder in the air.

"Right through the village bold as brass," Claud said. "Good old Bessie."

"She seems in rather a hurry to me."

Claud lit a new cigarette from the stub of the old one. "Bessie is never in a hurry," he said.

"She certainly isn't walking normal," I told him. "You look."

He squinted at her through the smoke of his cigarette. Then he took the cigarette out of his mouth and looked again.

"Well?" I said.

"She does seem to be going a tiny bit quick, doesn't she?" he said carefully.

"She s going damn quick

There was a pause. Claud was beginning to stare very hard at the approaching woman

"Perhaps she doesn't want to be caught in the rain, Gordon. I'll bet that s exactly what it is, she thinks it's going to rain and she don't want the baby to get wet '

"Why doesn't she put the hood up?

He didn't answer this.

"She's *running!*" I cried. "Look!" Bessie had suddenly broken into a full sprint

Claud stood very still, watching the woman; and in the silence that followed I fancied I could hear a baby screaming.

"What's up?"

He didn't answer

"There's something wrong with that baby, I said "Listen."

At this point, Bessie was about two hundred yards away from is but closing fast.

"Can you hear him now?' I said

'Yes.'

' He's yelling his head off '

The small shrill voice in the distance was growing louder every second, frantic, piercing, nonstop, almost hysterical

"He's having a fit," Claud announced.

"I think he must be."

"That's why she's running, Gordon She wants to get him in here quick and put him under a cold tap."

"I'm sure you're right," I said "In fact I know you're right. Just listen to that noise."

"If it isn't a fit, you can bet your life it s something like it."

'I quite agree."

Claud shifted his feet uneasily on the gravel of the driveway. There's a thousand and one different things keep happening every day to little babies like that," he said.

"Of course."

"I knew a baby once who caught his fingers in the spokes of the pram wheel. He lost the lot. It cut them clean off '

"Yes.'

"Whatever it is," Claud said, "I wish to Christ she'd stop running '

A long truck loaded with bricks came up behind Bessie and the driver slowed down and poked his head out the window to stare.

Bessie ignored him and flew on, and she was so close now I could see her big red face with the mouth wide open, panting for breath. I noticed she was wearing white gloves on her hands, very prim and dainty, and there was a funny little white hat to match perched right on the top of her head, like a mushroom.

Suddenly, out of the pram, straight up into the air, flew an enormous pheasant[1]

Claud let out a cry of horror

The fool in the truck going along beside Bessie started roaring with laughter.

The pheasant flapped around drunkenly for a few seconds, then it lost height and landed in the grass by the side of the road.

A grocer's van came up behind the truck and began hooting to get by. Bessie kept on running.

Then—*whoosh!*—a second pheasant flew up out of the pram.

Then a third, and a fourth. Then a fifth.

"My God!" I said. "It's the pills! They're wearing off!"

Claud didn't say anything.

Bessie covered the last fifty yards at a tremendous pace, and she came swinging into the driveway of the filling-station with birds flying up out of the pram in all directions.

"What the hell's going on?" she cried.

"Go round the back!" I shouted. "Go round the back!" But she pulled up sharp against the first pump in the line and before we could reach her she had seized the screaming infant in her arms and dragged him clear.

"No! No!" Claud cried, racing toward her. "Don't lift the baby[1] Put him back! Hold down the sheet!" But she wasn't even listening, and with the weight of the child suddenly lifted away, a great cloud of pheasants rose up out of the pram, fifty or sixty of them, at least, and the whole sky above us was filled with huge brown birds clapping their wings furiously to gain height.

Claud and I started running up and down the driveway waving our arms to frighten them off the premises. "Go away!" we shouted. "Shoo! Go away!" But they were too dopey still to take any notice of us and within half a minute down they came again and settled themselves like a swarm of locusts all over the front of my filling-station. The place was covered with them. They sat wing to wing along the edges of the roof and on the concrete canopy that came out over the pumps, and a dozen at least were clinging to the sill of the office window Some had flown down onto the rack that held the bottles of lubricating-oil, and others were sliding about on the bonnets of my second-hand cars. One cockbird with a fine tail was perched superbly on top of a petrol pump, and quite a number, those that were too drunk to stay aloft, simply squatted in the driveway at our feet, fluffing their feathers and blinking their small eyes.

Across the road, a line of cars had already started forming behind the brick-lorry and the grocery-van, and people were opening their doors and getting out and beginning to cross over to have a closer look. I glanced at my watch. It was twenty to nine. Any moment now, I thought, a large black car is going to come streaking along the road from the direction of the village, and the car will be a Rolls, and the face behind the wheel will be the great glistening butcher's face of Mr. Victor Hazel, maker of sausages and pies.

"They near pecked him to pieces!" Bessie was shouting, clasping the screaming baby to her bosom.

"You go on home, Bessie," Claud said, white in the face.

"Lock up," I said. "Put out the sign. We've gone for the day."

The Great Switcheroo

1964

THERE were about forty people at Jerry and Samantha's cock-tail-party that evening. It was the usual crowd, the usual discomfort, the usual appalling noise. People had to stand very close to one another and shout to make themselves heard. Many were grinning, showing capped white teeth. Most of them had a cigarette in the left hand, a drink in the right.

I moved away from my wife, Mary, and her group. I headed for the small bar in the far corner, and when I got there, I sat down on a bar-stool and faced the room. I did this so that I could look at the women. I settled back with my shoulders against the bar-rail, sipping my Scotch and examining the women one by one over the rim of my glass.

I was studying not their figures but their faces, and what inter-ested me there was not so much the face itself but the big red mouth in the middle of it all. And even then, it wasn't the whole mouth but only the lower lip. The lower lip, I had recently decided, was the great revealer. It gave away more than the eyes. The eyes hid their secrets. The lower lip hid very little. Take, for example, the lower lip of Jacinth Winkleman, who was standing nearest to me. Notice the wrinkles on that lip, how some were parallel and some radiated outward. No two people have the same pattern of lip-wrinkles, and come to think of it, you could catch a criminal that way if you had his lip-print on file and he had taken a drink at the scene of the crime. The lower lip is what you suck and nibble when you're ruffled, and Martha Sullivan was doing that right now as she watched from a distance her fatuous husband slobbering over Judy Martinson. You lick it when lecherous. I could see Ginny Lomax licking hers with the tip of her tongue as she stood beside Ted Dorling and gazed up into his face. It was a deliberate lick, the tongue coming out slowly and making a slow wet wipe along the entire length of the lower lip.

I saw Ted Dorling looking at Ginny's tongue, which was what she wanted him to do.

It really does seem to be a fact, I told myself, as my eyes wandered from lower lip to lower lip across the room, that all the less attractive traits of the human animal, arrogance, rapacity, gluttony, lasciviousness, and the rest of them, are clearly signalled in that little carapace of scarlet skin. But you have to know the code. The protuberant or bulging lower lip is supposed to signify sensuality. But this is only half true in men and wholly untrue in women. In women, it is the thin line you should look for, the narrow blade with the sharply delineated bottom edge. And in the nymphomaniac there is a tiny just visible crest of skin at the top centre of the lower lip.

Samantha, my hostess, had that.

Where was she now, Samantha?

Ah, there she was, taking an empty glass out of a guest's hand. Now she was heading my way to refill it.

"Hello, Vic," she said. "You all alone?"

She's a nympho-bird all right, I told myself. But a very rare example of the species, because she is entirely and utterly monogamous. She is a married monogamous nympho-bird who stays forever in her own nest.

She is also the fruitiest female I have ever set eyes upon in my whole life.

"Let me help you," I said, standing up and taking the glass from her hand. "What's wanted in here?"

"Vodka on the rocks," she said. "Thanks, Vic." She laid a lovely long white arm upon the top of the bar and she leaned forward so that her bosom rested on the bar-rail, squashing upward. "Oops," I said, pouring vodka outside the glass.

Samantha looked at me with huge brown eyes, but said nothing.

"I'll wipe it up," I said.

She took the refilled glass from me and walked away. I watched her go. She was wearing black pants. They were so tight around the buttocks that the smallest mole or pimple would have shown through the cloth. But Samantha Rainbow had not a blemish on her bottom. I caught myself licking my own lower lip. That's right, I thought. I want her. I lust after that woman. But it's too risky to try. It would be suicide to make a pass at a girl like that. First of all, she lives next door, which is too close. Secondly, as I have already said, she is monogamous. Thirdly, she is thick as a thief with Mary, my own wife. They exchange dark female secrets. Fourthly, her husband,

Jerry, is my very old and good friend, and not even I, Victor Hammond, though I am churning with lust, would dream of trying to seduce the wife of a man who is my very old and trusty friend.

Unless . . .

It was at this point, as I sat on the bar-stool letching over Samantha Rainbow, that an interesting idea began to filter quietly into the centre of my brain. I remained still, allowing the idea to expand. I watched Samantha across the room, and began fitting her into the framework of the idea. Oh, Samantha, my gorgeous and juicy little jewel, I shall have you yet.

But could anybody seriously hope to get away with a crazy lark like that?

No, not in a million nights.

One couldn't even *try* it unless Jerry agreed. So why think about it?

Samantha was standing about six yards away, talking to Gilbert Mackesy. The fingers of her right hand were curled around a tall glass. The fingers were long and almost certainly dexterous.

Assuming, just for the fun of it, that Jerry did agree, then even so, there would still be gigantic snags along the way. There was, for example, the little matter of physical characteristics. I had seen Jerry many times at the club having a shower after tennis, but right now I couldn't for the life of me recall the necessary details. It wasn't the sort of thing one noticed very much. Usually, one didn't even look.

Anyway, it would be madness to put the suggestion to Jerry point-blank. I didn't know him *that* well. He might be horrified. He might even turn nasty. There could be an ugly scene. I must test him out, therefore, in some subtle fashion.

"You know something?" I said to Jerry about an hour later when we were sitting together on the sofa having a last drink. The guests were drifting away and Samantha was by the door saying goodbye to them. My own wife, Mary, was out on the terrace talking to Bob Swain. I could see her through the open french windows. "You know something funny?" I said to Jerry as we sat together on the sofa.

"What's funny?" Jerry asked me.

"A fellow I had lunch with today told me a fantastic story. Quite unbelievable."

"What story?" Jerry said. The whisky had begun to make him sleepy.

"This man, the one I had lunch with, had a terrific letch after the wife of his friend who lived nearby. And his friend had an equally big letch after the wife of the man I had lunch with. Do you see what I mean?"

"You mean two fellers who lived close to each other both fancied each other's wives."

"Precisely," I said.

"Then there was no problem," Jerry said.

"There was a very big problem," I said. "The wives were both very faithful and honourable women."

"Samantha's the same," Jerry said. "She wouldn't look at another man."

"Nor would Mary," I said. "She's a fine girl."

Jerry emptied his glass and set it down carefully on the sofa-table. "So what happened in your story?" he said. "It sounds dirty."

"What happened," I said, "was that these two randy sods cooked up a plan which made it possible for each of them to ravish the other's wife without the wives ever knowing it. If you can believe such a thing."

"With chloroform?" Jerry said.

"Not at all. They were fully conscious."

"Impossible," Jerry said. "Someone's been pulling your leg."

"I don't think so," I said. "From the way this man told it to me, with all the little details and everything, I don't think he was making it up. In fact, I'm sure he wasn't. And listen, they didn't do it just once, either. They've been doing it every two or three weeks for months!"

"And the wives don't know?"

"They haven't a clue."

"I've got to hear this," Jerry said. "Let's get another drink first."

We crossed to the bar and refilled our glasses, then returned to the sofa.

"You must remember," I said, "that there had to be a tremendous lot of preparation and rehearsal beforehand. And many intimate details had to be exchanged to give the plan a chance of working. But the essential part of the scheme was simple:

"They fixed a night, call it Saturday. On that night the husbands and wives were to go up to bed as usual, at say eleven or eleven thirty.

"From then on, normal routine would be preserved. A little reading, perhaps, a little talking, then out with the lights.

"After lights out, the husbands would at once roll over and

pretend to go to sleep. This was to discourage their wives from getting fresh, which at this stage must on no account be permitted. So the wives went to sleep. But the husbands stayed awake. So far so good.

"Then at precisely one A.M., by which time the wives would be in a good deep sleep, each husband would slide quietly out of bed, put on a pair of bedroom slippers and creep downstairs in his pyjamas. He would open the front door and go out into the night, taking care not to close the door behind him.

"They lived," I went on, "more or less across the street from one another. It was a quiet suburban neighbourhood and there was seldom anyone about at that hour. So these two furtive pyjama-clad figures would pass each other as they crossed the street, each one heading for another house, another bed, another woman."

Jerry was listening to me carefully. His eyes were a little glazed from drink, but he was listening to every word.

"The next part," I said, "had been prepared very thoroughly by both men. Each knew the inside of his friend's house almost as well as he knew his own. He knew how to find his way in the dark both downstairs and up without knocking over the furniture. He knew his way to the stairs and exactly how many steps there were to the top and which of them creaked and which didn't. He knew on which side of the bed the woman upstairs was sleeping.

"Each took off his slippers and left them in the hall, then up the stairs he crept in his bare feet and pyjamas. This part of it, according to my friend, was rather exciting. He was in a dark silent house that wasn't his own, and on his way to the main bedroom he had to pass no less than three children's bedrooms where the doors were always left slightly open."

"Children!" Jerry cried. "My God, what if one of them had woken up and said, 'Daddy, is that you?' "

"That was all taken care of," I said. "Emergency procedure would then come into effect immediately. Also if the wife, just as he was creeping into her room, woke up and said, 'Darling, what's wrong? Why are you wandering about?'; then again, emergency procedure."

"What emergency procedure?" Jerry said.

"Simple," I answered. "The man would immediately dash downstairs and out the front door and across to his own house and ring the bell. This was a signal for the other character, no matter what he was doing at the time, also to rush downstairs at full speed and open the door and let the other fellow in while he went out. This would get them both back quickly to their proper houses."

"With egg all over their faces," Jerry said.

"Not at all," I said.

"That doorbell would have woken the whole house," Jerry said.

"Of course," I said. "And the husband, returning upstairs in his pyjamas, would merely say, 'I went to see who the hell was ringing the bell at this ungodly hour. Couldn't find anyone. It must have been a drunk.'"

"What about the other guy?" Jerry asked. "How does he explain why he rushed downstairs when his wife or child spoke to him?"

"He would say, 'I heard someone prowling about outside, so I rushed down to get him, but he escaped.' 'Did you actually see him?' his wife would ask anxiously. 'Of course I saw him,' the husband would answer. 'He ran off down the street. He was too damn fast for me.' Whereupon the husband would be warmly congratulated for his bravery."

"Okay," Jerry said. "That's the easy part. Everything so far is just a matter of good planning and good timing. But what happens when these two horny characters actually climb into bed with each other's wives?"

"They go right to it," I said.

"The wives are sleeping," Jerry said.

"I know," I said. "So they proceed immediately with some very gentle but very skilful love-play, and by the time these dames are fully awake, they're as randy as rattlesnakes."

"No talking, I presume," Jerry said.

"Not a word."

"Okay, so the wives are awake," Jerry said. "And their hands get to work. So just for a start, what about the simple question of body size? What about the difference between the new man and the husband? What about tallness and shortness and fatness and thinness? You're not telling me these men were physically identical?"

"Not identical, obviously," I said. "But they were more or less similar in build and height. That was essential. They were both clean-shaven and had roughly the same amount of hair on their heads. That sort of similarity is commonplace. Look at you and me, for instance. We're roughly the same height and build, aren't we?"

"Are we?" Jerry said.

"How tall are you?" I said.

"Six foot exactly."

"I'm five eleven," I said. "One inch difference. What do you weigh?"

"One hundred and eighty-seven."

"I'm a hundred and eighty-four," I said. "What's three pounds among friends?"

There was a pause, Jerry was looking out through the french windows onto the terrace where my wife, Mary, was standing. Mary was still talking to Bob Swain and the evening sun was shining in her hair. She was a dark pretty girl with a bosom. I watched Jerry. I saw his tongue come out and go sliding along the surface of his lower lip.

"I guess you're right," Jerry said, still looking at Mary. "I guess we are about the same size, you and me." When he turned back and faced me again, there was a little red rose high up on each cheek. "Go on about these two men," he said. "What about some of the other differences?"

"You mean faces?" I said. "No one's going to see faces in the dark."

"I'm not talking about faces," Jerry said.

"What are you talking about, then?"

"I'm talking about their cocks," Jerry said. "That's what it's all about, isn't it? And you're not going to tell me . . ."

"Oh yes, I am," I said. "Just so long as both men were either circumcised or uncircumcised, then there was really no problem."

"Are you seriously suggesting that all men have the same size in cocks?" Jerry said. "Because they don't."

"I know they don't," I said.

"Some are enormous," Jerry said. "And some are titchy."

"There are always exceptions," I told him. "But you'd be surprised at the number of men whose measurements are virtually the same, give or take a centimetre. According to my friend, ninety percent are normal. Only ten percent are notably large or small."

"I don't believe that," Jerry said.

"Check on it sometime," I said. "Ask some well-travelled girl."

Jerry took a long slow sip of his whisky, and his eyes over the top of his glass were looking again at Mary on the terrace. "What about the rest of it?" he said.

"No problem," I said.

"No problem, my arse," he said. "Shall I tell you why this is a phony story?"

"Go ahead."

"Everybody knows that a wife and husband who have been married for some years develop a kind of routine. It's inevitable. My God, a new operator would be spotted instantly. You know damn well he would. You can't suddenly wade in with a totally different style and expect the woman not to notice it, and I don't care how randy she was. She'd smell a rat in the first minute!"

"A routine can be duplicated," I said. "Just so long as every detail of that routine is described beforehand."

"A bit personal, that," Jerry said.

"The whole thing's personal," I said. "So each man tells his story. He tells precisely what he usually does. He tells everything. The lot. The works. The whole routine from beginning to end."

"Jesus," Jerry said.

"Each of these men," I said, "had to learn a new part. He had, in effect, to become an actor. He was impersonating another character."

"Not so easy, that," Jerry said.

"No problem at all, according to my friend. The only thing one had to watch out for was not to get carried away and start improvising. One had to follow the stage directions very carefully and stick to them."

Jerry took another pull at his drink. He also took another look at Mary on the terrace. Then he leaned back against the sofa, glass in hand.

"These two characters," he said. "You mean they actually pulled it off?"

"I'm damn sure they did," I said. "They're still doing it. About once every three weeks."

"Fantastic story," Jerry said. "And a damn crazy dangerous thing to do. Just imagine the sort of hell that would break loose if you were caught. Instant divorce. Two divorces, in fact. One on each side of the street. Not worth it."

"Takes a lot of guts," I said.

"The party's breaking up," Jerry said. "They're all going home with their goddamn wives."

I didn't say any more after that. We sat there for a couple of minutes sipping our drinks while the guests began drifting toward the hall.

"Did he say it was fun, this friend of yours?" Jerry asked suddenly.

"He said it was a gas," I answered. "He said all the normal pleasures got intensified one hundred percent because of the risk. He swore it was the greatest way of doing it in the world, impersonating the husband and the wife not knowing it."

At that point, Mary came in through the french windows with Bob Swain. She had an empty glass in one hand and a flame-coloured azalea in the other. She had picked the azalea on the terrace.

"I've been watching you," she said, pointing the flower at me like a pistol. "You've hardly stopped talking for the last ten minutes. What's he been telling you, Jerry?"

"A dirty story," Jerry said, grinning.

"He does that when he drinks," Mary said.

"Good story," Jerry said. "But totally impossible. Get him to tell it to you sometime."

"I don't like dirty stories," Mary said. "Come along, Vic. It's time we went."

"Don't go yet," Jerry said, fixing his eyes upon her splendid bosom. "Have another drink."

"No thanks," she said. "The children'll be screaming for their supper. I've had a lovely time."

"Aren't you going to kiss me goodnight?" Jerry said, getting up from the sofa. He went for her mouth, but she turned her head quickly and he caught only the edge of her cheek.

"Go away, Jerry," she said. "You're drunk."

"Not drunk," Jerry said. "Just lecherous."

"Don't you get lecherous with me, my boy," Mary said sharply. "I hate that sort of talk." She marched away across the room, carrying her bosom before her like a battering-ram.

"So long, Jerry," I said. "Fine party."

Mary, full of dark looks, was waiting for me in the hall. Samantha was there, too, saying goodbye to the last guests—Samantha with her dexterous fingers and her smooth skin and her smooth, dangerous thighs. "Cheer up, Vic," she said to me, her white teeth showing. She looked like the creation, the beginning of the world, the first morning. "Goodnight, Vic darling," she said, stirring her fingers in my vitals.

I followed Mary out of the house. "You feeling all right?" she asked.

"Yes," I said. "Why not?"

"The amount you drink is enough to make anyone feel ill," she said.

There was a scrubby old hedge dividing our place from Jerry's and there was a gap in it we always used. Mary and I walked through the gap in silence. We went into the house and she cooked up a big pile of scrambled eggs and bacon, and we ate it with the children.

After the meal, I wandered outside. The summer evening was clear and cool and because I had nothing else to do I decided to mow the grass in the front garden. I got the mower out of the shed and started it up. Then I began the old routine of marching back and forth behind it. I like mowing grass. It is a soothing operation, and on our front lawn I could always look at Samantha's house going one way and think about her going the other.

I had been at it for about ten minutes when Jerry came strolling through the gap in the hedge. He was smoking a pipe and had his hands in his pockets and he stood on the edge of the grass, watching me. I pulled up in front of him, but left the motor ticking over.

"Hi, sport," he said. "How's everything?"

"I'm in the doghouse," I said. "So are you."

"Your little wife," he said, "is just too goddamn prim and prissy to be true."

"Oh, I know that."

"She rebuked me in my own house," Jerry said.

"Not very much."

"It was enough," he said, smiling slightly.

"Enough for what?"

"Enough to make me want to get a little bit of my own back on her. So what would you think if I suggested you and I have a go at that thing your friend told you about at lunch?"

When he said this, I felt such a surge of excitement my stomach nearly jumped out of my mouth. I gripped the handles of the mower and started revving the engine.

"Have I said the wrong thing?" Jerry asked.

I didn't answer.

"Listen," he said. "If you think it's a lousy idea, let's just forget I ever mentioned it. You're not mad at me, are you?"

"I'm not mad at you, Jerry," I said. "It's just that it never entered my head that *we* should do it."

"It entered mine," he said. "The set-up is perfect. We wouldn't even have to cross the street." His face had gone suddenly bright and his eyes were shining like two stars. "So what do you say, Vic?"

"I'm thinking," I said.

"Maybe you don't fancy Samantha."

"I don't honestly know," I said.

"She's lots of fun," Jerry said. "I guarantee that."

At this point, I saw Mary come out onto the front porch. "There's Mary," I said. "She's looking for the children. We'll talk some more tomorrow."

"Then it's a deal?"

"It could be, Jerry. But only on condition we don't rush it. I want to be dead sure everything is right before we start. Damn it all, this is a whole brand-new can of beans!"

"No, it's not!" he said. "Your friend said it was a gas. He said it was easy."

"Ah, yes," I said. "My friend. Of course. But each case is different." I opened the throttle on the mower and went whirring away across the lawn. When I got to the far side and turned around, Jerry was already through the gap in the hedge and walking up to his front door.

The next couple of weeks was a period of high conspiracy for Jerry and me. We held secret meetings in bars and restaurants to discuss strategy, and sometimes he dropped into my office after work and we had a planning session behind the closed door. Whenever a doubtful point arose, Jerry would always say, "How did your friend do it?" And I would play for time and say, "I'll call him up and ask him about that one."

After many conferences and much talk, we agreed upon the following main points:

1. That D-Day should be a Saturday.
2. That on D-Day evening we should take our wives out to a good dinner, the four of us together.
3. That Jerry and I should leave our houses and cross over through the gap in the hedge at precisely one A.M. Sunday morning.
4. That instead of lying in bed in the dark until one A.M. came along, we should both, as soon as our wives were asleep, go quietly downstairs to the kitchen and drink coffee.
5. That we should use the front doorbell idea if an emergency arose.
6. That the return cross-over time was fixed for two A.M.
7. That while in the wrong bed, questions (if any) from the woman must be answered by an "Uh-uh" sounded with the lips closed tight.

8. That I myself must immediately give up cigarettes and take to a pipe so that I would "smell" the same as Jerry.

9. That we should at once start using the same brand of hair oil and after-shave lotion.

10. That as both of us normally wore our wrist-watches in bed, and they were much the same shape, it was decided not to exchange. Neither of us wore rings.

11. That each man must have something unusual about him that the woman would identify positively with her own husband. We therefore invented what became known as "The Sticking-Plaster Ploy." It worked like this: On D-Day evening, when the couples arrived back in their own homes immediately after the dinner, each husband would make a point of going to the kitchen to cut himself a piece of cheese. At the same time, he would carefully stick a large bit of plaster over the tip of the forefinger of his right hand. Having done this, he would hold up the finger and say to his wife, "I cut myself. It's nothing, but it was bleeding a bit." Thus, later on, when the men have switched beds, each woman will be made very much aware of the plaster-covered finger (the man would see to that), and will associate it directly with her own husband. An important psychological ploy, this, calculated to dissipate any tiny suspicion that might enter the mind of either female.

So much for the basic plans. Next came what we referred to in our notes as "Familiarisation with the Lay-out." Jerry schooled me first. He gave me three hours' training in his own house one Sunday afternoon when his wife and children were out. I had never been into their bedroom before. On the dressing table were Samantha's perfumes, her brushes, and all her other little things. A pair of her stockings was draped over the back of a chair. Her nightdress, white and blue, was hanging behind the door leading to the bathroom.

"Okay," Jerry said. "It'll be pitch dark when you come in. Samantha sleeps on this side, so you must tiptoe around the end of the bed and slide in on the other side, over there. I'm going to blindfold you and let you practise."

At first, with the blindfold on, I wandered all over the room like a drunk. But after about an hour's work, I was able to negotiate the course pretty well. But before Jerry would finally pass me out, I had to go blindfolded all the way from the front door through the hall, up the stairs, past the children's rooms, into Samantha's room and finish up in exactly the right place. And I had to do it silently, like a thief. All this took three hours of hard work, but I got it in the end.

The following Sunday morning when Mary had taken our children to church, I was able to give Jerry the same sort of work-out in my house. He learned the ropes faster than me, and within an hour he had passed the blindfold test without placing a foot wrong.

It was during this session that we decided to disconnect each woman's bedside lamp as we entered the bedroom. So Jerry practised finding the plug and pulling it out with his blindfold on, and the following weekend, I was able to do the same in Jerry's house.

Now came by far the most important part of our training. We called it "Spilling the Beans," and it was here that both of us had to describe in every detail the procedure we adopted when making love to our own wives. We agreed not to worry ourselves with any exotic variations that either of us might or might not occasionally practise. We were concerned only with teaching one another the most commonly used routine, the one least likely to arouse suspicion.

The session took place in my office at six o'clock on a Wednesday evening, after the staff had gone home. At first, we were both slightly embarrassed, and neither of us wanted to begin. So I got out the bottle of whisky, and after a couple of stiff drinks, we loosened up and the teach-in started. While Jerry talked I took notes, and vice versa. At the end of it all, it turned out that the only real difference between Jerry's routine and my own was one of tempo. But what a difference it was! He took things (if what he said was to be believed) in such a leisurely fashion and he prolonged the moments to such an extravagant degree that I wondered privately to myself whether his partner did not sometimes go to sleep in the middle of it all. My job, however, was not to criticise but to copy, and I said nothing.

Jerry was not so discreet. At the end of my personal description, he had the temerity to say, "Is that really what you do?"

"What do you mean?" I asked.

"I mean is it all over and done with as quickly as that?"

"Look," I said. "We aren't here to give each other lessons. We're here to learn the facts."

"I know that," he said. "But I'm going to feel a bit of an ass if I copy your style exactly. My God, you go through it like an express train whizzing through a country station!"

I stared at him, mouth open.

"Don't look so surprised," he said. "The way you told it to me, anyone would think . . ."

"Think what?" I said.

"Oh, forget it," he said.

"Thank you," I said. I was furious. There are two things in this world at which I happen to know I excel. One is driving an automobile and the other is you-know-what. So to have him sit there and tell me I didn't know how to behave with my own wife was a monstrous piece of effrontery. It was he who didn't know, not me. Poor Samantha. What she must have had to put up with over the years.

"I'm sorry I spoke," Jerry said. He poured more whisky into our glasses. "Here's to the great switcheroo!" he said. "When do we go?"

"Today is Wednesday," I said. "How about this coming Saturday?"

"Christ," Jerry said.

"We ought to do it while everything's still fresh in our minds," I said. "There's an awful lot to remember."

Jerry walked to the window and looked down at the traffic in the street below. "Okay," he said, turning around. "Saturday it shall be!" Then we drove home in our separate cars.

"Jerry and I thought we'd take you and Samantha out to dinner Saturday night," I said to Mary. We were in the kitchen and she was cooking hamburgers for the children.

She turned around and faced me, frying-pan in one hand, spoon in the other. Her blue eyes looked straight into mine. "My Lord, Vic," she said. "How nice. But what are we celebrating?"

I looked straight back at her and said, "I thought it would be a change to see some new faces. We're always meeting the same old bunch of people in the same old houses."

She took a step forward and kissed me on the cheek. "What a good man you are," she said. "I love you."

"Don't forget to phone the baby-sitter."

"No, I'll do it tonight," she said.

Thursday and Friday passed by very quickly, and suddenly it was Saturday. It was D-Day. I woke up feeling madly excited. After breakfast, I couldn't sit still, so I decided to go out and wash the car. I was in the middle of this when Jerry came strolling through the gap in the hedge, pipe in mouth.

"Hi, sport," he said. "This is the day."

"I know that," I said. I also had a pipe in my mouth. I was forcing myself to smoke it, but I had trouble keeping it alight, and the smoke burned my tongue.

"How're you feeling?" Jerry asked.

"Terrific," I said. "How about you?"

"I'm nervous," he said.

"Don't be nervous, Jerry."

"This is one hell of a thing we're trying to do," he said. "I hope we pull it off."

I went on polishing the windshield. I had never known Jerry to be nervous of anything before. It worried me a bit.

"I'm damn glad we're not the first people ever to try it," he said. "If no one had ever done it before, I don't think I'd risk it."

"I agree," I said.

"What stops me being too nervous," he said, "is the fact that your friend found it so fantastically easy."

"My friend said it was a cinch," I said. "But for Chrissake, Jerry, don't be nervous when the time comes. That would be disastrous."

"Don't worry," he said. "But Jesus, it's exciting, isn't it?"

"It's exciting all right," I said.

"Listen," he said. "We'd better go easy on the booze tonight."

"Good idea," I said. "See you at eight thirty."

At half past eight, Samantha, Jerry, Mary, and I drove in Jerry's car to Billy's Steak House. The restaurant, despite its name, was high-class and expensive, and the girls had put on long dresses for the occasion. Samantha was wearing something green that didn't start until it was halfway down her front, and I had never seen her looking lovelier. There were candles on our table. Samantha was seated opposite me and whenever she leaned forward with her face close to the flame, I could see that tiny crest of skin at the top centre of her lower lip. "Now," she said as she accepted a menu from the waiter, "I wonder what I'm going to have tonight."

Ho-ho-ho, I thought, that's a good question.

Everything went fine in the restaurant and the girls enjoyed themselves. When we arrived back at Jerry's house, it was eleven forty-five, and Samantha said, "Come in and have a nightcap."

"Thanks," I said, "but it's a bit late. And the baby-sitter has to be driven home." So Mary and I walked across to our house, and *now,* I told myself as I entered the front door, *from now on* the count-down begins. I must keep a clear head and forget nothing.

While Mary was paying the baby-sitter, I went to the fridge and found a piece of Canadian cheddar. I took a knife from the drawer and a strip of plaster from the cupboard. I stuck the plaster around the tip of the forefinger of my right hand and waited for Mary to turn around.

"I cut myself," I said holding up the finger for her to see. "It's nothing, but it was bleeding a bit."

"I'd have thought you'd had enough to eat for the evening," was all she said. But the plaster registered on her mind and my first little job had been done.

I drove the baby-sitter home and by the time I got back up to the bedroom it was round about midnight and Mary was already half asleep with her light out. I switched out the light on my side of the bed and went into the bathroom to undress. I pottered about in there for ten minutes or so and when I came out, Mary, as I had hoped, was well and truly sleeping. There seemed no point in getting into bed beside her. So I simply pulled back the covers a bit on my side to make it easier for Jerry, then with my slippers on, I went downstairs to the kitchen and switched on the electric kettle. It was now twelve seventeen. Forty-three minutes to go.

At twelve thirty-five, I went upstairs to check on Mary and the kids. Everyone was sound asleep.

At twelve fifty-five, five minutes before zero hour, I went up again for a final check. I went right up close to Mary's bed and whispered her name. There was no answer. Good. *That's it! Let's go!*

I put a brown raincoat over my pyjamas. I switched off the kitchen light so that the whole house was in darkness. I put the front door lock on the latch. And then, feeling an enormous sense of exhilaration, I stepped silently out into the night.

There were no lamps on our street to lighten the darkness. There was no moon or even a star to be seen. It was a black black night, but the air was warm and there was a little breeze blowing from somewhere.

I headed for the gap in the hedge. When I got very close, I was able to make out the hedge itself and find the gap. I stopped there, waiting. Then I heard Jerry's footsteps coming toward me.

"Hi, sport," he whispered. "Everything okay?"

"All ready for you," I whispered back.

He moved on. I heard his slippered feet padding softly over the grass as he went toward my house. I went toward his.

I opened Jerry's front door. It was even darker inside than out. I closed the door carefully. I took off my raincoat and hung it on the door knob. I removed my slippers and placed them against the wall by the door. I literally could not see my hands before my face. Everything had to be done by touch.

My goodness, I was glad Jerry had made me practise blindfolded for so long. It wasn't my feet that guided me now but my fingers. The fingers of one hand or another were never for a moment out of contact with something, a wall, the banister, a piece of furniture, a window-curtain. And I knew or thought I knew exactly where I was all the time. But it was an awesome eerie feeling trespassing on tiptoe through someone else's house in the middle of the night. As I fingered my way up the stairs, I found myself thinking of the burglars who had broken into our front room last winter and stolen the television set. When the police came next morning, I pointed out to them an enormous turd lying in the snow outside the garage. "They nearly always do that," one of the cops told me. "They can't help it. They're scared."

I reached the top of the stairs. I crossed the landing with my right fingertips touching the wall all the time. I started down the corridor, but paused when my hand found the door of the first children's-room. The door was slightly open. I listened. I could hear young Robert Rainbow, aged eight, breathing evenly inside. I moved on. I found the door to the second children's-bedroom. This one belonged to Billy, aged six, and Amanda, three. I stood listening. All was well.

The main bedroom was at the end of the corridor, about four yards on. I reached the door. Jerry had left it open, as planned. I went in. I stood absolutely still just inside the door, listening for any sign that Samantha might be awake. All was quiet. I felt my way around the wall until I reached Samantha's side of the bed. Immediately, I knelt on the floor and found the plug connecting her bedside lamp. I drew it from its socket and laid it on the carpet. Good. Much safer now. I stood up. I couldn't see Samantha, and at first I couldn't hear anything either. I bent low over the bed. Ah yes, I could hear her breathing. Suddenly I caught a whiff of the heavy musky perfume she had been using that evening, and I felt the blood rushing to my groin. Quickly I tiptoed around the big bed, keeping two fingers in gentle contact with the edge of the bed the whole way.

All I had to do now was get in. I did so, but as I put my weight upon the mattress, the creaking of the springs underneath sounded as though someone was firing a rifle in the room. I lay motionless, holding my breath. I could hear my heart thumping away like an engine in my throat. Samantha was facing away from me. She didn't move. I pulled the covers up over my chest and turned toward her. A female glow came out of her to me. Here we go, then! *Now!*

I slid a hand over and touched her body. Her nightdress was warm and silky. I rested the hand gently on her hip. Still she didn't move. I waited a minute or so, then I allowed the hand that lay upon the hip to steal onward and go exploring. Slowly, deliberately, and very accurately, my fingers began the process of setting her on fire.

She stirred. She turned onto her back. Then she murmured sleepily, "Oh, dear . . . Oh, my goodness me . . . Good heavens, darling!"

I, of course, said nothing. I just kept on with the job.

A couple of minutes went by.

She was lying quite still.

Another minute passed. Then another. She didn't move a muscle.

I began to wonder how much longer it would be before she caught alight.

I persevered.

But why the silence? Why this absolute and total immobility, this frozen posture?

Suddenly it came to me. I had forgotten completely about Jerry! I was so hotted up, I had forgotten all about his own personal routine! I was doing it my way, not his! His way was far more complex than mine. It was ridiculously elaborate. It was quite unnecessary. But it was what she was used to. And now she was noticing the difference and trying to figure out what on earth was going on.

But it was too late to change direction now. I must keep going.

I kept going. The woman beside me was like a coiled spring lying there. I could feel the tension under her skin. I began to sweat.

Suddenly, she uttered a queer little groan.

More ghastly thoughts rushed through my mind. Could she be ill? Was she having a heart attack? Ought I to get the hell out quick?

She groaned again, louder this time. Then all at once, she cried out, "Yes-yes-yes-yes-yes!" and like a bomb whose slow fuse has finally reached the dynamite, she exploded into life. She grabbed me in her arms and went for me with such incredible ferocity, I felt I was being set upon by a tiger.

Or should I say a tigress?

I never dreamed a woman could do the things Samantha did to

me then. She was a whirlwind, a dazzling frenzied whirlwind that tore me up by the roots and spun me around and carried me high into the heavens, to places I did not know existed.

I myself did not contribute. How could I? I was helpless. I was the palm-tree spinning in the heavens, the lamb in the claws of the tiger. It was as much as I could do to keep breathing.

Thrilling it was, all the same, to surrender to the hands of a violent woman, and for the next ten, twenty, thirty minutes—how would I know?—the storm raged on. But I have no intention here of regaling the reader with bizarre details. I do not approve of washing juicy linen in public. I am sorry, but there it is. I only hope that my reticence will not create too strong a sense of anticlimax. Certainly, there was nothing "anti" about my own climax, and in the final searing paroxysm I gave a shout which should have awakened the entire neighbourhood. Then I collapsed. I crumpled up like a drained wineskin.

Samantha, as though she had done no more than drink a glass of water, simply turned away from me and went right back to sleep.

Phew!

I lay still, recuperating slowly.

I had been right, you see, about that little thing on her lower lip, had I not?

Come to think of it, I had been right about more or less everything that had to do with this incredible escapade. What a triumph! I felt wonderfully relaxed and well-spent.

I wondered what time it was. My watch was not a luminous one. I'd better go. I crept out of bed. I felt my way, a trifle less cautiously this time, around the bed, out of the bedroom, along the corridor, down the stairs and into the hall of the house. I found my raincoat and slippers. I put them on. I had a lighter in the pocket of my raincoat. I used it and read the time. It was eight minutes before two. Later than I thought, I opened the front door and stepped out into the black night.

My thoughts now began to concentrate upon Jerry. Was he all right? Had he gotten away with it? I moved through the darkness toward the gap in the hedge.

"Hi, sport," a voice whispered beside me.

"Jerry!"

"Everything okay?" Jerry asked.

"Fantastic," I said. "Amazing. What about you?"

"Same with me," he said. I caught the flash of his white teeth grinning at me in the dark. "We made it, Vic!" he whispered, touching my arm. "You were right! It worked! It was sensational!"

"See you tomorrow," I whispered. "Go home."

We moved apart. I went through the hedge and entered my house. Three minutes later, I was safely back in my own bed, and my own wife was sleeping soundly alongside me.

The next morning was Sunday. I was up at eight thirty and went downstairs in pyjamas and dressing-gown, as I always do on a Sunday, to make breakfast for the family. I had left Mary sleeping. The two boys, Victor, aged nine, and Wally, seven, were already down.

"Hi, Daddy," Wally said.

"I've got a great new breakfast," I announced.

"What?" both boys said together. They had been into town and fetched the Sunday paper and were now reading the comics.

"We make some buttered toast and we spread orange marmalade on it," I said. "Then we put strips of crisp bacon on top of the marmalade."

"*Bacon!*" Victor said. "With *orange marmalade?*"

"I know. But you wait till you try it. It's wonderful."

I poured out the grapefruit juice and drank two glasses of it myself. I set another on the table for Mary when she came down. I switched on the electric kettle, put bread in the toaster, and started to fry the bacon. At this point, Mary came into the kitchen. She had a flimsy peach-coloured chiffon thing over her nightdress.

"Good morning," I said, watching her over my shoulder as I manipulated the frying-pan.

She did not answer. She went to her chair at the kitchen table and sat down. She started to sip her juice. She looked neither at me nor at the boys. I went on frying the bacon.

"Hi, Mummy," Wally said.

She didn't answer this either.

The smell of the bacon fat was beginning to turn my stomach.

"I'd like some coffee," Mary said, not looking around. Her voice was very odd.

"Coming right up," I said. I pushed the frying-pan away from the heat and quickly made a cup of black instant coffee. I placed it before her.

"Boys," she said, addressing the children, "would you please do your reading in the other room till breakfast is ready."

"Us?" Victor said. "Why?"

"Because I say so."

"Are we doing something wrong?" Wally asked.

"No, honey, you're not. I just want to be left alone for a moment with Daddy."

I felt myself shrink inside my skin. I wanted to run. I wanted to rush out the front door and go running down the street and hide.

"Get yourself a coffee, Vic," she said, "and sit down." Her voice was quite flat. There was no anger in it. There was just nothing. And she still wouldn't look at me. The boys went out, taking the comics section with them.

"Shut the door," Mary said to them.

I put a spoonful of powdered coffee into my cup and poured boiling water over it. I added milk and sugar. The silence was shattering. I crossed over and sat down in my chair opposite her. It might just as well have been an electric chair, the way I was feeling.

"Listen, Vic," she said, looking into her coffee cup. "I want to get this said before I lose my nerve and then I won't be able to say it."

"For heaven's sake, what's all the drama about?" I asked. "Has something happened?"

"Yes, Vic, it has."

"What?"

Her face was pale and still and distant, unconscious of the kitchen around her.

"Come on, then, out with it," I said bravely.

"You're not going to like this very much," she said, and her big blue haunted-looking eyes rested a moment on my face, then travelled away.

"What am I not going to like very much?" I said. The sheer terror of it all was beginning to stir my bowels. I felt the same way as those burglars the cops had told me about.

"You know I hate talking about love-making and all that sort of thing," she said. "I've never once talked to you about it all the time we've been married."

"That's true," I said.

She took a sip of her coffee, but she wasn't tasting it. "The point is this," she said. "I've never liked it. If you really want to know, I've hated it."

"Hated what?" I asked.

"Sex," she said. "Doing it."

"Good Lord!" I said.

"It's never given me even the slightest little bit of pleasure."

This was shattering enough in itself, but the real cruncher was still to come, I felt sure of that.

"I'm sorry if that surprises you," she added.

I couldn't think of anything to say, so I kept quiet.

Her eyes rose again from the coffee cup and looked into mine, watchful, as if calculating something, then fell again. "I wasn't ever going to tell you," she said. "And I never would have if it hadn't been for last night."

I said very slowly, "What about last night?"

"Last night," she said, "I suddenly found out what the whole crazy thing is all about."

"You did?"

She looked full at me now, and her face was as open as a flower. "Yes," she said. "I surely did."

I didn't move.

"Oh, darling!" she cried, jumping up and rushing over and giving me an enormous kiss. "Thank you so much for last night! You were marvellous! And I was marvellous! We were both marvellous! Don't look so embarrassed, my darling! You ought to be proud of yourself! You were fantastic! I love you! I do! I do!"

I just sat there.

She leaned close to me and put an arm around my shoulders. "And now," she said softly, "now that you have . . . I don't quite know how to say this . . . now that you have sort of discovered what it is I *need,* everything is going to be so marvellous from now on!"

I still sat there. She went slowly back to her chair. A big tear was running down one of her cheeks. I couldn't think why.

"I was right to tell you, wasn't I?" she said, smiling through her tears.

"Yes," I said. "Oh, yes." I stood up and went over to the cooker so that I wouldn't be facing her. Through the kitchen window, I caught sight of Jerry crossing his garden with the Sunday paper under his arm. There was a lilt in his walk, a little prance of triumph in each pace he took, and when he reached the steps of his front porch, he ran up them two at a time.

The Boy Who Talked
with Animals

1974

N︎OT so long ago, I decided to spend a few days in the West Indies. I was to go there for a short holiday. Friends had told me it was marvelous. I would laze around all day long, they said, sunning myself on the silver beaches and swimming in the warm green sea.

I chose Jamaica, and flew direct from London to Kingston. The drive from Kingston airport to my hotel on the north shore took two hours. My room in the hotel had a little balcony, and from there I could step straight down onto the beach. There were tall coconut palms growing all around, and every so often an enormous green nut the size of a football would fall out of the sky and drop with a thud on the sand. It was considered foolish to linger underneath a coconut palm because if one of those things landed on your head, it would smash your skull.

The Jamaican girl who came in to tidy my room told me that a wealthy American called Mr. Wasserman had met his end in precisely that manner only two months before.

"You're joking," I said to her.

"Not joking!" she cried. "No, *suh!* I sees it happening with my very own eyes!"

"But wasn't there a terrific fuss about it?" I asked.

"They hush it up," she answered darkly. "The hotel folks hush it up and so do the newspaper folks because things like that are very bad for the tourist business."

"And you say you actually saw it happen?"

"I actually saw it happen," she said. "Mr. Wasserman, he's standing right under that very tree over there on the beach. He's got his camera out and he's pointing it at the sunset. It's a red sunset that evening, and very pretty. Then all at once, down comes a big green nut right smack onto the top of his bald head, *wham!* And that," she added with a touch of relish, "is the very last sunset Mr. Wasserman ever did see."

"You mean it killed him instantly?"

"I don't know about *instantly*," she said. "I remember the next thing that happens the camera falls out of his hands onto the sand. Then his arms drop down to his sides and hang there. Then he starts swaying. He sways backward and forward several times ever so gentle, and I'm standing there watching him, and I says to myself the poor man's gone all dizzy and maybe he's going to faint any moment. Then very very slowly, he keels right over and down he goes."

"Was he dead?"

"Dead as a doornail," she said.

"Good heavens."

"That's right," she said. "It never pays to be standing under a coconut palm when there's a breeze blowing."

"Thank you," I said. "I'll remember that."

On the evening of my second day, I was sitting on my little balcony with a book on my lap and a tall glass of rum punch in my hand. I wasn't reading the book. I was watching a small green lizard stalking another small green lizard on the balcony floor about six feet away. The stalking lizard was coming up on the other one from behind, moving forward very slowly and very cautiously, and when he came within reach, he flicked out a long tongue and touched the other one's tail. The other one jumped round, and the two of them faced each other, motionless, glued to the floor, crouching, staring, and very tense. Then suddenly, they started doing a funny little hopping dance together. They hopped up in the air. They hopped backward. They hopped forward. They hopped sideways. They circled one another like two boxers, hopping and prancing and dancing all the time. It was a queer thing to watch, and I guessed it was some sort of a courtship ritual they were going through. I kept very still, waiting to see what was going to happen next.

But I never saw what happened next because at that moment I became aware of a great commotion on the beach below. I glanced over and saw a crowd of people clustering around something at the water's edge. There was a narrow canoe-type fisherman's boat pulled up on the sand nearby, and all I could think of was that the fisherman had come in with a lot of fish and that the crowd was looking at it.

A haul of fish is something that has always fascinated me. I put my book aside and stood up. More people were trooping down from the hotel veranda and hurrying over the beach to join the crowd on the edge of the water. The men were wearing those frightful Bermuda shorts that come down to the knees, and their shirts were bilious with pinks and oranges and every other clashing color you could think of. The women had better taste, and were dressed for the most part in pretty cotton dresses. Nearly everyone carried a drink in one hand.

I picked up my own drink and stepped down from the balcony onto the beach. I made a little detour around the coconut palm under which Mr. Wasserman had supposedly met his end and strode across the beautiful silvery sand to join the crowd.

But it wasn't a haul of fish they were staring at. It was a turtle, an upside-down turtle lying on its back in the sand. But what a turtle it was! It was a giant, a mammoth. I had not thought it possible for a turtle to be as enormous as this. How can I describe its size? Had it been the right way up, I think a tall man could have sat on its back without his feet touching the ground. It was perhaps five feet long and four feet across, with a high domed shell of great beauty.

The fisherman who had caught it had tipped it onto its back to stop it from getting away. There was also a thick rope tied around the middle of its shell, and one proud fisherman, slim and black and naked except for a small loincloth, stood a short way off holding the end of the rope with both hands.

Upside down it lay, this magnificent creature, with its four thick flippers waving frantically in the air, and its long wrinkled neck stretching far out of its shell. The flippers had large sharp claws on them.

"Stand back, ladies and gentlemen, please!" cried the fisherman. "Stand well back! Them claws is *dangerous,* man! They'll rip your arm clear away from your body!"

The crowd of hotel guests was thrilled and delighted by this spectacle. A dozen cameras were out and clicking away. Many of the women were squealing with pleasure and clutching onto the arms of their men, and the men were demonstrating their lack of fear and their masculinity by making foolish remarks in loud voices.

"Make yourself a nice pair of horn-rimmed spectacles out of that shell, hey Al?"

"Darn thing must weigh over a ton!"

"You mean to say it can actually float?"

"Sure it floats. Powerful swimmer, too. Pull a boat easy."

"He's a snapper, is he?"

"That's no snapper. Snapper turtles don't grow as big as that. But I'll tell you what. He'll snap your hand off quick enough if you get too close to him."

"Is that true?" one of the women asked the fisherman. "Would he snap off a person's hand?"

"He would right now," the fisherman said, smiling with brilliant white teeth. "He won't ever hurt you when he's in the ocean, but you catch him and pull him ashore and tip him up like this, then man alive, you'd better watch out! He'll snap at anything that comes in reach!"

"I guess I'd get a bit snappish myself," the woman said, "if I was in his situation."

One idiotic man had found a plank of driftwood on the sand, and he was carrying it toward the turtle. It was a fair-sized plank, about five feet long and maybe an inch thick. He started poking one end of it at the turtle's head.

"I wouldn't do that," the fisherman said. "You'll only make him madder than ever."

When the end of the plank touched the turtle's neck, the great beast whipped around and the mouth opened wide and *snap,* it took the plank in its mouth and bit through it as if it were made of cheese.

"Wow!" they shouted. "Did you see that! I'm glad it wasn't my arm!"

"Leave him alone," the fisherman said. "It don't help to get him all stirred up."

A paunchy man with wide hips and very short hairy legs came up to the fisherman and said, "Listen, feller. I want that shell. I'll buy it from you." And to his plump wife, he said, "You know what I'm going to do, Mildred? I'm going to take that shell home and have it polished up by an expert. Then I'm going to place it smack in the center of our living room! Won't that be something?"

"Fantastic," the plump wife said. "Go ahead and buy it, baby."

"Don't worry," he said. "It's mine already." And to the fisherman, he said, "How much for the shell?"

"I already sold him," the fisherman said. "I sold him shell and all."

"Not so fast, feller," the paunchy man said. "I'll bid you higher. Come on. What'd he offer you?"

"No can do," the fisherman said. "I already sold him."

"Who to?" the paunchy man said.

"To the manager."

"What manager?"

"The manager of the hotel."

"Did you hear that?" shouted another man. "He's sold it to the manager of our hotel! And you know what that means? It means turtle soup, that's what it means!"

"Right you are! And turtle steak! You ever have turtle steak, Bill?"

"I never have, Jack. But I can't wait."

"A turtle steak's better than a beefsteak if you cook it right. It's more tender and it's got one heck of a flavor."

"Listen," the paunchy man said to the fisherman. "I'm not trying to buy the meat. The manager can have the meat. He can have everything that's inside including the teeth and toenails. All I want is the shell."

"And if I know you, baby," his wife said, beaming at him, "you're going to get the shell."

I stood there listening to the conversation of these human beings. They were discussing the destruction, the consumption and the flavor of a creature who seemed, even when upside down, to be extraordinarily dignified. One thing was certain. He was senior to any of them in age. For probably one hundred and fifty years he had been cruising in the green waters of the West Indies. He was there when George Washington was President of the United States and Napoleon was being clobbered at Waterloo. He would have been a small turtle then, but he was most certainly there.

And now he was here, upside down on the beach, waiting to be translated into soup and steak. He was clearly alarmed by all the noise and the shouting around him. His old wrinkled neck was straining out of its shell, and the great head was twisting this way and that as though searching for someone who would explain the reason for all this ill-treatment.

"How are you going to get him up to the hotel?" the paunchy man asked.

"Drag him up the beach with the rope," the fisherman answered. "The staff'll be coming along soon to take him. It's going to need ten men, all pulling at once."

"Hey, listen!" cried a muscular young man. "Why don't *we* drag him up?" The muscular young man was wearing magenta and pea-green Bermuda shorts and no shirt. He had an exceptionally hairy chest, and the absence of a shirt was obviously a calculated touch. "What say we do a little work for our supper?" he cried, rippling his muscles. "Come on, fellers! Who's for some exercise?"

"Great idea!" they shouted. "Splendid scheme!"

The men handed their drinks to the women and rushed to catch hold of the rope. They ranged themselves along it as though for a tug-of-war, and the hairy-chested man appointed himself anchorman and captain of the team.

"Come on, now, fellers!" he shouted. "When I say *heave,* then all heave at once, you understand?"

The fisherman didn't like this much. "It's better you leave this job for the hotel," he said.

"Nonsense!" shouted hairy-chest. *"Heave,* boys, *heave!"*

They all heaved. The giant turtle wobbled on its back and nearly toppled over.

"Don't tip him!" yelled the fisherman. "You're going to tip him over if you do that! And if he gets back onto his legs again, he'll escape for sure!"

"Cool it, laddie," said hairy-chest in a patronizing voice. "How can he escape? We've got a rope round him, haven't we?"

"That old turtle will drag the whole lot of you away with him if you give him a chance!" cried the fisherman. "He'll drag you into the ocean, every one of you!"

"Heave!" shouted hairy-chest, ignoring the fisherman. *"Heave,* boys, *heave!"*

And now the gigantic turtle began very slowly to slide up the beach toward the hotel, toward the kitchens, toward the place where the big knives were kept. The womenfolk and the older, fatter, less athletic men followed alongside, shouting encouragement.

"Heave!" shouted the hairy-chested anchorman. "Put your back into it, fellers! You can pull harder than that!"

Suddenly I heard screams. Everyone heard them. They were screams so high-pitched, so shrill and so urgent they cut right through everything. "No-o-o-o-o!" screamed the scream. "No! No! No! No! No!"

The crowd froze. The tug-of-war men stopped tugging and the onlookers stopped shouting and every single person present turned toward the place where the screams were coming from.

Half walking, half running down the beach from the hotel were three people, a man, a woman and a small boy. They were half running because the boy was pulling the man along. The man had the boy by the wrist, trying to slow him down, but the boy kept pulling. At the same time, he was jumping and twisting and wriggling and trying to free himself from the father's grip. It was the boy who was screaming.

"Don't!" he screamed. "Don't do it! Let him go! Please let him go!"

The woman, his mother, was trying to catch hold of the boy's other arm to help restrain him, but the boy was jumping about so much, she didn't succeed.

"Let him go!" screamed the boy. "It's horrible what you're doing! Please let him go!"

"Stop that, David!" the mother said, still trying to catch his other arm. "Don't be so childish! You're making a perfect fool of yourself."

"Daddy!" the boy screamed. "Daddy! Tell them to let him go!"

"I can't do that, David," the father said. "It isn't any of our business."

The tug-of-war pullers remained motionless, still holding the rope with the gigantic turtle on the end of it. Everyone stood silent and surprised, staring at the boy. They were all a bit off balance now. They had the slightly hangdog air of people who have been caught doing something that was not entirely honorable.

"Come on now, David," the father said, pulling against the boy. "Let's go back to the hotel and leave these people alone."

"I'm not going back!" the boy shouted. "I don't want to go back! I want them to let it go!"

"Now, David," the mother said.

"Beat it, kid," the hairy-chested man told the boy.

"You're horrible and cruel!" the boy shouted. "All of you are horrible and cruel!" He threw the words high and shrill at the forty or fifty adults standing there on the beach, and nobody, not even the hairy-chested man, answered him this time. "Why don't you put him back in the sea?" the boy shouted. "He hasn't done anything to you! Let him go!"

The father was embarrassed by his son, but he was not ashamed of him. "He's crazy about animals," he said, addressing the crowd. "Back home he's got every kind of animal under the sun. He talks with them."

"He loves them," the mother said.

Several people began shuffling their feet around in the sand. Here and there in the crowd it was possible to sense a slight change of mood, a feeling of uneasiness, a touch even of shame. The boy, who could have been no more than eight or nine years old, had stopped struggling with his father now. The father still held him by the wrist, but he was no longer restraining him.

"Go on!" the boy called out. "Let him go! Undo the rope and let him go!" He stood very small and erect, facing the crowd, his eyes shining like two stars and the wind blowing in his hair. He was magnificent.

"There's nothing we can do, David," the father said gently. "Let's go on back."

"No!" the boy cried out, and at that moment he suddenly gave a twist and wrenched his wrist free from the father's grip. He was away like a streak, running across the sand toward the giant upturned turtle.

"David!" the father yelled, starting after him. "Stop! Come back!"

The boy dodged and swerved through the crowd like a player running with the ball, and the only person who sprang forward to intercept him was the fisherman. "Don't you go near that turtle, boy!" he shouted as he made a lunge for the swiftly running figure. But the boy dodged round him and kept going. "He'll bite you to pieces!" yelled the fisherman. "Stop, boy! Stop!"

But it was too late to stop him now, and as he came running straight at the turtle's head, the turtle saw him, and the huge upside-down head turned quickly to face him.

The voice of the boy's mother, the stricken, agonized wail of the mother's voice rose up into the evening sky. *"David!"* it cried. *"Oh, David!"* And a moment later, the boy was throwing himself onto his knees in the sand and flinging his arms around the wrinkled old neck and hugging the creature to his chest. The boy's cheek was pressing against the turtle's head, and his lips were moving, whispering soft words that nobody else could hear. The turtle became absolutely still. Even his giant flippers stopped waving in the air.

A great sigh, a long soft sigh of relief went up from the crowd. Many people took a pace or two backward, as though trying perhaps to get a little farther away from something that was beyond their understanding. But the father and mother came forward together and stood about ten feet away from their son.

"Daddy!" the boy cried out, still caressing the old brown head. "Please do something, Daddy! Please make them let him go!"

"Can I be of any help here?" said a man in a white suit who had just come down from the hotel. This, as everyone knew, was Mr. Edwards, the manager. He was a tall, beak-nosed Englishman with a long, pink face. *"What* an extraordinary thing!" he said, looking at the boy and the turtle. "He's lucky he hasn't had his head bitten off." And to the boy, he said, "You'd better come away from there now, sonny. That thing's dangerous."

"I want them to let him go!" cried the boy, still cradling the head in his arms. "Tell them to let him go!"

"You realize he could be killed any moment," the manager said to the boy's father.

"Leave him alone," the father said.

"Rubbish," the manager said. "Go in and grab him. But be quick. And be careful."

"No," the father said.

"What do you mean, no?" said the manager. "These things are lethal! Don't you understand that?"

"Yes," the father said.

"Then for heaven's sake, man, get him away!" cried the manager. "There's going to be a very nasty accident if you don't."

"Who owns it?" the father said. "Who owns the turtle?"

"We do," the manager said. "The hotel has bought it."

"Then do me a favor," the father said. "Let me buy it from you."

The manager looked at the father but said nothing.

"You don't know my son," the father said, speaking quietly. "He'll go crazy if it's taken up to the hotel and slaughtered. He'll become hysterical."

"Just pull him away," the manager said. "And be quick about it."

"He loves animals," the father said. "He really loves them. He communicates with them."

The crowd was silent, trying to hear what was being said. Nobody moved away. They stood as though hypnotized.

"If we let it go," the manager said, "they'll only catch it again."

"Perhaps they will," the father said. "But those things can swim."

"I know they can swim," the manager said. "They'll catch him all the same. This is a valuable item, you must realize that. The shell alone is worth a lot of money."

"I don't care about the cost," the father said. "Don't worry about that. I want to buy it."

The boy was still kneeling in the sand beside the turtle, caressing its head.

The manager took a handkerchief from his breast pocket and started wiping his fingers. He was not keen to let the turtle go. He probably had the dinner menu already planned. On the other hand, he didn't want another gruesome accident on his private beach this season. Mr. Wasserman and the coconut, he told himself, had been quite enough for one year, thank you very much.

The father said, "I would deem it a great personal favor, Mr. Edwards, if you would let me buy it. And I promise you won't regret it. I'll make quite sure of that."

The manager's eyebrows went up just a fraction of an inch. He had got the point. He was being offered a bribe. That was a different matter. For a few seconds he went on wiping his hands with the handkerchief. Then he shrugged his shoulders and said, "Well, I suppose if it will make your boy feel any better . . ."

"Thank you," the father said.

"Oh, thank you!" the mother cried. "Thank you so very much!"

"Willy," the manager said, beckoning to the fisherman.

The fisherman came forward. He looked thoroughly confused. "I never seen anything like this before in my whole life," he said. "This old turtle was the fiercest I ever caught! He fought like a devil when we brought him in! It took all six of us to land him! That boy's crazy!"

"Yes, I know," the manager said. "But now I want you to let him go."

"Let him go!" the fisherman cried, aghast. "You mustn't ever let this one go, Mr. Edwards! He's broke the record! He's the biggest turtle ever been caught on this island! Easy the biggest! And what about our money?"

"You'll get your money."

"I got the other five to pay off as well," the fisherman said, pointing down the beach.

About a hundred yards down, on the water's edge, five black-skinned almost naked men were standing beside a second boat. "All six of us are in on this, equal shares," the fisherman went on. "I can't let him go till we got the money."

"I guarantee you'll get it," the manager said. "Isn't that good enough for you?"

"I'll underwrite that guarantee," the father of the boy said, stepping forward. "And there'll be an extra bonus for all six of the fishermen just as long as you let him go at once. I mean immediately, this instant."

The fisherman looked at the father. Then he looked at the manager. "Okay," he said. "If that's the way you want it."

"There's one condition," the father said. "Before you get your money, you must promise you won't go straight out and try to catch him again. Not this evening, anyway. Is that understood?"

"Sure," the fisherman said. "That's a deal." He turned and ran down the beach, calling to the other five fishermen. He shouted something to them that we couldn't hear, and in a minute or two, all six of them came back together. Five of them were carrying long thick wooden poles.

The boy was still kneeling beside the turtle's head. "David," the father said to him gently. "It's all right now, David. They're going to let him go."

The boy looked round, but he didn't take his arms from the turtle's neck, and he didn't get up. "When?" he asked.

"Now," the father said. "Right now. So you'd better come away."

"You promise?" the boy said.

"Yes, David, I promise."

The boy withdrew his arms. He got to his feet. He stepped back a few paces.

"Stand back, everyone!" shouted the fisherman called Willy. "Stand right back, everybody, please!"

The crowd moved a few yards up the beach. The tug-of-war men let go the rope and moved back with the others.

Willy got down on his hands and knees and crept very cautiously up to one side of the turtle. Then he began untying the knot in the rope. He kept well out of the range of the big flippers as he did this.

When the knot was untied, Willy crawled back. Then the five other fishermen stepped forward with their poles. The poles were about seven feet long and immensely thick. They wedged them underneath the shell of the turtle and began to rock the great creature from side to side on its shell. The shell had a high dome and was well shaped for rocking.

"Up and down!" sang the fishermen as they rocked away. "Up and down! Up and down! Up and down!" The old turtle became thoroughly upset, and who could blame it? The big flippers lashed the air frantically, and the head kept shooting in and out of the shell.

"Roll him over!" sang the fishermen. "Up and over! Roll him over! One more time and over he goes!"

The turtle tilted high up onto its side and crashed down in the sand the right way up.

But it didn't walk away at once. The huge brown head came out and peered cautiously around.

"Go, turtle, go!" the small boy called out. "Go back to the sea!"

The two hooded black eyes of the turtle peered up at the boy. The eyes were bright and lively, full of the wisdom of great age. The boy looked back at the turtle, and this time when the boy spoke, his voice was soft and intimate. "Goodbye, old man," he said. "Go far away this time." The black eyes remained resting on the boy for a few seconds more. Nobody moved. Then, with great dignity, the massive beast turned away and began waddling toward the edge of the ocean. He didn't hurry. He moved sedately over the sandy beach, the big shell rocking gently from side to side as he went.

The crowd watched in silence.

He entered the water.

He kept going.

Soon he was swimming. He was in his element now. He swam gracefully and very fast, with the head held high. The sea was calm, and he made little waves that fanned out behind him on both sides, like the waves of a boat.

It was several minutes before we lost sight of him, and by then he was halfway to the horizon.

The guests began wandering back toward the hotel. They were curiously subdued. There was no joking or bantering now, no laughing. Something had happened. Something strange had come fluttering across the beach.

I walked back to my small balcony and sat down with a cigarette. I had an uneasy feeling that this was not the end of the affair.

The next morning at eight o'clock, the Jamaican girl, the one who had told me about Mr. Wasserman and the coconut, brought a glass of orange juice to my room.

"Big *big* fuss in the hotel this morning," she said as she placed the glass on the table and drew back the curtains. "Everyone flying about all over the place like they was crazy."

"Why? What's happened?"

"That little boy in number twelve, he's vanished. He disappeared in the night."

"You mean the turtle boy?"

"That's him," she said. "His parents is raising the roof and the manager's going mad."

"How long's he been missing?"

"About two hours ago his father found his bed empty. But he could've gone any time in the night I reckon."

"Yes," I said. "He could."

"Everybody in the hotel searching high and low," she said. "And a police car just arrived."

"Maybe he just got up early and went for a climb on the rocks," I said.

Her large, dark, haunted-looking eyes rested a moment on my

face, then traveled away. "I do not think so," she said, and out she went.

I slipped on some clothes and hurried down to the beach. On the beach itself, two native policemen in khaki uniforms were standing with Mr. Edwards, the manager. Mr. Edwards was doing the talking. The policemen were listening patiently. In the distance, at both ends of the beach, I could see small groups of people, hotel servants as well as hotel guests, spreading out and heading for the rocks. The morning was beautiful. The sky was smoke blue, faintly glazed with yellow. The sun was up and making diamonds all over the smooth sea. And Mr. Edwards was talking loudly to the two native policemen, and waving his arms.

I wanted to help. What should I do? Which way should I go? It would be pointless simply to follow the others. So I just kept walking toward Mr. Edwards.

About then, I saw the fishing boat. The long wooden canoe with a single mast and a flapping brown sail was still some way out to sea, but it was heading for the beach. The two natives aboard, one at either end, were paddling hard. They were paddling very hard. The paddles rose and fell at such a terrific speed they might have been in a race. I stopped and watched them. Why the great rush to reach the shore? Quite obviously they had something to tell. I kept my eyes on the boat. Over to my left, I could hear Mr. Edwards saying to the two policemen, "It is perfectly ridiculous. I can't have people disappearing just like that from the hotel. You'd better find him fast, you understand me? He's either wandered off somewhere and got lost or he's been kidnapped. Either way, it's the responsibility of the police. . . ."

The fishing boat skimmed over the sea and came gliding up onto the sand at the water's edge. Both men dropped their paddles and jumped out. They started running up the beach. I recognized the one in front as Willy. When he caught sight of the manager and the two policemen, he made straight for them.

"Hey, Mr. Edwards!" Willy called out. "We just seen a crazy thing!"

The manager stiffened and jerked back his neck. The two policemen remained impassive. They were used to excitable people. They met them every day.

Willy stopped in front of the group, his chest heaving in and out with heavy breathing. The other fisherman was close behind him. Their black skins were shining with sweat.

"We been paddling full speed for a long way," Willy said, excusing his out-of-breathness. "We thought we ought to come back and tell it as quick as we can."

"Tell what?" the manager said. "What did you see?"

"It was crazy man! Absolutely crazy!"

"Get on with it, Willy, for heaven's sake."

"You won't believe it," Willy said. "There ain't nobody going to believe it. Isn't that right, Tom?"

"That's right," the other fisherman said, nodding vigorously. "If Willy here hadn't been with me to prove it, I wouldn't have believed it myself!"

"Believed what?" Mr. Edwards said. "Just tell us what you saw."

"We'd gone off early," Willy said, "about four o'clock this morning, and we must've been a couple of miles out before it got light enough to see anything properly. Suddenly, as the sun comes up, we see right ahead of us, not more'n fifty yards away, we see something we couldn't believe not even with our own eyes. . . ."

"What?" snapped Mr. Edwards. "For heaven's sake, get on!"

"We sees that old monster turtle swimming away out there, the one on the beach yesterday, and we sees the boy sitting high up on the turtle's back and riding him over the sea like a horse!"

"You gotta believe it!" the other fisherman cried. "I sees it too, so you gotta believe it!"

Mr. Edwards looked at the two policemen. The two policemen looked at the fishermen. "You wouldn't be having us on, would you?" one of the policemen said.

"I swear it!" cried Willy. "It's the gospel truth! There's this tiny little boy riding high up on the old turtle's back and his feet isn't even touching the water! He's dry as a bone and sitting there comfy and easy as could be! So we go after them. Of course we go after them. At first we try creeping up on them very quietly, like we always do when we're catching a turtle, but the boy sees us. We aren't very far away at this time, you understand. No more than from here to the edge of the water. And when the boy sees us, he sort of leans forward as if he's saying something to that old turtle, and the turtle's head comes up and he starts swimming like the clappers of hell! Man, could that turtle go! Tom and me can paddle pretty quick when we want to, but we've no chance against that monster! No chance at all! He's going at least twice as fast as we are! Easy twice as fast, what you say, Tom?"

"I'd say he's going *three times* as fast," Tom said. "And I'll tell you why. In about ten or fifteen minutes, they're a mile ahead of us."

"Why on earth didn't you call out to the boy?" the manager asked. "Why didn't you speak to him earlier on, when you were closer?"

"We never *stop* calling out, man!" Willy cried. "As soon as the boy sees us and we're not trying to creep up on them any longer, then we start yelling. We yell everything under the sun at that boy to try and get him aboard. 'Hey boy!' I yell at him. 'You come on back with us! We'll give you a lift home! That ain't no good what you're doing there, boy! Jump off and swim while you got the chance and we'll pick you up! Go on, boy, jump! Your mammy must be waiting for you at home, boy, so why don't you come on in with us?' And once I shouted at him, 'Listen, boy! We're gonna make you a promise! We promise not to catch that old turtle if you come with us!' "

"Did he answer you at all?" the manager asked.

"He never even looks round!" Willy said. "He sits high up on that shell and he's sort of rocking backward and forward with his body just like he's urging the old turtle to go faster and faster! You're gonna lose that little boy, Mr. Edwards, unless someone gets out there real quick and grabs him away!"

The manager's normally pink face had turned white as paper. "Which way were they heading?" he asked sharply.

"North," Willy answered. "Almost due north."

"Right!" the manager said. "We'll take the speedboat! I want you with us, Willy. And you, Tom."

The manager, the two policemen and the two fishermen ran down to where the boat that was used for water skiing lay beached on the sand. They pushed the boat out, and even the manager lent a hand, wading up to his knees in his well-pressed white trousers. Then they all climbed in.

I watched them go zooming off.

Two hours later, I watched them coming back. They had seen nothing.

All through that day, speedboats and yachts from other hotels along the coast searched the ocean. In the afternoon, the boy's father hired a helicopter. He rode in it himself, and they were up there three hours. They found no trace of the turtle or the boy.

For a week, the search went on, but with no result.

And now, nearly a year has gone by since it happened. In that time, there has been only one significant bit of news. A party of Americans, out from Nassau in the Bahamas, were deep-sea fishing off a large island called Eleuthera. There are literally thousands of coral reefs and small uninhabited islands in this area, and upon one of these tiny islands, the captain of the yacht saw through his binoculars the figure of a small person. There was a sandy beach on the island, and the small person was walking on the beach. The binoculars were passed around, and everyone who looked through them agreed that it was a child of some sort. There was, of course, a lot of excitement on board, and the fishing lines were quickly reeled in. The captain steered the yacht straight for the island. When they were half a mile off, they were able, through the binoculars, to see clearly that the figure on the beach was a boy, and although sunburned, he was almost certainly white-skinned, not a native. At that point, the watchers on the yacht also spotted what looked like a giant turtle on the sand near the boy. What happened next happened very quickly. The boy, who had probably caught sight of the approaching yacht, jumped onto the turtle's back, and the huge creature entered the water and swam at great speed around the island and out of sight. The yacht searched for two hours, but nothing more was seen either of the boy or the turtle.

There is no reason to disbelieve this report. There were five people on the yacht. Four of them were Americans and the captain was a Bahamian from Nassau. All of them in turn saw the boy and the turtle through the binoculars.

To reach Eleuthera Island from Jamaica by sea, one must first travel northeast for two hundred and fifty miles and pass through the Windward Passage between Cuba and Haiti. Then one must go north-northwest for a further three hundred miles at least. This is a total distance of five hundred and fifty miles, which is a very long journey for a small boy to make on the shell of a giant turtle.

Who knows what to think of all this?

One day, perhaps, he will come back, though I personally doubt it. I have a feeling he's quite happy where he is.

The Hitchhiker

1975

I HAD a new car. It was an exciting toy, a big BMW 3.3 Li, which means 3.3 liter, long wheelbase, fuel injection. It had a top speed of 129 mph and terrific acceleration. The body was pale blue. The seats inside were darker blue and they were made of leather, genuine soft leather of the finest quality. The windows were electrically operated and so was the sunroof. The radio aerial popped up when I switched on the radio, and disappeared when I switched it off. The powerful engine growled and grunted impatiently at slow speeds, but at sixty miles an hour the growling stopped and the motor began to purr with pleasure.

I was driving up to London by myself. It was a lovely June day. They were haymaking in the fields and there were buttercups along both sides of the road. I was whispering along at 70 mph, leaning back comfortably in my seat, with no more than a couple of fingers resting lightly on the wheel to keep her steady. Ahead of me I saw a man thumbing a lift. I touched the brake and brought the car to a stop beside him. I always stopped for hitchhikers. I knew just how it used to feel to be standing on the side of a country road watching the cars go by. I hated the drivers for pretending they didn't see me, especially the ones in big cars with three empty seats. The large expensive cars seldom stopped. It was always the smaller ones that offered you a lift, or the old rusty ones or the ones that were already crammed full of children and the driver would say, "I think we can squeeze in one more."

The hitchhiker poked his head through the open window and said, "Going to London, guv'nor?"

"Yes," I said. "Jump in."

He got in and I drove on.

He was a small ratty-faced man with gray teeth. His eyes were dark and quick and clever, like rat's eyes, and his ears were slightly pointed at the top. He had a cloth cap on his head and he was wearing a grayish-colored jacket with enormous pockets. The gray jacket, together with the quick eyes and the pointed ears, made him look more than anything like some sort of a huge human rat.

"What part of London are you headed for?" I asked him.

"I'm goin' right through London and out the other side," he said. "I'm goin' to Epsom, for the races. It's Derby Day today."

"So it is," I said. "I wish I were going with you. I love betting on horses."

"I never bet on horses," he said. "I don't even watch 'em run. That's a stupid silly business."

"Then why do you go?" I asked.

He didn't seem to like that question. His little ratty face went absolutely blank and he sat there staring straight ahead at the road, saying nothing.

"I expect you help to work the betting machines or something like that," I said.

"That's even sillier," he answered. "There's no fun working them lousy machines and selling tickets to mugs. Any fool could do that."

There was a long silence. I decided not to question him any more. I remembered how irritated I used to get in my hitchhiking days when drivers kept asking *me* questions. Where are you going? Why are you going there? What's your job? Are you married? Do you have a girl friend? What's her name? How old are you? And so forth and so forth. I used to hate it.

"I'm sorry," I said. "It's none of my business what you do. The trouble is, I'm a writer, and most writers are terribly nosy."

"You write books?" he asked.

"Yes."

"Writin' books is okay," he said. "It's what I call a skilled trade. I'm in a skilled trade too. The folks I despise is them that spend all their lives doin' crummy old routine jobs with no skill in 'em at all. You see what I mean?"

"Yes."

"The secret of life," he said, "is to become very very good at somethin' that's very very 'ard to do."

"Like you," I said.

"Exactly. You and me both."

"What makes you think that *I'm* any good at my job?" I asked. "There's an awful lot of bad writers around."

"You wouldn't be drivin' about in a car like this if you weren't no good at it," he answered. "It must've cost a tidy packet, this little job."

"It wasn't cheap."

"What can she do flat out?" he asked.

"One hundred and twenty-nine miles an hour," I told him.

"I'll bet she won't do it."

"I'll bet she will."

"All car-makers is liars," he said. "You can buy any car you like and it'll never do what the makers say it will in the ads."

"This one will."

"Open 'er up then and prove it," he said. "Go on, guv'nor, open 'er right up and let's see what she'll do."

There is a traffic circle at Chalfont St. Peter and immediately beyond it there's a long straight section of divided highway. We came out of the circle onto the highway and I pressed my foot hard down on the accelerator. The big car leaped forward as though she'd been stung. In ten seconds or so, we were doing ninety.

"Lovely!" he cried. "Beautiful! Keep goin'!"

I had the accelerator jammed right down against the floor and I held it there.

"One hundred!" he shouted. "A hundred and five! A hundred and ten! A hundred and fifteen! Go on! Don't slack off!"

I was in the outside lane and we flashed past several cars as though they were standing still—a green Mini, a big cream-colored Citroen, a white Land Rover, a huge truck with a container on the back, an orange-colored Volkswagen Minibus. . . .

"A hundred and twenty!" my passenger shouted, jumping up and down. "Go on! Go on! Get 'er up to one-two-nine!"

At that moment, I heard the scream of a police siren. It was so loud it seemed to be right inside the car, and then a cop on a motorcycle loomed up alongside us on the inside lane and went past us and raised a hand for us to stop.

"Oh, my sainted aunt!" I said. "That's torn it!"

The cop must have been doing about a hundred and thirty when he passed us, and he took plenty of time slowing down. Finally, he pulled to the side of the road and I pulled in behind him. "I didn't know police motorcycles could go as fast as that," I said rather lamely.

"That one can," my passenger said. "It's the same make as yours. It's a BMW R90S. Fastest bike on the road. That's what they're usin' nowadays."

The cop got off his motorcycle and leaned the machine sideways onto its prop stand. Then he took off his gloves and placed them carefully on the seat. He was in no hurry now. He had us where he wanted us and he knew it.

"This is real trouble," I said. "I don't like it one little bit."

"Don't talk to 'im more than is necessary, you understand," my companion said. "Just sit tight and keep mum."

Like an executioner approaching his victim, the cop came strolling slowly toward us. He was a big meaty man with a belly, and his blue breeches were skin-tight around his enormous thighs. His goggles were pulled up onto the helmet, showing a smoldering red face with wide cheeks.

We sat there like guilty schoolboys, waiting for him to arrive.

"Watch out for this man," my passenger whispered, " 'e looks mean as the devil."

The cop came around to my open window and placed one meaty hand on the sill. "What's the hurry?" he said.

"No hurry, officer," I answered.

"Perhaps there's a woman in the back having a baby and you're rushing her to hospital? Is that it?"

"No, officer."

"Or perhaps your house is on fire and you're dashing home to rescue the family from upstairs?" His voice was dangerously soft and mocking.

"My house isn't on fire, officer."

"In that case," he said, "you've got yourself into a nasty mess, haven't you? Do you know what the speed limit is in this country?"

"Seventy," I said.

"And do you mind telling me exactly what speed you were doing just now?"

I shrugged and didn't say anything.

When he spoke next, he raised his voice so loud that I jumped. *"One hundred and twenty miles per hour!"* he barked. "That's *fifty* miles an hour over the limit!"

He turned his head and spat out a big gob of spit. It landed on the wing of my car and started sliding down over my beautiful blue paint. Then he turned back again and stared hard at my passenger. "And who are you?" he asked sharply.

"He's a hitchhiker," I said. "I'm giving him a lift."

"I didn't ask you," he said. "I asked him."

" 'Ave I done somethin' wrong?" my passenger asked. His voice was soft and oily as haircream.

"That's more than likely," the cop answered. "Anyway, you're a witness. I'll deal with you in a minute. Driver's license," he snapped, holding out his hand.

I gave him my driver's license.

He unbuttoned the left-hand breast pocket of his tunic and brought out the dreaded book of tickets. Carefully, he copied the name and address from my license. Then he gave it back to me. He strolled around to the front of the car and read the number from the license plate and wrote that down as well. He filled in the date, the time and the details of my offense. Then he tore out the top copy of the ticket. But before handing it to me, he checked that all the information had come through clearly on his own carbon copy. Finally, he replaced the book in his breast pocket and fastened the button.

"Now you," he said to my passenger, and he walked around to the other side of the car. From the other breast pocket he produced a small black notebook. "Name?" he snapped.

"Michael Fish," my passenger said.

"Address?"

"Fourteen, Windsor Lane, Luton."

"Show me something to prove this is your real name and address," the policeman said.

My passenger fished in his pockets and came out with a driver's license of his own. The policeman checked the name and address and handed it back to him. "What's your job?" he asked sharply.

"I'm an 'od carrier."

"A *what?*"

"An 'od carrier."

"Spell it."

"H-o-d c-a—"

"That'll do. And what's a hod carrier, may I ask?"

"An 'od carrier, officer, is a person 'oo carries the cement up the ladder to the bricklayer. And the 'od is what 'ee carries it in. It's got a long 'handle, and on the top you've got bits of wood set at an angle . . ."

"All right, all right. Who's your employer?"

"Don't 'ave one. I'm unemployed."

The cop wrote all this down in the black notebook. Then he returned the book to its pocket and did up the button.

"When I get back to the station I'm going to do a little checking up on you," he said to my passenger.

"Me? What've I done wrong?" the rat-faced man asked.

"I don't like your face, that's all," the cop said. "And we just might have a picture of it somewhere in our files." He strolled round the car and returned to my window.

"I suppose you know you're in serious trouble," he said to me.

"Yes, officer."

"You won't be driving this fancy car of yours again for a very long time, not after *we've* finished with you. You won't be driving *any* car again, come to that, for several years. And a good thing, too. I hope they lock you up for a spell into the bargain."

"You mean prison?" I asked, alarmed.

"Absolutely," he said, smacking his lips. "In the clink. Behind the bars. Along with all the other criminals who break the law. *And* a hefty fine into the bargain. Nobody will be more pleased about that than me. I'll see you in court, both of you. You'll be getting a summons to appear."

He turned away and walked over to his motorcycle. He flipped the prop stand back into position with his foot and swung his leg over the saddle. Then he kicked the starter and roared off up the road out of sight.

"Phew!" I gasped. "That's done it."

"We was caught," my passenger said. "We was caught good and proper."

"I was caught, you mean."

"That's right," he said. "What you goin' to do now, guv'nor?"

"I'm going straight up to London to talk to my solicitor," I said. I started the car and drove on.

"You mustn't believe what 'ee said to you about goin' to prison," my passenger said. "They don't put nobody in the clink just for speedin'."

"Are you sure of that?" I asked.

"I'm positive," he answered. "They can take your license away and they can give you a whoppin' big fine, but that'll be the end of it."

I felt tremendously relieved.

"By the way," I said, "why did you lie to him?"

"Who, me?" he said. "What makes you think I lied?"

"You told him you were an unemployed hod carrier. But you told *me* you were in a highly skilled trade."

"So I am," he said. "But it don't pay to tell everythin' to a copper."

"So what *do* you do?" I asked him.

"Ah," he said slyly. "That'd be tellin', wouldn't it?"

"Is it something you're ashamed of?"

"Ashamed?" he cried. "Me, ashamed of my job? I'm about as proud of it as anybody could be in the entire world!"

"Then why won't you tell me?"

"You writers really is nosy parkers, aren't you?" he said. "And you ain't goin' to be 'appy, I don't think, until you've found out exactly what the answer is?"

"I don't really care one way or the other," I told him, lying.

He gave me a crafty little ratty look out of the sides of his eyes. "I think you do care," he said. "I can see it on your face that you think I'm in some kind of a very peculiar trade and you're just achin' to know what it is."

I didn't like the way he read my thoughts. I kept quiet and stared at the road ahead.

"You'd be right, too," he went on. "I *am* in a very peculiar trade. I'm in the queerest peculiar trade of 'em all."

I waited for him to go on.

"That's why I 'as to be extra careful oo' I'm talkin' to, you see. 'Ow am I to know, for instance, you're not another copper in plain clothes?"

"Do I look like a copper?"

"No," he said. "You don't. And you ain't. Any fool could tell that."

He took from his pocket a tin of tobacco and a packet of cigarette papers and started to roll a cigarette. I was watching him out of the corner of one eye, and the speed with which he performed this rather difficult operation was incredible. The cigarette was rolled and ready in about five seconds. He ran his tongue along the edge of the paper, stuck it down and popped the cigarette between his lips. Then, as if from nowhere, a lighter appeared in his hand. The lighter flamed. The cigarette was lit. The lighter disappeared. It was altogether a remarkable performance.

"I've never seen anyone roll a cigarette as fast as that," I said.

"Ah," he said, taking a deep suck of smoke. "So you noticed."

"Of course I noticed. It was quite fantastic."

He sat back and smiled. It pleased him very much that I had noticed how quickly he could roll a cigarette. "You want to know what makes me able to do it?" he asked.

"Go on then."

"It's because I've got fantastic fingers. These fingers of mine," he said, holding up both hands high in front of him, "are quicker and cleverer than the fingers of the best piano player in the world!"

"Are you a piano player?"

"Don't be daft," he said. "Do I look like a piano player?"

I glanced at his fingers. They were so beautifully shaped, so slim and long and elegant, they didn't seem to belong to the rest of him at all. They looked more like the fingers of a brain surgeon or a watchmaker.

"My job," he went on, "is a hundred times more difficult than playin' the piano. Any twerp can learn to do that. There's titchy little kids learnin' to play the piano in almost any 'ouse you go into these days. That's right, ain't it?"

"More or less," I said.

"Of course it's right. But there's not one person in ten million can learn to do what I do. Not one in ten million! 'Ow about that?"

"Amazing," I said.

"You're darn right it's amazin'," he said.

"I think I know what you do," I said. "You do conjuring tricks. You're a conjuror."

"Me?" he snorted. "A conjuror? Can you picture me goin' round crummy kid's parties makin' rabbits come out of top 'ats?"

"Then you're a card player. You get people into card games and you deal yourself marvelous hands."

"Me! A rotten cardsharper!" he cried. "That's a miserable racket if ever there was one."

"All right. I give up."

I was taking the car along slowly now, at no more than forty miles an hour, to make quite sure I wasn't stopped again. We had come onto the main London-Oxford road and were running down the hill toward Denham.

Suddenly, my passenger was holding up a black leather belt in his hand. "Ever seen this before?" he asked. The belt had a brass buckle of unusual design.

"Hey!" I said. "That's mine, isn't it? It *is* mine! Where did you get it?"

He grinned and waved the belt gently from side to side. "Where d'you think I got it?" he said. "Off the top of your trousers, of course."

I reached down and felt for my belt. It was gone.

"You mean you took it off me while we've been driving along?" I asked flabbergasted.

He nodded, watching me all the time with those little black ratty eyes.

"That's impossible," I said. "You'd have had to undo the buckle and slide the whole thing out through the loops all the way round. I'd have seen you doing it. And even if I hadn't seen you, I'd have felt it."

"Ah, but you didn't, did you?" he said, triumphant. He dropped the belt on his lap, and now all at once there was a brown shoelace dangling from his fingers. "And what about this, then?" he exclaimed, waving the shoelace.

"What about it?" I said.

"Anyone around 'ere missin' a shoelace?" he asked, grinning.

I glanced down at my shoes. The lace of one of them was missing. "Good grief!" I said. "How did you do that? I never saw you bending down."

"You never saw nothin'," he said proudly. "You never even saw me move an inch. And you know why?"

"Yes," I said. "Because you've got fantastic fingers."

"Exactly right!" he cried. "You catch on pretty quick, don't you?" He sat back and sucked away at his homemade cigarette, blowing the smoke out in a thin stream against the windshield. He knew he had impressed me greatly with those two tricks, and this made him very happy. "I don't want to be late," he said. "What time is it?"

"There's a clock in front of you," I told him.

"I don't trust car clocks," he said. "What does your watch say?"

I hitched up my sleeve to look at the watch on my wrist. It wasn't there. I looked at the man. He looked back at me, grinning.

"You've taken that, too," I said.

He held out his hand and there was my watch lying in his palm. "Nice bit of stuff, this," he said. "Superior quality. Eighteen-carat gold. Easy to sell, too. It's never any trouble gettin' rid of quality goods."

"I'd like it back, if you don't mind," I said rather huffily.

He placed the watch carefully on the leather tray in front of him. "I wouldn't nick anything from you, guv'nor," he said. "You're my pal. You're givin' me a lift."

"I'm glad to hear it," I said.

"All I'm doin' is answerin' your question," he went on. "You asked me what I did for a livin' and I'm showin' you."

"What else have you got of mine?"

He smiled again, and now he started to take from the pocket of his jacket one thing after another that belonged to me—my driver's license, a key ring with four keys on it, some pound notes, a few coins, a letter from my publishers, my diary, a stubby old pencil, a cigarette lighter, and last of all, a beautiful old sapphire ring with pearls around it belonging to my wife. I was taking the ring up to a jeweler in London because one of the pearls was missing.

"Now *there's* another lovely piece of goods," he said, turning the ring over in his fingers. "That's eighteenth century, if I'm not mistaken, from the reign of King George the Third."

"You're right," I said, impressed. "You're absolutely right."

He put the ring on the leather tray with the other items.

"So you're a pickpocket," I said.

"I don't like that word," he answered. "It's a coarse and vulgar word. Pickpockets is coarse and vulgar people who only do easy little amateur jobs. They lift money from blind old ladies."

"What do you call yourself, then?"

"Me? I'm a fingersmith. I'm a professional fingersmith." He spoke the words solemnly and proudly, as though he were telling me he was the President of the Royal College of Surgeons or the Archbishop of Cantebury.

"I've never heard that word before," I said. "Did you invent it?"

"Of course I didn't invent it," he replied. "It's the name given to them who's risen to the very top of the profession. You've 'heard of a goldsmith and a silversmith, for instance. They're experts with gold and silver. I'm an expert with my fingers, so I'm a fingersmith."

"It must be an interesting job."

"It's a marvelous job," he answered. "It's lovely."

"And that's why you go to the races?"

"Race meetings is easy meat," he said. "You just stand around after the race, watchin' for the lucky ones to queue up and draw their money. And when you see someone collectin' a big bundle of notes, you simply follows after 'im and 'elps yourself. But don't get me wrong, guv'nor. I never takes nothin' from a loser. Nor from poor people neither. I only go after them as can afford it, the winners and the rich."

"That's very thoughtful of you," I said. "How often do you get caught?"

"Caught?" he cried, disgusted. "*Me* get caught! It's only pick-pockets get caught. Fingersmiths never. Listen, I could take the false teeth out of your mouth if I wanted to and you wouldn't even catch me!"

"I don't have false teeth," I said.

"I know you don't," he answered. "Otherwise I'd 'ave 'ad 'em out long ago!"

I believed him. Those long slim fingers of his seemed able to do anything.

We drove on for a while without talking.

"That policeman's going to check up on you pretty thoroughly," I said. "Doesn't that worry you a bit?"

"Nobody's checkin' up on me," he said.

"Of course they are. He's got your name and address written down most carefully in his black book."

The man gave me another of his sly ratty little smiles. "Ah," he said. "So 'ee 'as. But I'll bet 'ee ain't got it all written down in 'is memory as well. I've never known a copper yet with a decent memory. Some of 'em can't even remember their own names."

"What's memory got to do with it?" I asked. "It's written down in his book, isn't it?"

"Yes, guv'nor, it is. But the trouble is, 'ee's lost the book. 'Ee's lost both books, the one with my name in it *and* the one with yours."

In the long delicate fingers of his right hand, the man was holding up in triumph the two books he had taken from the policeman's pockets. "Easiest job I ever done," he announced proudly.

I nearly swerved the car into a milk truck, I was so excited.

"That copper's got nothin' on either of us now," he said.

"You're a genius!" I cried.

" 'Ee's got no names, no addresses, no car number, no nothin'," he said.

"You're brilliant!"

"I think you'd better pull in off this main road as soon as possible," he said. "Then we'd better build a little bonfire and burn these books."

"You're a fantastic fellow!" I exclaimed.

"Thank you, guv'nor," he said. "It's always nice to be appreciated."

The Wonderful Story
of Henry Sugar

1976

One

Henry Sugar was forty-one years old and unmarried. He
was also wealthy.

He was wealthy because he had had a rich father, who was now
dead. He was unmarried because he was too selfish to share any of
his money with a wife.

He was six feet two inches tall, but he wasn't really as good-
looking as he thought he was.

He paid a great deal of attention to his clothes. He went to an
expensive tailor for his suits, to a shirtmaker for his shirts, and to a
bootmaker for his shoes.

He used a costly aftershave on his face, and he kept his hands
soft with a cream that contained turtle oil.

His hairdresser trimmed his hair once every ten days, and he
always took a manicure at the same time.

His upper front teeth had been capped at incredible expense
because the originals had had a rather nasty yellowish tinge. A small
mole had been removed from his left cheek by a plastic surgeon.

He drove a Ferrari car that must have cost him about the same
as a country cottage.

He lived in London in the summer, but as soon as the first frosts
appeared in October, he was off to the West Indies or the South of
France, where he stayed with friends. All his friends were wealthy
from inherited money.

Henry had never done a day's work in his life, and his personal
motto, which he had invented himself, was this: *It is better to incur a
mild rebuke than to perform an onerous task.* His friends thought this was
hilarious.

Men like Henry Sugar are to be found drifting like seaweed all
over the world. They can be seen especially in London, New York,
Paris, Nassau, Montego Bay, Cannes and St. Tropez. They are not

particularly bad men. But they are not good men either. They are of no real importance. They are simply a part of the decoration.

All of them, all wealthy people of this type, have one peculiarity in common: they have a terrific urge to make themselves still wealthier than they already are. The million is never enough. Nor is the two million. Always, they have this insatiable longing to get more money. And that is because they live in constant terror of waking up one morning and finding there's nothing in the bank.

These people all employ the same methods for trying to increase their fortunes. They buy stocks and shares, and watch them going up and down. They play roulette and blackjack for high stakes in casinos. They bet on horses. They bet on just about everything. Henry Sugar had once staked a thousand pounds on the result of a tortoise race on Lord Liverpool's tennis lawn. And he had wagered double that sum with a man called Esmond Hanbury on an even sillier bet, which was as follows: They let Henry's dog out into the garden and watched it through the window. But before the dog was let out, each man had to guess beforehand what would be the first object the dog would lift its leg against. Would it be a wall, a post, a bush or a tree? Esmond chose a wall. Henry, who had been studying his dog's habits for days with a view to making this particular bet, chose a tree, and he won the money.

With ridiculous games such as these did Henry and his friends try to conquer the deadly boredom of being both idle and wealthy.

Henry himself, as you may have noticed, was not above cheating a little on these friends of his if he saw the chance. The bet with the dog was definitely not honest. Nor, if you want to know, was the bet on the tortoise race. Henry cheated on that one by secretly forcing a little sleeping-pill powder into the mouth of his opponent's tortoise an hour before the race.

And now that you've got a rough idea of the sort of person Henry Sugar was, I can begin my story.

One summer weekend, Henry drove down from London to Guildford to stay with Sir William Wyndham. The house was magnificent, and so were the grounds, but when Henry arrived on that Saturday afternoon, it was already pelting with rain. Tennis was out, croquet was out. So was swimming in Sir William's outdoor pool. The host and his guests sat glumly in the drawing room, staring at the rain splashing against the windows. The very rich are enormously resentful of bad weather. It is the one discomfort that their money cannot do anything about.

Somebody in the room said, "Let's have a game of canasta for lovely high stakes."

The others thought that a splendid idea, but as there were five people in all, one would have to sit out. They cut the cards. Henry drew the lowest, the unlucky card.

The other four sat down and began to play. Henry was annoyed at being out of the game. He wandered out of the drawing room into the great hall. He stared at the pictures for a few moments, then he walked on through the house, bored to death and having nothing to do. Finally, he mooched into the library.

Sir William's father had been a famous book collector, and all four walls of this huge room were lined with books from floor to ceiling. Henry Sugar was not impressed. He wasn't even interested. The only books he read were detective novels and thrillers. He ambled aimlessly round the room, looking to see if he could find any of the sort of books he liked. But the ones in Sir William's library were all leather-bound volumes with names on them like Balzac, Ibsen, Voltaire, Johnson and Pepys. Boring rubbish, the whole lot of it, Henry told himself. And he was just about to leave when his eye was caught and held by a book that was quite different from all the others. It was so slim he would never have noticed it if it hadn't been sticking out a little from the ones on either side. And when he pulled it from the shelf, he saw that it was actually nothing more than a cardboard-covered exercise book of the kind children use at school. The cover was dark blue, but there was nothing written on it. Henry opened the exercise book. On the first page, handprinted in ink, it said:

A REPORT ON AN INTERVIEW WITH IMHRAT KHAN,
THE MAN WHO COULD SEE WITHOUT HIS EYES
BY JOHN F. CARTWRIGHT, M.D.
BOMBAY, INDIA   DECEMBER 1934

That sounds mildly interesting, Henry told himself. He turned over a page. What followed was all handwritten in black ink. The writing was clear and neat. Henry read the first two pages standing up. Suddenly, he found himself wanting to read on. This was good stuff. It was fascinating. He carried the little book over to a leather armchair by the window and settled himself comfortably. Then he started reading again from the beginning.

Two

This is what Henry read in the little blue exercise book:

I, John Cartwright, am a surgeon at Bombay General Hospital. On the morning of the second of December, 1934, I was in the doctors' rest room having a cup of tea. There were three other doctors there with me, all having a well-earned tea break. They were Dr. Marshall, Dr. Phillips and Dr. Macfarlane. There was a knock on the door. "Come in," I said.

The door opened and an Indian came in who smiled at us and said, "Excuse me, please. Could I ask you gentlemen a favor?"

The doctors' rest room was a most private place. Nobody other than a doctor was allowed to enter it except in an emergency.

"This is a private room," Dr. Macfarlane said sharply.

"Yes, yes," he answered. "I know that and I am very sorry to be bursting in like this, sirs, but I have a most interesting thing to show you."

All four of us were pretty annoyed and we didn't say anything.

"Gentlemen," he said. "I am a man who can see without using his eyes."

We still didn't invite him to go on. But we didn't kick him out either.

"You can cover my eyes in any way you wish," he said. "You can bandage my head with fifty bandages and I will still be able to read you a book."

He seemed perfectly serious. I felt my curiosity beginning to stir. "Come here," I said. He came over to me. "Turn around." He turned around. I placed my hands firmly over his eyes, holding the lids closed. "Now," I said, "one of the other doctors in the room is going to hold up some fingers. Tell me how many he's holding up."

Dr. Marshall held up seven fingers.

"Seven," the Indian said.

"Once more," I said.

Dr. Marshall clenched both fists and hid all his fingers.

"No fingers," the Indian said.

I removed my hands from his eyes. "Not bad," I said.

"Hold on," Dr. Marshall said. "Let's try this." There was a doctor's white coat hanging from a peg on the door. Dr. Marshall took it down and rolled in into a sort of long scarf. He then wound it around the Indian's head and held the ends tight at the back. "Try him now," Dr. Marshall said.

I took a key from my pocket. "What is this?" I asked.

"A key," he answered.

I put the key back and held up an empty hand. "What is this object?" I asked him.

"There isn't any object," the Indian said. "Your hand is empty."

Dr. Marshall removed the covering from the man's eyes. "How do you do it?" he asked. "What's the trick?"

"There is no trick," the Indian said. "It is a genuine thing that I have managed after years of training."

"What sort of training?" I asked.

"Forgive me, sir," he said, "but that is a private matter."

"Then why did you come here?" I asked.

"I came to request a favor of you," he said.

The Indian was a tall man of about thirty with light brown skin the color of a coconut. He had a small black moustache. Also, there was a curious matting of black hair growing all over the outsides of his ears. He wore a white cotton robe, and he had sandals on his bare feet.

"You see, gentlemen," he went on. "I am at present earning my living by working in a traveling theater, and we have just arrived here in Bombay. Tonight we give our opening performance."

"Where do you give it?" I asked.

"In the Royal Palace Hall," he answered. "In Acacia Street. I am the star performer. I am billed on the program as 'Imhrat Khan, the man who sees without his eyes.' And it is my duty to advertise the show in a big way. If we don't sell tickets, we don't eat."

"What does this have to do with us?" I asked him.

"Very interesting for you," he said. "Lots of fun. Let me explain. You see, whenever our theater arrives in a new town, I myself go straight to the largest hospital and I ask the doctors there to bandage my eyes. I ask them to do it in the most expert fashion. They must make sure my eyes are completely covered many times over. It is important that this job is done by doctors, otherwise people will think I am cheating. Then, when I am fully bandaged, I go out into the street and I do a dangerous thing."

"What do you mean by that?" I asked.

"What I mean is that I do something that is extremely dangerous for someone who cannot see."

"What do you do?" I asked.

"It is very interesting," he said. "And you will see me do it if you will be so kind as to bandage me up first. It would be a great favor to me if you will do this little thing, sirs."

I looked at the other three doctors. Dr. Phillips said he had to go back to his patients. Dr. Macfarlane said the same. Dr. Marshall said, "Well, why not? It might be amusing. It won't take a minute."

"I'm with you," I said. "But let's do the job properly. Let's make absolutely sure he can't peep."

"You are extremely kind," the Indian said. "Please do whatever you wish."

Dr. Phillips and Dr. Macfarlane left the room.

"Before we bandage him," I said to Dr. Marshall, "let's first of all seal down his eyelids. When we've done that, we'll fill his eye sockets with something soft and solid and sticky."

"Such as what?" Dr. Marshall asked.

"What about dough?"

"Dough would be perfect," Dr. Marshall said.

"Right," I said. "If you will nip down to the hospital bakery and get some dough, I'll take him into the surgery and seal his lids."

I led the Indian out of the rest room and down the long hospital corridor to the surgery. "Lie down there," I said, indicating the high bed. He lay down. I took a small bottle from the cupboard. It had an eyedropper in the top. "This is something called colodion," I told him. "It will harden over your closed eyelids so that it is impossible for you to open them."

"How do I get it off afterward?" he asked me.

"Alcohol will dissolve it away quite easily," I said. "It's perfectly harmless. Close your eyes now."

The Indian closed his eyes. I applied colodion to both lids. "Keep them closed," I said. "Wait for it to harden."

In a couple of minutes, the colodion had made a hard film over the eyelids, sticking them down tight. "Try to open them," I said.

He tried but couldn't.

Dr. Marshall came in with a basin of dough. It was the ordinary white dough used for baking bread. It was nice and soft. I took a lump of the dough and plastered it over one of the Indian's eyes. I filled the whole socket and let the dough overlap onto the surrounding skin. Then I pressed the edges down hard. I did the same with the other eye.

"That isn't too uncomfortable, is it?" I asked.

"No," the Indian said. "It's fine."

"You do the bandaging," I said to Dr. Marshall. "My fingers are too sticky."

"A pleasure," Dr. Marshall said. "Watch this." He took a thick wad of cotton wool and laid it on top of the Indian's dough-filled eyes. The cotton wool stuck to the dough and stayed in place. "Sit down, please," Dr. Marshall said.

The Indian sat on the bed.

Dr. Marshall took a roll of three-inch bandage and proceeded to wrap it round and round the man's head. The bandage held the cotton wool and the dough firmly in place. Dr. Marshall pinned the bandage. After that, he took a second bandage and began to wrap that one not only around the man's eyes but around his entire face and head.

"Please to leave my nose free for breathing," the Indian said.

"Of course," Dr. Marshall answered. He finished the job and pinned down the end of the bandage. "How's that?" he asked.

"Splendid," I said. "There's no way he can possibly see through that."

The whole of the Indian's head was now swathed in thick white bandage, and the only thing you could see was the end of the nose sticking out. He looked like a man who had had some terrible brain operation.

"How does that feel?" Dr. Marshall asked him.

"It feels good," the Indian said. "I must compliment you gentlemen on doing such a fine job."

"Off you go, then," Dr. Marshall said, grinning at me. "Show us how clever you are at seeing things now."

The Indian got off the bed and walked straight to the door. He opened the door and went out.

"Great Scott!" I said. "Did you see that? He put his hand right on the doorknob!"

Dr. Marshall had stopped grinning. His face had suddenly gone white. "I'm going after him," he said, rushing for the door. I rushed for the door as well.

The Indian was walking quite normally along the hospital corridor. Dr. Marshall and I were about five yards behind him. And very spooky it was to watch this man with the enormous white and totally bandaged head strolling casually along the corridor just like anyone else. It was especially spooky when you knew for a certainty that his eyelids were sealed, that his eye sockets were filled with dough, and that there was a great wad of cotton wool and bandages on top of that.

I saw a native orderly coming along the corridor toward the Indian. He was pushing a food trolley. Suddenly the orderly caught sight of the man with the white head, and he froze. The bandaged Indian stepped casually to one side of the trolley and went on.

"He saw it!" I cried. "He must have seen that trolley! He walked right round it! This is absolutely unbelievable!"

Dr. Marshall didn't answer me. His cheeks were white, his whole face rigid with shocked disbelief.

The Indian came to the stairs and started to go down them. He went down with no trouble at all. He didn't even put a hand on the handrail. Several people were coming up the stairs. Each of them stopped, gasped, stared and quickly got out of the way.

At the bottom of the stairs, the Indian turned right and headed for the doors that led out into the street. Dr. Marshall and I kept close behind him.

The entrance to our hospital stands back a little from the street, and there is a rather grand series of steps leading down from the entrance into a small courtyard with acacia trees around it. Dr. Marshall and I came out into the blazing sunshine and stood at the top of the steps. Below us, in the courtyard, we saw a crowd of maybe a hundred people. At least half of them were barefoot children, and as our white-headed Indian walked down the steps, they all cheered and shouted and surged toward him. He greeted them by holding both hands above his head.

Suddenly I saw the bicycle. It was over to one side at the bottom of the steps, and a small boy was holding it. The bicycle itself was quite ordinary, but on the back of it, fixed somehow to the rear wheel frame, was a huge placard, about five feet square. On the placard were written the following words:

Imhrat Khan, The Man Who Sees Without His Eyes!
Today my eyes have been bandaged by hospital doctors!
Appearing Tonight and all this week at
The Royal Palace Hall, Acacia Street, at 7 P.M.
Don't miss it! You will see miracles performed!

Our Indian had reached the bottom of the steps and now he walked straight over to the bicycle. He said something to the boy, and the boy smiled. The Indian mounted the bicycle. The crowd made way for him. Then, lo and behold, this fellow with the blocked-up bandaged eyes now proceeded to ride across the court-yard and straight out into the bustling honking traffic of the street beyond! The crowd cheered louder than ever. The barefoot children ran after him, squealing and laughing. For a minute or so, we were able to keep him in sight. We saw him riding superbly down the busy street with cars whizzing past him and a bunch of children running in his wake. Then he turned a corner and was gone.

"I feel quite giddy," Dr. Marshall said. "I can't bring myself to believe it."

"We have to believe it," I said. "He couldn't possibly have removed the dough from under the bandages. We never let him out of our sight. And as for unsealing his eyelids, that job would take him five minutes with cotton wool and alcohol."

"Do you know what I think," Dr. Marshall said. "I think we have witnessed a miracle."

We turned and walked slowly back into the hospital.

Three

For the rest of the day, I was kept busy with patients in the hospital. At six in the evening, I came off duty and drove back to my flat for a shower and a change of clothes. It was the hottest time of year in Bombay, and even after sundown the heat was like an open furnace. If you sat still in a chair and did nothing, the sweat would come seeping out of your skin. Your face glistened with dampness all day long and your shirt stuck to your chest. I took a long cool shower. I drank a whiskey and soda sitting on the veranda, with only a towel around my waist. Then I put on some clean clothes.

At ten minutes to seven, I was outside the Royal Palace Hall in Acacia Street. It was not much of a place. It was one of those smallish seedy halls that can be hired inexpensively for meetings or dances. There was a fair-sized crowd of local Indians milling around outside the ticket office, and a large poster over the entrance proclaimed that THE INTERNATIONAL THEATER COMPANY was performing every night that week. It said there would be jugglers and conjurors and acrobats and sword swallowers and fire eaters and snake charmers and a one-act play entitled *The Rajah and the Tiger Lady.* But above all this and in by far the largest letters, it said IMHRAT KHAN, THE MIRACLE MAN WHO SEES WITHOUT HIS EYES.

I bought a ticket and went in.

The show lasted two hours. To my surprise, I thoroughly enjoyed it. All the performers were excellent. I liked the man who juggled with cooking utensils. He had a saucepan, a frying pan, a baking tray, a huge plate and a casserole pot all flying through the air at the same time. The snake charmer had a big green snake that stood almost on the tip of its tail and swayed to the music of his flute. The fire eater ate fire and the sword swallower pushed a thin-pointed rapier at least four feet down his throat and into his stomach. Last of all, to a great fanfare of trumpets, our friend Imhrat Khan came on to do his act. The bandages we had put on him at the hospital had now been removed.

Members of the audience were called onto the stage to blindfold him with sheets and scarves and turbans, and in the end there was so much material wrapped around his head he could hardly keep his balance. He was then given a revolver. A small boy came out and stood at the left of the stage. I recognized him as the one who had held the bicycle outside the hospital that morning. The boy placed a tin can on the top of his head and stood quite still. The audience became deathly silent as Imhrat Khan took aim. He fired. The bang made us all jump. The tin can flew off the boy's head and clattered to the floor. The boy picked it up and showed the bullet hole to the audience. Everyone clapped and cheered. The boy smiled.

Then the boy stood against a wooden screen and Imhrat Khan threw knives all around his body, most of them going very close indeed. This was a splendid act. Not many people could have thrown knives with such accuracy even with their eyes uncovered, but here he was, this extraordinary fellow, with his head so swathed in sheets it looked like a great snowball on a stick, and he was flicking the sharp knives into the screen within a hairsbreadth of the boy's head. The boy smiled all the way through the act, and when it was over the audience stamped its feet and screamed with excitement.

Imhrat Khan's last act, though not so spectacular, was even more impressive. A metal barrel was brought on stage. The audience was invited to examine it, to make sure there were no holes. There were no holes. The barrel was then placed over Imhrat Khan's already bandaged head. It came down over his shoulders and as far as his elbows, pinning the upper part of his arms to his sides. But he could still hold out his forearms and his hands. Someone put a needle in one of his hands and a length of cotton thread in the other. With no false moves, he neatly threaded the cotton through the eye of the needle. I was flabbergasted.

As soon as the show was over, I made my way backstage. I found Imrat Khan in a small but clean dressing room, sitting quietly on a wooden stool. The little Indian boy was unwinding the mass of scarves and sheets from around his head.

"Ah," he said. "It is my friend the doctor from the hospital. Come in, sir, come in."

"I saw the show," I said.

"And what did you think?"

"I liked it very much. I thought you were wonderful."

"Thank you," he said. "That is a high compliment."

"I must congratulate your assistant as well," I said, nodding to the small boy. "He is very brave."

"He cannot speak English," the Indian said. "But I will tell him what you said." He spoke rapidly to the boy in Hindustani, and the boy nodded solemnly but said nothing.

"Look," I said. "I did you a small favor this morning. Would you do me one in return? Would you consent to come out and have supper with me?"

All the wrappings were off his head now. He smiled at me and said, "I think you are feeling curious, doctor. Am I not right?"

"Very curious," I said. "I'd like to talk to you."

Once again, I was struck by the peculiarly thick matting of black hair growing on the outsides of his ears. I had not seen anything quite like it on another person. "I have never been questioned by a doctor before," he said. "But I have no objection. It would be a pleasure to have supper with you."

"Shall I wait in the car?"

"Yes, please," he said. "I must wash myself and get out of these dirty clothes."

I told him what my car looked like and said I would be waiting outside.

He emerged fifteen minutes later, wearing a clean white cotton robe and the usual sandals on his bare feet. And soon the two of us were sitting comfortably in a small restaurant that I sometimes went to because it made the best curry in the city. I drank beer with my curry. Imrat Khan drank lemonade.

"I am not a writer," I said to him, "I am a doctor. But if you will tell me your story from the beginning, if you will explain to me how you developed this magical power of being able to see without your eyes, I will write it down as faithfully as I can. And then, perhaps, I can get it published in the *British Medical Journal* or even in some famous magazine. And because I *am* a doctor and not just some writer trying to sell a story for money, people will be far more inclined to take seriously what I say. It would help you, wouldn't it, to become better known?"

"It would help me very much," he said. "But why should you want to do this?"

"Because I am madly curious," I answered. "That is the only reason."

Imhrat Khan took a mouthful of curried rice and chewed it slowly. Then he said, "Very well, my friend. I will do it."

"Splendid!" I cried. "Let's go back to my flat as soon as we've finished eating and then we can talk without anyone disturbing us."

We finished our meal. I paid the bill. Then I drove Imhrat Khan back to my flat.

Four

In the living room, I got out paper and pencils so that I could make notes. I have a sort of private shorthand of my own that I use for taking down the medical history of patients, and with it I am able to record most of what a person says if he doesn't speak too quickly. I think I got just about everything Imhrat Khan said to me that evening, word for word, and here it is. I give it to you exactly as he spoke it:

"I am an Indian, a Hindu," said Imhrat Khan, "and I was born in Akhnur, in Kashmir State, in 1905. My family is poor and my father worked as a ticket inspector on the railway. When I was a small boy of thirteen, an Indian conjuror comes to our school and gives a performance. His name, I remember, is Professor Moor—all conjurors in India call themselves 'professor'—and his tricks are very good. I am tremendously impressed. I think it is real magic. I feel— how shall I call it—I feel a powerful wish to learn about this magic myself, so two days later I run away from home determined to find and to follow my new hero, Professor Moor. I take all my savings, fourteen rupees, and only the clothes I am wearing. I am wearing a white dhoti and sandals. This is 1918 and I am thirteen years old.

"I find out that Professor Moor has gone to Lahore, two hundred miles away, so all alone, I take a ticket, third class, and I get on the train and follow him. In Lahore, I discover the Professor. He is working at his conjuring in a very cheap-type show. I tell him of my admiration and offer myself to him as assistant. He accepts me.

My pay? Ah yes, my pay is eight annas a day.

"The Professor teaches me to do the linking-rings trick and my job is to stand in the street before the theater dressed in funny clothes doing the linking rings and calling to the people to come in and see the show.

"For six whole weeks this is very fine. It is much better than going to school. But then what a terrible bombshell I receive when suddenly it comes to me that there is no real magic in Professor Moor, that all is trickery and quickness of the hand. Immediately the Professor is no longer my hero. I lose every bit of interest in my job, but at the same time my whole mind becomes filled with a very strong longing. I long above all things to find out about the real magic and to discover something about the strange power which is called yoga.

"To do this, I must find a yogi who is willing to let me become his disciple. This is not going to be easy. True yogis do not grow on trees. There are very few of them in the whole of India. Also, they are fanatically religious people. Therefore, if I am to have success in finding a teacher, I too would have to pretend to be a very religious man.

"No, I am actually not religious. And because of that, I am what you would call a bit of a cheat. I wanted to acquire yoga powers purely for selfish reasons. I wanted to use these powers to get fame and fortune.

"Now this was something the true yogi would despise more than anything in the world. In fact, the true yogi believes that any yogi who misuses his powers will die an early and sudden death. A yogi must never perform in public. He must practice his art only in absolute privacy and as a religious service, otherwise he will be smitten to death. This I did not believe and I still don't.

"So now my search for a yogi instructor begins. I leave Professor Moor and go to a town called Amritsar in the Punjab, where I join a traveling theater company. I have to make a living while I am searching for the secret, and already I have had success in amateur acting at my school. So for three years I travel with this theater group all over the Punjab and by the end of it, when I am sixteen and a half years old, I am playing top of the bill. All the time I am saving money and now I have altogether a very great sum, two thousand rupees.

"It is at that moment that I hear news of a man called Banerjee. This Banerjee, it is said, is one of the truly great yogis of India, and he possesses extraordinary yoga powers. Above all, people are telling of how he has acquired the rare power of levitation, so that when he prays his whole body leaves the ground and becomes suspended in the air eighteen inches from the soil.

"Ah-ha, I think. This surely is the man for me. This Banerjee is the one that I must seek. So at once I take my savings and leave the theater company and make my way to Rikhikesh, on the banks of the Ganges, where rumor says that Banerjee is living.

"For six months I search for Banerjee. Where is he? Where? Where is Banerjee? Ah yes, they say in Rikhikesh, Banerjee has certainly been in town, but that is a while ago, and even then no one saw him. And now? Now Banerjee has gone to another place. What other place? Ah well, they say, how can one know that. How indeed? How can one know about the movements of such a one as Banerjee. Does he not live a life of absolute seclusion? Does he not? And I say yes. Yes, yes, yes. Of course. That is obvious. Even to me.

"I spend all my savings trying to find this Banerjee, all except thirty-five rupees. But it is no good. However, I stay in Rikhikesh and make a living by doing ordinary conjuring tricks for small groups and suchlike. These are the tricks I have learned from Professor Moor and by nature my sleight of hand is very good.

"Then one day, there I am sitting in the small hotel in Rikhikesh and again I hear talk of the yogi Banerjee. A traveler is saying how he has heard that Banerjee is now living in the jungle, not so very far away, but in the dense jungle and all alone.

"But where?

"The traveler is not sure where. Possibly, he says, it is over there, in that direction, north of the town, and he points with his finger.

"Well, that is enough for me. I go to the market and begin to bargain for hiring a tonga, which is a horse and cart, and the transaction is just being completed with the driver when up comes a man who has been standing listening nearby and he says that he too is going in that direction. He asks can he come part of the way with me and share the cost. I answer, 'Delighted, of course,' and off we go, the man and me sitting in the cart, and the driver driving the horse. Off we go along a very small path which leads right through the jungle.

"And then what truly fantastic luck should happen! I am talking to my companion and I find that he is a disciple of none other than the great Banerjee himself and that he is going now on a visit to his

master. So straight out I tell him that I too would like to become a
disciple of the yogi.

"He turns and looks at me long and slow, and for perhaps three
minutes he does not speak. Then he says, quietly, 'No, that is impossible.'

"All right, I say to myself, we shall see. Then I ask if it is really
true that Banerjee levitates when he prays.

" 'Yes,' he says. 'That is true. But no one is allowed to observe
the thing happening. No one is ever allowed to come near Banerjee
when he is praying.'

"So we go on a little farther in the tonga, talking all the time
about Banerjee, and I manage by very careful casual questioning to
find out a number of small things about him, such as what time of
day he commences with his praying. Then soon the man says, 'I will
leave you here. This is where I dismount.'

"I drop him off and I pretend to drive on along my journey, but
around a corner I tell the driver to stop and wait. Quickly I jump
down and I sneak back along the road, looking for this man, the
disciple of Banerjee. He is not on the road. Already he has disappeared into the jungle. But which way? Which side of the road? I
stand very still and listen.

"I hear a sort of rustling in the undergrowth. That must be him,
I tell myself. If it is not him, then it is a tiger. But it is him. I see
him ahead. He is going forward through thick jungle. There is not
even a little path where he is walking, and he is having to push his
way between tall bamboos and every kind of heavy vegetation. I
creep after him. I keep about one hundred yards behind him because
I am frightened he may hear me. I can certainly hear him. It is
impossible to proceed in silence through very thick jungle, and
when I lose sight of him, which is most of the time, I am able to
follow his sound.

"For about half an hour this tense game of follow-the-leader
goes on. Then suddenly, I can no longer hear the man in front of
me. I stop and listen. The jungle is silent. I am terrified that I may
have lost him. I creep on a little way, and all at once, through the
thick undergrowth, I see before me a little clearing, and in the
middle of the clearing are two huts. They are small huts built entirely
of jungle leaves and branches. My heart jumps and I feel a great
surging of excitement inside me because this, I know for certain, is
the place of Banerjee, the yogi.

"The disciple has already disappeared. He must have gone into one of the huts. All is quiet. So now I proceed to make a most careful inspection of the trees and bushes and other things all around. There is a small waterhole beside the nearest hut, and I see a prayer mat beside it, and that, I say to myself, is where Banerjee meditates and prays. Close to this waterhole, not thirty yards away, there is a large tree, a great spreading baobab tree with beautiful thick branches which spread in such a way you can put a bed on them and lie on the bed and still not be seen from underneath. That will be my tree, I say to myself. I shall hide in that tree and wait until Banerjee comes out to pray. Then I will be able to see everything.

"But the disciple has told me that the time of prayer is not until five or six in the evening, so I have several hours to wait. Therefore I at once walk back through the jungle to the road and I speak to the tonga driver. I tell him he too must wait. For this, I have to pay him extra money, but it doesn't matter because now I am so excited I don't care about anything for the moment, not even money.

"And all through the great noontime heat of the jungle I wait beside the tonga, and on through the heavy wet heat of the afternoon, and then, as five o'clock approaches, I make my way quietly back through the jungle to the hut, my heart beating so I can feel it shaking my whole body. I climb up my tree and I hide among the leaves in such a way that I can see but cannot be seen. And I wait. I wait for forty-five minutes.

"A watch? Yes, I have on a wristwatch. I remember it clearly. It was a watch I won in a raffle and I was proud to own it. On the face of my watch it said the maker's name, The Islamia Watch Company, Ludhiana. And so with my watch I am careful to be timing everything that goes on because I want to get every single detail of this experience.

"I sit up in the tree, waiting.

"Then, all at once, a man is coming out of the hut. The man is tall and thin. He is dressed in an orange-colored dhoti and he carries before him a tray with brass pots and incense burners. He goes over and sits down cross-legged on the mat by the waterhole, putting the tray on the ground before him, and all the movements that he makes seem somehow very calm and gentle. He leans forward and scoops a handful of water from the pool and throws it over his shoulder. He takes the incense burner and passes it back and forth across his chest, slowly, in a gentle, flowing manner. He puts his hands palm downward on his knees. He pauses. He takes a long breath through his nostrils. I can see him take a long breath and suddenly I can see his face is changing. There is a sort of brightness coming over all his face, a sort of . . . well, a sort of brightness on his skin and I can see his face is changing.

"For fourteen minutes he remains quite still in that position, and then, as I look at him, I see, quite positively I see his body lifting slowly . . . slowly . . . slowly off the ground. He is still sitting cross-legged, the hands palm downward on the knees, and his whole body is lifting slowly off the ground, up into the air. Now I can see daylight underneath him. Twelve inches above the ground he is sitting . . . fifteen inches . . . eighteen . . . twenty . . . and soon he is at least two feet above the prayer mat.

"I stay quite still up there in the tree, watching, and I keep saying to myself, now look carefully, make sure, be certain that you are seeing correctly. There before you, thirty yards away, is a man sitting in great serenity upon the air. Are you seeing him? Yes, I am seeing him. But are you sure there is no illusion? Are you sure there is no deception? Are you sure you are not imagining? Are you sure? Yes, I am sure, I say. I am sure. I stare at him marveling. For a long while I keep staring, and then the body is coming slowly down again toward the earth. I see it coming. I see it moving gently downward, slowly downward, lowering to the earth until again his buttocks rest upon the mat.

"Forty-six minutes by my watch it had been suspended! I timed it.

"And then, for a long, long while, for over two hours, the man remains sitting absolutely still, like a stone person, with not the slightest movement. To me, it does not seem that he is breathing. His eyes are closed, and still there is this brightness on his face and also this slightly smiling look, a thing I have not seen on any other face in all my life since then.

"At last he stirs. He moves his hands. He stands up. He bends down again. He picks up the tray and goes slowly back into the hut. I am wonderstruck. I feel exalted. I forget all caution and I climb down quickly from the tree and run straight over to the hut and rush in through the door. Banerjee is bending over, washing his feet and hands in a basin. His back is toward me, but he hears me and he turns quickly and straightens up. There is great surprise on his face and the first thing he says is, 'How long have you been here?' He says it sharply, like he is not pleased.

"At once I tell the whole truth, the whole story about being up in the tree and watching him, and at the end I tell him there is nothing I want in life except to become his disciple. Please will he let me become his disciple?

"Suddenly he seems to explode. He becomes furious and he begins shouting at me. 'Get out!' he shouts. 'Get out of here! Get out! Get out! Get out!' And in his fury he picks up a small brick and flings it at me and it strikes my right leg just below the knee and tears the flesh. I have the scar still. I will show it to you. There, you see, just below the knee.

"Banerjee's anger is terrible and I am very frightened. I turn and run away. I run back through the jungle to where the tonga driver is waiting, and we drive home to Rikhiskesh. But that night I regain my courage. I make for myself a decision and it is this: that I will return every day to the hut of Banerjee, and I will keep on and on at him until at last he *has* to take me on as a disciple, just to get himself some peace.

"This I do. Each day I go to see him and each day his anger pours out upon me like a volcano, him shouting and yelling and me standing there frightened but also obstinate and repeating always to him my wish to become a disciple. For five days it is like this. Then, all at once, on my sixth visit, Banerjee seems to become quite calm, quite polite. He explains he cannot himself take me on as a disciple. But he will give me a note, he says, to another man, a friend, a great yogi, who lives in Hardawar. I am to go there and I will receive help and instruction."

Five

Imhrat Khan paused and asked me if he might have a glass of water. I fetched it for him. He took a long, slow drink, then he went on with his story:

"This is in 1922 and I am nearly seventeen years old. So I go to Hardawar. And there I find the yogi, and because I have a letter from the great Banerjee, he consents to give me instruction.

"Now what is this instruction?

"It is, of course, the critical part of the whole thing. It is what I have been yearning for and searching for, so you can be sure I am an eager pupil.

"The first instruction, the most elementary part, consists of having to practice the most difficult physical exercises, all of them concerned with muscle control and breathing. But after some weeks of this, even the eager pupil becomes impatient. I tell the yogi that it is my mental powers I wish to develop, not my physical ones.

"He replies, 'If you will develop control of your body, then the control of your mind will be an automatic thing.' But I want both at once, and I keep asking him, and in the end he says, 'Very well, I will give you some exercises to help you to concentrate the conscious mind.'

" 'Conscious mind?' I ask. 'Why do you say *conscious* mind?'

" 'Because each man has two minds, the conscious and the subconscious. The subconscious mind is highly concentrated, but the conscious mind, the one everyone uses, is a scattered, unconcentrated thing. It is concerning itself with thousands of different items, the things you are seeing around you and the things you are thinking about. So you must learn to concentrate it in such a way that you can visualize at will *one item*, one item only, and absolutely nothing else. If you work hard at this, you should be able to concentrate your mind, your conscious mind, upon any one object you select for at least three and a half minutes. But that will take about fifteen years.'

" 'Fifteen years!' I cry.

" 'It may take longer,' he says. 'Fifteen years is the usual time.'

" 'But I will be an old man by then!'

" 'Do not despair,' the yogi says. 'The time varies with different people. Some take ten years, a few can take less, and on extremely rare occasions a special person comes along who is able to develop the power in only one or two years. But that is one in a million.'

" 'Who are these special people?' I ask. 'Do they look different from other people?'

" 'They look the same,' he says. 'A special person might be a humble roadsweeper or a factory worker. Or he might be a rajah. There is no way of telling until the training begins.'

" 'Is it really so difficult,' I ask, 'to concentrate the mind upon a single object for three and a half minutes?'

" 'It is almost impossible,' he answers. 'Try it and see. Shut your eyes and think of something. Think of just one object. Visualize it. See it before you. And in a few seconds your mind will start wandering. Other little thoughts will creep in. Other visions will come to you. It is a very difficult thing.'

"Thus spoke the yogi of Hardawar.

"And so my real exercises begin. Each evening, I sit down and close my eyes and visualize the face of the person I love best, which is my brother. I concentrate upon visualizing his face. But the instant my mind begins to wander, I stop the exercise and rest for some minutes. Then I try again.

"After three years of daily practice, I am able to concentrate absolutely upon my brother's face for one and a half minutes. I am making progress. But an interesting thing happens. In doing these exercises, I lose my sense of smell absolutely. And never to this day does it come back to me.

"Then the necessity for earning my living to buy food forces me to leave Hardawar. I go to Calcutta, where there are greater opportunities, and there I soon begin to make quite good money by giving conjuring performances. But always I continue with the exercises. Every evening, wherever I am, I settle myself down in a quiet corner and practice the concentrating of the mind upon my brother's face. Occasionally, I choose something not so personal, like for example an orange or a pair of spectacles, and that makes it even more difficult.

"One day, I travel from Calcutta to Dacca in East Bengal to give a conjuring show at a college there, and while in Dacca, I happen to be present at a demonstration of walking on fire. There are many people watching. There is a big trench dug at the bottom of a sloping lawn. The spectators are sitting by the hundreds upon the slopes of the lawn looking down upon the trench.

"The trench is about twenty-five feet long. It has been filled with logs and firewood and charcoal, and a lot of paraffin has been poured on it. The paraffin has been lit, and after a while the whole trench has become a smoldering hot furnace. It is so hot that the men who are stoking it are obliged to wear goggles. There is a high wind and the wind fans the charcoal almost to white heat.

"The Indian firewalker then comes forward. He is naked except for a small loincloth, and his feet are bare. The crowd becomes silent. The firewalker enters the trench and walks the whole length of it, over the white-hot charcoal. He doesn't stop. Nor does he hurry. He simply walks over the white-hot coals and comes out at the other end, and his feet are not even singed. He shows the soles of his feet to the crowd. The crowd stares in amazement.

"Then the firewalker walks the trench once more. This time he goes even slower, and as he does it, I can see on his face a look of pure and absolute concentration. This man, I tell myself, has practiced yoga. He is a yogi.

"After the performance, the firewalker calls out to the crowd, asking if there is anyone brave enough to come down and walk on the fire. There is a hush in the crowd. I feel a sudden surge of excitement in my chest. This is my chance. I must take it. I must have faith and courage. I *must* try it. I have been doing my concentration exercises for over three years now and the time has come to give myself a severe test.

"While I am standing there thinking these thoughts, a volunteer comes forward from the crowd. It is a young Indian man. He announces that he would like to try the firewalk. This decides me, and I also step forward and make my announcement. The crowd gives us both a cheer.

"Now the real firewalker becomes the supervisor. He tells the other man he will go first. He makes him remove his dhoti, otherwise, he says, the hem will catch fire from the heat. And the sandals must be taken off.

"The young Indian does what he is told. But now that he is close to the trench and can feel the terrible heat coming from it, he begins to look frightened. He steps back a few paces, shielding his eyes from the heat with his hands.

" 'You don't have to do it if you don't want to,' the real firewalker says.

"The crowd waits and watches, sensing a drama.

"The young man, though scared out of his wits, wishes to prove how brave he is, and he says, 'Of course I'll do it.'

"With that, he runs toward the trench. He steps into it with one foot, then the other. He gives a fearful scream and leaps out again and falls to the ground. The poor man lies there screaming in pain. The soles of his feet are badly burned and some of the skin has come right away. Two of his friends run forward and carry him off.

" 'Now it is your turn,' says the firewalker. 'Are you ready?'

" 'I am ready,' I say. 'But please be silent while I prepare myself.'

"A great hush has come over the crowd. They have seen one man get badly burned. Is the second one going to be mad enough to do the same thing?

"Someone in the crowd shouts, 'Don't do it! You must be mad!' Others take up the shout, all telling me to give up. I turn and face them and raise my hands for silence. They stop shouting and stare at me. Every eye in that place is upon me now.

"I feel extraordinarily calm.

"I pull my dhoti off over my head. I take off my sandals. I stand there naked except for my underpants. I stand very still and close my eyes. I begin to concentrate my mind. I concentrate on the fire. I see nothing but the white-hot coals and I concentrate on them being not hot but cold. The coals are cold, I tell myself. They cannot burn me. It is impossible for them to burn me because there is no heat in them. I allow half a minute to go by. I know that I must not wait too long because I am only able to concentrate absolutely upon any one thing for a minute and a half.

"I keep concentrating. I concentrate so hard that I go into a sort of trance. I step out onto the coals. I walk fairly fast the whole length of the trench. And behold, I am not burned!

"The crowd goes mad. They yell and cheer. The original fire-walker rushes up to me and examines the soles of my feet. He can't believe what he sees. There is not a burn mark on them.

" 'Ayeee!' he cries. 'What is this? Are you a yogi?'

" 'I am on the way, sir,' I answer proudly. 'I am well on the way.'

"After that, I dress and leave quickly, avoiding the crowd.

"Of course I am excited. 'It is coming to me,' I say. 'Now at last the power is beginning to come.' And all the time I am remembering something else. I am remembering a thing that the old yogi of Hardawar said to me. He said, 'Certain holy people have been known to develop so great a concentration that they could see without using their eyes.' I keep remembering that saying and I keep longing for the power to do likewise myself. And after my success with the firewalking, I decide that I will concentrate everything upon this single aim—to see without the eyes.''

Six

For only the second time so far, Imhrat Khan broke off his story. He took another sip of water, then he leaned back in his chair and closed his eyes.

"I am trying to get everything in the correct order," he said. "I don't want to omit anything."

"You're doing fine," I told him. "Carry on."

"Very well," he said. "So I am still in Calcutta and I have just had success with firewalking. And now I have decided to concentrate all my energy on this one thing, which is to see without the eyes.

"The time has come, therefore, to make a slight change in the exercises. Each night now I light a candle and I begin by staring at the flame. A candle flame, you know, has three separate parts, the yellow at the top, the mauve lower down, and the black right inside. I place the candle sixteen inches away from my face. The flame is absolutely level with my eyes. It must not be above or below. It must be dead level because then I do not have to make even the tiniest little adjustment of the eye muscles by looking up or down. I settle myself comfortably and I begin to stare at the black part of the flame, right in the center. All this is merely to concentrate my conscious mind, to empty it of everything around me. So I stare at the black spot in the flame until everything around me has disappeared and I can see nothing else. Then slowly I shut my eyes and begin to concentrate as usual upon one single object of my choice, which as you know is usually my brother's face.

"I do this every night before bed and by 1929, when I am twenty-four years old, I can concentrate upon an object for three minutes without any wandering of my mind. So it is now, at this time, when I am twenty-four, that I begin to become aware of a slight ability to see an object with my eyes closed. It is a very slight ability, just a queer little feeling that when I close my eyes and look at something hard, with fierce concentration, then I can see the outline of the object I am looking at.

"Slowly I am beginning to develop my *inner* sense of sight.

"You ask me what I mean by that. I will explain it to you exactly as the yogi of Hardawar explained it to me.

"All of us, you see, have two senses of sight, just as we have two senses of smell and taste and hearing. There is the outer sense, the highly developed one which we all use, and there is the *inner* one also. If only we could develop these inner senses of ours, then we could smell without our noses, taste without our tongues, hear without our ears and see without our eyes. Do you not understand? Do you not see that our noses and tongues and ears and eyes are only . . . how shall I say it? . . . are only instruments which assist in conveying the sensation itself to the brain.

"And so it is that I am all the time striving to develop my inner sense of sight. Each night now I perform my usual exercises with the candle flame and my brother's face. After that I rest a little while. I drink a cup of coffee. Then I blindfold myself and I sit in my chair trying to visualize, trying to see, not just to imagine, but actually to *see* without my eyes every object in the room.

"And gradually success begins to come.

"Soon I am working with a pack of cards. I take a card from the top of the pack and hold it before me, back to front, trying to see through it. Then, with a pencil in my other hand, I write down what I think it is. I take another card and do the same again. I go through the whole of the pack like that and when it is over I check what I have written down against the pile of cards beside me. Almost at once I have a sixty to seventy percent success.

"I do other things. I buy maps and complicated navigating charts and pin them up all around my room. I spend hours looking at them blindfold, trying to see them, trying to read the small lettering of the place names and the rivers. Every evening for the next four years, I proceed with this kind of practice.

"By the year 1933—that is only last year—when I am twenty-eight years old, I can read a book. I can cover my eyes completely and I can read a book right through.

"So now at last I have it, this power. For certain I have it now, and at once, because I cannot wait with impatience, I include the blindfold act in my ordinary conjuring performance.

"The audience loves it. They applaud long and loud. But not one single person believes it to be genuine. Everyone thinks it is just another clever trick. And the fact that I am a conjuror makes them think more than ever that I am faking. Conjurors are men who trick you. They trick you with cleverness. And so no one believes me. Even the doctors who blindfold me in the most expert way refuse to believe that anyone can see without his eyes. They forget there may be other ways of sending the image to the brain."

"What other ways?" I asked him.

"Quite honestly, I don't know exactly how it is I can see without my eyes. But what I do know is this: When my eyes are bandaged, I am not using the eyes at all. The seeing is done by another part of my body."

"Which part?" I asked him.

"Any part at all as long as the skin is bare. For example, if you put a sheet of metal in front of me and put a book behind the metal, I cannot read the book. But if you allow me to put my hand around the sheet of metal so that the hand is seeing the book, then I can read it."

"Would you mind if I tested you on that?" I asked.

"Not at all," he answered.

"I don't have a sheet of metal," I said, "but the door will do just as well."

I stood up and went to the bookshelf. I took down the first book that came to hand. It was *Alice's Adventures in Wonderland*. I opened the door and asked my visitor to stand behind it, out of sight. I opened the book at random and propped it on a chair the other side of the door to him. Then I stationed myself in a position where I could see both him and the book.

"Can you read that book?" I asked him.

"No," he answered. "Of course not."

"All right. You may now put your hand around the door, but only the hand."

He slid his hand around the edge of the door until it was within sight of the book. Then I saw the fingers on the hand parting from one another, spreading wide, beginning to quiver slightly, feeling the air like the antennae of an insect. And the hand turned so that the back of it was facing the book.

"Try to read the left page from the top," I said.

There was silence for perhaps ten seconds, then smoothly, without pause, he began to read: " '*Have you guessed the riddle yet?' the Hatter said, turning to Alice again. 'No, I give it up' Alice replied. 'What's the answer?' 'I haven't the slightest idea,' said the Hatter. 'Nor I,' said the March Hare. Alice sighed wearily. 'I think you might do something better with the time,' she said, 'than wasting it in asking riddles that have no answers.' "*

"It's perfect!" I cried. "Now I believe you! You are a miracle!" I was enormously excited.

"Thank you, doctor," he said gravely. "What you say gives me great pleasure."

"One question," I said. "It's about the playing cards. When you held up the reverse side of one of them, did you put your hand around the other side to help you read it?"

"You are very perceptive," he said. "No, I did not. In the case of the cards, I was actually able to *see through* them in some way."

"How do you explain that?" I asked.

"I don't explain it," he said. "Except perhaps that a card is such a flimsy thing, it is so thin, and not solid like metal or thick like a door. That is all the explanation I can give. There are many things in this world, doctor, that we cannot explain."

"Yes," I said. "There certainly are."

"Would you be kind enough to take me home now," he said. "I feel very tired."

I drove him home in my car.

Seven

That night I didn't go to bed. I was far too worked up to sleep. I had just witnessed a miracle. This man would have doctors all over the world turning somersaults in the air! He could change the whole course of medicine! From a doctor's point of view, he must be the most valuable man alive! We doctors must get hold of him and keep him safe. We must look after him. We mustn't let him go. We must find out exactly how it is that an image can be sent to the brain without using the eyes. And if we do that, then blind people might be able to see and deaf people might be able to hear. Above all, this incredible man must not be ignored and left to wander around India, living in cheap rooms and playing in second-rate theaters.

I got so steamed up thinking about this that after a while I grabbed a notebook and a pen and started writing down with great care everything that Imhrat Khan had told me that evening. I used the notes I had made while he was talking. I wrote for five hours without stopping. And at eight o'clock the next morning, when it was time to go to the hospital, I had finished the most important part, the pages you have just read.

At the hospital that morning, I didn't see Dr. Marshall until we met in the doctors' rest room during our tea break.

I told him as much as I could in the ten minutes we had to spare. "I'm going back to the theater tonight," I said. "I *must* talk to him again. I must persuade him to stay here. We mustn't lose him now."

"I'll come with you," Dr. Marshall said.

"Right," I said. "We'll watch the show first and then we'll take him out to supper."

At a quarter to seven that evening, I drove Dr. Marshall in my car to Acacia Road. I parked the car, and the two of us walked over to the Royal Palace Hall.

"There's something wrong," I said. "Where is everybody?"

There was no crowd outside the hall and the doors were closed. The poster advertising the show was still in place, but I now saw that someone had written across it in large printed letters, using black paint, the words TONIGHT'S PERFORMANCE CANCELED. There was an old gatekeeper standing by the locked doors.

"What happened?" I asked him.

"Someone died," he said.

"Who?" I asked, knowing already who it was.

"The man who sees without his eyes," the gatekeeper answered.

"How did he die?" I cried. "When? Where?"

"They say he died in his bed," the gatekeeper said. "He went to sleep and never woke up. These things happen."

We walked slowly back to the car. I felt an overwhelming sense of grief and anger. I should never have allowed this precious man to go home last night. I should have kept him. I should have given him my bed and taken care of him. I shouldn't have let him out of my sight. Imhrat Khan was a maker of miracles. He had communicated with mysterious and dangerous forces that are beyond the reach of ordinary people. He had also broken all the rules. He had performed miracles in public. He had taken money for doing so. And, worst of all, he had told some of those secrets to an outsider—me. Now he was dead.

"So that's that," Dr. Marshall said.

"Yes," I said. "It's all over. Nobody will ever know how he did it."

This is a true and accurate report of everything that took place concerning my two meetings with Imhrat Khan.

(signed)   *John F. Cartwright, M.D.*
....

Bombay, December 4, 1934

Eight

"Well, well, well," said Henry Sugar. "Now *that* is extremely interesting."

He closed the exercise book and sat gazing at the rain splashing against the windows of the library.

"This," Henry Sugar went on, talking aloud to himself, "is a terrific piece of information. It could change my life."

The piece of information Henry was referring to was that Imhrat Khan had trained himself to read the value of a playing card from the reverse side. And Henry the gambler, the rather dishonest gambler, had realized at once that if only *he* could train himself to do the same thing, he could make a fortune.

For a few moments, Henry allowed his mind to dwell upon the marvelous things he would be able to do if he could read cards from the back. He would win every single time at canasta and bridge and poker. And better still, he would be able to go into any casino in the world and clean up at blackjack and all the other high-powered card games they played!

In gambling casinos, as Henry knew very well, nearly everything depended in the end upon the turn of a single card, and if you knew beforehand what the value of that card was, then you were home and dry!

But could he do it? Could he actually train himself to do this thing?

He didn't see why not. That stuff with the candle flame didn't appear to be particularly hard work. And according to the book, that was really all there was to it—just staring into the middle of the flame and trying to concentrate upon the face of the person you loved best.

It would probably take him several years to bring it off, but then who in the world wouldn't be willing to train for a few years in order to beat the casinos every time he went in?

"By golly," he said aloud, "I'll do it! I'm going to do it!"

He sat very still in the armchair in the library, working out a plan of campaign. Above all, he would tell nobody what he was up to. He would steal the little book from the library so that none of his friends might come upon it by chance and learn the secret. He would carry the book with him wherever he went. It would be his bible. He couldn't possibly go out and find a real live yogi to instruct him, so the book would be his yogi instead. It would be his teacher.

Henry stood up and slipped the slim blue exercise book under his jacket. He walked out of the library and went straight upstairs to the bedroom they had given him for the weekend. He got out his suitcase and hid the book underneath his clothes. He then went downstairs again and found his way to the butler's pantry.

"John," he said, addressing the butler, "can you find me a candle? Just an ordinary white candle."

Butlers were trained never to ask for reasons. They simply obeyed orders. "Do you wish a candleholder as well, sir?"

"Yes. A candle and a candleholder."

"Very good, sir. Shall I bring them to your room?"

"No. I'll hang around here till you find them."

The butler soon found a candle and a candleholder. Henry said, "And now could you find me a ruler?" The butler found him a ruler.

Henry thanked him and returned to his bedroom.

When he was inside the bedroom, he locked the door. He drew all the curtains so that the place was in twilight. He put the candle-holder with the candle in it on the dressing table and pulled up a chair. When he sat down, he noticed with satisfaction that his eyes were exactly level with the wick of the candle. Now, using the ruler, he positioned his face sixteen inches from the candle, which again was what the book had said must be done.

That Indian fellow had visualized the face of the person he loved best, which in his case was a brother. Henry didn't have a brother. He decided instead to visualize his own face. With his cigarette lighter, he lit the wick. A yellow flame appeared and burned steadily.

Henry sat quite still and stared into the candle flame. The book had been quite right. The flame, when you looked into it closely, did have three separate parts. There was the yellow outside. Then there was the mauve inner sheath. And right in the middle was the tiny magic area of absolute blackness. He stared at the tiny black area. He focused his eyes upon it and kept staring at it, and as he did so, an extraordinary thing happened. His mind went absolutely blank, and his brain ceased fidgeting around, and all at once it felt as though he himself, his whole body, was actually encased within the flame, sitting snug and cozy within the little black area of nothingness.

With no trouble at all, Henry allowed the image of his own face to swim into sight before him. He concentrated upon the face and nothing but the face. He blocked out all other thoughts. He succeeded completely in doing this, but only for about fifteen seconds. After that, his mind began to wander and he found himself thinking about gambling casinos and how much money he was going to win. At this point, he looked away from the candle and gave himself a rest.

This was his very first effort. He was thrilled. He had done it. Admittedly he hadn't kept it up for very long. But neither had that Indian fellow on the first attempt.

After a few minutes, he tried again. It went well. He had no stopwatch to time himself with, but he sensed that this was definitely a longer go than the first one.

"It's terrific!" he cried. "I'm going to succeed! I'm going to do it!" He had never been so excited by anything in his life.

From that day on, no matter where he was or what he was doing, Henry made a point of practicing with the candle every morning and every evening. Often he practiced at midday as well. For the first time in his life he was throwing himself into something with genuine enthusiasm. And the progress he made was remarkable. After six months, he could concentrate absolutely upon his own face for no less than three minutes without a single outside thought entering his mind.

The yogi of Hardawar had told the Indian fellow that a man would have to practice for fifteen years to get that sort of result!

But wait! The yogi had also said something else. He had said (and here Henry eagerly consulted the little blue exercise book for the hundredth time), he had said that on extremely rare occasions a special person comes along who is able to develop the power in only one or two years.

"That's me!" Henry cried. "It must be me! I am the one-in-a-million person who is gifted with the ability to acquire yoga powers at incredible speed! Whoopee and hurray! It won't be long now before I'm breaking the bank in every casino in Europe and America!"

But Henry at this point showed unusual patience and good sense. He didn't rush to get out a pack of cards to see if he could read them from the reverse side. In fact, he kept well away from card games of all kinds. He had given up bridge and canasta and poker as soon as he had started working with the candle. What's more he had given up razzing around to parties and weekends with his rich friends. He had become dedicated to this single aim of acquiring yoga powers, and everything else would have to wait until he had succeeded.

Sometime during the tenth month, Henry became aware, just as Imhrat Khan had done before him, of a slight ability to see an object with his eyes closed. When he closed his eyes and stared at something hard, with fierce concentration, he could actually see the outline of the object he was looking at.

"It's coming to me!" he cried. "I'm doing it! It's fantastic!"

Now he worked harder than ever at his exercises with the candle, and at the end of the first year he could actually concentrate upon the image of his own face for no less than five and a half minutes!

At this point, he decided the time had come to test himself with the cards. He was in the living room of his London flat when he made this decision, and it was near midnight. He got out a pack of cards and a pencil and paper. He was shaking with excitement. He placed the pack upside down before him and concentrated on the top card.

All he could see at first was the design on the back of the card. It was a very ordinary design of thin red lines, one of the commonest playing-card designs in the world. He now shifted his concentration from the pattern itself to the other side of the card. He concentrated with great intensity upon the invisible underneath of the card, and he allowed no other single thought to creep into his mind. Thirty seconds went by.

Then one minute . . .

Two minutes . . .

Three minutes . . .

Henry didn't move. His concentration was intense and absolute. He was visualizing the reverse side of the playing-card. No other thought of any kind was allowed to enter his head.

During the fourth minute, something began to happen. Slowly, magically, but very clearly, the black symbols became spades and alongside the spades appeared the figure five.

The five of spades!

Henry switched off his concentration. And now, with shaking fingers, he picked up the card and turned it over.

It *was* the five of spades!

"I've done it!" he cried aloud, leaping up from his chair. "I've seen through it! I'm on my way!"

After resting for a while, he tried again, and this time he used a stopwatch to see how long it took him. After three minutes and fifty-eight seconds, he read the card as the king of diamonds. He was right!

The next time he was right again and it took him three minutes and fifty-four seconds. That was four seconds less.

He was sweating with excitement and exhaustion. "That's enough for today," he told himself. He got up and poured himself an enormous drink of whiskey and sat down to rest and to gloat over his success.

His job now, he told himself, was to keep practicing and practicing with the cards until he could see through them instantly. He was convinced it could be done. Already, on the second try, he had knocked four seconds off his time. He would give up working with the candle and concentrate solely upon the cards. He would keep at it day and night.

And that is what he did. But now that he could smell real success in the offing, he became more fanatical than ever. He never left his flat except to buy food and drink. All day and often far into the night, he crouched over the cards with the stopwatch beside him, trying to reduce the time it took him to read from the reverse side.

Within a month, he was down to one and a half minutes.

And at the end of six months of fierce concentrated work, he could do it in twenty seconds. But even that was too long. When you are gambling in a casino and the dealer is waiting for you to say yes or no to the next card, you are not going to be allowed to stare at it for twenty seconds before making up your mind. Three or four seconds would be permissible. But no more.

Henry kept at it. But from now on, it became more and more difficult to improve his speed. To get down from twenty seconds to nineteen took him a week of very hard work. From nineteen to eighteen took him nearly two weeks. And seven more months went by before he could read through a card in ten seconds flat.

His target was four seconds. He knew that unless he could see through a card in a maximum of four seconds, he wouldn't be able to work the casinos successfully. Yet the nearer he got toward the target, the more difficult it became to reach it. It took four weeks to get his time down from ten seconds to nine, and five more weeks to go from nine to eight. But at this stage, hard work no longer bothered him. His powers of concentration had now developed to such a degree that he was able to work for twelve hours at a stretch with no trouble at all. And he knew with absolute certainty that he would get there in the end. He would not stop until he did. Day after day, night after night, he sat crouching over the cards with his stopwatch beside him, fighting with a terrible intensity to knock those last few stubborn seconds off his time.

The last three seconds were the worst of all. To get from seven seconds down to his target of four took him exactly eleven months!

The great moment came on a Saturday evening. A card lay facedown on the table in front of him. He clicked the stopwatch and began to concentrate. At once, he saw a blob of red. The blob swiftly took shape and became a diamond. And then, almost instantaneously, a figure six appeared in the top left-hand corner. He clicked the watch again. He checked the time. It was four seconds! He turned the card over. It was the six of diamonds! He had done it! He had it in four seconds flat!

He tried again with another card. In four seconds he read it as the queen of spades. He went right through the pack, timing himself with every card. Four seconds! Four seconds! Four seconds! It was always the same! He had done it at last! It was all over! He was ready to go!

And how long had it taken him? It had taken him exactly three years and three months of concentrated work.

And now for the casinos!

When should he start?

Why not tonight?

Tonight was Saturday. All the casinos were crowded on Saturday nights. So much the better. There'd be less chance of becoming conspicuous. He went into his bedroom to change into his dinner jacket and black tie. Saturday was a dressy night at the big London casinos.

He would go, he decided, to Lord's House. There are well over one hundred legitimate casinos in London, but none of them is open to the general public. You must become a member before you are allowed to walk in. Henry was a member of no less than ten casinos. Lord's House was his favorite. It was the finest and most exclusive in the country.

Nine

Lord's House was a magnificent Georgian mansion in the center of London, and for over two hundred years it had been the private residence of a duke. Now it was taken over by the bookmakers, and the superb high-ceilinged rooms where the aristocracy and often royalty used to gather and play a gentle game of whist were today filled with a new kind of people who played a very different sort of game.

Henry drove to Lord's House and pulled up outside the great entrance. He got out of the car but left the engine running. Immediately, an attendant in green uniform came forward to park it for him.

Along the curb on both sides of the street stood perhaps a dozen Rolls Royces. Only the very wealthy belonged to Lord's House.

"Why hello, Mr. Sugar!" said the man behind the desk whose job it was never to forget a face. "We haven't seen you for years!"

"I've been busy," Henry answered.

He went upstairs, up the marvelous wide staircase with its carved mahogany banisters, and entered the cashier's office. There he wrote a check for one thousand pounds. The cashier gave him ten large pink rectangular plaques made of plastic. On each it said £100. Henry slipped them into his pocket and spent a few minutes sauntering through the various gaming rooms to get the feel of things again after such a long absence. There was a big crowd here tonight. Well-fed women stood around the roulette wheel like plump hens around a feeding hopper. Jewels and gold were dripping over their bosoms and from their wrists. Many of them had blue hair. The men were in dinner jackets and there wasn't a tall one among them. Why, Henry wondered, did this particular kind of rich man always have short legs? Their legs all seemed to stop at the knees with no thighs above. Most of them had bellies coming out a long way, and crimson faces and cigars between their lips. Their eyes glittered with greed.

All this Henry noticed. It was the first time in his life that he had looked with distaste upon this type of wealthy gambling-casino person. Up until now, he had always regarded them as companions, as members of the same group and class as himself. Tonight they seemed vulgar.

Could it be, he wondered, that the yoga powers he had acquired over the last three years had altered him just a little bit?

He stood watching the roulette. Upon the long green table people were placing their money, trying to guess which little slot the small white ball would fall into on the next spin of the wheel. Henry looked at the wheel. And suddenly, perhaps more from habit than anything else, he found himself beginning to concentrate upon it. It was not difficult. He had been practicing the art of total concentration for so long that it had become something of a routine. In a fraction of a second, his mind had become completely and absolutely concentrated upon the wheel. Everything else in the room, the noise, the people, the lights, the smell of cigar smoke, all this was wiped out of his mind, and he saw only the round, polished roulette wheel with the small white numbers around the rim. The numbers went from 1 to 36, with a 0 between 1 and 36. Very quickly, all the numbers blurred and disappeared in front of his eyes, all except one, all except the number 18. The 18 was the only number he could see. At first it was slightly fuzzy and out of focus. Then the edges sharpened and the whiteness of it grew brighter, more brilliant, until it began to glow as though there was a bright light behind it. It grew bigger. It seemed to jump toward him. At that point, Henry switched off his concentration. The room swam back into vision.

"Have you all finished?" the croupier was saying.

Henry took a £100 plaque from his pocket and placed it on the square marked 18 on the green table. Although the table was covered all over with other people's bets, his was the only one on 18.

The croupier spun the wheel. The little white ball bounced and skittered around the rim. The people watched. All eyes were on the little ball. The wheel slowed. It came to rest. The ball jiggled a few more times, hesitated, then dropped neatly into slot 18.

"Eighteen!" called the croupier.

The crowd sighed. The croupier's assistant scooped up the piles of losing plaques with a long-handled wooden scooper. But he didn't take Henry's. They paid him thirty-six to one: £3600 for his £100. They gave it to him in three £1000 plaques and six £100s.

Henry began to feel an extraordinary sense of power. He felt he could break this place if he wanted to. He could ruin this fancy high-powered expensive joint in a matter of hours. He could take a million off them and all the stony-faced sleek gentlemen who stood around watching the money rolling in would be scurrying about like panicky rats.

Should he do that?

It was a great temptation.

But it would be the end of everything. He would become famous and would never be allowed into a casino again anywhere in the world. He mustn't do it. He must be very careful not to draw attention to himself.

Henry moved casually out of the roulette room and passed into the room where they were playing blackjack. He stood in the doorway watching the action. There were four tables. They were oddly shaped, these blackjack tables, each one curved like a crescent moon, with the players sitting on high stools around the outside of the half-circle and the dealer standing inside.

The packs of cards (at Lord's House they used four packs shuffled together) lay in an open-ended box known as a *shoe,* and the dealer pulled the cards out of the shoe one by one with his fingers. The reverse side of the first card in the shoe was always visible, but no others.

Blackjack, as the casinos call it, is a very simple game. You and I know it by one of three other names: pontoon, twenty-one or *vingt-et-un.* The player tries to get his cards to add up to as near twenty-one as possible, but if he goes over twenty-one, he's bust and the dealer takes the money. In nearly every hand, the player is faced with the problem of whether to draw another card and risk being bust, or whether to stick with what he's got. But Henry would not have that problem. In four seconds, he would have "seen through" the card the dealer was offering him, and he would know whether to say yes or no. Henry could turn blackjack into a farce.

In all casinos, they have an awkward rule about blackjack betting that we do not have at home. At home, we look at our first card before we make a bet, and if it's a good one we bet high. The casinos don't allow you to do this. They insist that everyone at the table makes his bet *before* the first card of the hand is dealt. What's more, you are not allowed to increase your bet later on by buying a card.

None of this would disturb Henry either. So long as he sat on the dealer's immediate left, then he would always receive the first card in the shoe at the beginning of each deal. The reverse side of this card would be clearly visible to him, and he would "read through" it before he made his bet.

Now, standing quietly just inside the doorway, Henry waited for a place to become vacant on the dealer's left at any of the four tables. He had to wait twenty minutes for this to happen, but he got what he wanted in the end.

He perched himself on the high stool and handed the dealer one of the £1000 plaques he had won at roulette. "All in twenty-fives, please," he said.

The dealer was a youngish man with black eyes and gray skin. He never smiled and he spoke only when necessary. His hands were exceptionally slim and there was arithmetic in his fingers. He took Henry's plaque and dropped it into a slot in the table. Rows of different-colored circular chips lay neatly in a wooden tray in front of him, chips for £25, £10 and £5, maybe a hundred of each. With his thumb and forefinger, the dealer picked up a wedge of £25 chips and placed them in a tall pile on the table. He didn't have to count them. He knew there were exactly twenty chips in the pile. Those nimble fingers could pick up with absolute accuracy any number of chips from one to twenty and never be wrong. The dealer picked up a second lot of twenty chips, making forty in all. He slid them over the table to Henry.

Henry stacked the chips in front of him, and as he did so, he glanced at the top card in the shoe. He switched on his concentration and in four seconds he read it as a ten. He pushed out eight of his chips, £200. This was the maximum stake allowed for blackjack at Lord's House.

He was dealt the ten, and for his second card he got a nine, nineteen altogether.

Everyone sticks on nineteen. You sit tight and hope the dealer won't get twenty or twenty-one.

So when the dealer came around again to Henry, he said,

"Nineteen," and passed on to the next player.

"Wait," Henry said.

The dealer paused and came back to Henry. He raised his brows and looked at him with those cool black eyes. "You wish to draw to nineteen?" he asked somewhat sarcastically. He spoke with an Italian accent, and there was scorn as well as sarcasm in his voice. There were only two cards in the pack that would not bust a nineteen, the ace (counting as a one) and the two. Only an idiot would risk drawing to nineteen, especially with £200 on the table.

The next card to be dealt lay clearly visible in the front of the shoe. At least, the reverse side of it was clearly visible. The dealer hadn't yet touched it.

"Yes," Henry said, "I think I'll have another card."

The dealer shrugged and flipped the card out of the shoe. The two of clubs landed neatly in front of Henry, alongside the ten and the nine.

"Thank you," Henry said. "That will do nicely."

"Twenty-one," the dealer said. His black eyes glanced up again into Henry's face, and they rested there, silent, watchful, puzzled. Henry had unbalanced him. He had never in his life seen anyone draw to a nineteen. This fellow had drawn to nineteen with a calmness and a certainty that was quite staggering. And he had won.

Henry caught the look in the dealer's eyes, and he realized at once that he had made a silly mistake. He had been too clever. He had drawn attention to himself. He must never do that again. He must be very careful in the future how he used his powers. He must even make himself lose occasionally, and every now and again he must do something a bit stupid.

The game went on. Henry's advantage was so enormous, he had difficulty keeping his winnings down to a reasonable sum. Every now and again, he would ask for a third card when he already knew it was going to bust him. And once, when he saw that his first card was going to be an ace, he put out his smallest stake, then made a great show of cursing himself aloud for not having made a bigger bet in the first place.

In an hour, he had won exactly £3000, and there he stopped. He pocketed his chips and made his way back to the cashier's office to turn them in for real money.

He had made £3000 from blackjack and £3600 from roulette, £6600 in all. It could just as easily have been £660,000. As a matter of fact, he told himself, he was now almost certainly able to make money faster than any other man in the entire world.

The cashier received Henry's pile of chips and plaques without twitching a muscle. He wore steel spectacles, and the pale eyes behind the spectacles were not interested in Henry. They looked only at the chips on the counter. This man also had arithmetic in his fingers. But he had more than that. He had arithmetic, trigonometry and calculus and algebra and Euclidean geometry in every nerve of his body. He was a human calculating machine with a hundred thousand electric wires in his brain. It took him five seconds to count Henry's one hundred and twenty chips.

"Would you like a cheque for this, Mr. Sugar?" he asked. The cashier, like the man at the desk downstairs, knew every member by name.

"No, thank you," Henry said, "I'll take it in cash."

"As you wish," said the voice behind the spectacles, and he turned away and went to a safe at the back of the office that must have contained millions.

By Lord's House standards, Henry's win was fairly small potatoes. The Arab oil boys were in London now, and they liked to gamble. So did the shady diplomats from the Far East and the Japanese businessmen and the British tax-dodging real-estate operators. Staggering sums of money were being won and lost, mostly lost, in the large London casinos every day.

The cashier returned with Henry's money and dropped the bundle of notes on the counter. Although there was enough there to buy a small house or a large automobile, the chief cashier at Lord's House was not impressed. He might just as well have been passing Henry a pack of chewing gum for all the notice he took of the money he was dishing out.

"You wait, my friend," Henry thought to himself as he pocketed the money. "You just wait." He walked away.

"Your car, sir?" said the man at the door in the green uniform.

"Not yet," Henry told him. "I think I'll take a bit of fresh air first."

He strolled away down the street. It was nearly midnight. The evening was cool and pleasant. The great city was still wide awake. Henry could feel the bulge in the inside pocket of his jacket where the big wad of money was lying. He touched the bulge with one hand. He patted it gently. It was a lot of money for an hour's work.

And what of the future?

What was the next move going to be?

He could make a million in a month.

He could make more if he wanted to.

There was no limit to what he could make.

Walking through the streets of London in the cool of the evening, Henry began to think about the next move.

Now, had this been a made-up story instead of a true one, it would have been necessary to invent some sort of a surprising and exciting end for it. It would not be difficult to do that. Something dramatic and unusual. So before telling you what really *did* happen to Henry in real life, let us pause here for a moment to see what a competent fiction writer would have done to wrap up this story. His notes would read something like this:

1. Henry must die. Like Imhrat Khan before him, he had violated the code of the yogi and had used his powers for personal gain.

2. It will be best if he dies in some unusual and interesting manner that will surprise the reader.

3. For example, he could go home to his flat and start counting his money and gloating over it. While doing this, he might suddenly begin to feel unwell. He has a pain in his chest.

4. He becomes frightened. He decides to go to bed immediately and rest. He takes off his clothes. He walks naked to the closet to get his pajamas. He passes the full-length mirror that stands against the wall. He stops. He stares at the reflection of his naked self in the mirror. Automatically, from force of habit he begins to concentrate. And then . . .

5. All at once, he is "seeing through" his own skin. He "sees through" it in the same way that he "saw through" those playing cards a while back. It is like an X-ray picture, only far better. An X-ray can see only the bones and the very dense areas. Henry can see everything. He sees his arteries and veins with the blood pumping through him. He can see his liver, his kidneys, his intestines and he can see his heart beating.

6. He looks at the place in his chest where the pain is coming from . . . and he sees . . . or thinks he sees . . . a small dark lump inside the big vein leading into the heart on the right hand side. What could a small dark lump be doing inside the vein? It must be a blockage of some kind. It must be a clot. A blood clot!

7. At first, the clot seems to be stationary. Then it moves. The movement is very slight, no more than a millimeter or two. The blood inside the vein is pumping up behind the clot and pushing past it and the little clot moves again. It jerks forward about half an inch. This time, up the vein, toward the heart. Henry watches in terror. He knows, as almost everyone else in the world knows, that a blood clot that has broken free and is traveling in a vein will ultimately reach the heart. When it reaches the heart, you often die. . . .

That wouldn't be such a bad ending for a work of fiction, but this story is not fiction. It is true. The only untrue things about it are Henry's name and the name of the gambling casino. Henry's name was not Henry Sugar. His name has to be protected. It still must be protected. And for obvious reasons, one cannot call the casino by its real name. Apart from that, it is a true story.

And because it is a true story, it must have the true ending. The true one may not be quite so dramatic or spooky as a made-up one could be, but it is nonetheless interesting. Here is what actually happened.

Ten

After walking the London streets for about an hour, Henry returned to Lord's House and collected his car. Then he drove back to his flat. He was a puzzled man. He couldn't understand why he felt so little excitement about his tremendous success. If this sort of thing had happened to him three years ago, before he'd started the yoga business, he'd have gone crazy with excitement. He'd have been dancing in the streets and rushing off to the nearest nightclub to celebrate with champagne.

The funny thing was that he didn't really feel excited at all. He felt melancholy. It had somehow all been too easy. Every time he'd made a bet, he'd been certain of winning. There was no thrill, no suspense, no danger of losing. He knew, of course, that from now on he could travel around the world and make millions. But was it going to be any fun doing it?

It was slowly beginning to dawn upon Henry that nothing is any fun if you can get as much of it as you want. Especially money.

Another thing. Was it not possible that the process he had gone through in order to acquire yoga powers had completely changed his outlook on life?

Certainly it was possible.

Henry drove home and went straight to bed.

The next morning he woke up late. But he didn't feel any more cheerful now than he had the night before. And when he got out of bed and saw the enormous bundle of money still lying on his dressing table, he felt a sudden and very acute revulsion toward it. He didn't want it. For the life of him, he couldn't explain why this was so, but the fact remained that he simply did not want any part of it.

He picked up the bundle. It was all in twenty-pound notes, three hundred and thirty of them to be exact. He walked onto the balcony of his flat, and there he stood in his dark-red silk pajamas looking down at the street below him.

Henry's flat was in Curzon Street, which is right in the middle of London's most fashionable and expensive district, known as Mayfair. One end of Curzon Street runs into Berkeley Square, the other into Park Lane. Henry lived three floors above street level, and outside his bedroom there was a small balcony with iron railings that overhung the street.

The month was June, the morning was full of sunshine, and the time was about eleven o'clock. Although it was a Sunday, there were quite a few people strolling about on the sidewalks.

Henry peeled off a single twenty-pound note from his wad and dropped it over the balcony. A breeze took hold of it and blew it sideways in the direction of Park Lane. Henry stood watching it. It fluttered and twisted in the air and eventually came to rest on the opposite side of the street, directly in front of an old man. The old man was wearing a long, brown, shabby overcoat and a floppy hat, and he was walking slowly, all by himself. He caught sight of the note as it fluttered past his face, and he stopped and picked it up. He held it with both hands and stared at it. He turned it over. He peered closer. Then he raised his head and looked up.

"Hey there!" Henry shouted, cupping a hand to his mouth. "That's for you! It's a present!"

The old man stood quite still, holding the note in front of him and gazing up at the figure on the balcony above.

"Put it in your pocket!" Henry shouted. "Take it home!" His voice carried far along the street, and many people stopped and looked up.

Henry peeled off another note and threw it down. The watchers below him didn't move. They simply watched. They had no idea what was going on. A man was up there on the balcony and he had shouted something, and now he had just thrown down what looked like a piece of paper. Everyone followed the piece of paper as it went fluttering down, and this one came near to a young couple who were standing arm in arm on the sidewalk across the street. The man unlinked his arm and tried to catch the paper as it went past him. He missed it but picked it up from the ground. He examined it closely. The watchers on both sides of the street all had their eyes on the young man now. To many of them, the paper had looked very much like a banknote of some kind, and they were waiting to find out.

"It's twenty pounds!" the man yelled, jumping up and down. "It's a twenty-pound note!"

"Keep it!" Henry shouted at him. "It's yours!"

"You mean it?" the man called back, holding the note out at arm's length. "Can I really keep it?"

Suddenly there was a rustle of excitement along both sides of the street, and everyone started moving at once. They ran out into the middle of the road and clustered underneath the balcony. They lifted their arms above their heads and started calling out, "Me! How about one for me! Drop us another one, guv'ner! Send down a few more!"

Henry peeled off another five or six notes and threw them down.

There were screams and yells as the pieces of paper fanned out in the wind and floated downward, and there was a good old-fashioned scrimmage in the streets as they reached the hands of the crowd. But it was all very good-natured. People were laughing. They thought it a fantastic joke. Here was a man standing three floors up, in his pajamas, slinging these enormously valuable notes into the air. Quite a few of those present had never even seen a twenty-pound note in their lives before this moment.

But now something else was beginning to happen.

The speed with which news will spread along the streets of a city is phenomenal. The news of what Henry was doing flashed like lightning up and down the length of Curzon Street and into the smaller and larger streets beyond. From all sides, people came running. Within a few minutes, about a thousand men and women and children were blocking the road underneath Henry's balcony. Drivers, who couldn't get through, got out of their cars and joined the crowd. And all of a sudden, there was chaos in Curzon Street.

At this point, Henry simply raised his arm and swung it out and flung the entire bundle of notes into the air. More than six thousand pounds went fluttering down toward the screaming crowd below.

The scramble that followed was really something to see. People were jumping up to catch the notes before they reached the ground, and everyone was pushing and jostling and yelling and falling over, and soon the whole place was a mass of tangled, yelling, fighting human beings.

Above the noise and behind him in his own flat, Henry suddenly heard his front-door bell ringing long and loud. He went in from the balcony and opened the door. A large policeman with a black moustache stood outside with his hands on his hips. "You!" he bellowed angrily. "You're the one! What the devil d'you think you're doing?"

"Good morning, officer," Henry said. "I'm sorry about the crowd. I didn't think it would turn out like that. I was just giving away some money."

"You are causing a nuisance!" the policeman bellowed. "You are creating an obstruction! You are inciting a riot and you are blocking the entire street!"

"I said I was sorry," Henry answered. "I won't do it again, I promise. They'll soon go away."

The policeman took one hand off his hip and from the inside of his palm he produced a twenty-pound note.

"Ah-ha!" Henry cried. "You got one yourself! I'm so glad! I'm so happy for you!"

"Now you just stop that larking about!" the policeman said, "because I have a few serious questions to ask you about these here twenty-pound notes." He took a notebook from his breast pocket. "In the first place," he went on, "where exactly did you get them from?"

"I won them," Henry said. "I had a lucky night." He went on to give the name of the club where he had won the money, and the policeman wrote it down in his little book. "Check it up," Henry added. "They'll tell you it's true."

The policeman lowered the notebook and looked Henry in the eye. "As a matter of fact," he said, "I believe your story. I think you're telling the truth. But that doesn't excuse what you did one little bit."

"I didn't do anything wrong," Henry said.

"You're a blithering young idiot!" the policeman shouted, beginning to work himself up all over again. "You're an ass and an imbecile! If you've been lucky enough to win yourself a tremendous big sum of money like that and you want to give it away, you don't throw it out the window!"

"Why not?" Henry asked, grinning. "It's as good a way of getting rid of it as any."

"It's a damned stupid silly way of getting rid of it!" the policeman cried. "Why didn't you give it where it would do some good? To a hospital, for instance? Or an orphanage? There's orphanages all over the country that hardly have enough money to buy the kids a present even for Christmas! And then along comes a little twit like you who's never even known what it's like to be hard up and you throw the stuff out into the street! It makes me mad, it really does!"

"An orphanage?" Henry said.

"Yes, an *orphanage!*" the policeman cried. "I was brought up in one so I ought to know what it's like!" With that, the policeman turned away and went quickly down the stairs toward the street.

Henry didn't move. The policeman's words, and more especially the genuine fury with which they had been spoken, smacked our hero right between the eyes.

"An orphanage?" he cried aloud. "That's quite a thought. But why only one orphanage? Why not lots of them?" And now, very quickly, there began to come to him the great and marvelous idea that was to change everything.

Henry shut the front door and went back into his flat. All at once, he felt a powerful excitement stirring in his belly. He started pacing up and down, ticking off the points that would make his marvelous idea possible.

"One," he said, "I can get hold of a very large sum of money each day of my life.

"Two. I must not go to the same casino more than once every twelve months.

"Three. I must not win too much from any one casino or somebody will get suspicious. I suggest I keep it down to twenty thousand pounds a night.

"Four. Twenty thousand pounds a night for three hundred and sixty-five days in the year comes to how much?"

Henry took a pencil and paper and worked this one out.

"It comes to seven million, three hundred thousand pounds," he said aloud.

"Very well. Point number five. I shall have to keep moving. No more than two or three nights at a stretch in any one city or the word will get around. Go from London to Monte Carlo. Then to Cannes. To Biarritz. To Deauville. To Las Vegas. To Mexico City. To Buenos Aires. To Nassau. And so on.

"Six. With the money I make, I will set up an absolutely first-class orphanage in every country I visit. I will become a Robin Hood. I will take money from the bookmakers and the gambling proprietors and give it to the children. Does that sound corny and sentimental? As a dream, it does. But as a reality, if I can really make it work, it won't be corny at all, or sentimental. It would be rather tremendous.

"Seven. I will need somebody to help me, a man who will sit at home and take care of all that money and buy the houses and organize the whole thing. A money man. Someone I can trust. What about John Winston?"

Eleven

John Winston was Henry's accountant. He handled his income-tax affairs, his investments and all other problems that had to do with money. Henry had known him for eighteen years, and a friendship had developed between the two men. Remember though, that up until now, John Winston had known Henry only as the wealthy idle playboy who had never done a day's work in his life.

"You must be mad," John Winston said when Henry told him his plan. "Nobody has ever devised a system for beating the casinos."

From his pocket, Henry produced a brand-new unopened pack of cards. "Come on," he said. "We'll play a little blackjack. You're the dealer. And don't tell me those cards are marked. It's a new pack."

Solemnly, for nearly an hour, sitting in Winston's office whose windows looked out over Berkeley Square, the two men played blackjack. They used matchsticks as counters, each match being worth twenty-five pounds. After fifty minutes, Henry was no less than thirty-four thousand pounds ahead!

John Winston couldn't believe it. "How do you do it?" he said.

"Put the pack on the table," Henry said. "Face down."

Winston obeyed.

Henry concentrated on the top card for four seconds. "That's a knave of hearts," he said. It was.

"The next one is . . . a three of hearts." It was. He went right through the entire pack, naming every card.

"Go on," John Winston said. "Tell me how you do it." This usually calm and mathematical man was leaning forward over his desk, staring at Henry with eyes as big and bright as two stars. "You do realize you are doing something completely impossible?" he said.

"It's not impossible," Henry said. "It is only very difficult. I am the one man in the world who can do it."

The telephone rang on John Winston's desk. He lifted the receiver and said to his secretary, "No more calls please, Susan, until I tell you. Not even my wife." He looked up, waiting for Henry to go on.

Henry then proceeded to explain to John Winston exactly how he had acquired the power. He told him how he had found the notebook and about Imhrat Khan and then he described how he had been working nonstop for the past three years, training his mind to concentrate.

When he had finished, John Winston said, "Have you tried walking on fire?"

"No," Henry said, "and I'm not going to."

"What makes you think you'll be able to do this thing with the cards in a casino?"

Henry then told him about his visit to Lord's House the night before.

"Six thousand, six hundred pounds!" John Winston cried. "Did you honestly win that much in real money?"

"Listen," Henry said. "I just won thirty-four thousand from you in less than an hour!"

"So you did."

"Six thousand was the very least I could win," Henry said. "It was a terrific effort not to win more."

"You will be the richest man on earth."

"I don't want to be the richest man on earth," Henry said. "Not anymore." He then told him about his plan for orphanages.

When he had finished, he said, "Will you join me, John? Will you be my money man, my banker, my administrator and everything else? There will be millions coming in every year."

John Winston, a cautious and prudent accountant, would not agree to anything at all on the spur of the moment. "I want to see you in action first," he said.

So that night, they went together to the Ritz Club on Curzon Street. "Can't go to Lord's House again now for some time," Henry said.

On the first spin of the roulette wheel, Henry staked £100 on number 27. It came up. The second time he put it on number 4; that came up too. A total of £7200 profit.

An Arab standing next to Henry said, "I have just lost fifty-five thousand pounds. How do you do it?"

"Luck," Henry said. "Just luck."

They moved into the blackjack room and there, in half an hour, Henry won a further £10,000. Then he stopped.

Outside in the street, John Winston said, "I believe you now. I'll come with you."

"We start tomorrow," Henry said.

"Do you really intend to do this every single night?"

"Yes," Henry said. "I shall move very fast from place to place, from country to country. And every day, I shall send the profits back to you through the banks."

"Do you realize how much it will add up to in a year?"

"Millions," Henry said cheerfully. "About seven million a year."

"In that case, I can't operate out of this country," John Winston said. "The taxman will have it all."

"Go anywhere you like," Henry said. "It makes no difference to me. I trust you completely."

"I shall go to Switzerland," John Winston said. "But not tomorrow. I can't just pull up and fly away. I'm not an unattached bachelor like you with no responsibilities. I must talk to my wife and children. I must give notice to my partners in the firm. I must sell my house. I must find another house in Switzerland. I must take the kids out of school. My dear man, these things take time!"

Henry drew from his pocket the £17,500 he had just won and handed them to the other man. "Here's some petty cash to tide you over until you get settled," he said. "But do hurry up. I want to get cracking."

Within a week, John Winston was in Lausanne, with an office high up on the lovely hillside above Lake Geneva. His family would follow him as soon as possible.

And Henry went to work in the casinos.

Twelve

One year later, he had sent a little over eight million pounds to John Winston in Lausanne. The money was sent five days a week to a Swiss company called ORPHANAGES S.A. Nobody except John Winston and Henry knew where the money came from or what was going to happen to it. As for the Swiss authorities, they never want to know where money comes from. Henry sent the money through the banks. The Monday remittance was always the biggest because it included Henry's take for Friday, Saturday and Sunday, when the banks were closed. He moved with astonishing speed, and often the only clue that John Winston had to his whereabouts was the address of the bank that had sent the money on a particular day. One day it would come perhaps from a bank in Manila. The next day from Bangkok. It came from Las Vegas, from Curaçao, from Freeport, from Grand Cayman, from San Juan, from Nassau, from London, from Biarritz. It came from anywhere and everywhere as long as there was a big casino in the city.

Thirteen

For seven years, all went well. Nearly fifty million pounds had arrived in Lausanne and had been safely banked away. Already, John Winston had got three orphanages established, one in France, one in England, and one in the United States. Five more were on the way.

Then came a bit of trouble. There is a grapevine among casino owners, and although Henry was always extraordinarily careful not to take too much from any one place on any one night, the news was bound to spread in the end.

They got wise to him one night in Las Vegas when Henry rather imprudently took one hundred thousand dollars from each of three separate casinos that all happened to be owned by the same mob.

What happened was this. The morning after, when Henry was in his hotel room packing to leave for the airport, there was a knock on his door. A bellhop came in and whispered to Henry that two men were waiting for him in the lobby. Other men, the bellhop said, were guarding the rear exit. These were very hard men, the bellhop said, and he did not give much for Henry's chances of survival if he were to go downstairs at this moment.

"Why do you come and tell me?" Henry asked him. "Why are you on my side?"

"I'm not on anyone's side," the bellhop said. "But we all know you won a lot of money last night and I figured you might give me a nice present for tipping you off."

"Thanks," Henry said. "But how do I get away? I'll give you a thousand dollars if you can get me out of here."

"That's easy," the bellhop said. "Take your own clothes off and put on my uniform. Then walk out through the lobby with your suitcase. But tie me up before you leave. I've gotta be lying here on the floor tied up hand and foot so they won't think I helped you. I'll say you had a gun and I couldn't do nothing."

"Where's the cord to tie you up with?" Henry asked.

"Right here in my pocket," the bellhop said, grinning.

Henry put on the bellhop's gold and green uniform, which wasn't too bad a fit. Then he tied the man up good and proper with the cord and stuffed a handkerchief in his mouth. Finally, he pushed ten one-hundred-dollar bills under the carpet for the bellhop to collect later.

Down in the lobby, two short, thick, black-haired thugs were watching the people as they came out of the elevators. But they hardly glanced at the man in the green and gold bellhop's uniform who came out carrying a suitcase and who walked smartly across the lobby and out through the revolving doors that led to the street.

At the airport, Henry changed his flight and took the next plane to Los Angeles. Things were not going to be quite so easy from now on, he told himself. But that bellhop had given him an idea.

In Los Angeles, and in nearby Hollywood and Beverly Hills, where all the film people live, Henry sought out the very best makeup man in the business. This was Max Engelman. Henry called on him. He liked him immediately.

"How much do you earn?" Henry asked him.

"Oh, about forty thousand dollars a year," Max told him.

"I'll give you a hundred thousand," Henry said, "if you will come with me and be my makeup artist."

"What's the big idea?" Max asked him.

"I'll tell you," Henry said. And he did.

Max was only the second person Henry had told. John Winston

was the first. And when Henry showed Max how he could read the cards, Max was flabbergasted.

"Great heavens, man!" he cried. "You could make a fortune!"

"I already have," Henry told him. "I've made ten fortunes. But I want to make ten more." He told Max about the orphanages. With John Winston's help, he had already set up seven of them in seven different countries.

Max was a small dark-skinned man who had escaped from Vienna when the Nazis went in. He had never married. He had no ties. He became wildly enthusiastic. "It's crazy!" he cried. "It's the craziest thing I've heard in my life! I'll join you, man! Let's go!"

From then on, Max Engelman traveled everywhere with Henry and carried with him in a trunk such an assortment of wigs, false beards, sideburns, moustaches and makeup materials as you have never seen. He could turn his master into any one of thirty or forty unrecognizable people, and the casino managers, who were all watching for Henry now, never once saw him again as Mr. Henry Sugar. As a matter of fact, only a year after the Las Vegas episode, Henry and Max actually went back to that dangerous city, and on a warm starry night Henry took a cool eighty thousand dollars from the first of the big casinos he had visited before. He went disguised as an elderly Brazilian diplomat, and they never knew what hit them.

Now that Henry no longer appeared as himself in the casinos, there were, of course, a number of other details that had to be taken care of, such as false identity cards and passports. In Monte Carlo, for example, a visitor must always show his passport before being allowed to enter the casino. Henry visited Monte Carlo eleven more times with Max's assistance, every time with a different passport and in a different disguise.

Max adored the work. He loved creating new characters for Henry. "I have an entirely fresh one for you today!" he would announce. "Just wait till you see it! Today you will be an Arab sheik from Kuwait!"

"Do we have an Arab passport?" Henry would ask. "And Arab papers?"

"We have everything," Max would answer. "John Winston has sent me a lovely passport in the name of His Royal Highness Sheik Abu Bin Bey!"

And so it went on. Over the years, Max and Henry became as brothers. They were crusading brothers, two men who moved swiftly through the skies, milking the casinos of the world and sending the money straight back to John Winston in Switzerland, where the company known as ORPHANAGES S.A. grew richer and richer.

Fourteen

Henry died last year, at the age of sixty-three, his work completed. He had been at it for just on twenty years.

His personal reference book listed three hundred and seventy-one major casinos in twenty-one different countries or islands. He had visited them all many times, and he had never lost.

According to John Winston's accounts, he had made altogether £144 million.

He left twenty-one well-established, well-run orphanages scattered about the world, one in each country he visited. All these were administered and financed from Lausanne by John and his staff.

But how do I, who am neither Max Engelman nor John Winston, happen to know all this? And how did I come to write the story in the first place?

I will tell you.

Soon after Henry's death, John Winston telephoned me from Switzerland. He introduced himself simply as the head of a company calling itself ORPHANAGES S.A., and asked me if I would come out to Lausanne to see him with a view to writing a brief history of the organization. I don't know how he got hold of my name. He probably had a list of writers and stuck a pin into it. He would pay me well, he said. And he added, "A remarkable man has died recently. His name was Henry Sugar. I think people ought to know a bit about what he has done."

In my ignorance, I asked whether the story was really interesting enough to merit being put on paper.

"All right," said the man who now controlled £144 million. "Forget it, I'll ask someone else. There are plenty of writers around."

That needled me. "No," I said. "Wait. Could you at least tell me who this Henry Sugar was and what he did? I've never even heard of him."

In five minutes on the phone, John Winston told me something about Henry Sugar's secret career. It was secret no longer. Henry was dead and would never gamble again. I listened, enthralled.

"I'll be on the next plane," I said.

"Thank you," John Winston said. "I would appreciate that."

In Lausanne, I met John Winston, now over seventy, and also Max Engleman, who was about the same age. They were both still shattered by Henry's death, Max even more so than John Winston, for Max had been beside him constantly for over thirteen years. "I loved him," Max said, a shadow falling over his face. "He was a great man. He never thought about himself. He never kept a penny of the money he won, except what he needed to travel and to eat. Listen, once we were in Biarritz and he had just been to the bank and given them half a million francs to send home to John. It was lunchtime. We went to a place and had a simple lunch, an omelette and a bottle of wine, and when the bill came, Henry hadn't got anything to pay it with. I hadn't either. He was a lovely man."

John Winston told me everything he knew. He showed me the original dark-blue notebook written by Dr. John Cartwright in Bombay in 1934 about Imhrat Khan, and I copied it out word for word.

"Henry always carried it with him," John Winston said. "In the end, he knew the whole thing by heart."

He showed me the account books of ORPHANAGES S.A. with Henry's winnings recorded in them day by day over twenty years, and a truly staggering sight they were.

When he had finished, I said to him, "There's a big gap in this story, Mr. Winston. You've told me almost nothing about Henry's travels and about his adventures in the casinos of the world."

"That's Max's story," John Winston said. "Max knows all about that because he was with him. But he says he wants to have a shot at writing it himself. He's already started."

"Then why not let Max write the whole thing?" I asked.

"He doesn't want to," John Winston said. "He only wants to write about Henry and Max. It should be a fantastic story if he ever gets it finished. But he is old now, like me, and I doubt he will manage it."

"One last question," I said. "You keep calling him Henry Sugar. And yet you tell me that wasn't his name. Don't you want me to say who he really was when I do the story?"

"No," John Winston said. "Max and I promised never to reveal it. Oh, it'll probably leak out sooner or later. After all, he was from a fairly well known English family. But I'd appreciate it if you don't try to find out. Just call him plain Mr. Henry Sugar."

And that is what I have done.

The Bookseller

1986

IF, in those days, you walked up from Trafalgar Square into Charing Cross Road, you would come in a few minutes to a shop on the right-hand side that had above the window the words WILLIAM BUGGAGE—RARE BOOKS.

If you peered through the window itself you would see that the walls were lined with books from floor to ceiling, and if you then pushed open the door and went in, you would immediately be assailed by that subtle odour of old cardboard and tea leaves that pervades the interiors of every second-hand bookshop in London. Nearly always, you would find two or three customers in there, silent shadowy figures in overcoats and trilby hats rummaging among the sets of Jane Austen and Trollope and Dickens and George Eliot, hoping to find a first edition.

No shop-keeper ever seemed to be hovering around to keep an eye on the customers, and if somebody actually wanted to pay for a book instead of pinching it and walking out, then he or she would have to push through a door at the back of the shop on which it said OFFICE—PAY HERE. If you went into the office you would find both Mr. William Buggage and his assistant, Miss Muriel Tottle, seated at their respective desks and very much preoccupied.

Mr. Buggage would be sitting behind a valuable eighteenth-century mahogany partners-desk, and Miss Tottle, a few feet away, would be using a somewhat smaller but no less elegant piece of furniture, a Regency writing-table with a top of faded green leather. On Mr. Buggage's desk there would invariably be one copy of the day's *London Times,* as well as *The Daily Telegraph, The Manchester Guardian, The Western Mail,* and *The Glasgow Herald.* There would also be a current edition of *Who's Who* close at hand, fat and red and well thumbed. Miss Tottle's writing-table would have on it an electric typewriter and a plain but very nice open box containing notepaper and envelopes, as well as a quantity of paper-clips and staplers and other secretarial paraphernalia.

Now and again, but not very often, a customer would enter the office from the shop and would hand his chosen volume to Miss Tottle, who checked the price written in pencil on the fly-leaf and accepted the money, giving change when necessary from somewhere in the left-hand drawer of her writing-table. Mr. Buggage never bothered even to glance up at those who came in and went out, and if one of them asked a question, it would be Miss Tottle who answered it.

Neither Mr. Buggage nor Miss Tottle appeared to be in the least concerned about what went on in the main shop. In point of fact, Mr. Buggage took the view that if someone was going to steal a book, then good luck to him. He knew very well that there was not a single valuable first edition out there on the shelves. There might be a moderately rare volume of Galsworthy or an early Waugh that had come in with a job lot bought at auction, and there were certainly some good sets of Boswell and Walter Scott and Robert Louis Stevenson and the rest, often very nicely bound in half or even whole calf. But those were not really the sort of things you could slip into your overcoat pocket. Even if a villain *did* walk out with half a dozen volumes, Mr. Buggage wasn't going to lose any sleep over it. Why should he when he knew that the shop itself earned less money in a whole year than the back-room business grossed in a couple of days. It was what went on in the back room that counted.

One morning in February when the weather was foul and sleet was slanting white and wet onto the window-panes of the office, Mr. Buggage and Miss Tottle were in their respective places as usual and each was engrossed, one might even say fascinated, by his and her own work. Mr. Buggage, with a gold Parker pen poised above a note-pad, was reading *The Times* and jotting things down as he went along. Every now and again, he would refer to *Who's Who* and make more jottings.

Miss Tottle, who had been opening the mail, was now examining some cheques and adding up totals.

"Three today," she said.

"What's it come to?" Mr. Buggage asked, not looking up.

"One thousand six hundred," Miss Tottle said.

Mr. Buggage said, "I don't suppose we've 'eard anything yet from that bishop's 'ouse in Chester, 'ave we?"

"A bishop lives in a palace, Billy, not a house," Miss Tottle said.

"I don't give a sod where 'ee lives," Mr. Buggage said. "But

I get just a little bit uneasy when there's no quick answer from somebody like that."

"As a matter of fact, the reply came this morning," Miss Tottle said.

"Coughed up all right?"

"The full amount."

"That's a relief," Mr. Buggage said. "We never done a bishop before and I'm not sure it was any too clever."

"The cheque came from some solicitors."

Mr. Buggage looked up sharply. "Was there a letter?" he asked.

"Yes."

"Read it."

Miss Tottle found the letter and began to read: "Dear Sir, With reference to your communication of the 4th Instant, we enclose herewith a cheque for £537 in full settlement. Yours faithfully, Smithson, Briggs and Ellis." Miss Tottle paused. "That seems all right, doesn't it?"

"It's all right this time," Mr. Buggage said. "But we don't want no more solicitors and let's not 'ave any more bishops either."

"I agree about bishops," Miss Tottle said. "But you're not suddenly ruling out earls and lords and all that lot, I hope?"

"Lords is fine," Mr. Buggage said. "We never 'ad no trouble with lords. Nor earls either. And didn't we do a duke once?"

"The Duke of Dorset," Miss Tottle said. "Did him last year. Over a thousand quid."

"Very nice," Mr. Buggage said. "I remember selectin' 'im myself straight off the front page." He stopped talking while he prised a bit of food out from between two front teeth with the nail of his little finger. "What I says is this," he went on. "The bigger the title, the bigger the twit. In fact, anyone's got a title on 'is name is almost certain to be a twit."

"Now that's not quite true, Billy," Miss Tottle said. "Some people are given titles because they've done absolutely brilliant things, like inventing penicillin or climbing Mount Everest."

"I'm talking about in'erited titles," Mr. Buggage said. "Anyone gets born with a title, it's odds-on 'ee's a twit."

"You're right there," Miss Tottle said. "We've never had the slightest trouble with the aristocracy."

Mr. Buggage leaned back in his chair and gazed solemnly at Miss Tottle. "You know what?" he said. "One of these days we might even 'ave a crack at royalty."

"Ooh, I'd *love* it," Miss Tottle said. "Sock them for a fortune."

Mr. Buggage continued to gaze at Miss Tottle's profile, and as he did so, a slightly lascivious glint crept into his eye. One is forced to admit that Miss Tottle's appearance, when judged by the highest standards, was disappointing. To tell the truth when judged by *any* standards, it was still disappointing. Her face was long and horsey and her teeth, which were also rather long, had a sulphurous tinge about them. So did her skin. The best you could say about her was that she had a generous bosom, but even that had its faults. It was the kind that makes a single long tightly bound bulge from one side of the chest to the other, and at first glance one got the impression that there were not two individual breasts growing out of her body but simply one big long loaf of bread.

Then again, Mr. Buggage himself was in no position to be overly finicky. When one saw him for the first time, the word that sprang instantly to mind was "grubby." He was squat, paunchy, bald and flaccid, and so far as his face was concerned, one could only make a guess at what it looked like because not much of it was visible to the eye. The major part was covered over by an immense thicket of black, bushy, slightly curly hair, a fashion, one fears, that is all too common these days, a foolish practice and incidentally a rather dirty habit. Why so many males wish to conceal their facial characteristics is beyond the comprehension of us ordinary mortals. One must presume that if it were possible for these people also to grow hair all over their noses and cheeks and eyes, then they would do so, ending up with no visible face at all but only an obscene and rather gamey ball of hair. The only possible conclusion one can arrive at when looking at one of these bearded males is that the vegetation is a kind of smoke-screen and is cultivated in order to conceal something unsightly or unsavory.

This was almost certainly true in Mr. Buggage's case, and it was therefore fortunate for all of us, and especially for Miss Tottle, that the beard was there. Mr. Buggage continued to gaze wistfully at his assistant. Then he said, "Now pet, why don't you 'urry up and get them cheques in the post because after you've done that I've got a little proposal to put to you."

Miss Tottle looked back over her shoulder at the speaker and gave him a smirk that showed the cutting edges of her sulphur teeth. Whenever he called her "pet," it was a sure sign that feelings of a carnal nature were beginning to stir within Mr. Buggage's breast, and in other parts as well.

"Tell it to me now, lover," she said.

"You get them cheques done first," he said. He could be very commanding at times, and Miss Tottle thought it was wonderful.

Miss Tottle now began what she called her Daily Audit. This involved examining all of Mr. Buggage's bank accounts and all of her own and then deciding into which of them the latest cheques should be paid. Mr. Buggage, you see, at this particular moment, had exactly sixty-six different accounts in his own name and Miss Tottle had twenty-two. These were scattered around among various branches of the big three banks, Barclays, Lloyds, and National Westminster, all over London and a few in the suburbs. There was nothing wrong with that. And it had not been difficult, as the business became more and more successful, for either of them to walk into any branch of these banks and open a Current Account, with an initial deposit of a few hundred pounds. They would then receive a cheque book, a paying-in book and the promise of a monthly statement.

Mr. Buggage had discovered early on that if a person has an account with several or even many different branches of a bank, this will cause no comment by the staff. Each branch deals strictly with its own customers and their names are not circulated to other branches or to Head Office, not even in these computerised times.

On the other hand, banks are required by law to notify the Inland Revenue of the names of all clients who have Deposit Accounts containing one thousand pounds or more. They must also report the amounts of interest earned. But no such law applies to Current Accounts because they earn no interest. Nobody takes any notice of a person's Current Account unless it is overdrawn or unless, and this seldom happens, the balance becomes ridiculously large. A Current Account containing let us say £100,000 might easily raise an eyebrow or two among the staff, and the client would almost certainly get a nice letter from the manager suggesting that some of the money be placed on deposit to earn interest. But Mr. Buggage didn't give a fig for interest and he wanted no raised eyebrows either. That is why he and Miss Tottle had eighty-eight different bank accounts between them. It was Miss Tottle's job to see that the amounts in each of these accounts never exceeded £20,000. Anything more than that might, in Mr. Buggage's opinion, cause an eyebrow to raise, especially if it were left lying untouched in a Current Account for months or years. The agreement between the two partners was seventy-five percent of the profits of the business to Mr. Buggage and twenty-five percent to Miss Tottle.

Miss Tottle's Daily Audit involved examining a list she kept of all the balances in all those eighty-eight separate accounts and then deciding into which of them the daily cheque or cheques should be deposited. She had in her filing-cabinet eighty-eight different files, one for each bank account, and eighty-eight different cheque books and eighty-eight different paying-in books. Miss Tottle's task was not a complicated one but she had to keep her wits about her and not muddle things up. Only the previous week they had to open four new accounts at four new branches, three for Mr. Buggage and one for Miss Tottle. "Soon we're goin' to 'ave over a 'undred accounts in our names," Mr. Buggage had said to Miss Tottle at the time.

"Why not two hundred?" Miss Tottle had said.

"A day will come," Mr. Buggage said, "when we'll 'ave used up all the banks in this part of the country and you and I is goin' to 'ave to travel all the way up to Sunderland or Newcastle to open new ones."

But now Miss Tottle was busy with her Daily Audit. "That's done," she said, putting the last cheque and the paying-in slip into its envelope.

" 'Ow much we got in our accounts all together at this very moment?" Mr. Buggage asked her.

Miss Tottle unlocked the middle drawer of her writing-table and took out a plain school exercise book. On the cover she had written the words *My old arithmetic book from school.* She considered this a rather ingenious ploy designed to put people off the scent should the book ever fall into the wrong hands. "Just let me add on today's deposit," she said, finding the right page and beginning to write down figures. "There we are. Counting today, *you* have got in all the sixty-six branches, one million, three hundred and twenty thousand, six hundred and forty-three pounds, unless you've been cashing any cheques in the last few days."

"I 'aven't," Mr. Buggage said. "And what've you got?"

"*I* have got . . . four hundred and thirty thousand, seven hundred and twenty-five pounds."

"Very nice," Mr. Buggage said. "And 'ow long's it taken us to gather in those tidy little sums?"

"Just eleven years," Miss Tottle said. "What was that teeny weeny proposal you were going to put to me, lover?"

"Ah," Mr. Buggage said, laying down his gold pencil and leaning back to gaze at her once again with that pale licentious eye. "I was just thinkin' . . . 'ere's exactly what I was thinkin' . . . why on earth should a millionaire like me be sittin' 'ere in this filthy freezin' weather when I could be reclinin' in the lap of luxury beside a swimmin' pool with a nice girl like you to keep me company and flunkeys bringin' us goblets of iced champagne every five minutes?''

"Why indeed?" Miss Tottle cried, grinning widely.

"Then get out the book and let's see where we 'aven't been?"

Miss Tottle walked over to a bookshelf on the opposite wall and took down a thickish paperback called *The 300 Best Hotels in the World chosen by Rene Lecler.* She returned to her chair and said, "Where to this time, lover?''

"Somewhere in North Africa," Mr. Buggage said. "This is February and you've got to go at least to North Africa to get it really warm. Italy's not 'ot enough yet, nor is Spain. And I don't want the flippin' West Indies. I've 'ad enough of them. Where 'aven't we been in North Africa?"

Miss Tottle was turning the pages of the book. "That's not so easy," she said. "We've done the Palais Jamai in Fez . . . and the Gazelle d'Or in Taroudant . . . and the Tunis Hilton in Tunis. We didn't like that one . . ."

" 'Ow many we done so far altogether in that book?" Mr. Buggage asked her.

"I think it was forty-eight the last time I counted."

"And I 'ave every intention of doin' all three 'undred of 'em before I'm finished," Mr. Buggage said. "That's my big ambition and I'll bet nobody else 'as ever done it."

"I think Mr. Rene Lecler must have done it," Miss Tottle said.

" 'Oo's 'ee?"

"The man who wrote the book."

" 'Ee don't count," Mr. Buggage said. He leaned sideways in his chair and began to scratch the left cheek of his rump in a slow meditative manner. "And I'll bet 'ee 'asn't anyway. These travel guides use any Tom, Dick and 'Arry to go round for 'em."

"Here's one!" Miss Tottle cried. "Hotel La Mamounia in Marrakech."

"Where's that?"

"In Morocco. Just round the top corner of Africa on the left-hand side."

"Go on then. What does it say about it?"

"It says," Miss Tottle read, *"This was Winston Churchill's favourite haunt and from his balcony he painted the Atlas sunset time and again."*

"I don't paint," Mr. Buggage said. "What else does it say?"

Miss Tottle read on: *"As the liveried Moorish servant shows you into the tiled and latticed colonaded court, you step decisively into an illustration of the 1001 Arabian nights . . ."*

"That's more like it," Mr. Buggage said. "Go on."

"Your next contact with reality will come when you pay your bill on leaving."

"That don't worry us millionaires," Mr. Buggage said. "Let's go. We'll leave tomorrow. Call that travel agent right away. First class. We'll shut the shop for ten days."

"Don't you want to do today's letters?"

"Bugger today's letters," Mr. Buggage said. "We're on 'oliday from now on. Get onto that travel agent quick." He leaned the other way now and started scratching his right buttock with the fingers of his right hand. Miss Tottle watched him and Mr. Buggage saw her watching him but he didn't care. "Call that travel agent," he said.

"And I'd better get us some Travellers Cheques," Miss Tottle said.

"Get five thousand quid's worth. I'll write the cheque. This one's on me. Give me a cheque book. Choose the nearest bank. And call that 'otel in wherever it was and ask for the biggest suite they've got. They're never booked up when you want the biggest suite."

Twenty-four hours later, Mr. Buggage and Miss Tottle were sunbathing beside the pool at La Mamounia in Marrakech and they were drinking champagne.

"This is the life," Miss Tottle said. "Why don't we retire altogether and buy a grand house in a climate like this?"

"What do we want to retire for?" Mr. Buggage said. "We got the best business in London goin' for us and personally I find that very enjoyable."

On the other side of the pool a dozen Moroccan servants were laying out a splendid buffet lunch for the guests. There were enormous cold lobsters and large pink hams and very small roast chickens and several kinds of rice and about ten different salads. A chef was grilling steaks over a charcoal fire. Guests were beginning to get up from deck-chairs and mattresses to mill around the buffet with plates in their hands. Some were in swimsuits, some in light summer clothes, and most had straw hats on their heads. Mr. Buggage was watching them. Almost without exception, they were English. They were the very rich English, smooth, well mannered, overweight, loud-voiced and infinitely dull. He had seen them before all around

Jamaica and Barbados and places like that. It was evident that quite a few of them knew one another because at home, of course, they moved in the same circles. But whether they knew each other or not, they certainly *accepted* each other because all of them belonged to the same nameless and exclusive club. Any member of this club could always, by some subtle social alchemy, recognise a fellow member at a glance. Yes, they say to themselves, he's one of us. She's one of us. Mr. Buggage was not one of them. He was not in the club and he never would be. He was a *nouveau* and that, regardless of how many millions he had, was unacceptable. He was also overtly vulgar and that was unacceptable, too. The very rich could be just as vulgar as Mr. Buggage, or even more so, but they did it in a different way.

"There they are," Mr. Buggage said, looking across the pool at the guests. "Them's our bread and butter. Every one of 'em's likely to be a future customer."

"How right you are," Miss Tottle said.

Mr. Buggage, lying on a mattress that was striped in blue, red, and green, was propped up on one elbow, staring at the guests. His stomach was bulging out in folds over his swimming-trunks and droplets of sweat were running out of the fatty crevices. Now he shifted his gaze to the recumbent figure of Miss Tottle lying beside him on her own mattress. Miss Tottle's loaf-of-bread bosom was encased in a strip of scarlet bikini. The bottom half of the bikini was daringly brief and possibly a shade too small and Mr. Buggage could see traces of black hair high up on the inside of her thighs.

"We'll 'ave our lunch, pet, then we'll go to our room and take a little nap, right?"

Miss Tottle displayed her sulphurous teeth and nodded her head.

"And after that we'll do some letters."

"Letters?" she cried. "I don't want to do letters! I thought this was going to be a holiday!"

"It *is* a 'oliday, pet, but I don't like lettin' good business go to waste. The 'otel will lend you a typewriter. I already checked on that. And they're lendin' me their *'Oo's 'Oo*. Every good 'otel in the world keeps an English *'Oo's 'Oo*. The manager likes to know 'oo's important so 'ee can kiss their backsides."

"They won't find *you* in it," Miss Tottle said, a bit huffy now.

"No," Mr. Buggage said. "I'll grant you that. But they won't find many in it that's got more money'n me neither. In this world, it's not 'oo you are, my girl. It's not even 'oo you know. It's what you *got* that counts."

"We've never done letters on holiday before," Miss Tottle said.

"There's a first time for everything, pet."

"How can we do letters without newspapers?"

"You know very well English papers always go airmail to places like this. I bought a *Times* in the foyer when we arrived. It's actually the same as I was workin' on in the office yesterday so I done most of my 'omework already. I'm beginning to fancy a piece of that lobster over there. You ever seen bigger lobsters than that?"

"But you're surely not going to *post* the letters from here, are you?" Miss Tottle said.

"Certainly not. We'll leave 'em undated and date 'em and post 'em as soon as we return. That way we'll 'ave a nice backlog up our sleeves."

Miss Tottle stared at the lobsters on the table across the pool, then at the people milling around, then she reached out and placed a hand on Mr. Buggage's thigh, high up under the bathing-shorts. She began to stroke the hairy thigh. "Come on, Billy," she said, "why don't we take a break from the letters same as we always do when we're on hols?"

"You surely don't want us throwing about a thousand quid away a day, do you?" Mr. Buggage said. "And quarter of it yours, don't forget that."

"We don't have the firm's notepaper and we can't use hotel paper, for God's sake."

"I brought the notepaper," Mr. Buggage said, triumphant. "I got a 'ole box of it. *And* envelopes."

"Oh, all *right,*" Miss Tottle said. "Are you going to fetch me some of that lobster, lover?"

"We'll go together," Mr. Buggage said, and he stood up and started waddling round the pool in those almost knee-length bathing-trunks he had bought a couple of years back in Honolulu. They had a pattern of green and yellow and white flowers on them. Miss Tottle got to her feet and followed him.

Mr. Buggage was busy helping himself at the buffet when he heard a man's voice behind him saying, "Fiona, I don't think you've met Mrs. Smith-Swithin . . . and this is Lady Hedgecock."

"How d'you do" . . . "How d'you do," the voices said.

Mr. Buggage glanced round at the speakers. There was a man and a woman in swimming-clothes and two elderly ladies wearing cotton dresses. Those names, he thought. I've heard those names before, I know I have . . . Smith-Swithin . . . Lady Hedgecock. He shrugged and continued to load food onto his plate.

A few minutes later, he was sitting with Miss Tottle at a small table under a sun-umbrella and each of them was tucking into an immense half lobster. "Tell me, does the name Lady 'Edgecock mean anything to you?" Mr. Buggage asked, talking with his mouth full.

"Lady Hedgecock? She's one of our clients. Or she was. I never forget names like that. Why?"

"And what about a Mrs. Smith-Swithin? Does that also ring a bell?"

"It does, actually," Miss Tottle said. "Both of them do. Why do you ask that suddenly?"

"Because both of 'em's 'ere."

"Good God! How d'you know?"

"And what's more, my girl, they're together! They're chums!"

"They're not!"

"Oh, yes they are!"

Mr. Buggage told her how he knew. "There they are," he said, pointing with a fork whose prongs were yellow with mayonnaise. "Those two fat old broads talkin' to the tall man and the woman."

Miss Tottle stared, fascinated. "You know," she said, "I've never actually seen a client of ours in the flesh before, not in all the years we've been in business."

"Nor me," Mr. Buggage said. "One thing's for sure. I picked 'em right, didn't I? They're rolling in it. That's obvious. And they're stupid. That's even more obvious."

"Do you think it could be dangerous, Billy, the two of them knowing each other?"

"It's a bloody queer coincidence," Mr. Buggage said, "but I don't think it's dangerous. Neither of 'em's ever goin' to say a word. That's the beauty of it."

"I guess you're right."

"The only possible danger," Mr. Buggage said, "would be if they saw my name on the register. I got a very unusual name just like theirs. It would ring bells at once."

"Guests don't see the register," Miss Tottle said.

"No, they don't," Mr. Buggage said. "No one's ever goin' to bother us. They never 'as and they never will."

"Amazing lobster," Miss Tottle said.

"Lobster is sex food," Mr. Buggage announced, eating more of it.

"You're thinking of oysters, lover."

"I am not thinking of oysters. Oysters is sex food, too, but lobsters is stronger. A dish of lobsters can drive some people crazy."

"Like you, perhaps?" she said, wriggling her rump in the chair.

"Maybe," Mr. Buggage said. "We shall just 'ave to wait and see about that, won't we, pet?"

"Yes," she said.

"It's a good thing they're so expensive," Mr. Buggage said. "If every Tom, Dick and 'Arry could afford to buy 'em, the 'ole world would be full of *sex maniacs.*"

"Keep eating it," she said.

After lunch, the two of them went upstairs to their suite, where they cavorted clumsily on the huge bed for a brief period. Then they took a nap.

And now they were in their private sitting-room and were wearing only dressing-gowns over their nakedness, Mr. Buggage in a plum-coloured silk one, Miss Tottle in pastel pink and pale green. Mr. Buggage was reclining on the sofa with a copy of yesterday's *Times* on his lap and a *Who's Who* on the coffee table.

Miss Tottle was at the writing-desk with a hotel typewriter before her and a notebook in her hand. Both were again drinking champagne.

"This is a prime one," Mr. Buggage was saying. "Sir Edward Leishman. Got the lead obit. Chairman of Aerodynamics Engineering. *One of our major industrialists,* it says.

"Nice," Miss Tottle said. "Make sure the wife's alive."

"Leaves a widow and three children," Mr. Buggage read out. "And . . . wait a minute . . . in *'Oo's 'Oo* it says, *Recreations, walkin' and fishin'. Clubs, White's and the Reform."*

"Address?" Miss Tottle asked.

"The Red House, Andover, Wilts."

"How d'you spell Leishman?" Miss Tottle asked. Mr. Buggage spelled it.

"How much shall we go for?"

"A lot," Mr. Buggage said. "He was loaded. Try around nine 'undred."

"You want to slip in *The Compleat Angler?* It says he was a fisherman."

"Yes. First edition. Four 'undred and twenty quid. You know

the rest of it by 'eart. Bang it out quick. I got another good one to come.''

Miss Tottle put a sheet of notepaper into the typewriter and very rapidly she began to type. She had done so many thousands of these letters over the years that she never had to pause for one word. She even knew how to compile the list of books so that it came out to around nine hundred pounds or three hundred and fifty pounds or five hundred and twenty or whatever. She could make it come out to any sum Mr. Buggage thought the client would stand. One of the secrets of this particular trade, as Mr. Buggage knew, was never to be too greedy. Never go over a thousand quid with anyone, not even a famous millionaire.

The letter, as Miss Tottle typed it, went like this:

WILLIAM BUGGAGE—RARE BOOKS

27a Charing Cross Road,
London.

Dear Lady Leishman,

It is with very great regret that I trouble you at this tragic time of your bereavement, but regretfully I am left with no alternative in the circumstances.

I had the pleasure of serving your late husband over a number of years and my invoices were always sent to him care of White's Club, as indeed were many of the little parcels of books that he collected with such enthusiasm.

He was always a prompt settler and a very pleasant gentleman to deal with. I am listing below his more recent purchases, those which, alas, he had ordered in more recent times before he passed away and which were delivered to him in the usual manner.

Perhaps I should explain to you that publications of this nature are often very rare and can therefore be rather costly. Some are privately printed, some are actually banned in this country and those are more costly still.

Rest assured, dear madam, that I always conduct business in the strictest confidence. My own reputation over many years in the trade is the best guarantee of my discretion. When the bill is paid, that is the last you will hear of the matter, unless of course you happen to be able to lay hands on your late husband's collection of erotica, in which case I should be happy to make you an offer for it.

To Books:

THE COMPLEAT ANGLER, Isaak Walton, First Edition.
   Good clean copy. Some rubbing of edges. Rare. £420
LOVE IN FURS, Leopold von Sacher-Masoch, 1920 edition.
   Slip cover. 75
SEXUAL SECRETS, Translation from Danish. 40
HOW TO PLEASURE YOUNG GIRLS WHEN YOU ARE
   OVER SIXTY, Illustrations. Private printing from Paris. 95
THE ART OF PUNISHMENT—THE CANE, THE WHIP
   AND THE LASH, Translated from German.
   Banned in U.K. 115
THREE NAUGHTY NUNS, Good clean edition. 60
RESTRAINT—SHACKLES AND SILKEN CORDS,
   Illustrations. 80
WHY TEENAGERS PREFER OLD MEN, Illustrations.
   American. 90
THE LONDON DIRECTORY OF ESCORTS AND
   HOSTESSES, Current edition. 20

                        Total now due £995

                            Yours faithfully,
                            William Buggage

"Right," Miss Tottle said, running the notepaper out of her typewriter. "Done that one. But you realise I don't have my 'Bible' here, so I'll have to check the names when I get home before posting the letters."

"You do that," Mr. Buggage said.

Miss Tottle's Bible was a massive index-card file in which were recorded the names and addresses of every client they had written to since the beginning of the business. The purpose of this was to try as nearly as possible to ensure that no two members of the same family received a Buggage invoice. If this were to happen, there would always be the danger that they might compare notes. It also served to guard against a case where a widow who had received one invoice upon the death of her first husband might be sent another invoice on the death of the second husband. That, of course, would let the cat right out of the bag. There was no guaranteed way of avoiding this perilous mistake because the widow would have changed her name when she remarried, but Miss Tottle had developed an instinct for sniffing out such pitfalls, and the Bible helped her to do it.

"What's next?" Miss Tottle asked.

"The next is Major General Lionel Anstruther. Here 'ee is. Got about six inches in *'Oo's 'Oo. Clubs, Army and Navy. Recreations, Ridin' to 'Ounds.'*"

"I suppose he fell off a horse and broke his flipping neck," Miss Tottle said. "I'll start with *Memoirs of a Foxhunting Man, first edition*, right?"

"Right. Two 'undred and twenty quid," Mr. Buggage said. "And make it between five and six 'undred altogether."

"Okay."

"And put in *The Sting of the Ridin' Crop.* Whips seem to come natural to these fox-huntin' folk."

And so it went on.

The holiday in Marrakech continued pleasantly enough and nine days later Mr. Buggage and Miss Tottle were back in the office in Charing Cross Road, both with sun-scorched skins as red as the shells of the many lobsters they had eaten. They quickly settled down again into their normal and stimulating routine. Day after day the letters went out and the cheques came in. It was remarkable how smoothly the business ran. The psychology behind it was, of course, very sound. Strike a widow at the height of her grief, strike her with something that is unbearably awful, something she wants to forget about and put behind her, something she wants nobody else to discover. What's more, the funeral is imminent. So she pays up fast to get the sordid little business out of the way. Mr. Buggage knew his onions. In all the years he had been operating, he had never once had a protest or an angry reply. Just a cheque in an envelope. Now and again, but not often, there was no reply at all. The disbelieving widow had been brave enough to sling his letter into the waste-paper basket and that was the end of it. None of them quite dared to challenge the invoice because they could never be absolutely positive that the late husband had been as pure as the wife believed and hoped. Men never are. In many cases, of course, the widow knew very well that her beloved had been a lecherous old bird and Mr. Buggage's invoice came as no surprise. So she paid up even faster.

About a month after their return from Marrakech, on a wet and rainy afternoon in March, Mr. Buggage was reclining comfortably in his office with his feet up on the top of his fine partner's-desk, dictating to Miss Tottle some details about a deceased and distinguished admiral. *"Recreations,"* he was saying, reading from *Who's Who, "Gardening, sailing and stamp-collecting . . . ."* At that point, the door from the main shop opened and a young man came in with a book in his hand. "Mr. Buggage?" he said.

Mr. Buggage looked up. "Over there," he said, waving toward Miss Tottle. "She'll deal with you."

The young man stood still. His navy-blue overcoat was wet from the weather and droplets of water were dripping from his hair. He didn't look at Miss Tottle. He kept his eyes on Mr. Buggage. "Don't you want the money?" he said, pleasantly enough.

"She'll take it."

"Why won't you take it?"

"Because she's the cashier," Mr. Buggage said. "You want to buy a book, go ahead. She'll deal with you."

"I'd rather deal with *you*," the young man said.

Mr. Buggage looked up at him. "Go on," he said. "Just do as you're told, there's a good lad."

"You *are* the proprietor?" the young man said. "You *are* Mr. William Buggage?"

"What if I am," Mr. Buggage said, his feet still up on the desk.

"Are you or aren't you?"

"What's it to you?" Mr. Buggage said.

"So that's settled," the young man said. "How d'you do, Mr. Buggage." There was a curious edge to his voice now, a mixture of scorn and mockery.

Mr. Buggage took his feet down from the desk-top and sat up a trifle straighter. "You're a bit of a cheeky young bugger, aren't you," he said. "If you want that book, I suggest you just pay your money over there and then you can 'op it. Right?"

The young man turned towards the still open door that led to the front of the shop. Just the other side of the door there were a couple of the usual kind of customers, men in raincoats, pulling out books and examining them.

"Mother," the young man called softly. "You can come in, Mother. Mr. Buggage is here."

A small woman of about sixty came in and stood beside the young man. She had a trim figure for her age and a face that must once have been ravishing, but now it showed traces of strain and exhaustion, and the pale blue eyes were dulled with grief. She was wearing a black coat and a simple black hat. She left the door open behind her.

"Mr. Buggage," the young man said. "This is my mother, Mrs. Northcote."

Miss Tottle, the rememberer of names, turned round quick and looked at Mr. Buggage and made little warning movements with her mouth. Mr. Buggage got the message and said as politely as he could, "And what can I do for you, madam?"

The woman opened her black handbag and took out a letter. She unfolded it carefully and held it out to Mr. Buggage. "Then it will be you who sent me this?" she said.

Mr. Buggage took the letter and examined it at some length. Miss Tottle, who had turned right round in her chair now, was watching Mr. Buggage.

"Yes," Mr. Buggage said. "This is my letter and my invoice. All correct and in order. What is your problem, madam?"

"What I came here to ask you," the woman said, "is, are you sure it's right?"

"I'm afraid it is, madam."

"But it is so unbelievable . . . I find it impossible to believe that my husband bought those books."

"Let's see now, your 'usband, Mr. . . . Mr. . . . er . . ."

"Northcote," Miss Tottle said.

"Yes, Mr. Northcote, yes, of course, Mr. Northcote. 'Ee wasn't in 'ere often, once or twice a year maybe, but a good customer and a very fine gentleman. May I offer you, madam, my sincere condolences on your sad loss."

"Thank you, Mr. Buggage. But are you really quite certain you haven't been mixing him up with somebody else?"

"Not a chance, madam. Not the slightest chance. My good secretary over there will confirm that there is no mistake."

"May I see it?" Miss Tottle said, getting up and crossing to take the letter from Mr. Buggage. "Yes," she said, examining it. "I typed this myself. There is no mistake."

"Miss Tottle's been with me a long time," Mr. Buggage said. "She knows the business inside out. I can't remember 'er ever makin' a mistake."

"I should hope not," Miss Tottle said.

"So there you are, madam," Mr. Buggage said.

"It simply isn't *possible*," the woman said.

"Ah, but men will be men," Mr. Buggage said. "They all 'ave their little bit of fun now and again and there's no 'arm in that, is there, madam?" He sat confident and unmoved in his chair, waiting now to have done with it. He felt himself master of the situation.

The woman stood very straight and still, and she was looking

Mr. Buggage directly in the eyes. "These curious books you list on your invoice," she said, "do they print them in Braille?"

"In what?"

"In Braille."

"I don't know what you're talking about, madam."

"I thought you wouldn't," she said. "That's the only way my husband could have read them. He lost his sight in the last war, in the Battle of Alamein more than forty years ago, and he was blind for ever after."

The office became suddenly very quiet. The mother and her son stood motionless, watching Mr. Buggage. Miss Tottle turned away and looked out of the window. Mr. Buggage cleared his throat as though to say something, but thought better of it. The two men in raincoats, who were close enough to have heard every word through the open door, came quietly into the office. One of them held out a plastic card and said to Mr. Buggage, "Inspector Richards, Serious Crimes Division, Scotland Yard." And to Miss Tottle, who was already moving back towards her desk, he said, "Don't touch any of those papers, please miss. Leave everything just where it is. You're both coming along with us."

The son took his mother gently by the arm and led her out of the office, through the shop and onto the street.